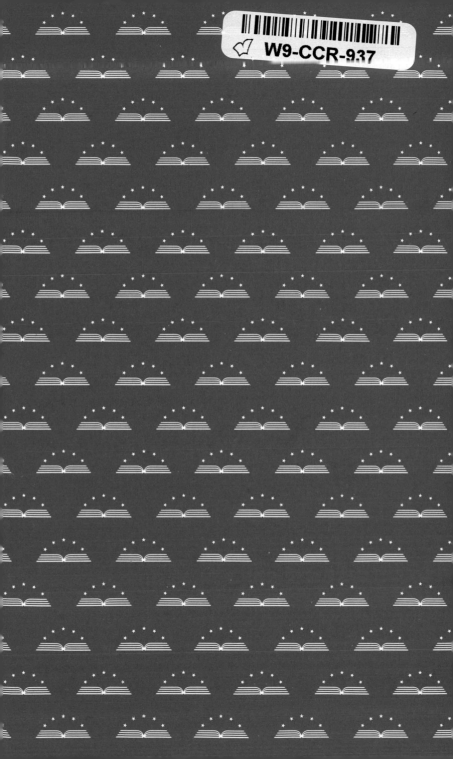

THEODORE DREISER

# THEODORE DREISER

## AN AMERICAN TRAGEDY

THE LIBRARY OF AMERICA

The paper used in this publication meets the
minimum requirements of the American National Standard for
Information Sciences—Permanence of Paper for Printed
Library Materials, ANSI Z39.48—1984.

Distributed to the trade in the United States
by Penguin Putnam Inc.
and in Canada by Penguin Books Canada Ltd.

Library of Congress Catalog Number: 2002030168
For cataloging information, see end of Notes.
ISBN 1–931082–31–6

First Printing
The Library of America—140

Manufactured in the United States of America

THOMAS P. RIGGIO
WROTE THE NOTES FOR THIS VOLUME

# Contents

# AN AMERICAN TRAGEDY

# *Chapter I*

Dusk—of a summer night.

And the tall walls of the commercial heart of an American city of perhaps 400,000 inhabitants—such walls as in time may linger as a mere fable.

And up the broad street, now comparatively hushed, a little band of six,—a man of about fifty, short, stout, with bushy hair protruding from under a round black felt hat, a most unimportant-looking person, who carried a small portable organ such as is customarily used by street preachers and singers. And with him a woman perhaps five years his junior, taller, not so broad, but solid of frame and vigorous, very plain in face and dress, and yet not homely, leading with one hand a small boy of seven and in the other carrying a Bible and several hymn books. With these three, but walking independently behind, was a girl of fifteen, a boy of twelve and another girl of nine, all following obediently, but not too enthusiastically, in the wake of the others.

It was hot, yet with a sweet languor about it all.

Crossing at right angles the great thoroughfare on which they walked, was a second canyon-like way, threaded by throngs and vehicles and various lines of cars which clanged their bells and made such progress as they might amid swiftly moving streams of traffic. Yet the little group seemed unconscious of anything save a set purpose to make its way between the contending lines of traffic and pedestrians which flowed by them.

Having reached an intersection this side of the second principal thoroughfare—really just an alley between two tall structures—now quite bare of life of any kind, the man put down the organ, which the woman immediately opened, setting up a music rack upon which she placed a wide flat hymn book. Then handing the Bible to the man, she fell back in line with him, while the twelve-year-old boy put down a small camp-stool in front of the organ. The man—the father, as he chanced to be—looked about him with seeming wide-eyed assurance, and announced, without appearing to care whether he had any auditors or not:

"We will first sing a hymn of praise, so that any who may wish to acknowledge the Lord may join us. Will you oblige, Hester?"

At this the eldest girl, who until now had attempted to appear as unconscious and unaffected as possible, bestowed her rather slim and as yet undeveloped figure upon the camp chair and turned the leaves of the hymn book, pumping the organ while her mother observed:

"I should think it might be nice to sing twenty-seven to-night—'How Sweet the Balm of Jesus' Love.'"

By this time various homeward-bound individuals of diverse grades and walks of life, noticing the small group disposing itself in this fashion, hesitated for a moment to eye them askance or paused to ascertain the character of their work. This hesitancy, construed by the man apparently to constitute attention, however mobile, was seized upon by him and he began addressing them as though they were specifically here to hear him.

"Let us all sing twenty-seven, then—'How Sweet the Balm of Jesus' Love.'"

At this the young girl began to interpret the melody upon the organ, emitting a thin though correct strain, at the same time joining her rather high soprano with that of her mother, together with the rather dubious baritone of the father. The other children piped weakly along, the boy and girl having taken hymn books from the small pile stacked upon the organ. As they sang, this nondescript and indifferent street audience gazed, held by the peculiarity of such an unimportant-looking family publicly raising its collective voice against the vast skepticism and apathy of life. Some were interested or moved sympathetically by the rather tame and inadequate figure of the girl at the organ, others by the impractical and materially inefficient texture of the father, whose weak blue eyes and rather flabby but poorly-clothed figure bespoke more of failure than anything else. Of the group the mother alone stood out as having that force and determination which, however blind or erroneous, makes for self-preservation, if not success in life. She, more than any of the others, stood up with an ignorant, yet somehow respectable air of conviction.

If you had watched her, her hymn book dropped to her side, her glance directed straight before her into space, you would have said: "Well, here is one who, whatever her defects, probably does what she believes as nearly as possible." A kind of hard, fighting faith in the wisdom and mercy of that definite overruling and watchful power which she proclaimed, was written in her every feature and gesture.

> "The love of Jesus saves me whole,
> The love of God my steps control,"

she sang resonantly, if slightly nasally, between the towering walls of the adjacent buildings.

The boy moved restlessly from one foot to the other, keeping his eyes down, and for the most part only half singing. A tall and as yet slight figure, surmounted by an interesting head and face—white skin, dark hair—he seemed more keenly observant and decidedly more sensitive than most of the others—appeared indeed to resent and even to suffer from the position in which he found himself. Plainly pagan rather than religious, life interested him, although as yet he was not fully aware of this. All that could be truly said of him now was that there was no definite appeal in all this for him. He was too young, his mind much too responsive to phases of beauty and pleasure which had little, if anything, to do with the remote and cloudy romance which swayed the minds of his mother and father.

Indeed the home life of which this boy found himself a part and the various contacts, material and psychic, which thus far had been his, did not tend to convince him of the reality and force of all that his mother and father seemed so certainly to believe and say. Rather, they seemed more or less troubled in their lives, at least materially. His father was always reading the Bible and speaking in meeting at different places, especially in the "mission," which he and his mother conducted not so far from this corner. At the same time, as he understood it, they collected money from various interested or charitably inclined business men here and there who appeared to believe in such philanthropic work. Yet the family was always "hard up," never very well clothed, and deprived of many comforts and pleasures which seemed common enough

to others. And his father and mother were constantly proclaiming the love and mercy and care of God for him and for
all. Plainly there was something wrong somewhere. He could
not get it all straight, but still he could not help respecting his
mother, a woman whose force and earnestness, as well as her
sweetness, appealed to him. Despite much mission work and
family cares, she managed to be fairly cheerful, or at least sustaining, often declaring most emphatically "God will provide"
or "God will show the way," especially in times of too great
stress about food or clothes. Yet apparently, in spite of this, as
he and all the other children could see, God did not show any
very clear way, even though there was always an extreme necessity for His favorable intervention in their affairs.

To-night, walking up the great street with his sisters and
brother, he wished that they need not do this any more, or at
least that he need not be a part of it. Other boys did not do
such things, and besides, somehow it seemed shabby and even
degrading. On more than one occasion, before he had been
taken on the street in this fashion, other boys had called to
him and made fun of his father, because he was always publicly emphasizing his religious beliefs or convictions. Thus in
one neighborhood in which they had lived, when he was but
a child of seven, his father, having always preluded every conversation with "Praise the Lord," he heard boys call "Here
comes old Praise-the-Lord Griffiths." Or they would call out
after him "Hey, you're the fellow whose sister plays the organ.
Is there anything else she can play?"

"What does he always want to go around saying, 'Praise the
Lord' for? Other people don't do it."

It was that old mass yearning for a likeness in all things that
troubled them, and him. Neither his father nor his mother
was like other people, because they were always making so
much of religion, and now at last they were making a business
of it.

On this night in this great street with its cars and crowds
and tall buildings, he felt ashamed, dragged out of normal
life, to be made a show and jest of. The handsome automobiles that sped by, the loitering pedestrians moving off to
what interests and comforts he could only surmise; the gay
pairs of young people, laughing and jesting and the "kids"

staring, all troubled him with a sense of something different, better, more beautiful than his, or rather their life.

And now units of this vagrom and unstable street throng, which was forever shifting and changing about them, seemed to sense the psychologic error of all this in so far as these children were concerned, for they would nudge one another, the more sophisticated and indifferent lifting an eyebrow and smiling contemptuously, the more sympathetic or experienced commenting on the useless presence of these children.

"I see these people around here nearly every night now—two or three times a week, anyhow," this from a young clerk who had just met his girl and was escorting her toward a restaurant. "They're just working some religious dodge or other, I guess."

"That oldest boy don't wanta be here. He feels outa place, I can see that. It ain't right to make a kid like that come out unless he wants to. He can't understand all this stuff, anyhow." This from an idler and loafer of about forty, one of those odd hangers-on about the commercial heart of a city, addressing a pausing and seemingly amiable stranger.

"Yeh, I guess that's so," the other assented, taking in the peculiar cast of the boy's head and face. In view of the uneasy and self-conscious expression upon the face whenever it was lifted, one might have intelligently suggested that it was a little unkind as well as idle to thus publicly force upon a temperament as yet unfitted to absorb their import, religious and psychic services best suited to reflective temperaments of maturer years.

Yet so it was.

As for the remainder of the family, both the youngest girl and boy were too small to really understand much of what it was all about or to care. The eldest girl at the organ appeared not so much to mind, as to enjoy the attention and comment her presence and singing evoked, for more than once, not only strangers, but her mother and father, had assured her that she had an appealing and compelling voice, which was only partially true. It was not a good voice. They did not really understand music. Physically, she was of a pale, emasculate and unimportant structure, with no real mental force or depth, and was easily made to feel that this was an excellent field in which to distinguish herself and attract a little attention. As for the parents, they were determined upon spiritualizing the world as much as possible, and, once the hymn was concluded, the father launched into one of those hackneyed descriptions of the delights of a release, via self-realization of the mercy of God and the love of Christ and the will of God toward sinners, from the burdensome cares of an evil conscience.

"All men are sinners in the light of the Lord," he declared. "Unless they repent, unless they accept Christ, His love and forgiveness of them, they can never know the happiness of being spiritually whole and clean. Oh, my friends! If you could but know the peace and content that comes with the knowledge, the inward understanding, that Christ lived and died for you and that He walks with you every day and hour, by light and by dark, at dawn and at dusk, to keep and strengthen you for the tasks and cares of the world that are ever before you. Oh, the snares and pitfalls that beset us all! And then the soothing realization that Christ is ever with us, to counsel, to aid, to hearten, to bind up our wounds and make us whole! Oh, the peace, the satisfaction, the comfort, the glory of that!"

"Amen!" asseverated his wife, and the daughter, Hester, or Esta, as she was called by the family, moved by the need of as much public support as possible for all of them—echoed it after her.

Clyde, the eldest boy, and the two younger children merely gazed at the ground, or occasionally at their father, with a feeling that possibly it was all true and important, yet somehow not as significant or inviting as some of the other things which life held. They heard so much of this, and to their young and eager minds life was made for something more than street and mission hall protestations of this sort.

Finally, after a second hymn and an address by Mrs. Griffiths, during which she took occasion to refer to the mission work jointly conducted by them in a near-by street, and their services to the cause of Christ in general, a third hymn was indulged in, and then some tracts describing the mission rescue work being distributed, such voluntary gifts as were forthcoming were taken up by Asa—the father. The small organ

was closed, the camp chair folded up and given to Clyde, the
Bible and hymn books picked up by Mrs. Griffiths, and with
the organ supported by a leather strap passed over the shoulder of Griffiths, senior, the missionward march was taken up.

During all this time Clyde was saying to himself that he did
not wish to do this any more, that he and his parents looked
foolish and less than normal—"cheap" was the word he
would have used if he could have brought himself to express
his full measure of resentment at being compelled to participate in this way—and that he would not do it any more if he
could help. What good did it do them to have him along? His
life should not be like this. Other boys did not have to do as
he did. He meditated now more determinedly than ever a rebellion by which he would rid himself of the need of going
out in this way. Let his elder sister go if she chose; she liked
it. His younger sister and brother might be too young to care.
But he——

"They seemed a little more attentive than usual to-night, I
thought," commented Griffiths to his wife as they walked
along, the seductive quality of the summer evening air soften-
ing him into a more generous interpretation of the customary
indifferent spirit of the passer-by.

"Yes; twenty-seven took tracts to-night as against eighteen
on Thursday."

"The love of Christ must eventually prevail," comforted the
father, as much to hearten himself as his wife. "The pleasures
and cares of the world hold a very great many, but when sorrow overtakes them, then some of these seeds will take root."

"I am sure of it. That is the thought which always keeps me
up. Sorrow and the weight of sin eventually bring some of
them to see the error of their way."

They now entered into the narrow side street from which
they had emerged, and walking as many as a dozen doors
from the corner, entered the door of a yellow single-story
wooden building, the large window and the two glass panes
in the central door of which had been painted a gray-white.
Across both windows and the smaller panels in the double
door had been painted: "The Door of Hope. Bethel Independent Mission. Meetings Every Wednesday and Saturday
night, 8 to 10. Sundays at 11, 3 and 8. Everybody Welcome."

Under this legend on each window were printed the words: "God is Love," and below this again, in smaller type: "How Long Since You Wrote to Mother?"

The small company entered the yellow unprepossessing door and disappeared.

# Chapter II

THAT such a family, thus cursorily presented, might have a different and somewhat peculiar history could well be anticipated, and it would be true. Indeed, this one presented one of those anomalies of psychic and social reflex and motivation such as would tax the skill of not only the psychologist but the chemist and physicist as well, to unravel. To begin with, Asa Griffiths, the father, was one of those poorly integrated and correlated organisms, the product of an environment and a religious theory, but with no guiding or mental insight of his own, yet sensitive and therefore highly emotional, and without any practical sense whatsoever. Indeed it would be hard to make clear just how life appealed to him, or what the true hue of his emotional responses was. On the other hand, as has been indicated, his wife was of a firmer texture but with scarcely any truer or more practical insight into anything.

The history of this man and his wife is of no particular interest here save as it affected their boy of twelve, Clyde Griffiths. This youth, aside from a certain emotionalism and exotic sense of romance which characterized him, and which he took more from his father than from his mother, brought a more vivid and intelligent imagination to things, and was constantly thinking of how he might better himself, if he had a chance; places to which he might go, things he might see, and how differently he might live, if only this, that and the other thing were true. The principal thing that troubled Clyde up to his fifteenth year, and for long after in retrospect, was that the calling or profession of his parents was the shabby thing that it appeared to be in the eyes of others. For so often throughout his youth in different cities in which his parents had conducted a mission or spoken on the streets—Grand Rapids, Detroit, Milwaukee, Chicago, lastly Kansas City—it had been obvious that people, at least the boys and girls he encountered, looked down upon him and his brothers and sisters for being the children of such parents. On several occasions, and much against the mood of his parents, who never countenanced such exhibitions of temper, he had stopped to fight with one or another of these boys. But always, beaten or victorious, he had been made conscious of the fact that the work his parents did was not satisfactory to others,—shabby, trivial. And always he was thinking of what he would do, once he reached the place where he could get away.

For Clyde's parents had proved impractical in the matter of the future of their children. They did not understand the importance or the essential necessity for some form of practical or professional training for each and every one of their young ones. Instead, being wrapped up in the notion of evangelizing the world, they had neglected to keep their children in school in any one place. They had moved here and there, sometimes in the very midst of an advantageous school season, because of a larger and better religious field in which to work. And there were times when, the work proving highly unprofitable and Asa being unable to make much money at the two things he most understood—gardening and canvassing for one invention or another—they were quite without sufficient food or decent clothes, and the children could not go to school. In the face of such situations as these, whatever the children might think, Asa and his wife remained as optimistic as ever, or they insisted to themselves that they were, and had unwavering faith in the Lord and His intention to provide.

The combination home and mission which this family occupied was dreary enough in most of its phases to discourage the average youth or girl of any spirit. It consisted in its entirety of one long store floor in an old and decidedly colorless and inartistic wooden building which was situated in that part of Kansas City which lies north of Independence Boulevard and west of Troost Avenue, the exact street or place being called Bickel, a very short thoroughfare opening off Missouri Avenue, a somewhat more lengthy but no less nondescript highway. And the entire neighborhood in which it stood was very faintly and yet not agreeably redolent of a commercial life which had long since moved farther south, if not west. It was some five blocks from the spot on which twice a week the open air meetings of these religious enthusiasts and proselytizers were held.

And it was the ground floor of this building, looking out into Bickel Street at the front and some dreary back yards of equally dreary frame houses, which was divided at the front into a hall forty by twenty-five feet in size, in which had been placed some sixty collapsible wood chairs, a lectern, a map of Palestine or the Holy Land, and for wall decorations some twenty-five printed but unframed mottoes which read, in part:

"Wine is a mocker, strong drink is raging and whosoever is deceived thereby is not wise."

"Take Hold of shield and buckler, and stand up for mine help." Psalms 35:2.

"And ye, my flock, the flock of my pasture, are men, and I am your God, saith the Lord God." Ezekiel 34:31.

"O God, thou knowest my foolishness, and my sins are not hid from Thee." Psalms 69:5.

"If ye have faith as a grain of mustard seed, ye shall say unto this mountain, Remove hence to yonder place; and it shall move; and nothing shall be impossible unto you." Matthew 17:20.

"For the day of the Lord is near." Obadiah 15.

"For there shall be no reward to the evil man." Proverbs 24:20.

"Look, then, not upon the wine when it is red: it biteth like a serpent, and stingeth like an adder." Proverbs 23:31, 32.

These mighty adjurations were as silver and gold plates set in a wall of dross.

The rear forty feet of this very commonplace floor was intricately and yet neatly divided into three small bedrooms, a living room which overlooked the backyard and wooden fences of yards no better than those at the back; also, a combination kitchen and dining room exactly ten feet square, and a store room for mission tracts, hymnals, boxes, trunks and whatever else of non-immediate use, but of assumed value, which the family owned. This particular small room lay immediately to the rear of the mission hall itself, and into it before or after speaking or at such times as a conference seemed important, both Mr. and Mrs. Griffiths were wont to retire— also at times to meditate or pray.

How often had Clyde and his sisters and younger brother seen his mother or father, or both, in conference with some derelict or semi-repentant soul who had come for advice or aid, most usually for aid. And here at times, when his mother's and father's financial difficulties were greatest, they were to be found thinking, or as Asa Griffiths was wont helplessly to say at times, "praying their way out," a rather ineffectual way, as Clyde began to think later.

And the whole neighborhood was so dreary and run-down that he hated the thought of living in it, let alone being part of a work that required constant appeals for aid, as well as constant prayer and thanksgiving to sustain it.

Mrs. Elvira Griffiths before she had married Asa had been nothing but an ignorant farm girl, brought up without much thought of religion of any kind. But having fallen in love with him, she had become inoculated with the virus of Evangelism and proselytizing which dominated him, and had followed him gladly and enthusiastically in all of his ventures and through all of his vagaries. Being rather flattered by the knowledge that she could speak and sing, her ability to sway and persuade and control people with the "word of God," as she saw it, she had become more or less pleased with herself on this account and so persuaded to continue.

Occasionally a small band of people followed the preachers to their mission, or learning of its existence through their street work, appeared there later—those odd and mentally disturbed or distrait souls who are to be found in every place. And it had been Clyde's compulsory duty throughout the years when he could not act for himself to be in attendance at these various meetings. And always he had been more irritated than favorably influenced by the types of men and

women who came here—mostly men—down-and-out laborers, loafers, drunkards, wastrels, the botched and helpless who
seemed to drift in, because they had no other place to go.
And they were always testifying as to how God or Christ or
Divine Grace had rescued them from this or that predicament—never how they had rescued any one else. And always
his father and mother were saying "Amen" and "Glory to
God," and singing hymns and afterward taking up a collection for the legitimate expenses of the hall—collections
which, as he surmised, were little enough—barely enough to
keep the various missions they had conducted in existence.

The one thing that really interested him in connection with
his parents was the existence somewhere in the east—in a
small city called Lycurgus, near Utica he understood—of an
uncle, a brother of his father's, who was plainly different
from all this. That uncle—Samuel Griffiths by name—was
rich. In one way and another, from casual remarks dropped
by his parents, Clyde had heard references to certain things
this particular uncle might do for a person, if he but would;
references to the fact that he was a shrewd, hard business
man; that he had a great house and a large factory in Lycurgus for the manufacture of collars and shirts, which employed
not less than three hundred people; that he had a son who
must be about Clyde's age, and several daughters, two at
least, all of whom must be, as Clyde imagined, living in luxury in Lycurgus. News of all this had apparently been
brought west in some way by people who knew Asa and his
father and brother. As Clyde pictured this uncle, he must be
a kind of Crœsus, living in ease and luxury there in the east,
while here in the west—Kansas City—he and his parents and
his brother and sisters were living in the same wretched and
hum-drum, hand-to-mouth state that had always characterized their lives.

But for this—apart from anything he might do for himself,
as he early began to see—there was no remedy. For at fifteen,
and even a little earlier, Clyde began to understand that his
education, as well as his sisters' and brother's, had been sadly
neglected. And it would be rather hard for him to overcome
this handicap, seeing that other boys and girls with more
money and better homes were being trained for special kinds

of work. How was one to get a start under such circumstances? Already when, at the age of thirteen, fourteen and fifteen, he began looking in the papers, which, being too worldly, had never been admitted to his home, he found that mostly skilled help was wanted, or boys to learn trades in which at the moment he was not very much interested. For true to the standard of the American youth, or the general American attitude toward life, he felt himself above the type of labor which was purely manual. What! Run a machine, lay bricks, learn to be a carpenter, or a plasterer, or a plumber, when boys no better than himself were clerks and druggists' assistants and bookkeepers and assistants in banks and real estate offices and such! Wasn't it menial, as miserable as the life he had thus far been leading, to wear old clothes and get up so early in the morning and do all the commonplace things such people had to do?

For Clyde was as vain and proud as he was poor. He was one of those interesting individuals who looked upon himself as a thing apart—never quite wholly and indissolubly merged with the family of which he was a member, and never with any profound obligations to those who had been responsible for his coming into the world. On the contrary, he was inclined to study his parents, not too sharply or bitterly, but with a very fair grasp of their qualities and capabilities. And yet, with so much judgment in that direction, he was never quite able—at least not until he had reached his sixteenth year—to formulate any policy in regard to himself, and then only in a rather fumbling and tentative way.

Incidentally by that time the sex lure or appeal had begun to manifest itself and he was already intensely interested and troubled by the beauty of the opposite sex, its attractions for him and his attraction for it. And, naturally and coincidentally, the matter of his clothes and his physical appearance had begun to trouble him not a little—how he looked and how other boys looked. It was painful to him now to think that his clothes were not right; that he was not as handsome as he might be, not as interesting. What a wretched thing it was to be born poor and not to have any one to do anything for you and not to be able to do so very much for yourself!

Casual examination of himself in mirrors whenever he

found them tended rather to assure him that he was not so bad-looking—a straight, well-cut nose, high white forehead, wavy, glossy, black hair, eyes that were black and rather melancholy at times. And yet the fact that his family was the unhappy thing that it was, that he had never had any real friends, and could not have any, as he saw it, because of the work and connection of his parents, was now tending more and more to induce a kind of mental depression or melancholia which promised not so well for his future. It served to make him rebellious and hence lethargic at times. Because of his parents, and in spite of his looks, which were really agreeable and more appealing than most, he was inclined to misinterpret the interested looks which were cast at him occasionally by young girls in very different walks of life from him—the contemptuous and yet rather inviting way in which they looked to see if he were interested or disinterested, brave or cowardly.

And yet, before he had ever earned any money at all, he had always told himself that if only he had a better collar, a nicer shirt, finer shoes, a good suit, a swell overcoat like some boys had! Oh, the fine clothes, the handsome homes, the watches, rings, pins that some boys sported; the dandies many youths of his years already were! Some parents of boys of his years actually gave them cars of their own to ride in. They were to be seen upon the principal streets of Kansas City flitting to and fro like flies. And pretty girls with them. And he had nothing. And he never had had.

And yet the world was so full of so many things to do—so many people were so happy and so successful. What was he to do? Which way to turn? What one thing to take up and master—something that would get him somewhere. He could not say. He did not know exactly. And these peculiar parents were in no way sufficiently equipped to advise him.

# Chapter III

ONE of the things that served to darken Clyde's mood just about the time when he was seeking some practical solution for himself, to say nothing of its profoundly disheartening effect on the Griffiths family as a whole, was the fact that his sister Esta, in whom he took no little interest (although they really had very little in common), ran away from home with an actor who happened to be playing in Kansas City and who took a passing fancy for her.

The truth in regard to Esta was that in spite of her guarded up-bringing, and the seeming religious and moral fervor which at times appeared to characterize her, she was just a sensuous, weak girl who did not by any means know yet what she thought. Despite the atmosphere in which she moved, essentially she was not of it. Like the large majority of those who profess and daily repeat the dogmas and creeds of the world, she had come into her practices and imagined attitude so insensibly from her earliest childhood on, that up to this time, and even later, she did not know the meaning of it all. For the necessity of thought had been obviated by advice and law, or "revealed" truth, and so long as other theories or situations and impulses of an external, or even internal, character did not arise to clash with these, she was safe enough. Once they did, however, it was a foregone conclusion that her religious notions, not being grounded on any conviction or temperamental bias of her own, were not likely to withstand the shock. So that all the while, and not unlike her brother Clyde, her thoughts as well as her emotions were wandering here and there—to love, to comfort—to things which in the main had little, if anything, to do with any self-abnegating and self-immolating religious theory. Within her was a chemism of dreams which somehow counteracted all they had to say.

Yet she had neither Clyde's force, nor, on the other hand, his resistance. She was in the main a drifter, with a vague yearning toward pretty dresses, hats, shoes, ribbons and the like, and superimposed above this, the religious theory or notion that she should not be. There were the long bright streets of a morning and afternoon after school or of an evening. The charm of certain girls swinging along together, arms locked, secrets a-whispering, or that of boys, clownish, yet revealing through their bounding ridiculous animality the force and meaning of that chemistry and urge toward mating which lies back of all youthful thought and action. And in herself, as from time to time she observed lovers or flirtation-seekers who lingered at street corners or about doorways, and who looked at her in a longing and seeking way, there was a stirring, a nerve plasm palpitation that spoke loudly for all the seemingly material things of life, not for the thin pleasantries of heaven.

And the glances drilled her like an invisible ray, for she was pleasing to look at and was growing more attractive hourly. And the moods in others awakened responsive moods in her, those rearranging chemisms upon which all the morality or immorality of the world is based.

And then one day, as she was coming home from school, a youth of that plausible variety known as "masher" engaged her in conversation, largely because of a look and a mood which seemed to invite it. And there was little to stay her, for she was essentially yielding, if not amorous. Yet so great had been her home drilling as to the need of modesty, circumspection, purity and the like, that on this occasion at least there was no danger of any immediate lapse. Only this attack once made, others followed, were accepted, or not so quickly fled from, and by degrees, these served to break down that wall of reserve which her home training had served to erect. She became secretive and hid her ways from her parents.

Youths occasionally walked and talked with her in spite of herself. They demolished that excessive shyness which had been hers, and which had served to put others aside for a time at least. She wished for other contacts—dreamed of some bright, gay, wonderful love of some kind, with some one.

Finally, after a slow but vigorous internal growth of mood and desire, there came this actor, one of those vain, handsome, animal personalities, all clothes and airs, but no morals (no taste, no courtesy or real tenderness even), but of compelling magnetism, who was able within the space of one brief week and a few meetings to completely befuddle and enmesh her so that she was really his to do with as he wished. And the truth was that he scarcely cared for her at all. To him, dull as he was, she was just another girl—fairly pretty, obviously sensuous and inexperienced, a silly who could be taken by a few soft words—a show of seemingly sincere affection, talk of the opportunity of a broader, freer life on the road, in other great cities, as his wife.

And yet his words were those of a lover who would be true forever. All she had to do, as he explained to her, was to come away with him and be his bride, at once—now. Delay was so vain when two such as they had met. There was difficulty about marriage here, which he could not explain—it related to friends—but in St. Louis he had a preacher friend who would wed them. She was to have new and better clothes than she had ever known, delicious adventures, love. She would travel with him and see the great world. She would never need to trouble more about anything save him; and while it was truth to her—the verbal surety of a genuine passion—to him it was the most ancient and serviceable type of blarney, often used before and often successful.

In a single week then, at odd hours, morning, afternoon and night, this chemic witchery was accomplished.

Coming home rather late one Saturday night in April from a walk which he had taken about the business heart, in order to escape the regular Saturday night mission services, Clyde found his mother and father worried about the whereabouts of Esta. She had played and sung as usual at this meeting. And all had seemed all right with her. After the meeting she had gone to her room, saying that she was not feeling very well and was going to bed early. But by eleven o'clock, when Clyde returned, her mother had chanced to look into her room and discovered that she was not there nor anywhere about the place. A certain bareness in connection with the room—some trinkets and dresses removed, an old and familiar suitcase gone—had first attracted her mother's attention. Then the house search proving that she was not there, Asa had gone outside to look up and down the street. She sometimes walked out alone, or sat or stood in front of the mission during its idle or closed hours.

This search revealing nothing, Clyde and he had walked to

a corner, then along Missouri Avenue. No Esta. At twelve
they returned and after that, naturally, the curiosity in regard
to her grew momentarily sharper.

At first they assumed that she might have taken an unex-
plained walk somewhere, but as twelve-thirty, and finally one,
and one-thirty, passed and no Esta, they were about to notify
the police, when Clyde, going into her room, saw a note
pinned to the pillow of her small wooden bed—a missive that
had escaped the eye of his mother. At once he went to it, curious and comprehending, for he had often wondered in what
way, assuming that he ever wished to depart surreptitiously,
he would notify his parents, for he knew they would never
countenance his departure unless they were permitted to supervise it in every detail. And now here was Esta missing, and
here was undoubtedly some such communication as he might
have left. He picked it up, eager to read it, but at that moment his mother came into the room and, seeing it in his
hand, exclaimed: "What's that? A note? Is it from her?" He
surrendered it and she unfolded it, reading it quickly. He
noted that her strong broad face, always tanned a reddish
brown, blanched as she turned away toward the outer room.
Her biggish mouth was now set in a firm, straight line. Her
large, strong hand shook the least bit as it held the small note
aloft.

"Asa!" she called, and then tramping into the next room
where he was, his frizzled grayish hair curling distractedly
above his round head, she said: "Read this."

Clyde, who had followed, saw him take it a little nervously
in his pudgy hand, his lips, always weak and beginning to
crinkle at the center with age, now working curiously. Any
one who had known his life's history would have said it was
the expression, slightly emphasized, with which he had received most of the untoward blows of his life in the past.

"Tst! Tst! Tst!" was the only sound he made at first, a suck-
ing sound of the tongue and palate—most weak and inadequate, it seemed to Clyde. Next there was another "Tst! Tst!
Tst!", his head beginning to shake from side to side. Then,
"Now, what do you suppose could have caused her to do
that?" Then he turned and gazed at his wife, who gazed
blankly in return. Then, walking to and fro, his hands behind

him, his short legs taking unconscious and queerly long steps, his head moving again, he gave vent to another ineffectual "Tst! Tst! Tst!"

Always the more impressive, Mrs. Griffiths now showed herself markedly different and more vital in this trying situation, a kind of irritation or dissatisfaction with life itself, along with an obvious physical distress, seeming to pass through her like a visible shadow. Once her husband had gotten up, she reached out and took the note, then merely glared at it again, her face set in hard yet stricken and disturbing lines. Her manner was that of one who is intensely disquieted and dissatisfied, one who fingers savagely at a material knot and yet cannot undo it, one who seeks restraint and freedom from complaint and yet who would complain bitterly, angrily. For behind her were all those years of religious work and faith, which somehow, in her poorly integrated conscience, seemed dimly to indicate that she should justly have been spared this. Where was her God, her Christ, at this hour when this obvious evil was being done? Why had He not acted for her? How was He to explain this? His Biblical promises! His perpetual guidance! His declared mercies!

In the face of so great a calamity, it was very hard for her, as Clyde could see, to get this straightened out, instantly at least. Although, as Clyde had come to know, it could be done eventually, of course. For in some blind, dualistic way both she and Asa insisted, as do all religionists, in disassociating God from harm and error and misery, while granting Him nevertheless supreme control. They would seek for something else—some malign, treacherous, deceiving power which, in the face of God's omniscience and omnipotence, still beguiles and betrays—and find it eventually in the error and perverseness of the human heart, which God has made, yet which He does not control, because He does not want to control it.

At the moment, however, only hurt and rage were with her, and yet her lips did not twitch as did Asa's, nor did her eyes show that profound distress which filled his. Instead she retreated a step and reëxamined the letter, almost angrily, then said to Asa: "She's run away with some one and she doesn't say——" Then she stopped suddenly, remembering the presence of the children—Clyde, Julia, and Frank, all present and all gazing curiously, intently, unbelievingly. "Come in here," she called to her husband, "I want to talk to you a minute. You children had better go on to bed. We'll be out in a minute."

With Asa then she retired quite precipitately to a small room back of the mission hall. They heard her click the electric bulb. Then their voices were heard in low converse, while Clyde and Julia and Frank looked at each other, although Frank, being so young—only ten—could scarcely be said to have comprehended fully. Even Julia hardly gathered the full import of it. But Clyde, because of his larger contact with life and his mother's statement ("She's run away with some one"), understood well enough. Esta had tired of all this, as had he. Perhaps there was some one, like one of those dandies whom he saw on the streets with the prettiest girls, with whom she had gone. But where? And what was he like? That note told something, and yet his mother had not let him see it. She had taken it away too quickly. If only he had looked first, silently and to himself!

"Do you suppose she's run away for good?" he asked Julia dubiously, the while his parents were out of the room, Julia herself looking so blank and strange.

"How should I know?" she replied a little irritably, troubled by her parents' distress and this secretiveness, as well as Esta's action. "She never said anything to me. I should think she'd be ashamed of herself if she has."

Julia, being colder emotionally than either Esta or Clyde, was more considerate of her parents in a conventional way, and hence sorrier. True, she did not quite gather what it meant, but she suspected something, for she had talked occasionally with girls, but in a very guarded and conservative way. Now, however, it was more the way in which Esta had chosen to leave, deserting her parents and her brothers and herself, that caused her to be angry with her, for why should she go and do anything which would distress her parents in this dreadful fashion. It was dreadful. The air was thick with misery.

And as his parents talked in their little room, Clyde brooded too, for he was intensely curious about life now. What was it Esta had really done? Was it, as he feared and thought, one of those dreadful runaway or sexually disagreeable affairs which the boys on the streets and at school were always slyly talking about? How shameful, if that were true! She might never come back. She had gone with some man. There was something wrong about that, no doubt, for a girl, anyhow, for all he had ever heard was that all decent contacts between boys and girls, men and women, led to but one thing—marriage. And now Esta, in addition to their other troubles, had gone and done this. Certainly this home life of theirs was pretty dark now, and it would be darker instead of brighter because of this.

Presently the parents came out, and then Mrs. Griffiths' face, if still set and constrained, was somehow a little different, less savage perhaps, more hopelessly resigned.

"Esta's seen fit to leave us, for a little while, anyhow," was all she said at first, seeing the children waiting curiously. "Now, you're not to worry about her at all, or think any more about it. She'll come back after a while, I'm sure. She has chosen to go her own way, for a time, for some reason. The Lord's will be done." ("Blessed be the name of the Lord!" interpolated Asa.) "I thought she was happy here with us, but apparently she wasn't. She must see something of the world for herself, I suppose." (Here Asa put in another Tst! Tst! Tst!) "But we mustn't harbor hard thoughts. That won't do any good now—only thoughts of love and kindness." Yet she said this with a kind of sternness that somehow belied it—a click of the voice, as it were. "We can only hope that she will soon see how foolish she has been, and unthinking, and come back. She can't prosper on the course she's going now. It isn't the Lord's way or will. She's too young and she's made a mistake. But we can forgive her. We must. Our hearts must be kept open, soft and tender." She talked as though she were addressing a meeting, but with a hard, sad, frozen face and voice. "Now, all of you go to bed. We can only pray now, and hope, morning, noon and night, that no evil will befall her. I wish she hadn't done that," she added, quite out of keeping with the rest of her statement and really not thinking of the children as present at all—just of Esta.

But Asa!

Such a father, as Clyde often thought, afterwards.

Apart from his own misery, he seemed only to note and be impressed by the more significant misery of his wife. During all this, he had stood foolishly to one side—short, gray, frizzled, inadequate.

"Well, blessed be the name of the Lord," he interpolated from time to time. "We must keep our hearts open. Yes, we mustn't judge. We must only hope for the best. Yes, yes! Praise the Lord—we must praise the Lord! Amen! Oh, yes! Tst! Tst! Tst!"

"If any one asks where she is," continued Mrs. Griffiths after a time, quite ignoring her spouse and addressing the children, who had drawn near her, "we will say that she has gone on a visit to some of my relatives back in Tonawanda. That won't be the truth, exactly, but then we don't know where she is or what the truth is—and she may come back. So we must not say or do anything that will injure her until we know."

"Yes, praise the Lord!" called Asa, feebly.

"So if any one should inquire at any time, until we know, we will say that."

"Sure," put in Clyde, helpfully, and Julia added, "All right."

Mrs. Griffiths paused and looked firmly and yet apologetically at her children. Asa, for his part, emitted another "Tst! Tst! Tst!" and then the children were waved to bed.

At that, Clyde, who really wanted to know what Esta's letter had said, but was convinced from long experience that his mother would not let him know unless she chose, returned to his room again, for he was tired. Why didn't they search more if there was hope of finding her? Where was she now—at this minute? On some train somewhere? Evidently she didn't want to be found. She was probably dissatisfied, just as he was. Here he was, thinking so recently of going away somewhere himself, wondering how the family would take it, and now she had gone before him. How would that affect his point of view and action in the future? Truly, in spite of his father's and mother's misery, he could not see that her going was such a calamity, not from the *going* point of view, at any rate. It was only another something which hinted that things were not right here. Mission work was nothing. All this religious emotion and talk was not so much either. It hadn't saved Esta. Evidently, like himself, she didn't believe so much in it, either.

# Chapter IV

THE EFFECT of this particular conclusion was to cause Clyde to think harder than ever about himself. And the principal result of his thinking was that he must do something for himself and soon. Up to this time the best he had been able to do was to work at such odd jobs as befall all boys between their twelfth and fifteenth years: assisting a man who had a paper route during the summer months of one year, working in the basement of a five-and-ten cent store all one summer long, and on Saturdays, for a period during the winter, opening boxes and unpacking goods, for which he received the munificent sum of five dollars a week, a sum which at the time seemed almost a fortune. He felt himself rich and, in the face of the opposition of his parents, who were opposed to the theater and motion pictures also, as being not only worldly, but sinful, he could occasionally go to one or another of those—in the gallery—a form of diversion which he had to conceal from his parents. Yet that did not deter him. He felt that he had a right to go with his own money; also to take his younger brother Frank, who was glad enough to go with him and say nothing.

Later in the same year, wishing to get out of school because he already felt himself very much belated in the race, he secured a place as an assistant to a soda water clerk in one of the cheaper drug stores of the city, which adjoined a theater and enjoyed not a little patronage of this sort. A sign—"Boy Wanted"—since it was directly on his way to school, first interested him. Later, in conversation with the young man whose assistant he was to be, and from whom he was to learn the trade, assuming that he was sufficiently willing and facile, he gathered that if he mastered this art, he might make as much as fifteen and even eighteen dollars a week. It was rumored that Stroud's at the corner of 14th and Baltimore Streets paid that much to two of their clerks. The particular store to which he was applying paid only twelve, the standard salary of most places.

But to acquire this art, as he was now informed, required

time and the friendly help of an expert. If he wished to come
here and work for five to begin with—well, six, then, since his
face fell—he might soon expect to know a great deal about
the art of mixing sweet drinks and decorating a large variety
of ice-creams with liquid sweets, thus turning them into sun-
daes. For the time being apprenticeship meant washing and
polishing all the machinery and implements of this particular
counter, to say nothing of opening and sweeping out the
store at so early an hour as seven-thirty, dusting, and deliver-
ing such orders as the owner of this drug store chose to send
out by him. At such idle moments as his immediate superior—a Mr. Sieberling—twenty, dashing, self-confident, talka-
tive, was too busy to fill all the orders, he might be called
upon to mix such minor drinks—lemonades, coca-colas and
the like—as the trade demanded.

Yet this interesting position, after due consultation with his
mother, he decided to take. For one thing, it would provide
him, as he suspected, with all the ice-cream sodas he desired,
free—an advantage not to be disregarded. In the next place,
as he saw it at the time, it was an open door to a trade—
something which he lacked. Further, and not at all disadvan-
tageously as he saw it, this store required his presence at night
as late as twelve o'clock, with certain hours off during the day
to compensate for this. And this took him out of his home at
night—out of the ten-o'clock-boy class at last. They could
not ask him to attend any meetings save on Sunday, and not
even then, since he was supposed to work Sunday afternoons
and evenings.

Next, the clerk who manipulated this particular soda fountain, quite regularly received passes from the manager of the
theater next door, and into the lobby of which one door to
the drug-store gave—a most fascinating connection to Clyde.
It seemed so interesting to be working for a drug store thus
intimately connected with a theater.

And best of all, as Clyde now found to his pleasure, and yet
despair at times, the place was visited, just before and after the
show on matinée days, by bevies of girls, single and en suite,
who sat at the counter and giggled and chattered and gave
their hair and their complexions last perfecting touches before
the mirror. And Clyde, callow and inexperienced in the ways

of the world, and those of the opposite sex, was never weary
of observing the beauty, the daring, the self-sufficiency and
the sweetness of these, as he saw them. For the first time in
his life, while he busied himself with washing glasses, filling
the ice-cream and syrup containers, arranging the lemons and
oranges in the trays, he had an almost uninterrupted opportunity of studying these girls at close range. The wonder of
them! For the most part, they were so well-dressed and
smart-looking—the rings, pins, furs, delightful hats, pretty
shoes they wore. And so often he overheard them discussing
such interesting things—parties, dances, dinners, the shows
they had seen, the places in or near Kansas City to which they
were soon going, the difference between the styles of this year
and last, the fascination of certain actors and actresses—principally actors—who were now playing or soon coming to the
city. And to this day, in his own home he had heard nothing
of all this.

And very often one or another of these young beauties was
accompanied by some male in evening suit, dress shirt, high
hat, bow tie, white kid gloves and patent leather shoes, a costume which at that time Clyde felt to be the last word in all
true distinction, beauty, gallantry and bliss. To be able to
wear such a suit with such ease and air! To be able to talk to
a girl after the manner and with the sang-froid of some of
these gallants! What a true measure of achievement! No
good-looking girl, as it then appeared to him, would have
anything to do with him if he did not possess this standard of
equipment. It was plainly necessary—the thing. And once he
did attain it—was able to wear such clothes as these—well,
then was he not well set upon the path that leads to all the
blisses? All the joys of life would then most certainly be spread
before him. The friendly smiles! The secret handclasps,
maybe—an arm about the waist of some one or another—a
kiss—a promise of marriage—and then, and then!

And all this as a revealing flash after all the years of walking
through the streets with his father and mother to public
prayer meeting, the sitting in chapel and listening to queer
and nondescript individuals—depressing and disconcerting
people—telling how Christ had saved them and what God
had done for them. You bet he would get out of that now. He

would work and save his money and be somebody. Decidedly this simple and yet idyllic compound of the commonplace had all the luster and wonder of a spiritual transfiguration, the true mirage of the lost and thirsting and seeking victim of the desert.

However, the trouble with this particular position, as time speedily proved, was that much as it might teach him of mixing drinks and how to eventually earn twelve dollars a week, it was no immediate solvent for the yearnings and ambitions that were already gnawing at his vitals. For Albert Sieberling, his immediate superior, was determined to keep as much of his knowledge, as well as the most pleasant parts of the tasks, to himself. And further he was quite at one with the druggist for whom they worked in thinking that Clyde, in addition to assisting him about the fountain, should run such errands as the druggist desired, which kept Clyde industriously employed for nearly all the hours he was on duty.

Consequently there was no immediate result to all this. Clyde could see no way to dressing better than he did. Worse, he was haunted by the fact that he had very little money and very few contacts and connections—so few that, outside his own home, he was lonely and not so very much less than lonely there. The flight of Esta had thrown a chill over the religious work there, and because, as yet, she had not returned—the family, as he now heard, was thinking of breaking up here and moving, for want of a better idea, to Denver, Colorado. But Clyde, by now, was convinced that he did not wish to accompany them. What was the good of it, he asked himself? There would be just another mission there, the same as this one.

He had always lived at home—in the rooms at the rear of the mission in Bickel Street, but he hated it. And since his eleventh year, during all of which time his family had been residing in Kansas City, he had been ashamed to bring boy friends to or near it. For that reason he had always avoided boy friends, and had walked and played very much alone—or with his brothers and sisters.

But now that he was sixteen and old enough to make his own way, he ought to be getting out of this. And yet he was earning almost nothing—not enough to live on, if he were alone—and he had not as yet developed sufficient skill or courage to get anything better.

Nevertheless when his parents began to talk of moving to Denver, and suggested that he might secure work out there, never assuming for a moment that he would not want to go, he began to throw out hints to the effect that it might be better if he did not. He liked Kansas City. What was the use of changing? He had a job now and he might get something better. But his parents, bethinking themselves of Esta and the fate that had overtaken her, were not a little dubious as to the outcome of such early adventuring on his part alone. Once they were away, where would he live? With whom? What sort of influence would enter his life, who would be at hand to aid and council and guide him in the straight and narrow path, as they had done? It was something to think about.

But spurred by this imminence of Denver, which now daily seemed to be drawing nearer, and the fact that not long after this Mr. Sieberling, owing to his too obvious gallantries in connection with the fair sex, lost his place in the drug store, and Clyde came by a new and bony and chill superior who did not seem to want him as an assistant, he decided to quit—not at once, but rather to see, on such errands as took him out of the store, if he could not find something else. Incidentally in so doing, looking here and there, he one day thought he would speak to the manager of the fountain which was connected with the leading drug store in the principal hotel of the city—the latter a great twelve-story affair, which represented, as he saw it, the quintessence of luxury and ease. Its windows were always so heavily curtained; the main entrance (he had never ventured to look beyond that) was a splendiferous combination of a glass and iron awning, coupled with a marble corridor lined with palms. Often he had passed here, wondering with boyish curiosity what the nature of the life of such a place might be. Before its doors, so many taxis and automobiles were always in waiting.

To-day, being driven by the necessity of doing something for himself, he entered the drug store which occupied the principal corner, facing 14th street at Baltimore, and finding a girl cashier in a small glass cage near the door, asked of her who was in charge of the soda fountain. Interested by his tentative and uncertain manner, as well as his deep and rather appealing eyes, and instinctively judging that he was looking for something to do, she observed: "Why, Mr. Secor, there, the manager of the store." She nodded in the direction of a short, meticulously dressed man of about thirty-five, who was arranging an especial display of toilet novelties on the top of a glass case. Clyde approached him, and being still very dubious as to how one went about getting anything in life, and finding him engrossed in what he was doing, stood first on one foot and then on the other, until at last, sensing some one was hovering about for something, the man turned: "Well?" he queried.

"You don't happen to need a soda fountain helper, do you?" Clyde cast at him a glance that said as plain as anything could, "If you have any such place, I wish you would please give it to me. I need it."

"No, no, no," replied this individual, who was blond and vigorous and by nature a little irritable and contentious. He was about to turn away, but seeing a flicker of disappointment and depression pass over Clyde's face, he turned and added, "Ever work in a place like this before?"

"No place as fine as this. No, sir," replied Clyde, rather fancifully moved by all that was about him. "I'm working now down at Mr. Klinkle's store at 7th and Brooklyn, but it isn't anything like this one and I'd like to get something better if I could."

"Uh," went on his interviewer, rather pleased by the innocent tribute to the superiority of his store. "Well, that's reasonable enough. But there isn't anything here right now that I could offer you. We don't make many changes. But if you'd like to be a bell-boy, I can tell you where you might get a place. They're looking for an extra boy in the hotel inside there right now. The captain of the boys was telling me he was in need of one. I should think that would be as good as helping about a soda fountain, any day."

Then seeing Clyde's face suddenly brighten, he added: "But you mustn't say that I sent you, because I don't know you. Just ask for Mr. Squires inside there, under the stairs, and he can tell you all about it."

At the mere mention of work in connection with so imposing an institution as the Green-Davidson, and the possibility
of his getting it, Clyde first stared, felt himself tremble the
least bit with excitement, then thanking his advisor for his
kindness, went direct to a green-marbled doorway which
opened from the rear of this drug-store into the lobby of the
hotel. Once through it, he beheld a lobby, the like of which,
for all his years but because of the timorous poverty that had
restrained him from exploring such a world, was more arresting, quite, than anything he had seen before. It was all so
lavish. Under his feet was a checkered black-and-white marble
floor. Above him a coppered and stained and gilded ceiling.
And supporting this, a veritable forest of black marble
columns as highly polished as the floor—glassy smooth. And
between the columns which ranged away toward three separate entrances, one right, one left and one directly forward toward Dalrymple Avenue—were lamps, statuary, rugs, palms,
chairs, divans, tête-à-têtes—a prodigal display. In short it was
compact, of all that gauche luxury of appointment which, as
some one once sarcastically remarked, was intended to supply
"exclusiveness to the masses." Indeed, for an essential hotel in
a great and successful American commercial city, it was almost
too luxurious. Its rooms and hall and lobbies and restaurants
were entirely too richly furnished, without the saving grace of
either simplicity or necessity.

As Clyde stood, gazing about the lobby, he saw a large
company of people—some women and children, but principally men as he could see—either walking or standing about
and talking or idling in the chairs, side by side or alone. And
in heavily draped and richly furnished alcoves where were
writing-tables, newspaper files, a telegraph office, a haberdasher's shop, and a florist's stand, were other groups. There
was a convention of dentists in the city, not a few of whom,
with their wives and children, were gathered here; but to
Clyde, who was not aware of this nor of the methods and
meanings of conventions, this was the ordinary, everyday appearance of this hotel.

He gazed about in awe and amazement, then remembering
the name of Squires, he began to look for him in his office
"under the stairs." To his right was a grand double-winged

black-and-white staircase which swung in two separate flights and with wide, generous curves from the main floor to the one above. And between these great flights was evidently the office of the hotel, for there were many clerks there. But behind the nearest flight, and close to the wall through which he had come, was a tall desk, at which stood a young man of about his own age in a maroon uniform bright with many brass buttons. And on his head was a small, round, pill-box cap, which was cocked jauntily over one ear. He was busy making entries with a lead pencil in a book which lay open before him. Various other boys about his own age, and uniformed as he was, were seated upon a long bench near him, or were to be seen darting here and there, sometimes returning to this one with a slip of paper or a key or note of some kind, and then seating themselves upon the bench to await another call apparently, which seemed to come swiftly enough. A telephone upon the small desk at which stood the uniformed youth was almost constantly buzzing, and after ascertaining what was wanted, this youth struck a small bell before him, or called "front," to which the first boy on the bench, responded. Once called, they went hurrying up one or the other stairs or toward one of the several entrances or elevators, and almost invariably were to be seen escorting individuals whose bags and suitcases and overcoats and golf sticks they carried. There were others who disappeared and returned, carrying drinks on trays or some package or other, which they were taking to one of the rooms above. Plainly this was the work that he should be called upon to do, assuming that he would be so fortunate as to connect himself with such an institution as this.

And it was all so brisk and enlivening that he wished that he might be so fortunate as to secure a position here. But would he be? And where was Mr. Squires? He approached the youth at the small desk: "Do you know where I will find Mr. Squires?" he asked.

"Here he comes now," replied the youth, looking up and examining Clyde with keen, gray eyes.

Clyde gazed in the direction indicated, and saw approaching a brisk and dapper and decidedly sophisticated-looking person of perhaps twenty-nine or thirty years of age. He was so very slender, keen, hatchet-faced and well-dressed that Clyde was not only impressed but overawed at once—a very shrewd and cunning-looking person. His nose was so long and thin, his eyes so sharp, his lips thin, and chin pointed.

"Did you see that tall, gray-haired man with the Scotch plaid shawl who went through here just now?" he paused to say to his assistant at the desk. The assistant nodded. "Well, they tell me that's the Earl of Landreil. He just came in this morning with fourteen trunks and four servants. Can you beat it! He's somebody in Scotland. That isn't the name he travels under, though, I hear. He's registered as Mr. Blunt. Can you beat that English stuff? They can certainly lay on the class, eh?"

"You said it!" replied his assistant deferentially.

He turned for the first time, glimpsing Clyde, but paying no attention to him. His assistant came to Clyde's aid.

"That young fella there is waiting to see you," he explained.

"You want to see me?" queried the captain of the bell-hops, turning to Clyde, and observing his none-too-good clothes, at the same time making a comprehensive study of him.

"The gentleman in the drug store," began Clyde, who did not quite like the looks of the man before him, but was determined to present himself as agreeably as possible, "was saying—that is, he said that I might ask you if there was any chance here for me as a bell-boy. I'm working now at Klinkle's drug-store at 7th and Brooklyn, as a helper, but I'd like to get out of that and he said you might—that is—he thought you had a place open now." Clyde was so flustered and disturbed by the cool, examining eyes of the man before him that he could scarcely get his breath properly, and swallowed hard.

For the first time in his life, it occurred to him that if he wanted to get on he ought to insinuate himself into the good graces of people—do or say something that would make them like him. So now he contrived an eager, ingratiating smile, which he bestowed on Mr. Squires, and added: "If you'd like to give me a chance, I'd try very hard and I'd be very willing."

The man before him merely looked at him coldly, but being the soul of craft and self-acquisitiveness in a petty way, and rather liking anybody who had the skill and the will to be diplomatic, he now put aside an impulse to shake his head negatively, and observed: "But you haven't had any training in this work."

"No, sir, but couldn't I pick it up pretty quick if I tried hard?"

"Well, let me see," observed the head of the bell-hops, scratching his head dubiously. "I haven't any time to talk to you now. Come around Monday afternoon. I'll see you then." He turned on his heel and walked away.

Clyde, left alone in this fashion, and not knowing just what it meant, stared, wondering. Was it really true that he had been invited to come back on Monday? Could it be possible that—— He turned and hurried out, thrilling from head to toe. The idea! He had asked this man for a place in the very finest hotel in Kansas City and he had asked him to come back and see him on Monday. Gee! what would that mean? Could it be possible that he would be admitted to such a grand world as this—and that so speedily? Could it really be?

# Chapter V

THE imaginative flights of Clyde in connection with all this—his dreams of what it might mean for him to be connected with so glorious an institution—can only be suggested. For his ideas of luxury were in the main so extreme and mistaken and gauche—mere wanderings of a repressed and unsatisfied fancy, which as yet had had nothing but imaginings to feed it.

He went back to his old duties at the drug-store—to his home after hours in order to eat and sleep—but now for the balance of this Friday and Saturday and Sunday and Monday until late in the day, he walked on air, really. His mind was not on what he was doing, and several times his superior at the drug-store had to remind him to "wake-up." And after hours, instead of going directly home, he walked north to the corner of 14th and Baltimore, where stood this great hotel, and looked at it. There, at midnight even, before each of the three principal entrances—one facing each of three streets—was a doorman in a long maroon coat with many buttons and a high-rimmed and long-visored maroon cap. And inside, behind looped and fluted French silk curtains, were the still blazing lights, the à la carte dining-room and the American grill in the basement near one corner still open. And about them were many taxis and cars. And there was music always—from somewhere.

After surveying it all this Friday night and again on Saturday and Sunday morning, he returned on Monday afternoon at the suggestion of Mr. Squires and was greeted by that individual rather crustily, for by then he had all but forgotten him. But seeing that at the moment he was actually in need of help, and being satisfied that Clyde might be of service, he led him into his small office under the stair, where, with a very superior manner and much actual indifference, he proceeded to question him as to his parentage, where he lived, at what he had worked before and where, what his father did for a living—a poser that for Clyde, for he was proud and so ashamed to admit that his parents conducted a mission and preached on the streets. Instead he replied (which was true at times) that his father canvassed for a washing machine and wringer company—and on Sundays preached—a religious revelation, which was not at all displeasing to this master of boys who were inclined to be anything but home-loving and conservative. Could he bring a reference from where he now was? He could.

Mr. Squires proceeded to explain that this hotel was very strict. Too many boys, on account of the scenes and the show here, the contact with undue luxury to which they were not accustomed—though these were not the words used by Mr. Squires—were inclined to lose their heads and go wrong. He was constantly being forced to discharge boys who, because they made a little extra money, didn't know how to conduct themselves. He must have boys who were willing, civil, prompt, courteous to everybody. They must be clean and neat about their persons and clothes and show up promptly— on the dot—and in good condition for the work every day. And any boy who got to thinking that because he made a little money he could flirt with anybody or talk back, or go off on parties at night, and then not show up on time or too tired to be quick and bright, needn't think that he would be here long. He would be fired, and that promptly. He would not tolerate any nonsense. That must be understood now, once and for all.

Clyde nodded assent often and interpolated a few eager "yes, sirs" and "no, sirs," and assured him at the last that it was the furtherest thing from his thoughts and temperament to dream of any such high crimes and misdemeanors as he had outlined. Mr. Squires then proceeded to explain that this hotel only paid fifteen dollars a month and board—at the servant's table in the basement—to any bell-boy at any time. But, and this information came as a most amazing revelation to Clyde, every guest for whom any of these boys did anything—carried a bag or delivered a pitcher of water or did anything—gave him a tip, and often quite a liberal one—a dime, fifteen cents, a quarter, sometimes more. And these tips, as Mr. Squires explained, taken all together, averaged from four to six dollars a day—not less and sometimes more —most amazing pay, as Clyde now realized. His heart gave an enormous bound and was near to suffocating him at the mere mention of so large a sum. From four to six dollars! Why, that was twenty-eight to forty-two dollars a week! He could scarcely believe it. And that in addition to the fifteen dollars a month and board. And there was no charge, as Mr. Squires now explained, for the handsome uniforms the boys wore. But it might not be worn or taken out of the place. His hours, as Mr. Squires now proceeded to explain, would be as follows: On Mondays, Wednesdays, Fridays and Sundays, he was to work from six in the morning until noon, and then, with six hours off, from six in the evening until midnight. On Tuesdays, Thursdays and Saturdays, he need only work from noon until six, thus giving him each alternate afternoon or evening to himself. But all his meals were to be taken outside his working hours and he was to report promptly in uniform for line-up and inspection by his superior exactly ten minutes before the regular hours of his work began at each watch.

As for some other things which were in his mind at the time, Mr. Squires said nothing. There were others, as he knew, who would speak for him. Instead he went on to add, and then quite climactically for Clyde at that time, who had been sitting as one in a daze: "I suppose you are ready to go to work now, aren't you?"

"Yes, sir, yes, sir," he replied.

"Very good!" Then he got up and opened the door which had shut them in. "Oscar," he called to a boy seated at the head of the bell-boy bench, to which a tallish, rather oversized youth in a tight, neat-looking uniform responded with alacrity. "Take this young man here—Clyde Griffiths is your name, isn't it?— up to the wardrobe on the twelfth and see if Jacobs can find a suit to fit. But if he can't, tell him to alter it by to-morrow. I think the one Silsbee wore ought to be about right for him."

Then he turned to his assistant at the desk who was at the moment looking on. "I'm giving him a trial, anyhow," he commented. "Have one of the boys coach him a little to-night or whenever he starts in. Go ahead, Oscar," he called to the boy in charge of Clyde. "He's green at this stuff, but I think he'll do," he added to his assistant, as Clyde and Oscar disappeared in the direction of one of the elevators. Then he walked off to have Clyde's name entered upon the payroll.

In the meantime, Clyde, in tow of this new mentor, was listening to a line of information such as never previously had come to his ears anywhere.

"You needn't be frightened, if you ain't never worked at anything like dis before," began this youth, whose last name was Hegglund as Clyde later learned, and who hailed from Jersey City, New Jersey, exotic lingo, gestures and all. He was tall, vigorous, sandy-haired, freckled, genial and voluble. They had entered upon an elevator labeled "employees." "It ain't so hard. I got my first job in Buffalo t'ree years ago and I never knowed a t'ing about it up to dat time. All you gotta do is to watch de udders an' see how dey do, see. Yu get dat, do you?"

Clyde, whose education was not a little superior to that of his guide, commented quite sharply in his own mind on the use of such words as "knowed," and "gotta"—also upon "t'ing," "dat," "udders," and so on, but so grateful was he for any courtesy at this time that he was inclined to forgive his obviously kindly mentor anything for his geniality.

"Watch whoever's doin' anyt'ing, at first, see, till you git to know, see. Dat's de way. When de bell rings, if you're at de head of de bench, it's your turn, see, an' you jump up and go quick. Dey like you to be quick around here, see. An' whenever you see any one come in de door or out of an elevator wit a bag, an' you're at de head of de bench, you jump, wedder de captain rings de bell or calls 'front' or not. Sometimes he's busy or ain't lookin' an' he wants you to do dat, see. Look sharp, cause if you don't get no bags, you don't get no tips, see. Everybody dat has a bag or anyt'ing has to have it carried for 'em, unless dey won't let you have it, see.

"But be sure and wait somewhere near de desk for whoever comes in until dey sign up for a room," he rattled on as they ascended in the elevator. "Most every one takes a room. Den de clerk'll give you de key an' after dat all you gotta do is to carry up de bags to de room. Den all you gotta do is to turn on de lights in de batroom and closet, if dere is one, so dey'll know where dey are, see. An' den raise de curtains in de day time or lower 'em at night, an' see if dere's towels in de room, so you can tell de maid if dere ain't, and den if dey don't give you no tip, you gotta go, only most times, unless you draw a stiff, all you gotta do is hang back a little—make a stall, see—fumble wit de door-key or try de transom, see. Den, if dey're any good, dey'll hand you a tip. If dey don't, you're out, dat's all, see. You can't even look as dough you was sore, dough—nottin' like dat, see. Den you come down an' unless dey wants ice-water or somepin, you're troo, see. It's back to de bench, quick. Dere ain't much to it. Only you gotta be quick all de time, see, and not let any one get by you comin' or goin'—dat's de main t'ing.

"An' after dey give you your uniform, an' you go to work, don't forgit to give de captain a dollar after every watch before you leave, see—two dollars on de day you has two watches, and a dollar on de day you has one, see? Dat's de way it is here. We work togedder like dat, here, an' you gotta do dat if you wanta hold your job. But dat's all. After dat all de rest is yours."

Clyde saw.

A part of his twenty-four or thirty-two dollars as he figured it was going glimmering, apparently—eleven or twelve all told—but what of it! Would there not be twelve or fifteen or even more left? And there were his meals and his uniform. Kind Heaven! What a realization of paradise! What a consummation of luxury!

Mr. Hegglund of Jersey City escorted him to the twelfth floor and into a room where they found on guard a wizened and grizzled little old man of doubtful age and temperament, who forthwith outfitted Clyde with a suit that was so near a fit that, without further orders, it was not deemed necessary to alter it. And trying on various caps, there was one that fitted him—a thing that sat most rakishly over one ear—only, as Hegglund informed him, "You'll have to get dat hair of yours cut. Better get it clipped behind. It's too long." And with that Clyde himself had been in mental agreement before he spoke. His hair certainly did not look right in the new cap. He hated it now. And going downstairs, and reporting to Mr. Whipple, Mr. Squires' assistant, the latter had said: "Very well. It fits all right, does it? Well, then, you go on here at six. Report at five-thirty and be here in your uniform at five-forty-five for inspection."

Whereupon Clyde, being advised by Hegglund to go then

and there to get his uniform and take it to the dressing-room in the basement, and get his locker from the locker-man, he did so, and then hurried most nervously out—first to get a hair-cut and afterwards to report to his family on his great luck.

He was to be a bell-boy in the great Hotel Green-Davidson. He was to wear a uniform and a handsome one. He was to make—but he did not tell his mother at first what he was to make, truly—but more than eleven or twelve at first, anyhow, he guessed—he could not be sure. For now, all at once, he saw economic independence ahead for himself, if not for his family, and he did not care to complicate it with any claims which a confession as to his real salary would most certainly inspire. But he did say that he was to have his meals free—because that meant eating away from home, which was what he wished. And in addition he was to live and move always in the glorious atmosphere of this hotel—not to have to go home ever before twelve, if he did not wish—to have good clothes—interesting company, maybe—a good time, gee!

And as he hurried on about his various errands now, it occurred to him as a final and shrewd and delicious thought that he need not go home on such nights as he wished to go to a theater or anything like that. He could just stay down-town and say he had to work. And that with free meals and good clothes—think of that!

The mere thought of all this was so astonishing and entrancing that he could not bring himself to think of it too much. He must wait and see. He must wait and see just how much he would make here in this perfectly marvelous-marvelous realm.

# Chapter VI

A<small>ND</small> as conditions stood, the extraordinary economic and
social inexperience of the Griffiths—Asa and Elvira—
dovetailed all too neatly with his dreams. For neither Asa nor
Elvira had the least knowledge of the actual character of the
work upon which he was about to enter, scarcely any more
than he did, or what it might mean to him morally, imagina-
tively, financially, or in any other way. For neither of them had
ever stopped in a hotel above the fourth class in all their days.
Neither one had ever eaten in a restaurant of a class that
catered to other than individuals of their own low financial
level. That there could be any other forms of work or contact
than those involved in carrying the bags of guests to and from
the door of a hotel to its office, and back again, for a boy of
Clyde's years and temperament, never occurred to them. And
it was naïvely assumed by both that the pay for such work
must of necessity be very small anywhere, say five or six dollars a week, and so actually below Clyde's deserts and his
years.

And in view of this, Mrs. Griffiths, who was more practical
than her husband at all times, and who was intensely interested in Clyde's economic welfare, as well as that of her other
children, was actually wondering why Clyde should of a sudden become so enthusiastic about changing to this new situation, which, according to his own story, involved longer
hours and not so very much more pay, if any. To be sure, he
had already suggested that it might lead to some superior position in the hotel, some clerkship or other, but he did not
know when that would be, and the other had promised rather
definite fulfillment somewhat earlier—as to money, anyhow.

But seeing him rush in on Monday afternoon and announce that he had secured the place and that forthwith he
must change his tie and collar and get his hair cut and go
back and report, she felt better about it. For never before had
she seen him so enthusiastic about anything, and it was something to have him more content with himself—not so moody,
as he was at times.

Yet, the hours which he began to maintain now—from six in the morning until midnight—with only an occasional early return on such evenings as he chose to come home when he was not working—and when he troubled to explain that he had been let off a little early—together with a certain eager and restless manner—a desire to be out and away from his home at nearly all such moments as he was not in bed or dressing or undressing, puzzled his mother and Asa, also. The hotel! The hotel! He must always hurry off to the hotel, and all that he had to report was that he liked it ever so much, and that he was doing all right, he thought. It was nicer work than working around a soda fountain, and he might be making more money pretty soon—he couldn't tell—but as for more than that he either wouldn't or couldn't say.

And all the time the Griffiths—father and mother—were feeling that because of the affair in connection with Esta, they should really be moving away from Kansas City—should go to Denver. And now more than ever, Clyde was insisting that he did not want to leave Kansas City. They might go, but he had a pretty good job now and wanted to stick to it. And if they left, he could get a room somewhere—and would be all right—a thought which did not appeal to them at all.

But in the meantime what an enormous change in Clyde's life. Beginning with that first evening, when at 5:45, he appeared before Mr. Whipple, his immediate superior, and was approved—not only because of the fit of his new uniform, but for his general appearance—the world for him had changed entirely. Lined up with seven others in the servants' hall, immediately behind the general offices in the lobby, and inspected by Mr. Whipple, the squad of eight marched at the stroke of six through a door that gave into the lobby on the other side of the staircase from where stood Mr. Whipple's desk, then about and in front of the general registration office to the long bench on the other side. A Mr. Barnes, who alternated with Mr. Whipple, then took charge of the assistant captain's desk, and the boys seated themselves—Clyde at the foot—only to be called swiftly and in turn to perform this, that and the other service—while the relieved squad of Mr. Whipple was led away into the rear servants' hall as before, where they disbanded.

"Cling!"

The bell on the room clerk's desk had sounded and the first boy was going.

"Cling!" It sounded again and a second boy leaped to his feet.

"Front!"—"Center door!" called Mr. Barnes, and a third boy was skidding down the long marble floor toward that entrance to seize the bags of an incoming guest, whose white whiskers and youthful, bright tweed suit were visible to Clyde's uninitiated eyes a hundred feet away. A mysterious and yet sacred vision—a tip!

"Front!" It was Mr. Barnes calling again. "See what 913 wants—ice-water, I guess." And a fourth boy was gone.

Clyde, steadily moving up along the bench and adjoining Hegglund, who had been detailed to instruct him a little, was all eyes and ears and nerves. He was so tense that he could hardly breathe, and fidgeted and jerked until finally Hegglund exclaimed: "Now, don't git excited. Just hold your horses, will yuh? You'll be all right. You're jist like I was when I begun—all noives. But dat ain't de way. Easy's what you gotta be aroun' here. An' you wants to look as dough you wasn't seein' nobody nowhere—just lookin' to what ya got before ya."

"Front!" Mr. Barnes again. Clyde was scarcely able to keep his mind on what Hegglund was saying. "115 wants some writing paper and pens." A fifth boy had gone.

"Where do you get writing paper and pens if they want em?" He pleaded of his instructor, as one who was about to die might plead.

"Off'n de key desk, I toldja. He's to de left over dere. He'll give 'em to ya. An' you gits ice-water in de hall we lined up in just a minute ago—at dat end over dere, see—you'll see a little door. You gotta give dat guy in dere a dime oncet in a while or he'll get sore."

"Cling!" The room clerk's bell. A sixth boy had gone without a word to supply some order in that direction.

"And now remember," continued Hegglund, seeing that he himself was next, and cautioning him for the last time, "if dey wants drinks of any kind, you get 'em in de grill over dere off'n de dining-room. An' be sure and git de names of de drinks straight or dey'll git sore. An' if it's a room you're showing, pull de shades down to-night and turn on de lights. An' if it's anyt'ing from de dinin'-room you gotta see de head-waiter—he gets de tip, see."

"Front!" He was up and gone.

And Clyde was number one. And number four was already seating himself again by his side—but looking shrewdly around to see if anybody was wanted anywhere.

"Front!" It was Mr. Barnes. Clyde was up and before him, grateful that it was no one coming in with bags, but worried for fear it might be something that he would not understand or could not do quickly.

"See what 882 wants." Clyde was off toward one of the two elevators marked, "employees," the proper one to use, he thought, because he had been taken to the twelfth floor that way, but another boy stepping out from one of the fast passenger elevators cautioned him as to his mistake.

"Goin' to a room?" he called. "Use the guest elevators. Them's for the servants or anybody with bundles."

Clyde hastened to cover his mistake. "Eight," he called. There being no one else on the elevator with them, the negro elevator boy in charge of the car saluted him at once.

"You'se new, ain't you? I ain't seen you around here befo'."

"Yes, I just came on," replied Clyde.

"Well, you won't hate it here," commented this youth in the most friendly way. "No one hates this house, I'll say. Eight did you say?" He stopped the car and Clyde stepped out. He was too nervous to think to ask the direction and now began looking at room numbers, only to decide after a moment that he was in the wrong corridor. The soft brown carpet under his feet; the soft, cream-tinted walls; the snow-white bowl lights set in the ceiling—all seemed to him parts of a perfection and a social superiority which was almost unbelievable—so remote from all that he had ever known.

And finally, finding 882, he knocked timidly and was greeted after a moment by a segment of a very stout and vigorous body in a blue and white striped union suit and a related segment of a round and florid head in which was set one eye and some wrinkles to one side of it.

"Here's a dollar bill, son," said the eye seemingly—and now a hand appeared holding a paper dollar. It was fat and red. "You go out to a haberdasher's and get me a pair of garters—Boston Garters—silk—and hurry back."

"Yes, sir," replied Clyde, and took the dollar. The door closed and he found himself hustling along the hall toward the elevator, wondering what a haberdasher's was. As old as he was—seventeen—the name was new to him. He had never even heard it before, or noticed it at least. If the man had said a "gents' furnishing store," he would have understood at once, but now here he was told to go to a haberdasher's and he did not know what it was. A cold sweat burst out upon his forehead. His knees trembled. The devil! What would he do now? Could he ask any one, even Hegglund, and not seem——

He pushed the elevator button. The car began to descend. A haberdasher. A haberdasher. Suddenly a same thought reached him. Supposing he didn't know what a haberdasher was? After all the man wanted a pair of silk Boston garters. Where did one get silk Boston garters—at a store, of course, a place where they sold things for men. Certainly. A gents' furnishing store. He would run out to a store. And on the way down, noting another friendly negro in charge, he asked: "Do you know if there's a gents' furnishing store anywhere around here?"

"One in the building, captain, right outside the south lobby," replied the negro, and Clyde hurried there, greatly relieved. Yet he felt odd and strange in his close-fitting uniform and his peculiar hat. All the time he was troubled by the notion that his small round, tight-fitting hat might fall off. And he kept pressing it furtively and yet firmly down. And bustling into the haberdasher's, which was blazing with lights outside, he exclaimed, "I want to get a pair of Boston silk garters."

"All right, son, here you are," replied a sleek, short man with bright, bald head, pink face and gold-rimmed glasses. "For some one in the hotel, I presume? Well, we'll make that seventy-five cents, and here's a dime for you," he remarked as he wrapped up the package and dropped the dollar in the cash register. "I always like to do the right thing by you boys in there because I know you come to me whenever you can."

Clyde took the dime and the package, not knowing quite

what to think. The garters must be seventy-five cents—he said so. Hence only twenty-five cents need to be returned to the man. Then the dime was his. And now, maybe—would the man really give him another tip?

He hurried back into the hotel and up to the elevators. The strains of a string orchestra somewhere were filling the lobby with delightful sounds. People were moving here and there— so well-dressed, so much at ease, so very different from most of the people in the streets or anywhere, as he saw it.

An elevator door flew open. Various guests entered. Then Clyde and another bell-boy who gave him an interested glance. At the sixth floor the boy departed. At the eight Clyde and an old lady stepped forth. He hurried to the door of his guest and tapped. The man opened it, somewhat more fully dressed than before. He had on a pair of trousers and was shaving.

"Back, eh," he called.

"Yes, sir," replied Clyde, handing him the package and change. "He said it was seventy-five cents."

"He's a damned robber, but you can keep the change, just the same," he replied, handing him the quarter and closing the door. Clyde stood there, quite spellbound for the fraction of a second. "Thirty-five cents"—he thought—"thirty-five cents." And for one little short errand. Could that really be the way things went here? It couldn't be, really. It wasn't possible—not always.

And then, his feet sinking in the soft nap of the carpet, his hand in one pocket clutching the money, he felt as if he could squeal or laugh out loud. Why, thirty-five cents—and for a little service like that. This man had given him a quarter and the other a dime and he hadn't done anything at all.

He hurried from the car at the bottom—the strains of the orchestra once more fascinated him, the wonder of so well-dressed a throng thrilling him—and made his way to the bench from which he had first departed.

And following this he had been called to carry the three bags and two umbrellas of an aged farmer-like couple, who had engaged a parlor, bedroom and bath on the fifth floor. En route they kept looking at him, as he could see, but said nothing. Yet once in their room, and after he had promptly turned on the lights near the door, lowered the blinds and placed the bags upon the bag racks, the middle-aged and rather awkward husband—a decidedly solemn and be-whiskered person—studied him and finally observed: "Young fella, you seem to be a nice, brisk sort of boy—rather better than most we've seen so far, I must say."

"I certainly don't think that hotels are any place for boys," chirped up the wife of his bosom—a large and rotund person, who by this time was busily employed inspecting an adjoining room. "I certainly wouldn't want any of my boys to work in 'em—the way people act."

"But here, young man," went on the elder, laying off his overcoat and fishing in his trousers pocket. "You go down and get me three or four evening papers if there are that many and a pitcher of ice-water, and I'll give you fifteen cents when you get back."

"This hotel's better'n the one in Omaha, Pa," added the wife sententiously. "It's got nicer carpets and curtains."

And as green as Clyde was, he could not help smiling se-cretly. Openly, however, he preserved a masklike solemnity, seemingly effacing all facial evidence of thought, and took the change and went out. And in a few moments he was back with the ice-water and all the evening papers and departed smilingly with his fifteen cents.

But this, in itself, was but a beginning in so far as this par-ticular evening was concerned, for he was scarcely seated upon the bench again, before he was called to room 529, only to be sent to the bar for drinks—two ginger ales and two syphons of soda—and this by a group of smartly-dressed young men and girls who were laughing and chattering in the room, one of whom opened the door just wide enough to in-struct him as to what was wanted. But because of a mirror over the mantel, he could see the party and one pretty girl in a white suit and cap, sitting on the edge of a chair in which reclined a young man who had his arm about her.

Clyde stared, even while pretending not to. And in his state of mind, this sight was like looking through the gates of Paradise. Here were young fellows and girls in this room, not so much older than himself, laughing and talking and drink-ing even—not ice-cream sodas and the like, but such drinks

no doubt as his mother and father were always speaking
against as leading to destruction, and apparently nothing was
thought of it.

He bustled down to the bar, and having secured the drinks
and a charge slip, returned—and was paid—a dollar and a half
for the drinks and a quarter for himself. And once more he
had a glimpse of the appealing scene. Only now one of the
couples was dancing to a tune sung and whistled by the other
two.

But what interested him as much as the visits to and
glimpses of individuals in the different rooms, was the moving panorama of the main lobby—the character of the clerks
behind the main desk—room clerk, key clerk, mail clerk,
cashier and assistant cashier. And the various stands about the
place—flower stand, news stand, cigar stand, telegraph office,
taxicab office, and all manned by individuals who seemed to
him curiously filled with the atmosphere of this place. And
then around and between all these walking or sitting were
such imposing men and women, young men and girls all so
fashionably dressed, all so ruddy and contented looking. And
the cars or other vehicles in which some of them appeared
about dinner time and later. It was possible for him to see
them in the flare of the lights outside. The wraps, furs, and
other belongings in which they appeared, or which were often carried by these other boys and himself across the great
lobby and into the cars or the dining-room or the several elevators. And they were always of such gorgeous textures, as
Clyde saw them. Such grandeur. This, then, most certainly
was what it meant to be rich, to be a person of consequence
in the world—to have money. It meant that you did what you
pleased. That other people, like himself, waited upon you.
That you possessed all of these luxuries. That you went how,
where and when you pleased.

# Chapter VII

Aᴺᴰ ꜱᴏ, of all the influences which might have come to Clyde at this time, either as an aid or an injury to his development, perhaps the most dangerous for him, considering his temperament, was this same Green-Davidson, than which no more materially affected or gaudy a realm could have been found anywhere between the two great American mountain ranges. Its darkened and cushioned tea-room, so somber and yet tinted so gayly with colored lights, was an ideal rendezvous, not only for such inexperienced and eager flappers of the period who were to be taken by a show of luxury, but also for those more experienced and perhaps a little faded beauties, who had a thought for their complexions and the advantages of dim and uncertain lights. Also, like most hotels of its kind, it was frequented by a certain type of eager and ambitious male of no certain age or station in life, who counted upon his appearance here at least once, if not twice a day, at certain brisk and interesting hours, to establish for himself the reputation of man-about-town, or rounder, or man of wealth, or taste, or attractiveness, or all.

And it was not long after Clyde had begun to work here that he was informed by these peculiar boys with whom he was associated, one or more of whom was constantly seated with him upon the "hop-bench," as they called it, as to the evidence and presence even here—it was not long before various examples of the phenomena were pointed out to him—of a certain type of social pervert, morally disarranged and socially taboo, who sought to arrest and interest boys of their type, in order to come into some form of illicit relationship with them, which at first Clyde could not grasp. The mere thought of it made him ill. And yet some of these boys, as he was now informed—a certain youth in particular, who was not on the same watch with him at this time—were supposed to be of the mind that "fell for it," as one of the other youths phrased it.

And the talk and the palaver that went on in the lobby and the grill, to say nothing of the restaurants and rooms, were sufficient to convince any inexperienced and none-too-discerning mind that the chief business of life for any one with a little money or social position was to attend a theater, a ball-game in season, or to dance, motor, entertain friends at dinner, or to travel to New York, Europe, Chicago, California. And there had been in the lives of most of these boys such a lack of anything that approached comfort or taste, let alone luxury, that not unlike Clyde, they were inclined to not only exaggerate the import of all that they saw, but to see in this sudden transition an opportunity to partake of it all. Who were these people with money, and what had they done that they should enjoy so much luxury, where others as good seemingly as themselves had nothing? And wherein did these latter differ so greatly from the successful? Clyde could not see. Yet these thoughts flashed through the minds of every one of these boys.

At the same time the admiration, to say nothing of the private overtures of a certain type of woman or girl, who inhibited perhaps by the social milieu in which she found herself, but having means, could invade such a region as this, and by wiles and smiles and the money she possessed, ingratiate herself into the favor of some of the more attractive of these young men here, was much commented upon.

Thus a youth named Ratterer—a hall-boy here—sitting beside him the very next afternoon, seeing a trim, well-formed blonde woman of about thirty enter with a small dog upon her arm, and much bedecked with furs, first nudged him and, with a faint motion of the head indicating her vicinity, whispered, "See her? There's a swift one. I'll tell you about her sometime when I have time. Gee, the things she don't do!"

"What about her?" asked Clyde, keenly curious, for to him she seemed exceedingly beautiful, most fascinating.

"Oh, nothing, except she's been in with about eight different men around here since I've been here. She fell for Doyle"—another hall-boy whom by this time Clyde had already observed as being the quintessence of Chesterfieldian grace and airs and looks, a youth to imitate—"for a while, but now she's got some one else."

"Really?" inquired Clyde, very much astonished and wondering if such luck would ever come to him.

"Surest thing you know," went on Ratterer. "She's a bird that way—never gets enough. Her husband, they tell me, has a big lumber business somewhere over in Kansas, but they don't live together no more. She has one of the best suites on the sixth, but she ain't in it half the time. The maid told me."

This same Ratterer, who was short and stocky but good-looking and smiling, was so smooth and bland and generally agreeable that Clyde was instantly drawn to him and wished to know him better. And Ratterer reciprocated that feeling, for he had the notion that Clyde was innocent and inexperienced and that he would like to do some little thing for him if he could.

The conversation was interrupted by a service call, and never resumed about this particular woman, but the effect on Clyde was sharp. The woman was pleasing to look upon and exceedingly well-groomed, her skin clear, her eyes bright. Could what Ratterer had been telling him really be true? She was so pretty. He sat and gazed, a vision of something which he did not care to acknowledge even to himself tingling the roots of his hair.

And then the temperaments and the philosophy of these boys—Kinsella, short and thick and smooth-faced and a little dull, as Clyde saw it, but good-looking and virile, and reported to be a wizard at gambling, who, throughout the first three days at such times as other matters were not taking his attention, had been good enough to continue Hegglund's instructions in part. He was a more suave, better spoken youth than Hegglung, though not so attractive as Ratterer, Clyde thought, without the latter's sympathetic outlook, as Clyde saw it.

And again, there was Doyle—Eddie—whom Clyde found intensely interesting from the first, and of whom he was not a little jealous, because he was so very good-looking, so trim of figure, easy and graceful of gesture, and with so soft and pleasing a voice. He went about with an indescribable air which seemed to ingratiate him instantly with all with whom he came in contact—the clerks behind the counter no less than the strangers who entered and asked this or that question of him. His shoes and collar were so clean and trim, and his hair cut and brushed and oiled after a fashion which would have become a moving-picture actor. From the first Clyde was utterly fascinated by his taste in the matter of dress—the nearest of brown suits, caps, with ties and socks to match. He should wear a brown-belted coat just like that. He should have a brown cap. And a suit as well cut and attractive.

Similarly, a not unrelated and yet different effect was produced by that same youth who had first introduced Clyde to the work here—Hegglund—who was one of the older and more experienced bell-hops, and of considerable influence with the others because of his genial and devil-may-care attitude toward everything, outside the exact line of his hotel duties. Hegglund was neither as schooled nor as attractive as some of the others, yet by reason of a most avid and dynamic disposition—plus a liberality where money and pleasure were concerned, and a courage, strength and daring which neither Doyle nor Ratterer nor Kinsella could match—a strength and daring almost entirely divested of reason at times—he interested and charmed Clyde immensely. As he himself related to Clyde, after a time, he was the son of a Swedish journeyman baker who some years before in Jersey City had deserted his mother and left her to make her way as best she could. In consequence neither Oscar nor his sister Martha had had any too much education or decent social experience of any kind. On the contrary, at the age of fourteen he had left Jersey City in a box car and had been making his way ever since as best he could. And like Clyde, also, he was insanely eager for all the pleasures which he had imagined he saw swirling around him, and was for prosecuting adventures in every direction, lacking, however, the nervous fear of consequence which characterized Clyde. Also he had a friend, a youth by the name of Sparser, somewhat older than himself, who was chauffeur to a wealthy citizen of Kansas City, and who occasionally managed to purloin a car and so accommodate Hegglund in the matter of brief outings here and there; which courtesy, unconventional and dishonest though it might be, still caused Hegglund to feel that he was a wonderful fellow and of much more importance than some of these others, and to lend him in their eyes a luster which had little of the reality which it suggested to them.

Not being as attractive as Doyle, it was not so easy for him to win the attention of girls, and those he did succeed in interesting were not of the same charm or import by any means. Yet he was inordinately proud of such contacts as he could effect and not a little given to boasting in regard to them, a thing which Clyde took with more faith than would most, being of less experience. For this reason Hegglund liked Clyde, almost from the very first, sensing in him perhaps a pleased and willing auditor.

So, finding Clyde on the bench beside him from time to time, he had proceeded to continue his instructions. Kansas City was a fine place to be if you knew how to live. He had worked in other cities—Buffalo, Cleveland, Detroit, St. Louis—before he came here, but he had not liked any of them any better, principally—which was a fact which he did not trouble to point out at the time—because he had not done as well in those places as he had here. He had been a dish-washer, car-cleaner, plumber's helper and several other things before finally, in Buffalo, he had been inducted into the hotel business. And then a youth, working there, but who was now no longer here, had persuaded him to come on to Kansas City. But here:

"Say—de tips in dis hotel is as big as you'll git anywhere, I know dat. An' what's more, dey's nice people workin' here. You do your bit by dem and dey'll do right by you. I been here now over a year an' I ain't got no complaint. Dat guy Squires is all right if you don't cause him no trouble. He's hard, but he's got to look out for hisself, too—dat's natural. But he don't fire nobody unless he's got a reason. I know dat, too. And as for de rest dere's no trouble. An' when your work's troo, your time's your own. Dese fellows here are good sports, all o' dem. Dey're no four-flushers an' no tightwads, eider. Whenever dere's anyting on—a good time or sumpin' like dat, dere on—nearly all of 'em. An' dey don't mooch or grouch in case tings don't work out right, neider. I know dat, cause I been wit 'em now, lots o' times."

He gave Clyde the impression that these youths were all the best of friends—close—all but Doyle, who was a little stand-offish, but not coldly so. "He's got too many women chasin' him, dat's all." Also that they went here and there together on occasion—to a dance hall, a dinner, a certain gambling joint down near the river, a certain pleasure resort—"Kate

Sweeney's"—where were some peaches of girls—and so on and so forth, a world of such information as had never previously been poured into Clyde's ear, and that set him meditating, dreaming, doubting, worrying and questioning as to the wisdom, charm, delight to be found in all this—also the permissibility of it in so far as he was concerned. For had he not been otherwise instructed in regard to all this all his life long? There was a great thrill and yet a great question involved in all to which he was now listening so attentively.

Again there was Thomas Ratterer, who was of a type which at first glance, one would have said, could scarcely prove either inimical or dangerous to any of the others. He was not more than five feet four, plump, with black hair and olive skin, and with an eye that was as limpid as water and as genial as could be. He, too, as Clyde learned after a time, was of a nondescript family, and so had profited by no social or financial advantages of any kind. But he had a way, and was liked by all of these youths—so much so that he was consulted about nearly everything. A native of Wichita, recently moved to Kansas City, he and his sister were the principal support of a widowed mother. During their earlier and formative years, both had seen their very good-natured and sympathetic mother, of whom they were honestly fond, spurned and abused by a faithless husband. There had been times when they were quite without food. On more than one occasion they had been ejected for non-payment of rent. None too continuously Tommy and his sister had been maintained in various public schools. Finally, at the age of fourteen he had decamped to Kansas City, where he had secured different odd jobs, until he succeeded in connecting himself with the Green-Davidson, and was later joined by his mother and sister who had removed from Wichita to Kansas City to be with him.

But even more than by the luxury of the hotel or these youths, whom swiftly and yet surely he was beginning to decipher, Clyde was impressed by the downpour of small change that was tumbling in upon him and making a small lump in his right-hand pants pocket—dimes, nickels, quarters and half-dollars even, which increased and increased even on the first day until by nine o'clock he already had over four dollars in his pocket, and by twelve, at which hour he went off duty, he had over six and a half—as much as previously he had earned in a week.

And of all this, as he then knew, he need only hand Mr. Squires one—no more, Hegglund had said—and the rest, five dollars and a half, for one evening's interesting—yes, delightful and fascinating—work, belonged to himself. He could scarcely believe it. It seemed fantastic, Aladdinish, really. Nevertheless, at twelve, exactly, of that first day a gong had sounded somewhere—a shuffle of feet had been heard and three boys had appeared—one to take Barnes' place at the desk, the other two to answer calls. And at the command of Barnes, the eight who were present were ordered to rise, right dress and march away. And in the hall outside, and just as he was leaving, Clyde approached Mr. Squires and handed him a dollar in silver. "That's right," Mr. Squires remarked. No more. Then, Clyde, along with the others, descended to his locker, changed his clothes and walked out into the darkened streets, a sense of luck and a sense of responsibility as to future luck so thrilling him as to make him rather tremulous—giddy, even.

To think that now, at last, he actually had such a place. To think that he could earn this much every day, maybe. He began to walk toward his home, his first thought being that he must sleep well and so be fit for his duties in the morning. But thinking that he would not need to return to the hotel before 11:30 the next day, he wandered into an all-night beanery to have a cup of coffee and some pie. And now all he was thinking was that he would only need to work from noon until six, when he should be free until the following morning at six. And then he would make more money. A lot of it to spend on himself.

# Chapter VIII

THE THING that most interested Clyde at first was how, if at all, he was to keep the major portion of all this money he was making for himself. For ever since he had been working and earning money, it had been assumed that he would contribute a fair portion of all that he received—at least three-fourths of the smaller salaries he had received up to this time—toward the upkeep of the home. But now, if he announced that he was receiving at least twenty-five dollars a week and more—and this entirely apart from the salary of fifteen a month and board—his parents would assuredly expect him to pay ten or twelve.

But so long had he been haunted by the desire to make himself as attractive looking as any other well-dressed boy that, now that he had the opportunity, he could not resist the temptation to equip himself first and as speedily as possible. Accordingly, he decided to say to his mother that all of the tips he received aggregated no more than a dollar a day. And, in order to give himself greater freedom of action in the matter of disposing of his spare time, he announced that frequently, in addition to the long hours demanded of him every other day, he was expected to take the place of other boys who were sick or set to doing other things. And also, he explained that the management demanded of all boys that they look well outside as well as inside the hotel. He could not long be seen coming to the hotel in the clothes that he now wore. Mr. Squires, he said, had hinted as much. But, as if to soften the blow, one of the boys at the hotel had told him of a place where he could procure quite all the things that he needed on time.

And so unsophisticated was his mother in these matters that she believed him.

But that was not all. He was now daily in contact with a type of youth who, because of his larger experience with the world and with the luxuries and vices of such a life as this, had already been inducted into certain forms of libertinism and vice even which up to this time were entirely foreign to

57

Clyde's knowledge and set him agape with wonder and at first with even a timorous distaste. Thus, as Hegglund had pointed out, a certain percentage of this group, of which Clyde was now one, made common cause in connection with quite regular adventures which usually followed their monthly pay night. These adventures, according to their moods and their cash at the time, led them usually either to one of two rather famous and not too respectable all-night restaurants. In groups, as he gathered by degrees from hearing them talk, they were pleased to indulge in occasional late showy suppers with drinks, after which they were wont to go to either some flashy dance hall of the downtown section to pick up a girl, or that failing as a source of group interest, to visit some notorious—or as they would have deemed it reputed—brothel, very frequently camouflaged as a boarding house, where for much less than the amount of cash in their possession they could, as they often boasted, "have any girl in the house." And here, of course, because of their known youth, ignorance, liberality, and uniform geniality and good looks, they were made much of, as a rule, being made most welcome by the various madames and girls of these places who sought, for commercial reasons of course, to interest them to come again.

And so starved had been Clyde's life up to this time and so eager was he for almost any form of pleasure, that from the first he listened with all too eager ears to any account of anything that spelled adventure or pleasure. Not that he approved of these types of adventures. As a matter of fact at first it offended and depressed him, seeing as he did that it ran counter to all he had heard and been told to believe these many years. Nevertheless so sharp a change and relief from the dreary and repressed work in which he had been brought up was it, that he could not help thinking of all this with an itch for the variety and color it seemed to suggest. He listened sympathetically and eagerly, even while at times he was mentally disapproving of what he heard. And seeing him so sympathetic and genial, first one and then another of these youths made overtures to him to go here, there or the other place— to a show, a restaurant, one of their homes, where a card game might be indulged in by two or three of them, or even to one of the shameless houses, contact with which Clyde at first resolutely refused. But by degrees, becoming familiar with Hegglund and Ratterer, both of whom he liked very much, and being invited by them to a joy-night supper—a "blow-out" as they termed it, at Frissell's—he decided to go.

"There's going to be another one of our monthly blow-outs to-morrow night, Clyde, around at Frissell's," Ratterer had said to him. "Don't you want to come along? You haven't been yet."

By this time, Clyde, having acclimated himself to this caloric atmosphere, was by no means as dubious as he was at first. For by now, in imitation of Doyle, whom he had studied most carefully and to great advantage, he had outfitted himself with a new brown suit, cap, overcoat, socks, stickpin and shoes as near like those of his mentor as possible. And the costume became him well—excellently well—so much so that he was far more attractive than he had ever been in his life, and now, not only his parents, but his younger brother and sister, were not a little astonished and even amazed by the change.

How could Clyde have come by all this grandeur so speedily? How much could all this that he wore now have cost? Was he not hypothecating more of his future earnings for this temporary grandeur than was really wise? He might need it in the future. The other children needed things, too. And was the moral and spiritual atmosphere of a place that made him work such long hours and kept him out so late every day, and for so little pay, just the place to work?

To all of which, he had replied, rather artfully for him, that it was all for the best, he was not working too hard. His clothes were not too fine, by any means—his mother should see some of the other boys. He was not spending too much money. And, anyhow, he had a long while in which to pay for all he had bought.

But now, as to this supper. That was a different matter, even to him. How, he asked himself, in case the thing lasted until very late as was expected, could he explain to his mother and father his remaining out so very late. Ratterer had said it might last until three or four, anyhow, although he might go, of course, any time. But how would that look, deserting the crowd? And yet hang it all, most of them did not live at home as he did, or if they did like Ratterer, they had parents who didn't mind what they did. Still, a late supper like that—was it wise? All these boys drank and thought nothing of it—Hegglund, Ratterer, Kinsella, Shiel. It must be silly for him to think that there was so much danger in drinking a little, as they did on these occasions. On the other hand it was true that he need not drink unless he wanted to. He could go, and if anything was said at home, he would say that he had to work late. What difference did it make if he stayed out late once in a while? Wasn't he a man now? Wasn't he making more money than any one else in the family? And couldn't he begin to do as he pleased?

He began to sense the delight of personal freedom—to sniff the air of personal and delicious romance—and he was not to be held back by any suggestion which his mother could now make.

# Chapter IX

A ND SO the interesting dinner, with Clyde attending, came to pass. And it was partaken of at Frissell's, as Ratterer had said. And by now Clyde, having come to be on genial terms with all of these youths, was in the gayest of moods about it all. Think of his new state in life, anyhow. Only a few weeks ago he was all alone, not a boy friend, scarcely a boy acquaintance in the world! And here he was, so soon after, going to this fine dinner with this interesting group.

And true to the illusions of youth, the place appeared far more interesting than it really was. It was little more than an excellent chop-house of the older American order. Its walls were hung thick with signed pictures of actors and actresses, together with playbills of various periods. And because of the general excellence of the food, to say nothing of the geniality of its present manager, it had become the hangout of passing actors, politicians, local business men, and after them, the generality of followers who are always drawn by that which presents something a little different to that with which they are familiar.

And these boys, having heard at one time and another from cab and taxi drivers that this was one of the best places in town, fixed upon it for their monthly dinners. Single plates of anything cost from sixty cents to a dollar. Coffee and tea were served in pots only. You could get anything you wanted to drink. To the left of the main room as you went in was a darker and low-ceilinged room, with a fireplace, to which only men resorted and sat and smoked, and read papers after dinner, and it was for this room that these youths reserved their greatest admiration. Eating here, they somehow felt older, wiser, more important—real men of the world. And both Ratterer and Hegglund, to whom by now Clyde had become very much attached, as well as most of the others, were satisfied that there was not another place in all Kansas City that was really as good.

And so this day, having drawn their pay at noon, and being off at six for the night, they gathered outside the hotel at the corner nearest the drug store at which Clyde had originally applied for work, and were off in a happy, noisy frame of mind—Hegglund, Ratterer, Paul Shiel, Davis Higby, another youth, Arthur Kinsella and Clyde.

"Didja hear de trick de guy from St. Louis pulled on de main office yesterday?" Hegglund inquired of the crowd generally, as they started walking. "Wires last Saturday from St. Louis for a parlor, bedroom and bat for himself and wife, an' orders flowers put in de room. Jimmy, the key clerk, was just tellin' me. Den he comes on here and registers himself an' his girl, see, as man and wife, an', gee, a peach of a lookin' girl, too—I saw 'em. Listen, you fellows, cantcha? Den, on Wednesday, after he's been here tree days and dey're beginnin' to wonder about him a little—meals sent to de room and all dat—he comes down and says dat his wife's gotta go back to St. Louis, and dat he won't need no suite, just one room, and dat dey can transfer his trunk and her bags to de new room until train time for her. But de trunk ain't his at all, see, but hers. And she ain't goin', don't know nuttin about it. But he is. Den he beats it, see, and leaves her and de trunk in de room. And widout a bean, see? Now, dey're holdin' her and her trunk, an' she's cryin' and wirin' friends, and dere's hell to pay all around. Can ya beat dat? An' de flowers, too. Roses. An' six different meals in de room and drinks for him, too."

"Sure, I know the one you mean," exclaimed Paul Shiel. "I took up some drinks myself. I felt there was something phony about that guy. He was too smooth and loud-talking. An' he only come across with a dime at that."

"I remember him, too," exclaimed Ratterer. "He sent me down for all the Chicago papers Monday an' only give me a dime. He looked like a bluff to me."

"Well, dey fell for him up in front, all right." It was Hegglund talking. "An' now dey're tryin' to gouge it outa her. Can you beat it?"

"She didn't look to me to be more than eighteen or twenty, if she's that old," put in Arthur Kinsella, who up to now had said nothing.

"Did you see either of 'em, Clyde?" inquired Ratterer, who was inclined to favor and foster Clyde and include him in everything.

"No," replied Clyde. "I must have missed those two. I don't remember seeing either of 'em."

"Well, you missed seein' a bird when you missed that one. Tall, long black cut-a-way coat, wide, black derby pulled low over his eyes, pearl-gray spats, too. I thought he was an English duke or something at first, the way he walked, and with a cane, too. All they gotta do is pull that English stuff, an' talk loud an' order everybody about an' they git by with it every time."

"That's right," commented Davis Higby. "That's good stuff, that English line. I wouldn't mind pulling some of it myself sometime."

They had now turned two corners, crossed two different streets and, in group formation, were making their way through the main door of Frissell's, which gave in on the reflection of lights upon china and silverware and faces, and the buzz and clatter of a dinner crowd. Clyde was enormously impressed. Never before, apart from the Green-Davidson, had he been in such a place. And with such wise, experienced youths.

They made their way to a group of tables which faced a leather wall-seat. The head-waiter, recognizing Ratterer and Hegglund and Kinsella as old patrons, had two tables put together and butter and bread and glasses brought. About these they arranged themselves, Clyde with Ratterer and Higby occupying the wall-seat; Hegglund, Kinsella and Sheil sitting opposite.

"Now, me for a good old Manhattan, to begin wit'," exclaimed Hegglund avidly, looking about on the crowd in the room and feeling that now indeed he was a person. Of a reddish-tan hue, his eyes keen and blue, his reddish-brown hair brushed straight up from his forehead, he seemed not unlike a large and overzealous rooster.

And similarly, Arthur Kinsella, once he was in here, seemed to perk up and take heart of his present glory. In a sort of ostentatious way, he drew back his coat sleeves, seized a bill of fare, and scanning the drink-list on the back, exclaimed: "Well, a dry Martini is good enough for a start."

"Well, I'm going to begin with a Scotch and soda," observed Paul Sheil, solemnly, examining at the same time the meat orders.

"None of your cocktails for me to-night," insisted Ratterer, genially, but with a note of reserve in his voice. "I said I wasn't going to drink much to-night, and I'm not. I think a glass of Rhine wine and seltzer will be about my speed."

"For de love o' Mike, will you listen to dat, now," exclaimed Hegglund, deprecatingly. "He's goin' to begin on Rhine wine. And him dat likes Manhattans always. What's gettin' into you all of a sudden, Tommy? I tought you said you wanted a good time to-night."

"So I do," replied Ratterer, "but can't I have a good time without lappin' up everything in the place? I want to stay sober to-night. No more call-downs for me in the morning, if I know what I'm about. I came pretty near not showing up last time."

"That's true, too," exclaimed Arthur Kinsella. "I don't want to drink so much I don't know where I'm at, but I'm not going to begin worrying about it now."

"How about you, Higby?" Hegglund now called to the round-eyed youth.

"I'm having a Manhattan, too," he replied, and then, looking up at the waiter who was beside him, added, "How's tricks, Dennis?"

"Oh, I can't complain," replied the waiter. "They're breakin' all right for me these days. How's everything over to the hotel?"

"Fine, fine," replied Higby, cheerfully, studying the bill-of-fare.

"An' you, Griffiths? What are you goin' to have?" called Hegglund, for, as master-of-ceremonies, delegated by the others to look after the orders and pay the bill and tip the waiter, he was now fulfilling the rôle.

"Who, me? Oh, me," exclaimed Clyde, not a little disturbed by this inquiry, for up to now—this very hour, in fact—he had never touched anything stronger than coffee or ice-cream soda. He had been not a little taken back by the brisk and sophisticated way in which these youths ordered cocktails and whisky. Surely he could not go so far as that, and yet, so well had he known long before this, from the conversation of these youths, that on such occasions as this they did drink, that he did not see how he could very well hold back. What would they think of him if he didn't drink something? For ever since he had been among them, he had been trying to appear as much of a man of the world as they were. And yet back of him, as he could plainly feel, lay all of the years in which he had been drilled in the "horrors" of drink and evil companionship. And even though in his heart this long while he had secretly rebelled against nearly all the texts and maxims to which his parents were always alluding, deeply resenting really as worthless and pointless the ragamuffin crew of wasters and failures whom they were always seeking to save, still, now he was inclined to think and hesitate. Should he or should he not drink?

For the fraction of an instant only, while all these things in him now spoke, he hesitated, then added: "Why, I, oh—I think I'll take Rhine wine and seltzer, too." It was the easiest and safest thing to say, as he saw it. Already the rather temperate and even innocuous character of Rhine wine and seltzer had been emphasized by Hegglund and all the others. And yet Ratterer was taking it—a thing which made his choice less conspicuous and, as he felt, less ridiculous.

"Will you listen to dis now?" exclaimed Hegglund, dramatically. "He says he'll have Rhine wine and seltzer, too. I see where dis party breaks up at half-past eight, all right, unless some of de rest of us do something."

And Davis Higby, who was far more trenchant and roistering than his pleasant exterior gave any indication of, turned to Ratterer and said: "Whatja want to start this Rhine wine and seltzer stuff for, so soon, Tom? Dontcha want us to have any fun at all to-night?"

"Well, I told you why," said Ratterer. "Besides, the last time I went down to that joint I had forty bucks when I went in and not a cent when I came out. I want to know what's goin' on this time."

"That joint," thought Clyde on hearing it. Then, after this supper, when they had all drunk and eaten enough, they were going down to one of those places called a "joint"—a bad-house, really. There was no doubt of it—he knew what the word meant. There would be women there—bad women— evil women. And he would be expected—could he—would he?

For the first time in his life now, he found himself confronted by a choice as to his desire for the more accurate knowledge of the one great fascinating mystery that had for so long confronted and fascinated and baffled and yet frightened him a little. For, despite all his many thoughts in regard to all this and women in general, he had never been in contact with any one of them in this way. And now—now—

All of a sudden he felt faint thrills of hot and cold racing up and down his back and all over him. His hands and face grew hot and then became moist—then his cheeks and forehead flamed. He could feel them. Strange, swift, enticing and yet disturbing thoughts raced in and out of his consciousness. His hair tingled and he saw pictures—bacchanalian scenes—which swiftly, and yet in vain, he sought to put out of his mind. They would keep coming back. And he wanted them to come back. Yet he did not. And through it all he was now a little afraid. Pshaw! Had he no courage at all? These other fellows were not disturbed by the prospects of what was before them. They were very gay. They were already beginning to laugh and kid one another in regard to certain funny things that had happened the last time they were all out together. But what would his mother think if she knew? His mother! He dared not think of his mother or his father either at this time, and put them both resolutely out of his mind.

"Oh, say, Kinsella," called Higby. "Do you remember that little red head in that Pacific Street joint that wanted you to run away to Chicago with her?"

"Do I?" replied the amused Kinsella, taking up the Martini that was just then served him. "She even wanted me to quit the hotel game and let her start me in a business of some kind. 'I wouldn't need to work at all if I stuck by her,' she told me."

"Oh, no, you wouldn't need to work at all, except one way," called Ratterer.

The waiter put down Clyde's glass of Rhine wine and seltzer beside him and, interested and intense and troubled and fascinated by all that he heard, he picked it up, tasted it and, finding it mild and rather pleasing, drank it all down at once. And yet so wrought up were his thoughts that he scarcely realized then that he had drunk it.

"Good for you," observed Kinsella, in a most cordial tone. "You must like that stuff."

"Oh, it's not so bad," said Clyde.

And Hegglund, seeing how swiftly it had gone, and feeling that Clyde, new to this world and green, needed to be cheered and strengthened, called to the waiter: "Here, Jerry! One more of these, and make it a big one," he whispered behind his hand.

And so the dinner proceeded. And it was nearly eleven before they had exhausted the various matters of interest to them—stories of past affairs, past jobs, past feats of daring. And by then Clyde had had considerable time to meditate on all of these youths—and he was inclined to think that he was not nearly as green as they thought, or if so, at least shrewder than most of them—of a better mentality, really. For who were they and what were their ambitions? Hegglund, as he could see, was vain and noisy and foolish—a person who could be taken in and conciliated by a little flattery. And Higby and Kinsella, interesting and attractive boys both, were still vain of things he could not be proud of—Higby of knowing a little something about automobiles—he had an uncle in the business—Kinsella of gambling, rolling dice even. And as for Ratterer and Shiel, he could see and had noticed for some time, that they were content with the bell-hop business—just continuing in that and nothing more—a thing which he could not believe, even now, would interest him forever.

At the same time, being confronted by this problem of how soon they would be wanting to go to a place into which he had never ventured before, and to be doing things which he had never let himself think he would do in just this way, he was just a little disturbed. Had he not better excuse himself after they got outside, or perhaps, after starting along with them in whatsoever direction they chose to go, quietly slip away at some corner and return to his own home? For had he not already heard that the most dreadful of diseases were occasionally contracted in just such places—and that men died miserable deaths later because of low vices begun in this fashion? He could hear his mother lecturing concerning all this—yet with scarcely any direct knowledge of any kind. And yet, as an argument per contra, here were all of these boys in nowise disturbed by what was in their minds or moods to do. On the contrary, they were very gay over it all and amused—nothing more.

In fact, Ratterer, who was really very fond of Clyde by now, more because of the way he looked and inquired and listened than because of anything Clyde did or said, kept nudging him with his elbow now and then, asking laughingly, "How about it, Clyde? Going to be initiated to-night?" and then smiling broadly. Or finding Clyde quite still and thinking at times, "They won't do more than bite you, Clyde."

And Hegglund, taking his cue from Ratterer and occasionally desisting from his own self-glorifying diatribes, would add: "You won't ever be de same, Clyde. Dey never are. But we'll all be wid you in case of trouble."

And Clyde, nervous and irritated, would retort: "Ah, cut it out, you two. Quit kidding. What's the use of trying to make out that you know so much more than I do?"

And Ratterer would signal Hegglund with his eyes to let up and would occasionally whisper to Clyde: "That's all right, old man, don't get sore. You know we were just fooling, that's all." And Clyde, very much drawn to Ratterer, would relent and wish he were not so foolish as to show what he actually was thinking about.

At last, however, by eleven o'clock, they had had their fill of conversation and food and drink and were ready to depart, Hegglund leading the way. And instead of the vulgar and secretive mission producing a kind of solemnity and mental or moral self-examination and self-flagellation, they laughed and talked as though there was nothing but a delicious form of amusement before them. Indeed, much to Clyde's disgust and amazement, they now began to reminisce concerning other ventures into this world—of one particular one which seemed to amuse them all greatly, and which seemed to concern some "joint," as they called it, which they had once visited—a place called "Bettina's." They had been led there originally by a certain wild youth by the name of "Pinky" Jones of the staff of another local hotel. And this boy and one other by the name of Birmingham, together with Hegglund, who had become wildly intoxicated, had there indulged in wild pranks which all but led to their arrest—pranks which to Clyde, as he listened to them, seemed scarcely possible to boys of this caliber and cleanly appearance—pranks so crude and disgusting as to sicken him a little.

"Oh, ho, and de pitcher of water de girl on de second floor doused on me as I went out," called Hegglund, laughing heartily.

"And the big fat guy on the second floor that came to the door to see. Remember?" laughed Kinsella. "He thought there was a fire or a riot, I bet."

"And you and that little fat girl, Piggy. 'Member, Ratterer?" squealed Shiel, laughing and choking as he tried to tell of it.

"And Ratterer's legs all bent under his load. Yoo-hoo!" yelled Hegglund. "And de way de two of 'em finally slid down de steps."

"That was all your fault, Hegglund," called Higby from Kinsella's side. "If you hadn't tried that switching stuff we never woulda got put out."

"I tell you I was drunk," protested Ratterer. "It was the red-eye they sold in there."

"And that long, thin guy from Texas with the big mustache, will you ever forget him, an' the way he laughed?" added Kinsella. "He wouldn't help nobody 'gainst us. 'Member?"

"It's a wonder we weren't all thrown in the street or locked up. Oh, gee, what a night!" reminisced Ratterer.

By now Clyde was faintly dizzy with the nature of these revelations. "Switchin'." That could mean but one thing.

And they expected him to share in revels such as these, maybe. It could not be. He was not that sort of person. What would his mother and father think if they were to hear of such dreadful things? And yet——

Even as they talked, they had reached a certain house in a dark and rather wide street, the curbs of which for a block or more on either side were sprinkled with cabs and cars. And at the corner, only a little distance away, were some young men standing and talking. And over the way, more men. And not a half a block farther on, they passed two policemen, idling and conversing. And although there was no light visible in any window, nor over any transom, still, curiously, there was a sense of vivid, radiant life. One could feel it in this dark street. Taxis spun and honked and two old-time closed carriages still in use rolled here and there, their curtains drawn. And doors slammed or opened and closed. And now and then a segment of bright inward light pierced the outward gloom and then disappeared again. Overhead on this night were many stars.

Finally, without any comment from any one, Hegglund, accompanied by Higby and Sheil, marched up the steps of this house and rang the bell. Almost instantly the door was opened by a black girl in a red dress. "Good evening. Walk right in, won't you?" was the affable greeting, and the six, having pushed past her and through the curtains of heavy velvet, which separated this small area from the main chambers, Clyde found himself in a bright and rather gaudy general parlor or reception room, the walls of which were ornamented with gilt-framed pictures of nude or semi-nude girls and some very high pier mirrors. And the floor was covered by a bright red thick carpet, over which were strewn many gilt chairs. At the back, before some very bright red hangings, was a gilded upright piano. But of guests or inmates there seemed to be none, other than the black girl.

"Jest be seated, won't you? Make yourselves at home. I'll call the madam." And, running upstairs to the left, she began calling: "Oh, Marie! Sadie! Caroline! They is some young gentlemen in the parlor."

And at that moment, from a door in the rear, there emerged a tall, slim and rather pale-faced woman of about thirty-eight or forty—very erect, very executive, very intelligent and graceful-looking—diaphanously and yet modestly garbed, who said, with a rather wan and yet encouraging smile: "Oh, hello, Oscar, it's you, is it? And you too, Paul. Hello! Hello, Davis! Just make yourselves at home anywhere, all of you. Fannie will be in in a minute. She'll bring you something to drink. I've just hired a new pianist from St. Joe—a negro. Wait'll you hear him. He's awfully clever."

She returned to the rear and called, "Oh, Sam!"

As she did so, nine girls of varying ages and looks, but none apparently over twenty-four or five—came trooping down the stairs at one side in the rear, and garbed as Clyde had never seen any women dressed anywhere. And they were all laughing and talking as they came—evidently very well pleased with themselves and in nowise ashamed of their appearance, which in some instances was quite extraordinary, as Clyde saw it, their costumes ranging from the gayest and flimsiest of boudoir negligées to the somewhat more sober, if no less revealing, dancing and ballroom gowns. And they were of such varied types and sizes and complexions—slim and stout and medium—tall or short—and dark or light or betwixt. And, whatever their ages, all seemed young. And they smiled so warmly and enthusiastically.

"Oh, hello, sweetheart! How are you? Don't you want to dance with me?" or "Wouldn't you like something to drink?"

# Chapter X

PREPARED as Clyde was to dislike all this, so steeped had he been in moods and maxims antipathetic to anything of its kind, still so innately sensual and romantic was his own disposition and so starved where sex was concerned, that instead of being sickened, he was quite fascinated. The very fleshly sumptuousness of most of these figures, dull and unromantic as might be the brains that directed them, interested him for the time being. After all, here was beauty of a gross, fleshy character, revealed and purchasable. And there were no difficulties of mood or inhibitions to overcome in connection with any of these girls. One of them, a quite pretty brunette in a black and red costume, with a band of red ribbon across her forehead, seemed to be decidedly at home with Higby, for already she was dancing with him in the back room to a jazz melody most irrationally hammered out upon the piano.

And Ratterer, to Clyde's surprise, was already seated upon one of the gilt chairs and upon his knees was lounging a tall young girl with very light hair and blue eyes. And she was smoking a cigarette and tapping her gold slippers to the melody of the piano. It was really quite an amazing and Aladdin-like scene to him. And here was Hegglund, before whom was standing a German or Scandinavian type, plump and pretty, her arms akimbo and her feet wide apart. And she was asking—with an upward swell of the voice, as Clyde could hear: "You make love to me to-night?" But Hegglund, apparently not very much taken with these overtures, calmly shook his head, after which she went on to Kinsella.

And even as he was looking and thinking, a quite attractive blonde girl of not less than twenty-four, but who seemed younger to Clyde, drew up a chair beside him and seating herself, said: "Don't you dance?" He shook his head nervously. "Want me to show you?"

"Oh, I wouldn't want to try here," he said.

"Oh, it's easy," she continued. "Come on!" But since he would not, though he was rather pleased with her for being agreeable to him, she added: "Well, how about something to drink then?"

"Sure," he agreed, gallantly, and forthwith she signaled the young negress who had returned as waitress, and in a moment a small table was put before them and a bottle of whisky with soda on the side—a sight that so astonished and troubled Clyde that he could scarcely speak. He had forty dollars in his pocket, and the cost of drinks here, as he had heard from the others, would not be less than two dollars each, but even so, think of him buying drinks for such a woman at such a price! And his mother and sisters and brother at home with scarcely the means to make ends meet. And yet he bought and paid for several, feeling all the while that he had let himself in for a terrifying bit of extravagance, if not an orgy, but now that he was here, he must go through with it.

And besides, as he now saw, this girl was really pretty. She had on a Delft blue evening gown of velvet, with slippers and stockings to match. In her ears were blue earrings and her neck and shoulders and arms were plump and smooth. The most disturbing thing about her was that her bodice was cut very low—he dared scarcely look at her there—and her cheeks and lips were painted—most assuredly the marks of the scarlet woman. Yet she did not seem very aggressive, in fact quite human, and she kept looking rather interestedly at his deep and dark and nervous eyes.

"You work over at the Green-Davidson, too, don't you?" she asked.

"Yes," replied Clyde, trying to appear as if all this were not new to him—as if he had been often in just such a place as this, amid such scenes. "How did you know?"

"Oh, I know Oscar Hegglund," she replied. "He comes around here once in a while. Is he a friend of yours?"

"Yes. That is, he works over at the hotel with me."

"But you haven't been here before."

"No," said Clyde, swiftly, and yet with a trace of inquiry in his own mood. Why should she say he hadn't been here before?

"I thought you hadn't. I've seen most of these other boys before, but I never saw you. You haven't been working over at the hotel very long, have you?"

"No," said Clyde, a little irritated by this, his eyebrows and the skin of his forehead rising and falling as he talked—a form of contraction and expansion that went on involuntarily whenever he was nervous or thought deeply. "What of it?"

"Oh, nothing. I just knew you hadn't. You don't look very much like these other boys—you look different." She smiled oddly and rather ingratiatingly, a smile and a mood which Clyde failed to interpret.

"How different?" he inquired, solemnly and contentiously, taking up a glass and drinking from it.

"I'll bet you one thing," she went on, ignoring his inquiry entirely. "You don't care for girls like me very much, do you?"

"Oh, yes, I do, too," he said, evasively.

"Oh, no, you don't either. I can tell. But I like you just the same. I like your eyes. You're not like those other fellows. You're more refined, kinda. I can tell. You don't look like them."

"Oh, I don't know," replied Clyde, very much pleased and flattered, his forehead wrinkling and clearing as before. This girl was certainly not as bad as he thought, maybe. She was more intelligent—a little more refined than the others. Her costume was not so gross. And she hadn't thrown herself upon him as had these others upon Hegglund, Higby, Kinsella and Ratterer. Nearly all of the group by now were seated upon chairs or divans about the room and upon their knees were girls. And in front of every couple was a little table with a bottle of whisky upon it.

"Look who's drinking whisky!" called Kinsella to such of the others as would pay any attention to him, glancing in Clyde's direction.

"Well, you needn't be afraid of me," went on the girl, while Clyde glanced at her arms and neck, at her too much revealed bosom, which quite chilled and yet enticed him. "I haven't been so very long in this business. And I wouldn't be here now if it hadn't been for all the bad luck I've had. I'd rather live at home with my family if I could, only they wouldn't have me, now." She looked rather solemnly at the floor, thinking mainly of the little inexperienced dunce Clyde was—so raw and green. Also of the money she had seen him take out of his pocket—plainly quite a sum. Also how really good-looking he was, not handsome or vigorous, but pleasing. And he was thinking at the instant of Esta, as to where she had gone or was now. What might have befallen her—who could say? What might have been done to her? Had this girl, by any chance, ever had any such unfortunate experience as she had had? He felt a growing, if somewhat grandiose, sympathy, and looked at her as much as to say: "You poor thing." Yet for the moment he would not trust himself to say anything or make any further inquiry.

"You fellows who come into a place like this always think so hard of everybody. I know how you are. But we're not as bad as you think."

Clyde's brows knit and smoothed again. Perhaps she was not as bad as he thought. She was a low woman, no doubt—evil but pretty. In fact, as he looked about the room from time to time, none of the girls appealed to him more. And she thought him better than these other boys—more refined—she had detected that. The compliment stuck. Presently she was filling his glass for him and urging him to drink with her. Another group of young men arrived about then—and other girls coming out of the mysterious portals at the rear to greet them—Hegglund and Ratterer and Kinsella and Higby, as he saw, mysteriously disappeared up that back stairs that was heavily curtained from the general room. And as these others came in, this girl invited him to come and sit upon a divan in the back room where the lights were dimmer.

And now, seated here, she had drawn very close to him and touched his hands and finally linking an arm in his and pressing close to him, inquired if he didn't want to see how pretty some of the rooms on the second floor were furnished. And seeing that he was quite alone now—not one of all the group with whom he had come around to observe him—and that this girl seemed to lean to him warmly and sympathetically, he allowed himself to be led up that curtained back stair and into a small pink and blue furnished room, while he kept saying to himself that this was an outrageous and dangerous proceeding on his part, and that it might well end in misery for him. He might contract some dreadful disease. She might charge him more than he could afford. He was afraid of her—

himself—everything, really—quite nervous and almost dumb with his several fears and qualms. And yet he went, and, the door locked behind him, this interestingly well-rounded and graceful Venus turned the moment they were within and held him to her, then calmly, and before a tall mirror which revealed her fully to herself and him, began to disrobe. . . .

# Chapter XI

THE EFFECT of this adventure on Clyde was such as might have been expected in connection with one so new and strange to such a world as this. In spite of all that deep and urgent curiosity and desire that had eventually led him to that place and caused him to yield, still, because of the moral precepts with which he had so long been familiar, and also because of the nervous esthetic inhibitions which were characteristic of him, he could not but look back upon all this as decidedly degrading and sinful. His parents were probably right when they preached that this was all low and shameful. And yet this whole adventure and the world in which it was laid, once it was all over, was lit with a kind of gross, pagan beauty or vulgar charm for him. And until other and more interesting things had partially effaced it, he could not help thinking back upon it with considerable interest and pleasure, even.

In addition he kept telling himself that now, having as much money as he was making, he could go and do about as he pleased. He need not go there any more if he did not want to, but he could go to other places that might not be as low, maybe—more refined. He wouldn't want to go with a crowd like that again. He would rather have just one girl somewhere if he could find her—a girl such as those with whom he had seen Sieberling and Doyle associate. And so, despite all of his troublesome thoughts of the night before, he was thus won quickly over to this new source of pleasure if not its primary setting. He must find a free pagan girl of his own somewhere if he could, like Doyle, and spend his money on her. And he could scarcely wait until opportunity should provide him with the means of gratifying himself in this way.

But more interesting and more to his purpose at the time was the fact that both Hegglund and Ratterer, in spite of, or possibly because of, a secret sense of superiority which they detected in Clyde, were inclined to look upon him with no little interest and to court him and to include him among all their thoughts of affairs and pleasures. Indeed, shortly after this first adventure, Ratterer invited him to come to his home, where, as Clyde most quickly came to see, was a life very different from his own. At the Griffiths all was so solemn and reserved, the still moods of those who feel the pressure of dogma and conviction. In Ratterer's home, the reverse of this was nearly true. The mother and sister with whom he lived, while not without some moral although no particular religious convictions, were inclined to view life with a great deal of generosity or, as a moralist would have seen it, laxity. There had never been any keen moral or characterful direction there at all. And so it was that Ratterer and his sister Louise, who was two years younger than himself, now did about as they pleased, and without thinking very much about it. But his sister chanced to be shrewd or individual enough not to wish to cast herself away on just any one.

The interesting part of all this was that Clyde, in spite of a certain strain of refinement which caused him to look askance at most of this, was still fascinated by the crude picture of life and liberty which it offered. Among such as these, at least, he could go, do, be as he had never gone or done or been before. And particularly was he pleased and enlightened—or rather dubiously liberated—in connection with his nervousness and uncertainty in regard to his charm or fascination for girls of his own years. For up to this very time, and in spite of his recent first visit to the erotic temple to which Hegglund and the others had led him, he was still convinced that he had no skill with or charm where girls were concerned. Their mere proximity or approach was sufficient to cause him to recede mentally, to chill or palpitate nervously, and to lose what little natural skill he had for conversation or poised banter such as other youths possessed. But now, in his visits to the home of Ratterer, as he soon discovered, he was to have ample opportunity to test whether this shyness and uncertainty could be overcome.

For it was a center for the friends of Ratterer and his sister, who were more or less of one mood in regard to life. Dancing, card-playing, love-making rather open and unashamed, went on there. Indeed, up to this time, Clyde would not have imagined that a parent like Mrs. Ratterer could have been as lackadaisical or indifferent as she was, apparently, to conduct and morals generally. He would not have imagined that any mother would have countenanced the easy camaraderie that existed between the sexes in Mrs. Ratterer's home.

And very soon, because of several cordial invitations which were extended to him by Ratterer, he found himself part and parcel of this group—a group which from one point of view—the ideas held by its members, the rather wretched English they spoke—he looked down upon. From another point of view—the freedom they possessed, the zest with which they managed to contrive social activities and exchanges—he was drawn to them. Because, for the first time, these permitted him, if he chose, to have a girl of his own, if only he could summon the courage. And this, owing to the well-meant ministrations of Ratterer and his sister and their friends, he soon sought to accomplish. Indeed the thing began on the occasion of his first visit to the Ratterers.

Louise Ratterer worked in a dry-goods store and often came home a little late for dinner. On this occasion she did not appear until seven, and the eating of the family meal was postponed accordingly. In the meantime, two girl friends of Louise arrived to consult her in connection with something, and finding her delayed, and Ratterer and Clyde there, they made themselves at home, rather impressed and interested by Clyde and his new finery. For he, at once girl-hungry and girl-shy, held himself nervously aloof, a manifestation which they mistook for a conviction of superiority on his part. And in consequence, arrested by this, they determined to show how really interesting they were—vamp him—no less. And he found their crude briskness and effrontery very appealing—so much so that he was soon taken by the charms of one, a certain Hortense Briggs, who, like Louise, was nothing more than a crude shop girl in one of the large stores, but pretty and dark and self-appreciative. And yet from the first, he realized that she was not a little coarse and vulgar—a very long way removed from the type of girl he had been imagining in his dreams that he would like to have.

"Oh, hasn't she come in yet?" announced Hortense, on first being admitted by Ratterer and seeing Clyde near one of the front windows, looking out. "Isn't that too bad? Well, we'll just have to wait a little bit if you don't mind"—this last with a switch and a swagger that plainly said, who would mind having us around? And forthwith she began to primp and admire herself before a mirror which surmounted an ocher-colored mantelpiece that graced a fireless grate in the dining-room. And her friend, Greta Miller, added: "Oh, dear, yes. I hope you won't make us go before she comes. We didn't come to eat. We thought your dinner would be all over by now."

"Where do you get that stuff—'put you out'?" replied Ratterer cynically. "As though anybody could drive you two outa here if you didn't want to go. Sit down and play the victrola or do anything you like. Dinner'll soon be ready and Louise'll be here any minute." He returned to the dining-room to look at a paper which he had been reading, after pausing to introduce Clyde. And the latter, because of the looks and the airs of these two, felt suddenly as though he had been cast adrift upon a chartless sea in an open boat.

"Oh, don't say eat to me!" exclaimed Greta Miller, who was surveying Clyde calmly as though she were debating with herself whether he was worth-while game or not, and deciding that he was: "With all the ice-cream and cake and pie and sandwiches we'll have to eat yet to-night. We was just going to warn Louise not to fill up too much. Kittie Keane's givin' a birthday party, you know, Tom, and she'll have a big cake an' everythin'. You're comin' down, ain't you, afterwards?" she concluded, with a thought of Clyde and his possible companionship in mind.

"I wasn't thinkin' of it," calmly observed Ratterer. "Me and Clyde was thinkin' of goin' to a show after dinner."

"Oh, how foolish," put in Hortense Briggs, more to attract attention to herself and take it away from Greta than anything else. She was still in front of the mirror, but turned now to cast a fetching smile on all, particularly Clyde, for whom she fancied her friend might be angling, "When you could come along and dance. I call that silly."

"Sure, dancing is all you three ever think of—you and Louise," retorted Ratterer. "It's a wonder you don't give yourselves a rest once in a while. I'm on my feet all day an' I like to sit down once in a while." He could be most matter-of-fact at times.

"Oh, don't say sit down to me," commented Greta Miller, with a lofty smile and a gliding, dancing motion of her left foot, "with all the dates we got ahead of us this week. Oh, gee!" Her eyes and eyebrows went up and she clasped her hands dramatically before her. "It's just terrible, all the dancin' we gotta do yet this winter, don't we, Hortense? Thursday night and Friday night and Saturday and Sunday nights." She counted on her fingers most archly. "Oh, gee! It is terrible, really." She gave Clyde an appealing, sympathy-seeking smile. "Guess where we were the other night, Tom. Louise and Ralph Thorpe and Hortense and Bert Gettler, me and Willie Bassick—out to Pegrain's on Webster Avenue. Oh, an' you oughta seen the crowd out there. Sam Shaffer and Tillie Burns was there. And we danced until four in the morning. I thought my knees would break. I ain't been so tired in I don't know when."

"Oh, gee!" broke in Hortense, seizing her turn and lifting her arms dramatically. "I thought I never would get to work the next morning. I could just barely see the customers moving around. And, wasn't my mother fussy! Gee! She hasn't gotten over it yet. She don't mind so much about Saturdays and Sundays, but all these week nights and when I have to get up the next morning at seven—gee—how she can pick!"

"An' I don't blame her, either," commented Mrs. Ratterer, who was just then entering with a plate of potatoes and some bread. "You two'll get sick and Louise, too, if you don't get more rest. I keep tellin' her she won't be able to keep her place or stand it if she don't get more sleep. But she don't pay no more attention to me than Tom does, and that's just none at all."

"Oh, well, you can't expect a fellow in my line to get in early, always, Ma," was all Ratterer said. And Hortense Briggs added: "Gee, I'd die if I had to stay in one night. You gotta have a little fun when you work all day."

What an easy household, thought Clyde. How liberal and indifferent. And the sexy, gay way in which these two girls posed about. And their parents thought nothing of it, evidently. If only he could have a girl as pretty as this Hortense Briggs, with her small, sensuous mouth and her bright hard eyes.

"To bed twice a week early is all I need," announced Greta Miller archly. "My father thinks I'm crazy, but more'n that would do me harm." She laughed jestingly, and Clyde, in spite of the "we was'es" and "I seen's," was most vividly impressed. Here was youth and geniality and freedom and love of life.

And just then the front door opened and in hurried Louise Ratterer, a medium-sized, trim, vigorous little girl in a red-lined cape and a soft blue felt hat pulled over her eyes. Unlike her brother, she was brisk and vigorous and more lithe and as pretty as either of these others.

"Oh, look who's here!" she exclaimed. "You two birds beat me home, didnja? Well, I got stuck to-night on account of some mix-up in my sales-book. And I had to go up to the cashier's office. You bet it wasn't my fault, though. They got my writin' wrong," then noting Clyde for the first time, she announced: "I bet I know who this is—Mr. Griffiths. Tom's talked about you a lot. I wondered why he didn't bring you around here before." And Clyde, very much flattered, mumbled that he wished he had.

But the two visitors, after conferring with Louise in a small front bedroom to which they all retired, reappeared presently and because of strenuous invitations, which were really not needed, decided to remain. And Clyde, because of their presence, was now intensely wrought up and alert—eager to make a pleasing impression and to be received upon terms of friendship here. And these three girls, finding him attractive, were anxious to be agreeable to him, so much so that for the first time in his life they put him at his ease with the opposite sex and caused him to find his tongue.

"We was just going to warn you not to eat so much," laughed Greta Miller, turning to Louise, "and now, see, we are all trying to eat again." She laughed heartily. "And they'll have pies and cakes and everythin' at Kittie's."

"Oh, gee, and we're supposed to dance, too, on top of all this. Well, heaven help me, is all I have to say," put in Hortense.

The peculiar sweetness of her mouth, as he saw it, as well as the way she crinkled it when she smiled, caused Clyde to be quite beside himself with admiration and pleasure. She looked quite delightful—wonderful to him. Indeed her effect on him made him swallow quickly and half choke on the coffee he had just taken. He laughed and felt irrepressibly gay.

At that moment she turned on him and said: "See, what I've done to him now."

"Oh, that ain't all you've done to me," exclaimed Clyde, suddenly being seized with an inspiration and a flow of thought and courage. Of a sudden, because of her effect on him, he felt bold and courageous, albeit a little foolish and added, "Say, I'm gettin' kinda woozy with all the pretty faces I see around here."

"Oh, gee, you don't want to give yourself away that quick around here, Clyde," cautioned Ratterer, genially. "These high-binders'll be after you to make you take 'em wherever they want to go. You better not begin that way." And, sure enough, Louise Ratterer, not to be abashed by what her brother had just said, observed: "You dance, don't you, Mr. Griffiths?"

"No, I don't," replied Clyde, suddenly brought back to reality by this inquiry and regretting most violently the handicap this was likely to prove in this group. "But you bet I wish I did now," he added gallantly and almost appealingly, looking first at Hortense and then at Greta Miller and Louise. But all pretended not to notice his preference, although Hortense titillated with her triumph. She was not convinced that she was so greatly taken with him, but it was something to triumph thus easily and handsomely over these others. And the others felt it. "Ain't that too bad?" she commented, a little indifferently and superiorly now that she realized that she was his preference. "You might come along with us, you and Tom, if you did. There's goin' to be mostly dancing at Kittie's."

Clyde began to feel and look crushed at once. To think that this girl, to whom of all those here he was most drawn, could dismiss him and his dreams and desires thus easily, and all because he couldn't dance. And his accursed home training was responsible for all this. He felt broken and cheated. What a boob he must seem not to be able to dance. And Louise Ratterer looked a little puzzled and indifferent, too. But Greta Miller, whom he liked less than Hortense, came to his rescue with: "Oh, it ain't so hard to learn. I could show you in a few minutes after dinner if you wanted to. It's only a few steps you have to know. And then you could go, anyhow, if you wanted to."

Clyde was grateful and said so—determined to learn here or elsewhere at the first opportunity. Why hadn't he gone to a dancing school before this, he asked himself. But the thing that pained him most was the seeming indifference of Hortense now that he had made it clear that he liked her. Perhaps it was that Bert Gettler, previously mentioned, with whom she had gone to the dance, who was making it impossible for him to interest her. So he was always to be a failure this way. Oh, gee!

But the moment the dinner was over and while the others were still talking, the first to put on a dance record and come over with hands extended was Hortense, who was determined not to be outdone by her rival in this way. She was not particularly interested or fascinated by Clyde, at least not to the extent of troubling about him as Greta did. But if her friend was going to attempt a conquest in this manner, was it not just as well to forestall her? And so, while Clyde misread her change of attitude to the extent of thinking that she liked him better than he had thought, she took him by the hands, thinking at the same time that he was too bashful. However, placing his right arm about her waist, his other clasped in hers at her shoulder, she directed his attention to her feet and his and began to illustrate the few primary movements of the dance. But so eager and grateful was he—almost intense and ridiculous—she did not like him very much, thought him a little unsophisticated and too young. At the same time, there was a charm about him which caused her to wish to assist him. And soon he was moving about with her quite easily— and afterwards with Greta and then Louise, but wishing always it was Hortense. And finally he was pronounced sufficiently skillful to go, if he would.

And now the thought of being near her, being able to dance with her again, drew him so greatly that, despite the fact that three youths, among them that same Bert Gettler, appeared on the scene to escort them, and although he and Ratterer had previously agreed to go to a theater together, he could not help showing how much he would prefer to follow these others—so much so that Ratterer finally agreed to abandon the theater idea. And soon they were off, Clyde grieving that he could not walk with Hortense, who was with Gettler, and hating his rival because of this; but still attempting to be civil to Louise and Greta, who bestowed sufficient attention on him to make him feel at ease. Ratterer, having noticed his extreme preference and being alone with him for a moment, said: "You better not get too stuck on that Hortense Briggs. I don't think she's on the level with anybody. She's got that fellow Gettler and others. She'll only work you an' you might not get anything, either."

But Clyde, in spite of this honest and well-meant caution, was not to be dissuaded. On sight, and because of the witchery of a smile, the magic and vigor of motion and youth, he was completely infatuated and would have given or done anything for an additional smile or glance or hand pressure. And that despite the fact that he was dealing with a girl who no more knew her own mind than a moth, and who was just reaching the stage where she was finding it convenient and profitable to use boys of her own years or a little older for whatever pleasures or clothes she desired.

The party proved nothing more than one of those ebullitions of the youthful mating period. The house of Kittie Keane was little more than a cottage in a poor street under bare December trees. But to Clyde, because of the passion for a pretty face that was suddenly lit in him, it had the color and the form and gayety of romance itself. And the young girls and boys that he met there—girls and boys of the Ratterer, Hegglund, Hortense stripe—were still of the very substance and texture of that energy, ease and forwardness which he would have given his soul to possess. And curiously enough, in spite of a certain nervousness on his part, he was by reason of his new companions made an integral part of the gayeties.

And on this occasion, he was destined to view a type of girl and youth in action such as previously it had not been his fortune or misfortune, as you will, to see. There was, for instance, a type of sensual dancing which Louise and Hortense

and Greta indulged in with the greatest nonchalance and assurance. At the same time, many of these youths carried
whisky in a hip flask, from which they not only drank themselves, but gave others to drink—boys and girls indiscrimi-
nately.

And the general hilarity for this reason being not a little
added to, they fell into more intimate relations—spooning
with one and another—Hortense and Louise and Greta included. Also to quarreling at times. And it appeared to be
nothing out of the ordinary, as Clyde saw, for one youth or
another to embrace a girl behind a door, to hold her on his
lap in a chair in some secluded corner, to lie with her on a
sofa, whispering intimate and unquestionably welcome things
to her. And although at no time did he espy Hortense doing
this—still, as he saw, she did not hesitate to sit on the laps of
various boys or to whisper with rivals behind doors. And this
for a time so discouraged and at the same time incensed him
that he felt he could not and would not have anything more
to do with her—she was too cheap, vulgar, inconsiderate.

At the same time, having partaken of the various drinks
offered him—so as not to seem less worldly wise than the
others—until brought to a state of courage and daring not
ordinarily characteristic of him, he ventured to half plead with
and at the same time half reproach her for her too lax conduct.

"You're a flirt, you are. You don't care who you jolly, do
you?" This as they were dancing together after one o'clock to
the music of a youth named Wilkens, at the none too toneful
piano. She was attempting to show him a new step in a genial
and yet coquettish way, and with an amused, sensuous look.

"What do you mean, flirt? I don't get you."

"Oh, don't you?" replied Clyde, a little crossly and still attempting to conceal his real mood by a deceptive smile. "I've
heard about you. You jolly 'em all."

"Oh, do I?" she replied quite irritably. "Well, I haven't
tried to jolly you very much, have I?"

"Well, now, don't get mad," he half pleaded and half
scolded, fearing, perhaps, that he had ventured too far and
might lose her entirely now. "I don't mean anything by it.
You don't deny that you let a lot of these fellows make love
to you. They seem to like you, anyway."

"Oh, well, of course they like me, I guess. I can't help that, can I?"

"Well, I'll tell you one thing," he blurted boastfully and passionately. "I could spend a lot more on you than they could. I got it." He had been thinking only the moment before of fifty-five dollars in bills that snuggled comfortably in his pocket.

"Oh, I don't know," she retorted, not a little intrigued by this cash offer, as it were, and at the same time not a little set up in her mood by the fact that she could thus inflame nearly all youths in this way. She was really a little silly, very light-headed, who was infatuated by her own charms and looked in every mirror, admiring her eyes, her hair, her neck, her hands, her figure, and practising a peculiarly fetching smile.

At the same time, she was not unaffected by the fact that Clyde was not a little attractive to look upon, although so very green. She liked to tease such beginners. He was a bit of a fool, as she saw him. But he was connected with the Green-Davidson, and he was well-dressed, and no doubt he had all the money he said and would spend it on her. Some of those whom she liked best did not have much money to spend.

"Lots of fellows with money would like to spend it on me." She tossed her head and flicked her eyes and repeated her coyest smile.

At once Clyde's countenance darkened. The witchery of her look was too much for him. The skin of his forehead crinkled and then smoothed out. His eyes burned lustfully and bitterly, his old resentment of life and deprivation showing. No doubt all she said was true. There were others who had more and would spend more. He was boasting and being ridiculous and she was laughing at him.

After a moment, he added, weakly, "I guess that's right, too. But they couldn't want you more than I do."

The uncalculated honesty of it flattered her not a little. He wasn't so bad after all. They were gracefully gliding about as the music continued.

"Oh, well, I don't flirt everywhere like I do here. These fellows and girls all know each other. We're always going around together. You mustn't mind what you see here."

She was lying artfully, but it was soothing to him none the

less. "Gee, I'd give anything if you'd only be nice to me," he pleaded, desperately and yet ecstatically. "I never saw a girl I'd rather have than you. You're swell. I'm crazy about you. Why won't you come out to dinner with me and let me take you to a show afterwards? Don't you want to do that, to-morrow night or Sunday? Those are my two nights off. I work other nights."

She hesitated at first, for even now she was not so sure that she wished to continue this contact. There was Gettler, to say nothing of several others, all jealous and attentive. Even though he spent money on her, she might not wish to bother with him. He was already too eager and he might become troublesome. At the same time, the natural coquetry of her nature would not permit her to relinquish him. He might fall into the hands of Greta or Louise. In consequence she finally arranged a meeting for the following Tuesday. But he could not come to the house, or take her home to-night—on account of her escort, Mr. Gettler. But on the following Tuesday, at six-thirty, near the Green-Davidson. And he assured her that they would dine first at Frissell's, and then see "The Corsair," a musical comedy at Libby's, only two blocks away.

# Chapter XII

NOW TRIVIAL as this contact may seem to some, it was of the utmost significance to Clyde. Up to this he had never seen a girl with so much charm who would deign to look at him, or so he imagined. And now he had found one, and she was pretty and actually interested sufficiently to accompany him to dinner and to a show. It was true, perhaps, that she was a flirt, and not really sincere with any one, and that maybe at first he could not expect her to center her attentions on him, but who knew—who could tell?

And true to her promise on the following Tuesday she met him at the corner of 14th Street and Wyandotte, near the Green-Davidson. And so excited and flattered and enraptured was he that he could scarcely arrange his jumbled thoughts and emotions in any seemly way. But to show that he was worthy of her, he had made an almost exotic toilet—hair pomaded, a butterfly tie, new silk muffler and silk socks to emphasize his bright brown shoes, purchased especially for the occasion.

But once he had reëncountered Hortense, whether all this was of any import to her he could not tell. For, after all, it was her own appearance, not his, that interested her. And what was more—a trick with her—she chose to keep him waiting until nearly seven o'clock, a delay which brought about in him the deepest dejection of spirit for the time being. For supposing, after all, in the interval, she had decided that she did not care for him and did not wish to see him any more. Well, then he would have to do without her, of course. But that would prove that he was not interesting to a girl as pretty as she was, despite all the nice clothes he was now able to wear and the money he could spend. He was determined that, girl or no girl, he would not have one who was not pretty. Ratterer and Hegglund did not seem to mind whether the girl they knew was attractive or not, but with him it was a passion. The thought of being content with one not so attractive almost nauseated him.

And yet here he was now, on the street corner in the dark— the flare of many signs and lights about, hundreds of pedestrians hurrying hither and thither, the thought of pleasurable

intentions and engagements written upon the faces of many—
and he, he alone, might have to turn and go somewhere
else—eat alone, go to a theater alone, go home alone, and
then to work again in the morning. He had just about concluded that he was a failure when out of the crowd, a little
distance away, emerged the face and figure of Hortense. She
was smartly dressed in a black velvet jacket with a reddish
brown collar and cuffs, and a bulgy, round tam of the same
material with a red leather buckle on the side. And her cheeks
and lips were rouged a little. And her eyes sparkled. And as
usual she gave herself all the airs of one very well content with
herself.

"Oh, hello, I'm late, ain't I? I couldn't help it. You see, I
forgot I had another appointment with a fella, a friend of
mine—gee, a peach of a boy, too, and it was only at six I remembered that I had the two dates. Well, I was in a mess
then. So I had to do something about one of you. I was just
about to call you up and make a date for another night, only
I remembered you wouldn't be at your place after six. Tom
never is. And Charlie always is in his place till six-thirty, anyhow, sometimes later, and he's a peach of a fella that way—
never grouchy or nothing. And he was goin' to take me to
the theater and to dinner, too. He has charge of the cigar
stand over here at the Orphia. So I called him up. Well, he
didn't like it so very much. But I told him I'd make it another
night. Now, aintcha glad? Dontcha think I'm pretty nice to
you, disappointin' a good-lookin' fella like Charlie for you?"

She had caught a glimpse of the disturbed and jealous and
yet fearsome look in Clyde's eyes as she talked of another.
And the thought of making him jealous was a delight to her.
She realized that he was very much smitten with her. So she
tossed her head and smiled, falling into step with him as he
moved up the street.

"You bet it was nice of you to come," he forced himself to
say, even though the reference to Charlie as a "peach of a
fella" seemed to affect his throat and his heart at the same
time. What chance had he to hold a girl who was so pretty
and self-willed? "Gee, you look swell to-night," he went on,
forcing himself to talk and surprising himself a little with his
ability to do so. "I like the way that hat looks on you, and

your coat too." He looked directly at her, his eyes lit with admiration, an eager yearning filling them. He would have liked to have kissed her—her pretty mouth—only he did not dare here, or anywhere as yet.

"I don't wonder you have to turn down engagements. You're pretty enough. Don't you want some roses to wear?" They were passing a flower store at the moment and the sight of them put the thought of the gift in his mind. He had heard Hegglund say that women liked fellows who did things for them.

"Oh, sure, I would like some roses," she replied, turning into the place. "Or maybe some of those violets. They look pretty. They go better with this jacket, I think."

She was pleased to think that Clyde was sporty enough to think of flowers. Also that he was saying such nice things about her. At the same time she was convinced that he was a boy who had had little, if anything, to do with girls. And she preferred youths and men who were more experienced, not so easily flattered by her—not so easy to hold. Yet she could not help thinking that Clyde was a better type of boy or man than she was accustomed to—more refined. And for that reason, in spite of his gaucheness (in her eyes) she was inclined to tolerate him—to see how he would do.

"Well, these are pretty nifty," she exclaimed, picking up a rather large bouquet of violets and pinning them on. "I think I'll wear these." And while Clyde paid for them, she posed before the mirror, adjusting them to her taste. At last, being satisfied as to their effect, she turned and exclaimed, "Well, I'm ready," and took him by the arm.

Clyde, being not a little overawed by her spirit and mannerisms, was at a loss what else to say for the moment, but he need not have worried—her chief interest in life was herself.

"Gee, I tell you I had a swift week of it last week. Out every night until three. An' Sunday until nearly morning. My, that was some rough party I was to last night, all right. Ever been down to Burkett's at Gifford's Ferry? Oh, a nifty place, all right, right over the Big Blue at 39th. Dancing in summer and you can skate outside when it's frozen in winter or dance on the ice. An' the niftiest little orchestra."

Clyde watched the play of her mouth and the brightness of her eyes and the swiftness of her gestures without thinking so much of what she said—very little.

"Wallace Trone was along with us—gee, he's a scream of a kid—and afterwards when we was sittin' down to eat ice cream, he went out in the kitchen and blacked up an' put on a waiter's apron and coat and then comes back and serves us. That's one funny boy. An' he did all sorts of funny stuff with the dishes and spoons." Clyde sighed because he was by no means as gifted as the gifted Trone.

"An' then, Monday morning, when we all got back it was nearly four, and I had to get up again at seven. I was all in. I coulda chucked my job, and I woulda, only for the nice people down at the store and Mr. Beck. He's the head of my department, you know, and say, how I do plague that poor man. I sure am hard on that store. One day I comes in late after lunch; one of the other girls punched the clock for me with my key, see, and he was out in the hall and he saw her, and he says to me afterwards, about two in the afternoon, 'Say look here, Miss Briggs' (he always calls me Miss Briggs, 'cause I won't let him call me nothing else. He'd try to get fresh if I did), 'that loanin' that key stuff don't go. Cut that stuff out now. This ain't no Follies.' I had to laugh. He does get so sore at times at all of us. But I put him in his place just the same. He's kinda soft on me, you know—he wouldn't fire me for worlds, not him. So I says to him, 'See here, Mr. Beck, you can't talk to me in any such style as that. I'm not in the habit of comin' late often. An' wot's more, this ain't the only place I can work in K.C. If I can't be late once in a while without hearin' about it, you can just send up for my time, that's all, see.' I wasn't goin' to let him get away with that stuff. And just as I thought, he weakened. All he says was, 'Well, just the same, I'm warnin' you. Next time maybe Mr. Tierney'll see you an' then you'll get a chance to try some other store, all right.' He knew he was bluffing and that I did, too. I had to laugh. An' I saw him laughin' with Mr. Scott about two minutes later. But, gee, I certainly do pull some raw stuff around there at times."

By then she and Clyde, with scarcely a word on his part,

and much to his ease and relief, had reached Frissell's. And
for the first time in his life he had the satisfaction of escorting
a girl to a table in such a place. Now he really was beginning
to have a few experiences worthy of the name. He was quite
on edge with the romance of it. Because of her very high estimate of herself, her very emphatic picture of herself as one
who was intimate with so many youths and girls who were
having a good time, he felt that up to this hour he had not
lived at all. Swiftly he thought of the different things she had
told him—Burkett's on the Big Blue, skating and dancing on
the ice—Charlie Trone—the young tobacco clerk with whom
she had had the engagement for to-night—Mr. Beck at the
store who was so struck on her that he couldn't bring himself
to fire her. And as he saw her order whatever she liked, without any thought of his purse, he contemplated quickly her
face, figure, the shape of her hands, so suggestive always of
the delicacy or roundness of the arm, the swell of her bust, already very pronounced, the curve of her eyebrows, the
rounded appeal of her smooth cheeks and chin. There was
something also about the tone of her voice, unctuous,
smooth, which somehow appealed to and disturbed him. To
him it was delicious. Gee, if he could only have such a girl all
for himself!

And in here, as without, she clattered on about herself, not
at all impressed, apparently, by the fact that she was dining
here, a place that to him had seemed quite remarkable. When
she was not looking at herself in a mirror, she was studying
the bill of fare and deciding what she liked—lamb with mint
jelly—no omelette, no beef—oh, yes, filet of mignon with
mushrooms. She finally compromised on that with celery and
cauliflower. And she would like a cocktail. Oh, yes, Clyde had
heard Hegglund say that no meal was worth anything without a few drinks, so now he had mildly suggested a cocktail.
And having secured that and a second, she seemed warmer
and gayer and more gossipy than ever.

But all the while, as Clyde noticed, her attitude in so far as
he was concerned was rather distant—impersonal. If for so
much as a moment, he ventured to veer the conversation ever
so slightly to themselves, his deep personal interest in her,

whether she was really very deeply concerned about any other youth, she threw him off by announcing that she liked all the boys, really. They were all so lovely—so nice to her. They had to be. When they weren't, she didn't have anything more to do with them. She "tied a can to them," as she once expressed it. Her quick eyes clicked and she tossed her head defiantly.

And Clyde was captivated by all this. Her gestures, her poses, moues and attitudes were sensuous and suggestive. She seemed to like to tease, promise, lay herself open to certain charges and conclusions and then to withhold and pretend that there was nothing to all of this—that she was very unconscious of anything save the most reserved thoughts in regard to herself. In the main, Clyde was thrilled and nourished by this mere proximity to her. It was torture, and yet a sweet kind of torture. He was full of the most tantalizing thoughts about how wonderful it would be if only he were permitted to hold her close, kiss her mouth, bite her, even. To cover her mouth with his! To smother her with kisses! To crush and pet her pretty figure! She would look at him at moments with deliberate, swimming eyes, and he actually felt a little sick and weak—almost nauseated. His one dream was that by some process, either of charm or money, he could make himself interesting to her.

And yet after going with her to the theater and taking her home again, he could not see that he had made any noticeable progress. For throughout the performance of "The Corsair" at Libby's, Hortense, who, because of her uncertain interest in him was really interested in the play, talked of nothing but similar shows she had seen, as well as of actors and actresses and what she thought of them, and what particular youth had taken her. And Clyde, instead of leading her in wit and defiance and matching her experiences with his own, was compelled to content himself with approving of her.

And all the time she was thinking that she had made another real conquest. And because she was no longer virtuous, and she was convinced that he had some little money to spend, and could be made to spend it on her, she conceived the notion of being sufficiently agreeable—nothing more—to hold him, keep him attentive, if possible, while at the same time she went her own way, enjoying herself as much as possible with others and getting Clyde to buy and do such things for her as might fill gaps—when she was not sufficiently or amusingly enough engaged elsewhere.

# Chapter XIII

FOR A PERIOD of four months at least this was exactly the way it worked out. After meeting her in this fashion, he was devoting not an inconsiderable portion of his free time to attempting to interest her to the point where she would take as much interest in him as she appeared to take in others. At the same time he could not tell whether she could be made to entertain a singular affection for any one. Nor could he believe that there was only an innocent camaraderie involved in all this. Yet she was so enticing that he was deliriously moved by the thought that if his worst suspicions were true, she might ultimately favor him. So captivated was he by this savor of sensuality and varietism that was about her, the stigmata of desire manifest in her gestures, moods, voice, the way she dressed, that he could not think of relinquishing her.

Rather, he foolishly ran after her. And seeing this, she put him off, at times evaded him, compelled him to content himself with little more than the crumbs of her company, while at the same time favoring him with descriptions or pictures of other activities and contacts which made him feel as though he could no longer endure to merely trail her in this fashion. It was then he would announce to himself in anger that he was not going to see her any more. She was no good to him, really. But on seeing her again, a cold indifference in everything she said and did, his courage failed him and he could not think of severing the tie.

She was not at all backward at the same time in speaking of things that she needed or would like to have—little things, at first—a new powder puff, a lip stick, a box of powder or a bottle of perfume. Later, and without having yielded anything more to Clyde than a few elusive and evasive endearments—intimate and languorous reclinings in his arms which promised much but always came to nothing—she made so bold as to indicate to him at different times and in different ways, purses, blouses, slippers, stockings, a hat, which she would like to buy if only she had the money. And he, in order to hold her favor and properly ingratiate himself, proceeded to buy them, though at times and because of some other developments in connection with his family, it pressed him hard to do so. And yet, as he was beginning to see toward the end of the fourth month, he was apparently little farther advanced in her favor than he had been in the beginning. In short, he was conducting a feverish and almost painful pursuit without any definite promise of reward.

In the meantime, in so far as his home ties went, the irritations and the depressions which were almost inextricably involved with membership in the Griffiths family were not different from what they had ever been. For, following the disappearance of Esta, there had settled a period of dejection which still endured. Only, in so far as Clyde was concerned, it was complicated with a mystery which was tantalizing and something more—irritating; for when it came to anything which related to sex in the Griffiths family, no parents could possibly have been more squeamish.

And especially did this apply to the mystery which had now surrounded Esta for some time. She had gone. She had not returned. And so far as Clyde and the others knew, no word of any kind had been received from her. However, Clyde had noted that after the first few weeks of her absence, during which time both his mother and father had been most intensely wrought up and troubled, worrying greatly as to her whereabouts and why she did not write, suddenly they had ceased their worries, and had become very much more resigned—at least not so tortured by a situation that previously had seemed to offer no hope whatsoever. He could not explain it. It was quite noticeable, and yet nothing was said. And then one day a little later, Clyde had occasion to note that his mother was in communication with some one by mail—something rare for her. For so few were her social or business connections that she rarely received or wrote a letter.

One day, however, very shortly after he had connected himself with the Green-Davidson, he had come in rather earlier than usual in the afternoon and found his mother bending over a letter which evidently had just arrived and which appeared to interest her greatly. Also it seemed to be connected with something which required concealment. For, on seeing him, she stopped reading at once, and, flustered and apparently nervous, arose and put the letter away without commenting in any way upon what she had been reading. But Clyde for some reason, intuition perhaps, had the thought that it might be from Esta. He was not sure. And he was too far away to detect the character of the handwriting. But whatever it was, his mother said nothing afterwards concerning it. She looked as though she did not want him to inquire, and so reserved were their relations that he would not have thought of inquiring. He merely wondered, and then dismissed it partially, but not entirely, from his mind.

A month or five weeks after this, and just about the time that he was becoming comparatively well-schooled in his work at the Green-Davidson, and was beginning to interest himself in Hortense Briggs, his mother came to him one afternoon with a very peculiar proposition for her. Without explaining what it was for, or indicating directly that now she felt that he might be in a better position to help her, she called him into the mission hall when he came in from work and, looking at him rather fixedly and nervously for her, said: "You wouldn't know, Clyde, would you, how I could raise a hundred dollars right away?"

Clyde was so astonished that he could scarcely believe his ears, for only a few weeks before the mere mention of any sum above four or five dollars in connection with him would have been preposterous. His mother knew that. Yet here she was asking him and apparently assuming that he might be able to assist her in this way. And rightly, for both his clothes and his general air had indicated a period of better days for him.

At the same time his first thought was, of course, that she had observed his clothes and goings-on and was convinced that he was deceiving her about the amount he earned. And in part this was true, only so changed was Clyde's manner of late, that his mother had been compelled to take a very different attitude toward him and was beginning to be not a little dubious as to her further control over him. Recently, or since he had secured this latest place, for some reason he had seemed to her to have grown wiser, more assured, less dubious of himself, inclined to go his own way and keep his own counsel. And while this had troubled her not a little in one sense, it rather pleased her in another. For to see Clyde, who had always seemed because of his sensitiveness and unrest so much of a problem to her, developing in this very interesting way was something; though at times, and in view of his very recent finery, she had been wondering and troubled as to the nature of the company he might be keeping. But since his hours were so long and so absorbing, and whatever money he made appeared to be going into clothes, she felt that she had no real reason to complain. Her one other thought was that perhaps he was beginning to act a little selfish—to think too much of his own comfort—and yet in the face of his long deprivations she could not very well begrudge him any temporary pleasure, either.

Clyde, not being sure of her real attitude, merely looked at her and exclaimed: "Why, where would I get a hundred dollars, Ma?" He had visions of his new-found source of wealth being dissipated by such unheard of and inexplicable demands as this, and distress and distrust at once showed on his countenance.

"I didn't expect that you could get it all for me," Mrs. Griffiths suggested tactfully. "I have a plan to raise the most of it, I think. But I did want you to help me try to think how I would raise the rest. I didn't want to go to your father with this if I could help it, and you're getting old enough now to be of some help." She looked at Clyde approvingly and interestedly enough. "Your father is such a poor hand at business," she went on, "and he gets so worried at times."

She passed a large and weary hand over her face and Clyde was moved by her predicament, whatever it was. At the same time, apart from whether he was willing to part with so much or not, or had it to give, he was decidedly curious about what all this was for. A hundred dollars! Gee whiz!

After a moment or two, his mother added: "I'll tell you what I've been thinking. I must have a hundred dollars, but I can't tell you for what now, you nor any one, and you mustn't ask me. There's an old gold watch of your father's in my desk and a solid gold ring and pin of mine. Those things ought to be worth twenty-five dollars at least, if they were sold or pawned. Then there is that set of solid silver knives and forks and that silver platter and pitcher in there"—Clyde knew the keepsakes well—"that platter alone is worth twenty-five dollars. I believe they ought to bring at least twenty or twenty-five together. I was thinking if I could get you to go to some good pawnshop with them down near where you work, and then if you would let me have five more a week for a while" (Clyde's countenance fell)—"I could get a friend of mine—Mr. Murch who comes here, you know—to advance me enough to make up the hundred, and then I could pay him back out of what you pay me. I have about ten dollars myself."

She looked at Clyde as much as to say: "Now, surely, you won't desert me in my hour of trouble," and Clyde relaxed, in spite of the fact that he had been counting upon using quite all that he earned for himself. In fact, he agreed to take the trinkets to the pawnshop, and to advance her five more for the time being until the difference between whatever the trinkets brought and one hundred dollars was made up. And yet in spite of himself, he could not help resenting this extra strain, for it had only been a very short time that he had been earning so much. And here was his mother demanding more and more, as he saw it—ten dollars a week now. Always something wrong, thought Clyde, always something needed, and with no assurance that there would not be more such demands later.

He took the trinkets, carried them to the most presentable pawnshop he could find, and being offered forty-five dollars for the lot, took it. This, with his mother's ten, would make fifty-five, and with forty-five she could borrow from Mr. Murch, would make a hundred. Only now, as he saw, it would mean that for nine weeks he would have to give her ten dollars instead of five. And that, in view of his present aspirations to dress, live and enjoy himself in a way entirely different from what he previously considered necessary, was by no means a pleasure to contemplate. Nevertheless he decided to do it. After all he owed his mother something. She had made many sacrifices for him and the others in days past and he could not afford to be too selfish. It was not decent.

But the most enduring thought that now came to him was that if his mother and father were going to look to him for financial aid, they should be willing to show him more consideration than had previously been shown him. For one thing he ought to be allowed to come and go with more freedom, in so far as his night hours were concerned. And at the same time he was clothing himself and eating his meals at the hotel, and that was no small item, as he saw it.

However, there was another problem that had soon arisen and it was this. Not so long after the matter of the hundred dollars, he encountered his mother in Montrose Street, one of the poorest streets which ran north from Bickel, and which consisted entirely of two unbroken lines of wooden houses and two-story flats and many unfurnished apartments. Even the Griffiths, poor as they were, would have felt themselves demeaned by the thought of having to dwell in such a street. His mother was coming down the front steps of one of the less tatterdemalion houses of this row, a lower front window of which carried a very conspicuous card which read "Furnished Rooms." And then, without turning or seeing Clyde across the street; she proceeded to another house a few doors away, which also carried a furnished rooms card and, after surveying the exterior interestedly, mounted the steps and rang the bell.

Clyde's first impression was that she was seeking the whereabouts of some individual in whom she was interested and of whose address she was not certain. But crossing over to her at about the moment the proprietress of the house put her head out of the door, he heard his mother say: "You have a room for rent?" "Yes." "Has it a bath?" "No, but there's a bath on the second floor." "How much is it a week?" "Four dollars." "Could I see it?" "Yes, just step in."

Mrs. Griffiths appeared to hesitate while Clyde stood below, not twenty-five feet away, and looked up at her, waiting for her to turn and recognize him. But she stepped in without turning. And Clyde gazed after her curiously, for while it was by no means inconceivable that his mother might be looking for a room for some one, yet why should she be looking for it in this street when as a rule she usually dealt with the Salvation Army or the Young Women's Christian Association. His first impulse was to wait and inquire of her what she was doing here, but being interested in several errands of his own, he went on.

That night, returning to his own home to dress and seeing

his mother in the kitchen, he said to her: "I saw you this morning, Ma, in Montrose Street."

"Yes," his mother replied, after a moment, but not before he had noticed that she had started suddenly as though taken aback by this information. She was paring potatoes and looked at him curiously. "Well, what of it?" she added, calmly, but flushing just the same—a thing decidedly unusual in connection with her where he was concerned. Indeed, that start of surprise interested and arrested Clyde. "You were going into a house there—looking for a furnished room, I guess."

"Yes, I was," replied Mrs. Griffiths, simply enough now. "I need a room for some one who is sick and hasn't much money, but it's not so easy to find either." She turned away as though she were not disposed to discuss this any more, and Clyde, while sensing her mood, apparently, could not resist adding: "Gee, that's not much of a street to have a room in." His new work at the Green-Davidson had already caused him to think differently of how one should live—any one. She did not answer him and he went to his room to change his clothes.

A month or so after this, coming east on Missouri Avenue late one evening, he again saw his mother in the near distance coming west. In the light of one of the small stores which ranged in a row on this street, he saw that she was carrying a rather heavy old-fashioned bag, which had long been about the house but had never been much used by any one. On sight of him approaching (as he afterwards decided) she had stopped suddenly and turned into a hallway of a three-story brick apartment building, and when he came up to it, he found the outside door was shut. He opened it, and saw a flight of steps dimly lit, up which she might have gone. However, he did not trouble to investigate, for he was uncertain, once he reached this place, whether she had gone in to call on some one or not, it had all happened so quickly. But waiting at the next corner, he finally saw her come out again. And then to his increasing curiosity, she appeared to look cautiously about before proceeding as before. It was this that caused him to think that she must have been endeavoring to conceal herself from him. But why?

His first impulse was to turn and follow her, so interested

was he by her strange movements. But he decided later that if she did not want him to know what she was doing, perhaps it was best that he should not. At the same time he was made intensely curious by this evasive gesture. Why should his mother not wish him to see her carrying a bag anywhere? Evasion and concealment formed no part of her real disposition (so different from his own). Almost instantly his mind proceeded to join this coincidence with the time he had seen her descending the steps of the rooming house in Montrose Street, together with the business of the letter he had found her reading, and the money she had been compelled to raise—the hundred dollars. Where could she be going? What was she hiding?

He speculated on all this, but he could not decide whether it had any definite connection with him or any member of the family until about a week later, when, passing along Eleventh near Baltimore, he thought he saw Esta, or at least a girl so much like her that she would be taken for her anywhere. She had the same height, and she was moving along as Esta used to walk. Only, now he thought as he saw her, she looked older. Yet, so quickly had she come and gone in the mass of people that he had not been able to make sure. It was only a glance, but on the strength of it, he had turned and sought to catch up with her, but upon reaching the spot she was gone. So convinced was he, however, that he had seen her that he went straight home, and, encountering his mother in the mission, announced that he was positive he had seen Esta. She must be back in Kansas City again. He could have sworn to it. He had seen her near Eleventh and Baltimore, or thought he had. Had his mother heard anything from her?

And then curiously enough he observed that his mother's manner was not exactly what he thought it should have been under the circumstances. His own attitude had been one of commingled astonishment, pleasure, curiosity and sympathy because of the sudden disappearance and now sudden reappearance of Esta. Could it be that his mother had used that hundred dollars to bring her back? The thought had come to him—why or from where, he could not say. He wondered. But if so, why had she not returned to her home, at least to notify the family of her presence here?

He expected his mother would be as astonished and puzzled as he was—quick and curious for details. Instead, she appeared to him to be obviously confused and taken aback by this information, as though she was hearing about something that she already knew and was puzzled as to just what her attitude should be.

"Oh, did you? Where? Just now, you say? At Eleventh and Baltimore? Well, isn't that strange? I must speak to Asa about this. It's strange that she wouldn't come here if she is back." Her eyes, as he saw, instead of looking astonished, looked puzzled, disturbed. Her mouth, always the case when she was a little embarrassed and disconcerted, worked oddly—not only the lips but the jaw itself.

"Well, well," she added, after a pause. "That is strange. Perhaps it was just some one who looked like her."

But Clyde, watching her out of the corner of his eye, could not believe that she was as astonished as she pretended. And, thereafter, Asa coming in, and Clyde not having as yet departed for the hotel, he heard them discussing the matter in some strangely inattentive and unillumined way, as if it was not quite as startling as it had seemed to him. And for some time he was not called in to explain what he had seen.

And then, as if purposely to solve this mystery for him, he encountered his mother one day passing along Spruce Street, this time carrying a small basket on her arm. She had, as he had noticed of late, taken to going out regularly mornings and afternoons or evenings. On this occasion, and long before she had had an opportunity to see him, he had discerned her peculiarly heavy figure draped in the old brown coat which she always wore, and had turned into Myrkel Street and waited for her to pass, a convenient news stand offering him shelter. Once she had passed, he dropped behind her, allowing her to precede him by half a block. And at Dalrymple, she crossed to Beaudry, which was really a continuation of Spruce, but not so ugly. The houses were quite old—quondam residences of an earlier day, but now turned into boarding and rooming houses. Into one of these he saw her enter and disappear, but before doing so she looked inquiringly about her.

After she had entered, Clyde approached the house and

studied it with great interest. What was his mother doing in there? Who was it she was going to see? He could scarcely have explained his intense curiosity to himself, and yet, since having thought that he had seen Esta on the street, he had an unconvinced feeling that it might have something to do with her. There were the letters, the one hundred dollars, the furnished room in Montrose Street.

Diagonally across the way from the house in Beaudry Street there was a large-trunked tree, leafless now in the winter wind, and near it a telegraph pole, close enough to make a joint shadow with it. And behind these he was able to stand unseen, and from this vantage point to observe the several windows, side and front and ground and second floor. Through one of the front windows above, he saw his mother moving about as though she were quite at home there. And a moment later, to his astonishment he saw Esta come to one of the two windows and put a package down on the sill. She appeared to have on only a light dressing gown or a wrap drawn about her shoulders. He was not mistaken this time. He actually started as he realized that it was she, also that his mother was in there with her. And yet what had she done that she must come back and hide away in this manner? Had her husband, the man she had run away with, deserted her?

He was so intensely curious that he decided to wait a while outside here to see if his mother might not come out, and then he himself would call on Esta. He wanted so much to see her again—to know what this mystery was all about. He waited, thinking how he had always liked Esta and how strange it was that she should be here, hiding away in this mysterious way.

After an hour, his mother came out, her basket apparently empty, for she held it lightly in her hand. And just as before, she looked cautiously about her, her face wearing that same stolid and yet care-stamped expression which it always wore these days—a cross between an uplifting faith and a troublesome doubt.

Clyde watched her as she proceeded to walk south on Beaudry Street toward the Mission. After she was well out of sight, he turned and entered the house. Inside, as he had surmised, he found a collection of furnished rooms, name plates some of which bore the names of the roomers pasted upon them. Since he knew that the southeast front room upstairs contained Esta, he proceeded there and knocked. And true enough, a light footstep responded within, and presently, after some little delay which seemed to suggest some quick preparation within, the door opened slightly and Esta peeped out—quizzically at first, then with a little cry of astonishment and some confusion. For, as inquiry and caution disappeared, she realized that she was looking at Clyde. At once she opened the door wide.

"Why, Clyde," she called. "How did you come to find me? I was just thinking of you."

Clyde at once put his arms around her and kissed her. At the same time he realized, and with a slight sense of shock and dissatisfaction, that she was considerably changed. She was thinner—paler—her eyes almost sunken, and not any better dressed than when he had seen her last. She appeared nervous and depressed. One of the first thoughts that came to him now was where her husband was. Why wasn't he here? What had become of him? As he looked about and at her, he noticed that Esta's look was one of confusion and uncertainty, not unmixed with a little satisfaction at seeing him. Her mouth was partly open because of a desire to smile and to welcome him, but her eyes showed that she was contending with a problem.

"I didn't expect you here," she added, quickly, the moment he released her. "You didn't see—" Then she paused, catching herself at the brink of some information which evidently she didn't wish to impart.

"Yes, I did, too—I saw Ma," he replied. "That's how I came to know you were here. I saw her coming out just now and I saw you up here through the window." (He did not care to confess that he had been following and watching his mother for an hour.) "But when did you get back?" he went on. "It's a wonder you wouldn't let the rest of us know something about you. Gee, you're a dandy, you are—going away and staying months and never letting any one of us know anything. You might have written me a little something, anyhow. We always got along pretty well, didn't we?"

His glance was quizzical, curious, imperative. She, for her

part, felt recessive and thence evasive—uncertain, quite, what to think or say or tell.

She uttered: "I couldn't think who it might be. No one comes here. But, my, how nice you look, Clyde. You've got such nice clothes, now. And you're getting taller. Mamma was telling me you are working at the Green-Davidson."

She looked at him admiringly and he was properly impressed by her notice of him. At the same time he could not get his mind off her condition. He could not cease looking at her face, her eyes, her thin-fat body. And as he looked at her waist and her gaunt face, he came to a very keen realization that all was not well with her. She was going to have a child. And hence the thought recurred to him—where was her husband—or at any rate, the man she had eloped with. Her original note, according to her mother, had said that she was going to get married. Yet now he sensed quite clearly that she was not married. She was deserted, left in this miserable room here alone. He saw it, felt it, understood it.

And he thought at once that this was typical of all that seemed to occur in his family. Here he was just getting a start, trying to be somebody and get along in the world and have a good time. And here was Esta, after her first venture in the direction of doing something for herself, coming to such a finish as this. It made him a little sick and resentful.

"How long have you been back, Esta?" he repeated dubiously, scarcely knowing just what to say now, for now that he was here and she was as she was he began to scent expense, trouble, distress and to wish almost that he had not been so curious. Why need he have been? It could only mean that he must help.

"Oh, not so very long, Clyde. About a month, now, I guess. Not more than that."

"I thought so. I saw you up on Eleventh near Baltimore about a month ago, didn't I? Sure I did," he added a little less joyously—a change that Esta noted. At the same time she nodded her head affirmatively. "I knew I did. I told Ma so at the time, but she didn't seem to think so. She wasn't as surprised as I thought she would be, though. I know why, now. She acted as though she didn't want me to tell her about it either. But I knew I wasn't wrong." He stared at Esta oddly, quite proud of his prescience in this case. He paused though, not knowing quite what else to say and wondering whether what he had just said was of any sense or import. It didn't seem to suggest any real aid for her.

And she, not quite knowing how to pass over the nature of her condition, or to confess it, either, was puzzled what to say. Something had to be done. For Clyde could see for himself that her predicament was dreadful. She could scarcely bear the look of his inquiring eyes. And more to extricate herself than her mother, she finally observed, "Poor Mamma. You mustn't think it strange of her, Clyde. She doesn't know what to do, you see, really. It's all my fault, of course. If I hadn't run away, I wouldn't have caused her all this trouble. She has so little to do with and she's always had such a hard time." She turned her back to him suddenly, and her shoulders began to tremble and her sides to heave. She put her hands to her face and bent her head low—and then he knew that she was silently crying.

"Oh, come now, sis," exclaimed Clyde, drawing near to her instantly and feeling intensely sorry for her at the moment. "What's the matter? What do you want to cry for? Didn't that man that you went away with marry you?"

She shook her head negatively and sobbed the more. And in that instant there came to Clyde the real psychological as well as sociological and biological import of his sister's condition. She was in trouble, pregnant—and with no money and no husband. That was why his mother had been looking for a room. That was why she had tried to borrow a hundred dollars from him. She was ashamed of Esta and her condition. She was ashamed of not only what people outside the family would think, but of what he and Julia and Frank might think—the effect of Esta's condition upon them perhaps—because it was not right, unmoral, as people saw it. And for that reason she had been trying to conceal it, telling stories about it—a most amazing and difficult thing for her, no doubt. And yet, because of poor luck, she hadn't succeeded very well.

And now he was again confused and puzzled, not only by his sister's condition and what it meant to him and the other members of the family here in Kansas City, but also by his mother's disturbed and somewhat unmoral attitude in regard to deception in this instance. She had evaded it not actually deceived him in regard to all this, for she knew Esta was here all the time. At the same time he was not inclined to be too unsympathetic in that respect toward her—far from it. For such deception in such an instance had to be, no doubt, even where people were as religious and truthful as his mother, or so he thought. You couldn't just let people know. He certainly wouldn't want to let people know about Esta, if he could help it. What would they think? What would they say about her and him? Wasn't the general state of his family low enough, as it was? And so, now he stood, staring and puzzled the while Esta cried. And she realizing that he was puzzled and ashamed, because of her, cried the more.

"Gee, that is tough," said Clyde, troubled, and yet fairly sympathetic after a time. "You wouldn't have run away with him unless you cared for him though—would you?" (He was thinking of himself and Hortense Briggs.) "I'm sorry for you, Ess. Sure, I am, but it won't do you any good to cry about it now, will it? There's lots of other fellows in the world beside him. You'll come out of it all right."

"Oh, I know," sobbed Esta, "but I've been so foolish. And I've had such a hard time. And now I've brought all this trouble on Mamma and all of you." She choked and hushed a moment. "He went off and left me in a hotel in Pittsburgh without any money," she added. "And if it hadn't been for Mamma, I don't know what I would have done. She sent me a hundred dollars when I wrote her. I worked for a while in a restaurant—as long as I could. I didn't want to write home and say that he had left me. I was ashamed to. But I didn't know what else to do there toward the last, when I began feeling so bad."

She began to cry again; and Clyde, realizing all that his mother had done and sought to do to assist her, felt almost as sorry now for his mother as he did for Esta—more so, for Esta had her mother to look after her and his mother had almost no one to help her.

"I can't work yet, because I won't be able to for a while," she went on. "And Mamma doesn't want me to come home now because she doesn't want Julia or Frank or you to know. And that's right, too, I know. Of course it is. And she hasn't got anything and I haven't. And I get so lonely here, some-times." Her eyes filled and she began to choke again. "And I've been so foolish."

And Clyde felt for the moment as though he could cry too. For life was so strange, so hard at times. See how it had treated him all these years. He had had nothing until re-cently and always wanted to run away. But Esta had done so, and see what had befallen her. And somehow he recalled her between the tall walls of the big buildings here in the busi-ness district, sitting at his father's little street organ and singing and looking so innocent and good. Gee, life was tough. What a rough world it was anyhow. How queer things went!

He looked at her and the room, and finally, telling her that she wouldn't be left alone, and that he would come again, only she mustn't tell his mother he had been there, and that if she needed anything she could call on him although he wasn't making so very much, either—and then went out. And then, walking toward the hotel to go to work, he kept dwelling on the thought of how miserable it all was—how sorry he was that he had followed his mother, for then he might not have known. But even so, it would have come out. His mother could not have concealed it from him indefinitely. She would have asked for more money eventually maybe. But what a dog that man was to go off and leave his sister in a big strange city without a dime. He puzzled, thinking now of the girl who had been deserted in the Green-Davidson some months before with a room and board bill unpaid. And how comic it had seemed to him and the other boys at the time—highly colored with a sensual interest in it.

But this, well, this was his own sister. A man had thought so little of his sister as that. And yet, try as he would, he could no longer think that it was as terrible as when he heard her crying in the room. Here was this brisk, bright city about him running with people and effort, and this gay hotel in which he worked. That was not so bad. Besides there was his own love affair, Hortense, and pleasures. There must be some way out for Esta. She would get well again and be all right. But to think of his being part of a family that was always so poor and so little thought of that things like this could happen to it—

one thing and another—like street preaching, not being able to pay the rent at times, his father selling rugs and clocks for a living on the streets—Esta running away and coming to an end like this. Gee!

# Chapter XIV

THE RESULT of all this on Clyde was to cause him to think more specifically on the problem of the sexes than he ever had before, and by no means in any orthodox way. For while he condemned his sister's lover for thus ruthlessly deserting her, still he was not willing to hold her entirely blameless by any means. She had gone off with him. As he now learned from her, he had been in the city for a week the year before she ran away with him, and it was then that he had introduced himself to her. The following year when he returned for two weeks, it was she who looked him up, or so Clyde suspected, at any rate. And in view of his own interest in and mood regarding Hortense Briggs, it was not for him to say that there was anything wrong with the sex relation in itself.

Rather, as he saw it now, the difficulty lay, not in the deed itself, but in the consequences which followed upon not thinking or not knowing. For had Esta known more of the man in whom she was interested, more of what such a relationship with him meant, she would not be in her present pathetic plight. Certainly such girls as Hortense Briggs, Greta and Louise, would never have allowed themselves to be put in any such position as Esta. Or would they? They were too shrewd. And by contrast with them in his mind, at least at this time, she suffered. She ought, as he saw it, to have been able to manage better. And so, by degrees, his attitude toward her hardened in some measure, though his feeling was not one of indifference either.

But the one influence that was affecting and troubling and changing him now was his infatuation for Hortense Briggs—than which no more agitating influence could have come to a youth of his years and temperament. She seemed, after his few contacts with her, to be really the perfect realization of all that he had previously wished for in a girl. She was so bright, vain, engaging, and so truly pretty. Her eyes, as they seemed to him, had a kind of dancing fire in them. She had a most entrancing way of pursing and parting her lips and at the same time looking straightly and indifferently before her, as though

she were not thinking of him, which to him was both flame
and fever. It caused him, actually, to feel weak and dizzy, at
times, cruelly seared in his veins with minute and wriggling
threads of fire, and this could only be described as conscious
lust, a torturesome and yet unescapable thing which yet in her
case he was unable to prosecute beyond embracing and kissing, a form of reserve and respect in regard to her which she
really resented in the very youths in whom she sought to inspire it. The type of boy for whom she really cared and was always seeking was one who could sweep away all such
psuedo-ingenuousness and superiorities in her and force her,
even against herself, to yield to him.

In fact she was constantly wavering between actual like and
dislike of him. And in consequence, he was in constant doubt
as to where he stood, a state which was very much relished by
her and yet which was never permitted to become so fixed in
his mind as to cause him to give her up entirely. After some
party or dinner or theater to which she had permitted him to
take her, and throughout which he had been particularly tactful—not too assertive—she could be as yielding and enticing
in her mood as the most ambitious lover would have liked.
And this might last until the evening was nearly over, when
suddenly, and at her own door or the room or house of some
girl with whom she was spending the night, she would turn,
and without rhyme or reason, endeavor to dismiss him with a
mere handclasp or a thinly flavored embrace or kiss. At such
times, if Clyde was foolish enough to endeavor to force her to
yield the favors he craved, she would turn on him with the
fury of a spiteful cat, would tear herself away, developing for
the moment, seemingly, an intense mood of opposition which
she could scarcely have explained to herself. Its chief mental
content appeared to be one of opposition to being compelled
by him to do anything. And, because of his infatuation and
his weak overtures due to his inordinate fear of losing her, he
would be forced to depart, usually in a dark and despondent
mood.

But so keen was her attraction for him that he could not
long remain away, but must be going about to where most
likely he would encounter her. Indeed, for the most part these
days, and in spite of the peculiar climax which had eventuated

in connection with Esta, he lived in a keen, sweet and sensual dream in regard to her. If only she would really come to care for him. At night, in his bed at home, he would lie and think of her—her face—the expressions of her mouth and eyes, the lines of her figure, the motions of her body in walking or dancing—and she would flicker before him as upon a screen. In his dreams, he found her deliciously near him, pressing against him—her delightful body all his—and then in the moment of crisis, when seemingly she was about to yield herself to him completely, he would awake to find her vanished—an illusion only.

Yet there were several things in connection with her which seemed to bode success for him. In the first place, like himself, she was part of a poor family—the daughter of a machinist and his wife, who up to this very time had achieved little more than a bare living. From her childhood she had had nothing, only such gew-gaws and fripperies as she could secure for herself by her wits. And so low had been her social state until very recently that she had not been able to come in contact with anything better than butcher and baker boys— the rather commonplace urchins and small job aspirants of her vicinity. Yet even here she had early realized that she could and should capitalize her looks and charm—and had. Not a few of these had even gone so far as to steal in order to get money to entertain her.

After reaching the age where she was old enough to go to work, and thus coming in contact with the type of boy and man in whom she was now interested, she was beginning to see that without yielding herself too much, but in acting discreetly, she could win a more interesting equipment than she had before. Only, so truly sensual and pleasure-loving was she that she was by no means always willing to divorce her self-advantages from her pleasures. On the contrary, she was often troubled by a desire to like those whom she sought to use, and per contra, not to obligate herself to those whom she could not like.

In Clyde's case, liking him but a little, she still could not resist the desire to use him. She liked his willingness to buy her any little thing in which she appeared interested—a bag, a scarf, a purse, a pair of gloves—anything that she could reasonably ask or take without obligating herself too much. And yet from the first, in her smart, tricky way, she realized that unless she could bring herself to yield to him—at some time or other offer him the definite reward which she knew he craved—she could not hold him indefinitely.

One thought that stirred her more than anything else was that the way Clyde appeared to be willing to spend his money on her she might easily get some quite expensive things from him—a pretty and rather expensive dress, perhaps, or a hat, or even a fur coat such as was then being shown and worn in the city, to say nothing of gold earrings, or a wrist watch, all of which she was constantly and enviously eyeing in the different shop windows.

One day not so long after Clyde's discovery of his sister Esta, Hortense, walking along Baltimore Street near its junction with Fifteenth—the smartest portion of the shopping section of the city—at the noon hour—with Doris Trine, another shop girl in her department store, saw in the window of one of the smaller and less exclusive fur stores of the city, a fur jacket of beaver that to her, viewed from the eye-point of her own particular build, coloring and temperament, was exactly what she needed to strengthen mightily her very limited personal wardrobe. It was not such an expensive coat, worth possibly a hundred dollars—but fashioned in such an individual way as to cause her to imagine that, once invested with it, her own physical charm would register more than it ever had.

Moved by this thought, she paused and exclaimed: "Oh, isn't that just the classiest, darlingest little coat you ever saw! Oh, do look at those sleeves, Doris." She clutched her companion violently by the arm. "Lookit the collar. And the lining! And those pockets! Oh, dear!" She fairly vibrated with the intensity of her approval and delight. "Oh, isn't that just too sweet for words? And the very kind of coat I've been thinking of since I don't know when. Oh, you pitty sing!" she exclaimed, affectedly, thinking all at once as much of her own pose before the window and its effect on the passer-by as of the coat before her. "Oh, if I could only have 'oo."

She clapped her hands admiringly, while Isadore Rubenstein, the elderly son of the proprietor, who was standing somewhat out of the range of her gaze at the moment, noted the gesture and her enthusiasm and decided forthwith that the coat must be worth at least twenty-five or fifty dollars more to her, anyhow, in case she inquired for it. The firm had been offering it at one hundred. "Oh, ha!" he grunted. But being of a sensual and somewhat romantic turn, he also speculated to himself rather definitely as to the probable trading value, affectionally speaking, of such a coat. What, say, would the poverty and vanity of such a pretty girl as this cause her to yield for such a coat?

In the meantime, however, Hortense, having gloated as long as her noontime hour would permit, had gone away, still dreaming and satiating her flaming vanity by thinking of how devastating she would look in such a coat. But she had not stopped to ask the price. Hence, the next day, feeling that she must look at it once more, she returned, only this time alone, and yet with no idea of being able to purchase it herself. On the contrary, she was only vaguely revolving the problem of how, assuming that the coat was sufficiently low in price, she could get it. At the moment she could think of no one. But seeing the coat once more, and also seeing Mr. Rubenstein, Jr., inside eyeing her in a most propitiatory and genial manner, she finally ventured in.

"You like the coat, eh?" was Rubenstein's ingratiating comment as she opened the door. "Well, that shows you have good taste, I'll say. That's one of the nobbiest little coats we've ever had to show in this store yet. A real beauty, that. And how it would look on such a beautiful girl as you!" He took it out of the window and held it up. "I seen you when you was looking at it yesterday." A gleam of greedy admiration was in his eye.

And noting this, and feeling that a remote and yet not wholly unfriendly air would win her more consideration and courtesy than a more intimate one, Hortense merely said, "Yes?"

"Yes, indeed. And I said right away, there's a girl that knows a really swell coat when she sees it."

The flattering unction soothed, in spite of herself.

"Look at that! Look at that!" went on Mr. Rubinstein, turning the coat about and holding it before her. "Where in Kansas City will you find anything to equal that to-day? Look at this silk lining here—genuine Mallinson silk—and these slant pockets. And the buttons. You think those things don't make a different-looking coat? There ain't another one like it in Kansas City to-day—not one. And there won't be. We designed it ourselves and we never repeat our models. We protect our customers. But come back here." (He led the way to a triple mirror at the back.) "It takes the right person to wear a coat like this—to get the best effect out of it. Let me try it on you."

And by the artificial light Hortense was now privileged to see how really fetching she did look in it. She cocked her head and twisted and turned and buried one small ear in the fur, while Mr. Rubenstein stood by, eyeing her with not a little admiration and almost rubbing his hands.

"There now," he continued. "Look at that. What do you say to that, eh? Didn't I tell you it was the very thing for you? A find for you. A pick-up. You'll never get another coat like that in this city. If you do, I'll make you a present of this one." He came very near, extending his plump hands, palms up.

"Well, I must say it does look smart on me," commented Hortense, her vainglorious soul yearning for it. "I can wear anything like this, though." She twisted and turned the more, forgetting him entirely and the effect her interest would have on his cost price. Then she added: "How much is it?"

"Well, it's really a two-hundred-dollar coat," began Mr. Rubenstein artfully. Then noting a shadow of relinquishment pass swiftly over Hortense's face, he added quickly: "That sounds like a lot of money, but of course we don't ask so much for it down here. One hundred and fifty is our price. But if that coat was at Jarek's, that's what you'd pay for it and more. We haven't got the location here and we don't have to pay the high rents. But it's worth every cent of two hundred."

"Why, I think that's a terrible price to ask for it, just awful," exclaimed Hortense sadly, beginning to remove the coat. She was feeling as though life were depriving her of nearly all that was worth while. "Why, at Biggs and Becks, they have lots of three-quarter mink and beaver coats for that much, and classy styles, too."

"Maybe, maybe. But not that coat," insisted Mr. Rubenstein stubbornly. "Just look at it again. Look at the collar. You mean to say you can find a coat like that up there? If you can, I'll buy the coat for you and sell it to you again for a hundred dollars. Actually, this is a special coat. It's copied from one of the smartest coats that was in New York last summer before the season opened. It has class. You won't find no coat like this coat."

"Oh, well, just the same, a hundred and fifty dollars is more than I can pay," commented Hortense dolefully, at the same time slipping on her old broadcloth jacket with the fur collar and cuffs, and edging toward the door.

"Wait! You like the coat?" wisely observed Mr. Rubenstein, after deciding that even a hundred dollars was too much for her purse, unless it could be supplemented by some man's. "It's really a two-hundred-dollar coat. I'm telling you that straight. Our regular price is one hundred and fifty. But if you could bring me a hundred and twenty-five dollars, since you want it so much, well, I'll let you have it for that. And that's like finding it. A stunning-looking girl like you oughtn't to have no trouble in finding a dozen fellows who would be glad to buy that coat and give it to you. I know I would, if I thought you would be nice to me."

He beamed ingratiatingly up at her, and Hortense, sensing the nature of the overture and resenting it—from him—drew back slightly. At the same time she was not wholly displeased by the compliment involved. But she was not coarse enough, as yet, to feel that just any one should be allowed to give her anything. Indeed not. It must be some one she liked, or at least some one that was enslaved by her.

And yet, even as Mr. Rubenstein spoke, and for some time afterwards, her mind began running upon possible individuals—favorites—who, by the necromancy of her charm for them, might be induced to procure this coat for her. Charlie Wilkens for instance—he of the Orphia cigar store—who was most certainly devoted to her after his fashion, but a fashion, however, which did not suggest that he might do much for her without getting a good deal in return.

And then there was Robert Kain, another youth—very tall, very cheerful and very ambitious in regard to her, who was connected with one of the local electric company's branch offices, but his position was not sufficiently lucrative—a mere entry clerk. Also he was too saving—always talking about his future.

And again, there was Bert Gettler, the youth who had escorted her to the dance the night Clyde first met her, but who was little more than a giddy-headed dancing soul, one not to be relied upon in a crisis like this. He was only a shoe salesman, probably twenty dollars a week, and most careful with his pennies.

But there was Clyde Griffiths, the person who seemed to have real money and to be willing to spend it on her freely. So ran her thoughts swiftly at the time. But could she now, she asked herself, offhand, inveigle him into making such an expensive present as this? She had not favored him so very much—had for the most part treated him indifferently. Hence she was not sure, by any means. Nevertheless as she stood there, debating the cost and the beauty of the coat, the thought of Clyde kept running through her mind. And all the while Mr. Rubenstein stood looking at her, vaguely sensing, after his fashion, the nature of the problem that was confronting her.

"Well, little girl," he finally observed, "I see you'd like to have this coat, all right, and I'd like to have you have it, too. And now I'll tell you what I'll do, and better than that I can't do, and wouldn't for nobody else—not a person in this city. Bring me a hundred and fifteen dollars any time within the next few days—Monday or Wednesday or Friday, if the coat is still here, and you can have it. I'll do even better. I'll save it for you. How's that? Until next Wednesday or Friday. More'n that no one would do for you, now, would they?"

He smirked and shrugged his shoulders and acted as though he were indeed doing her a great favor. And Hortense, going away, felt that if only—only she could take that coat at one hundred and fifteen dollars, she would be capturing a marvelous bargain. Also that she would be the smartest-dressed girl in Kansas City beyond the shadow of a doubt. If only she could in some way get a hundred and fifteen dollars before next Wednesday, or Friday.

# Chapter XV

As Hortense well knew Clyde was pressing more and more hungrily toward that ultimate condescension on her part, which, though she would never have admitted it to him, was the privilege of two others. They were never together any more without his insisting upon the real depth of her regard for him. Why was it, if she cared for him the least bit, that she refused to do this, that or the other—would not let him kiss her as much as he wished, would not let him hold her in his arms as much as he would like. She was always keeping dates with other fellows and breaking them or refusing to make them with him. What was her exact relationship toward these others? Did she really care more for them than she did for him? In fact, they were never together anywhere but what this problem of union was uppermost—and but thinly veiled.

And she liked to think that he was suffering from repressed desire for her all of the time; that she tortured him, and that the power to allay his suffering lay wholly in her—a sadistic trait which had for its soil Clyde's own masochistic yearning for her.

However, in the face of her desire for the coat, his stature and interest for her were beginning to increase. In spite of the fact that only the morning before she had informed Clyde, with quite a flourish, that she could not possibly see him until the following Monday—that all her intervening nights were taken—nevertheless, the problem of the coat looming up before her, she now most eagerly planned to contrive an immediate engagement with him without appearing too eager. For by then she had definitely decided to endeavor to persuade him, if possible, to buy the coat for her. Only, of course, she would have to alter her conduct toward him radically. She would have to be much sweeter—more enticing. Although she did not actually say to herself that now she might even be willing to yield herself to him, still basically that was what was in her mind.

For quite a little while she was unable to think how to proceed. How was she to see him this day, or the next at the very latest? How should she go about putting before him the need of this gift, or loan, as she finally worded it to herself? She might hint that he could loan her enough to buy the coat and that later she would pay him back by degrees (yet once in possession of the coat she well knew that that necessity would never confront her). Or, if he did not have so much money on hand at one time, she could suggest that she might arrange with Mr. Rubenstein for a series of time payments which could be met by Clyde. In this connection her mind suddenly turned and began to consider how she could flatter and cajole Mr. Rubenstein into letting her have the coat on easy terms. She recalled that he had said he would be glad to buy the coat for her if he thought she would be nice to him.

Her first scheme in connection with all this was to suggest to Louise Ratterer to invite her brother, Clyde and a third youth by the name of Scull, who was dancing attendance upon Louise, to come to a certain dance hall that very evening to which she was already planning to go with the more favored cigar clerk. Only now she intended to break that engagement and appear alone with Louise and Greta and announce that her proposed partner was ill. That would give her an opportunity to leave early with Clyde and with him walk past the Rubenstein store.

But having the temperament of a spider that spins a web for flies, she foresaw that this might involve the possibility of Louise's explaining to Clyde or Ratterer that it was Hortense who had instigated the party. It might even bring up some accidental mention of the coat on the part of Clyde to Louise later, which, as she felt, would never do. She did not care to let her friends know how she provided for herself. In consequence, she decided that it would not do for her to appeal to Louise nor to Greta in this fashion.

And she was actually beginning to worry as to how to bring about this encounter, when Clyde, who chanced to be in the vicinity on his way home from work, walked into the store where she was working. He was seeking for a date on the following Sunday. And to his intense delight, Hortense greeted him most cordially with a most engaging smile and a wave of the hand. She was busy at the moment with a customer. She soon finished, however, and drawing near, and keeping one eye on her floor-walker who resented callers, exclaimed: "I was just thinking about you. You wasn't thinking about me, was you? Trade last." Then she added, sotto voce, "Don't act like you are talking to me. I see our floor-walker over there."

Arrested by the unusual sweetness in her voice, to say nothing of the warm smile with which she greeted him, Clyde was enlivened and heartened at once. "Was I thinking of you?" he returned gayly. "Do I ever think of any one else? Say! Ratterer says I've got you on the brain "

"Oh, him," replied Hortense, pouting spitefully and scornfully, for Ratterer, strangely enough, was one whom she did not interest very much, and this she knew. "He thinks he's so smart," she added. "I know a lotta girls don't like him."

"Oh, Tom's all right," pleaded Clyde, loyally. "That's just his way of talking. He likes you."

"Oh, no, he don't, either," replied Hortense. "But I don't want to talk about him. Whatcha doin' around six o'clock to-night?"

"Oh, gee!" exclaimed Clyde disappointedly. "You don't mean to say you got to-night free, have you? Well, ain't that tough? I thought you were all dated up. I got to work!" He actually sighed, so depressed was he by the thought that she might be willing to spend the evening with him and he not able to avail himself of the opportunity, while Hortense, noting his intense disappointment, was pleased.

"Well, I gotta date, but I don't want to keep it," she went on with a contemptuous gathering of the lips. "I don't have to break it. I would though if you was free." Clyde's heart began to beat rapidly with delight.

"Gee, I wish I didn't have to work now," he went on, looking at her. "You're sure you couldn't make it to-morrow night? I'm off then. And I was just coming up here to ask you if you didn't want to go for an automobile ride next Sunday afternoon, maybe. A friend of Hegglund's got a car—a Packard—and Sunday we're all off. And he wanted me to get a bunch to run out to Excelsior Springs. He's a nice fellow" (this because Hortense showed signs of not being so very much interested). "You don't know him very well, but he is. But say, I can talk to you about that later. How about to-morrow night? I'm off then."

Hortense, who, because of the hovering floor-walker, was pretending to show Clyde some handkerchiefs, was now thinking how unfortunate that a whole twenty-four hours must intervene before she could bring him to view the coat with her—and so have an opportunity to begin her machinations. At the same time she pretended that the proposed meeting for the next night was a very difficult thing to bring about—more difficult than he could possibly appreciate. She even pretended to be somewhat uncertain as to whether she wanted to do it.

"Just pretend you're examining these handkerchiefs here," she continued, fearing the floor-walker might interrupt. "I gotta nother date for then," she continued thoughtfully, "and I don't know whether I can break it or not. Let me see." She feigned deep thought. "Well, I guess I can," she said finally. "I'll try, anyhow. Just for this once. You be here at Fifteenth and Main at 6.15—no, 6.30's the best you can do, ain't it?— and I'll see if I can't get there. I won't promise, but I'll see and I think I can make it. Is that all right?" She gave him one of her sweetest smiles and Clyde was quite beside himself with satisfaction. To think that she would break a date for him, at last. Her eyes were warm with favor and her mouth wreathed with a smile.

"Surest thing you know," he exclaimed, voicing the slang of the hotel boys. "You bet I'll be there. Will you do me a favor?"

"What is it?" she asked cautiously.

"Wear that little black hat with the red ribbon under your chin, will you? You look so cute in that."

"Oh, you," she laughed. It was so easy to kid Clyde. "Yes, I'll wear it," she added. "But you gotta go now. Here comes that old fish. I know he's going to kick. But I don't care. Six-thirty, eh? So long." She turned to give her attention to a new customer, an old lady who had been patiently waiting to inquire if she could tell her where the muslins were sold. And Clyde, tingling with pleasure because of this unexpected delight vouchsafed him, made his way most elatedly to the nearest exit.

He was not made unduly curious because of this sudden favor, and the next evening, promptly at six-thirty, and in the glow of the overhanging arc-lights showering their glistening radiance like rain, she appeared. As he noted, at once, she had worn the hat he liked. Also she was enticingly ebullient and friendly, more so than at any time he had known her. Before he had time to say that she looked pretty, or how pleased he was because she wore that hat, she began:

"Some favorite you're gettin' to be, *I'll say*, when *I'll* break an engagement and then wear an old hat I don't like just to please you. How do I get that way is what I'd like to know."

He beamed as though he had won a great victory. Could it be that at last he might be becoming a favorite with her?

"If you only knew how cute you look in that hat, Hortense, you wouldn't knock it," he urged admiringly. "You don't know how sweet you do look."

"Oh, ho. In this old thing?" she scoffed. "You certainly are easily pleased, I'll say."

"An' your eyes are just like soft, black velvet," he persisted eagerly. "They're wonderful." He was thinking of an alcove in the Green-Davidson hung with black velvet.

"Gee, you certainly have got 'em to-night," she laughed teasingly. "I'll have to do something about you." Then, before he could make any reply to this, she went off into an entirely fictional account of how, having had a previous engagement with a certain alleged young society man—Tom Keary by name—who was dogging her steps these days in order to get her to dine and dance, she had only this evening decided to "ditch" him, preferring Clyde, of course, for this occasion, anyhow. And she had called Keary up and told him that she could not see him to-night—called it all off, as it were. But just the same, on coming out of the employee's entrance, who should she see there waiting for her but this same Tom Keary, dressed to perfection in a bright gray raglan and spats, and with his closed sedan, too. And he would have taken her to the Green-Davidson, if she had wanted to go. He was a real sport. But she didn't. Not to-night, anyhow. Yet, if she had not contrived to avoid him, he would have delayed her. But she espied him first and ran the other way.

"And you should have just seen my little feet twinkle up Sargent and around the corner into Bailey Place," was the way she narcistically painted her flight. And so infatuated was

Clyde by this picture of herself and the wonderful Keary that he accepted all of her petty fabrications as truth.

And then, as they were walking in the direction of Gaspie's, a restaurant in Wyandotte near Tenth which quite lately he had learned was much better than Frissell's, Hortense took occasion to pause and look in a number of windows, saying as she did so that she certainly did wish that she could find a little coat that was becoming to her—that the one she had on was getting worn and that she must have another soon—a predicament which caused Clyde to wonder at the time whether she was suggesting to him that he get her one. Also whether it might not advance his cause with her if he were to buy her a little jacket, since she needed it.

But Rubenstein's coming into view on this same side of the street, its display window properly illuminated and the coat in full view, Hortense paused as she had planned.

"Oh, do look at that darling little coat there," she began, ecstatically, as though freshly arrested by the beauty of it, her whole manner suggesting a first and unspoiled impression. "Oh, isn't that the dearest, sweetest, cutest little thing you ever did see?" she went on, her histrionic powers growing with her desire for it. "Oh, just look at the collar, and those sleeves and those pockets. Aren't they the snappiest things you ever saw? Couldn't I just warm my little hands in those?" She glanced at Clyde out of the tail of her eye to see if he was being properly impressed.

And he, aroused by her intense interest, surveyed the coat with not a little curiosity. Unquestionably it was a pretty coat—very. But, gee, what would a coat like that cost, anyhow? Could it be that she was trying to interest him in the merits of a coat like that in order that he might get it for her? Why, it must be a two-hundred-dollar coat at least. He had no idea as to the value of such things, anyhow. He certainly couldn't afford a coat like that. And especially at this time when his mother was taking a good portion of his extra cash for Esta. And yet something in her manner seemed to bring it to him that that was exactly what she was thinking. It chilled and almost numbed him at first.

And yet, as he now told himself sadly, if Hortense wanted it, she could most certainly find some one who would get it for her—that young Tom Keary, for instance, whom she had just been describing. And, worse luck, she was just that kind of a girl. And if he could not get it for her, some one else could and she would despise him for not being able to do such things for her.

To his intense dismay and dissatisfaction she exclaimed: "Oh, what wouldn't I give for a coat like that!" She had not intended at the moment to put the matter so bluntly, for she wanted to convey the thought that was deepest in her mind to Clyde tactfully.

And Clyde, inexperienced as he was, and not subtle by any means, was nevertheless quite able to gather the meaning of that. It meant—it meant—for the moment he was not quite willing to formulate to himself what it did mean. And now—now—if only he had the price of that coat. He could feel that she was thinking of some one certain way to get the coat. And yet how was he to manage it? How? If he could only arrange to get this coat for her—if he only could promise her that he would get it for her by a certain date, say, if it didn't cost too much, then what? Did he have the courage to suggest to her to-night, or to-morrow, say, after he had learned the price of the coat, that if she would—why then—why then, well, he would get her the coat or anything else she really wanted. Only he must be sure that she was not really fooling him as she was always doing in smaller ways. He wouldn't stand for getting her the coat and then get nothing in return—never!

As he thought of it, he actually thrilled and trembled beside her. And she, standing there and looking at the coat, was thinking that unless he had sense enough now to get her this thing and to get what she meant—how she intended to pay for it—well then, this was the last. He need not think she was going to fool around with any one who couldn't or wouldn't do that much for her. Never.

They resumed their walk toward Gaspie's. And throughout the dinner, she talked of little else—how attractive the coat was, how wonderful it would look on her.

"Believe me," she said at one point, defiantly, feeling that Clyde was perhaps uncertain at the moment about his ability to buy it for her, "I'm going to find some way to get that coat. I think, maybe, that Rubenstein store would let me have it on time if I were to go in there and see him about it, make a big enough payment down. Another girl out of our store got a coat that way once," she lied promptly, hoping thus to induce Clyde to assist her with it. But Clyde, disturbed by the fear of some extraordinary cost in connection with it, hesitated to say just what he would do. He could not even guess the price of such a thing—it might cost two or three hundred, even—and he feared to obligate himself to do something which later he might not be able to do.

"You don't know what they might want for that, do you?" he asked, nervously, at the same time thinking if he made any cash gift to her at this time without some guarantee on her part, what right would he have to expect anything more in return than he had ever received? He knew how she cajoled him into getting things for her and then would not even let him kiss her. He flushed and churned a little internally with resentment at the thought of how she seemed to feel that she could play fast and loose with him. And yet, as he now recalled, she had just said she would do anything for any one who would get that coat for her—or nearly that.

"No-o," she hesitated at first, for the moment troubled as to whether to give the exact price or something higher. For if she asked for time, Mr. Rubenstein might want more. And yet if she said much more, Clyde might not want to help her. "But I know it wouldn't be more than a hundred and twenty-five. I wouldn't pay more than that for it."

Clyde heaved a sigh of relief. After all, it wasn't two or three hundred. He began to think now that if she could arrange to make any reasonable down payment—say, fifty or sixty dollars—he might manage to bring it together within the next two or three weeks anyhow. But if the whole hundred and twenty-five were demanded at once, Hortense would have to wait, and besides he would have to know whether he was to be rewarded or not—definitely.

"That's a good idea, Hortense," he exclaimed without, however, indicating in any way why it appealed to him so much. "Why don't you do that? Why don't you find out first what they want for it, and how much they want down? Maybe I could help you with it."

"Oh, won't that be just too wonderful!" Hortense

clapped her hands. "Oh, will you? Oh, won't that be just dandy? Now I just know I can get that coat. I just know they'll let me have it, if I talk to them right."

She was, as Clyde saw and feared, quite forgetting the fact that he was the one who was making the coat possible, and now it would be just as he thought. The fact that he was paying for it would be taken for granted.

But a moment later, observing his glum face, she added: "Oh, aren't you the sweetest, dearest thing, to help me in this way. You just bet I won't forget this either. You just wait and see. You won't be sorry. Now you just wait." Her eyes fairly snapped with gayety and even generosity toward him.

He might be easy and young, but he wasn't mean, and she would reward him, too, she now decided. Just as soon as she got the coat, which must be in a week or two at the latest, she was going to be very nice to him—do something for him. And to emphasize her own thoughts and convey to him what she really meant, she allowed her eyes to grow soft and swimming and to dwell on him promisingly—a bit of romantic acting which caused him to become weak and nervous. The gusto of her favor frightened him even a little, for it suggested, as he fancied, a disturbing vitality which he might not be able to match. He felt a little weak before her now—a little cowardly—in the face of what he assumed her real affection might mean.

Nevertheless, he now announced that if the coat did not cost more than one hundred and twenty-five dollars, that sum to be broken into one payment of twenty-five dollars down and two additional sums of fifty dollars each, he could manage it. And she on her part replied that she was going the very next day to see about it. Mr. Rubenstein might be induced to let her have it at once on the payment of twenty-five dollars down; if not that, then at the end of the second week, when nearly all would be paid.

And then in real gratitude to Clyde she whispered to him, coming out of the restaurant and purring like a cat, that she would never forget this and that he would see—and that she would wear it for him the very first time. If he were not working they might go somewhere to dinner. Or, if not that, then she would have it surely in time for the day of the proposed

automobile ride which he, or rather Hegglund, had suggested
for the following Sunday, but which might be postponed.

She suggested that they go to a certain dance hall, and
there she clung to him in the dances in a suggestive way and
afterwards hinted of a mood which made Clyde a little quivery and erratic.

He finally went home, dreaming of the day, satisfied that he
would have no trouble in bringing together the first payment,
if it were so much as fifty, even. For now, under the spur of
this promise, he proposed to borrow as much as twenty-five
from either Ratterer or Hegglund, and to repay it after the
coat was paid for.

But, ah, the beautiful Hortense. The charm of her, the
enormous, compelling, weakening delight. And to think that
at last, and soon, she was to be his. It was, plainly, of such
stuff as dreams are made of—the unbelievable become real.

# Chapter XVI

TRUE to her promise, the following day Hortense returned to Mr. Rubenstein, and with all the cunning of her nature placed before him, with many reservations, the nature of the dilemma which confronted her. Could she, by any chance, have the coat for one hundred and fifteen dollars on an easy payment plan? Mr. Rubenstein's head forthwith began to wag a solemn negative. This was not an easy payment store. If he wanted to do business that way he could charge two hundred for the coat and easily get it.

"But I could pay as much as fifty dollars when I took the coat," argued Hortense.

"Very good. But who is to guarantee that I get the other sixty-five, and when?"

"Next week twenty-five, and the week after that twenty-five and the week after that fifteen."

"Of course. But supposin' the next day after you take the coat an automobile runs you down and kills you. Then what? How do I get my money?"

Now that was a poser. And there was really no way that she could prove that any one would pay for the coat. And before that there would have to be all the bother of making out a contract, and getting some really responsible person—a banker, say—to endorse it. No, no, this was not an easy payment house. This was a cash house. That was why the coat was offered to her at one hundred and fifteen, but not a dollar less. Not a dollar.

Mr. Rubenstein sighed and talked on. And finally Hortense asked him if she could give him seventy-five dollars cash in hand, the other forty to be paid in one week's time. Would he let her have the coat then—to take home with her?

"But a week—a week—what is a week then?" argued Mr. Rubenstein. "If you can bring me seventy-five next week or to-morrow, and forty more in another week or ten days, why not wait a week and bring the whole hundred and fifteen? Then the coat is yours and no bother. Leave the coat. Come back to-morrow and pay me twenty-five or thirty dollars on account and I take the coat out of the window and lock it up for you. No one can even see it then. In another week bring me the balance or in two weeks. Then it is yours." Mr. Rubenstein explained the process as though it were a difficult matter to grasp.

But the argument once made was sound enough. It really left Hortense little to argue about. At the same time it reduced her spirit not a little. To think of not being able to take it now. And yet, once out of the place, her vigor revived. For, after all, the time fixed would soon pass and if Clyde performed his part of the agreement promptly, the coat would be hers. The important thing now was to make him give her twenty-five or thirty dollars wherewith to bind this wonderful agreement. Only now, because of the fact that she felt that she needed a new hat to go with the coat, she decided to say that it cost one hundred and twenty-five instead of one hundred and fifteen.

And once this conclusion was put before Clyde, he saw it as a very reasonable arrangement—all things considered—quite a respite from the feeling of strain that had settled upon him after his last conversation with Hortense. For, after all, he had not seen how he was to raise more than thirty-five dollars this first week anyhow. The following week would be somewhat easier, for then, as he told himself, he proposed to borrow twenty or twenty-five from Ratterer if he could, which, joined with the twenty or twenty-five which his tips would bring him, would be quite sufficient to meet the second payment. The week following he proposed to borrow at least ten or fifteen from Hegglund—maybe more—and if that did not make up the required amount to pawn his watch for fifteen dollars, the watch he had bought for himself a few months before. It ought to bring that at least; it cost fifty.

But, he now thought, there was Esta in her wretched room awaiting the most unhappy result of her one romance. How was she to make out, he asked himself, even in the face of the fact that he feared to be included in the financial problem which Esta as well as the family presented. His father was not now, and never had been, of any real financial service to his mother. And yet, if the problem were on this account to be shifted to him, how would he make out? Why need his father always peddle clocks and rugs and preach on the streets? Why couldn't his mother and father give up the mission idea, anyhow?

But, as he knew, the situation was not to be solved without his aid. And the proof of it came toward the end of the second week of his arrangement with Hortense, when, with fifty dollars in his pocket, which he was planning to turn over to her on the following Sunday, his mother, looking into his bedroom where he was dressing, said: "I'd like to see you for a minute, Clyde, before you go out." He noted she was very grave as she said this. As a matter of fact, for several days past, he had been sensing that she was undergoing a strain of some kind. At the same time he had been thinking all this while that with his own resources hypothecated as they were, he could do nothing. Or, if he did it meant the loss of Hortense. He dared not.

And yet what reasonable excuse could he give his mother for not helping her a little, considering especially the clothes he wore, and the manner in which he had been running here and there, always giving the excuse of working, but probably not deceiving her as much as he thought. To be sure, only two months before, he had obligated himself to pay her ten dollars a week more for five weeks, and had. But that only proved to her very likely that he had so much extra to give, even though he had tried to make it clear at the time that he was pinching himself to do it. And yet, however much he chose to waver in her favor, he could not, with his desire for Hortense directly confronting him.

He went out into the living-room after a time, and as usual his mother at once led the way to one of the benches in the mission—a cheerless, cold room these days.

"I didn't think I'd have to speak to you about this, Clyde, but I don't see any other way out of it. I haven't any one but you to depend upon now that you're getting to be a man. But you must promise not to tell any of the others—Frank or Julia or your father. I don't want them to know. But Esta's back here in Kansas City and in trouble, and I don't know quite what to do about her. I have so very little money to do with, and your father's not very much of a help to me any more."

She passed a weary, reflective hand across her forehead and

Clyde knew what was coming. His first thought was to pretend that he did not know that Esta was in the city, since he had been pretending this way for so long. But now, suddenly, in the face of his mother's confession and the need of pretended surprise on his part, if he were to keep up the fiction, he said, "Yes, I know."

"You know?" queried his mother, surprised.

"Yes, I know," Clyde repeated. "I saw you going in that house in Beaudry Street one morning as I was going along there," he announced calmly enough now. "And I saw Esta looking out of the window afterwards, too. So I went in after you left."

"How long ago was that?" she asked, more to gain time than anything else.

"Oh, about five or six weeks ago, I think. I been around to see her a coupla times since then, only Esta didn't want me to say anything about that either."

"Tst! Tst! Tst!" clicked Mrs. Griffiths, with her tongue. "Then you know what the trouble is."

"Yes," replied Clyde.

"Well, what is to be will be," she said resignedly. "You haven't mentioned it to Frank or Julia, have you?"

"No," replied Clyde, thoughtfully, thinking of what a failure his mother had made of her attempt to be secretive. She was no one to deceive any one, or his father, either. He thought himself far, far shrewder.

"Well, you mustn't," cautioned his mother solemnly. "It isn't best for them to know, I think. It's bad enough as it is this way," she added with a kind of wry twist to her mouth, the while Clyde thought of himself and Hortense.

"And to think," she added, after a moment, her eyes filling with a sad, all-enveloping gray mist, "she should have brought all this on herself and on us. And when we have so little to do with, as it is. And after all the instruction she has had—the training. 'The way of the transgressor——'"

She shook her head and put her two large hands together and gripped them firmly, while Clyde stared, thinking of the situation and all that it might mean to him.

She sat there, quite reduced and bewildered by her own peculiar part in all this. She had been as deceiving as any one, really. And here was Clyde, now, fully informed as to her falsehoods and strategy, and herself looking foolish and untrue. But had she not been trying to save him from all this—him and the others? And he was old enough to understand that now. Yet she now proceeded to explain why, and to say how dreadful she felt it all to be. At the same time, as she also explained, now she was compelled to come to him for aid in connection with it.

"Esta's about to be very sick," she went on suddenly and stiffly, not being able, or at least willing, apparently, to look at Clyde as she said it, and yet determined to be as frank as possible. "She'll need a doctor very shortly and some one to be with her all the time when I'm not there. I must get money somewhere—at least fifty dollars. You couldn't get me that much in some way, from some of your young men friends, could you, just a loan for a few weeks? You could pay it back, you know, soon, if you would. You wouldn't need to pay me anything for your room until you had."

She looked at Clyde so tensely, so urgently, that he felt quite shaken by the force and the cogency of the request. And before he could add anything to the nervous gloom which shadowed her face, she added: "That other money was for her, you know, to bring her back here after her—her"—she hesitated over the appropriate word but finally added—"husband left her there in Pittsburgh. I suppose she told you that."

"Yes, she did," replied Clyde, heavily and sadly. For after all, Esta's condition was plainly critical, which was something that he had not stopped to meditate on before.

"Gee, Ma," he exclaimed, the thought of the fifty dollars in his pocket and its intended destination troubling him considerably—the very sum his mother was seeking. "I don't know whether I can do that or not. I don't know any of the boys down there well enough for that. And they don't make any more than I do, either. I might borrow a little something, but it won't look very good." He choked and swallowed a little, for lying to his mother in this way was not easy. In fact, he had never had occasion to lie in connection with anything so trying—and so despicably. For here was fifty dollars in his pocket at the moment, with Hortense on the one hand and his mother and sister on the other, and the money would solve his mother's problem as fully as it would Hortense's, and more respectably. How terrible it was not to help her. How could he refuse her, really? Nervously he licked his lips and passed a hand over his brow, for a nervous moisture had broken out upon his face. He felt strained and mean and incompetent under the circumstances.

"And you haven't any money of your own right now that you could let me have, have you?" his mother half pleaded. For there were a number of things in connection with Esta's condition which required immediate cash and she had so little.

"No, I haven't, Ma," he said, looking at his mother shamefacedly, for a moment, then away, and if it had not been that she herself was so distrait, she might have seen the falsehood on his face. As it was, he suffered a pang of commingled self-commiseration and self-contempt, based on the distress he felt for his mother. He could not bring himself to think of losing Hortense. He must have her. And yet his mother looked so lone and so resourceless. It was shameful. He was low, really mean. Might he not, later, be punished for a thing like this?

He tried to think of some other way—some way of getting a little money over and above the fifty that might help. If only he had a little more time—a few weeks longer. If only Hortense had not brought up this coat idea just now.

"I'll tell you what I might do," he went on, quite foolishly and dully the while his mother gave vent to a helpless "Tst! Tst! Tst!" "Will five dollars do you any good?"

"Well, it will be something, anyhow," she replied. "I can use it."

"Well, I can let you have that much," he said, thinking to replace it out of his next week's tips and trust to better luck throughout the week. "And I'll see what I can do next week. I might let you have ten then. I can't say for sure. I had to borrow some of that other money I gave you, and I haven't got through paying for that yet, and if I come around trying to get more, they'll think—well, you know how it is."

His mother sighed, thinking of the misery of having to fall back on her one son thus far. And just when he was trying to get a start, too. What would he think of all this in after years? What would he think of her—of Esta—the family? For, for all his ambition and courage and desire to be out and doing, Clyde always struck her as one who was not any too powerful physically or rock-ribbed morally or mentally. So far as his nerves and emotions were concerned, at times he seemed to take after his father more than he did after her. And for the most part it was so easy to excite him—to cause him to show tenseness and strain—as though he were not so very well fit ted for either. And it was she, because of Esta and her husband and their joint and unfortunate lives, that was and had been heaping the greater part of this strain on him.

"Well, if you can't, you can't," she said. "I must try and think of some other way." But she saw no clear way at the moment.

# Chapter XVII

I N CONNECTION with the automobile ride suggested and arranged for the following Sunday by Hegglund through his chauffeur friend, a change of plan was announced. The car—an expensive Packard, no less—could not be had for that day, but must be used by this Thursday or Friday, or not at all. For, as had been previously explained to all, but not with the strictest adherence to the truth, the car belonged to a certain Mr. Kimbark, an elderly and very wealthy man who at the time was traveling in Asia. Also, what was not true was that this particular youth was not Mr. Kimbark's chauffeur at all, but rather the rakish, ne'er-do-well son of Sparser, the superintendent of one of Mr. Kimbark's stock farms. This son being anxious to pose as something more than the son of a superintendent of a farm, and as an occasional watchman, having access to the cars, had decided to take the very finest of them and ride in it.

It was Hegglund who proposed that he and his hotel friends be included on some interesting trip. But since the general invitation had been given, word had come that within the next few weeks Mr. Kimbark was likely to return. And because of this, Willard Sparser had decided at once that it might be best not to use the car any more. He might be taken unawares, perhaps, by Mr. Kimbark's unexpected arrival. Laying this difficulty before Hegglund, who was eager for the trip, the latter had scouted the idea. Why not use it once more anyhow? He had stirred up the interest of all of his friends in this and now hated to disappoint them. The following Friday, between noon and six o'clock, was fixed upon as the day. And since Hortense had changed in her plans she now decided to accompany Clyde, who had been invited, of course.

But as Hegglund had explained to Ratterer and Higby since it was being used without the owner's consent, they must meet rather far out—the men in one of the quiet streets near Seventeenth and West Prospect, from which point they could proceed to a meeting place more convenient for the girls, namely, Twentieth and Washington. From thence they would speed via the west Parkway and the Hannibal Bridge north and east to Harlem, North Kansas City, Minaville and so through Liberty and Moseby to Excelsior Springs. Their chief objective there was a little inn—the Wigwam—a mile or two this side of Excelsior which was open the year round. It was really a combination of restaurant and dancing parlor and hotel. A Victrola and Wurlitzer player-piano furnished the necessary music. Such groups as this were not infrequent, and Hegglund as well as Higby, who had been there on several occasions, described it as dandy. The food was good and the road to it excellent. There was a little river just below it where in the summer time at least there was rowing and fishing. In winter some people skated when there was ice. To be sure, at this time—January—the road was heavily packed with snow, but easy to get over, and the scenery fine. There was a little lake not so far from Excelsior, at this time of year also frozen over, and according to Hegglund, who was always unduly imaginative and high-spirited, they might go there and skate.

"Will you listen to who's talkin' about skatin' on a trip like this?" commented Ratterer, rather cynically, for to his way of thinking this was no occasion for any such side athletics, but for love-making exclusively.

"Aw, hell, can't a fellow have a funny idea even widout bein' roasted for it?" retorted the author of the idea.

The only one, apart from Sparser, who suffered any qualms in connection with all this was Clyde himself. For to him, from the first, the fact that the car to be used did not belong to Sparser, but to his employer, was disturbing, almost irritatingly so. He did not like the idea of taking anything that belonged to any one else, even for temporary use. Something might happen. They might be found out.

"Don't you think it's dangerous for us to be going out in this car?" he asked of Ratterer a few days before the trip and when he fully understood the nature of the source of the car.

"Oh, I don't know," replied Ratterer, who being accustomed to such ideas and devices as this was not much disturbed by them. "I'm not taking the car and you're not, are you? If he wants to take it, that's his lookout, ain't it? If he wants me to go, I'll go. Why wouldn't I? All I want is to be brought back here on time. That's the only thing that would ever worry me."

And Higby, coming up at the moment, had voiced exactly the same sentiments. Yet Clyde remained troubled. It might not work out right; he might lose his job through a thing like this. But so fascinated was he by the thought of riding in such a fine car with Hortense and with all these other girls and boys that he could not resist the temptation to go.

Immediately after noon on the Friday of this particular week the several participants of the outing were gathered at the points agreed upon. Hegglund, Ratterer, Higby and Clyde at Eighteenth and West Prospect near the railroad yards. Maida Axelrod, Hegglund's girl, Lucille Nickolas, a friend of Ratterer's, and Tina Kogel, a friend of Higby's, also Laura Sipe, another girl who was brought by Tina Kogel to be introduced to Sparser for the occasion, at Twentieth and Washington. Only since Hortense had sent word at the last moment to Clyde that she had to go out to her house for something, and that they were to run out to Forty-ninth and Genesee, where she lived, they did so, but not without grumbling.

The day, a late January one, was inclined to be smoky with lowering clouds, especially within the environs of Kansas City. It even threatened snow at times—a most interesting and picturesque prospect to those within. They liked it.

"Oh, gee, I hope it does," Tina Kogel exclaimed when some one commented on the possibility, and Lucille Nickolas added: "Oh, I just love to see it snow at times." Along the West Bluff Road, Washington and Second Streets, they finally made their way across the Hannibal Bridge to Harlem, and from thence along the winding and hill-sentineled river road to Randolph Heights and Minaville. And beyond that came Moseby and Liberty, to and through which the road bed was better, with interesting glimpses of small homesteads and the bleak snow-covered hills of January.

Clyde, who for all his years in Kansas City had never ventured much beyond Kansas City, Kansas, on the west or the primitive and natural woods of Swope Parks on the east, nor farther along the Kansas or Missouri Rivers than Argentine on the one side and Randolph Heights on the other, was quite

fascinated by the idea of travel which appeared to be suggested by all this—distant travel. It was all so different from
his ordinary routine. And on this occasion Hortense was inclined to be very genial and friendly. She snuggled down beside him on the seat, and when he, noting that the others had
already drawn their girls to them in affectionate embraces, put
his arm about her and drew her to him, she made no particular protest. Instead she looked up and said: "I'll have to take
my hat off, I guess." The others laughed. There was something about her quick, crisp way which was amusing at times.
Besides she had done her hair in a new way which made her
look decidedly prettier, and she was anxious to have the others see it.

"Can we dance anywhere out here?" she called to the others, without looking around.

"Surest thing you know," said Higby, who by now had persuaded Tina Kogel to take her hat off and was holding her
close. "They got a player-piano and a Victrola out there. If
I'd 'a' thought, I'd 'a' brought my cornet. I can play Dixie on
that."

The car was speeding at breakneck pace over a snowy white
road and between white fields. In fact, Sparser, considering
himself a master of car manipulation as well as the real owner
of it for the moment, was attempting to see how fast he could
go on such a road.

Dark vignettes of woods went by to right and left. Fields
away, sentinel hills rose and fell like waves. A wide-armed
scarecrow fluttering in the wind, its tall decayed hat awry,
stood near at hand in one place. And from near it a flock of
crows rose and winged direct toward a distant wood lightly
penciled against a foreground of snow.

In the front seat sat Sparser, guiding the car beside Laura
Sipe with the air of one to whom such a magnificent car was
a commonplace thing. He was really more interested in
Hortense, yet felt it incumbent on him, for the time being,
anyhow, to show some attention to Laura Sipe. And not to be
outdone in gallantry by the others, he now put one arm
about Laura Sipe while he guided the car with the other, a
feat which troubled Clyde, who was still dubious about the
wisdom of taking the car at all. They might all be wrecked by

such fast driving. Hortense was only interested by the fact that Sparser had obviously manifested his interest in her; that he had to pay some attention to Laura Sipe whether he wanted to or not. And when she saw him pull her to him and asked her grandly if she had done much automobiling about Kansas City, she merely smiled to herself.

But Ratterer, noting the move, nudged Lucille Nickolas, and she in turn nudged Higby, in order to attract his attention to the affectional development ahead.

"Getting comfortable up front there, Willard?" called Ratterer, genially, in order to make friends with him.

"I'll say I am," replied Sparser, gayly and without turning. "How about you, girlie?"

"Oh, I'm all right," Laura Sipe replied.

But Clyde was thinking that of all the girls present none was really so pretty as Hortense—not nearly. She had come garbed in a red and black dress with a very dark red poke bonnet to match. And on her left cheek, just below her small rouged mouth, she had pasted a minute square of black court plaster in imitation of some picture beauty she had seen. In fact, before the outing began, she had been determined to outshine all the others present, and distinctly she was now feeling that she was succeeding. And Clyde, for himself, was agreeing with her.

"You're the cutest thing here," whispered Clyde, hugging her fondly.

"Gee, but you can pour on the molasses, kid, when you want to," she called out loud, and the others laughed. And Clyde flushed slightly.

Beyond Minaville about six miles the car came to a bend in a hollow where there was a country store and here Hegglund, Higby and Ratterer got out to fetch candy, cigarettes and ice cream cones and ginger ale. And after that came Liberty, and then several miles this side of Excelsior Springs, they sighted the Wigwam which was nothing more than an old two-story farmhouse snuggled against a rise of ground behind it. There was, however, adjoining it on one side a newer and larger one-story addition consisting of the dining-room, the dance floor, and concealed by a partition at one end, a bar. An open fire flickered cheerfully here in a large fireplace. Down in a hollow across the road might be seen the Benton River or creek, now frozen solid.

"There's your river," called Higby cheerfully as he helped Tina Kogel out of the car, for he was already very much warmed by several drinks he had taken en route. They all paused for a moment to admire the stream, winding away among the trees. "I wanted dis bunch to bring dere skates and go down dere," sighed Hegglund, "but dey wouldn't. Well, dat's all right."

By then Lucille Nickolas, seeing a flicker of flame reflected in one of the small windows of the inn, called, "Oh, see, they gotta fire."

The car was parked, and they all trooped into the inn, and at once Higby briskly went over and started the large, noisy, clattery, tinny Nickelodeon with a nickel. And to rival him, and for a prank, Hegglund ran to the victrola which stood in one corner and put on a record of "The Grizzly Bear," which he found lying there.

At the first sounds of this strain, which they all knew, Tina Kogel called: "Oh, let's all dance to that, will you? Can't you stop that other old thing?" she added.

"Sure, after it runs down," explained Ratterer, laughingly. "The only way to stop that thing is not to feed it any nickels."

But now a waiter coming in, Higby began to inquire what everybody wanted. And in the meantime, to show off her charms, Hortense had taken the center of the floor and was attempting to imitate a grizzly bear walking on its hind legs, which she could do amusingly enough—quite gracefully. And Sparser, seeing her alone in the center of the floor and anxious to interest her now, followed her and tried to imitate her motions from behind. Finding him clever at it, and anxious to dance, she finally abandoned the imitation and giving him her arms went one-stepping about the room most vividly. At once, Clyde, who was by no means as good a dancer, became jealous—painfully so. In his eagerness for her, it seemed unfair to him that he should be deserted by her so early—at the very beginning of things. But she, becoming interested in Sparser, who seemed more worldly-wise, paid no attention at all to Clyde for the time being, but went dancing with her new conquest, his rhythmic skill seeming charmingly to match her own. And then, not to be out of it, the others at once chose partners, Hegglund dancing with Maida, Ratterer with Lucille and Higby with Tina Kogel. This left Laura Sipe for Clyde, who did not like her very much. She was not as perfect as she might be—a plump, pudgy-faced girl with inadequate sensual blue eyes—and Clyde, lacking any exceptional skill, they danced nothing but the conventional one-step while the others were dipping and lurching and spinning.

In a kind of sick fury, Clyde noticed that Sparser, who was still with Hortense, was by now holding her close and looking straight into her eyes. And she was permitting him. It gave him a feeling of lead at the pit of his stomach. Was it possible she was beginning to like this young upstart who had this car? And she had promised to like him for the present. It brought to him a sense of her fickleness—the probability of her real indifference to him. He wanted to do something— stop dancing and get her away from Sparser, but there was no use until this particular record ran out.

And then, just at the end of this, the waiter returned with a tray and put down cocktails, ginger ale and sandwiches upon three small tables which had been joined together. All but Sparser and Hortense quit and came toward it—a fact which Clyde was quick to note. She was a heartless flirt! She really did not care for him after all. And after making him think that she did, so recently—and getting him to help her with that coat. She could go to the devil now. He would show her. And he waiting for her! Wasn't that the limit? Yet, finally, seeing that the others were gathering about the tables, which had been placed near the fire, Hortense and Sparser ceased dancing and approached. Clyde was white and glum. He stood to one side, seemingly indifferent. And Laura Sipe, who had already noted his rage and understood the reason now moved away from him to join Tina Kogel, to whom she explained why he was so angry.

And then noting his glumness, Hortense came over, executing a phase of the "Grizzly" as she did so.

"Gee, wasn't that swell?" she began. "Gee, how I do love to dance to music like that!"

"Sure, it's swell for you," returned Clyde, burning with envy and disappointment.

"Why, what's the trouble?" she asked, in a low and almost

injured tone, pretending not to guess, yet knowing quite well why he was angry. "You don't mean to say that you're mad because I danced with him first, do you? Oh, how silly! Why didn't you come over then and dance with me? I couldn't refuse to dance with him when he was right there, could I?"

"Oh, no, of course, you couldn't," replied Clyde sarcastically, and in a low, tense tone, for he, no more than Hortense, wanted the others to hear. "But you didn't have to fall all over him and dream in his eyes, either, did you?" He was fairly blazing. "You needn't say you didn't, because I saw you."

At this she glanced at him oddly, realizing not only the sharpness of his mood, but that this was the first time he had shown so much daring in connection with her. It must be that he was getting to feel too sure of her. She was showing him too much attention. At the same time she realized that this was not the time to show him that she did not care for him as much as she would like to have him believe, since she wanted the coat, already agreed upon.

"Oh, gee, well, ain't that the limit?" she replied angrily, yet more because she was irritated by the fact that what he said was true than anything else. "If you aren't the grouch. Well, I can't help it, if you're going to be as jealous as that. I didn't do anything but dance with him just a little. I didn't think you'd be mad." She moved as if to turn away, but realizing that there was an understanding between them, and that he must be placated if things were to go on, she drew him by his coat lapels out of the range of the hearing of the others, who were already looking and listening, and began.

"Now, see here, you. Don't go acting like this. I didn't mean anything by what I did. Honest, I didn't. Anyhow, everybody dances like that now. And nobody means anything by it. Aren't you goin' to let me be nice to you like I said, or are you?"

And now she looked him coaxingly and winsomely and calculatingly straight in the eye, as though he were the one person among all these present whom she really did like. And deliberately, and of a purpose, she made a pursy, sensuous mouth—the kind she could make—and practised a play of the lips that caused them to seem to want to kiss him—a mouth that tempted him to distraction.

"All right," he said, looking at her weakly and yieldingly. "I suppose I am a fool, but I saw what you did, all right. You know I'm crazy about you, Hortense—just wild! I can't help it. I wish I could sometimes. I wish I wouldn't be such a fool." And he looked at her and was sad. And she, realizing her power over him and how easy it was to bring him around, replied: "Oh, you—you don't, either. I'll kiss you after a while, when the others aren't looking if you'll be good." At the same time she was conscious of the fact that Sparser's eyes were upon her. Also that he was intensely drawn to her and that she liked him more than any one she had recently encountered.

# Chapter XVIII

THE CLIMAX of the afternoon was reached, however, when
after several more dances and drinks, the small river and
its possibilities was again brought to the attention of all by
Hegglund, who, looking out of one of the windows, suddenly
exclaimed: "What's de matter wit de ice down dere? Look at
de swell ice. I dare dis crowd to go down dere and slide."

They were off pell-mell—Ratterer and Tina Kogel, running
hand in hand, Sparser and Lucille Nickolas, with whom he
had just been dancing, Higby and Laura Sipe, whom he was
finding interesting enough for a change, and Clyde and
Hortense. But once on the ice, which was nothing more than
a narrow, winding stream, blown clean in places by the wind,
and curving among thickets of leafless trees, the company
were more like young satyrs and nymphs of an older day.
They ran here and there, slipping and sliding—Higby, Lucille
and Maida immediately falling down, but scrambling to their
feet with bursts of laughter.

And Hortense, aided by Clyde at first, minced here and
there. But soon she began to run and slide, squealing in pretended fear. And now, not only Sparser but Higby, and this in
spite of Clyde, began to show Hortense attention. They
joined her in sliding, ran after her and pretended to try to trip
her up, but caught her as she fell. And Sparser, taking her by
the hand, dragged her, seemingly in spite of herself and the
others, far upstream and about a curve where they could not
be seen. Determined not to show further watchfulness or jealousy Clyde remained behind. But he could not help feeling
that Sparser might be taking this occasion to make a date,
even to kiss her. She was not incapable of letting him, even
though she might pretend to him that she did not want him
to. It was agonizing.

In spite of himself, he began to tingle with helpless pain—
to begin to wish that he could see them. But Hegglund,
having called every one to join hands and crack the whip, he
took the hand of Lucille Nickolas, who was holding on to
Hegglund's, and gave his other free hand to Maida Axelrod,

who in turn gave her free hand to Ratterer. And Higby and Laura Sipe were about to make up the tail when Sparser and Hortense came gliding back—he holding her by the hand. And they now tacked on at the foot. Then Hegglund and the others began running and doubling back and forth until all beyond Maida had fallen and let go. And, as Clyde noted, Hortense and Sparser, in falling, skidded and rolled against each other to the edge of the shore where were snow and leaves and twigs. And Hortense's skirts, becoming awry in some way, moved up to above her knees. But instead of showing any embarrassment, as Clyde thought and wished she might, she sat there for a few moments without shame and even laughing heartily—and Sparser with her and still holding her hand. And Laura Sipe, having fallen in such a way as to trip Higby, who had fallen across her, they also lay there laughing and yet in a most suggestive position, as Clyde thought. He noted, too, that Laura Sipe's skirts had been worked above her knees. And Sparser, now sitting up, was pointing to her pretty legs and laughing loudly, showing most of his teeth. And all the others were emitting peals and squeals of laughter.

"Hang it all!" thought Clyde. "Why the deuce does he always have to be hanging about her? Why didn't he bring a girl of his own if he wanted to have a good time? What right have they got to go where they can't be seen? And she thinks I think she means nothing by all this. She never laughs that heartily with me, you bet. What does she think I am that she can put that stuff over on me, anyhow?" He glowered darkly for the moment, but in spite of his thoughts the line or whip was soon re-formed and this time with Lucille Nickolas still holding his hand. Sparser and Hortense at the tail end again. But Hegglund, unconscious of the mood of Clyde and thinking only of the sport, called: "Better let some one else take de end dere, hadn'tcha?" And feeling the fairness of this, Ratterer and Maida Axelrod and Clyde and Lucille Nickolas now moved down with Higby and Laura Sipe and Hortense and Sparser above them. Only, as Clyde noted, Hortense still held Sparser by the hand, yet she moved just above him and took his hand, he being to the right, with Sparser next above to her left, holding her other hand firmly, which infuriated Clyde.

Why couldn't he stick to Laura Sipe, the girl brought out here for him? And Hortense was encouraging him.

He was very sad, and he felt so angry and bitter that he could scarcely play the game. He wanted to stop and quarrel with Sparser. But so brisk and eager was Hegglund that they were off before he could even think of doing so.

And then, try as he would, to keep his balance in the face of this, he and Lucille and Ratterer and Maida Axelrod were thrown down and spun around on the ice like curling irons. And Hortense, letting go of him at the right moment, seemed to prefer deliberately to hang on to Sparser. Entangled with these others, Clyde and they spun across forty feet of smooth, green ice and piled against a snow bank. At the finish, as he found, Lucille Nickolas was lying across his knees face down in such a spanking position that he was compelled to laugh. And Maida Axelrod was on her back, next to Ratterer, her legs straight up in the air; on purpose he thought. She was too coarse and bold for him. And there followed, of course, squeals and guffaws of delight—so loud that they could be heard for half a mile. Hegglund, intensely susceptible to humor at all times, doubled to the knees, slapped his thighs and bawled. And Sparser opened his big mouth and chortled and grimaced until he was scarlet. So infectious was the result that for the time being Clyde forgot his jealousy. He too looked and laughed. But Clyde's mood had not changed really. He still felt that she wasn't playing fair.

At the end of all this playing Lucille Nickolas and Tina Kogel being tired, dropped out. And Hortense, also. Clyde at once left the group to join her. Ratterer then followed Lucille. Then the others separating, Hegglund pushed Maida Axelrod before him down stream out of sight around a bend. Higby, seemingly taking his cue from this, pulled Tina Kogel up stream, and Ratterer and Lucille, seeming to see something of interest, struck into a thicket, laughing and talking as they went. Even Sparser and Laura, left to themselves, now wandered off, leaving Clyde and Hortense alone.

And then, as these two wandered toward a fallen log which here paralleled the stream, she sat down. But Clyde, smarting from his fancied wounds, stood silent for the time being, while she, sensing as much, took him by the belt of his coat and began to pull at him.

"Giddap, horsey," she played. "Giddap. My horsey has to skate me now on the ice."

Clyde looked at her glumly, glowering mentally, and not to be diverted so easily from the ills which he felt to be his.

"Whadd'ye wanta let that fellow Sparser always hang around you for?" he demanded. "I saw you going up the creek there with him a while ago. What did he say to you up there?"

"He didn't say anything."

"Oh, no, of course not," he replied cynically and bitterly. "And maybe he didn't kiss you, either."

"I should say not," she replied definitely and spitefully, "I'd like to know what you think I am, anyhow. I don't let people kiss me the first time they see me, smarty, and I want you to know it. I didn't let you, did I?"

"Oh, that's all right, too," answered Clyde; "but you didn't like me as well as you do him, either."

"Oh, didn't I? Well, maybe I didn't, but what right have you to say I like him, anyhow. I'd like to know if I can't have a little fun without you watching me all the time. You make me tired, that's what you do." She was quite angry now because of the proprietary air he appeared to be assuming.

And now Clyde, repulsed and somewhat shaken by this sudden counter on her part, decided on the instant that perhaps it might be best for him to modify his tone. After all, she had never said that she had really cared for him, even in the face of the implied promise she had made him.

"Oh, well," he observed glumly after a moment, and not without a little of sadness in his tone, "I know one thing. If I let on that I cared for any one as much as you say you do for me at times, I wouldn't want to flirt around with others like you are doing out here."

"Oh, wouldn't you?"

"No, I wouldn't."

"Well, who's flirting anyhow, I'd like to know?"

"You are."

"I'm not either, and I wish you'd just go away and let me alone if you can't do anything else but quarrel with me. Just

because I danced with him up there in the restaurant, is no
reason for you to think I'm flirting. Oh, you make me tired,
that's what you do."

"Do I?"

"Yes, you do."

"Well, maybe I better go off and not bother you any more
at all then," he returned, a trace of his mother's courage
welling up in him.

"Well, maybe you had, if that's the way you're going to feel
about me all the time," she answered, and kicked viciously
with her toes at the ice. But Clyde was beginning to feel that
he could not possibly go through with this—that after all he
was too eager about her—too much at her feet. He began to
weaken and gaze nervously at her. And she, thinking of her
coat again, decided to be civil.

"You didn't look in his eyes, did you?" he asked weakly, his
thoughts going back to her dancing with Sparser.

"When?"

"When you were dancing with him?"

"No, I didn't, not that I know of, anyhow. But supposing
I did. What of it? I didn't mean anything by it. Gee, criminy,
can't a person look in anybody's eyes if they want to?"

"In the way you looked in his? Not if you claim to like anybody else, I say." And the skin of Clyde's forehead lifted and
sank, and his eyelids narrowed. Hortense merely clicked impatiently and indignantly with her tongue.

"Tst! Tst! Tst! If you ain't the limit!"

"And a while ago back there on the ice," went on Clyde
determinedly and yet pathetically. "When you came back from
up there, instead of coming up to where I was you went to
the foot of the line with him. I saw you. And you held his
hand, too, all the way back. And then when you fell down,
you had to sit there with him holding your hand. I'd like to
know what you call that if it ain't flirting. What else is it? I'll
bet he thinks it is, all right."

"Well, I wasn't flirting with him just the same and I don't
care what you say. But if you want to have it that way, have it
that way. I can't stop you. You're so darn jealous you don't
want to let anybody else do anything, that's all the matter
with you. How else can you play on the ice if you don't hold

hands, I'd like to know? Gee, criminy! What about you and
that Lucille Nickolas? I saw her laying across your lap and you
laughing. And I didn't think anything of that. What do you
want me to do—come out here and sit around like a bump on
a log?—follow you around like a tail? Or you follow me?
What-a-yuh think I am anyhow? A nut?"

She was being ragged by Clyde, as she thought, and she
didn't like it. She was thinking of Sparser who was really more
appealing to her at the time than Clyde. He was more mate-
rialistic, less romantic, more direct.

He turned and, taking off his cap, rubbed his head
gloomily while Hortense, looking at him, thought first of him
and then of Sparser. Sparser was more manly, not so much of
a crybaby. He wouldn't stand around and complain this way,
you bet. He'd probably leave her for good, have nothing
more to do with her. Yet Clyde, after his fashion, was interesting and useful. Who else would do for her what he had?
And at any rate, he was not trying to force her to go off with
him now as these others had gone and as she had feared he
might try to do—ahead of her plan and wish. This quarrel
was obviating that.

"Now, see here," she said after a time, having decided that
it was best to assuage him and that it was not so hard to manage him after all. "Are we goin' t' fight all the time, Clyde?
What's the use, anyhow? Whatja want me to come out here
for if you just want to fight with me all the time? I wouldn't
have come if I'd 'a' thought you were going to do that all day."

She turned and kicked at the ice with the minute toe of her
shoes, and Clyde, always taken by her charm again, put his
arms about her, and crushed her to him, at the same time
fumbling at her breasts and putting his lips to hers and endeavoring to hold and fondle her. But now, because of her
suddenly developed liking for Sparser, and partially because of
her present mood towards Clyde, she broke away, a dissatisfaction with herself and him troubling her. Why should she let
him force her to do anything she did not feel like doing, just
now, anyhow, she now asked herself. She hadn't agreed to be
as nice to him to-day as he might wish. Not yet. At any rate
just now she did not want to be handled in this way by him,
and she would not, regardless of what he might do. And

Clyde, sensing by now what the true state of her mind in regard to him must be, stepped back and yet continued to gaze gloomily and hungrily at her. And she in turn merely stared at him.

"I thought you said you liked me," he demanded almost savagely now, realizing that his dreams of a happy outing this day were fading into nothing.

"Well, I do when you're nice," she replied, sly and evasively, seeking some way to avoid complication in connection with her original promises to him.

"Yes, you do," he grumbled. "I see how you do. Why, here we are out here now and you won't even let me touch you. I'd like to know what you meant by all that you said, anyhow."

"Well, what did I say?" she countered, merely to gain time.

"As though you didn't know."

"Oh, well. But that wasn't to be right away, either, was it? I thought we said"—she paused dubiously.

"I know what you said," he went on. "But I notice now that you don't like me an' that's all there is to it. What difference would it make if you really cared for me whether you were nice to me now or next week or the week after? Gee whiz, you'd think it was something that depended on what I did for you, not whether you cared for me." In his pain he was quite intense and courageous.

"That's not so!" she snapped, angrily and bitterly, irritated by the truth of what he said. "And I wish you wouldn't say that to me, either. I don't care anything about the old coat now, if you want to know it. And you can just let me alone from now on, too," she added. "I'll get all the coats I want without any help from you." At this, she turned and walked away.

But Clyde, now anxious to mollify her as usual, ran after her. "Don't go, Hortense," he pleaded. "Wait a minute. I didn't mean that either, honest I didn't. I'm crazy about you. Honest I am. Can't you see that? Oh, gee, don't go now. I'm not giving you the money to get something for it. You can have it for nothing if you want it that way. There ain't anybody else in the world like you to me, and there never has been. You can have the money for all I care, all of it. I don't want it back. But, gee, I did think you liked me a little. Don't you care for me at all, Hortense?" He looked cowed and frightened, and she, sensing her mastery over him, relented a little.

"Of course I do," she announced. "But just the same, that don't mean that you can treat me any old way, either. You don't seem to understand that a girl can't do everything you want her to do just when you want her to do it."

"Just what do you mean by that?" asked Clyde, not quite sensing just what she did mean. "I don't get you."

"Oh, yes, you do, too." She could not believe that he did not know.

"Oh, I guess I know what you're talkin' about. I know what you're going to say now," he went on disappointedly. "That's that old stuff they all pull. I know."

He was now reciting almost verbatim the words and intonations even of the other boys at the hotel— Higby, Ratterer, Eddie Doyle—who, having narrated the nature of such situations to him, and how girls occasionally lied out of pressing dilemmas in this way, had made perfectly clear to him what was meant. And Hortense knew now that he did know.

"Gee, but you're mean," she said in an assumed hurt way. "A person can never tell you anything or expect you to believe it. Just the same, it's true, whether you believe it or not."

"Oh, I know how you are," he replied, sadly yet a little loftily, as though this were an old situation to him. "You don't like me, that's all. I see that now, all right."

"Gee, but you're mean," she persisted, affecting an injured air. "It's the God's truth. Believe me or not, I swear it. Honest it is."

Clyde stood there. In the face of this small trick there was really nothing much to say as he saw it. He could not force her to do anything. If she wanted to lie and pretend, he would have to pretend to believe her. And yet a great sadness settled down upon him. He was not to win her after all—that was plain. He turned, and she, being convinced that he felt that she was lying now, felt it incumbent upon herself to do something about it—to win him around to her again.

"Please, Clyde, please," she began now, most artfully, "I

mean that. Really, I do. Won't you believe me? But I will next week, sure. Honest, I will. Won't you believe that? I meant everything I said when I said it. Honest, I did. I do like you— a lot. Won't you believe that, too—please?"

And Clyde, thrilled from head to toe by this latest phase of her artistry, agreed that he would. And once more he began to smile and recover his gayety. And by the time they reached the car, to which they were all called a few minutes after by Hegglund, because of the time, and he had held her hand and kissed her often, he was quite convinced that the dream he had been dreaming was as certain of fulfillment as anything could be. Oh, the glory of it when it should come true!

# Chapter XIX

FOR the major portion of the return trip to Kansas City, there was nothing to mar the very agreeable illusion under which Clyde rested. He sat beside Hortense, who leaned her head against his shoulder. And although Sparser, who had waited for the others to step in before taking the wheel, had squeezed her arm and received an answering and promising look, Clyde had not seen that.

But the hour being late and the admonitions of Hegglund, Ratterer and Higby being all for speed, and the mood of Sparser, because of the looks bestowed upon him by Hortense, being the gayest and most drunken, it was not long before the outlying lamps of the environs began to show. For the car was rushed along the road at break-neck speed. At one point, however, where one of the eastern trunk lines approached the city, there was a long and unexpected and disturbing wait at a grade crossing where two freight trains met and passed. Farther in, at North Kansas City, it began to snow, great soft slushy flakes, feathering down and coating the road surface with a slippery layer of mud which required more caution than had been thus far displayed. It was then half past five. Ordinarily, an additional eight minutes at high speed would have served to bring the car within a block or two of the hotel. But now, with another delay near Hannibal Bridge owing to grade crossing, it was twenty minutes to six before the bridge was crossed and Wyandotte Street reached. And already all four of these youths had lost all sense of the delight of the trip and the pleasure the companionship of these girls had given them. For already they were worrying as to the probability of their reaching the hotel in time. The smug and martinetish figure of Mr. Squires loomed before them all.

"Gee, if we don't do better than this," observed Ratterer to Higby, who was nervously fumbling with his watch, "we're not goin' to make it. We'll hardly have time, as it is, to change."

Clyde, hearing him, exclaimed: "Oh, crickets! I wish we

could hurry a little. Gee, I wish now we hadn't come to-day. It'll be tough if we don't get there on time."

And Hortense, noting his sudden tenseness and unrest, added: "Don't you think you'll make it all right?"

"Not this way," he said. But Hegglund, who had been studying the flaked air outside, a world that seemed dotted with falling bits of cotton, called: "Eh, dere Willard. We certainly gotta do better dan dis. It means de razoo for us if we don't get dere on time."

And Higby, for once stirred out of a gambler-like effrontery and calm, added: "We'll walk the plank all right unless we can put up some good yarn. Can't anybody think of anything?" As for Clyde, he merely sighed nervously.

And then, as though to torture them the more, an unexpected crush of vehicles appeared at nearly every intersection. And Sparser, who was irritated by this particular predicament, was contemplating with impatience the warning hand of a traffic policeman, which, at the intersection of Ninth and Wyandotte, had been raised against him. "There goes his mit again," he exclaimed. "What can I do about that! I might turn over to Washington, but I don't know whether we'll save any time by going over there."

A full minute passed before he was signaled to go forward. Then swiftly he swung the car to the right and three blocks over into Washington Street.

But here the conditions were no better. Two heavy lines of traffic moved in opposite directions. And at each succeeding corner several precious moments were lost as the cross-traffic went by. Then the car would tear on to the next corner, weaving its way in and out as best it could.

At Fifteenth and Washington, Clyde exclaimed to Ratterer: "How would it do if we got out at Seventeenth and walked over?"

"You won't save any time if I can turn over there," called Sparser. "I can get over there quicker than you can."

He crowded the other cars for every inch of available space. At Sixteenth and Washington, seeing what he considered a fairly clear block to the left, he turned the car and tore along that thoroughfare to as far as Wyandotte once more. Just as he neared the corner and was about to turn at high speed, swinging in close to the curb to do so, a little girl of about nine, who was running toward the crossing, jumped directly in front of the moving machine. And because there was no opportunity given him to turn and avoid her, she was struck and dragged a number of feet before the machine could be halted. At the same time, there arose piercing screams from at least half a dozen women, and shouts from as many men who had witnessed the accident.

Instantly they all rushed toward the child, who had been thrown under and passed over by the wheels. And Sparser, looking out and seeing them gathering about the fallen figure, was seized with an uninterpretable mental panic which conjured up the police, jail, his father, the owner of the car, severe punishment in many forms. And though by now all the others in the car were up and giving vent to anguished exclamations such as "Oh, God! He hit a little girl"; "Oh, gee, he's killed a kid!" "Oh, mercy!" "Oh, Lord!" "Oh, heavens, what'll we do now?" he turned and exclaimed: "Jesus, the cops! I gotta get outa this with this car."

And, without consulting the others, who were still half standing, but almost speechless with fear, he shot the lever into first, second and then high, and giving the engine all the gas it would endure, sped with it to the next corner beyond.

But there, as at the other corners in this vicinity, a policeman was stationed, and having already seen some commotion at the corner west of him, had already started to leave his post in order to ascertain what it was. As he did so, cries of "Stop that car"—"Stop that car"—reached his ears. And a man, running toward the sedan from the scene of the accident, pointed to it, and called: "Stop that car, stop that car. They've killed a child."

Then gathering what was meant, he turned toward the car, putting his police whistle to his mouth as he did so. But Sparser, having by this time heard the cries and seen the policeman leaving, dashed swiftly past him into Seventeenth Street, along which he sped at almost forty miles an hour, grazing the hub of a truck in one instance, scraping the fender of an automobile in another, and missing by inches and quarter inches vehicles or pedestrians, while those behind him in the car were for the most part sitting bolt upright and tense, their eyes wide, their hands clenched, their faces and lips set—or, as in the case of Hortense and Lucille Nickolas and Tina Kogel, giving voice to repeated, "Oh, Gods!" "Oh, what's going to happen now?"

But the police and those who had started to pursue were not to be outdone so quickly. Unable to make out the license plate number and seeing from the first motions of the car that it had no intention of stopping, the officer blew a loud and long blast on his police whistle. And the policeman at the next corner seeing the car speed by and realizing what it meant, blew on his whistle, then stopped, and springing on the running board of a passing touring car ordered it to give chase. And at this, seeing what was amiss or awind, three other cars, driven by adventurous spirits, joined in the chase, all honking loudly as they came.

But the Packard had far more speed in it than any of its pursuers, and although for the first few blocks of the pursuit there were cries of "Stop that car!" "Stop that car!" still, owing to the much greater speed of the car, these soon died away, giving place to the long wild shrieks of distant horns in full cry.

Sparser by now having won a fair lead and realizing that a straight course was the least baffling to pursue, turned swiftly into McGee, a comparatively quiet thoroughfare along which he tore for a few blocks to the wide and winding Gillham Parkway, whose course was southward. But having followed that at terrific speed for a short distance, he again—at Thirty-first—decided to turn—the houses in the distance confusing him and the suburban country to the north seeming to offer the best opportunity for evading his pursuers. And so now he swung the car to the left into that thoroughfare, his thought here being that amid these comparatively quiet streets it was possible to wind in and out and so shake off pursuit—at least long enough to drop his passengers somewhere and return the car to the garage.

And this he would have been able to do had it not been for the fact that in turning into one of the more outlying streets of this region, where there were scarcely any houses and no pedestrians visible, he decided to turn off his lights, the better to conceal the whereabouts of the car. Then, still speeding east, north, and east and south by turns, he finally dashed into one street where, after a few hundred feet, the pavement suddenly ended. But because another cross street was visible a hundred feet or so further on, and he imagined that by turning into that he might find a paved thoroughfare again, he sped on and then swung sharply to the left, only to crash roughly into a pile of paving stones left by a contractor who was preparing to pave the way. In the absence of the lights he had failed to distinguish this. And diagonally opposite to these, lengthwise of a prospective sidewalk, had been laid a pile of lumber for a house.

Striking the edge of the paving stones at high speed, he caromed, and all but upsetting the car, made directly for the lumber pile opposite, into which he crashed. Only instead of striking it head on, the car struck one end, causing it to give way and spread out, but only sufficiently to permit the right wheels to mount high upon it and so throw the car completely over onto its left side in the grass and snow beyond the walk. Then there, amid a crash of glass and the impacts of their own bodies, the occupants were thrown down in a heap, forward and to the left.

What happened afterwards was more or less of a mystery and a matter of confusion, not only to Clyde, but to all the others. For Sparser and Laura Sipe, being in front, were dashed against the wind-shield and the roof and knocked senseless, Sparser, having his shoulder, hip and left knee wrenched in such a way as to make it necessary to let him lie in the car as he was until an ambulance arrived. He could not possibly be lifted out through the door, which was in the roof as the car now lay. And in the second seat, Clyde, being nearest the door to the left and next to him Hortense, Lucille Nickolas and Ratterer, was pinioned under and yet not crushed by their combined weights. For Hortense in falling had been thrown completely over him on her side against the roof, which was now the left wall. And Lucille, next above her, fell in such a way as to lie across Clyde's shoulders only, while Ratterer, now topmost of the four, had, in falling, been thrown over the seat in front of him. But grasping the steering wheel in front of him as he fell, the same having been wrenched from Sparser's hands, he had broken his fall in part by clinging to it. But even so, his face and hands were cut and bruised and his shoulder, arm and hip slightly wrenched, yet not sufficiently to prevent his being of assistance to the others. For at once, realizing the plight of the others as well as his own, and stirred by their screams, Ratterer was moved to draw himself up and out through the top or side door which he now succeeded in opening, scrambling over the others to reach it.

Once out, he climbed upon the chassis beam of the toppled car, and, reaching down, caught hold of the struggling and moaning Lucille, who like the others was trying to climb up but could not. And exerting all his strength and exclaiming, "Be still, now, honey, I gotcha. You're all right, I'll getcha out," he lifted her to a sitting position on the side of the door, then down in the snow, where he placed her and where she sat crying and feeling her arms and her head. And after her he helped Hortense, her left cheek and forehead and both hands badly bruised and bleeding, but not seriously, although she did not know that at the time. She was whimpering and shivering and shaking—a nervous chill having succeeded the dazed and almost unconscious state which had followed the first crash.

At that moment, Clyde, lifting his bewildered head above the side door of the car, his left cheek, shoulder and arm bruised, but not otherwise injured, was thinking that he too must get out of this as quickly as possible. A child had been killed; a car stolen and wrecked; his job was most certainly lost; the police were in pursuit and might even find them there at any minute. And below him in the car was Sparser, prone where he fell, but already being looked to by Ratterer. And beside him Laura Sipe, also unconscious. He felt called upon to do something—to assist Ratterer, who was reaching down and trying to lay hold of Laura Sipe without injuring her. But so confused were his thoughts that he would have stood there without helping any one had it not been for Ratterer, who called most irritably, "Give us a hand here, Clyde, will you? Let's see if we can get her out. She's fainted." And Clyde, turning now instead of trying to climb out, began to seek to lift her from within, standing on the broken glass window of the side beneath his feet and attempting to draw her body back and up off the body of Sparser. But this was not possible. She was too limp—too heavy. He could only draw her back—off the body of Sparser—and then let her rest there, between the second and first seats on the car's side.

But, meanwhile, at the back, Hegglund, being nearest the top and only slightly stunned, had managed to reach the door nearest him and throw it back. Thus, by reason of his athletic body, he was able to draw himself up and out, saying as he did so: "Oh, Jesus, what a finish! Oh, Christ, dis is de limit! Oh, Jesus, we better beat it outa dis before de cops git here."

At the same time, however, seeing the others below him and hearing their cries, he could not contemplate anything so desperate as desertion. Instead, once out, he turned and making out Maida below him, exclaimed: "Here, for Christ's sake, gimme your hand. We gotta get outa dis, and dam quick, I tell ya." Then turning from Maida, who for the moment was feeling her wounded and aching head, he mounted the top chassis beam again and, reaching down, caught hold of Tina Kogel, who, only stunned, was trying to push herself to a sitting position while resting heavily on top of Higby. But he, relieved of the weight of the others, was already kneeling, and feeling his head and face with his hands.

"Gimme your hand, Dave," called Hegglund. "Hurry! For Christ's sake! We ain't got no time to lose around here. Are ya hurt? Christ, we gotta git outa here, I tellya. I see a guy comin' acrost dere now an' I doughno wedder he's a cop or not." He started to lay hold of Higby's left hand, but as he did so Higby repulsed him.

"Huh, uh," he exclaimed. "Don't pull. I'm all right. I'll get out by myself. Help the others." And standing up, his head above the level of the door, he began to look about within the car for something on which to place his foot. The back cushion having fallen out and forward, he got his foot on that and raised himself up to the door level on which he sat and drew out his leg. Then looking about, and seeing Hegglund attempting to assist Ratterer and Clyde with Sparser, he went to their aid.

Outside, some odd and confusing incidents had already occurred. For Hortense, who had been lifted out before Clyde, and had suddenly begun to feel her face, had as suddenly realized that her left cheek and forehead were not only scraped

but bleeding. And being seized by the notion that her beauty
might have been permanently marred by this accident, she
was at once thrown into a state of selfish panic which caused
her to become completely oblivious, not only to the misery
and injury of the others, but to the danger of discovery by the
police, the injury to the child, the wreck of this expensive
car—in fact everything but herself and the probability or possibility that her beauty had been destroyed. She began to
whimper on the instant and wave her hands up and down.
"Oh, goodness, goodness, goodness!" she exclaimed desperately. "Oh, how dreadful! Oh, how terrible! Oh, my face is all
cut." And feeling an urgent compulsion to do something
about it, she suddenly set off (and that without a word to any
one and while Clyde was still inside helping Ratterer) south
along 35th Street, toward the city where were lights and more
populated streets. Her one thought was to reach her own
home as speedily as possible in order that she might be able
to do something for herself.

Of Clyde, Sparser, Ratterer and the other girls—she really
thought nothing. What were they now? It was only intermit-
tently and between thoughts of her marred beauty that she
could even bring herself to think of the injured child—the
horror of which, as well as the pursuit by the police, maybe,
the fact that the car did not belong to Sparser or that it was
wrecked, and that they were all liable to arrest in consequence, affecting her but slightly. Her one thought in regard
to Clyde was that he was the one who had invited her to this
ill-fated journey—hence that he was to blame, really. Those
beastly boys—to think they should have gotten her into this
and then didn't have brains enough to manage better.

The other girls, apart from Laura Sipe, were not seriously
injured—any of them. They were more frightened than anything else, but now that this had happened they were in a
panic, lest they be overtaken by the police, arrested, exposed
and punished. And accordingly they stood about, exclaiming
"Oh, gee, hurry, can't you? Oh, dear, we ought all of us to
get away from here. Oh, it's all so terrible." Until at last Hegglund exclaimed: "For Christ's sake, keep quiet, cantcha?
We're doin' de best we can, cantcha see? You'll have de cops
down on us in a minute as it is."

And then, as if in answer to his comment, a lone suburbanite who lived some four blocks from the scene across the fields and who, hearing the crash and the cries in the night, had ambled across to see what the trouble was, now drew near and stood curiously looking at the stricken group and the car.

"Had an accident, eh?" he exclaimed, genially enough. "Any one badly hurt? Gee, that's too bad. And that's a swell car, too. Can I help any?"

Clyde, hearing him talk and looking out and not seeing Hortense anywhere, and not being able to do more for Sparser than stretch him in the bottom of the car, glanced agonizingly about. For the thought of the police and their certain pursuit was strong upon him. He must get out of this. He must not be caught here. Think of what would happen to him if he were caught—how he would be disgraced and punished probably—all his fine world stripped from him before he could say a word really. His mother would hear—Mr. Squires—everybody. Most certainly he would go to jail. Oh, how terrible that thought was—grinding really like a macerating wheel to his flesh. They could do nothing more for Sparser, and they only laid themselves open to being caught by lingering. So asking, "Where'd Miss Briggs go?" he now began to climb out, then started looking about the dark and snowy fields for her. His thought was that he would first assist her to wherever she might desire to go.

But just then in the distance was heard the horns and the hum of at least two motorcycles speeding swiftly in the direction of this very spot. For already the wife of the suburbanite, on hearing the crash and the cries in the distance, had telephoned the police that an accident had occurred here. And now the suburbanite was explaining: "That's them. I told the wife to telephone for an ambulance." And hearing this, all these others now began to run, for they all realized what that meant. And in addition, looking across the fields one could see the lights of these approaching machines. They reached Thirty-first and Cleveland together. Then one turned south toward this very spot, along Cleveland Avenue. And the other continued east on Thirty-first, reconnoitering for the accident.

"Beat it, for God's sake, all of youse," whispered Hegglund, excitedly. "Scatter!" And forthwith, seizing Maida Axelrod by the hand, he started to run east along Thirty-fifth Street, in which the car then lay—toward the outlying eastern suburbs. But after a moment, deciding that that would not do either, that it would be too easy to pursue him along a street, he cut northeast, directly across the open fields and away from the city.

And now, Clyde, as suddenly sensing what capture would mean—how all his fine thoughts of pleasure would most certainly end in disgrace and probably prison, began running also. Only in his case, instead of following Hegglund or any of the others, he turned south along Cleveland Avenue toward the southern limits of the city. But like Hegglund, realizing that that meant an easy avenue of pursuit for any one who chose to follow, he too took to the open fields. Only instead of running away from the city as before, he now turned southwest and ran toward those streets which lay to the south of Fortieth. Only much open space being before him before he should reach them, and a clump of bushes showing in the near distance, and the light of the motorcycle already sweeping the road behind him, he ran to that and for the moment dropped behind it.

Only Sparser and Laura Sipe were left within the car, she at that moment beginning to recover consciousness. And the visiting stranger, much astounded, was left standing outside.

"Why, the very idea!" he suddenly said to himself. "They must have stolen that car. It couldn't have belonged to them at all."

And just then the first motorcycle reaching the scene, Clyde from his not too distant hiding place was able to overhear. "Well, you didn't get away with it after all, did you? You thought you were pretty slick, but you didn't make it. You're the one we want, and what's become of the rest of the gang, eh? Where are they, eh?"

And hearing the suburbanite declare quite definitely that he had nothing to do with it, that the real occupants of the car had but then run away and might yet be caught if the police wished, Clyde, who was still within earshot of what was being said, began crawling upon his hands and knees at first in the snow south, south and west, always toward some of those distant streets which, lamplit and faintly glowing, he saw to the southwest of him, and among which presently, if he were not captured, he hoped to hide—to lose himself and so escape—if the fates were only kind—the misery and the punishment and the unending dissatisfaction and disappointment which now, most definitely, it all represented to him.

# BOOK TWO

# *Chapter I*

---

T HE HOME of Samuel Griffiths in Lycurgus, New York, a city of some twenty-five thousand inhabitants midway between Utica and Albany. Near the dinner hour and by degrees the family assembling for its customary meal. On this occasion the preparations were of a more elaborate nature than usual, owing to the fact that for the past four days Mr. Samuel Griffiths, the husband and father, had been absent attending a conference of shirt and collar manufacturers in Chicago, price-cutting by upstart rivals in the west having necessitated compromise and adjustment by those who manufactured in the east. He was but now returned and had telephoned earlier in the afternoon that he had arrived, and was going to his office in the factory where he would remain until dinner time.

Being long accustomed to the ways of a practical and convinced man who believed in himself and considered his judgment and his decision sound—almost final—for the most part, anyhow, Mrs. Griffiths thought nothing of this. He would appear and greet her in due order.

Knowing that he preferred leg of lamb above many other things, after due word with Mrs. Truesdale, her homely but useful housekeeper, she ordered lamb. And the appropriate vegetables and dessert having been decided upon, she gave herself over to thoughts of her eldest daughter Myra, who, having graduated from Smith College several years before, was still unmarried. And the reason for this, as Mrs. Griffiths well understood, though she was never quite willing to admit it openly, was that Myra was not very good looking. Her nose was too long, her eyes too close-set, her chin not sufficiently rounded to give her a girlish and pleasing appearance. For the most part she seemed too thoughtful and studious—as a rule not interested in the ordinary social life of that city. Neither did she possess that savoir faire, let alone that peculiar appeal for men, that characterized some girls even when they were not pretty. As her mother saw it, she was really too critical and

too intellectual, having a mind that was rather above the
world in which she found herself.

Brought up amid comparative luxury, without having to
worry about any of the rough details of making a living, she
had been confronted, nevertheless, by the difficulties of making her own way in the matter of social favor and love—two
objectives which, without beauty or charm, were about as difficult as the attaining to extreme wealth by a beggar. And the
fact that for twelve years now—ever since she had been fourteen—she had seen the lives of other youths and maidens in
this small world in which she moved passing gayly enough,
while hers was more or less confined to reading, music, the
business of keeping as neatly and attractively arrayed as possible, and of going to visit friends in the hope of possibly encountering somewhere, somehow, the one temperament who
would be interested in her, had saddened, if not exactly
soured her. And that despite the fact that the material comfort of her parents and herself was exceptional.

Just now she had gone through her mother's room to her
own, looking as though she were not very much interested in
anything. Her mother had been trying to think of something
to suggest that would take her out of herself, when the
younger daughter, Bella, fresh from a passing visit to the home
of the Finchleys, wealthy neighbors where she had stopped on
her way from the Snedeker School, burst in upon her.

Contrasted with her sister, who was tall and dark and rather
sallow, Bella, though shorter, was far more gracefully and vigorously formed. She had thick brown—almost black—hair, a
brown and olive complexion tinted with red, and eyes brown
and genial, that blazed with an eager, seeking light. In addition to her sound and lithe physique, she possessed vitality
and animation. Her arms and legs were graceful and active.
Plainly she was given to liking things as she found them—enjoying life as it was—and hence, unlike her sister, she was unusually attractive to men and boys—to men and women, old
and young—a fact which her mother and father well knew.
No danger of any lack of marriage offers for her when the
time came. As her mother saw it, too many youths and men
were already buzzing around, and so posing the question of a
proper husband for her. Already she had displayed a tendency

to become thick and fast friends, not only with the scions of the older and more conservative families who constituted the ultra-respectable element of the city, but also, and this was more to her mother's distaste, with the sons and daughters of some of those later and hence socially less important families of the region—the sons and daughters of manufacturers of bacon, canning jars, vacuum cleaners, wooden and wicker ware, and typewriters, who constituted a solid enough financial element in the city, but who made up what might be considered the "fast set" in the local life.

In Mrs. Griffiths' opinion, there was too much dancing, cabareting, automobiling to one city and another, without due social supervision. Yet, as a contrast to her sister, Myra, what a relief. It was only from the point of view of proper surveillance, or until she was safely and religiously married, that Mrs. Griffiths troubled or even objected to most of her present contacts and yearnings and gayeties. She desired to protect her.

"Now, where have you been?" she demanded, as her daughter burst into the room, throwing down her books and drawing near to the open fire that burned there.

"Just think, Mamma," began Bella most unconcernedly and almost irrelevantly. "The Finchleys are going to give up their place out at Greenwood Lake this coming summer and go up to Twelfth Lake near Pine Point. They're going to build a new bungalow up there. And Sondra says that this time it's going to be right down at the water's edge—not away from it, as it is out here. And they're going to have a great big verandah with a hardwood floor. And a boathouse big enough for a thirty-foot electric launch that Mr. Finchley is going to buy for Stuart. Won't that be wonderful? And she says that if you will let me, that I can come up there for all summer long, or for as long as I like. And Gil, too, if he will. It's just across the lake from the Emery Lodge, you know, and the East Gate Hotel. And the Phants' place, you know, the Phants of Utica, is just below theirs near Sharon. Isn't that just wonderful? Won't that be great? I wish you and Dad would make up your minds to build up there now sometime, Mamma. It looks to me now as though nearly everybody that's worth anything down here is moving up there."

She talked so fast and swung about so, looking now at the open fire burning in the grate, then out of the two high windows that commanded the front lawn and a full view of Wykeagy Avenue, lit by the electric lights in the winter dusk, that her mother had no opportunity to insert any comment until this was over. However, she managed to observe: "Yes? Well, what about the Anthonys and the Nicholsons and the Taylors? I haven't heard of their leaving Greenwood yet."

"Oh, I know, not the Anthonys or the Nicholsons or the Taylors. Who expects them to move? They're too old fashioned. They're not the kind that would move anywhere, are they? No one thinks they are. Just the same Greenwood isn't like Twelfth Lake. You know that yourself. And all the people that are anybody down on the South Shore are going up there for sure. The Cranstons next year, Sondra says. And after that, I bet the Harriets will go, too."

"The Cranstons and the Harriets and the Finchleys and Sondra," commented her mother, half amused and half irritated. "The Cranstons and you and Bertine and Sondra— that's all I hear these days." For the Cranstons, and the Finchleys, despite a certain amount of local success in connection with this newer and faster set, were, much more than any of the others, the subject of considerable unfavorable comment. They were the people who, having moved the Cranston Wickwire Company from Albany, and the Finchley Electric Sweeper from Buffalo, and built large factories on the south bank of the Mohawk River, to say nothing of new and grandiose houses in Wykeagy Avenue and summer cottages at Greenwood, some twenty miles northwest, were setting a rather showy, and hence disagreeable, pace to all of the wealthy residents of this region. They were given to wearing the smartest clothes, to the latest novelties in cars and entertainments, and constituted a problem to those who with less means considered their position and their equipment about as fixed and interesting and attractive as such things might well be. The Cranstons and the Finchleys were in the main a thorn in the flesh of the remainder of the elite of Lycurgus—too showy and too aggressive.

"How often have I told you that I don't want you to have so much to do with Bertine or that Letta Harriet or her brother either? They're too forward. They run around and talk and show off too much. And your father feels the same as I do in regard to them. As for Sondra Finchley, if she expects to go with Bertine and you, too, then you're not going to go with her either much longer. Besides I'm not sure that your father approves of your going anywhere without some one to accompany you. You're not old enough yet. And as for your going to Twelfth Lake to the Finchleys, well, unless we all go together, there'll be no going there, either." And now Mrs. Griffiths, who leaned more to the manner and tactics of the older, if not less affluent families, stared complainingly at her daughter.

Nevertheless Bella was no more abashed than she was irritated by this. On the contrary she knew her mother and knew that she was fond of her; also that she was intrigued by her physical charm as well as her assured local social success as much as was her father, who considered her perfection itself and could be swayed by her least, as well as her much practised, smile.

"Not old enough, not old enough," commented Bella reproachfully. "Will you listen? I'll be eighteen in July. I'd like to know when you and Papa are going to think I'm old enough to go anywhere without you both. Wherever you two go, I have to go, and wherever I want to go, you two have to go, too."

"Bella," censured her mother. Then after a moment's silence, in which her daughter stood there impatiently, she added, "Of course, what else would you have us do? When you are twenty-one or two, if you are not married by then, it will be time enough to think of going off by yourself. But at your age, you shouldn't be thinking of any such thing." Bella cocked her pretty head, for at the moment the side door down stairs was thrown open, and Gilbert Griffiths, the only son of this family and who very much in face and build, if not in manner or lack of force, resembled Clyde, his western cousin, entered and ascended.

He was at this time a vigorous, self-centered and vain youth of twenty-three who, in contrast with his two sisters, seemed much sterner and far more practical. Also, probably much more intelligent and aggressive in a business way—a field in which neither of the two girls took the slightest interest. He

was brisk in manner and impatient. He considered that his social position was perfectly secure, and was utterly scornful of
anything but commercial success. Yet despite this he was really deeply interested in the movements of the local society, of
which he considered himself and his family the most important part. Always conscious of the dignity and social standing
of his family in this community, he regulated his action and
speech accordingly. Ordinarily he struck the passing observer
as rather sharp and arrogant, neither as youthful or as playful
as his years might have warranted. Still he was young, attractive and interesting. He had a sharp, if not brilliant, tongue in
his head—a gift at times for making crisp and cynical remarks.
On account of his family and position he was considered also
the most desirable of all the young eligible bachelors in Lycurgus. Nevertheless he was so much interested in himself
that he scarcely found room in his cosmos for a keen and
really intelligent understanding of anyone else.

Hearing him ascend from below and enter his room, which
was at the rear of the house next to hers, Bella at once left her
mother's room, and coming to the door, called: "Oh, Gil, can
I come in?"

"Sure." He was whistling briskly and already, in view of
some entertainment somewhere, preparing to change to
evening clothes.

"Where are you going?"

"Nowhere, for dinner. To the Wynants afterwards."

"Oh, Constance to be sure."

"No, not Constance, to be sure. Where do you get that
stuff?"

"As though I didn't know."

"Lay off. Is that what you came in here for?"

"No, that isn't what I came in here for. What do you think?
The Finchleys are going to build a place up at Twelfth Lake
next summer, right on the lake, next to the Phants, and Mr.
Finchley's going to buy Stuart a thirty-foot launch and build
a boathouse with a sun-parlor right over the water to hold it.
Won't that be swell, huh?"

"Don't say 'swell.' And don't say 'huh.' Can't you learn to
cut out the slang? You talk like a factory girl. Is that all they
teach you over at that school?"

"Listen to who's talking about cutting out slang. How about yourself? You set a fine example around here, I notice."

"Well, I'm five years older than you are. Besides I'm a man. You don't notice Myra using any of that stuff."

"Oh, Myra. But don't let's talk about that. Only think of that new house they're going to build and the fine time they're going to have up there next summer. Don't you wish we could move up there, too? We could if we wanted to—if only Papa and Mamma would agree to it."

"Oh, I don't know that it would be so wonderful," replied her brother, who was really very much interested just the same. "There are other places besides Twelfth Lake."

"Who said there weren't? But not for the people that we know around here. Where else do the best people from Albany and Utica go but there now, I'd like to know. It's going to become a regular center, Sondra says, with all the finest houses along the west shore. Just the same, the Cranstons, the Lamberts and the Harriets are going to move up there pretty soon, too," Bella added most definitely and defiantly. "That won't leave so many out at Greenwood Lake, nor the very best people, either, even if the Anthonys and Nicholsons do stay here."

"Who says the Cranstons are going up there?" asked Gilbert, now very much interested.

"Why, Sondra!"

"Who told her?"

"Bertine."

"Gee, they're getting gayer and gayer," commented her brother oddly and a little enviously. "Pretty soon Lycurgus'll be too small to hold 'em." He jerked at a bow tie he was attempting to center and grimaced oddly as his tight neck-band pinched him slightly.

For although Gilbert had recently entered into the collar and shirt industry with his father as general supervisor of manufacturing, and with every prospect of managing and controlling the entire business eventually, still he was jealous of young Grant Cranston, a youth of his own age, very appealing and attractive physically, who was really more daring with and more attractive to the girls of the younger set. Cranston seemed to be satisfied that it was possible to combine a certain amount of social pleasure with working for his father with which Gilbert did not agree. In fact, young Griffiths would have preferred, had it been possible, so to charge young Cranston with looseness, only thus far the latter had managed to keep himself well within the bounds of sobriety. And the Cranston Wickwire Company was plainly forging ahead as one of the leading industries of Lycurgus.

"Well," he added, after a moment, "they're spreading out faster than I would if I had their business. They're not the richest people in the world, either." Just the same he was thinking that, unlike himself and his parents, the Cranstons were really more daring if not socially more avid of life. He envied them.

"And what's more," added Bella interestedly, "the Finchleys are to have a dance floor over the boathouse. And Sondra says that Stuart was hoping that you would come up there and spend a lot of time this summer."

"Oh, did he?" replied Gilbert, a little enviously and sarcastically. "You mean he said he was hoping you would come up and spend a lot of time. I'll be working this summer."

"He didn't say anything of the kind, smarty. Besides it wouldn't hurt us any if we did go up there. There's nothing much out at Greenwood any more that I can see. A lot of old hen parties."

"Is that so? Mother would like to hear that."

"And you'll tell her, of course."

"Oh, no, I won't either. But I don't think we're going to follow the Finchleys or the Cranstons up to Twelfth Lake just yet, either. You can go up there if you want, if Dad'll let you."

Just then the lower door clicked again, and Bella, forgetting her quarrel with her brother, ran down to greet her father.

# Chapter II

THE HEAD of the Lycurgus branch of the Griffiths, as contrasted with the father of the Kansas City family, was most arresting. Unlike his shorter and more confused brother of the Door of Hope, whom he had not even seen for thirty years, he was a little above the average in height, very well-knit, although comparatively slender, shrewd of eye, and incisive both as to manner and speech. Long used to contending for himself, and having come by effort as well as results to know that he was above the average in acumen and commercial ability, he was inclined at times to be a bit intolerant of those who were not. He was not ungenerous or unpleasant in manner, but always striving to maintain a calm and judicial air. And he told himself by way of excuse for his mannerisms that he was merely accepting himself at the value that others placed upon him and all those who, like himself, were successful.

Having arrived in Lycurgus about twenty-five years before with some capital and a determination to invest in a new collar enterprise which had been proposed to him, he had succeeded thereafter beyond his wildest expectations. And naturally he was vain about it. His family at this time—twenty-five years later—unquestionably occupied one of the best, as well as the most tastefully constructed residences in Lycurgus. They were also esteemed as among the few best families of this region—being, if not the oldest, at least among the most conservative, respectable and successful in Lycurgus. His two younger children, if not the eldest, were much to the front socially in the younger and gayer set and so far nothing had happened to weaken or darken his prestige.

On returning from Chicago on this particular day, after having concluded several agreements there which spelled trade harmony and prosperity for at least one year, he was inclined to feel very much at ease and on good terms with the world. Nothing had occurred to mar his trip. In his absence the Griffiths Collar and Shirt Company had gone on as though he had been present. Trade orders at the moment were large.

Now as he entered his own door he threw down a heavy bag and fashionably made coat and turned to see what he rather expected—Bella hurrying toward him. Indeed she was his pet, the most pleasing and different and artistic thing, as he saw it, that all his years had brought to him—youth, health, gayety, intelligence and affection—all in the shape of a pretty daughter.

"Oh, Daddy," she called most sweetly and enticingly as she saw him enter. "Is that you?"

"Yes At least it feels a little like me at the present moment. How's my baby girl?" And he opened his arms and received the bounding form of his last born. "There's a good, strong, healthy girl, I'll say," he announced as he withdrew his affectionate lips from hers. "And how's the bad girl been behaving herself since I left? No fibbing this time."

"Oh, just fine, Daddy. You can ask any one. I couldn't be better."

"And your mother?"

"She's all right, Daddy. She's up in her room. I don't think she heard you come in."

"And Myra? Is she back from Albany yet?"

"Yes. She's in her room. I heard her playing just now. I just got in myself a little while ago."

"Ay, hai. Gadding about again. I know you." He held up a genial forefinger, warningly, while Bella swung onto one of his arms and kept pace with him up the stairs to the floor above.

"Oh, no, I wasn't either, now," she cooed shrewdly and sweetly. "Just see how you pick on me, Daddy. I was only over with Sondra for a little while. And what do you think, Daddy? They're going to give up the place at Greenwood and build a big handsome bungalow up on Twelfth Lake right away. And Mr. Finchley's going to buy a big electric launch for Stuart and they're going to live up there next summer, maybe all the time, from May until October. And so are the Cranstons, maybe."

Mr. Griffiths, long used to his younger daughter's wiles, was interested at the moment not so much by the thought that she wished to convey—that Twelfth Lake was more desirable socially than Greenwood—as he was by the fact that the Finchleys were able to make this sudden and rather heavy expenditure for social reasons only.

Instead of answering Bella he went on upstairs and into his wife's room. He kissed Mrs. Griffiths, looked in upon Myra, who came to the door to embrace him, and spoke of the successful nature of the trip. One could see by the way he embraced his wife that there was an agreeable understanding between them—no disharmony—by the way he greeted Myra that if he did not exactly sympathize with her temperament and point of view, at least he included her within the largess of his affection.

As they were talking Mrs. Truesdale announced that dinner was ready, and Gilbert, having completed his toilet, now entered.

"I say, Dad," he called, "I have an interesting thing I want to see you about in the morning. Can I?"

"All right, I'll be there. Come in about noon."

"Come on all, or the dinner will be getting cold," admonished Mrs. Griffiths earnestly, and forthwith Gilbert turned and went down, followed by Griffiths, who still had Bella on his arm. And after him came Mrs. Griffiths and Myra, who now emerged from her room and joined them.

Once seated at the table, the family forthwith began discussing topics of current local interest. For Bella, who was the family's chief source of gossip, gathering the most of it from the Snedeker School, through which all the social news appeared to percolate most swiftly, suddenly announced: "What do you think, Mamma? Rosetta Nicholson, that niece of Mrs. Disston Nicholson, who was over here last summer from Albany—you know, she came over the night of the Alumnæ Garden Party on our lawn—you remember—the young girl with the yellow hair and squinty blue eyes—her father owns that big wholesale grocery over there—well, she's engaged to that Herbert Tickham of Utica, who was visiting Mrs. Lambert last summer. You don't remember him, but I do. He was tall and dark and sorta awkward, and awfully pale, but very handsome—oh, a regular movie hero."

"There you go, Mrs. Griffiths," interjected Gilbert shrewdly and cynically to his mother. "A delegation from the Misses

Snedeker's Select School sneaks off to the movies to brush up on heroes from time to time."

Griffiths senior suddenly observed: "I had a curious experience in Chicago this time, something I think the rest of you will be interested in." He was thinking of an accidental encounter two days before in Chicago between himself and the eldest son, as it proved to be, of his younger brother Asa. Also of a conclusion he had come to in regard to him.

"Oh, what is it, Daddy?" pleaded Bella at once. "Do tell me about it."

"Spin the big news, Dad," added Gilbert, who, because of the favor of his father, felt very free and close to him always.

"Well, while I was in Chicago at the Union League Club, I met a young man who is related to us, a cousin of you three children, by the way, the eldest son of my brother Asa, who is out in Denver now, I understand. I haven't seen or heard from him in thirty years." He paused and mused dubiously.

"Not the one who is a preacher somewhere, Daddy?" inquired Bella, looking up.

"Yes, the preacher. At least I understand he was for a while after he left home. But his son tells me he has given that up now. He's connected with something in Denver—a hotel, I think."

"But what's his son like?" interrogated Bella, who only knew such well groomed and ostensibly conservative youths and men as her present social status and supervision permitted, and in consequence was intensely interested. The son of a western hotel proprietor!

"A cousin? How old is he?" asked Gilbert instantly, curious as to his character and situation and ability.

"Well, he's a very interesting young man, I think," continued Griffiths tentatively and somewhat dubiously, since up to this hour he had not truly made up his mind about Clyde. "He's quite good-looking and well-mannered, too—about your own age, I should say, Gil, and looks a lot like you—very much so—same eyes and mouth and chin." He looked at his son examiningly. "He's a little bit taller, if anything, and looks a little thinner, though I don't believe he really is."

At the thought of a cousin who looked like him—possibly as attractive in every way as himself—and bearing his own

name, Gilbert chilled and bristled slightly. For here in Lycurgus, up to this time, he was well and favorably known as the
only son and heir presumptive to the managerial control of
his father's business, and to at least a third of the estate, if not
more. And now, if by any chance it should come to light that
there was a relative, a cousin of his own years and one who
looked and acted like him, even—he bridled at the thought.
Forthwith (a psychic reaction which he did not understand
and could not very well control) he decided that he did not
like him—could not like him.

"What's he doing now?" he asked in a curt and rather sour
tone, though he attempted to avoid the latter element in his
voice.

"Well, he hasn't much of a job, I must say," smiled Samuel
Griffiths, meditatively. "He's only a bell-hop in the Union
League Club in Chicago, at present, but a very pleasant and
gentlemanly sort of a boy, I will say. I was quite taken with
him. In fact, because he told me there wasn't much opportunity for advancement where he was, and that he would like to
get into something where there was more chance to do something and be somebody, I told him that if he wanted to come
on here and try his luck with us, we might do a little something for him—give him a chance to show what he could do,
at least."

He had not intended to set forth at once the fact that he
became interested in his nephew to this extent, but—rather to
wait and thrash it out at different times with both his wife and
son, but the occasion having seemed to offer itself, he had
spoken. And now that he had, he felt rather glad of it, for because Clyde so much resembled Gilbert he did want to do a
little something for him.

But Gilbert bristled and chilled, the while Bella and Myra,
if not Mrs. Griffiths, who favored her only son in everything—even to preferring him to be without a blood relation
or other rival of any kind, rather warmed to the idea. A cousin
who was a Griffiths and good-looking and about Gilbert's
age—and who, as their father reported, was rather pleasant
and well mannered—that pleased Bella and Myra while Mrs.
Griffiths, noting Gilbert's face darken, was not so moved. He
would not like him. But out of respect for her husband's

authority and general ability in all things, she now remained silent. But not so, Bella.

"Oh, you're going to give him a place, are you, Dad?" she commented. "That's interesting. I hope he's better-looking than the rest of our cousins."

"Bella," chided Mrs. Griffiths, while Myra, recalling a gauche uncle and cousin who had come on from Vermont several years before to visit them a few days, smiled wisely. At the same time Gilbert, deeply irritated, was mentally fighting against the idea. He could not see it at all. "Of course we're not turning away applicants who want to come in and learn the business right along now, as it is," he said sharply.

"Oh, I know," replied his father, "but not cousins and nephews exactly. Besides he looks very intelligent and ambitious to me. It wouldn't do any great harm if we let at least one of our relatives come here and show what he can do. I can't see why we shouldn't employ him as well as another."

"I don't believe Gil likes the idea of any other fellow in Lycurgus having the same name and looking like him," suggested Bella, slyly, and with a certain touch of malice due to the fact that her brother was always criticizing her.

"Oh, what rot!" Gilbert snapped irritably. "Why don't you make a sensible remark once in a while? What do I care whether he has the same name or not—or looks like me, either?" His expression at the moment was particularly sour.

"Gilbert!" pleaded his mother, reprovingly, "How can you talk so? And to your sister, too?"

"Well, I don't want to do anything in connection with this young man if it's going to cause any hard feelings here," went on Griffiths senior. "All I know is that his father was never very practical and I doubt if Clyde has ever had a real chance." (His son winced at this friendly and familiar use of his cousin's first name.) "My only idea in bringing him on here was to give him a start. I haven't the faintest idea whether he would make good or not. He might and again he might not. If he didn't—" He threw up one hand as much as to say, "If he doesn't, we will have to toss him aside, of course."

"Well, I think that's very kind of you, father," observed

Mrs. Griffiths, pleasantly and diplomatically. "I hope he proves satisfactory."

"And there's another thing," added Griffiths wisely and sententiously. "I don't expect this young man, so long as he is in my employ and just because he's a nephew of mine, to be treated differently to any other employee in the factory. He's coming here to work—not play. And while he is here, trying, I don't expect any of you to pay him any social attention—not the slightest. He's not the sort of boy anyhow, that would want to put himself on us—at least he didn't impress me that way, and he wouldn't be coming down here with any notion that he was to be placed on an equal footing with any of us. That would be silly. Later on, if he proves that he is really worth while, able to take care of himself, knows his place and keeps it, and any of you wanted to show him any little attention, well, then it will be time enough to see, but not before then."

By then, the maid, Amanda, assistant to Mrs. Truesdale, was taking away the dinner plates and preparing to serve the dessert. But as Mr. Griffiths rarely ate dessert, and usually chose this period, unless company was present, to look after certain stock and banking matters which he kept in a small desk in the library, he now pushed back his chair, arose, excusing himself to his family, and walked into the library adjoining. The others remained.

"I would like to see what he's like, wouldn't you?" Myra asked her mother.

"Yes. And I do hope he measures up to all of your father's expectations. He will not feel right if he doesn't."

"I can't get this," observed Gilbert, "bringing people on now when we can hardly take care of those we have. And besides, imagine what the bunch around here will say if they find out that our cousin was only a bell-hop before coming here!"

"Oh, well, they won't have to know that, will they?" said Myra.

"Oh, won't they? Well, what's to prevent him from speaking about it—unless we tell him not to—or some one coming along who has seen him there." His eyes snapped viciously.

"At any rate, I hope he doesn't. It certainly wouldn't do us any good around here."

And Bella added, "I hope he's not as dull as Uncle Allen's two boys. They're the most uninteresting boys I ever did see."

"Bella," cautioned her mother once more.

# Chapter III

THE Clyde whom Samuel Griffiths described as having
met at the Union League Club in Chicago, was a somewhat modified version of the one who had fled from Kansas
City three years before. He was now twenty, a little taller and
more firmly but scarcely any more robustly built, and considerably more experienced, of course. For since leaving his
home and work in Kansas City and coming in contact with
some rough usage in the world—humble tasks, wretched
rooms, no intimates to speak of, plus the compulsion to
make his own way as best he might—he had developed a
kind of self-reliance and smoothness of address such as one
would scarcely have credited him with three years before.
There was about him now, although he was not nearly so
smartly dressed as when he left Kansas City, a kind of conscious gentility of manner which pleased, even though it did
not at first arrest attention. Also, and this was considerably
different from the Clyde who had crept away from Kansas
City in a box car, he had much more of an air of caution and
reserve.

For ever since he had fled from Kansas City, and by one
humble device and another forced to make his way, he had
been coming to the conclusion that on himself alone depended his future. His family, as he now definitely sensed,
could do nothing for him. They were too impractical and too
poor—his mother, father, Esta, all of them.

At the same time, in spite of all their difficulties, he could
not now help but feel drawn to them, his mother in particular, and the old home life that had surrounded him as a boy—
his brother and sisters, Esta included, since she, too, as he
now saw it, had been brought no lower than he by circumstances over which she probably had no more control. And
often, his thoughts and mood had gone back with a definite
and disconcerting pang because of the way in which he had
treated his mother as well as the way in which his career in
Kansas City had been suddenly interrupted—his loss of
Hortense Briggs—a severe blow; the troubles that had come

to him since; the trouble that must have come to his mother and Esta because of him.

On reaching St. Louis two days later after his flight, and after having been most painfully bundled out into the snow a hundred miles from Kansas City in the gray of a winter morning, and at the same time relieved of his watch and overcoat by two brakemen who had found him hiding in the car, he had picked up a Kansas City paper—*The Star*—only to realize that his worst fear in regard to all that had occurred had come true. For there, under a two-column head, and with fully a column and a half of reading matter below, was the full story of all that had happened: a little girl, the eleven-year-old daughter of a well-to-do Kansas City family, knocked down and almost instantly killed—she had died an hour later; Sparser and Miss Sipe in a hospital and under arrest at the same time, guarded by a policeman sitting in the hospital awaiting their recovery; a splendid car very seriously damaged; Sparser's father, in the absence of the owner of the car for whom he worked, at once incensed and made terribly unhappy by the folly and seeming criminality and recklessness of his son.

But what was worse, the unfortunate Sparser had already been charged with larceny and homicide, and wishing, no doubt, to minimize his own share in this grave catastrophe, had not only revealed the names of all who were with him in the car—the youths in particular and their hotel address—but had charged that they along with him were equally guilty, since they had urged him to make speed at the time and against his will—a claim, which was true enough, as Clyde knew. And Mr. Squires, on being interviewed at the hotel, had furnished the police and the newspapers with the names of their parents and their home addresses.

This last was the sharpest blow of all. For there followed disturbing pictures of how their respective parents or relatives had taken it on being informed of their sins. Mrs. Ratterer, Tom's mother, had cried and declared her boy was a good boy, and had not meant to do any harm, she was sure. And Mrs. Hegglund—Oscar's devoted but aged mother—had said that there was not a more honest or generous soul and that he must have been drinking. And at his own home—*The Star* had described his mother as standing, pale, very startled and very distressed, clasping and unclasping her hands and looking as though she were scarcely able to grasp what was meant, unwilling to believe that her son had been one of the party and assuring all that he would most certainly return soon and explain all, and that there must be some mistake.

However, he had not returned. Nor had he heard anything more after that. For, owing to his fear of the police, as well as of his mother—her sorrowful, hopeless eyes, he had not written for months, and then a letter to his mother only to say that he was well and that she must not worry. He gave neither name nor address. Later, after that he had wandered on, essaying one small job and another, in St. Louis, Peoria, Chicago, Milwaukee—dishwashing in a restaurant, soda-clerking in a small outlying drug-store, attempting to learn to be a shoe clerk, a grocer's clerk, and what not; and being discharged and laid off and quitting because he did not like it. He had sent her ten dollars once—another time five, having, as he felt, that much to spare. After nearly a year and a half he had decided that the search must have lessened, his own part in the crime being forgotten, possibly, or by then not deemed sufficiently important to pursue—and when he was once more making a moderate living as the driver of a delivery wagon in Chicago, a job that paid him fifteen dollars a week, he resolved that he would write his mother, because now he could say that he had a decent place and had conducted himself respectably for a long time, although not under his own name.

And so at that time, living in a hall bedroom on the West Side of Chicago—Paulina Street—he had written his mother the following letter:

DEAR MOTHER:

Are you still in Kansas City? I wish you would write and tell me. I would so like to hear from you again and to write you again, too, if you really want me to. Honestly I do, Ma. I have been so lonely here. Only be careful and don't let any one know where I am yet. It won't do any good and might do a lot of harm just when I am trying so hard to get a start again. I didn't do anything wrong that time, myself. Really I didn't, although the papers said so—just went along. But I was afraid they would punish me for something that I didn't do. I just couldn't come back then. I wasn't to blame and then I was afraid of what you and father might think. But they invited me, Ma. I didn't tell him to go any faster or to take that car like he said. He took it himself and invited me and the others to go along. Maybe we were all to blame for running down that little girl, but we didn't mean to. None of us. And I have been so terribly sorry ever since. Think of all the trouble I have caused you! And just at the time when you most needed me. Gee! Mother, I hope you can forgive me. Can you?

I keep wondering how you are. And Esta and Julia and Frank and Father. I wish I knew where you are and what you are doing. You know how I feel about you, don't you, Ma? I've got a lot more sense now, anyhow, I see things different than I used to. I want to do something in this world. I want to be successful. I only have a fair place now, not as good as I had in K.C., but fair, and not in the same line. But I want something better, though I don't want to go back in the hotel business either if I can help it. It's not so very good for a young man like me—too high-flying, I guess. You see I know a lot more than I did back there. They like me all right where I am, but I got to get on in this world. Besides I am not really making more than my expenses here now, just my room and board and clothes, but I am trying to save a little in order to get into some line where I can work up and learn something. A person has to have a line of some kind these days. I see that now.

Won't you write me and tell me how you all are and what you are doing? I'd like to know. Give my love to Frank and Julia and Father and Esta, if they are all still there. I love you just the same and I guess you care for me a little, anyhow, don't you? I won't sign my real name, because it may be dangerous yet. (I haven't been using it since I left K.C.) But I'll give you my other one, which I'm going to leave off pretty soon and take up my old one. Wish I could do it now, but I'm afraid to yet. You can address me, if you will, as

HARRY TENET,
General Delivery, Chicago.

I'll call for it in a few days. I sign this way so as not to cause you or me any more trouble, see? But as soon as I feel more sure that this other thing has blown over, I'll use my own name again, sure.

Lovingly,

YOUR SON.

He drew a line where his real name should be and underneath wrote "you know" and mailed the letter.

Following that, because his mother had been anxious about him all this time and wondering where he was, he soon received a letter, postmarked Denver, which surprised him very much, for he had expected to hear from her as still in Kansas City.

DEAR SON:

I was surprised and so glad to get my boy's letter and to know that you were alive and safe. I had hoped and prayed so that you would return to the straight and narrow path—the only path that will ever lead you to success and happiness of any kind, and that God would let me hear from you as safe and well and working somewhere and doing well. And now he has rewarded my prayers. I knew he would. Blessed be His holy name.

Not that I blame you altogether for all that terrible trouble you got into and bringing so much suffering and disgrace on yourself and us—for well I know how the devil tempts and pursues all of us mortals and particularly just such a child as you. Oh, my son, if you only knew how you must be on your guard to avoid these pitfalls. And you have such a long road ahead of you. Will you be ever watchful and try always to cling to the teachings of our Savior that your mother has always tried to impress upon the minds and hearts of all you dear children? Will you stop and listen to the voice of our Lord that is ever with us, guiding our footsteps safely up the rocky path that leads to a heaven more beautiful than we can ever imagine here? Promise me, my child, that you will hold fast to all your early teachings and always bear in mind that "right is might," and my boy, never, never, take a drink of any kind no matter who offers it to you. There is where the devil reigns in all his glory and is ever ready to triumph over the weak one. Remember always what I have told you so often "Strong drink is raging and wine is a mocker," and it is my earnest prayer that these words will ring in your ears every time you are tempted—for I am sure now that that was perhaps the real cause of that terrible accident.

I suffered terribly over that, Clyde, and just at the time when I had such a dreadful ordeal to face with Esta. I almost lost her. She had such an awful time. The poor child paid dearly for her sin. We had to go in debt so deep and it took so long to work it out—but finally we did and now things are not as bad as they were, quite.

As you see, we are now in Denver. We have a mission of our own here now with housing quarters for all of us. Besides we have a few rooms to rent which Esta, and you know she is now Mrs. Nixon, of course, takes care of. She has a fine little boy who reminds your father and me of you so much when you were a baby. He does little things that are you all over again so many times that we almost feel that you are with us again—as you were. It is comforting, too, sometimes.

Frank and Julie have grown so and are quite a help to me. Frank has a paper route and earns a little money which helps. Esta wants to keep them in school just as long as we can.

Your father is not very well, but of course, he is getting older, and he does the best he can.

I am awful glad, Clyde, that you are trying so hard to better yourself in every way and last night your father was saying again that your uncle, Samuel Griffiths, of Lycurgus, is so rich and successful and I thought that maybe if you wrote him and asked him to give you something there so that you could learn the business, perhaps he would. I don't see why he wouldn't. After all you are his nephew. You know he has a great collar business there in Lycurgus and he is very rich, so they say. Why don't you write him and see? Somehow I feel that perhaps he would find a place for you and then you would have something sure to work for. Let me know if you do and what he says.

I want to hear from you often, Clyde. Please write and let us know all about you and how you are getting along. Won't you? Of course we love you as much as ever, and will do our best always to try to guide you right. We want you to succeed more than you know, but we also want you to be a good boy, and live a clean, righteous life, for, my son, what matter it if a man gaineth the whole world and loseth his own soul?

Write your mother, Clyde, and bear in mind that her love is always with you—guiding you—pleading with you to do right in the name of the Lord.

Affectionately,

MOTHER.

And so it was that Clyde had begun to think of his uncle Samuel and his great business long before he encountered him. He had also experienced an enormous relief in learning that his parents were no longer in the same financial difficulties they were when he left, and safely housed in a hotel, or at least a lodging house, probably connected with this new mission.

Then two months after he had received his mother's first letter and while he was deciding almost every day that he must do something, and that forthwith, he chanced one day to deliver to the Union League Club on Jackson Boulevard a package of ties and handkerchiefs which some visitor to

Chicago had purchased at the store, for which he worked. Upon entering, who should he come in contact with but Ratterer in the uniform of a club employee. He was in charge of inquiry and packages at the door. Although neither he nor Ratterer quite grasped immediately the fact that they were confronting one another again, after a moment Ratterer had exclaimed: "Clyde!" And then, seizing him by an arm, he added enthusiastically and yet cautiously in a very low tone: "Well, of all things! The devil! Whaddya know? Put 'er there. Where do you come from anyhow?" And Clyde, equally excited, exclaimed, "Well, by jing, if it ain't Tom. Whaddya know? You working here?"

Ratterer, who (like Clyde) had for the moment quite forgotten the troublesome secret which lay between them, added: "That's right. Surest thing you know. Been here for nearly a year, now." Then with a sudden pull at Clyde's arm, as much as to say, "Silence!" he drew Clyde to one side, out of the hearing of the youth to whom he had been talking as Clyde came in, and added: "Ssh! I'm working here under my own name, but I'd rather not let 'em know I'm from K.C., see. I'm supposed to be from Cleveland."

And with that he once more pressed Clyde's arm genially and looked him over. And Clyde, equally moved, added: "Sure. That's all right. I'm glad you were able to connect. My name's Tenet, Harry Tenet. Don't forget that." And both were radiantly happy because of old times' sake.

But Ratterer, noticing Clyde's delivery uniform, observed: "Driving a delivery, eh? Gee, that's funny. You driving a delivery. Imagine. That kills me. What do you want to do that for?" Then seeing from Clyde's expression that his reference to his present position might not be the most pleasing thing in the world, since Clyde at once observed: "Well, I've been up against it, sorta," he added: "But say, I want to see you. Where are you living?" (Clyde told him.) "That's all right. I get off here at six. Why not drop around after you're through work. Or, I'll tell you—suppose we meet at—well, how about Henrici's on Randolph Street? Is that all right? At seven, say. I get off at six and I can be over there by then if you can."

Clyde, who was happy to the point of ecstasy in meeting Ratterer again, nodded a cheerful assent.

He boarded his wagon and continued his deliveries, yet for the rest of the afternoon his mind was on his approaching meeting with Ratterer. And at five-thirty he hurried to his barn and then to his boarding house on the west side, where he donned his street clothes, then hastened to Henrici's. He had not been standing on the corner a minute before Ratterer appeared, very genial and friendly and dressed, if anything, more neatly than ever.

"Gee, it's good to have a look at you, old socks!" he began. "Do you know you're the only one of that bunch that I've seen since I left K.C.? That's right. My sister wrote me after we left home that no one seemed to know what became of either Higby or Heggie, or you, either. They sent that fellow Sparser up for a year—did you hear that? Tough, eh? But not so much for killing the little girl, but for taking the car and running it without a license and not stopping when signaled. That's what they got him for. But say,"—he lowered his voice most significantly at this point. "We'da got that if they'd got us. Oh, gee, I was scared. And run?" And once more he began to laugh, but rather hysterically at that. "What a wallop, eh? An' us leavin' him and that girl in the car. Oh, say. Tough, what? Just what else could a fellow do, though? No need of all of us going up, eh? What was her name? Laura Sipe. An' you cut out before I saw you, even. And that little Briggs girl of yours did, too. Did you go home with her?"

Clyde shook his head negatively.

"I should say I didn't," he exclaimed.

"Well, where did you go then?" he asked.

Clyde told him. And after he had set forth a full picture of his own wayfarings, Ratterer returned with: "Gee, you didn't know that that little Briggs girl left with a guy from out there for New York right after that, did you? Some fellow who worked in a cigar store, so Louise told me. She saw her afterwards just before she left with a new fur coat and all." (Clyde winced sadly.) "Gee, but you were a sucker to fool around with her. She didn't care for you or nobody. But you was pretty much gone on her, I guess, eh?" And he grinned at Clyde amusedly, and chucked him under the arm, in his old teasing way.

But in regard to himself, he proceeded to unfold a tale of only modest adventure, which was very different from the one Clyde had narrated, a tale which had less of nerves and worry and more of a sturdy courage and faith in his own luck and possibilities. And finally he had "caught on" to this, because, as he phrased it, "you can always get something in Chi."

And here he had been ever since—"very quiet, of course," but no one had ever said a word to him.

And forthwith, he began to explain that just at present there wasn't anything in the Union League, but that he would talk to Mr. Haley who was superintendent of the club—and that if Clyde wanted to, and Mr. Haley knew of anything, he would try and find out if there was an opening anywhere, or likely to be, and if so, Clyde could slip into it.

"But can that worry stuff," he said to Clyde toward the end of the evening. "It don't get you nothing."

And then only two days after this most encouraging conversation, and while Clyde was still debating whether he would resign his job, resume his true name and canvass the various hotels in search of work, a note came to his room, brought by one of the bell-boys of the Union League which read: "See Mr. Lightall at the Great Northern before noon to-morrow. There's a vacancy over there. It ain't the very best, but it'll get you something better later."

And accordingly Clyde, after telephoning his department manager that he was ill and would not be able to work that day, made his way to this hotel in his very best clothes. And on the strength of what references he could give, was allowed to go to work; and much to his relief under his own name. Also, to his gratification, his salary was fixed at twenty dollars a month, meals included. But the tips, as he now learned, aggregated not more than ten a week—yet that, counting meals was far more than he was now getting as he comforted himself; and so much easier work, even if it did take him back into the old line, where he still feared to be seen and arrested.

It was not so very long after this—not more than three months—before a vacancy occurred in the Union League staff. Ratterer, having some time before established himself as day assistant to the club staff captain, and being on good terms with him, was able to say to the latter that he knew exactly the man for the place—Clyde Griffiths—then employed at the Great Northern. And accordingly, Clyde was sent for, and being carefully coached beforehand by Ratterer as to how to approach his new superior, and what to say, he was given the place.

And here, very different from the Great Northern and superior from a social and material point of view, as Clyde saw it, to even the Green-Davidson, he was able once more to view at close range a type of life that most affected, unfortunately, his bump of position and distinction. For to this club from day to day came or went such a company of seemingly mentally and socially worldly elect as he had never seen anywhere before, the self-integrated and self-centered from not only all of the states of his native land but from all countries and continents. American politicians from the north, south, east, west—the principal politicians and bosses, or alleged statesmen of their particular regions—surgeons, scientists, arrived physicians, generals, literary and social figures, not only from America but from the world over.

Here also, a fact which impressed and even startled his sense of curiosity and awe, even—there was no faintest trace of that sex element which had characterized most of the phases of life to be seen in the Green-Davidson, and more recently the Great Northern. In fact, in so far as he could remember, had seemed to run through and motivate nearly, if not quite all of the phases of life that he had thus far contacted. But here was no sex—no trace of it. No women were admitted to this club. These various distinguished individuals came and went, singly as a rule, and with the noiseless vigor and reserve that characterizes the ultra successful. They often ate alone, conferred in pairs and groups, noiselessly—read their papers or books, or went here and there in swiftly driven automobiles—but for the most part seemed to be unaware of, or at least unaffected by, that element of passion which, to his immature mind up to this time, had seemed to propel and disarrange so many things in those lesser worlds with which up to now he had been identified.

Probably one could not attain to or retain one's place in so remarkable a world as this unless one were indifferent to sex, a disgraceful passion, of course. And hence in the presence or under the eyes of such people one had to act and seem as though such thoughts as from time to time swayed one were far from one's mind.

After he had worked here a little while, under the influence of this organization and various personalities who came here, he had taken on a most gentlemanly and reserved air. When he was within the precincts of the club itself, he felt himself different from what he really was—more subdued, less romantic, more practical, certain that if he tried now, imitated the soberer people of the world, and those only, that some day he might succeed, if not greatly, at least much better than he had thus far. And who knows? What if he worked very steadily and made only the right sort of contacts and conducted himself with the greatest care here, one of these very remarkable men whom he saw entering or departing from here might take a fancy to him and offer him a connection with something important somewhere, such as he had never had before, and that might lift him into a world such as he had never known.

For to say the truth, Clyde had a soul that was not destined to grow up. He lacked decidedly that mental clarity and inner directing application that in so many permits them to sort out from the facts and avenues of life the particular thing or things that make for their direct advancement.

# Chapter IV

HOWEVER, as he now fancied, it was because he lacked an education that he had done so poorly. Because of those various moves from city to city in his early youth, he had never been permitted to collect such a sum of practical training in any field as would permit him, so he thought, to aspire to the great worlds of which these men appeared to be a part. Yet his soul now yearned for this. The people who lived in fine houses, who stopped at great hotels, and had men like Mr. Squires, and the manager of the bell-hops here, to wait on them and arrange for their comfort. And he was still a bell-hop. And close to twenty-one. At times it made him very sad. He wished and wished that he could get into some work where he could rise and be somebody—not always remain a bell-hop, as at times he feared he might.

About the time that he reached this conclusion in regard to himself and was meditating on some way to improve and safeguard his future, his uncle, Samuel Griffiths, arrived in Chicago. And having connections here which made a card to this club an obvious civility, he came directly to it and for several days was about the place conferring with individuals who came to see him, or hurrying to and fro to meet people and visit concerns whom he deemed it important to see.

And it was not an hour after he arrived before Ratterer, who had charge of the pegboard at the door by day and who had but a moment before finished posting the name of this uncle on the board, signaled to Clyde, who came over.

"Didn't you say you had an uncle or something by the name of Griffiths in the collar business somewhere in New York State?"

"Sure," replied Clyde. "Samuel Griffiths. He has a big collar factory in Lycurgus. That's his ad you see in all the papers and that's his fire sign over there on Michigan Avenue."

"Would you know him if you saw him?"

"No," replied Clyde. "I never saw him in all my life."

"I'll bet anything it's the same fellow," commented Ratterer, consulting a small registry slip that had been handed him.

"Looka here—Samuel Griffiths, Lycurgus, N.Y. That's proba-bly the same guy, eh?"

"Surest thing you know," added Clyde, very much inter-ested and even excited, for this was the identical uncle about whom he had been thinking so long.

"He just went through here a few minutes ago," went on Ratterer. "Devoy took his bags up to K. Swell-looking man, too. You better keep your eye open and take a look at him when he comes down again. Maybe it's your uncle. He's only medium tall and kinda thin. Wears a small gray mustache and a pearl gray hat. Good-lookin'. I'll point him out to you. If it is your uncle you better shine up to him. Maybe he'll do somepin' for you—give you a collar or two," he added, laughing.

Clyde laughed too as though he very much appreciated this joke, although in reality he was flustered. His uncle Samuel! And in this club! Well, then this was his opportunity to intro-duce himself to his uncle. He had intended writing him be-fore ever he secured this place, but now he was here in this club and might speak to him if he chose.

But hold! What would his uncle think of him, supposing he chose to introduce himself? For he was a bell-boy again and acting in that capacity in this club. What, for instance, might be his uncle's attitude toward boys who worked as bell-boys, particularly at his—Clyde's—years. For he was over twenty now, and getting to be pretty old for a bell-boy, that is, if one ever intended to be anything else. A man of his wealth and high position might look on bell-hopping as menial, particu-larly bell-boys who chanced to be related to him. He might not wish to have anything to do with him—might not even wish him to address him in any way. It was in this state that he remained for fully twenty-four hours after he knew that his uncle had arrived at this club.

The following afternoon, however, after he had seen him at least half a dozen times and had been able to formulate the most agreeable impressions of him, since his uncle appeared to be so very quick, alert, incisive—so very different from his father in every way, and so rich and respected by every one here—he began to wonder, to fear even at times, whether he was going to let this remarkable opportunity slip. For after all, his uncle did not look to him to be at all unkindly—quite the reverse—very pleasant. And when, at the suggestion of Ratterer, he had gone to his uncle's room to secure a letter which was to be sent by special messenger, his uncle had scarcely looked at him, but instead had handed him the letter and half a dollar. "See that a boy takes that right away and keep the money for yourself," he had remarked.

Clyde's excitement was so great at the moment that he wondered that his uncle did not guess that he was his nephew. But plainly he did not. And he went away a little crestfallen.

Later some half dozen letters for his uncle having been put in the key-box, Ratterer called Clyde's attention to them. "If you want to run in on him again, here's your chance. Take those up to him. He's in his room, I think." And Clyde, after some hesitation, had finally taken the letters and gone to his uncle's suite once more.

His uncle was writing at the time and merely called: "Come!" Then Clyde, entering and smiling rather enigmatically, observed: "Here's some mail for you, Mr. Griffiths."

"Thank you very much, my son," replied his uncle and proceeded to finger his vest pocket for change. But Clyde, seizing this opportunity, exclaimed: "Oh, no, I don't want anything for that." And then before his uncle could say anything more, although he proceeded to hold out some silver to him, he added: "I believe I'm related to you, Mr. Griffiths. You're Mr. Samuel Griffiths of the Griffiths Collar Company of Lycurgus, aren't you?"

"Yes, I have a little something to do with it, I believe. Who are you?" returned his uncle, looking at him sharply.

"My name's Clyde Griffiths. My father, Asa Griffiths, is your brother, I believe."

At the mention of this particular brother, who, to the knowledge of all the members of this family, was distinctly not a success materially, the face of Samuel Griffiths clouded the least trifle. For the mention of Asa brought rather unpleasingly before him the stocky and decidedly not well-groomed figure of his younger brother, whom he had not seen in so many years. His most recent distinct picture of him was as a young man of about Clyde's age about his father's house near

Bertwick, Vermont. But how different! Clyde's father was then short, fat and poorly knit mentally as well as physically—oleaginous and a bit mushy, as it were. His chin was not firm, his eyes a pale watery blue, and his hair frizzled. Whereas this son of his was neat, alert, good-looking and seemingly well-mannered and intelligent, as most bell-hops were inclined to be as he noted. And he liked him.

However, Samuel Griffiths, who along with his elder brother Allen had inherited the bulk of his father's moderate property, and this because of Joseph Griffiths' prejudice against his youngest son, had always felt that perhaps an injustice had been done Asa. For Asa, not having proved very practical or intelligent, his father had first attempted to drive and then later ignore him, and finally had turned him out at about Clyde's age, and had afterward left the bulk of his property, some thirty thousand dollars, to these two elder brothers, share and share alike—willing Asa but a petty thousand.

It was this thought in connection with this younger brother that now caused him to stare at Clyde rather curiously. For Clyde, as he could see, was in no way like the younger brother who had been harried from his father's home so many years before. Rather he was more like his own son, Gilbert, whom, as he now saw he resembled. Also in spite of all of Clyde's fears he was obviously impressed by the fact that he should have any kind of place in this interesting club. For to Samuel Griffiths, who was more than less confined to the limited activities and environment of Lycurgus, the character and standing of this particular club was to be respected. And those young men who served the guests of such an institution as this, were, in the main, possessed of efficient and unobtrusive manners. Therefore to see Clyde standing before him in his neat gray and black uniform and with the air of one whose social manners at least were excellent, caused him to think favorably of him.

"You don't tell me!" he exclaimed interestedly. "So you're Asa's son. I do declare! Well, now, this is a surprise. You see I haven't seen or heard from your father in at least—well, say, twenty-five or six years, anyhow. The last time I did hear from him he was living in Grand Rapids, Michigan, I think, or here. He isn't here now, I presume."

"Oh, no, sir," replied Clyde, who was glad to be able to say this. "The family live in Denver. I'm here all alone."

"Your father and mother are living, I presume."

"Yes, sir. They're both alive."

"Still connected with religious work, is he—your father?"

"Well, yes, sir," answered Clyde, a little dubiously, for he was still convinced that the form of religious work his father essayed was of all forms the poorest and most inconsequential socially. "Only the church he has now," he went on, "has a lodging house connected with it. About forty rooms, I believe. He and my mother run that and the mission too."

"Oh, I see."

He was so anxious to make a better impression on his uncle than the situation seemed to warrant that he was quite willing to exaggerate a little.

"Well, I'm glad they're doing so well," continued Samuel Griffiths, rather impressed with the trim and vigorous appearance of Clyde. "You like this kind of work, I suppose?"

"Well, not exactly. No, Mr. Griffiths, I don't," replied Clyde quickly, alive at once to the possibilities of this query. "It pays well enough. But I don't like the way you have to make the money you get here. It isn't my idea of a salary at all. But I got in this because I didn't have a chance to study any particular work or get in with some company where there was a real chance to work up and make something of myself. My mother wanted me to write you once and ask whether there was any chance in your company for me to begin and work up, but I was afraid maybe that you might not like that exactly, and so I never did."

He paused, smiling, and yet with an inquiring look in his eye.

His uncle looked solemnly at him for a moment, pleased by his looks and his general manner of approach in this instance, and then replied: "Well, that is very interesting. You should have written, if you wanted to——" Then, as was his custom in all matters, he cautiously paused. Clyde noted that he was hesitating to encourage him.

"I don't suppose there is anything in your company that you would let me do?" he ventured boldly, after a moment.

Samuel Griffiths merely stared at him thoughtfully. He

liked and he did not like this direct request. However, Clyde appeared at least a very adaptable person for the purpose. He seemed bright and ambitious—so much like his own son, and he might readily fit into some department as head or assistant under his son, once he had acquired a knowledge of the various manufacturing processes. At any rate he might let him try it. There could be no real harm in that. Besides, there was his younger brother, to whom, perhaps, both he and his older brother Allen owed some form of obligation, if not exactly restitution.

"Well," he said, after a moment, "that is something I would have to think over a little. I wouldn't be able to say, offhand, whether there is or not. We wouldn't be able to pay you as much as you make here to begin with," he warned.

"Oh, that's all right," exclaimed Clyde, who was far more fascinated by the thought of connecting himself with his uncle than anything else. "I wouldn't expect very much until I was able to earn it, of course."

"Besides, it might be that you would find that you didn't like the collar business once you got into it, or we might find we didn't like you. Not every one is suited to it by a long way."

"Well, all you'd have to do then would be to discharge me," assured Clyde. "I've always thought I would be, though, ever since I heard of you and your big company."

This last remark pleased Samuel Griffiths. Plainly he and his achievements had stood in the nature of an ideal to this youth.

"Very well," he said. "I won't be able to give any more time to this now. But I'll be here for a day or two more, anyhow, and I'll think it over. It may be that I will be able to do something for you. I can't say now." And he turned quite abruptly to his letters.

And Clyde, feeling that he had made as good an impression as could be expected under the circumstances and that something might come of it, thanked him profusely and beat a hasty retreat.

The next day, having thought it over and deciding that Clyde, because of his briskness and intelligence, was likely to prove as useful as another, Samuel Griffiths, after due deliberation as to the situation at home, informed Clyde that in case any small opening in the home factory occurred he would be glad to notify him. But he would not even go so far as to guarantee him that an opening would immediately be forthcoming. He must wait.

Accordingly Clyde was left to speculate as to how soon, if ever, a place in his uncle's factory would be made for him.

In the meanwhile Samuel Griffiths had returned to Lycurgus. And after a later conference with his son, he decided that Clyde might be inducted into the very bottom of the business at least—the basement of the Griffiths plant, where the shrinking of all fabrics used in connection with the manufacture of collars was brought about, and where beginners in this industry who really desired to acquire the technique of it were placed, for it was his idea that Clyde by degrees was to be taught the business from top to bottom. And since he must support himself in some form not absolutely incompatible with the standing of the Griffiths family here in Lycurgus, it was decided to pay him the munificent sum of fifteen dollars to begin.

For while Samuel Griffiths, as well as his son Gilbert, realized that this was small pay (not for an ordinary apprentice but for Clyde, since he was a relative) yet so inclined were both toward the practical rather than the charitable in connection with all those who worked for them, that the nearer the beginner in this factory was to the clear mark of necessity and compulsion, the better. Neither could tolerate the socialistic theory relative to capitalistic exploitation. As both saw it, there had to be higher and higher social orders to which the lower social classes could aspire. One had to have castes. One was foolishly interfering with and disrupting necessary and unavoidable social standards when one tried to unduly favor any one—even a relative. It was necessary when dealing with the classes and intelligences below one, commercially or financially, to handle them according to the standards to which they were accustomed. And the best of these standards were those which held these lower individuals to a clear realization of how difficult it was to come by money—to an understanding of how very necessary it was for all who were engaged in what both considered the only really important constructive work of the world—that of material manufacture—to understand how very essential it was to be drilled, and that sharply and systematically, in all the details and processes which comprise that constructive work. And so to become inured to a narrow and abstemious life in so doing. It was good for their characters. It informed and strengthened the minds and spirits of those who were destined to rise. And those who were not should be kept right where they were.

Accordingly, about a week after that, the nature of Clyde's work having been finally decided upon, a letter was dispatched to him to Chicago by Samuel Griffiths himself in which he set forth that if he chose he might present himself any time now within the next few weeks. But he must give due notice in writing of at least ten days in advance of his appearance in order that he might be properly arranged for. And upon his arrival he was to seek out Mr. Gilbert Griffiths at the office of the mill, who would look after him.

And upon receipt of this Clyde was very much thrilled and at once wrote to his mother that he had actually secured a place with his uncle and was going to Lycurgus. Also that he was going to try to achieve a real success now. Whereupon she wrote him a long letter, urging him to be, oh, so careful of his conduct and associates. Bad companionship was at the root of nearly all of the errors and failures that befell an ambitious youth such as he. If he would only avoid evil-minded or foolish and headstrong boys and girls, all would be well. It was so easy for a young man of his looks and character to be led astray by an evil woman. He had seen what had befallen him in Kansas City. But now he was still young and he was going to work for a man who was very rich and who could do so much for him, if he would. And he was to write her frequently as to the outcome of his efforts here.

And so, after having notified his uncle as he had requested, Clyde finally took his departure for Lycurgus. But on his arrival there, since his original notification from his uncle had called for no special hour at which to call at the factory, he did not go at once, but instead sought out the one important hotel of Lycurgus, the Lycurgus House.

Then finding himself with ample time on his hands, and very curious about the character of this city in which he was to work, and his uncle's position in it, he set forth to look it over, his thought being that once he reported and began work he might not soon have the time again. He now ambled out into Central Avenue, the very heart of Lycurgus, which in this section was crossed by several business streets, which together with Central Avenue for a few blocks on either side, appeared to constitute the business center—all there was to the life and gayety of Lycurgus.

# Chapter V

B UT ONCE in this and walking about, how different it all
seemed to the world to which so recently he had been accustomed. For here, as he had thus far seen, all was on a so
much smaller scale. The depot, from which only a half hour
before he had stepped down, was so small and dull, untrou-
bled, as he could plainly see, by much traffic. And the factory
section which lay opposite the small city—across the Mohawk—was little more than a red and gray assemblage of
buildings with here and there a smokestack projecting upward, and connected with the city by two bridges—a half
dozen blocks apart—one of them directly at this depot, a
wide traffic bridge across which traveled a car-line following
the curves of Central Avenue, dotted here and there with
stores and small homes.

But Central Avenue was quite alive with traffic, pedestrians
and automobiles. Opposite diagonally from the hotel, which
contained a series of wide plate-glass windows, behind which
were many chairs interspersed with palms and pillars, was the
dry-goods emporium of Stark and Company, a considerable
affair, four stories in height, and of white brick, and at least a
hundred feet long, the various windows of which seemed
bright and interesting, crowded with as smart models as
might be seen anywhere. Also there were other large concerns, a second hotel, various automobile showrooms, a
moving picture theater.

He found himself ambling on and on until suddenly he was
out of the business district again and in touch with a wide and
tree-shaded thoroughfare of residences, the houses of which,
each and every one, appeared to possess more room space,
lawn space, general ease and repose and dignity even than any
with which he had ever been in contact. In short, as he sensed
it from this brief inspection of its very central portion, it
seemed a very exceptional, if small city street—rich, luxurious
even. So many imposing wrought-iron fences, flower-bordered
walks, grouped trees and bushes, expensive and handsome
automobiles either beneath porte-cochères within or speeding

along the broad thoroughfare without. And in some neigh-boring shops—those nearest Central Avenue and the business heart where this wide and handsome thoroughfare began, were to be seen such expensive-looking and apparently smart displays of the things that might well interest people of means and comfort—motors, jewels, lingerie, leather goods and fur-niture.

But where now did his uncle and his family live? In which house? What street? Was it larger and finer than any of these he had seen in this street?

He must return at once, he decided, and report to his uncle. He must look up the factory address, probably in that region beyond the river, and go over there and see him. What would he say, how act, what would his uncle set him to doing? What would his cousin Gilbert be like? What would he be likely to think of him? In his last letter his uncle had men-tioned his son Gilbert. He retraced his steps along Central Avenue to the depot and found himself quickly before the walls of the very large concern he was seeking. It was of red brick, six stories high—almost a thousand feet long. It was nearly all windows—at least that portion which had been most recently added and which was devoted to collars. An older section, as Clyde later learned, was connected with the newer building by various bridges. And the south walls of both these two structures, being built at the water's edge, paralleled the Mohawk. There were also, as he now found, various entrances along River Street, a hundred feet or more apart—and each one, guarded by an employee in uniform—entrances numbered one, two and three—which were labeled "for employees only"—an entrance numbered four which read "office"—and entrances five and six appeared to be de-voted to freight receipts and shipments.

Clyde made his way to the office portion and finding no one to hinder him, passed through two sets of swinging doors and found himself in the presence of a telephone girl seated at a telephone desk behind a railing, in which was set a small gate—the only entrance to the main office apparently. And this she guarded. She was short, fat, thirty-five and unattractive.

"Well?" she called as Clyde appeared.

"I want to see Mr. Gilbert Griffiths," Clyde began a little nervously.

"What about?"

"Well, you see, I'm his cousin. Clyde Griffiths is my name. I have a letter here from my uncle, Mr. Samuel Griffiths. He'll see me, I think."

As he laid the letter before her, he noticed that her quite severe and decidedly indifferent expression changed and became not so much friendly as awed. For obviously she was very much impressed not only by the information but his looks, and began to examine him slyly and curiously.

"I'll see if he's in," she replied much more civilly, and plugging at the same time a switch which led to Mr. Gilbert Griffiths' private office. Word coming back to her apparently that Mr. Gilbert Griffiths was busy at the moment and could not be disturbed, she called back: "It's Mr. Gilbert's cousin, Mr. Clyde Griffiths. He has a letter from Mr. Samuel Griffiths." Then she said to Clyde: "Won't you sit down? I'm sure Mr. Gilbert Griffiths will see you in a moment. He's busy just now."

And Clyde, noting the unusual deference paid him—a form of deference that never in his life before had been offered him—was strangely moved by it. To think that he should be a full cousin to this wealthy and influential family! This enormous factory! So long and wide and high—as he had seen—six stories. And walking along the opposite side of the river just now, he had seen through several open windows whole rooms full of girls and women hard at work. And he had been thrilled in spite of himself. For somehow the high red walls of the building suggested energy and very material success, a type of success that was almost without flaw, as he saw it.

He looked at the gray plaster walls of this outer waiting chamber—at some lettering on the inner door which read: "The Griffiths Collar & Shirt Company, Inc. Samuel Griffiths, Pres. Gilbert Griffiths, Sec'y."—and wondered what it was all like inside—what Gilbert Griffiths would be like—cold or genial, friendly or unfriendly.

And then, as he sat there meditating, the woman suddenly turned to him and observed: "You can go in now. Mr. Gilbert Griffiths' office is at the extreme rear of this floor, over toward the river. Any one of the clerks inside will show you."

She half rose as if to open the door for him, but Clyde, sensing the intent, brushed by her. "That's all right. Thanks," he said most warmly, and opening the glass-plated door he gazed upon a room housing many over a hundred employees—chiefly young men and young women. And all were apparently intent on their duties before them. Most of them had green shades over their eyes. Quite all of them had on short alpaca office coats or sleeve protectors over their shirt sleeves. Nearly all of the young women wore clean and attractive gingham dresses or office slips. And all about this central space, which was partitionless and supported by round white columns, were offices labeled with the names of the various minor officials and executives of the company—Mr. Smillie, Mr. Latch, Mr. Gotboy, Mr. Burkey.

Since the telephone girl had said that Mr. Gilbert Griffiths was at the extreme rear, Clyde, without much hesitation, made his way along the railed-off aisle to that quarter, where upon a half-open door he read: "Mr. Gilbert Griffiths, Sec'y." He paused, uncertain whether to walk in or not, and then proceeded to tap. At once a sharp, penetrating voice called: "Come," and he entered and faced a youth who looked, if anything, smaller and a little older and certainly much colder and shrewder than himself—such a youth, in short, as Clyde would have liked to imagine himself to be—trained in an executive sense, apparently authoritative and efficient. He was dressed, as Clyde noted at once, in a bright gray suit of a very pronounced pattern, for it was once more approaching spring. His hair, of a lighter shade than Clyde's, was brushed and glazed most smoothly back from his temples and forehead, and his eyes, which Clyde, from the moment he had opened the door had felt drilling him, were of a clear, liquid, grayish-green blue. He had on a pair of large horn-rimmed glasses which he wore at his desk only, and the eyes that peered through them went over Clyde swiftly and notatively, from his shoes to the round brown felt hat which he carried in his hand.

"You're my cousin, I believe," he commented, rather icily, as Clyde came forward and stopped—a thin and certainly not very favorable smile playing about his lips.

"Yes, I am," replied Clyde, reduced and confused by this calm and rather freezing reception. On the instant, as he now saw, he could not possibly have the same regard and esteem for this cousin, as he could and did have for his uncle, whose very great ability had erected this important industry. Rather, deep down in himself he felt that this young man, an heir and nothing more to this great industry, was taking to himself airs and superiorities which, but for his father's skill before him, would not have been possible.

At the same time so groundless and insignificant were his claims to any consideration here, and so grateful was he for anything that might be done for him, that he felt heavily obligated already and tried to smile his best and most ingratiating smile. Yet Gilbert Griffiths at once appeared to take this as a bit of presumption which ought not to be tolerated in a mere cousin, and particularly one who was seeking a favor of him and his father.

However, since his father had troubled to interest himself in him and had given him no alternative, he continued his wry smile and mental examination, the while he said: "We thought you would be showing up to-day or to-morrow. Did you have a pleasant trip?"

"Oh, yes, very," replied Clyde, a little confused by this inquiry.

"So you think you'd like to learn something about the manufacture of collars, do you?" Tone and manner were infiltrated by the utmost condescension.

"I would certainly like to learn something that would give me a chance to work up, have some future in it," replied Clyde, genially and with a desire to placate his young cousin as much as possible.

"Well, my father was telling me of his talk with you in Chicago. From what he told me I gather that you haven't had much practical experience of any kind. You don't know how to keep books, do you?"

"No, I don't," replied Clyde a little regretfully.

"And you're not a stenographer or anything like that?"

"No, sir, I'm not."

Most sharply, as Clyde said this, he felt that he was dreadfully lacking in every training. And now Gilbert Griffiths looked at him as though he were rather a hopeless proposition indeed from the viewpoint of this concern.

"Well, the best thing to do with you, I think," he went on, as though before this his father had not indicated to him exactly what was to be done in this case, "is to start you in the shrinking room. That's where the manufacturing end of this business begins, and you might as well be learning that from the ground up. Afterwards, when we see how you do down there, we can tell a little better what to do with you. If you had any office training it might be possible to use you up here." (Clyde's face fell at this and Gilbert noticed it. It pleased him.) "But it's just as well to learn the practical side of the business, whatever you do," he added rather coldly, not that he desired to comfort Clyde any but merely to be saying it as a fact. And seeing that Clyde said nothing, he continued: "The best thing, I presume, before you try to do anything around here is for you to get settled somewhere. You haven't taken a room anywhere yet, have you?"

"No, I just came in on the noon train," replied Clyde. "I was a little dirty and so I just went up to the hotel to brush up a little. I thought I'd look for a place afterwards."

"Well, that's right. Only don't look for any place. I'll have our superintendent see that you're directed to a good boarding house. He knows more about the town than you do." His thought here was that after all Clyde was a full cousin and that it wouldn't do to have him live just anywhere. At the same time he was greatly concerned lest Clyde get the notion that the family was very much concerned as to where he did live, which most certainly it was *not*, as he saw it. His final feeling was that he could easily place and control Clyde in such a way as to make him not very important to any one in any way—his father, the family, all the people who worked here.

He reached for a button on his desk and pressed it. A trim girl, very severe and reserved in a green gingham dress, appeared.

"Ask Mr. Whiggam to come here."

She disappeared and presently there entered a medium-sized and nervous, yet moderately stout, man who looked as though he were under a great strain. He was about forty years of age—repressed and noncommittal—and looked curiously and suspiciously about as though wondering what new trouble impended. His head, as Clyde at once noticed, appeared chronically to incline forward, while at the same time he lifted his eyes as though actually he would prefer not to look up.

"Whiggam," began young Griffiths authoritatively, "this is Clyde Griffiths, a cousin of ours. You remember I spoke to you about him."

"Yes, sir."

"Well, he's to be put in the shrinking department for the present. You can show him what he's to do. Afterwards you had better have Mrs. Braley show him where he can get a room." (All this had been talked over and fixed upon the week before by Gilbert and Whiggam, but now he gave it the ring of an original suggestion.) "And you'd better give his name in to the timekeeper as beginning to-morrow morning, see?"

"Yes, sir," bowed Whiggam deferentially. "Is that all?"

"Yes, that's all," concluded Gilbert smartly. "You go with Whiggam, Mr. Griffiths. He'll tell you what to do."

Whiggam turned. "If you'll just come with me, Mr. Griffiths," he observed deferentially, as Clyde could see—and that for all of his cousin's apparently condescending attitude—and marched out with Clyde at his heels. And young Gilbert as briskly turned to his own desk, but at the same time shaking his head. His feeling at the moment was that mentally Clyde was not above a good bell-boy in a city hotel probably. Else why should he come on here in this way. "I wonder what he thinks he's going to do here," he continued to think, "where he thinks he's going to get?"

And Clyde, as he followed Mr. Whiggam, was thinking what a wonderful place Mr. Gilbert Griffiths enjoyed. No doubt he came and went as he chose—arrived at the office late, departed early, and somewhere in this very interesting city dwelt with his parents and sisters in a very fine house—of course. And yet here he was—Gilbert's own cousin, and the nephew of his wealthy uncle, being escorted to work in a very minor department of this great concern.

Nevertheless, once they were out of the sight and hearing of Mr. Gilbert Griffiths, he was somewhat diverted from this mood by the sights and sounds of the great manufactory it-self. For here on this very same floor, but beyond the im-mense office room through which he had passed, was another much larger room filled with rows of bins, facing aisles not more than five feet wide, and containing, as Clyde could see, enormous quantities of collars boxed in small paper boxes, according to sizes. These bins were either being refilled by stock boys who brought more boxed collars from the boxing room in large wooden trucks, or were being as rapidly emptied by order clerks who, trundling small box trucks in front of them, were filling orders from duplicate check lists which they carried in their hands.

"Never worked in a collar factory before, Mr. Griffiths, I presume?" commented Mr. Whiggam with somewhat more spirit, once he was out of the presence of Gilbert Griffiths. Clyde noticed at once the Mr. Griffiths.

"Oh, no," he replied quickly. "I never worked at anything like this before."

"Expect to learn all about the manufacturing end of the game in the course of time, though, I suppose." He was walking briskly along one of the long aisles as he spoke, but Clyde noticed that he shot sly glances in every direction.

"I'd like to," he answered.

"Well, there's a little more to it than some people think, although you often hear there isn't very much to learn." He opened another door, crossed a gloomy hall and entered still another room which, filled with bins as was the other, was piled high in every bin with bolts of white cloth.

"You might as well know a little about this as long as you're going to begin in the shrinking room. This is the stuff from which the collars are cut, the collars and the lining. They are called webs. Each of these bolts is a web. We take these down in the basement and shrink them because they can't be used this way. If they are, the collars would shrink after they were cut. But you'll see. We tub them and then dry them afterwards."

He marched solemnly on and Clyde sensed once more that this man was not looking upon him as an ordinary employee by any means. His *Mr.* Griffiths, his supposition to the effect that Clyde was to learn all about the manufacturing end of the business, as well as his condescension in explaining about these webs of cloth, had already convinced Clyde that he was looked upon as one to whom some slight homage at least must be paid.

He followed Mr. Whiggam, curious as to the significance of this, and soon found himself in an enormous basement which had been reached by descending a flight of steps at the end of a third hall. Here, by the help of four long rows of incandescent lamps, he discerned row after row of porcelain tubs or troughs, lengthwise of the room, and end to end, which reached from one exterior wall to the other. And in these, under steaming hot water apparently, were any quantity of those same webs he had just seen upstairs, soaking. And near-by, north and south of these tubs, and paralleling them for the length of this room, all of a hundred and fifty feet in length, were enormous drying racks or moving skeleton platforms, boxed, top and bottom and sides, with hot steam pipes, between which on rolls, but festooned in such a fashion as to take advantage of these pipes, above, below and on either side, were more of these webs, but unwound and wet and draped as described, yet moving along slowly on these rolls from the east end of the room to the west. This movement, as Clyde could see, was accompanied by an enormous rattle and clatter of ratchet arms which automatically shook and moved these lengths of cloth forward from east to west. And as they moved they dried, and were then automatically rewound at the west end of these racks into bolt form once more upon a wooden spool and then lifted off by a youth whose duty it was to "take" from these moving platforms. One youth, as Clyde saw, "took" from two of these tracks at the west end; while at the east end another youth of about his own years "fed." That is, he took bolts of this now partially shrunk yet still wet cloth and attaching one end of it to some moving hooks, saw that it slowly and properly unwound and fed itself over the drying racks for the entire length of these tracks. As fast as it had gone the way of all webs, another was attached.

Between each two rows of tubs in the center of the room were enormous whirling separators or dryers, into which these webs of cloth, as they came from the tubs in which they had been shrinking for twenty-four hours, were piled and as much water as possible centrifugally extracted before they were spread out on the drying racks.

Primarily little more than this mere physical aspect of the

room was grasped by Clyde—its noise, its heat, its steam, the energy with which a dozen men and boys were busying themselves with various processes. They were, without exception, clothed only in armless undershirts, a pair of old trousers belted in at the waist, and with canvas-topped and rubber-soled sneakers on their bare feet. The water and the general dampness and the heat of the room seemed obviously to necessitate some such dressing as this.

"This is the shrinking room," observed Mr. Whiggam, as they entered. "It isn't as nice as some of the others, but it's where the manufacturing process begins. Kemerer!" he called.

A short, stocky, full-chested man, with a pale, full face and white, strong-looking arms, dressed in a pair of dirty and wrinkled trousers and an armless flannel shirt, now appeared. Like Whiggam in the presence of Gilbert, he appeared to be very much overawed in the presence of Whiggam.

"This is Clyde Griffiths, the cousin of Gilbert Griffiths. I spoke to you about him last week, you remember?"

"Yes, sir."

"He's to begin down here. He'll show up in the morning."

"Yes, sir."

"Better put his name down on your check list. He'll begin at the usual hour."

"Yes, sir."

Mr. Whiggam, as Clyde noticed, held his head higher and spoke more directly and authoritatively than at any time so far. He seemed to be master, not underling, now.

"Seven-thirty is the time every one goes to work here in the morning," went on Mr. Whiggam to Clyde informatively, "but they all ring in a little earlier—about seven-twenty or so, so as to have time to change their clothes and get to the machines.

"Now, if you want to," he added, "Mr. Kemerer can show you what you'll have to do to-morrow before you leave to-day. It might save a little time. Or, you can leave it until then if you want to. It don't make any difference to me. Only, if you'll come back to the telephone girl at the main entrance about five-thirty I'll have Mrs. Braley there for you. She's to show you about your room, I believe. I won't be there myself, but you just ask the telephone girl for her. She'll know." He turned and added, "Well, I'll leave you now."

He lowered his head and started to go away just as Clyde began. "Well, I'm very much obliged to you, Mr. Whiggam." Instead of answering, he waved one fishy hand slightly upward and was gone—down between the tubs toward the west door. And at once Mr. Kemerer—still nervous and overawed apparently—began.

"Oh, that's all right about what you have to do, Mr. Griffiths. I'll just let you bring down webs on the floor above to begin with to-morrow. But if you've got any old clothes, you'd better put 'em on. A suit like that wouldn't last long here." He eyed Clyde's very neat, if inexpensive suit, in an odd way. His manner, quite like that of Mr. Whiggam before him, was a mixture of uncertainty and a very small authority here in Clyde's case—of extreme respect and yet some private doubt, which only time might resolve. Obviously it was no small thing to be a Griffiths here, even if one were a cousin and possibly not as welcome to one's powerful relatives as one might be.

At first sight, and considering what his general dreams in connection with this industry were, Clyde was inclined to rebel. For the type of youth and man he saw here were in his estimation and at first glance rather below the type of individuals he hoped to find here—individuals neither so intelligent nor alert as those employed by the Union League and the Green-Davidson by a long distance. And still worse he felt them to be much more subdued and sly and ignorant—mere clocks, really. And their eyes, as he entered with Mr. Whiggam, while they pretended not to be looking, were very well aware, as Clyde could feel, of all that was going on. Indeed, he and Mr. Whiggam were the center of all their secret looks. At the same time, their spare and practical manner of dressing struck dead at one blow any thought of refinement in connection with the work in here. How unfortunate that his lack of training would not permit his being put to office work or something like that upstairs.

He walked with Mr. Kemerer, who troubled to say that these were the tubs in which the webs were shrunk over night—these the centrifugal dryers—these the rack dryers. Then he was told that he could go. And by then it was only three o'clock.

He made his way out of the nearest door and once outside he congratulated himself on being connected with this great company, while at the same time wondering whether he was going to prove satisfactory to Mr. Kemerer and Mr. Whiggam. Supposing he didn't. Or supposing he couldn't stand all this? It was pretty rough. Well, if worst came to worst, as he now thought, he could go back to Chicago, or on to New York, maybe, and get work.

But why hadn't Samuel Griffiths had the graciousness to receive and welcome him? Why had that young Gilbert Griffiths smiled so cynically? And what sort of a woman was this Mrs. Braley? Had he done wisely to come on here? Would this family do anything for him now that he was here?

It was thus that, strolling west along River Street on which were a number of other kinds of factories, and then north through a few other streets that held more factories—tinware, wickwire, a big vacuum carpet cleaning plant, a rug manufacturing company, and the like—that he came finally upon a miserable slum, the like of which, small as it was, he had not seen outside of Chicago or Kansas City. He was so irritated and depressed by the poverty and social angularity and crudeness of it—all spelling but one thing, social misery, to him—that he at once retraced his steps and recrossing the Mohawk by a bridge farther west soon found himself in an area which was very different indeed—a region once more of just such homes as he had been admiring before he left for the factory. And walking still farther south, he came upon that same wide and tree-lined avenue—which he had seen before—the exterior appearance of which alone identified it as the principal residence thoroughfare of Lycurgus. It was so very broad and well-paved and lined by such an arresting company of houses. At once he was very much alive to the personnel of this street, for it came to him immediately that it must be in this street very likely that his uncle Samuel lived. The houses were nearly all of French, Italian or English design, and excellent period copies at that, although he did not know it.

Impressed by their beauty and spaciousness, however, he walked along, now looking at one and another, and wondering which, if any, of these was occupied by his uncle, and deeply impressed by the significance of so much wealth. How superior and condescending his cousin Gilbert must feel, walking out of some such place as this in the morning.

Then pausing before one which, because of trees, walks, newly-groomed if bloomless flower beds, a large garage at the rear, a large fountain to the left of the house as he faced it, in the center of which was a boy holding a swan in his arms, and to the right of the house one lone cast iron stag pursued by some cast iron dogs, he felt especially impelled to admire, and charmed by the dignity of this place, which was a modified form of old English, he now inquired of a stranger who was passing—a middle-aged man of a rather shabby working type, "Whose house is that, mister?" and the man replied: "Why, that's Samuel Griffiths' residence. He's the man who owns the big collar factory over the river."

At once Clyde straightened up, as though dashed with cold water. His uncle's! His residence! Then that was one of his automobiles standing before the garage at the rear there. And there was another visible through the open door of the garage.

Indeed in his immature and really psychically unilluminated mind it suddenly evoked a mood which was as of roses, perfumes, lights and music. The beauty! The ease! What member of his own immediate family had ever even dreamed that his uncle lived thus! The grandeur! And his own parents so wretched—so poor, preaching on the streets of Kansas City and no doubt Denver. Conducting a mission! And although thus far no single member of this family other than his chill cousin had troubled to meet him, and that at the factory only, and although he had been so indifferently assigned to the menial type of work that he had, still he was elated and uplifted. For, after all, was he not a Griffiths, a full cousin as well as a full nephew to the two very important men who lived here, and now working for them in some capacity at least? And must not that spell a future of some sort, better than any he had known as yet? For consider who the Griffiths were here, as opposed to "who" the Griffiths were in Kansas City, say— or Denver. The enormous difference! A thing to be as carefully concealed as possible. At the same time, he was immediately reduced again, for supposing the Griffiths here— his uncle or his cousin or some friend or agent of theirs— should now investigate his parents and his past? Heavens! The matter of that slain child in Kansas City! His parents' miserable makeshift life! Esta! At once his face fell, his dreams being so thickly clouded over. If they should guess! If they should sense!

Oh, the devil—who was he anyway? And what did he really amount to? What could he hope for from such a great world as this really, once they knew why he had troubled to come here?

A little disgusted and depressed he turned to retrace his steps, for all at once he felt himself very much of a nobody.

# Chapter VI

THE ROOM which Clyde secured this same day with the aid of Mrs. Braley, was in Thorpe Street, a thoroughfare enormously removed in quality if not in distance from that in which his uncle resided. Indeed the difference was sufficient to decidedly qualify his mounting notions of himself as one who, after all, was connected with him. The commonplace brown or gray or tan colored houses, rather smoked or decayed which fronted it—the leafless and winter harried trees which in spite of smoke and dust seemed to give promise of the newer life so near at hand—the leaves and flowers of May. Yet as he walked into it with Mrs. Braley, many drab and commonplace figures of men and girls, and elderly spinsters resembling Mrs. Braley in kind, were making their way home from the several factories beyond the river. And at the door Mrs. Braley and himself were received by a none-too-polished woman in a clean gingham apron over a dark brown dress, who led the way to a second floor room, not too small or uncomfortably furnished—which she assured him he could have for four dollars without board or seven and one-half dollars with—a proposition which, seeing that he was advised by Mrs. Braley that this was somewhat better than he would get in most places for the same amount, he decided to take. And here, after thanking Mrs. Braley, he decided to remain—later sitting down to dinner with a small group of milltown store and factory employees, such as partially he had been accustomed to in Paulina Street in Chicago, before moving to the better atmosphere of the Union League. And after dinner he made his way out into the principal thoroughfares of Lycurgus, only to observe such a crowd of nondescript mill-workers as, judging these streets by day, he would not have fancied swarmed here by night—girls and boys, men and women of various nationalities, and types—Americans, Poles, Hungarians, French, English—and for the most part—if not entirely touched with a peculiar something—ignorance or thickness of mind or body, or with a certain lack of taste and alertness or daring, which seemed to mark them one and all as of the basement world which he had seen only this afternoon. Yet in some streets and stores, particularly those nearer Wykeagy Avenue, a better type of girl and young man who might have been and no doubt were of the various office groups of the different companies over the river—neat and active.

And Clyde, walking to and fro, from eight until ten, when as though by pre-arrangement, the crowd in the more congested streets seemed suddenly to fade away, leaving them quite vacant. And throughout this time contrasting it all with Chicago and Kansas City. (What would Ratterer think if he could see him now—his uncle's great house and factory?) And perhaps because of its smallness, liking it—the Lycurgus Hotel, neat and bright and with a brisk local life seeming to center about it. And the post-office and a handsomely spired church, together with an old and interesting graveyard, cheek by jowl with an automobile salesroom. And a new moving picture theater just around the corner in a side street. And various boys and girls, men and women, walking here and there, some of them flirting as Clyde could see. And with a suggestion somehow hovering over it all of hope and zest and youth—the hope and zest and youth that is at the bottom of all the constructive energy of the world everywhere. And finally returning to his room in Thorpe Street with the conclusion that he did like the place and would like to stay here. That beautiful Wykeagy Avenue! His uncle's great factory! The many pretty and eager girls he had seen hurrying to and fro!

In the meantime, in so far as Gilbert Griffiths was concerned, and in the absence of his father, who was in New York at the time (a fact which Clyde did not know and of which Gilbert did not trouble to inform him) he had conveyed to his mother and sisters that he had met Clyde, and if he were not the dullest, certainly he was not the most interesting person in the world, either. Encountering Myra, as he first entered at five-thirty, the same day that Clyde had appeared, he troubled to observe: "Well, that Chicago cousin of ours blew in to-day."

"Yes!" commented Myra, "What's he like?" The fact that her father had described Clyde as gentlemanly and intelligent had interested her, although knowing Lycurgus and the nature of the mill life here and its opportunities for those who worked in factories such as her father owned, she had wondered why Clyde had bothered to come.

"Well, I can't see that he's so much," replied Gilbert. "He's fairly intelligent and not bad-looking, but he admits that he's never had any business training of any kind. He's like all those young fellows who work for hotels. He thinks clothes are the whole thing, I guess. He had on a light brown suit and a brown tie and hat to match and brown shoes. His tie was too bright and he had on one of those bright pink striped shirts like they used to wear three or four years ago. Besides his clothes aren't cut right. I didn't want to say anything because he's just come on, and we don't know whether he'll hold out or not. But if he does, and he's going to pose around as a relative of ours, he'd better tone down, or I'd advise the governor to have a few words with him. Outside of that I guess he'll do well enough in one of the departments after a while, as foreman or something. He might even be made into a salesman later on, I suppose. But what he sees in all that to make it worth while to come here is more than I can guess. As a matter of fact, I don't think the governor made it clear to him just how few the chances are here for any one who isn't really a wizard or something."

He stood with his back to the large open fireplace.

"Oh, well, you know what Mother was saying the other day about his father. She thinks Daddy feels that he's never had a chance in some way. He'll probably do something for him whether he wants to keep him in the mill or not. She told me that she thought that Dad felt that his father hadn't been treated just right by their father."

Myra paused, and Gilbert, who had had this same hint from his mother before now, chose to ignore the implication of it.

"Oh, well, it's not my funeral," he went on. "If the governor wants to keep him on here whether he's fitted for anything special or not, that's his look-out. Only he's the one that's always talking about efficiency in every department and cutting and keeping out dead timber."

Meeting his mother and Bella later, he volunteered the

same news and much the same ideas. Mrs. Griffiths sighed; for after all, in a place like Lycurgus and established as they were, any one related to them and having their name ought to be most circumspect and have careful manners and taste and judgment. It was not wise for her husband to bring on any one who was not all of that and more.

On the other hand, Bella was by no means satisfied with the accuracy of her brother's picture of Clyde. She did not know Clyde, but she did know Gilbert, and as she knew he could decide very swiftly that this or that person was lacking in almost every way, when, as a matter of fact, they might not be at all as she saw it.

"Oh, well," she finally observed, after hearing Gilbert comment on more of Clyde's peculiarities at dinner, "if Daddy wants him, I presume he'll keep him, or do something with him eventually." At which Gilbert winced internally for this was a direct slap at his assumed authority in the mill under his father, which authority he was eager to make more and more effective in every direction, as his younger sister well knew.

In the meanwhile on the following morning, Clyde, returning to the mill, found that the name, or appearance, or both perhaps—his resemblance to Mr. Gilbert Griffiths—was of some peculiar advantage to him which he could not quite sufficiently estimate at present. For on reaching number one entrance, the doorman on guard there looked as though startled.

"Oh, you're Mr. Clyde Griffiths?" he queried. "You're goin' to work under Mr. Kemerer? Yes, I know. Well, that man there will have your key," and he pointed to a stodgy, stuffy old man whom later Clyde came to know as "Old Jeff," the time-clock guard, who, at a stand farther along this same hall, furnished and reclaimed all keys between seven-thirty and seven-forty.

When Clyde approached him and said: "My name's Clyde Griffiths and I'm to work downstairs with Mr. Kemerer," he too started and then said: "Sure, that's right. Yes, sir. Here you are, Mr. Griffiths. Mr. Kemerer spoke to me about you yesterday. Number seventy-one is to be yours. I'm giving you Mr. Duveny's old key." When Clyde had gone down the stairs into the shrinking department, he turned to the doorman who had drawn near and exclaimed: "Don't it beat all how much that fellow looks like Mr. Gilbert Griffiths? Why, he's almost his spittin' image. What is he, do you suppose, a brother or a cousin, or what?"

"Don't ask me," replied the doorman. "I never saw him before. But he's certainly related to the family all right. When I seen him first, I thought it was Mr. Gilbert. I was just about to tip my hat to him when I saw it wasn't."

And in the shrinking room when he entered, as on the day before, he found Kemerer as respectful and evasive as ever. For, like Whiggam before him, Kemerer had not as yet been able to decide what Clyde's true position with this company was likely to be. For, as Whiggam had informed Kemerer the day before, Mr. Gilbert had said no least thing which tended to make Mr. Whiggam believe that things were to be made especially easy for him, nor yet hard, either. On the contrary, Mr. Gilbert had said: "He's to be treated like all the other employees as to time and work. No different." Yet in introducing Clyde he had said: "This is my cousin, and he's going to try to learn this business," which would indicate that as time went on Clyde was to be transferred from department to department until he had surveyed the entire manufacturing end of the business.

Whiggam, for this reason, after Clyde had gone, whispered to Kemerer as well as to several others, that Clyde might readily prove to be some one who was a protégé of the chief—and therefore they determined to "watch their step," at least until they knew what his standing here was to be. And Clyde, noticing this, was quite set up by it, for he could not help but feel that this in itself, and apart from whatever his cousin Gilbert might either think or wish to do, might easily presage some favor on the part of his uncle that might lead to some good for him. So when Kemerer proceeded to explain to him that he was not to think that the work was so very hard or that there was so very much to do for the present, Clyde took it with a slight air of condescension. And in consequence Kemerer was all the more respectful.

"Just hang up your hat and coat over there in one of those lockers," he proceeded mildly and ingratiatingly even. "Then you can take one of those crate trucks back there and go up to the next floor and bring down some webs. They'll show you where to get them."

The days that followed were diverting and yet troublesome enough to Clyde, who to begin with was puzzled and disturbed at times by the peculiar social and workaday worlds and position in which he found himself. For one thing, those by whom now he found himself immediately surrounded at the factory were not such individuals as he would ordinarily select for companions—far below bell-boys or drivers or clerks anywhere. They were, one and all, as he could now clearly see, meaty or stodgy mentally and physically. They wore such clothes as only the most common laborers would wear—such clothes as are usually worn by those who count their personal appearance among the least of their troubles—their work and their heavy material existence being all. In addition, not knowing just what Clyde was, or what his coming might mean to their separate and individual positions, they were inclined to be dubious and suspicious.

After a week or two, however, coming to understand that Clyde was a nephew of the president, a cousin of the secretary of the company, and hence not likely to remain here long in any menial capacity, they grew more friendly, but inclined in the face of the sense of subserviency which this inspired in them, to become jealous and suspicious of him in another way. For, after all, Clyde was not one of them, and under such circumstances could not be. He might smile and be civil enough—yet he would always be in touch with those who were above them, would he not—or so they thought. He was, as they saw it, part of the rich and superior class and every poor man knew what that meant. The poor must stand together everywhere.

For his part, however, and sitting about for the first few days in this particular room eating his lunch, he wondered how these men could interest themselves in what were to him such dull and uninteresting items—the quality of the cloth that was coming down in the webs—some minute flaws in the matter of weight or weave—the last twenty webs hadn't looked so closely shrunk as the preceding sixteen; or the Cranston Wickwire Company was not carrying as many men as it had the month before—or the Anthony Woodenware

Company had posted a notice that the Saturday half-holiday would not begin before June first this year as opposed to the middle of May last year. They all appeared to be lost in the humdrum and routine of their work.

In consequence his mind went back to happier scenes. He wished at times he were back in Chicago or Kansas City. He thought of Ratterer, Hegglund, Higby, Louise Ratterer, Larry Doyle, Mr. Squires, Hortense—all of the young and thoughtless company of which he had been a part, and wondered what they were doing. What had become of Hortense? She had got that fur coat after all—probably from that cigar clerk and then had gone away with him after she had protested so much feeling for him—the little beast. After she had gotten all that money out of him. The mere thought of her and all that she might have meant to him if things had not turned as they had, made him a little sick at times. To whom was she being nice now? How had she found things since leaving Kansas City? And what would she think if she saw him here now or knew of his present high connections? Gee! That would cool her a little. But she would not think much of his present position. That was sure. But she might respect him more if she could see his uncle and his cousin and this factory and their big house. It would be like her then to try to be nice to him. Well, he would show her, if he ever ran into her again—snub her, of course, as no doubt he very well could by then.

# Chapter VII

IN SO FAR as his life at Mrs. Cuppy's went, he was not so very happily placed there, either. For that was but a commonplace rooming and boarding house, which drew to it, at best, such conservative mill and business types as looked on work and their wages, and the notions of the middle class religious world of Lycurgus as most essential to the order and well being of the world. From the point of view of entertainment or gayety, it was in the main a very dull place.

At the same time, because of the presence of one Walter Dillard—a brainless sprig who had recently come here from Fonda, it was not wholly devoid of interest for Clyde. The latter—a youth of about Clyde's own age and equally ambitious socially—but without Clyde's tact or discrimination anent the governing facts of life, was connected with the men's furnishing department of Stark and Company. He was spry, avid, attractive enough physically, with very light hair, a very light and feeble mustache, and the delicate airs and ways of a small town Beau Brummell. Never having had any social standing or the use of any means whatsoever—his father having been a small town dry goods merchant before him, who had failed—he was, because of some atavistic spur or filip in his own blood, most anxious to attain some sort of social position.

But failing that so far, he was interested in and envious of those who had it—much more so than Clyde, even. The glory and activity of the leading families of this particular city had enormous weight with him—the Nicholsons, the Starks, the Harriets, Griffiths, Finchleys, et cetera. And learning a few days after Clyde's arrival of his somewhat left-handed connection with this world, he was most definitely interested. What? A Griffiths! The nephew of the rich Samuel Griffiths of Lycurgus! And in this boarding house! Beside him at this table! At once his interest rose to where he decided that he must cultivate this stranger as speedily as possible. Here was a real social opportunity knocking at his very door—a connecting link to one of the very best families! And besides was he not young, attractive and probably ambitious like himself—a fellow to play around with if one could? He proceeded at once to make overtures to Clyde. It seemed almost too good to be true.

In consequence he was quick to suggest a walk, the fact that there was a certain movie just on at the Mohawk, which was excellent—very snappy. Didn't Clyde want to go? And because of his neatness, smartness—a touch of something that was far from humdrum or the heavy practicality of the mill and the remainder of this boarding house world, Clyde was inclined to fall in with him.

But, as he now thought, here were his great relatives and he must watch his step here. Who knew but that he might be making a great mistake in holding such free and easy contacts as this. The Griffiths—as well as the entire world of which they were a part—as he guessed from the general manner of all those who even contacted him, must be very removed from the commonalty here. More by instinct than reason, he was inclined to stand off and look very superior—more so since those, including this very youth on whom he practised this seemed to respect him the more. And although upon eager—and even—after its fashion, supplicating request, he now went with this youth—still he went cautiously. And his aloof and condescending manner Dillard at once translated as "class" and "connection." And to think he had met him in this dull, dubby boarding house here. And on his arrival—at the very inception of his career here.

And so his manner was that of the sycophant—although he had a better position and was earning more money than Clyde was at this time, twenty-two dollars a week.

"I suppose you'll be spending a good deal of your time with your relatives and friends here," he volunteered on the occasion of their first walk together, and after he had extracted as much information as Clyde cared to impart, which was almost nothing, while he volunteered a few, most decidedly furbished bits from his own history. His father owned a dry goods store *now*. He had come over here to study other methods, et cetera. He had an uncle here—connected with Stark and Company. He had met a few—not so many as yet—nice people here, since he hadn't been here so very long himself—four months all told.

But Clyde's relatives!

"Say, your uncle must be worth over a million, isn't he? They say he is. Those houses in Wykeagy Avenue are certainly the cats'. You won't see anything finer in Albany or Utica or Rochester either. Are you Samuel Griffiths' own nephew? You don't say! Well, that'll certainly mean a lot to you here. I wish I had a connection like that. You bet I'd make it count."

He beamed on Clyde eagerly and hopefully, and through him Clyde sensed even more how really important this blood relation was. Only think how much it meant to this strange youth.

"Oh, I don't know," replied Clyde dubiously, and yet very much flattered by this assumption of intimacy. "I came on to learn the collar business, you know. Not to play about very much. My uncle wants me to stick to that, pretty much."

"Sure, sure. I know how that is," replied Dillard, "that's the way my uncle feels about me, too. He wants me to stick close to the work here and not play about very much. He's the buyer for Stark and Company, you know. But still a man can't work all the time, either. He's got to have a little fun."

"Yes, that's right," said Clyde—for the first time in his life a little condescendingly.

They walked along in silence for a few moments. Then: "Do you dance?"

"Yes," answered Clyde.

"Well, so do I. There are a lot of cheap dance halls around here, but I never go to any of those. You can't do it and keep in with the nice people. This is an awfully close town that way, they say. The best people won't have anything to do with you unless you go with the right crowd. It's the same way up at Fonda. You have to 'belong' or you can't go out anywhere at all. And that's right, I guess. But still there are a lot of nice girls here that a fellow can go with—girls of right nice families—not in society, of course—but still, they're not talked about, see. And they're not so slow, either. Pretty hot stuff, some of them. And you don't have to marry any of 'em, either." Clyde began to think of him as perhaps a little too lusty for this new life here, maybe. At the same time he liked him some. "By the way," went on Dillard, "what are you doing next Sunday afternoon?"

"Well, nothing in particular, that I know of just now," replied Clyde, sensing a new problem here. "I don't know just what I may have to do by then, but I don't know of anything now."

"Well, how'd you like to come with me, if you're not too busy. I've come to know quite a few girls since I've been here. Nice ones. I can take you out and introduce you to my uncle's family, if you like. They're nice people. And afterwards— I know two girls we can go and see—peaches. One of 'em did work in the store, but she don't now—she's not doing anything now. The other is her pal. They have a victrola and they can dance. I know it isn't the thing to dance here on Sundays but no one need know anything about that. The girls' parents don't mind. Afterwards we might take 'em to a movie or something—if you want to—not any of those things down near the mill district but one of the better ones—see?"

There formulated itself in Clyde's mind the question as to what, in regard to just such proposals as this, his course here was to be. In Chicago, and recently—because of what happened in Kansas City—he had sought to be as retiring and cautious as possible. For—after that and while connected with the club, he had been taken with the fancy of trying to live up to the ideals with which the seemingly stern face of that institution had inspired him—conservatism—hard work—saving one's money—looking neat and gentlemanly. It was such an Eveless paradise, that.

In spite of his quiet surroundings here, however, the very air of the city seemed to suggest some such relaxation as this youth was now suggesting—a form of diversion that was probably innocent enough but still connected with girls and their entertainment—there were so many of them here, as he could see. These streets, after dinner, here, were so alive with good-looking girls, and young men, too. But what might his new found relatives think of him in case he was seen stepping about in the manner and spirit which this youth's suggestions seemed to imply? Hadn't he just said that this was an awfully close town and that everybody knew nearly everything about everybody else? He paused in doubt. He must decide now. And then, being lonely and hungry for companionship, he replied: "Yes,—well—I think that's all right." But he added a little dubiously: "Of course my relatives here——"

"Oh, sure, that's all right," replied Dillard smartly. "You have to be careful, of course. Well, so do I." If he could only go around with a Griffiths, even if he was new around here and didn't know many people—wouldn't it reflect a lot of credit on him? It most certainly would—did already, as he saw it.

And forthwith he offered to buy Clyde some cigarettes—a soda—anything he liked. But Clyde, still feeling very strange and uncertain, excused himself, after a time, because this youth with his complacent worship of society and position, annoyed him a little, and made his way back to his room. He had promised his mother a letter and he thought he had better go back and write it, and incidentally to think a little on the wisdom of this new contact.

# Chapter VIII

NEVERTHELESS, the next day being a Saturday and a half holiday the year round in this concern, Mr. Whiggam came through with the pay envelopes.

"Here you are, Mr. Griffiths," he said, as though he were especially impressed with Clyde's position.

Clyde, taking it, was rather pleased with this mistering, and going back toward his locker, promptly tore it open and pocketed the money. After that, taking his hat and coat, he wandered off in the direction of his room, where he had his lunch. But, being very lonely, and Dillard not being present because he had to work, he decided upon a trolley ride to Gloversville, which was a city of some twenty thousand inhabitants and reported to be as active, if not as beautiful, as Lycurgus. And that trip amused and interested him because it took him into a city very different from Lycurgus in its social texture.

But the next day—Sunday—he spent idly in Lycurgus, wandering about by himself. For, as it turned out, Dillard was compelled to return to Fonda for some reason and could not fulfill the Sunday understanding. Encountering Clyde, however, on Monday evening, he announced that on the following Wednesday evening, in the basement of the Diggby Avenue Congregational Church, there was to be held a social with refreshments. And according to young Dillard, at least this promised to prove worth while.

"We can just go out there," was the way he put it to Clyde, "and buzz the girls a little. I want you to meet my uncle and aunt. They're nice people all right. And so are the girls. They're no slouches. Then we can edge out afterwards, about ten, see, and go around to either Zella or Rita's place. Rita has more good records over at her place, but Zella has the nicest place to dance. By the way, you didn't chance to bring along your dress suit with you, did you?" he inquired. For having already inspected Clyde's room, which was above his own on the third floor, in Clyde's absence and having discovered that he had only a dress suit case and no trunk, and apparently no dress suit anywhere, he had decided that in spite

229

of Clyde's father conducting a hotel and Clyde having worked in the Union League Club in Chicago, he must be very indifferent to social equipment. Or, if not, must be endeavoring to make his own way on some character-building plan without help from any one. This was not to his liking, exactly. A man should never neglect these social essentials. Nevertheless, Clyde was a Griffiths and that was enough to cause him to overlook nearly anything, for the present anyhow.

"No, I didn't," replied Clyde, who was not exactly sure as to the value of this adventure—even yet—in spite of his own loneliness,—"but I intend to get one." He had already thought since coming here of his lack in this respect, and was thinking of taking at least thirty-five of his more recently hard-earned savings and indulging in a suit of this kind.

Dillard buzzed on about the fact that while Zella Shuman's family wasn't rich—they owned the house they lived in—still she went with a lot of nice girls here, too. So did Rita Dickerman. Zella's father owned a little cottage upon Eckert Lake, near Fonda. When next summer came—and with it the holidays and pleasant week-ends, he and Clyde, supposing that Clyde liked Rita, might go up there some time for a visit, for Rita and Zella were inseparable almost. And they were pretty, too. "Zella's dark and Rita's light," he added enthusiastically.

Clyde was interested by the fact that the girls were pretty and that out of a clear sky and in the face of his present loneliness, he was being made so much of by this Dillard. But, was it wise for him to become very much involved with him? That was the question—for, after all, he really knew nothing of him. And he gathered from Dillard's manner, his flighty enthusiasm for the occasion, that he was far more interested in the girls as girls—a certain freedom or concealed looseness that characterized them—than he was in the social phase of the world which they represented. And wasn't that what brought about his downfall in Kansas City? Here in Lycurgus, of all places, he was least likely to forget it—aspiring to something better as he now did.

None-the-less, at eight-thirty on the following Wednesday evening—they were off, Clyde full of eager anticipation. And by nine o'clock they were in the midst of one of those semi-religious, semi-social and semi-emotional church affairs, the object of which was to raise money for the church—the general service of which was to furnish an occasion for gossip among the elders, criticism and a certain amount of enthusiastic, if disguised courtship and flirtation among the younger members. There were booths for the sale of quite everything from pies, cakes and ice cream to laces, dolls and knickknacks of every description, supplied by the members and parted with for the benefit of the church. The Reverend Peter Isreals, the minister, and his wife were present. Also Dillard's uncle and aunt, a pair of brisk and yet uninteresting people whom Clyde could sense were of no importance socially here. They were too genial and altogether social in the specific neighborhood sense, although Grover Wilson, being a buyer for Stark and Company, endeavored to assume a serious and important air at times.

He was an undersized and stocky man who did not seem to know how to dress very well or could not afford it. In contrast to his nephew's almost immaculate garb, his own suit was far from perfect-fitting. It was unpressed and slightly soiled. And his tie the same. He had a habit of rubbing his hands in a clerkly fashion, of wrinkling his brows and scratching the back of his head at times, as though something he was about to say had cost him great thought and was of the utmost importance. Whereas, nothing that he uttered, as even Clyde could see, was of the slightest importance.

And so, too, with the stout and large Mrs. Wilson, who stood beside him while he was attempting to rise to the importance of Clyde. She merely beamed a fatty beam. She was almost ponderous, and pink, with a tendency to a double chin. She smiled and smiled, largely because she was naturally genial and on her good behavior here, but incidentally because Clyde was who he was. For as Clyde himself could see, Walter Dillard had lost no time in impressing his relatives with the fact that he was a Griffiths. Also that he had encountered and made a friend of him and that he was now chaperoning him locally.

"Walter has been telling us that you have just come on here to work for your uncle. You're at Mrs. Cuppy's now, I understand. I don't know her but I've always heard she keeps such a nice, refined place. Mr. Parsley, who lives here with her, used to go to school with me. But I don't see much of him any more. Did you meet him yet?"

"No, I didn't," said Clyde in return.

"Well, you know, we expected you last Sunday to dinner, only Walter had to go home. But you must come soon. Any time at all. I would love to have you." She beamed and her small grayish brown eyes twinkled.

Clyde could see that because of the fame of his uncle he was looked upon as a social find, really. And so it was with the remainder of this company, old and young—the Rev. Peter Isreals and his wife; Mr. Micah Bumpus, a local vendor of printing inks, and his wife and son; Mr. and Mrs. Maximilian Pick, Mr. Pick being a wholesale and retail dealer in hay, grain and feed; Mr. Witness, a florist, and Mrs. Throop, a local real estate dealer. All knew Samuel Griffiths and his family by reputation and it seemed not a little interesting and strange to all of them that Clyde, a real nephew of so rich a man, should be here in their midst. The only trouble with this was that Clyde's manner was very soft and not as impressive as it should be—not so aggressive and contemptuous. And most of them were of that type of mind that respects insolence even where it pretends to condemn it.

In so far as the young girls were concerned, it was even more noticeable. For Dillard was making this important relationship of Clyde's perfectly plain to every one. "This is Clyde Griffiths, the nephew of Samuel Griffiths, Mr. Gilbert Griffiths' cousin, you know. He's just come on here to study the collar business in his uncle's factory." And Clyde, who realized how shallow was this pretense, was still not a little pleased and impressed by the effect of it all. This Dillard's effrontery. The brassy way in which, because of Clyde, he presumed to patronize these people. On this occasion, he kept guiding Clyde here and there, refusing for the most part to leave him alone for an instant. In fact he was determined that all whom he knew and liked among these girls and young men should know who and what Clyde was and that he was presenting him. Also that those whom he did not like should see as little of him as possible—not be introduced at all. "She don't amount to anything. Her father only keeps a small garage here. I wouldn't bother with her if I were you." Or,

"He isn't much around here. Just a clerk in our store." At the same time, in regard to some others, he was all smiles and compliments, or at worst apologetic for their social lacks.

And then he was introduced to Zella Shuman and Rita Dickerman, who, for reasons of their own, not the least among which was a desire to appear a little wise and more sophisticated than the others here, came a little late. And it was true, as Clyde was to find out soon afterwards, that they were different, too—less simple and restricted than quite all of the girls whom Dillard had thus far introduced him to. They were not as sound religiously and morally as were these others. And as even Clyde noted on meeting them, they were as keen for as close an approach to pagan pleasure without admitting it to themselves, as it was possible to be and not be marked for what they were. And in consequence, there was something in their manner, the very spirit of the introduction, which struck him as different from the tone of the rest of this church group – not exactly morally or religiously unhealthy but rather much freer, less repressed, less reserved than were these others.

"Oh, so you're Mr. Clyde Griffiths," observed Zella Shuman. "My, you look a lot like your cousin, don't you? I see him driving down Central Avenue ever so often. Walter has been telling us all about you. Do you like Lycurgus?"

The way she said "Walter," together with something intimate and possessive in the tone of her voice, caused Clyde to feel at once that she must feel rather closer to and freer with Dillard than he himself had indicated. A small scarlet bow of velvet ribbon at her throat, two small garnet earrings in her ears, a very trim and tight-fitting black dress, with a heavily flounced skirt, seemed to indicate that she was not opposed to showing her figure, and prized it, a mood which except for a demure and rather retiring poise which she affected, would most certainly have excited comment in such a place as this.

Rita Dickerman, on the other hand, was lush and blonde, with pink cheeks, light chestnut hair, and bluish gray eyes. Lacking the aggressive smartness that characterized Zella Shuman, she still radiated a certain something which to Clyde seemed to harmonize with the liberal if secret mood of her friend. Her manner, as Clyde could see, while much less suggestive of masked bravado was yielding and to him designedly so, as well as naturally provocative. It had been arranged that she was to intrigue him. Very much fascinated by Zella Shuman and in tow of her, they were inseparable. And when Clyde was introduced to her, she beamed upon him in a melting and sensuous way which troubled him not a little. For here in Lycurgus, as he was telling himself at the time, he must be very careful with whom he became familiar. And yet, unfortunately, as in the case of Hortense Briggs, she evoked thoughts of intimacy, however unproblematic or distant, which troubled him. But he must be careful. It was just such a free attitude as this suggested by Dillard as well as these girls' manners that had gotten him into trouble before.

"Now we'll just have a little ice cream and cake," suggested Dillard, after the few preliminary remarks were over, "and then we can get out of here. You two had better go around together and hand out a few hellos. Then we can meet at the ice cream booth. After that, if you say so, we'll leave, eh? What do you say?"

He looked at Zella Shuman as much as to say: "You know what is the best thing to do," and she smiled and replied: "That's right. We can't leave right away. I see my cousin Mary over there. And Mother. And Fred Bruckner. Rita and I'll just go around by ourselves for a while and then we'll meet you, see." And Rita Dickerman forthwith bestowed upon Clyde an intimate and possessive smile.

After about twenty minutes of drifting and browsing, Dillard received some signal from Zella, and he and Clyde paused near the ice cream booth with its chairs in the center of the room. In a few moments they were casually joined by Zella and Rita, with whom they had some ice cream and cake. And then, being free of all obligations and as some of the others were beginning to depart, Dillard observed: "Let's beat it. We can go over to your place, can't we?"

"Sure, sure," whispered Zella, and together they made their way to the coat room. Clyde was still so dubious as to the wisdom of all this that he was inclined to be a little silent. He did not know whether he was fascinated by Rita or not. But once out in the street out of view of the church and the homing amusement seekers, he and Rita found themselves together, Zella and Dillard having walked on ahead. And al-

though Clyde had taken her arm, as he thought fit, she maneuvered it free and laid a warm and caressing hand on his
elbow. And she nudged quite close to him, shoulder to
shoulder, and half leaning on him, began pattering of the life
of Lycurgus.

There was something very furry and caressing about her
voice now. Clyde liked it. There was something heavy and
languorous about her body, a kind of ray or electron that intrigued and lured him in spite of himself. He felt that he
would like to caress her arm and might if he wished—that he
might even put his arm around her waist, and so soon. Yet
here he was, a Griffiths, he was shrewd enough to think—a
Lycurgus Griffiths—and that was what now made a difference—that made all those girls at this church social seem so
much more interested in him and so friendly. Yet in spite of
this thought, he did squeeze her arm ever so slightly and
without reproach or comment from her.

And once in the Shuman home, which was a large old-fashioned square frame house with a square cupola, very retired
among some trees and a lawn, they made themselves at home
in a general living room which was much more handsomely
furnished than any home with which Clyde had been identified heretofore. Dillard at once began sorting the records,
with which he seemed most familiar, and to pull two rather
large rugs out of the way, revealing a smooth, hardwood
floor.

"There's one thing about this house and these trees and
these soft-toned needles," he commented for Clyde's benefit,
of course, since he was still under the impression that Clyde
might be and probably was a very shrewd person who was
watching his every move here. "You can't hear a note of this
victrola out in the street, can you, Zell? Nor upstairs, either,
really, not with the soft needles. We've played it down here
and danced to it several times, until three and four in the
morning and they didn't even know it upstairs, did they,
Zell?"

"That's right. But then Father's a little hard of hearing.
And Mother don't hear anything, either, when she gets in her
room and gets to reading. But it is hard to hear at that."

"Why, do people object so to dancing here?" asked Clyde.

"Oh, they don't—not the factory people—not at all," put in Dillard, "but most of the church people do. My uncle and aunt do. And nearly everyone else we met at the church to-night, except Zell and Rita." He gave them a most approving and encouraging glance. "And they're too broadminded to let a little thing like that bother them. Ain't that right, Zell?"

This young girl, who was very much fascinated by him, laughed and nodded, "You bet, that's right. I can't see any harm in it."

"Nor me, either," put in Rita, "nor my father and mother. Only they don't like to say anything about it or make me feel that they want me to do too much of it."

Dillard by then had started a piece entitled "Brown Eyes" and immediately Clyde and Rita and Dillard and Zella began to dance, and Clyde found himself insensibly drifting into a kind of intimacy with this girl which boded he could scarcely say what. She danced so warmly and enthusiastically—a kind of weaving and swaying motion which suggested all sorts of repressed enthusiasms. And her lips were at once wreathed with a kind of lyric smile which suggested a kind of hunger for this thing. And she was very pretty, more so dancing and smiling than at any other time.

"She is delicious," thought Clyde, "even if she is a little soft. Any fellow would do almost as well as me, but she likes me because she thinks I'm somebody." And almost at the same moment she observed: "Isn't it just too gorgeous? And you're such a good dancer, Mr. Griffiths."

"Oh, no," he replied, smiling into her eyes, "you're the one that's the dancer. I can dance because you're dancing with me."

He could feel now that her arms were large and soft, her bosom full for one so young. Exhilarated by dancing, she was quite intoxicating, her gestures almost provoking.

"Now we'll put on 'The Love Boat,'" called Dillard the moment "Brown Eyes" was ended, "and you and Zella can dance together and Rita and I will have a spin, eh, Rita?"

He was so fascinated by his own skill as a dancer, however, as well as his natural joy in the art, that he could scarcely wait to begin another, but must take Rita by the arms before putting on another record, gliding here and there, doing steps and executing figures which Clyde could not possibly achieve and which at once established Dillard as the superior dancer. Then, having done so, he called to Clyde to put on "The Love Boat."

But as Clyde could see, after dancing with Zella once, this was planned to be a happy companionship of two mutually mated couples who would not interfere with each other in any way, but rather would aid each other in their various schemes to enjoy one another's society. For while Zella danced with Clyde, and danced well and talked to him much, all the while he could feel that she was interested in Dillard and Dillard only and would prefer to be with him. For, after a few dances, and while he and Rita lounged on a settee and talked, Zella and Dillard left the room to go to the kitchen for a drink. Only, as Clyde observed, they stayed much longer than any single drink would have required.

And similarly, during this interval, it seemed as though it was intended even, by Rita, that he and she should draw closer to one another. For, finding the conversation on the settee lagging for a moment, she got up and apropos of nothing—no music and no words—motioned to him to dance some more with her. She had danced certain steps with Dillard which she pretended to show Clyde. But because of their nature, these brought her and Clyde into closer contact than before—very much so. And standing so close together and showing Clyde by elbow and arm how to do, her face and cheek came very close to him—too much for his own strength of will and purpose. He pressed his cheek to hers and she turned smiling and encouraging eyes upon him. On the instant, his self-possession was gone and he kissed her lips. And then again—and again. And instead of withdrawing them, as he thought she might, she let him—remained just as she was in order that he might kiss her more.

And suddenly now, as he felt this yielding of her warm body so close to him, and the pressure of her lips in response to his own, he realized that he had let himself in for a relationship which might not be so very easy to modify or escape. Also that it would be a very difficult thing for him to resist, since he now liked her and obviously she liked him.

# Chapter IX

APART FROM the momentary thrill and zest of this, the effect was to throw Clyde, as before, speculatively back
upon the problem of his proper course here. For here was this
girl, and she was approaching him in this direct and suggestive way. And so soon after telling himself and his mother that
his course was to be so different here—no such approaches or
relationships as had brought on his downfall in Kansas City.
And yet—and yet——

He was sorely tempted now, for in his contact with Rita he
had the feeling that she was expecting him to suggest a further step—and soon. But just how and where? Not in connection with this large, strange house. There were other
rooms apart from the kitchen to which Dillard and Zella had
ostensibly departed. But even so, such a relationship once established! What then? Would he not be expected to continue
it, or let himself in for possible complications in case he did
not? He danced with and fondled her in a daring and aggressive fashion, yet thinking as he did so, "But this is not what I
should be doing either, is it? This is Lycurgus. I am a Griffiths, here. I know how these people feel toward me—their
parents even. Do I really care for her? Is there not something
about her quick and easy availability which, if not exactly dangerous in so far as my future here is concerned, is not quite
satisfactory,—too quickly intimate?" He was experiencing a
sensation not unrelated to his mood in connection with the
lupanar in Kansas City—attracted and yet repulsed. He could
do no more than kiss and fondle her here in a somewhat restrained way until at last Dillard and Zella returned, whereupon the same degree of intimacy was no longer possible.

A clock somewhere striking two, it suddenly occurred to
Rita that she must be going—her parents would object to her
staying out so late. And since Dillard gave no evidence of deserting Zella, it followed, of course, that Clyde was to see her
home, a pleasure that now had been allayed by a vague suggestion of disappointment or failure on the part of both. He
had not risen to her expectations, he thought. Obviously he

lacked the courage yet to follow up the proffer of her favors, was the way she explained it to herself.

At her own door, not so far distant, and after a conversation which was still tinctured with intimations of some future occasions which might prove more favorable,—her attitude was decidedly encouraging, even here. They parted, but with Clyde still saying to himself that this new relationship was developing much too swiftly. He was not sure that he should undertake a relationship such as this here—so soon, anyhow. Where now were all his fine decisions made before coming here? What was he going to decide? And yet because of the sensual warmth and magnetism of Rita, he was irritated by his resolution and his inability to proceed as he otherwise might.

Two things which eventually decided him in regard to this came quite close together. One related to the attitude of the Griffiths themselves, which, apart from that of Gilbert, was not one of opposition or complete indifference, so much as it was a failure on the part of Samuel Griffiths in the first instance and the others largely because of him to grasp the rather anomalous, if not exactly lonely position in which Clyde would find himself here unless the family chose to show him at least some little courtesy or advise him cordially from time to time. Yet Samuel Griffiths, being always very much pressed for time, had scarcely given Clyde a thought during the first month, at least. He was here, properly placed, as he heard, would be properly looked after in the future,—what more, just now, at least?

And so for all of five weeks before any action of any kind was taken, and with Gilbert Griffiths comforted thereby, Clyde was allowed to drift along in his basement world wondering what was being intended in connection with himself. The attitude of others, including Dillard and these girls, finally made his position here seem strange.

However, about a month after Clyde had arrived, and principally because Gilbert seemed so content to say nothing regarding him, the elder Griffiths inquired one day:

"Well, what about your cousin? How's he doing by now?" And Gilbert, only a little worried as to what this might bode, replied, "Oh, he's all right. I started him off in the shrinking room. Is that all right?"

"Yes, I think so. That's as good a place as any for him to begin, I believe. But what do you think of him by now?"

"Oh," answered Gilbert very conservatively and decidedly independently—a trait for which his father had always admired him—"Not so much. He's all right, I guess. He may work out. But he doesn't strike me as a fellow who would ever make much of a stir in this game. He hasn't had much of an education of any kind, you know. Any one can see that. Besides, he's not so very aggressive or energetic-looking. Too soft, I think. Still I don't want to knock him. He may be all right. You like him and I may be wrong. But I can't help but think that his real idea in coming here is that you'll do more for him than you would for someone else, just because he is related to you."

"Oh, you think he does. Well, if he does, he's wrong." But at the same time, he added, and that with a bantering smile: "He may not be as impractical as you think, though. He hasn't been here long enough for us to really tell, has he? He didn't strike me that way in Chicago. Besides there are a lot of little corners into which he might fit, aren't there, without any great waste, even if he isn't the most talented fellow in the world? If he's content to take a small job in life, that's his business. I can't prevent that. But at any rate, I don't want him sent away yet, anyhow, and I don't want him put on piece work. It wouldn't look right. After all, he is related to us. Just let him drift along for a little while and see what he does for himself."

"All right, governor," replied his son, who was hoping that his father would absent-mindedly let him stay where he was—in the lowest of all the positions the factory had to offer.

But, now, and to his dissatisfaction, Samuel Griffiths proceeded to add, "We'll have to have him out to the house for dinner pretty soon, won't we? I have thought of that but I haven't been able to attend to it before. I should have spoken to Mother about it before this. He hasn't been out yet, has he?"

"No, sir, not that I know of," replied Gilbert dourly. He did not like this at all, but was too tactful to show his opposition just here. "We've been waiting for you to say something about it, I suppose."

"Very well," went on Samuel, "you'd better find out where he's stopping and have him out. Next Sunday wouldn't be a bad time, if we haven't anything else on." Noting a flicker of doubt or disapproval in his son's eyes, he added: "After all, Gil, he's my nephew and your cousin, and we can't afford to ignore him entirely. That wouldn't be right, you know, either. You'd better speak to your mother to-night, or I will, and arrange it." He closed the drawer of a desk in which he had been looking for certain papers, got up and took down his hat and coat and left the office.

In consequence of this discussion, an invitation was sent to Clyde for the following Sunday at six-thirty to appear and participate in a Griffiths family meal. On Sunday at one-thirty was served the important family dinner to which usually was invited one or another of the various local or visiting friends of the family. At six-thirty nearly all of these guests had departed, and sometimes one or two of the Griffiths themselves, the cold collation served being partaken of by Mr. and Mrs. Griffiths and Myra—Bella and Gilbert usually having appointments elsewhere.

On this occasion, however, as Mrs. Griffiths and Myra and Bella decided in conference, they would all be present with the exception of Gilbert, who, because of his opposition as well as another appointment, explained that he would stop in for only a moment before leaving. Thus Clyde as Gilbert was pleased to note would be received and entertained without the likelihood of contacts, introductions and explanations to such of their more important connections who might chance to stop in during the afternoon. They would also have an opportunity to study him for themselves and see what they really did think without committing themselves in any way.

But in the meantime in connection with Dillard, Rita and Zella there had been a development which, because of the problem it had posed, was to be affected by this very decision on the part of the Griffiths. For following the evening at the Shuman home, and because, in spite of Clyde's hesitation at the time, all three including Rita herself, were still convinced that he must or would be smitten with her charms, there had been various hints, as well as finally a direct invitation or proposition on the part of Dillard to the effect that because of the camaraderie which had been established between himself and Clyde and these two girls, they make a week-end trip somewhere—preferably to Utica or Albany. The girls would

go, of course. He could fix that through Zella with Rita for
Clyde if he had any doubts or fears as to whether it could be
negotiated or not. "You know she likes you. Zell was telling
me the other day that she said she thought you were the
candy. Some ladies' man, eh?" And he nudged Clyde genially
and intimately,—a proceeding in this newer and grander
world in which he now found himself,—and considering who
he was here, was not as appealing to Clyde as it otherwise
might have been. These fellows who were so pushing where
they thought a fellow amounted to something more than they
did! He could tell.

At the same time, the proposition he was now offering—as
thrilling and intriguing as it might be from one point of
view—was likely to cause him endless trouble—was it not? In
the first place he had no money—only fifteen dollars a week
here so far—and if he was going to be expected to indulge in
such expensive outings as these, why, of course, he could not
manage. Carfare, meals, a hotel bill, maybe an automobile
ride for two. And after that he would be in close contact with
this Rita whom he scarcely knew. And might she not take it
on herself to become intimate here in Lycurgus, maybe—expect him to call on her regularly—and go places—and then—
well, gee—supposing the Griffiths—his cousin Gilbert, heard
of or saw this. Hadn't Zella said that she saw him often on
the street here and there in Lycurgus? And wouldn't they be
likely to encounter him somewhere—sometime—when they
were all together? And wouldn't that fix him as being intimate
with just another store clerk like Dillard who didn't amount
to so much after all? It might even mean the end of his career
here! Who could tell what it might lead to?

He coughed and made various excuses. Just now he had a
lot of work to do. Besides—a venture like that—he would
have to see first. His relatives, you know. Besides next Sunday
and the Sunday after, some extra work in connection with the
factory was going to hold him in Lycurgus. After that time he
would see. Actually, in his wavering way—and various disturbing thoughts as to Rita's charm returning to him at moments, he was wondering if it was not desirable—his other
decision to the contrary notwithstanding, to skimp himself as
much as possible over two or three weeks and so go anyhow.

He had been saving something toward a new dress suit and collapsible silk hat. Might he not use some of that—even though he knew the plan to be all wrong?

The fair, plump, sensuous Rita!

But then, not at that very moment—but in the interim following, the invitation from the Griffiths. Returning from his work one evening very tired and still cogitating this gay adventure proposed by Dillard, he found lying on the table in his room a note written on very heavy and handsome paper which had been delivered by one of the servants of the Griffiths in his absence. It was all the more arresting to him because on the flap of the envelope was embossed in high relief the initials "E.G." He at once tore it open and eagerly read:

"MY DEAR NEPHEW:

"Since your arrival my husband has been away most of the time, and although we have wished to have you with us before, we have thought it best to await his leisure. He is freer now and we will be very glad if you can find it convenient to come to supper with us at six o'clock next Sunday. We dine very informally—just ourselves—so in case you can or cannot come, you need not bother to write or telephone. And you need not dress for this occasion either. But come if you can. We will be happy to see you.

"Sincerely, your aunt,
"ELIZABETH GRIFFITHS."

On reading this Clyde, who, during all this silence and the prosecution of a task in the shrinking room which was so eminently distasteful to him, was being more and more weighed upon by the thought that possibly, after all, this quest of his was going to prove a vain one and that he was going to be excluded from any real contact with his great relatives, was most romantically and hence impractically heartened. For only see—here was this grandiose letter with its "very happy to see you," which seemed to indicate that perhaps, after all, they did not think so badly of him. Mr. Samuel Griffiths had been away all the time. That was it. Now he would get to see his aunt and cousins and the inside of that great house. It must be very wonderful. They might even take him up after this— who could tell? But how remarkable that he should be taken up now, just when he had about decided that they would not.

And forthwith his interest in, as well as his weakness for, Rita, if not Zella and Dillard began to evaporate. What! Mix with people so far below him—a Griffiths—in the social scale here and at the cost of endangering his connection with that important family. Never! It was a great mistake. Didn't this letter coming just at this time prove it? And fortunately—(how fortunately!)—he had had the good sense not to let himself in for anything as yet. And so now, without much trouble, and because, most likely from now on it would prove necessary for him so to do he could gradually eliminate himself from this contact with Dillard—move away from Mrs. Cuppy's—if necessary, or say that his uncle had cautioned him—anything, but not go with this crowd any more, just the same. It wouldn't do. It would endanger his prospects in connection with this new development. And instead of troubling over Rita and Utica now, he began to formulate for himself once more the essential nature of the private life of the Griffiths, the fascinating places they must go, the interesting people with whom they must be in contact. And at once he began to think of the need of a dress suit, or at least a tuxedo and trousers. Accordingly the next morning, he gained permission from Mr. Kemerer to leave at eleven and not return before one, and in that time he managed to find coat, trousers and a pair of patent leather shoes, as well as a white silk muffler for the money he had already saved. And so arrayed he felt himself safe. He must make a good impression.

And for the entire time between then and Sunday evening, instead of thinking of Rita or Dillard or Zella any more, he was thinking of this opportunity. Plainly it was an event to be admitted to the presence of such magnificence.

The only drawback to all this, as he well sensed now, was this same Gilbert Griffiths, who surveyed him always whenever he met him anywhere with such hard, cold eyes. He might be there, and then he would probably assume that superior attitude, to make him feel his inferior position, if he could—and Clyde had the weakness at times of admitting to himself that he could. And no doubt, if he (Clyde) sought to carry himself with too much of an air in the presence of this family, Gilbert most likely would seek to take it out of him in some way later in connection with the work in the factory. He might see to it, for instance, that his father heard only unfavorable things about him. And, of course, if he were retained in this wretched shrinking room, and given no show of any kind, how could he expect to get anywhere or be anybody? It was just his luck that on arriving here he should find this same Gilbert looking almost like him and being so opposed to him for obviously no reason at all.

However, despite all his doubts, he decided to make the best of this opportunity, and accordingly on Sunday evening at six set out for the Griffiths' residence, his nerves decidedly taut because of the ordeal before him. And when he reached the main gate, a large, arched wrought iron affair which gave in on a wide, winding, brick walk which led to the front entrance, he lifted the heavy latch which held the large iron gates in place, with almost a quaking sense of adventure. And as he approached along the walk, he felt as though he might well be the object of observant and critical eyes. Perhaps Mr. Samuel or Mr. Gilbert Griffiths or one or the other of the two sisters was looking at him now from one of those heavily curtained windows. On the lower floor several lights glowed with a soft and inviting radiance.

This mood, however, was brief. For soon the door was opened by a servant who took his coat and invited him into the very large living room, which was very impressive. To Clyde, even after the Green-Davidson and the Union League, it seemed a very beautiful room. It contained so many handsome pieces of furniture and such rich rugs and hangings. A fire burned in the large, high fireplace before which was circled a number of divans and chairs. There were lamps, a tall clock, a great table. No one was in the room at the moment, but presently as Clyde fidgeted and looked about he heard a rustling of silk to the rear, where a great staircase descended from the rooms above. And from there he saw Mrs. Griffiths approaching him, a bland and angular and faded-looking woman. But her walk was brisk, her manner courteous, if non-committal, as was her custom always, and after a few moments of conversation he found himself peaceful and fairly comfortable in her presence.

"My nephew, I believe," she smiled.

"Yes," replied Clyde simply, and because of his nervousness, with unusual dignity. "I am Clyde Griffiths."

"I'm very glad to see you and to welcome you to our home," began Mrs. Griffiths with a certain amount of aplomb which years of contact with the local high world had given her at last. "And my children will be, too, of course. Bella is not here just now or Gilbert, either, but then they will be soon, I believe. My husband is resting, but I heard him stirring just now, and he'll be down in a moment. Won't you sit here?" She motioned to a large divan between them. "We dine nearly always alone here together on Sunday evening, so I thought it would be nice if you came just to be alone with us. How do you like Lycurgus now?"

She arranged herself on one of the large divans before the fire and Clyde rather awkwardly seated himself at a respectful distance from her.

"Oh, I like it very much," he observed, exerting himself to be congenial and to smile. "Of course I haven't seen so very much of it yet, but what I have I like. This street is one of the nicest I have ever seen anywhere," he added enthusiastically. "The houses are so large and the grounds so beautiful."

"Yes, we here in Lycurgus pride ourselves on Wykeagy Avenue," smiled Mrs. Griffiths, who took no end of satisfaction in the grace and rank of her own home in this street. She and her husband had been so long climbing up to it. "Every one who sees it seems to feel the same way about it. It was laid out many years ago when Lycurgus was just a village. It is only within the last fifteen years that it has come to be as handsome as it is now.

"But you must tell me something about your mother and father. I never met either of them, you know, though, of course, I have heard my husband speak of them often—that is, of his brother, anyhow," she corrected. "I don't believe he ever met your mother. How is your father?"

"Oh, he's quite well," replied Clyde, simply. "And Mother, too. They're living in Denver now. We did live for a while in Kansas City, but for the last three years they've been out there. I had a letter from Mother only the other day. She says everything is all right."

"Then you keep up a correspondence with her, do you?

That's nice." She smiled, for by now she had become interested by and, on the whole, rather taken with Clyde's appearance. He looked so neat and generally presentable, so much like her own son that she was a little startled at first and intrigued on that score. If anything, Clyde was taller, better built and hence better looking, only she would never have been willing to admit that. For to her Gilbert, although he was intolerant and contemptuous even to her at times, simulating an affection which was as much a custom as a reality, was still a dynamic and aggressive person putting himself and his conclusions before everyone else. Whereas Clyde was more soft and vague and fumbling. Her son's force must be due to the innate ability of her husband as well as the strain of some relatives in her own line who had not been unlike Gilbert, while Clyde probably drew his lesser force from the personal unimportance of his parents.

But having settled this problem in her son's favor, Mrs. Griffiths was about to ask after his sisters and brothers, when they were interrupted by Samuel Griffiths who now approached. Measuring Clyde, who had risen, very sharply once more, and finding him very satisfactory in appearance at least, he observed: "Well, so here you are, eh? They've placed you, I believe, without my ever seeing you."

"Yes, sir," replied Clyde, very deferentially and half bowing in the presence of so great a man.

"Well, that's all right. Sit down! Sit down! I'm very glad they did. I hear you're working down in the shrinking room at present. Not exactly a pleasant place, but not such a bad place to begin, either—at the bottom. The best people start there sometimes." He smiled and added: "I was out of the city when you came on or I would have seen you."

"Yes, sir," replied Clyde, who had not ventured to seat himself again until Mr. Griffiths had sunk into a very large stuffed chair near the divan. And the latter, now that he saw Clyde in an ordinary Tuxedo with a smart pleated shirt and black tie, as opposed to the club uniform in which he had last seen him in Chicago, was inclined to think him even more attractive than before—not quite as negligible and unimportant as his son Gilbert had made out. Still, not being dead to the need of force and energy in business and sensing that Clyde was undoubtedly lacking in these qualities, he did now wish that Clyde had more vigor and vim in him. It would reflect more handsomely on the Griffiths end of the family and please his son more, maybe.

"Like it where you are now?" he observed condescendingly.

"Well, yes, sir, that is, I wouldn't say that I like it exactly," replied Clyde quite honestly. "But I don't mind it. It's as good as any other way to begin, I suppose." The thought in his mind at the moment was that he would like to impress on his uncle that he was cut out for something better. And the fact that his cousin Gilbert was not present at the moment gave him the courage to say it.

"Well, that's the proper spirit," commented Samuel Griffiths, pleased. "It isn't the most pleasant part of the process, I will admit, but it's one of the most essential things to know, to begin with. And it takes a little time, of course, to get anywhere in any business these days."

From this Clyde wondered how long he was to be left in that dim world below stairs.

But while he was thinking this Myra came forward, curious about him and what he would be like, and very pleased to see that he was not as uninteresting as Gilbert had painted him. There was something, as she now saw, about Clyde's eyes—nervous and somewhat furtive and appealing or seeking—that at once interested her, and reminded her, perhaps, since she was not much of a success socially either, of something in herself.

"Your cousin, Clyde Griffiths, Myra," observed Samuel rather casually, as Clyde arose. "My daughter Myra," he added, to Clyde. "This is the young man I've been telling you about."

Clyde bowed and then took the cool and not very vital hand that Myra extended to him, but feeling it just the same to be more friendly and considerate than the welcome of the others.

"Well, I hope you'll like it, now that you're here," she began, genially. "We all like Lycurgus, only after Chicago I suppose it will not mean so very much to you." She smiled and Clyde, feeling very formal and stiff in the presence of all these very superior relatives, now returned a stiff "thank you," and was just about to seat himself when the outer door opened and Gilbert Griffiths strode in. The whirring of a motor had preceded this—a motor that had stopped outside the large east side entrance. "Just a minute, Dolge," he called to some one outside. "I won't be long." Then turning to the family, he added: "Excuse me, folks, I'll be back in a minute." He dashed up the rear stairs, only to return after a time and confront Clyde, if not the others, with that same rather icy and inconsiderate air that had so far troubled him at the factory. He was wearing a light, belted motoring coat of a very pronounced stripe, and a dark leather cap and gauntlets which gave him almost a military air. After nodding to Clyde rather stiffly, and adding, "How do you do," he laid a patronizing hand on his father's shoulder and observed: "Hi, Dad. Hello, Mother. Sorry I can't be with you to-night. But I just came over from Amsterdam with Dolge and Eustis to get Constance and Jacqueline. There's some doings over at the Bridgemans'. But I'll be back again before morning. Or at the office, anyhow. Everything all right with you, Mr. Griffiths?" he observed to his father.

"Yes, I have nothing to complain of," returned his father. "But it seems to me you're making a pretty long night of it, aren't you?"

"Oh, I don't mean that," returned his son, ignoring Clyde entirely. "I just mean that if I can't get back by two, I'll stay over, that's all, see." He tapped his father genially on the shoulder again.

"I hope you're not driving that car as fast as usual," complained his mother. "It's not safe at all."

"Fifteen miles an hour, Mother. Fifteen miles an hour. I know the rules." He smiled loftily.

Clyde did not fail to notice the tone of condescension and authority that went with all this. Plainly here, as at the factory, he was a person who had to be reckoned with. Apart from his father, perhaps, there was no one here to whom he offered any reverence. What a superior attitude, thought Clyde!

How wonderful it must be to be a son who, without having had to earn all this, could still be so much, take oneself so seriously, exercise so much command and authority. It might be, as it plainly was, that this youth was very superior and indifferent in tone toward him. But think of being such a youth, having so much power at one's command!

# Chapter X

A T THIS POINT a maid announced that supper was served and instantly Gilbert took his departure. At the same time the family arose and Mrs. Griffiths asked the maid: "Has Bella telephoned yet?"

"No, ma'am," replied the servant, "not yet."

"Well, have Mrs. Truesdale call up the Finchleys and see if she's there. You tell her I said that she is to come home at once."

The maid departed for a moment while the group proceeded to the dining room, which lay to the west of the stairs at the rear. Again, as Clyde saw, this was another splendidly furnished room done in a very light brown, with a long center table of carved walnut, evidently used only for special occasions. It was surrounded by high-backed chairs and lighted by candelabras set at even spaces upon it. In a lower ceilinged and yet ample circular alcove beyond this, looking out on the garden to the south, was a smaller table set for six. It was in this alcove that they were to dine, a different thing from what Clyde had expected for some reason.

Seated in a very placid fashion, he found himself answering questions principally as to his own family, the nature of its life, past and present; how old was his father now? His mother? What had been the places of their residence before moving to Denver? How many brothers and sisters had he? How old was his older sister, Esta? What did she do? And the others? Did his father like managing a hotel? What had been the nature of his father's work in Kansas City? How long had the family lived there?

Clyde was not a little troubled and embarrassed by this chain of questions which flowed rather heavily and solemnly from Samuel Griffiths or his wife. And from Clyde's hesitating replies, especially in regard to the nature of the family life in Kansas City, both gathered that he was embarrassed and troubled by some of the questions. They laid it to the extreme poverty of their relatives, of course. For having asked, "I suppose you began your hotel work in Kansas City, didn't you, after you left school?" Clyde blushed deeply, bethinking himself of the incident of the stolen car and of how little real schooling he had had. Most certainly he did not like the thought of having himself identified with hotel life in Kansas City, and more especially the Green-Davidson.

But fortunately at this moment, the door opened and Bella entered, accompanied by two girls such as Clyde would have assumed at once belonged to this world. How different to Rita and Zella with whom his thought so recently had been disturbedly concerned. He did not know Bella, of course, until she proceeded most familiarly to address her family. But the others—one was Sondra Finchley, so frequently referred to by Bella and her mother—as smart and vain and sweet a girl as Clyde had ever laid his eyes upon—so different to any he had ever known and so superior. She was dressed in a close-fitting tailored suit which followed her form exactly and which was enhanced by a small dark leather hat, pulled fetchingly low over her eyes. A leather belt of the same color encircled her neck. By a leather leash she led a French bull and over one arm carried a most striking coat of black and gray checks—not too pronounced and yet having the effect of a man's modish overcoat. To Clyde's eyes she was the most adorable feminine thing he had seen in all his days. Indeed her effect on him was electric—thrilling—arousing in him a curiously stinging sense of what it was to want and not to have—to wish to win and yet to feel, almost agonizingly, that he was destined not even to win a glance from her. It tortured and flustered him. At one moment he had a keen desire to close his eyes and shut her out—at another to look only at her constantly—so truly was he captivated.

Yet, whether she saw him or not, she gave no sign at first, exclaiming to her dog: "Now, Bissell, if you're not going to behave, I'm going to take you out and tie you out there. Oh, I don't believe I can stay a moment if he won't behave better than this." He had seen a family cat and was tugging to get near her.

Beside her was another girl whom Clyde did not fancy nearly so much, and yet who, after her fashion, was as smart as Sondra and perhaps as alluring to some. She was blonde—tow-headed—with clear almond-shaped, greenish-gray eyes, a small, graceful, catlike figure, and a slinky feline manner. At once, on entering, she sidled across the room to the end of the table where Mrs. Griffiths sat and leaning over her at once began to purr.

"Oh, how are you, Mrs. Griffiths? I'm so glad to see you again. It's been some time since I've been over here, hasn't it? But then Mother and I have been away. She and Grant are over at Albany to-day. And I just picked up Bella and Sondra here at the Lamberts'. You're just having a quiet little supper by yourselves, aren't you? How are you, Myra?" she called, and reaching over Mrs. Griffiths' shoulder touched Myra quite casually on the arm, as though it were more a matter of form than anything else.

In the meantime Bella, who next to Sondra seemed to Clyde decidedly the most charming of the three, was exclaiming: "Oh, I'm late. Sorry, Mamma and Daddy. Won't that do this time?" Then noting Clyde, and as though for the first time, although he had risen as they entered and was still standing, she paused in semi-mock modesty as did the others. And Clyde, over-sensitive to just such airs and material distinctions, was fairly tremulous with a sense of his own inadequacy, as he waited to be introduced. For to him, youth and beauty in such a station as this represented the ultimate triumph of the female. His weakness for Hortense Briggs, to say nothing of Rita, who was not so attractive as either of these, illustrated the effect of trim femininity on him, regardless of merit.

"Bella," observed Samuel Griffiths, heavily, noting Clyde still standing, "your cousin, Clyde."

"Oh, yes," replied Bella, observing that Clyde looked exceedingly like Gilbert. "How are you? Mother has been saying that you were coming to call one of these days." She extended a finger or two, then turned toward her friends. "My friends, Miss Finchley and Miss Cranston, Mr. Griffiths."

The two girls bowed, each in the most stiff and formal manner, at the same time studying Clyde most carefully and rather directly, "Well, he does look like Gil a lot, doesn't he?" whispered Sondra to Bertine, who had drawn near to her. And Bertine replied: "I never saw anything like it. He's really better-looking, isn't he—a lot?"

Sondra nodded, pleased to note in the first instance that he was somewhat better-looking than Bella's brother, whom she did not like—next that he was obviously stricken with her, which was her due, as she invariably decided in connection with youths thus smitten with her. But having thus decided, and seeing that his glance was persistently and helplessly drawn to her, she concluded that she need pay no more attention to him, for the present anyway. He was too easy.

But now Mrs. Griffiths, who had not anticipated this visitation and was a little irritated with Bella for introducing her friends at this time since it at once raised the question of Clyde's social position here, observed: "Hadn't you two better lay off your coats and sit down? I'll just have Nadine lay extra plates at this end. Bella, you can sit next to your father."

"Oh, no, not at all," and "No, indeed, we're just on our way home ourselves. I can't stay a minute," came from Sondra and Bertine. But now that they were here and Clyde had proved to be as attractive as he was, they were perversely interested to see what, if any, social flare there was to him. Gilbert Griffiths, as both knew, was far from being popular in some quarters—their own in particular, however much they might like Bella. He was, for two such self-centered beauties as these, too aggressive, self-willed and contemptuous at times. Whereas Clyde, if one were to judge by his looks, at least was much more malleable. And if it were to prove now that he was of equal station, or that the Griffiths thought so, decidedly he would be available locally, would he not? At any rate, it would be interesting to know whether he was rich. But this thought was almost instantly satisfied by Mrs. Griffiths, who observed rather definitely and intentionally to Bertine: "Mr. Griffiths is a nephew of ours from the West who has come on to see if he can make a place for himself in my husband's factory. He's a young man who has to make his own way in the world and my husband has been kind enough to give him an opportunity."

Clyde flushed, since obviously this was a notice to him that his social position here was decidedly below that of the Griffiths or these girls. At the same time, as he also noticed, the look of Bertine Cranston, who was only interested in youths of means and position, changed from one of curiosity to marked indifference. On the other hand, Sondra Finchley, by no means so practical as her friend, though of a superior station in her set, since she was so very attractive and her parents possessed of even more means—re-surveyed Clyde with one thought written rather plainly on her face, that it was too bad. He really was so attractive.

At the same time Samuel Griffiths, having a peculiar fondness for Sondra, if not Bertine, whom Mrs. Griffiths also disliked as being too tricky and sly, was calling to her: "Here, Sondra, tie up your dog to one of the dining-room chairs and come and sit by me. Throw your coat over that chair. Here's room for you." He motioned to her to come.

"But I can't, Uncle Samuel!" called Sondra, familiarly and showily and yet somehow sweetly, seeking to ingratiate herself by this affected relationship. "We're late now. Besides Bissell won't behave. Bertine and I are just on our way home, truly."

"Oh, yes, Papa," put in Bella, quickly, "Bertine's horse ran a nail in his foot yesterday and is going lame to-day. And neither Grant nor his father is home. She wants to know if you know anything that's good for it."

"Which foot is it?" inquired Griffiths, interested, while Clyde continued to survey Sondra as best he might. She was so delicious, he thought—her nose so tiny and tilted—her upper lip arched so roguishly upward toward her nose.

"It's the left fore. I was riding out on the East Kingston road yesterday afternoon. Jerry threw a shoe and must have picked up a splinter, but John doesn't seem to be able to find it."

"Did you ride him much with the nail, do you think?"

"About eight miles—all the way back."

"Well, you had better have John put on some liniment and a bandage and call a veterinary. He'll come around all right, I'm sure."

The group showed no signs of leaving and Clyde, left quite to himself for the moment, was thinking what an easy, delightful world this must be—this local society. For here they were without a care, apparently, between any of them. All their talk was of houses being built, horses they were riding, friends they had met, places they were going to, things they were going to do. And there was Gilbert, who had left only a little while before—motoring somewhere with a group of young men. And Bella, his cousin, trifling around with these girls in the beautiful homes of this street, while he was shunted away in a small third-floor room at Mrs. Cuppy's with no place to go. And with only fifteen dollars a week to live on. And in the morning he would be working in the basement again, while these girls were rising to more pleasure. And out in Denver were his parents with their small lodging house and mission, which he dared not even describe accurately here.

Suddenly the two girls declaring they must go, they took themselves off. And he and the Griffiths were once more left to themselves—he with the feeling that he was very much out of place and neglected here, since Samuel Griffiths and his wife and Bella, anyhow, if not Myra, seemed to be feeling that he was merely being permitted to look into a world to which he did not belong; also, that because of his poverty it would be impossible to fit him into—however much he might dream of associating with three such wonderful girls as these. And at once he felt sad—very—his eyes and his mood darkening so much that not only Samuel Griffiths, but his wife as well as Myra noticed it. If he could enter upon this world, find some way. But of the group it was only Myra, not any of the others, who sensed that in all likelihood he was lonely and depressed. And in consequence as all were rising and returning to the large living room (Samuel chiding Bella for her habit of keeping her family waiting) it was Myra who drew near to Clyde to say: "I think after you've been here a little while you'll probably like Lycurgus better than you do now, even. There are quite a number of interesting places to go and see around here—lakes and the Adirondacks are just north of here, about seventy miles. And when the summer comes and we get settled at Greenwood, I'm sure Father and Mother will like you to come up there once in a while."

She was by no means sure that this was true, but under the circumstances, whether it was or not, she felt like saying it to Clyde. And thereafter, since he felt more comfortable with her, he talked with her as much as he could without neglecting either Bella or the family, until about half-past nine, when, suddenly feeling very much out of place and alone, he arose saying that he must go, that he had to get up early in the morning. And as he did so, Samuel Griffiths walked with him to the front door and let him out. But he, too, by now, as had Myra before him, feeling that Clyde was rather attractive and yet, for reasons of poverty, likely to be neglected from now on, not only by his family, but by himself as well, observed most pleasantly, and, as he hoped, compensatively: "It's rather nice out, isn't it? Wykeagy Avenue hasn't begun to show what it can do yet because the spring isn't quite here. But in a few weeks," and he looked up most inquiringly at the sky and sniffed the late April air, "we must have you out. All the trees and flowers will be in bloom then and you can see how really nice it is. Good-night."

He smiled and put a very cordial note into his voice, and once more Clyde felt that, whatever Gilbert Griffiths' attitude might be, most certainly his father was not wholly indifferent to him.

# Chapter XI

THE DAYS lapsed and, although no further word came from the Griffiths, Clyde was still inclined to exaggerate the importance of this one contact and to dream from time to time of delightful meetings with those girls and how wonderful if a love affair with one of them might eventuate for him. The beauty of that world in which they moved. The luxury and charm as opposed to this of which he was a part. Dillard! Rita! Tush! They were really dead for him. He aspired to this other or nothing as he saw it now and proceeded to prove as distant to Dillard as possible, an attitude which by degrees tended to alienate that youth entirely for he saw in Clyde a snob which potentially he was if he could have but won to what he desired. However, as he began to see afterwards, time passed and he was left to work until, depressed by the routine, meager pay and commonplace shrinking-room contacts, he began to think not so much of returning to Rita or Dillard,—he could not quite think of them now with any satisfaction, but of giving up this venture here and returning to Chicago or going to New York, where he was sure that he could connect himself with some hotel if need be. But then, as if to revive his courage and confirm his earlier dreams, a thing happened which caused him to think that certainly he was beginning to rise in the estimation of the Griffiths—father and son—whether they troubled to entertain him socially or not. For it chanced that one Saturday in spring, Samuel Griffiths decided to make a complete tour of inspection of the factory with Joshua Whiggam at his elbow. Reaching the shrinking department about noon, he observed for the first time with some dismay, Clyde in his undershirt and trousers working at the feeding end of two of the shrinking racks, his nephew having by this time acquired the necessary skill to "feed" as well as "take." And recalling how very neat and generally presentable he had appeared at his house but a few weeks before, he was decidedly disturbed by the contrast. For one thing he had felt about Clyde, both in Chicago and here at his home, was that he had presented a neat and pleasing appearance. And he, almost as much as his son, was jealous, not only of the name, but the general social appearance of the Griffiths before the employees of this factory as well as the community at large. And the sight of Clyde here, looking so much like Gilbert and in an armless shirt and trousers working among these men, tended to impress upon him more sharply than at any time before the fact that Clyde was his nephew, and that he ought not to be compelled to continue at this very menial form of work any longer. To the other employees it might appear that he was unduly indifferent to the meaning of such a relationship.

Without, however, saying a word to Whiggam or anyone else at the time, he waited until his son returned on Monday morning, from a trip that he had taken out of town, when he called him into his office and observed: "I made a tour of the factory Saturday and found young Clyde still down in the shrinking room."

"What of it, Dad?" replied his son, curiously interested as to why his father should at this time wish to mention Clyde in this special way. "Other people before him have worked down there and it hasn't hurt them."

"All true enough, but they weren't nephews of mine. And they didn't look as much like you as he does"—a comment which irritated Gilbert greatly. "It won't do, I tell you. It doesn't look quite right to me, and I'm afraid it won't look right to other people here who see how much he looks like you and know that he is your cousin and my nephew. I didn't realize that at first, because I haven't been down there, but I don't think it wise to keep him down there any longer doing that kind of thing. It won't do. We'll have to make a change, switch him around somewhere else where he won't look like that."

His eyes darkened and his brow wrinkled. The impression that Clyde made in his old clothes and with beads of sweat standing out on his forehead had not been pleasant.

"But I'll tell you how it is, Dad," Gilbert persisted, anxious and determined because of his innate opposition to Clyde to keep him there if possible. "I'm not so sure that I can find just the right place for him now anywhere else—at least not without moving someone else who has been here a long time and worked hard to get there. He hasn't had any training in anything so far, but just what he's doing."

"Don't know or don't care anything about that," replied Griffiths senior, feeling that his son was a little jealous and in consequence disposed to be unfair to Clyde. "That's no place for him and I won't have him there any longer. He's been there long enough. And I can't afford to have the name of any of this family come to mean anything but just what it does around here now—reserve and ability and energy and good judgment. It's not good for the business. And anything less than that is a liability. You get me, don't you?"

"Yes, I get you all right, governor."

"Well, then, do as I say. Get hold of Whiggam and figure out some other place for him around here, and not as piece worker or a hand either. It was a mistake to put him down there in the first place. There must be some little place in one of the departments where he can be fitted in as the head of something, first or second or third assistant to some one, and where he can wear a decent suit of clothes and look like somebody. And, if necessary, let him go home on full pay until you find something for him. But I want him changed. By the way, how much is he being paid now?"

"About fifteen, I think," replied Gilbert blandly.

"Not enough, if he's to make the right sort of an appearance here. Better make it twenty-five. It's more than he's worth, I know, but it can't be helped now. He has to have enough to live on while he's here, and from now on, I'd rather pay him that than have any one think we were not treating him right."

"All right, all right, governor. Please don't be cross about it, will you?" pleaded Gilbert, noting his father's irritation. "I'm not entirely to blame. You agreed to it in the first place when I suggested it, didn't you? But I guess you're right at that. Just leave it to me. I'll find a decent place for him," and turning, he proceeded in search of Whiggam, although at the same time thinking how he was to effect all this without permitting Clyde to get the notion that he was at all important here—to make him feel that this was being done as a favor to him and not for any reasons of merit in connection with himself.

And at once, Whiggam appearing, he, after a very diplomatic approach on the part of Gilbert, racked his brains, scratched his head, went away and returned after a time to say that the only thing he could think of, since Clyde was obviously lacking in technical training, was that of assistant to Mr. Liggett, who was foreman in charge of five big stitching rooms on the fifth floor, but who had under him one small and very special, though by no means technical, department which required the separate supervision of either an assistant forelady or man.

This was the stamping room—a separate chamber at the west end of the stitching floor, where were received daily from the cutting room above from seventy-five to one hundred thousand dozen unstitched collars of different brands and sizes. And here they were stamped by a group of girls according to the slips or directions attached to them with the size and brand of the collar. The sole business of the assistant foreman in charge here, as Gilbert well knew, after maintaining due decorum and order, was to see that this stamping process went uninterruptedly forward. Also that after the seventy-five to one hundred thousand dozen collars were duly stamped and transmitted to the stitchers, who were just outside in the larger room, to see that they were duly credited in a book of entry. And that the number of dozens stamped by each girl was duly recorded in order that her pay should correspond with her services.

For this purpose a little desk and various entry books, according to size and brand, were kept here. Also the cutters' slips, as taken from the bundles by the stampers were eventually delivered to this assistant in lots of a dozen or more and filed on spindles. It was really nothing more than a small clerkship, at times in the past held by young men or girls or old men or middle-aged women, according to the exigencies of the life of the place.

The thing that Whiggam feared in connection with Clyde and which he was quick to point out to Gilbert on this occasion was that because of his inexperience and youth Clyde might not, at first, prove as urgent and insistent a master of this department as the work there required. There were nothing but young girls there—some of them quite attractive.

Also was it wise to place a young man of Clyde's years and looks among so many girls? For, being susceptible, as he might well be at that age, he might prove too easy—not stern enough. The girls might take advantage of him. If so, it wouldn't be possible to keep him there very long. Still there was this temporary vacancy, and it was the only one in the whole factory at the moment. Why not, for the time being, send him upstairs for a tryout? It might not be long before either Mr. Liggett or himself would know of something else or whether or not he was suited for the work up there. In that case it would be easy to make a re-transfer.

Accordingly, about three in the afternoon of this same Monday, Clyde was sent for and after being made to wait for some fifteen minutes, as was Gilbert's method, he was admitted to the austere presence.

"Well, how are you getting along down where you are now?" asked Gilbert coldly and inquisitorially. And Clyde, who invariably experienced a depression whenever he came anywhere near his cousin, replied, with a poorly forced smile, "Oh, just about the same, Mr. Griffiths. I can't complain. I like it well enough. I'm learning a little something, I guess."

"You guess?"

"Well, I know I've learned a few things, of course," added Clyde, flushing slightly and feeling down deep within himself a keen resentment at the same time that he achieved a half-ingratiating and half-apologetic smile.

"Well, that's a little better. A man could hardly be down there as long as you've been and not know whether he had learned anything or not." Then deciding that he was being too severe, perhaps, he modified his tone slightly, and added: "But that's not why I sent for you. There's another matter I want to talk to you about. Tell me, did you ever have charge of any people or any other person than yourself, at any time in your life?"

"I don't believe I quite understand," replied Clyde, who, because he was a little nervous and flustered, had not quite registered the question accurately.

"I mean have you ever had any people work under you—been given a few people to direct in some department somewhere? Been a foreman or an assistant foreman in charge of anything?"

"No, sir, I never have," answered Clyde, but so nervous that he almost stuttered. For Gilbert's tone was very severe and cold—highly contemptuous. At the same time, now that the nature of the question was plain, its implication came to him. In spite of his cousin's severity, his ill manner toward him, still he could see his employers were thinking of making a foreman of him—putting him in charge of somebody—people. They must be! At once his ears and fingers began to titillate—the roots of his hair to tingle: "But I've seen how it's done in clubs and hotels," he added at once. "And I think I might manage if I were given a trial." His cheeks were now highly colored—his eyes crystal clear.

"Not the same thing. Not the same thing," insisted Gilbert sharply. "Seeing and doing are two entirely different things. A person without any experience can think a lot, but when it comes to doing, he's not there. Anyhow, this is one business that requires people who do know."

He stared at Clyde critically and quizzically while Clyde, feeling that he must be wrong in his notion that something was going to be done for him, began to quiet himself. His cheeks resumed their normal pallor and the light died from his eyes.

"Yes, sir, I guess that's true, too," he commented.

"But you don't need to guess in this case," insisted Gilbert. "You know. That's the trouble with people who don't know. They're always guessing."

The truth was that Gilbert was so irritated to think that he must now make a place for his cousin, and that despite his having done nothing at all to deserve it, that he could scarcely conceal the spleen that now colored his mood.

"You're right, I know," said Clyde placatingly, for he was still hoping for this hinted-at promotion.

"Well, the fact is," went on Gilbert, "I might have placed you in the accounting end of the business when you first came if you had been technically equipped for it." (The phrase "technically equipped" overawed and terrorized Clyde, for he scarcely understood what that meant.) "As it was," went on Gilbert, nonchalantly, "we had to do the best we could for you. We knew it was not very pleasant down there, but we couldn't do anything more for you at the time." He drummed on his desk with his fingers. "But the reason I called you up here to-day is this. I want to discuss with you a temporary vacancy that has occurred in one of our departments upstairs and which we are wondering—my father and I—whether you might be able to fill." Clyde's spirits rose amazingly. "Both my father and I," he went on, "have been thinking for some little time that we would like to do a little something for you, but as I say, your lack of practical training of any kind makes it very difficult for both of us. You haven't had either a commercial or a trade education of any kind, and that makes it doubly hard." He paused long enough to allow that to sink in—give Clyde the feeling that he was an interloper indeed. "Still," he added after a moment, "so long as we have seen fit to bring you on here, we have decided to give you a tryout at something better than you are doing. It won't do to let you stay down there indefinitely. Now, let me tell you a little something about what I have in mind," and he proceeded to explain the nature of the work on the fifth floor.

And when after a time Whiggam was sent for and appeared and had acknowledged Clyde's salutation, he observed: "Whiggam, I've just been telling my cousin here about our conversation this morning and what I told you about our plan to try him out as the head of that department. So if you'll just take him up to Mr. Liggett and have him or some one explain the nature of the work up there, I'll be obliged to you." He turned to his desk. "After that you can send him back to me," he added. "I want to talk to him again."

Then he arose and dismissed them both with an air, and Whiggam, still somewhat dubious as to the experiment, but now very anxious to be pleasant to Clyde since he could not tell what he might become, led the way to Mr. Liggett's floor. And there, amid a thunderous hum of machines, Clyde was led to the extreme west of the building and into a much smaller department which was merely railed off from the greater chamber by a low fence. Here were about twenty-five girls and their assistants with baskets, who apparently were doing their best to cope with a constant stream of unstitched collar bundles which fell through several chutes from the floor above.

And now at once, after being introduced to Mr. Liggett, he

was escorted to a small railed-off desk at which sat a short, plump girl of about his own years, not so very attractive, who arose as they approached. "This is Miss Todd," began Whiggam. "She's been in charge for about ten days now in the absence of Mrs. Angier. And what I want you to do now, Miss Todd, is to explain to Mr. Griffiths here just as quickly and clearly as you can what it is you do here. And then later in the day when he comes up here, I want you to help him to keep track of things until he sees just what is wanted and can do it himself. You'll do that, won't you?"

"Why, certainly, Mr. Whiggam. I'll be only too glad to," complied Miss Todd, and at once she began to take down the books of records and to show Clyde how the entry and discharge records were kept—also later how the stamping was done—how the basket girls took the descending bundles from the chutes and distributed them evenly according to the needs of the stamper and how later, as fast as they were stamped, other basket girls carried them to the stitchers outside. And Clyde, very much interested, felt that he could do it, only among so many women on a floor like this he felt very strange. There were so very, very many women—hundreds of them—stretching far and away between white walls and white columns to the eastern end of the building. And tall windows that reached from floor to ceiling let in a veritable flood of light. These girls were not all pretty. He saw them out of the tail of his eye as first Miss Todd and later Whiggam, and even Liggett, volunteered to impress points on him.

"The important thing," explained Whiggam after a time, "is to see that there is no mistake as to the number of thousands of dozens of collars that come down here and are stamped, and also that there's no delay in stamping them and getting them out to the stitchers. Also that the records of these girls' work is kept accurately so that there won't be any mistakes as to their time."

At last Clyde saw what was required of him and the conditions under which he was about to work and said so. He was very nervous but quickly decided that if this girl could do the work, he could. And because Liggett and Whiggam, interested by his relationship to Gilbert, appeared very friendly and persisted in delaying here, saying that there was nothing he could not manage they were sure, he returned after a time with Whiggam to Gilbert who, on seeing him enter, at once observed: "Well, what's the answer? Yes or no. Do you think you can do it or do you think you can't?"

"Well, I know that I can do it," replied Clyde with a great deal of courage for him, yet with the private feeling that he might not make good unless fortune favored him some even now. There were so many things to be taken into consideration—the favor of those above as well as about him—and would they always favor him?

"Very good, then. Just be seated for a moment," went on Gilbert. "I want to talk to you some more in connection with that work up there. It looks easy to you, does it?"

"No, I can't say that it looks exactly easy," replied Clyde, strained and a little pale, for because of his inexperience he felt the thing to be a great opportunity—one that would require all his skill and courage to maintain. "Just the same I think I can do it. In fact I know I can and I'd like to try."

"Well, now, that sounds a little better," replied Gilbert crisply and more graciously. "And now I want to tell you something more about it. I don't suppose you ever thought there was a floor with that many women on it, did you?"

"No, sir, I didn't," replied Clyde. "I knew they were somewhere in the building, but I didn't know just where."

"Exactly," went on Gilbert. "This plant is practically operated by women from cellar to roof. In the manufacturing department, I venture to say there are ten women to every man. On that account every one in whom we entrust any responsibility around here must be known to us as to their moral and religious character. If you weren't related to us, and if we didn't feel that because of that we knew a little something about you, we wouldn't think of putting you up there or anywhere in this factory over anybody until we did know. But don't think because you're related to us that we won't hold you strictly to account for everything that goes on up there and for your conduct. We will, and all the more so because you are related to us. You understand that, do you? And why—the meaning of the Griffiths name here?"

"Yes, sir," replied Clyde.

"Very well, then," went on Gilbert. "Before we place any

one here in any position of authority, we have to be absolutely sure that they're going to behave themselves as gentlemen always—that the women who are working here are going to receive civil treatment always. If a young man, or an old one for that matter, comes in here at any time and imagines that because there are women here he's going to be allowed to play about and neglect his work and flirt or cut up, that fellow is doomed to a short stay here. The men and women who work for us have got to feel that they are employees first, last and all the time—and they have to carry that attitude out into the street with them. And unless they do it, and we hear anything about it, that man or woman is done for so far as we are concerned. We don't want 'em and we won't have 'em. And once we're through with 'em, we're through with 'em."

He paused and stared at Clyde as much as to say: "Now I hope I have made myself clear. Also that we will never have any trouble in so far as you are concerned."

And Clyde replied: "Yes, I understand. I think that's right. In fact I know that's the way it has to be."

"And ought to be," added Gilbert.

"And ought to be," echoed Clyde.

At the same time he was wondering whether it was really true as Gilbert said. Had he not heard the mill girls already spoken about in a slighting way? Yet consciously at the moment he did not connect himself in thought with any of these girls upstairs. His present mood was that, because of his abnormal interest in girls, it would be better if he had nothing to do with them at all, never spoke to any of them, kept a very distant and cold attitude, such as Gilbert was holding toward him. It must be so, at least if he wished to keep his place here. And he was now determined to keep it and to conduct himself always as his cousin wished.

"Well, now, then," went on Gilbert as if to supplement Clyde's thoughts in this respect, "what I want to know of you is, if I trouble to put you in that department, even temporarily, can I trust you to keep a level head on your shoulders and go about your work conscientiously and not have your head turned or disturbed by the fact that you're working among a lot of women and girls?"

"Yes, sir, I know you can," replied Clyde very much impressed by his cousin's succinct demand, although, after Rita, a little dubious.

"If I can't, now is the time to say so," persisted Gilbert. "By blood you're a member of this family. And to our help here, and especially in a position of this kind, you represent us. We can't have anything come up in connection with you at any time around here that won't be just right. So I want you to be on your guard and watch your step from now on. Not the least thing must occur in connection with you that any one can comment on unfavorably. You understand, do you?"

"Yes, sir," replied Clyde most solemnly. "I understand that. I'll conduct myself properly or I'll get out." And he was thinking seriously at the moment that he could and would. The large number of girls and women upstairs seemed very remote and of no consequence just then.

"Very good. Now, I'll tell you what else I want you to do. I want you to knock off for the day and go home and sleep on this and think it over well. Then come back in the morning and go to work up there, if you still feel the same. Your salary from now on will be twenty-five dollars, and I want you to dress neat and clean so that you will be an example to the other men who have charge of departments."

He arose coldly and distantly, but Clyde, very much encouraged and enthused by the sudden jump in salary, as well as the admonition in regard to dressing well, felt so grateful toward his cousin that he longed to be friendly with him. To be sure, he was hard and cold and vain, but still he must think something of him, and his uncle too, or they would not choose to do all this for him and so speedily. And if ever he were able to make friends with him, win his way into his good graces, think how prosperously he would be placed here, what commercial and social honors might not come to him?

So elated was he at the moment that he bustled out of the great plant with a jaunty stride, resolved among other things that from now on, come what might, and as a test of himself in regard to life and work, he was going to be all that his uncle and cousin obviously expected of him—cool, cold even, and if necessary severe, where these women or girls of this department were concerned. No more relations with Dillard or Rita or anybody like that for the present anyhow.

# Chapter XII

THE IMPORT of twenty-five dollars a week! Of being the head of a department employing twenty-five girls! Of wearing a good suit of clothes again! Sitting at an official desk in a corner commanding a charming river view and feeling that at last, after almost two months in that menial department below stairs, he was a figure of some consequence in this enormous institution! And because of his relationship and new dignity, Whiggam, as well as Liggett, hovering about with advice and genial and helpful comments from time to time. And some of the managers of the other departments including several from the front office—an auditor and an advertising man occasionally pausing in passing to say hello. And the details of the work sufficiently mastered to permit him to look about him from time to time, taking an interest in the factory as a whole, its processes and supplies, such as where the great volume of linen and cotton came from, how it was cut in an enormous cutting room above this one, holding hundreds of experienced cutters receiving very high wages; how there was an employment bureau for recruiting help, a company doctor, a company hospital, a special dining room in the main building, where the officials of the company were allowed to dine—but no others—and that he, being an accredited department head could now lunch with those others in that special restaurant if he chose and could afford to. Also he soon learned that several miles out from Lycurgus, on the Mohawk, near a hamlet called Van Troup, was an interfactory country club, to which most of the department heads of the various factories about belonged, but, alas, as he also learned, Griffiths and Company did not really favor their officials mixing with those of any other company, and for that reason few of them did. Yet he, being a member of the family, as Liggett once said to him, could probably do as he chose as to that. But he decided, because of the strong warnings of Gilbert, as well as his high blood relations with this family, that he had better remain as aloof as possible. And so smiling and being as genial as possible to all, nevertheless for the most part, and in order to avoid Dillard and others of his ilk, and although he was much more lonely than otherwise he would have been, returning to his room or the public squares of this and near-by cities on Saturday and Sunday afternoons, and even, since he thought this might please his uncle and cousin and so raise him in their esteem, beginning to attend one of the principal Presbyterian churches—the Second or High Street Church, to which on occasion, as he had already learned, the Griffiths themselves were accustomed to resort. Yet without ever coming in contact with them in person, since from June to September they spent their week-ends at Greenwood Lake, to which most of the society life of this region as yet resorted.

In fact the summer life of Lycurgus, in so far as its society was concerned, was very dull. Nothing in particular ever eventuated then in the city, although previous to this, in May, there had been various affairs in connection with the Griffiths and their friends which Clyde had either read about or saw at a distance—a graduation reception and dance at the Snedeker School, a lawn fête upon the Griffiths' grounds, with a striped marquee tent on one part of the lawn and Chinese lanterns hung in among the trees. Clyde had observed this quite by accident one evening as he was walking alone about the city. It raised many a curious and eager thought in regard to this family, its high station and his relation to it. But having placed him comfortably in a small official position which was not arduous, the Griffiths now proceeded to dismiss him from their minds. He was doing well enough, and they would see something more of him later, perhaps.

And then a little later he read in the Lycurgus *Star* that there was to be staged on June twentieth the annual inter-city automobile floral parade and contest (Fonda, Gloversville, Amsterdam and Schenectady), which this year was to be held in Lycurgus and which was the last local social affair of any consequence, as *The Star* phrased it, before the annual hegira to the lakes and mountains of those who were able to depart for such places. And the names of Bella, Bertine and Sondra, to say nothing of Gilbert, were mentioned as contestants or defendants of the fair name of Lycurgus. And since this occurred on a Saturday afternoon, Clyde, dressed in his best, yet decidedly wishing to obscure himself as an ordinary spectator, was able to see once more the girl who had so infatuated him on sight, obviously breasting a white rose-surfaced stream and guiding her craft with a paddle covered with yellow daffodils—a floral representation of some Indian legend in connection with the Mohawk River. With her dark hair filleted Indian fashion with a yellow feather and brown-eyed susans, she was arresting enough not only to capture a prize, but to recapture Clyde's fancy. How marvelous to be of that world.

In the same parade he had seen Gilbert Griffiths accompanied by a very attractive girl chauffeuring one of four floats representing the four seasons. And while the one he drove was winter, with this local society girl posed in ermine with white roses for snow all about, directly behind came another float, which presented Bella Griffiths as spring, swathed in filmy draperies and crouching beside a waterfall of dark violets. The effect was quite striking and threw Clyde into a mood in regard to love, youth and romance which was delicious and yet very painful to him. Perhaps he should have retained Rita, after all.

In the meantime he was living on as before, only more spaciously in so far as his own thoughts were concerned. For his first thought after receiving this larger allowance was that he had better leave Mrs. Cuppy's and secure a better room in some private home which, if less advantageously situated for him, would be in a better street. It took him out of all contact with Dillard. And now, since his uncle had promoted him, some representative of his or Gilbert's might wish to stop by to see him about something. And what would one such think if he found him living in a small room such as he now occupied?

Ten days after his salary was raised, therefore, and because of the import of his name, he found it possible to obtain a room in one of the better houses and streets—Jefferson Avenue, which paralleled Wykeagy Avenue, only a few blocks farther out. It was the home of a widow whose husband had been a mill manager and who let out two rooms without board in order to be able to maintain this home, which was above the average for one of such position in Lycurgus. And Mrs. Peyton, having long been a resident of the city and knowing much about the Griffiths, recognized not only the

name but the resemblance of Clyde to Gilbert. And being intensely interested by this, as well as his general appearance,
she at once offered him an exceptional room for so little as
five dollars a week, which he took at once.

In connection with his work at the factory, however, and in
spite of the fact that he had made such drastic resolutions in
regard to the help who were beneath him, still it was not always possible for him to keep his mind on the mere mechan-
ical routine of the work or off of this company of girls as girls,
since at least a few of them were attractive. For it was summer—late June. And over all the factory, especially around
two, three and four in the afternoon, when the endless repe-
tition of the work seemed to pall on all, a practical indifference not remote from languor and in some instances
sensuality, seemed to creep over the place. There were so
many women and girls of so many different types and moods.
And here they were so remote from men or idle pleasure in
any form, all alone with just him, really. Again the air within
the place was nearly always heavy and physically relaxing, and
through the many open windows that reached from floor to
ceiling could be seen the Mohawk swirling and rippling, its
banks carpeted with green grass and in places shaded by trees.
Always it seemed to hint of pleasures which might be found
by idling along its shores. And since these workers were employed so mechanically as to leave their minds free to roam
from one thought of pleasure to another, they were for the
most part thinking of themselves always and what they would
do, assuming that they were not here chained to this routine.

And because their moods were so brisk and passionate, they
were often prone to fix on the nearest object. And since Clyde
was almost always the only male present—and in these days in
his best clothes—they were inclined to fix on him. They were,
indeed, full of all sorts of fantastic notions in regard to his private relations with the Griffiths and their like, where he lived
and how, whom in the way of a girl he might be interested in.
And he, in turn, when not too constrained by the memory of
what Gilbert Griffiths had said to him, was inclined to think
of them—certain girls in particular—with thoughts that bordered on the sensual. For, in spite of the wishes of the Griffiths Company, and the discarded Rita or perhaps because of

her, he found himself becoming interested in three different girls here. They were of a pagan and pleasure-loving turn—this trio—and they thought Clyde very handsome. Ruza Nikoforitch—a Russian-American girl—big and blonde and animal, with swimming brown eyes, a snub fat nose and chin, was very much drawn to him. Only, such was the manner with which he carried himself always, that she scarcely dared to let herself think so. For to her, with his hair so smoothly parted, torsoed in a bright-striped shirt, the sleeves of which in this weather were rolled to the elbows, he seemed almost too perfect to be real. She admired his clean, brown polished shoes, his brightly buckled black leather belt, and the loose four-in-hand tie he wore.

Again there was Martha Bordaloue, a stocky, brisk Canadian-French girl of trim, if rotund, figure and ankles, hair of a reddish gold and eyes of greenish blue with puffy pink cheeks and hands that were plump and yet small. Ignorant and pagan, she saw in Clyde some one whom, even for so much as an hour, assuming that he would, she would welcome—and that most eagerly. At the same time, being feline and savage, she hated all or any who even so much as presumed to attempt to interest him, and despised Ruza for that reason. For as she could see Ruza tried to nudge or lean against Clyde whenever he came sufficiently near. At the same time she herself sought by every single device known to her—her shirtwaist left open to below the borders of her white breast, her outer skirt lifted trimly above her calves when working, her plump round arms displayed to the shoulders to show him that physically at least she was worth his time. And the sly sighs and languorous looks when he was near, which caused Ruza to exclaim one day: "That French cat! He should look at her!" And because of Clyde she had an intense desire to strike her.

And yet again there was the stocky and yet gay Flora Brandt, a decidedly low class American type of coarse and yet enticing features, black hair, large, swimming and heavily-lashed black eyes, a snub nose and full and sensuous and yet pretty lips, and a vigorous and not ungraceful body, who, from day to day, once he had been there a little while, had continued to look at him as if to say—"What! You don't think

I'm attractive?" And with a look which said: "How can you continue to ignore me? There are lots of fellows who would be delighted to have your chance, I can tell you."

And, in connection with these three, the thought came to him after a time that since they were so different, more common as he thought, less well-guarded and less sharply interested in the conventional aspects of their contacts, it might be possible and that without detection on the part of any one for him to play with one or another of them—or all three in turn if his interest should eventually carry him so far—without being found out, particularly if beforehand he chose to impress on them the fact that he was condescending when he noticed them at all. Most certainly, if he could judge by their actions, they would willingly reward him by letting him have his way with them somewhere, and think nothing of it afterward if he chose to ignore them, as he must to keep his position here. Nevertheless, having given his word as he had to Gilbert Griffiths, he was still in no mood to break it. These were merely thoughts which from time to time were aroused in him by a situation which for him was difficult in the extreme. His was a disposition easily and often intensely inflamed by the chemistry of sex and the formula of beauty. He could not easily withstand the appeal, let alone the call, of sex. And by the actions and approaches of each in turn he was surely tempted at times, especially in these warm and languorous summer days, with no place to go and no single intimate to commune with. From time to time he could not resist drawing near to these very girls who were most bent on tempting him, although in the face of their looks and nudges, not very successfully concealed at times, he maintained an aloofness and an assumed indifference which was quite remarkable for him.

But just about this time there was a rush of orders, which necessitated, as both Whiggam and Liggett advised, Clyde taking on a few extra "try-out" girls who were willing to work for the very little they could earn at the current piece work rate until they had mastered the technique, when of course they would be able to earn more. There were many such who applied at the employment branch of the main office on the ground floor. In slack times all applications were rejected or the sign hung up "No Help Wanted."

And since Clyde was relatively new to this work, and thus far had neither hired nor discharged any one, it was agreed between Whiggam and Liggett that all the help thus sent up should first be examined by Liggett, who was looking for extra stitchers also. And in case any were found who promised to be satisfactory as stampers, they were to be turned over to Clyde with the suggestion that he try them. Only before bringing any one back to Clyde, Liggett was very careful to explain that in connection with this temporary hiring and discharging there was a system. One must not ever give a new employee, however well they did, the feeling that they were doing anything but moderately well until their capacity had been thoroughly tested. It interfered with their proper development as piece workers, the greatest results that could be obtained by any one person. Also one might freely take on as many girls as were needed to meet any such situation, and then, once the rush was over, as freely drop them—unless, occasionally, a very speedy worker was found among the novices. In that case it was always advisable to try to retain such a person, either by displacing a less satisfactory person or transferring some one from some other department, to make room for new blood and new energy.

The next day, after this notice of a rush, back came four girls at different times and escorted always by Liggett, who in each instance explained to Clyde: "Here's a girl who might do for you. Miss Tyndal is her name. You might give her a try-out." Or, "You might see if this girl will be of any use to you." And Clyde, after he had questioned them as to where they had worked, what the nature of the general working experiences were, and whether they lived at home here in Lycurgus or alone (the bachelor girl was not much wanted by the factory) would explain the nature of the work and pay, and then call Miss Todd, who in her turn would first take them to the rest room where were lockers for their coats, and then to one of the tables where they would be shown what the process was. And later it was Miss Todd's and Clyde's business to discover how well they were getting on and whether it was worth while to retain them or not.

Up to this time, apart from the girls to whom he was so definitely drawn, Clyde was not so very favorably impressed with the type of girl who was working here. For the most part, as he saw them, they were of a heavy and rather unintelligent company, and he had been thinking that smarter-looking girls might possibly be secured. Why not? Were there none in Lycurgus in the factory world? So many of these had fat hands, broad faces, heavy legs and ankles. Some of them even spoke with an accent, being Poles or the children of Poles, living in that slum north of the mill. And they were all concerned with catching a "feller," going to some dancing place with him afterwards, and little more. Also, Clyde had noticed that the American types who were here were of a decidedly different texture, thinner, more nervous and for the most part more angular, and with a general reserve due to prejudices, racial, moral and religious, which would not permit them to mingle with these others or with any men, apparently.

But among the extras or try-outs that were brought to him during this and several succeeding days, finally came one who interested Clyde more than any girl whom he had seen here so far. She was, as he decided on sight, more intelligent and pleasing—more spiritual—though apparently not less vigorous, if more gracefully proportioned. As a matter of fact, as he saw her at first, she appeared to him to possess a charm which no one else in this room had, a certain wistfulness and wonder combined with a kind of self-reliant courage and determination which marked her at once as one possessed of will and conviction to a degree. Nevertheless, as she said, she was inexperienced in this kind of work, and highly uncertain as to whether she would prove of service here or anywhere.

Her name was Roberta Alden, and, as she at once explained, previous to this she had been working in a small hosiery factory in a town called Trippetts Mills fifty miles north of Lycurgus. She had on a small brown hat that did not look any too new, and was pulled low over a face that was small and regular and pretty and that was haloed by bright, light brown hair. Her eyes were of a translucent gray blue. Her little suit was commonplace, and her shoes were not so very new-looking and quite solidly-soled. She looked practical and serious and yet so bright and clean and willing and possessed of so much hope and vigor that along with Liggett, who had first talked with her, he was at once taken with her.

Distinctly she was above the average of the girls in this room. And he could not help wondering about her as he talked to her, for she seemed so tense, a little troubled as to the outcome of this interview, as though this was a very great adventure for her.

She explained that up to this time she had been living with her parents near a town called Biltz, but was now living with friends here. She talked so honestly and simply that Clyde was very much moved by her, and for this reason wished to help her. At the same time he wondered if she were not really above the type of work she was seeking. Her eyes were so round and blue and intelligent—her lips and nose and ears and hands so small and pleasing.

"You're going to live in Lycurgus, then, if you can get work here?" he said, more to be talking to her than anything else.

"Yes," she said, looking at him most directly and frankly.

"And the name again?" He took down a record pad.

"Roberta Alden."

"And your address here?"

"228 Taylor Street."

"I don't even know where that is myself," he informed her because he liked talking to her. "I haven't been here so very long, you see." He wondered just why afterwards he had chosen to tell her as much about himself so swiftly. Then he added: "I don't know whether Mr. Liggett has told you all about the work here. But it's piece work, you know, stamping collars. I'll show you if you'll just step over here," and he led the way to a near-by table where the stampers were. After letting her observe how it was done, and without calling Miss Todd, he picked up one of the collars and proceeded to explain all that had been previously explained to him.

At the same time, because of the intentness with which she observed him and his gestures, the seriousness with which she appeared to take all that he said, he felt a little nervous and embarrassed. There was something quite searching and penetrating about her glance. After he had explained once more what the bundle rate was, and how much some made and how little others, and she had agreed that she would like to try, he called Miss Todd, who took her to the locker room to

hang up her hat and coat. Then presently he saw her returning, a fluff of light hair about her forehead, her cheeks slightly
flushed, her eyes very intent and serious. And as advised by
Miss Todd, he saw her turn back her sleeves, revealing a
pretty pair of forearms. Then she fell to, and by her gestures
Clyde guessed that she would prove both speedy and accurate. For she seemed most anxious to obtain and keep this
place.

After she had worked a little while, he went to her side and
watched her as she picked up and stamped the collars piled
beside her and threw them to one side. Also the speed and
accuracy with which she did it. Then, because for a second
she turned and looked at him, giving him an innocent and
yet cheerful and courageous smile, he smiled back, most
pleased.

"Well, I guess you'll make out all right," he ventured to
say, since he could not help feeling that she would. And instantly, for a second only, she turned and smiled again. And
Clyde, in spite of himself, was quite thrilled. He liked her on
the instant, but because of his own station here, of course, as
he now decided, as well as his promise to Gilbert, he must be
careful about being congenial with any of the help in this
room—even as charming a girl as this. It would not do. He
had been guarding himself in connection with the others and
must with her too, a thing which seemed a little strange to
him then, for he was very much drawn to her. She was so
pretty and cute. Yet she was a working girl, as he remembered
now, too—a factory girl, as Gilbert would say, and he was her
superior. But she *was* so pretty and cute.

Instantly he went on to others who had been put on this
same day, and finally coming to Miss Todd asked her to report pretty soon on how Miss Alden was getting along—that
he wanted to know.

But at the same time that he had addressed Roberta, and
she had smiled back at him, Ruza Nikoforitch, who was working two tables away, nudged the girl working next her, and
without any one noting it, first winked, then indicated with a
slight movement of the head both Clyde and Roberta. Her
friend was to watch them. And after Clyde had gone away and
Roberta was working as before, she leaned over and whis-

pered: "He says she'll do already." Then she lifted her eyebrows and compressed her lips. And her friend replied, so softly that no one could hear her: "Pretty quick, eh? And he didn't seem to see any one else at all before."

Then the twain smiled most wisely, a choice bit between them. Ruza Nikoforitch was jealous.

# Chapter XIII

THE REASONS why a girl of Roberta's type should be seeking employment with Griffiths and Company at this time and in this capacity are of some point. For, somewhat after the fashion of Clyde in relation to his family and his life, she too considered her life a great disappointment. She was the daughter of Titus Alden, a farmer—of near Biltz, a small town in Mimico County, some fifty miles north. And from her youth up she had seen little but poverty. Her father—the youngest of three sons of Ephraim Alden, a farmer in this region before him—was so unsuccessful that at forty-eight he was still living in a house which, though old and much in need of repair at the time his father willed it to him, was now bordering upon a state of dilapidation. The house itself, while primarily a charming example of that excellent taste which produced those delightful gabled homes which embellish the average New England town and street, had been by now so reduced for want of paint, shingles, and certain flags which had once made a winding walk from a road gate to the front door, that it presented a decidedly melancholy aspect to the world, as though it might be coughing and saying: "Well, things are none too satisfactory with me."

The interior of the house corresponded with the exterior. The floor boards and stair boards were loose and creaked most eerily at times. Some of the windows had shades—some did not. Furniture of both an earlier and a later date, but all in a somewhat decayed condition, intermingled and furnished it in some nondescript manner which need hardly be described.

As for the parents of Roberta, they were excellent examples of that native type of Americanism which resists facts and reveres illusion. Titus Alden was one of that vast company of individuals who are born, pass through and die out of the world without ever quite getting any one thing straight. They appear, blunder, and end in a fog. Like his two brothers, both older and almost as nebulous, Titus was a farmer solely because his father had been a farmer. And he was here on this farm because it had been willed to him and because it was

easier to stay here and try to work this than it was to go elsewhere. He was a Republican because his father before him
was a Republican and because this county was Republican. It
never occurred to him to be otherwise. And, as in the case of
his politics and his religion, he had borrowed all his notions
of what was right and wrong from those about him. A single,
serious, intelligent or rightly informing book had never been
read by any member of this family—not one. But they were
nevertheless excellent, as conventions, morals and religions
go—honest, upright, God-fearing and respectable.

In so far as the daughter of these parents was concerned,
and in the face of natural gifts which fitted her for something
better than this world from which she derived, she was still, in
part, at least, a reflection of the religious and moral notions
there and then prevailing,—the views of the local ministers
and the laity in general. At the same time, because of a warm,
imaginative, sensuous temperament, she was filled—once she
reached fifteen and sixteen—with the world-old dream of all
of Eve's daughters from the homeliest to the fairest—that her
beauty or charm might some day and ere long smite bewitchingly and so irresistibly the soul of a given man or men.

So it was that although throughout her infancy and girl-
hood she was compelled to hear of and share a depriving and
toilsome poverty, still, because of her innate imagination, she
was always thinking of something better. Maybe, some day,
who knew, a larger city like Albany or Utica! A newer and
greater life.

And then what dreams! And in the orchard of a spring day
later, between her fourteenth and eighteenth years when the
early May sun was making pink lamps of every aged tree and
the ground was pinkly carpeted with the falling and odorous
petals, she would stand and breathe and sometimes laugh, or
even sigh, her arms upreached or thrown wide to life. To be
alive! To have youth and the world before one. To think of
the eyes and the smile of some youth of the region who by
the merest chance had passed her and looked, and who might
never look again, but who, nevertheless, in so doing, had
stirred her young soul to dreams.

None the less she was shy, and hence recessive—afraid of
men, especially the more ordinary types common to this re-

gion. And these in turn, repulsed by her shyness and refinement, tended to recede from her, for all of her physical charm, which was too delicate for this region. Nevertheless, at the age of sixteen, having repaired to Biltz in order to work in Appleman's Dry Goods Store for five dollars a week, she saw many young men who attracted her. But here because of her mood in regard to her family's position, as well as the fact that to her inexperienced eyes they appeared so much better placed than herself, she was convinced that they would not be interested in her. And here again it was her own mood that succeeded in alienating them almost completely. Nevertheless she remained working for Mr. Appleman until she was between eighteen and nineteen, all the while sensing that she was really doing nothing for herself because she was too closely identified with her home and her family, who appeared to need her.

And then about this time, an almost revolutionary thing for this part of the world occurred. For because of the cheapness of labor in such an extremely rural section, a small hosiery plant was built at Trippetts Mills. And though Roberta, because of the views and standards that prevailed hereabout, had somehow conceived of this type of work as beneath her, still she was fascinated by the reports of the high wages to be paid. Accordingly she repaired to Trippetts Mills, where, boarding at the house of a neighbor who had previously lived in Biltz, and returning home every Saturday afternoon, she planned to bring together the means for some further form of practical education—a course at a business college at Homer or Lycurgus or somewhere which might fit her for something better—bookkeeping or stenography.

And in connection with this dream and this attempted saving two years went by. And in the meanwhile, although she earned more money (eventually twelve dollars a week), still, because various members of her family required so many little things and she desired to alleviate to a degree the privations of these others from which she suffered, nearly all that she earned went to them.

And again here, as at Biltz, most of the youths of the town who were better suited to her intellectually and temperamentally—still looked upon the mere factory type as beneath them in many ways. And although Roberta was far from being that type, still having associated herself with them she was inclined to absorb some of their psychology in regard to themselves. Indeed by then she was fairly well satisfied that no one of these here in whom she was interested would be interested in her—at least not with any legitimate intentions.

And then two things occurred which caused her to think, not only seriously of marriage, but of her own future, whether she married or not. For her sister, Agnes, now twenty, and three years her junior, having recently reëncountered a young schoolmaster who some time before had conducted the district school near the Alden farm, and finding him more to her taste now than when she had been in school, had decided to marry him. And this meant, as Roberta saw it, that she was about to take on the appearance of a spinster unless she married soon. Yet she did not quite see what was to be done until the hosiery factory at Trippetts Mills suddenly closed, never to reopen. And then, in order to assist her mother, as well as help with her sister's wedding, she returned to Biltz.

But then there came a third thing which decidedly affected her dreams and plans. Grace Marr, a girl whom she had met at Trippetts Mills, had gone to Lycurgus and after a few weeks there had managed to connect herself with the Finchley Vacuum Cleaner Company at a salary of fifteen dollars a week and at once wrote to Roberta telling her of the opportunities that were then present in Lycurgus. For in passing the Griffiths Company, which she did daily, she had seen a large sign posted over the east employment door reading "Girls Wanted." And inquiry revealed the fact that girls at this company were always started at nine or ten dollars, quickly taught some one of the various phases of piece work and then, once they were proficient, were frequently able to earn as much as from fourteen to sixteen dollars, according to their skill. And since board and room were only consuming seven of what she earned, she was delighted to communicate to Roberta, whom she liked very much, that she might come and room with her if she wished.

Roberta, having reached the place where she felt that she could no longer endure farm life but must act for herself once more, finally arranged with her mother to leave in order that she might help her more directly with her wages.

But once in Lycurgus and employed by Clyde, her life, after the first flush of self-interest which a change so great implied for her, was not so much more enlarged socially or materially either, for that matter, over what it had been in Biltz and Trippetts Mills. For, despite the genial intimacy of Grace Marr—a girl not nearly as attractive as Roberta, and who, because of Roberta's charm and for the most part affected gayety, counted on her to provide a cheer and companionship which otherwise she would have lacked—still the world into which she was inducted here was scarcely any more liberal or diversified than that from which she sprang.

For, to begin with, the Newtons, sister and brother-in-law of Grace Marr, with whom she lived, and who, despite the fact that they were not unkindly, proved to be, almost more so than were the types with whom, either in Biltz or Trippetts Mills, she had been in constant contact, the most ordinary small town mill workers—religious and narrow to a degree. George Newton, as every one could see and feel, was a pleasant if not very emotional or romantic person who took his various small plans in regard to himself and his future as of the utmost importance. Primarily he was saving what little cash he could out of the wages he earned as threadman in the Cranston Wickwire factory to enable him to embark upon some business for which he thought himself fitted. And to this end, and to further enhance his meager savings, he had joined with his wife in the scheme of taking over an old house in Taylor Street which permitted the renting of enough rooms to carry the rent and in addition to supply the food for the family and five boarders, counting their labor and worries in the process as nothing. And on the other hand, Grace Marr, as well as Newton's wife, Mary, were of that type that here as elsewhere find the bulk of their social satisfaction in such small matters as relate to the organization of a small home, the establishing of its import and integrity in a petty and highly conventional neighborhood and the contemplation of life and conduct through the lens furnished by a purely sectarian creed.

And so, once part and parcel of this particular household,

Roberta found after a time, that it, if not Lycurgus, was narrow and restricted—not wholly unlike the various narrow and restricted homes at Biltz. And these lines, according to the Newtons and their like, to be strictly observed. No good could come of breaking them. If you were a factory employee you should accommodate yourself to the world and customs of the better sort of Christian factory employees. Every day therefore—and that not so very long after she had arrived—she found herself up and making the best of a not very satisfactory breakfast in the Newton dining room, which was usually shared by Grace and two other girls of nearly their own age—Opal Feliss and Olive Pope—who were connected with the Cranston Wickwire Company. Also by a young electrician by the name of Fred Shurlock, who worked for the City Lighting Plant. And immediately after breakfast joining a long procession that day after day at this hour made for the mills across the river. For just outside her own door she invariably met with a company of factory girls and women, boys and men, of the same relative ages, to say nothing of many old and weary-looking women who looked more like wraiths than human beings, who had issued from the various streets and houses of this vicinity. And as the crowd, because of the general inpour into it from various streets, thickened at Central Avenue, there was much ogling of the prettier girls by a certain type of factory man, who, not knowing any of them, still sought, as Roberta saw it, unlicensed contacts and even worse. Yet there was much giggling and simpering on the part of girls of a certain type who were by no means as severe as most of those she had known elsewhere. Shocking!

And at night the same throng, re-forming at the mills, crossing the bridge at the depot and returning as it had come. And Roberta, because of her social and moral training and mood, and in spite of her decided looks and charm and strong desires, feeling alone and neglected. Oh, how sad to see the world so gay and she so lonely. And it was always after six when she reached home. And after dinner there was really nothing much of anything to do unless she and Grace attended one or another of the moving picture theaters or she could bring herself to consent to join the Newtons and Grace at a meeting of the Methodist Church.

None the less once part and parcel of this household and working for Clyde she was delighted with the change. This big city. This fine Central Avenue with its stores and moving picture theaters. These great mills. And again this Mr. Griffiths, so young, attractive, smiling and interested in her.

# Chapter XIV

IN the same way Clyde, on encountering her, was greatly stirred. Since the abortive contact with Dillard, Rita and Zella, and afterwards the seemingly meaningless invitation to the Griffiths with its introduction to and yet only passing glimpse of such personages as Bella, Sondra Finchley and Bertine Cranston, he was lonely indeed. That high world! But plainly he was not to be allowed to share in it. And yet because of his vain hope in connection with it, he had chosen to cut himself off in this way. And to what end? Was he not if anything more lonely than ever? Mrs. Peyton! Going to and from his work but merely nodding to people or talking casually—or however sociably with one or another of the storekeepers along Central Avenue who chose to hail him—or even some of the factory girls here in whom he was not interested or with whom he did not dare to develop a friendship. What was that? Just nothing really. And yet as an offset to all this, of course, was he not a Griffiths and so entitled to their respect and reverence even on this account? What a situation really! What to do!

And at the same time, this Roberta Alden, once she was placed here in this fashion and becoming more familiar with local conditions, as well as the standing of Clyde, his charm, his evasive and yet sensible interest in her, was becoming troubled as to her state too. For once part and parcel of this local home she had joined she was becoming conscious of various local taboos and restrictions which made it seem likely that never at any time here would it be possible to express an interest in Clyde or any one above her officially. For there was a local taboo in regard to factory girls aspiring toward or allowing themselves to become interested in their official superiors. Religious, moral and reserved girls didn't do it. And again, as she soon discovered, the lines of demarcation and stratification between the rich and the poor in Lycurgus was as sharp as though cut by a knife or divided by a high wall. And another taboo in regard to all the foreign family girls and men,—ignorant, low, immoral, un-American! One should—above all—have nothing to do with them.

But among these people as she could see—the religious and moral, lower middle-class group to which she and all of her intimates belonged—dancing or local adventurous gayety, such as walking the streets or going to a moving picture theater—was also taboo. And yet she, herself, at this time, was becoming interested in dancing. Worse than this, the various young men and girls of the particular church which she and Grace Marr attended at first, were not inclined to see Roberta or Grace as equals, since they, for the most part, were members of older and more successful families of the town. And so it was that after a very few weeks of attendance of church affairs and services, they were about where they had been when they started—conventional and acceptable, but without the amount of entertainment and diversion which was normally reaching those who were of their same church but better placed.

And so it was that Roberta, after encountering Clyde and sensing the superior world in which she imagined he moved, and being so taken with the charm of his personality, was seized with the very virus of ambition and unrest that afflicted him. And every day that she went to the factory now she could not help but feel that his eyes were upon her in a quiet, seeking and yet doubtful way. Yet she also felt that he was too uncertain as to what she would think of any overture that he might make in her direction to risk a repulse or any offensive interpretation on her part. And yet at times, after the first two weeks of her stay here, she wishing that he would speak to her—that he would make some beginning—at other times that he must not dare—that it would be dreadful and impossible. The other girls there would see at once. And since they all plainly felt that he was too good or too remote for them, they would at once note that he was making an exception in her case and would put their own interpretation on it. And she knew the type of a girl who worked in the Griffiths stamping room would put but one interpretation on it,—that of looseness.

At the same time in so far as Clyde and his leaning toward her was concerned there was that rule laid down by Gilbert. And although, because of it, he had hitherto appeared not to notice or to give any more attention to one girl than another,

still, once Roberta arrived, he was almost unconsciously inclined to drift by her table and pause in her vicinity to see
how she was progressing. And, as he saw from the first, she
was a quick and intelligent worker, soon mastering without
much advice of any kind all the tricks of the work, and thereafter earning about as much as any of the others—fifteen dollars a week. And her manner was always that of one who
enjoyed it and was happy to have the privilege of working
here. And pleased to have him pay any little attention to her.

At the same time he noted to his surprise and especially
since to him she seemed so refined and different, a certain ex-
uberance and gayety that was not only emotional, but in a
delicate poetic way, sensual. Also that despite her difference
and reserve she was able to make friends with and seemed to
be able to understand the viewpoint of most of the foreign
girls who were essentially so different from her. For, listening
to her discuss the work here, first with Lena Schlict, Hoda
Petkanas, Angelina Pitti and some others who soon chose to
speak to her, he reached the conclusion that she was not
nearly so conventional or standoffish as most of the other
American girls. And yet she did not appear to lose their respect either.

Thus, one noontime, coming back from the office lunch
down stairs a little earlier than usual, he found her and several
of the foreign-family girls, as well as four of the American
girls, surrounding Polish Mary, one of the gayest and rough-
est of the foreign-family girls, who was explaining in rather a
high key how a certain "feller" whom she had met the night
before had given her a beaded bag, and for what purpose.

"I should go with heem to be his sweetheart," she announced with a flourish, the while she waved the bag before
the interested group. "And I say, I tack heem an' think on
heem. Pretty nice bag, eh?" she added, holding it aloft and
turning it about. "Tell me," she added with provoking and
yet probably only mock serious eyes and waving the bag toward Roberta, "what shall I do with heem? Keep heem an' go
with heem to be his sweetheart or give heem back? I like
heem pretty much, that bag, you bet."

And although, according to the laws of her upbringing, as
Clyde suspected, Roberta should have been shocked by all

this, she was not, as he noticed—far from it. If one might
have judged from her face, she was very much amused.

Instantly she replied with a gay smile: "Well, it all depends
on how handsome he is, Mary. If he's very attractive, I think
I'd string him along for a while, anyhow, and keep the bag as
long as I could."

"Oh, but he no wait," declared Mary archly, and with
plainly a keen sense of the riskiness of the situation, the while
she winked at Clyde who had drawn near. "I got to give heem
bag or be sweetheart to-night, and so swell bag I never can
buy myself." She eyed the bag archly and roguishly, her own
nose crinkling with the humor of the situation. "What I do
then?"

"Gee, this is pretty strong stuff for a little country girl like
Miss Alden. She won't like this, maybe," thought Clyde to
himself.

However, Roberta, as he now saw, appeared to be equal to
the situation, for she pretended to be troubled. "Gee, you are
in a fix," she commented. "I don't know what you'll do
now." She opened her eyes wide and pretended to be greatly
concerned. However, as Clyde could see, she was merely acting, but carrying it off very well.

And frizzled-haired Dutch Lena now leaned over to say: "I
take it and him too, you bet, if you don't want him. Where is
he? I got no feller now." She reached over as if to take the bag
from Mary, who as quickly withdrew it. And there were
squeals of delight from nearly all the girls in the room, who
were amused by this eccentric horseplay. Even Roberta
laughed loudly, a fact which Clyde noted with pleasure, for he
liked all this rough humor, considering it mere innocent play.

"Well, maybe you're right, Lena," he heard her add just as
the whistle blew and the hundreds of sewing machines in the
next room began to hum. "A good man isn't to be found
every day." Her blue eyes were twinkling and her lips, which
were most temptingly modeled, were parted in a broad smile.
There was much banter and more bluff in what she said than
anything else, as Clyde could see, but he felt that she was not
nearly as narrow as he had feared. She was human and gay
and tolerant and good-natured. There was decidedly a very
liberal measure of play in her. And in spite of the fact that her

clothes were poor, the same little round brown hat and blue cloth dress that she had worn on first coming to work here, she was prettier than anyone else. And she never needed to paint her lips and cheeks like the foreign girls, whose faces at times looked like pink-frosted cakes. And how pretty were her arms and neck—plump and gracefully designed! And there was a certain grace and abandon about her as she threw herself into her work as though she really enjoyed it. As she worked fast during the hottest portions of the day, there would gather on her upper lip and chin and forehead little beads of perspiration which she was always pausing in her work to touch with her handkerchief, while to him, like jewels, they seemed only to enhance her charm.

Wonderful days, these, now for Clyde. For once more and here, where he could be near her the long day through, he had a girl whom he could study and admire and by degrees proceed to crave with all of the desire of which he seemed to be capable—and with which he had craved Hortense Briggs—only with more satisfaction, since as he saw it she was simpler, more kindly and respectable. And though for quite a while at first Roberta appeared or pretended to be quite indifferent to or unconscious of him, still from the very first this was not true. She was only troubled as to the appropriate attitude for her. The beauty of his face and hands—the blackness and softness of his hair, the darkness and melancholy and lure of his eyes. He was attractive—oh, very. Beautiful, really, to her.

And then one day shortly thereafter, Gilbert Griffiths walking through here and stopping to talk to Clyde, she was led to imagine by this that Clyde was really much more of a figure socially and financially than she had previously thought. For just as Gilbert was approaching, Lena Schlict, who was working beside her, leaned over to say: "Here comes Mr. Gilbert Griffiths. His father owns this whole factory and when he dies, he'll get it, they say. And he's his cousin," she added, nodding toward Clyde. "They look a lot alike, don't they?"

"Yes, they do," replied Roberta, slyly studying not only Clyde but Gilbert, "only I think Mr. Clyde Griffiths is a little nicer looking, don't you?"

Hoda Petkanas, sitting on the other side of Roberta and overhearing this last remark, laughed. "That's what every one here thinks. He's not stuck up like that Mr. Gilbert Griffiths, either."

"Is he rich, too?" inquired Roberta, thinking of Clyde.

"I don't know. They say not," she pursed her lips dubiously, herself rather interested in Clyde along with the others. "He worked down in the shrinking room before he came up here. He was just working by the day, I guess. But he only came on here a little while ago to learn the business. Maybe he won't work in here much longer."

Roberta was suddenly troubled by this last remark. She had not been thinking, or so she had been trying to tell herself, of Clyde in any romantic way, and yet the thought that he might suddenly go at any moment, never to be seen by her any more, disturbed her now. He was so youthful, so brisk, so attractive. And so interested in her, too. Yes, that was plain. It was wrong to think that he would be interested in her—or to try to attract him by any least gesture of hers, since he was so important a person here—far above her.

For, true to her complex, the moment she heard that Clyde was so highly connected and might even have money, she was not so sure that he could have any legitimate interest in her. For was she not a poor working girl? And was he not a very rich man's nephew? He would not marry her, of course. And what other legitimate thing would he want with her? She must be on her guard in regard to him.

# Chapter XV

THE THOUGHTS of Clyde at this time in regard to Roberta and his general situation in Lycurgus were for the most part confused and disturbing. For had not Gilbert warned him against associating with the help here? On the other hand, in so far as his actual daily life was concerned, his condition was socially the same as before. Apart from the fact that his move to Mrs. Peyton's had taken him into a better street and neighborhood, he was really not so well off as he had been at Mrs. Cuppy's. For there at least he had been in touch with those young people who would have been diverting enough had he felt that it would have been wise to indulge them. But now, aside from a bachelor brother who was as old as Mrs. Peyton herself, and a son thirty—slim and reserved, who was connected with one of the Lycurgus banks—he saw no one who could or would trouble to entertain him. Like the others with whom he came in contact, they thought him possessed of relationships which would make it unnecessary and even a bit presumptuous for them to suggest ways and means of entertaining him.

On the other hand, while Roberta was not of that high world to which he now aspired, still there was that about her which enticed him beyond measure. Day after day and because so much alone, and furthermore because of so strong a chemic or temperamental pull that was so definitely asserting itself, he could no longer keep his eyes off her—or she hers from him. There were evasive and yet strained and feverish eye-flashes between them. And after one such in his case—a quick and furtive glance on her part at times—by no means intended to be seen by him, he found himself weak and then feverish. Her pretty mouth, her lovely big eyes, her radiant and yet so often shy and evasive smile. And, oh, she had such pretty arms—such a trim, lithe, sentient, quick figure and movements. If he only dared be friendly with her—venture to talk with and then see her somewhere afterwards—if she only would and if he only dared.

Confusion. Aspiration. Hours of burning and yearning. For

indeed he was not only puzzled but irritated by the anomalous and paradoxical contrasts which his life here presented—loneliness and wistfulness as against the fact that it was being generally assumed by such as knew him that he was rather pleasantly and interestingly employed socially.

Therefore in order to enjoy himself in some way befitting his present rank, and to keep out of the sight of those who were imagining that he was being so much more handsomely entertained than he was, he had been more recently, on Saturday afternoons and Sundays, making idle sightseeing trips to Gloversville, Fonda, Amsterdam and other places, as well as Gray and Crum Lakes, where there were boats, beaches and bathhouses, with bathing suits for rent. And there, because he was always thinking that if by chance he should be taken up by the Griffiths, he would need as many social accomplishments as possible, and by reason of encountering a man who took a fancy to him and who could both swim and dive, he learned to do both exceedingly well. But canoeing fascinated him really. He was pleased by the picturesque and summery appearance he made in an outing shirt and canvas shoes paddling about Crum Lake in one of the bright red or green or blue canoes that were leased by the hour. And at such times these summer scenes appeared to possess an airy, fairy quality, especially with a summer cloud or two hanging high above in the blue. And so his mind indulged itself in day dreams as to how it would feel to be a member of one of the wealthy groups that frequented the more noted resorts of the north— Racquette Lake—Schroon Lake—Lake George and Champlain—dance, golf, tennis, canoe with those who could afford to go to such places—the rich of Lycurgus.

But it was about this time that Roberta with her friend Grace found Crum Lake and had decided on it, with the approval of Mr. and Mrs. Newton, as one of the best and most reserved of all the smaller watering places about here. And so it was that they, too, were already given to riding out to the pavilion on a Saturday or Sunday afternoon, and once there following the west shore along which ran a well-worn footpath which led to clumps of trees, underneath which they sat and looked at the water, for neither could row a boat or swim. Also there were wild flowers and berry bushes to be plundered. And from certain marshy spots, to be reached by venturing out for a score of feet or more, it was possible to reach and take white lilies with their delicate yellow hearts. They were decidedly tempting and on two occasions already the marauders had brought Mrs. Newton large armfuls of blooms from the fields and shore line here.

On the third Sunday afternoon in July, Clyde, as lonely and rebellious as ever, was paddling about in a dark blue canoe along the south bank of the lake about a mile and a half from the boathouse. His coat and hat were off, and in a seeking and half resentful mood he was imagining vain things in regard to the type of life he would really like to lead. At different points on the lake in canoes, or their more clumsy companions, the row-boats, were boys and girls, men and women. And over the water occasionally would come their laughter or bits of their conversation. And in the distance would be other canoes and other dreamers, happily in love, as Clyde invariably decided, that being to him the sharpest contrast to his own lorn state.

At any rate, the sight of any other youth thus romantically engaged with his girl was sufficient to set dissonantly jangling the repressed and protesting libido of his nature. And this would cause his mind to paint another picture in which, had fortune favored him in the first place by birth, he would now be in some canoe on Schroon or Racquette or Champlain Lake with Sondra Finchley or some such girl, paddling and looking at the shores of a scene more distingué than this. Or might he not be riding or playing tennis, or in the evening dancing or racing from place to place in some high-powered car, Sondra by his side? He felt so out of it, so lonely and restless and tortured by all that he saw here, for everywhere that he looked he seemed to see love, romance, contentment. What to do? Where to go? He could not go on alone like this forever. He was too miserable.

In memory as well as mood his mind went back to the few gay happy days he had enjoyed in Kansas City before that dreadful accident—Ratterer, Hegglund, Higby, Tina Kogel, Hortense, Ratterer's sister Louise—in short, the gay company of which he was just beginning to be a part when that terrible accident had occurred. And next to Dillard, Rita, Zella,—

a companionship that would have been better than this, certainly. Were the Griffiths never going to do any more for him than this? Had he only come here to be sneered at by his cousin, pushed aside, or rather completely ignored by all the bright company of which the children of his rich uncle were a part? And so plainly, from so many interesting incidents, even now in this dead summertime, he could see how privileged and relaxed and apparently decidedly happy were those of that circle. Notices in the local papers almost every day as to their coming and going here and there, the large and expensive cars of Samuel as well as Gilbert Griffiths parked outside the main office entrance on such days as they were in Lycurgus—an occasional group of young society figures to be seen before the grill of the Lycurgus Hotel, or before one of the fine homes in Wykeagy Avenue, some one having returned to the city for an hour or a night.

And in the factory itself, whenever either was there— Gilbert or Samuel—in the smartest of summer clothes and attended by either Messrs. Smillie, Latch, Gotboy or Burkey, all high officials of the company, making a most austere and even regal round of the immense plant and consulting with or listening to the reports of the various minor department heads. And yet here was he—a full cousin to this same Gilbert, a nephew to this distinguished Samuel—being left to drift and pine by himself, and for no other reason than, as he could now clearly see, he was not good enough. His father was not as able as this, his great uncle—his mother (might Heaven keep her) not as distinguished or as experienced as his cold, superior, indifferent aunt. Might it not be best to leave? Had he not made a foolish move, after all, in coming on here? What, if anything, did these high relatives ever intend to do for him?

In loneliness and resentment and disappointment, his mind now wandered from the Griffiths and their world, and particularly that beautiful Sondra Finchley, whom he recalled with a keen and biting thrill, to Roberta and the world which she as well as he was occupying here. For although a poor factory girl, she was still so much more attractive than any of these other girls with whom he was every day in contact.

How unfair and ridiculous for the Griffiths to insist that a man in his position should not associate with a girl such as Roberta, for instance, and just because she worked in the mill. He might not even make friends with her and bring her to some such lake as this or visit her in her little home on account of that. And yet he could not go with others more worthy of him, perhaps, for lack of means or contacts. And besides she was so attractive—very—and especially enticing to him. He could see her now as she worked with her swift, graceful movements at her machine. Her shapely arms and hands, her smooth skin and her bright eyes as she smiled up at him. And his thoughts were played over by exactly the same emotions that swept him so regularly at the factory. For poor or not—a working girl by misfortune only—he could see how he could be very happy with her if only he did not need to marry her. For now his ambitions toward marriage had been firmly magnetized by the world to which the Griffiths belonged. And yet his desires were most colorfully inflamed by her. If only he might venture to talk to her more—to walk home with her some day from the mill—to bring her out here to this lake on a Saturday or Sunday, and row about—just to idle and dream with her.

He rounded a point studded with a clump of trees and bushes and covering a shallow where were scores of water lilies afloat, their large leaves resting flat upon the still water of the lake. And on the bank to the left was a girl standing and looking at them. She had her hat off and one hand to her eyes for she was facing the sun and was looking down in the water. Her lips were parted in careless inquiry. She was very pretty, he thought, as he paused in his paddling to look at her. The sleeves of a pale blue waist came only to her elbows. And a darker blue skirt of flannel reconveyed to him the trimness of her figure. It wasn't Roberta! It couldn't be! Yes, it was!

Almost before he had decided, he was quite beside her, some twenty feet from the shore, and was looking up at her, his face lit by the radiance of one who had suddenly, and beyond his belief, realized a dream. And as though he were a pleasant apparition suddenly evoked out of nothing and nowhere, a poetic effort taking form out of smoke or vibrant energy, she in turn stood staring down at him, her lips unable to resist the wavy line of beauty that a happy mood always brought to them.

"My, Miss Alden! It is you, isn't it?" he called. "I was wondering whether it was. I couldn't be sure from out there."

"Why, yes it is," she laughed, puzzled, and again just the least bit abashed by the reality of him. For in spite of her obvious pleasure at seeing him again, only thinly repressed for the first moment or two, she was on the instant beginning to be troubled by her thoughts in regard to him—the difficulties that contact with him seemed to prognosticate. For this meant contact and friendship, maybe, and she was no longer in any mood to resist him, whatever people might think. And yet here was her friend, Grace Marr. Would she want her to know of Clyde and her interest in him? She was troubled. And yet she could not resist smiling and looking at him in a frank and welcoming way. She had been thinking of him so much and wishing for him in some happy, secure, commendable way. And now here he was. And there could be nothing more innocent than his presence here—nor hers.

"Just out for a walk?" he forced himself to say, although, because of his delight and his fear of her really, he felt not a little embarrassed now that she was directly before him. At the same time he added, recalling that she had been looking so intently at the water: "You want some of these water lilies? Is that what you're looking for?"

"Uh, huh," she replied, still smiling and looking directly at him, for the sight of his dark hair blown by the wind, the pale blue outing shirt he wore open at the neck, his sleeves rolled up and the yellow paddle held by him above the handsome blue boat, quite thrilled her. If only she could win such a youth for her very own self—just hers and no one else's in the whole world. It seemed as though this would be paradise—that if she could have him she would never want anything else in all the world. And here at her very feet he sat now in this bright canoe on this clear July afternoon in this summery world—so new and pleasing to her. And now he was laughing up at her so directly and admiringly. Her girl friend was far in the rear somewhere looking for daisies. Could she? Should she?

"I was seeing if there was any way to get out to any of

them," she continued a little nervously, a tremor almost revealing itself in her voice. "I haven't seen any before just here on this side."

"I'll get you all you want," he exclaimed briskly and gayly. "You just stay where you are. I'll bring them." But then, bethinking him of how much more lovely it would be if she were to get in with him, he added: "But see here—why don't you get in here with me? There's plenty of room and I can take you anywhere you want to go. There's lots nicer lilies up the lake here a little way and on the other side too. I saw hundreds of them over there just beyond that island."

Roberta looked. And as she did, another canoe paddled by, holding a youth of about Clyde's years and a girl no older than herself. She wore a white dress and a pink hat and the canoe was green. And far across the water at the point of the very island about which Clyde was talking was another canoe—bright yellow with a boy and a girl in that. She was thinking she would like to get in without her companion, if possible—with her, if need be. She wanted so much to have him all to herself. If she had only come out here alone. For if Grace Marr were included, she would know and later talk, maybe, or think, if she heard anything else in regard to them ever. And yet if she did not, there was the fear that he might not like her any more—might even come to dislike her or give up being interested in her, and that would be dreadful.

She stood staring and thinking, and Clyde, troubled and pained by her doubt on this occasion and his own loneliness and desire for her, suddenly called: "Oh, please don't say no. Just get in, won't you? You'll like it. I want you to. Then we can find all the lilies you want. I can let you out anywhere you want to get out—in ten minutes if you want to."

She marked the "I want you to." It soothed and strengthened her. He had no desire to take any advantage of her as she could see.

"But I have my friend with me here," she exclaimed almost sadly and dubiously, for she still wanted to go alone—never in her life had she wanted any one less than Grace Marr at this moment. Why had she brought her? She wasn't so very pretty and Clyde might not like her, and that might spoil the occasion. "Besides," she added almost in the same breath and with many thoughts fighting her, "maybe I'd better not. Is it safe?"

"Oh, yes, but maybe you better had," laughed Clyde seeing that she was yielding. "It's perfectly safe," he added eagerly. Then maneuvering the canoe next to the bank, which was a foot above the water, and laying hold of a root to hold it still, he said: "Of course you won't be in any danger. Call your friend then, if you want to, and I'll row the two of you. There's room for two and there are lots of water lilies everywhere over there." He nodded toward the east side of the lake.

Roberta could no longer resist and seized an overhanging branch by which to steady herself. At the same time she began to call: "Oh, Gray-ace! Gray-ace! Where are you?" for she had at last decided that it was best to include her.

A far-off voice as quickly answered: "Hello-o! What do you want?"

"Come up here. Come on. I got something I want to tell you."

"Oh, no, you come on down here. The daisies are just wonderful."

"No, you come on up here. There's some one here that wants to take us boating." She intended to call this loudly, but somehow her voice failed and her friend went on gathering flowers. Roberta frowned. She did not know just what to do. "Oh, very well, then," she suddenly decided, and straightening up added: "We can row down to where she is, I guess."

And Clyde, delighted, exclaimed: "Oh, that's just fine. Sure. Do get in. We'll pick these here first and then if she hasn't come, I'll paddle down nearer to where she is. Just step square in the center and that will balance it."

He was leaning back and looking up at her and Roberta was looking nervously and yet warmly into his eyes. Actually it was as though she were suddenly diffused with joy, enveloped in a rosy mist.

She balanced one foot. "Will it be perfectly safe?"

"Sure, sure," emphasized Clyde. "I'll hold it safe. Just take hold of that branch there and steady yourself by that." He held the boat very still as she stepped. Then, as the canoe careened slightly to one side, she dropped to the cushioned seat with a little cry. It was like that of a baby to Clyde.

"It's all right," he reassured her. "Just sit in the center there. It won't tip over. Gee, but this is funny. I can't make it out quite. You know just as I was coming around that point I was thinking of you—how maybe you might like to come out to a place like this sometime. And now here you are and here I am, and it all happened just like that." He waved his hand and snapped his fingers.

And Roberta, fascinated by this confession and yet a little frightened by it, added: "Is that so?" She was thinking of her own thoughts in regard to him.

"Yes, and what's more," added Clyde, "I've been thinking of you all day, really. That's the truth. I was wishing I might see you somewhere this morning and bring you out here."

"Oh, now, Mr. Griffiths. You know you don't mean that," pleaded Roberta, fearful lest this sudden contact should take too intimate and sentimental a turn too quickly. She scarcely liked that because she was afraid of him and herself, and now she looked at him, trying to appear a little cold or at least disinterested, but it was a very weak effort.

"That's the truth, though, just the same," insisted Clyde.

"Well, I think it is beautiful myself," admitted Roberta. "I've been out here, too, several times now. My friend and I." Clyde was once more delighted. She was smiling now and full of wonder.

"Oh, have you?" he exclaimed, and there was more talk as to why he liked to come out and how he had learned to swim here. "And to think I turned in here and there you were on the bank, looking at those water lilies. Wasn't that queer? I almost fell out of the boat. I don't think I ever saw you look as pretty as you did just now standing there."

"Oh, now, Mr. Griffiths," again pleaded Roberta cautiously. "You mustn't begin that way. I'll be afraid you're a dreadful flatterer. I'll have to think you are if you say anything like that so quickly."

Clyde once more gazed at her weakly, and she smiled because she thought he was more handsome than ever. But what would he think, she added to herself, if she were to tell him that just before he came around that point she was thinking of him too, and wishing that he were there with her, and not Grace. And how they might sit and talk, and hold hands

perhaps. He might even put his arms around her waist, and
she might let him. That would be terrible, as some people
here would see it, she knew. And it would never do for him
to know that—never. That would be too intimate—too bold.
But just the same it was so. Yet what would these people here
in Lycurgus think of her and him now if they should see her,
letting him paddle her about in this canoe! He a factory manager and she an employee in his department. The conclusion!
The scandal, maybe, even. And yet Grace Marr was along—or
soon would be. And she could explain to her—surely. He was
out rowing and knew her, and why shouldn't he help her get
some lilies if he wanted to? It was almost unavoidable—this
present situation, wasn't it?

Already Clyde had maneuvered the canoe around so that
they were now among the water lilies. And as he talked, having laid his paddle aside, he had been reaching over and
pulling them up, tossing them with their long, wet stems at
her feet as she lay reclining in the seat, one hand over the side
of the canoe in the water, as she had seen other girls holding
theirs. And for the moment her thoughts were allayed and
modified by the beauty of his head and arms and the tousled
hair that now fell over his eyes. How handsome he was!

# Chapter XVI

THE OUTCOME of that afternoon was so wonderful for both that for days thereafter neither could cease thinking about it or marveling that anything so romantic and charming should have brought them together so intimately when both were considering that it was not wise for either to know the other any better than employee and superior.

After a few moments of badinage in the boat in which he had talked about the beauty of the lilies and how glad he was to get them for her, they picked up her friend, Grace, and eventually returned to the boathouse.

Once on the land again there developed not a little hesitation on her part as well as his as to how farther to proceed, for they were confronted by the problem of returning into Lycurgus together. As Roberta saw it, it would not look right and might create talk. And on his part, he was thinking of Gilbert and other people he knew. The trouble that might come of it. What Gilbert would say if he did hear. And so both he and she, as well as Grace, were dubious on the instant about the wisdom of riding back together. Grace's own reputation, as well as the fact that she knew Clyde was not interested in her, piqued her. And Roberta, realizing this from her manner, said: "What do you think we had better do, excuse ourselves?"

At once Roberta tried to think just how they could extricate themselves gracefully without offending Clyde. Personally she was so enchanted that had she been alone she would have preferred to have ridden back with him. But with Grace here and in this cautious mood, never. She must think up some excuse.

And at the same time, Clyde was wondering just how he was to do now—ride in with them and brazenly face the possibility of being seen by some one who might carry the news to Gilbert Griffiths or evade doing so on some pretext or other. He could think of none, however, and was about to turn and accompany them to the car when the young electrician, Shurlock, who lived in the Newton household and who had been on the balcony of the pavilion, hailed them. He was with a friend who had a small car, and they were ready to return to the city.

"Well, here's luck," he exclaimed. "How are you, Miss Alden? How do you do, Miss Marr? You two don't happen to be going our way, do you? If you are, we can take you in with us."

Not only Roberta but Clyde heard. And at once she was about to say that, since it was a little late and she and Grace were scheduled to attend church services with the Newtons, it would be more convenient for them to return this way. She was, however, half hoping that Shurlock would invite Clyde and that he would accept. But on his doing so, Clyde instantly refused. He explained that he had decided to stay out a little while longer. And so Roberta left him with a look that conveyed clearly enough the gratitude and delight she felt. They had had such a good time. And he in turn, in spite of many qualms as to the wisdom of all this, fell to brooding on how sad it was that just he and Roberta might not have remained here for hours longer. And immediately after they had gone, he returned to the city alone.

The next morning he was keener than ever to see Roberta again. And although the peculiarly exposed nature of the work at the factory made it impossible for him to demonstrate his feelings, still by the swift and admiring and seeking smiles that played over his face and blazed in his eyes, she knew that he was as enthusiastic, if not more so, as on the night before. And on her part, although she felt that a crisis of some sort was impending, and in spite of the necessity of a form of secrecy which she resented, she could not refrain from giving him a warm and quite yielding glance in return. The wonder of his being interested in her! The wonder and the thrill!

Clyde decided at once that his attentions were still welcome. Also that he might risk saying something to her, supposing that a suitable opportunity offered. And so, after waiting an hour and seeing two fellow workers leave from either side of her, he seized the occasion to drift near and to pick up one of the collars she had just stamped, saying, as though talking about that: "I was awfully sorry to have to leave you last night. I wish we were out there again to-day instead of here, just you and me, don't you?"

Roberta turned, conscious that now was the time to decide whether she would encourage or discourage any attention on his part. At the same time she was almost faintingly eager to accept his attentions regardless of the problem in connection with them. His eyes! His hair! His hands! And then instead of rebuking or chilling him in any way, she only looked, but with eyes too weak and melting to mean anything less than yielding and uncertainty. Clyde saw that she was hopelessly and helplessly drawn to him, as indeed he was to her. On the instant he was resolved to say something more, when he could, as to where they could meet when no one was along, for it was plain that she was no more anxious to be observed than he was. He well knew more sharply to-day than ever before that he was treading on dangerous ground.

He began to make mistakes in his calculations, to feel that, with her so near him, he was by no means concentrating on the various tasks before him. She was too enticing, too compelling in so many ways to him. There was something so warm and gay and welcome about her that he felt that if he could persuade her to love him he would be among the most fortunate of men. Yet there was that rule, and although on the lake the day before he had been deciding that his position here was by no means as satisfactory as it should be, still with Roberta in it, as now it seemed she well might be, would it not be much more delightful for him to stay? Could he not, for the time being at least, endure the further indifference of the Griffiths? And who knows, might they not yet become interested in him as a suitable social figure if only he did nothing to offend them? And yet here he was attempting to do exactly the thing he had been forbidden to do. What kind of an injunction was this, anyhow, wherewith Gilbert had enjoined him? If he could come to some understanding with her, perhaps she would meet him in some clandestine way and thus obviate all possibility of criticism.

It was thus that Clyde, seated at his desk or walking about, was thinking. For now his mind, even in the face of his duties, was almost entirely engaged by her, and he could think of nothing else. He had decided to suggest that they meet for the first time, if she would, in a small park which was just west of the first outlying resort on the Mohawk. But throughout the day, so close to each other did the girls work, he had no opportunity to communicate with her. Indeed noontime came and he went below to his lunch, returning a little early in the hope of finding her sufficiently detached to permit him to whisper that he wished to see her somewhere. But she was surrounded by others at the time and so the entire afternoon went by without a single opportunity.

However, as he was going out, he bethought him that if he should chance to meet her alone somewhere in the street, he would venture to speak to her. For she wanted him to—that he knew, regardless of what she might say at any time. And he must find some way that would appear as accidental and hence as innocent to her as to others. But as the whistle blew and she left the building she was joined by another girl, and he was left to think of some other way.

That same evening, however, instead of lingering about the Peyton house or going to a moving picture theater, as he so often did now, or walking alone somewhere in order to allay his unrest and loneliness, he chose now instead to seek out the home of Roberta on Taylor Street. It was not a pleasing house, as he now decided, not nearly so attractive as Mrs. Cuppy's or the house in which he now dwelt. It was too old and brown, the neighborhood too nondescript, if conservative. But the lights in different rooms glowing at this early hour gave it a friendly and genial look. And the few trees in front were pleasant. What was Roberta doing now? Why couldn't she have waited for him in the factory? Why couldn't she sense now that he was outside and come out? He wished intensely that in some way he could make her feel that he was out here, and so cause her to come out. But she didn't. On the contrary, he observed Mr. Shurlock issue forth and disappear toward Central Avenue. And, after that, pedestrian after pedestrian making their way out of different houses along the street and toward Central, which caused him to walk briskly about the block in order to avoid being seen. At the same time he sighed often, because it was such a fine night—a full moon rising about nine-thirty and hanging heavy and yellow over the chimney tops. He was so lonely.

But at ten, the moon becoming too bright, and no Roberta appearing, he decided to leave. It was not wise to be hanging about here. But the night being so fine he resented the thought of his room and instead walked up and down Wykeagy Avenue, looking at the fine houses there—his uncle Samuel's among them. Now, all their occupants were away at their summer places. The houses were dark. And Sondra Finchley and Bertine Cranston and all that company—what were they doing on a night like this? Where dancing? Where speeding? Where loving? It was so hard to be poor, not to have money and position and to be able to do in life exactly as you wished.

And the next morning, more eager than usual, he was out of Mrs. Peyton's by six-forty-five, anxious to find some way of renewing his attentions to Roberta. For there was that crowd of factory workers that proceeded north along Central Avenue. And she would be a unit in it, of course, at about 7.10. But his trip to the factory was fruitless. For, after swallowing a cup of coffee at one of the small restaurants near the post-office and walking the length of Central Avenue toward the mill, and pausing at a cigar store to see if Roberta should by any chance come along alone, he was rewarded by the sight of her with Grace Marr again. What a wretched, crazy world this was, he at once decided, and how difficult it was in this miserable town for anyone to meet anyone else alone. Everyone, nearly, knew everyone else. Besides, Roberta knew that he was trying to get a chance to talk to her. Why shouldn't she walk alone then? He had looked at her enough yesterday. And yet here she was walking with Grace Marr and appeared seemingly contented. What was the matter with her anyhow?

By the time he reached the factory he was very sour. But the sight of Roberta taking her place at her bench and tossing him a genial "good morning" with a cheerful smile, caused him to feel better and that all was not lost.

It was three o'clock in the afternoon and a lull due to the afternoon heat, the fag of steadily continued work, and the flare of reflected light from the river outside was over all. The tap, tap, tap of metal stamps upon scores of collars at once—nearly always slightly audible above the hum and whirr of the sewing machines beyond was, if anything, weaker than usual. And there was Ruza Nikoforitch, Hoda Petkanas, Martha Bordaloue, Angelina Pitti and Lena Schlict, all joining in a song called "Sweethearts" which some one had started. And Roberta, perpetually conscious of Clyde's eyes, as well as his mood, was thinking how long it would be before he would come around with some word in regard to something. For she wished him to—and because of his whispered words of the day before, she was sure that it would not be long, because he would not be able to resist it. His eyes the night before had told her that. Yet because of the impediments of this situation she knew that he must be having a difficult time thinking of any way by which he could say anything to her. And still at certain moments she was glad, for there were such moments when she felt she needed the security which the presence of so many girls gave her.

And as she thought of all this, stamping at her desk along with the others, she suddenly discovered that a bundle of collars which she had already stamped as sixteens were not of that size but smaller. She looked at it quickly and nervously, then decided that there was but one thing to do—lay the bundle aside and await comment from one of the foremen, including Clyde, or take it directly to him now—really the better way, because it prevented any of the foremen seeing it before he did. That was what all the girls did when they made mistakes of any kind. And all trained girls were supposed to catch all possible errors of that kind.

And yet now and in the face of all her very urgent desires she hesitated, for this would take her direct to Clyde and give him the opportunity he was seeking. But, more terrifying, it was giving her the opportunity she was seeking. She wavered between loyalty to Clyde as a superintendent, loyalty to her old conventions as opposed to her new and dominating desire and her repressed wish to have Clyde speak to her—then went over with the bundle and laid it on his desk. But her hands, as she did so, trembled. Her face was white—her throat taut. At the moment, as it chanced, he was almost vainly trying to calculate the scores of the different girls from the stubs laid before him, and was having a hard time of it because his mind was not on what he was doing. And then he looked up. And there was Roberta bending toward him. His nerves became very taut, his throat and lips dry, for here and now was his opportunity. And, as he could see, Roberta was almost suffocating from the strain which her daring and self-deception was putting upon her nerves and heart.

"There's been a distake" (she meant to say mistake) "in regard to this bundle upstairs," she began. "I didn't notice it either until I'd stamped nearly all of them. They're fifteen-and-a-half and I've stamped nearly all of them sixteen. I'm sorry."

Clyde noticed, as she said this, that she was trying to smile a little and appear calm, but her cheeks were quite blanched and her hand, particularly the one that held the bundle, trembled. On the instant he realized that although loyalty and order were bringing her with this mistake to him, still there was more than that to it. In a weak, frightened, and yet love-driven way, she was courting him, giving him the opportunity he was seeking, wishing him to take advantage of it. And he, embarrassed and shaken for the moment by this sudden visitation, was still heartened and hardened into a kind of effrontery and gallantry such as he had not felt as yet in regard to her. She was seeking him—that was plain. She was interested, and clever enough to make the occasion which permitted him to speak. Wonderful! The sweetness of her daring.

"Oh, that's all right," he said, pretending a courage and a daring in regard to her which he did not feel even now. "I'll just send them down to the wash room and then we'll see if we can't restamp them. It's not our mistake, really."

He smiled most warmly and she met his look with a repressed smile of her own, already turning and fearing that she had manifested too clearly what had brought her.

"But don't go," he added quickly. "I want to ask you something. I've been trying to get a word with you ever since Sunday. I want you to meet me somewhere, will you? There's a rule here that says a head of a department can't have anything to do with a girl who works for him—outside I mean. But I want you to see me just the same, won't you? You know," and he smiled winsomely and coaxingly into her eyes, "I've been just nearly crazy over you ever since you came in here and Sunday made it worse. And now I'm not going to let any old rule come between me and you, if I can help it. Will you?"

"Oh, I don't know whether I can do that or not," replied Roberta, who, now that she had succeeded in accomplishing what she had wished, was becoming terrorized by her own daring. She began looking around nervously and feeling that every eye in the room must be upon her. "I live with Mr. and Mrs. Newton, my friend's sister and brother-in-law, you know, and they're very strict. It isn't the same as if—" She was going to add "I was home" but Clyde interrupted her.

"Oh, now please don't say no, will you? Please don't. I want to see you. I don't want to cause you any trouble, that's all. Otherwise I'd be glad to come round to your house. You know how it is."

"Oh, no, you mustn't do that," cautioned Roberta. "Not yet anyhow." She was so confused that quite unconsciously she was giving Clyde to understand that she was expecting him to come around some time later.

"Well," smiled Clyde, who could see that she was yielding in part. "We could just walk out near the end of some street here—that street you live in, if you wish. There are no houses out there. Or there's a little park—Mohawk—just west of Dreamland on the Mohawk Street line. It's right on the river. You might come out there. I could meet you where the car stops. Will you do that?"

"Oh, I'd be afraid to do that I think—go so far, I mean. I never did anything like that before." She looked so innocent and frank as she said this that Clyde was quite carried away by the sweetness of her. And to think he was making a clandestine appointment with her. "I'm almost afraid to go anywhere here alone, you know. People talk so here, they say, and some one would be sure to see me. But——"

"Yes, but what?"

"I'm afraid I'm staying too long at your desk here, don't you think?" She actually gasped as she said it. And Clyde realizing the openness of it, although there was really nothing very unusual about it, now spoke quickly and forcefully.

"Well, then, how about the end of that street you live in? Couldn't you come down there for just a little while to-night—a half hour or so, maybe?"

"Oh, I couldn't make it to-night, I think—not so soon. I'll have to see first, you know. Arrange, that is. But another day." She was so excited and troubled by this great adventure of hers that her face, like Clyde's at times, changed from a half smile to a half frown without her realizing that it was registering these changes.

"Well, then, how about Wednesday night at eight-thirty or nine? Couldn't you do that? Please, now."

Roberta considered most sweetly, nervously. Clyde was enormously fascinated by her manner at the moment, for she looked around, conscious, or so she seemed, that she was being observed and that her stay here for a first visit was very long.

"I suppose I'd better be going back to my work now," she replied without really answering him.

"Wait a minute," pled Clyde. "We haven't fixed on the time for Wednesday. Aren't you going to meet me? Make it nine or eight-thirty, or any time you want to. I'll be there waiting for you after eight if you wish. Will you?"

"All right, then, say eight-thirty or between eight-thirty and nine, if I can. Is that all right? I'll come if I can, you know, and if anything does happen I'll tell you the next morning, you see." She flushed and then looked around once more, a foolish, flustered look, then hurried back to her bench, fairly tingling from head to toe, and looking as guilty as though she had been caught red-handed in some dreadful crime. And Clyde at his desk was almost choking with excitement. The wonder of her agreeing, of his talking to her like that, of her venturing to make a date with him at all here in Lycurgus, where he was so well-known! Thrilling!

For her part, she was thinking how wonderful it would be just to walk and talk with him in the moonlight, to feel the pressure of his arm and hear his soft appealing voice.

# Chapter XVII

I T WAS quite dark when Roberta stole out on Wednesday
night to meet Clyde. But before that what qualms and
meditations in the face of her willingness and her agreement
to do so. For not only was it difficult for her to overcome her
own mental scruples within, but in addition there was all the
trouble in connection with the commonplace and religious
and narrow atmosphere in which she found herself imbedded
at the Newtons. For since coming here she had scarcely gone
anywhere without Grace Marr. Besides on this occasion—a
thing she had forgotten in talking to Clyde—she had agreed
to go with the Newtons and Grace to the Gideon Baptist
Church, where a Wednesday prayer meeting was to be followed by a social with games, cake, tea and ice cream.

In consequence she was troubled severely as to how to
manage, until it came back to her that a day or two before
Mr. Liggett, in noting how rapid and efficient she was, had
observed that at any time she wanted to learn one phase of
the stitching operations going on in the next room, he would
have her taken in hand by Mrs. Braley, who would teach her.
And now that Clyde's invitation and this church affair fell on
the same night, she decided to say that she had an appointment with Mrs. Braley at her home. Only, as she also decided,
she would wait until just before dinner Wednesday and then
say that Mrs. Braley had invited her to come to her house.
Then she could see Clyde. And by the time the Newtons and
Grace returned she could be back. Oh, how it would feel to
have him talk to her—say again as he did in the boat that he
never had seen any one look so pretty as she did standing on
the bank and looking for water lilies. Many, many thoughts—
vague, dreadful, colorful, came to her—how and where they
might go—be—do—from now on, if only she could arrange
to be friends with him without harm to her or him. If need
be, she now decided, she could resign from the factory and
get a place somewhere else—a change which would absolve
Clyde from any responsibility in regard to her.

There was, however, another mental as well as emotional

phase in regard to all this and that related to her clothes. For since coming to Lycurgus she had learned that the more intelligent girls here dressed better than did those about Biltz and Trippetts Mills. At the same time she had been sending a fair portion of her money to her mother—sufficient to have equipped her exceptionally well, as she now realized, had she retained it. But now that Clyde was swaying her so greatly she was troubled about her looks, and on the evening after her conversation with him at the mill, she had gone through her small wardrobe, fixing upon a soft blue hat which Clyde had not yet seen, together with a checkered blue and white flannel skirt and a pair of white canvas shoes purchased the previous summer at Biltz. Her plan was to wait until the Newtons and Grace had departed for church and then swiftly dress and leave.

At eight-thirty, when night had finally fallen, she went east along Taylor to Central Avenue, then by a circuitous route made her way west again to the trysting place. And Clyde was already there. Against an old wooden fence that enclosed a five-acre cornfield, he was leaning and looking back toward the interesting little city, the lights in so many of the homes of which were aglow through the trees. The air was laden with spices—the mingled fragrance of many grasses and flowers. There was a light wind stirring in the long swords of the corn at his back—in the leaves of the trees overhead. And there were stars—the big dipper and the little dipper and the milky way—sidereal phenomena which his mother had pointed out to him long ago.

And he was thinking how different was his position here to what it had been in Kansas City. There he had been so nervous in regard to Hortense Briggs or any girl, really—afraid almost to say a word to any of them. Whereas here, and especially since he had had charge of this stamping room, he had seemed to become aware of the fact that he was more attractive than he had ever thought he was before. Also that the girls were attracted to him and that he was not so much afraid of them. The eyes of Roberta herself showed him this day how much she was drawn to him. She was his girl. And when she came, he would put his arms around her and kiss her. And she would not be able to resist him.

He stood listening, dreaming and watching, the rustling corn behind him stirring an old recollection in him, when suddenly he saw her coming. She looked trim and brisk and yet nervous, and paused at the street end and looked about like a frightened and cautious animal. At once Clyde hurried forward toward her and called softly: "Hello. Gee, it's nice to have you meet me. Did you have any trouble?" He was thinking how much more pleasing she was than either Hortense Briggs or Rita Dickerman, the one so calculating, the other so sensually free and indiscriminate.

"Did I have any trouble? Oh, didn't I though?" And at once she plunged into a full and picturesque account, not only of the mistake in regard to the Newtons' church night and her engagement with them, but of a determination on the part of Grace Marr not to go to the church social without her, and how she had to fib, oh, so terribly, about going over to Mrs. Braley's to learn to stitch—a Liggett-Roberta development of which Clyde had heard nothing so far and concerning which he was intensely curious, because at once it raised the thought that already Liggett might be intending to remove her from under his care. He proceeded to question her about that before he would let her go on with her story, an interest which Roberta noticed and because of which she was very pleased.

"But I can't stay very long, you know," she explained briskly and warmly at the first opportunity, the while Clyde laid hold of her arm and turned toward the river, which was to the north and untenanted this far out. "The Baptist Church socials never last much beyond ten-thirty or eleven, and they'll be back soon. So I'll have to manage to be back before they are."

Then she gave many reasons why it would be unwise for her to be out after ten, reasons which annoyed yet convinced Clyde by their wisdom. He had been hoping to keep her out longer. But seeing that the time was to be brief, he was all the keener for a closer contact with her now, and fell to complimenting her on her pretty hat and cape and how becoming they were. At once he tried putting his arm about her waist, but feeling this to be a too swift advance she removed his arm, or tried to, saying in the softest and most coaxing voice

"Now, now—that's not nice, is it? Can't you just hold my arm or let me hold yours?" But he noted, once she persuaded him to disengage her waist, she took his arm in a clinging, snuggling embrace and measured her stride to his. On the instant he was thinking how natural and unaffected her manner was now that the ice between them had been broken.

And how she went on babbling! She liked Lycurgus, only she thought it was the most religious town she had ever been in—worse than Biltz or Trippetts Mills that way. And then she had to explain to Clyde what Biltz and Trippetts Mills were like—and her home—a very little, for she did not care to talk about that. And then back to the Newtons and Grace Marr and how they watched her every move. Clyde was thinking as she talked how different she was from Hortense Briggs or Rita, or any other girl he had ever known—so much more simple and confiding—not in any way mushy as was Rita, or brash or vain or pretentious, as was Hortense, and yet really as pretty and so much sweeter. He could not help thinking if she were smartly dressed how sweet she would be. And again he was wondering what she would think of him and his attitude toward Hortense in contrast to his attitude toward her now, if she knew.

"You know," he said at the very first opportunity, "I've been trying to talk to you ever since you came to work at the factory but you see how very watchful every one is. They're the limit. They told me when I came up there that I mustn't interest myself in any girl working there and so I tried not to. But I just couldn't help this, could I?" He squeezed her arm affectionately, then stopped suddenly and, disengaging his arm from hers, put both his about her. "You know, Roberta, I'm crazy about you. I really am. I think you're the dearest, sweetest thing. Oh, say! Do you mind my telling you? Ever since you showed up there, I haven't been able to sleep, nearly. That's the truth—honest it is. I think and think of you. You've got such nice eyes and hair. To-night you look just too cute—lovely, I think. Oh, Roberta," suddenly he caught her face between his two hands and kissed her, before really she could evade him. Them having done this he held her while she resisted him, although it was almost impossible for her to do so. Instead she felt as though she wanted to put her arms around him or have him told her tight, and this mood in regard to him and herself puzzled and troubled her. It was awful. What would people think—say—if they knew? She was a bad girl, really, and yet she wanted to be this way—near him—now as never before.

"Oh, you mustn't, Mr. Griffiths," she pleaded. "You really mustn't, you know. Please. Some one might see us. I think I hear some one coming. Please, now." She looked about quite frightened, apparently, while Clyde laughed ecstatically. Life had presented him a delicious sweet at last. "You know I never did anything like this before," she went on. "Honest, I didn't. Please. It's only because you said——"

Clyde was pressing her close, not saying anything in reply—his pale face and dark hungry eyes held very close to hers. He kissed her again and again despite her protests, her little mouth and chin and cheeks seeming too beautiful—too irresistible—then murmured pleadingly, for he was too overcome to speak vigorously.

"Oh, Roberta, dearest, please, please, say that you love me. Please do! I know that you do, Roberta. I can tell. Please, tell me now. I'm so crazy about you. We have so little time."

He kissed her again upon the cheek and mouth, and suddenly he felt her relax. She stood quite still and unresisting in his arms. He felt a wonder of something—he could not tell what. All of a sudden he felt tears upon her face, her head sunk to his shoulder, and then he heard her say: "Yes, yes, yes. I do love you. Yes, yes. I do. I do."

There was a sob—half of misery, half of delight—in her voice and Clyde caught that. He was so touched by her honesty and simplicity that tears sprang to his own eyes. "It's all right, Roberta. It's all right. Please don't cry. Oh, I think you're so sweet. I do. I do, Roberta."

He looked up and before him in the east over the low roofs of the city was the thinnest, yellowest topmost arc of the rising July moon. It seemed at the moment as though life had given him all—all—that he could possibly ask of it.

# Chapter XVIII

THE CULMINATION of this meeting was but the prelude, as both Clyde and Roberta realized, to a series of contacts and rejoicings which were to extend over an indefinite period. They had found love. They were deliciously happy, whatever the problems attending its present realization might be. But the ways and means of continuing with it were a different matter. For not only was her connection with the Newtons a bar to any normal procedure in so far as Clyde was concerned, but Grace Marr herself offered a distinct and separate problem. Far more than Roberta she was chained, not only by the defect of poor looks, but by the narrow teachings and domestic training of her early social and religious life. Yet she wanted to be gay and free, too. And in Roberta, who, while gay and boastful at times, was still well within the conventions that chained Grace, she imagined that she saw one who was not so bound. And so it was that she clung to her closely and as Roberta saw it a little wearisomely. She imagined that they could exchange ideas and jests and confidences in regard to the love life and their respective dreams without injury to each other. And to date this was her one solace in an otherwise gray world.

But Roberta, even before the arrival of Clyde in her life, did not want to be so clung to. It was a bore. And afterwards she developed an inhibition in regard to him where Grace was concerned. For she not only knew that Grace would resent this sudden desertion, but also that she had no desire to face out within herself the sudden and revolutionary moods which now possessed her. Having at once met and loved him, she was afraid to think what, if anything, she proposed to permit herself to do in regard to him. Were not such contacts between the classes banned here? She knew they were. Hence she did not care to talk about him at all.

In consequence on Monday evening following the Sunday on the lake when Grace had inquired most gayly and familiarly after Clyde, Roberta had as instantly decided not to appear nearly as interested in him as Grace might already be imagining. Accordingly, she said little other than that he was very pleasant to her and had inquired after Grace, a remark which caused the latter to eye her slyly and to wonder if she were really telling what had happened since. "He was so very friendly I was beginning to think he was struck on you."

"Oh, what nonsense!" Roberta replied shrewdly, and a bit alarmed. "Why, he wouldn't look at me. Besides, there's a rule of the company that doesn't permit him to, as long as I work there."

This last, more than anything else, served to allay Grace's notions in regard to Clyde and Roberta, for she was of that conventional turn of mind which would scarcely permit her to think of any one infringing upon a company rule. Nevertheless Roberta was nervous lest Grace should be associating her and Clyde in her mind in some clandestine way, and she decided to be doubly cautious in regard to Clyde—to feign a distance she did not feel.

But all this was preliminary to troubles and strains and fears which had nothing to do with what had gone before, but took their rise from difficulties which sprang up immediately afterwards. For once she had come to this complete emotional understanding with Clyde, she saw no way of meeting him except in this very clandestine way and that so very rarely and uncertainly that she could not say when there was likely to be another meeting.

"You see, it's this way," she explained to Clyde when, a few evenings later, she had managed to steal out for an hour and they walked from the region at the end of Taylor Street down to the Mohawk, where were some open fields and a low bank rising above the pleasant river. "The Newtons never go any place much without inviting me. And even if they didn't, Grace'd never go unless I went along. It's just because we were together so much in Trippetts Mills that she feels that way, as though I were a part of the family. But now it's different, and yet I don't see how I am going to get out of it so soon. I don't know where to say I'm going or whom I am going with."

"I know that, honey," he replied softly and sweetly. "That's all true enough. But how is that going to help us now? You can't expect me to get along with just looking at you in the factory, either, can you?"

He gazed at her so solemnly and yearningly that she was moved by her sympathy for him, and in order to assuage his depression added: "No, I don't want you to do that, dear. You know I don't. But what am I to do?" She laid a soft and pleading hand on the back of one of Clyde's thin, long and nervous ones.

"I'll tell you what, though," she went on after a period of reflection, "I have a sister living in Homer, New York. That's about thirty-five miles north of here. I might say I was going up there some Saturday afternoon or Sunday. She's been writing me to come up, but I hadn't thought of it before. But I might go—that is—I might——"

"Oh, why not do that?" exclaimed Clyde eagerly. "That's fine! A good idea!"

"Let me see," she added, ignoring his exclamation. "If I remember right you have to go to Fonda first, then change cars there. But I could leave here any time on the trolley and there are only two trains a day from Fonda, one at two, and one at seven on Saturday. So I might leave here any time before two, you see, and then if I didn't make the two o'clock train, it would be all right, wouldn't it? I could go on the seven. And you could be over there, or meet me on the way, just so no one here saw us. Then I could go on and you could come back. I could arrange that with Agnes, I'm sure. I would have to write her."

"How about all the time between then and now, though?" he queried peevishly. "It's a long time till then, you know."

"Well, I'll have to see what I can think of, but I'm not sure, dear. I'll have to see. And you think too. But I ought to be going back now," she added nervously. She at once arose, causing Clyde to rise, too, and consult his watch, thereby discovering that it was already near ten.

"But what about us!" he continued persistently. "Why couldn't you pretend next Sunday that you're going to some other church than yours and meet me somewhere instead? Would they have to know?"

At once Clyde noted Roberta's face darken slightly, for here he was encroaching upon something that was still too closely identified with her early youth and convictions to permit infringement.

"Hump, uh," she replied quite solemnly. "I wouldn't want to do that. I wouldn't feel right about it. And it wouldn't be right, either."

Immediately Clyde sensed that he was treading on dangerous ground and withdrew the suggestion because he did not care to offend or frighten her in any way. "Oh, well. Just as you say. I only thought since you don't seem to be able to think of any other way."

"No, no, dear," she pleaded softly, because she noted that he felt that she might be offended. "It's all right, only I wouldn't want to do that. I couldn't."

Clyde shook his head. A recollection of his own youthful inhibitions caused him to feel that perhaps it was not right for him to have suggested it.

They returned in the direction of Taylor Street without, apart from the proposed trip to Fonda, either having hit upon any definite solution. Instead, after kissing her again and again and just before letting her go, the best he could suggest was that both were to try and think of some way by which they could meet before, if possible. And she, after throwing her arms about his neck for a moment, ran east along Taylor Street, her little figure swaying in the moonlight.

However, apart from another evening meeting which was made possible by Roberta's announcing a second engagement with Mrs. Braley, there was no other encounter until the following Saturday when Roberta departed for Fonda. And Clyde, having ascertained the exact hour, left by the car ahead, and joined Roberta at the first station west. From that point on until evening, when she was compelled to take the seven o'clock train, they were unspeakably happy together, loitering near the little city comparatively strange to both.

For outside of Fonda a few miles they came to a pleasure park called Starlight where, in addition to a few clap-trap pleasure concessions such as a ring of captive aeroplanes, a Ferris wheel, a merry-go-round, an old mill and a dance floor, was a small lake with boats. It was after its fashion an idyllic spot with a little band-stand out on an island near the center of the lake and on the shore a grave and captive bear in a cage. Since coming to Lycurgus Roberta had not ventured to visit any of the rougher resorts near there, which were very much like

this, only much more strident. On sight of this both exclaimed: "Oh, look!" And Clyde added at once: "Let's get off
here, will you—shall we? What do you say? We're almost to
Fonda anyhow. And we can have more fun here."

At once they climbed down. And having disposed of her
bag for the time being, he led the way first to the stand of a
man who sold frankfurters. Then, since the merry-go-round
was in full blast, nothing would do but that Roberta should
ride with him. And in the gayest of moods, they climbed on,
and he placed her on a zebra, and then stood close in order
that he might keep his arm about her, and both try to catch
the brass ring. And as commonplace and noisy and gaudy as
it all was, the fact that at last he had her all to himself unseen,
and she him, was sufficient to evoke in both a kind of ecstasy
which was all out of proportion to the fragile, gimcrack scene.
Round and round they spun on the noisy, grinding machine,
surveying now a few idle pleasure seekers who were in boats
upon the lake, now some who were flying round in the gaudy
green and white captive aeroplanes or turning upward and
then down in the suspended cages of the Ferris wheel.

Both looked at the woods and sky beyond the lake; the
idlers and dancers in the dancing pavilion dreaming and
thrilling, and then suddenly Clyde asked: "You dance, don't
you, Roberta?"

"Why, no, I don't," she replied, a little sadly, for at the very
moment she had been looking at the happy dancers rather
ruefully and thinking how unfortunate it was that she had
never been allowed to dance. It might not be right or nice,
perhaps—her own church said it was not—but still, now that
they were here and in love like this—these others looked so
gay and happy—a pretty medley of colors moving round and
round in the green and brown frame—it did not seem so bad
to her. Why shouldn't people dance, anyway? Girls like herself
and boys like Clyde? Her younger brother and sister, in spite
of the views of her parents, were already declaring that when
the opportunity offered, they were going to learn.

"Oh, isn't that too bad!" he exclaimed, thinking how delightful it would be to hold Roberta in his arms. "We could
have such fun now if you could. I could teach you in a few
minutes if you wanted me to."

"I don't know about that," she replied quizzically, her eyes showing that his suggestion appealed to her. "I'm not so clever that way. And you know dancing isn't considered so very nice in my part of the country. And my church doesn't approve of it, either. And I know my parents wouldn't like me to."

"Oh, shucks," replied Clyde foolishly and gayly, "what nonsense, Roberta. Why, everybody dances these days or nearly everybody. How can you think there's anything wrong with it?"

"Oh, I know," replied Roberta oddly and quaintly, "maybe they do in your set. I know most of those factory girls do, of course. And I suppose where you have money and position, everything's right. But with a girl like me, it's different. I don't suppose your parents were as strict as mine, either."

"Oh, weren't they, though?" laughed Clyde who had not failed to catch the "your set"; also the "where you have money and position."

"Well, that's all you know about it," he went on. "They were as strict as yours and stricter, I'll bet. But I danced just the same. Why, there's no harm in it, Roberta. Come on, let me teach you. It's wonderful, really. Won't you, dearest?"

He put his arm around her and looked into her eyes and she half relented, quite weakened by her desire for him.

Just then the merry-go-round stopped and without any plan or suggestion they seemed instinctively to drift to the side of the pavilion where the dancers—not many but avid— were moving briskly around. Fox-trots and one-steps were being supplied by an orchestrelle of considerable size. At a turnstile, all the remaining portions of the pavilion being screened in, a pretty concessionaire was sitting and taking tickets—ten cents per dance per couple. But the color and the music and the motions of the dancers gliding rhythmically here and there quite seized upon both Clyde and Roberta.

The orchestrelle stopped and the dancers were coming out. But no sooner were they out than five-cent admission checks were once more sold for the new dance.

"I don't believe I can," pleaded Roberta, as Clyde led her to the ticket-stile. "I'm afraid I'm too awkward, maybe. I never danced, you know."

"You awkward, Roberta," he exclaimed. "Oh, how crazy. Why, you're as graceful and pretty as you can be. You'll see. You'll be a wonderful dancer."

Already he had paid the coin and they were inside.

Carried away by a bravado which was three-fourths her conception of him as a member of the Lycurgus upper crust and possessor of means and position, he led the way into a corner and began at once to illustrate the respective movements. They were not difficult and for a girl of Roberta's natural grace and zest, easy. Once the music started and Clyde drew her to him, she fell into the positions and steps without effort, and they moved rhythmically and instinctively together. It was the delightful sensation of being held by him and guided here and there that so appealed to her—the wonderful rhythm of his body coinciding with hers.

"Oh, you darling," he whispered. "Aren't you the dandy little dancer, though. You've caught on already. If you aren't the wonderful kid. I can hardly believe it."

They went about the floor once more, then a third time, before the music stopped and by the time it did, Roberta was lost in a sense of delight such as had never come to her before. To think she had been dancing! And it should be so wonderful! And with Clyde! He was so slim, graceful—quite the handsomest of any of the young men on the floor, she thought. And he, in turn, was now thinking that never had he known any one as sweet as Roberta. She was so gay and winsome and yielding. She would not try to work him for anything. And as for Sondra Finchley, well, she had ignored him and he might as well dismiss her from his mind—and yet even here, and with Roberta, he could not quite forget her.

At five-thirty when the orchestrelle was silenced for lack of customers and a sign reading "Next Concert 7.30" hung up, they were still dancing. After that they went for an ice-cream soda, then for something to eat, and by then, so swiftly had sped the time, it was necessary to take the very next car for the depot at Fonda.

As they neared this terminal, both Clyde and Roberta were full of schemes as to how they were to arrange for to-morrow. For Roberta would be coming back then and if she could arrange to leave her sister's a little early Sunday he could come over from Lycurgus to meet her. They could linger around Fonda until eleven at least, when the last train south from Homer was due. And pretending she had arrived on that they could then, assuming there was no one whom they knew on the Lycurgus car, journey to that city.

And as arranged so they met. And in the dark outlying streets of that city, walked and talked and planned, and Roberta told Clyde something—though not much—of her home life at Biltz.

But the great thing, apart from their love for each other and its immediate expression in kisses and embraces, was the how and where of further contacts. They must find some way, only, really, as Roberta saw it, she must be the one to find the way, and that soon. For while Clyde was obviously very impatient and eager to be with her as much as possible, still he did not appear to be very ready with suggestions—available ones.

But that, as she also saw, was not easy. For the possibility of another visit to her sister in Homer or her parents in Biltz was not even to be considered under a month. And apart from them what other excuses were there? New friends at the factory—the post-office—the library—the Y.W.C.A.—all suggestions of Clyde's at the moment. But these spelled but an hour or two together at best, and Clyde was thinking of other week-ends like this. And there were so few remaining summer week-ends.

# Chapter XIX

THE RETURN of Roberta and Clyde, as well as their outing together, was quite unobserved, as they thought. On the car from Fonda they recognized no one. And at the Newtons' Grace was already in bed. She merely awakened sufficiently to ask a few questions about the trip—and those were casual and indifferent. How was Roberta's sister? Had she stayed all day in Homer or had she gone to Biltz or Trippetts Mills? (Roberta explained that she had remained at her sister's.) She herself must be going up pretty soon to see her parents at Trippetts Mills. Then she fell asleep.

But at dinner the next night the Misses Opal Feliss and Olive Pope, who had been kept from the breakfast table by a too late return from Fonda and the very region in which Roberta had spent Saturday afternoon, now seated themselves and at once, as Roberta entered, interjected a few genial and well-meant but, in so far as Roberta was concerned, decidedly troubling observations.

"Oh, there you are! Look who's back from Starlight Park. Howja like the dancing over there, Miss Alden? We saw you, but you didn't see us." And before Roberta had time to think what to reply, Miss Feliss had added: "We tried to get your eye, but you couldn't see any one but him, I guess. I'll say you dance swell."

At once Roberta, who had never been on very intimate terms with either of these girls and who had neither the effrontery nor the wit to extricate herself from so swift and complete and so unexpected an exposure, flushed. She was all but speechless and merely stared, bethinking her at once that she had explained to Grace that she was at her sister's all day. And opposite sat Grace, looking directly at her, her lips slightly parted as though she would exclaim: "Well, of all things! And dancing! A man!" And at the head of the table, George Newton, thin and meticulous and curious, his sharp eyes and nose and pointed chin now turned in her direction.

But on the instant, realizing that she must say something, Roberta replied: "Oh, yes, that's so. I did go over there for a little while. Some friends of my sister's were coming over and I went with them." She was about to add, "We didn't stay very long," but stopped herself. For at that moment a certain fighting quality which she had inherited from her mother, and which had asserted itself in the case of Grace before this, now came to her rescue. After all, why shouldn't she be at Starlight Park if she chose? And what right had the Newtons or Grace or anyone else to question her for that matter? She was paying her way. Nevertheless, as she realized, she had been caught in a deliberate lie and all because she lived here and was constantly being questioned and looked after in regard to her very least move. Miss Pope added curiously, "I don't suppose he's a Lycurgus boy. I don't remember ever seeing him around here."

"No, he isn't from here," returned Roberta shortly and coldly, for by now she was fairly quivering with the realization that she had been caught in a falsehood before Grace. Also that Grace would resent intensely this social secrecy and desertion of her. At once she felt as though she would like to get up from the table and leave and never return. But instead she did her best to compose herself, and now gave the two girls with whom she had never been familiar, a steady look. At the same time she looked at Grace and Mr. Newton with defiance. If anything more were said she proposed to give a fictitious name or two—friends of her brother-in-law in Homer, or better yet to refuse to give any information whatsoever. Why should she?

Nevertheless, as she learned later that evening, she was not to be spared the refusing of it. Grace, coming to their room immediately afterward, reproached her with: "I thought you said you stayed out at your sister's all the time you were gone?"

"Well, what if I did say it?" replied Roberta defiantly and even bitterly, but without a word in extenuation, for her thought was now that unquestionably Grace was pretending to catechize her on moral grounds, whereas in reality the real source of her anger and pique was that Roberta was slipping away from and hence neglecting her.

"Well, you don't have to lie to me in order to go anywhere or see anybody without me in the future. I don't want to go

with you. And what's more I don't want to know where you
go or who you go with. But I do wish you wouldn't tell me
one thing and then have George and Mary find out that it
ain't so, and that you're just trying to slip away from me or
that I'm lying to them in order to protect myself. I don't
want you to put me in that position."

She was very hurt and sad and contentious and Roberta
could see for herself that there was no way out of this trying
situation other than to move. Grace was a leech a hanger-
on. She had no life of her own and could contrive none. As
long as she was anywhere near her she would want to devote
herself to her—to share her every thought and mood with
her. And yet if she told her about Clyde she would be
shocked and critical and would unquestionably eventually
turn on her or even expose her. So she merely replied: "Oh,
well, have it that way if you want to. I don't care. I don't propose to tell anything unless I choose to."

And at once Grace conceived the notion that Roberta did
not like her any more and would have nothing to do with her.
She arose immediately and walked out of the room—her head
very high and her spine very stiff. And Roberta, realizing that
she had made an enemy of her, now wished that she was out
of here. They were all too narrow here anyway. They would
never understand or tolerate this clandestine relationship with
Clyde—so necessary to him apparently, as he had explained—
so troublesome and even disgraceful to her from one point of
view, and yet so precious. She did love him, so very, very
much. And she must now find some way to protect herself
and him—move to another room.

But that in this instance required almost more courage and
decision than she could muster. The anomalous and unprotected nature of a room where one was not known. The look
of it. Subsequent explanation to her mother and sister maybe.
Yet to remain here after this was all but impossible, too, for
the attitude of Grace as well as the Newtons—particularly
Mrs. Newton, Grace's sister—was that of the early Puritans or
Friends who had caught a "brother" or "sister" in a great sin.
She was dancing—and secretly! There was the presence of
that young man not quite adequately explained by her trip
home, to say nothing of her presence at Starlight Park. Be-

sides, in Roberta's mind was the thought that under such definite espionage as must now follow, to say nothing of the unhappy and dictatorial attitude of Grace, she would have small chance to be with Clyde as much as she now most intensely desired. And accordingly, after two days of unhappy thought and then a conference with Clyde who was all for her immediate independence in a new room where she would not be known or spied upon, she proceeded to take an hour or two off; and having fixed upon the southeast section of the city as one most likely to be free from contact with either the Newtons or those whom thus far she had encountered at the Newtons', she inquired there, and after little more than an hour's search found one place which pleased her. This was in an old brick house in Elm Street occupied by an upholsterer and his wife and two daughters, one a local milliner and another still in school. The room offered was on the ground floor to the right of a small front porch and overlooking the street. A door off this same porch gave into a living room which separated this room from the other parts of the house and permitted ingress and egress without contact with any other portion of the house. And since she was still moved to meet Clyde clandestinely this as she now saw was important.

Besides, as she gathered from her one conversation with Mrs. Gilpin, the mother of this family, the character of this home was neither so strict nor inquisitive as that of the Newtons. Mrs. Gilpin was large, passive, cleanly, not so very alert and about fifty. She informed Roberta that as a rule she didn't care to take boarders or roomers at all, since the family had sufficient means to go on. However, since the family scarcely ever used the front room, which was rather set off from the remainder of the house, and since her husband did not object, she had made up her mind to rent it. And again she preferred some one who worked like Roberta—a girl, not a man—and one who would be glad to have her breakfast and dinner along with her family. Since she asked no questions as to her family or connections, merely looking at her interestedly and seeming to be favorably impressed by her appearance, Roberta gathered that here were no such standards as prevailed at the Newtons.

And yet what qualms in connection with the thought of

moving thus. For about this entire clandestine procedure there hung, as she saw it, a sense of something untoward and even sinful, and then on top of it all, quarreling and then breaking with Grace Marr, her one girl friend here thus far, and the Newtons on account of it, when, as she well knew, it was entirely due to Grace that she was here at all. Supposing her parents or her sister in Homer should hear about this through some one whom Grace knew and think strangely of her going off by herself in Lycurgus in this way? Was it right? Was it possible that she could do things like this—and so soon after her coming here? She was beginning to feel as though her hitherto impeccable standards were crumbling.

And yet there was Clyde now. Could she give him up?

After many emotional aches she decided that she could not. And accordingly after paying a deposit and arranging to occupy the room within the next few days, she returned to her work and after dinner the same evening announced to Mrs. Newton that she was going to move. Her premeditated explanation was that recently she had been thinking of having her younger brother and sister come and live with her and since one or both were likely to come soon, she thought it best to prepare for them.

And the Newtons, as well as Grace, feeling that this was all due to the new connections which Roberta had recently been making and which were tending to alienate her from Grace, were now content to see her go. Plainly she was beginning to indulge in a type of adventure of which they could not approve. Also it was plain that she was not going to prove as useful to Grace as they had at first imagined. Possibly she knew what she was doing. But more likely she was being led astray by notions of a good time not consistent with the reserved life led by her at Trippetts Mills.

And Roberta herself, once having made this move and settled herself in this new atmosphere (apart from the fact that it gave her much greater freedom in connection with Clyde) was dubious as to her present course. Perhaps—perhaps—she had moved hastily and in anger and might be sorry. Still she had done it now, and it could not be helped. So she proposed to try it for a while.

To salve her own conscience more than anything else, she

at once wrote her mother and her sister a very plausible version of why she had been compelled to leave the Newtons.
Grace had grown too possessive, domineering and selfish. It
had become unendurable. However, her mother need not
worry. She was satisfactorily placed. She had a room to herself
and could now entertain Tom and Emily or her mother or
Agnes, in case they should ever visit her here. And she would
be able to introduce them to the Gilpins whom she proceeded to describe.

Nevertheless, her underlying thought in connection with
all this, in so far as Clyde and his great passion for her was
concerned—and hers for him—was that she was indeed trifling with fire and perhaps social disgrace into the bargain.
For, although consciously at this time she was scarcely willing
to face the fact that this room—its geometric position in relation to the rest of the house—had been of the greatest import
to her at the time she first saw it, yet subconsciously she knew
it well enough. The course she was pursuing was dangerous—
that she knew. And yet how, as she now so often asked herself
at moments when she was confronted by some desire which
ran counter to her sense of practicability and social morality,
was she to do?

# Chapter XX

H OWEVER, as both Roberta and Clyde soon found, after several weeks in which they met here and there, such spots as could be conveniently reached by interurban lines, there were still drawbacks and the principal of these related to the attitude of both Roberta and Clyde in regard to this room, and what, if any, use of it was to be made by them jointly. For in spite of the fact that thus far Clyde had never openly agreed with himself that his intentions in relation to Roberta were in any way different to those normally entertained by any youth toward any girl for whom he had a conventional social regard, still, now that she had moved into this room, there was that ineradicable and possibly censurable, yet very human and almost unescapable, desire for something more—the possibility of greater and greater intimacy with and control of Roberta and her thoughts and actions in everything so that in the end she would be entirely his. But how *his*? By way of marriage and the ordinary conventional and durable existence which thereafter must ordinarily ensue? He had never said so to himself thus far. For in flirting with her or any girl of a lesser social position than that of the Griffiths here (Sondra Finchley, Bertine Cranston, for instance) he would not—and that largely due to the attitude of his newly-found relatives, their very high position in this city—have deemed marriage advisable. And what would they think if they should come to know? For socially, as he saw himself now, if not before coming here, he was supposed to be above the type of Roberta and should of course profit by that notion. Besides there were all those that knew him here, at least to speak to. On the other hand, because of the very marked pull that her temperament had for him, he had not been able to say for the time being that she was not worthy of him or that he might not be happy in case it were possible or advisable for him to marry her.

And there was another thing now that tended to complicate matters. And that was that fall with its chilling winds and frosty nights was drawing near. Already it was near October first and most of those out-of-door resorts which, up to the middle of September at least, had provided diversion, and that at a fairly safe distance from Lycurgus, were already closed for the season. And dancing, except in the halls of the near-by cities and which, because of a mood of hers in regard to them, were unacceptable, was also for the time being done away with. As for the churches, moving pictures, and restaurants of Lycurgus, how under the circumstances, owing to Clyde's position here, could they be seen in them? They could not, as both reasoned between them. And so now, while her movements were unrestrained, there was no place to go unless by some readjustment of their relations he might be permitted to call on her at the Gilpins'. But that, as he knew, she would not think of and, at first, neither had he the courage to suggest it.

However they were at a street-end one early October night about six weeks after she had moved to her new room. The stars were sharp. The air cool. The leaves were beginning to turn. Roberta had returned to a three-quarter green-and-cream-striped winter coat that she wore at this season of the year. Her hat was brown, trimmed with brown leather and of a design that became her. There had been kisses over and over—that same fever that had been dominating them continuously since first they met—only more pronounced if anything.

"It's getting cold, isn't it?" It was Clyde who spoke. And it was eleven o'clock and chill.

"Yes, I should say it is. I'll soon have to get a heavier coat."

"I don't see how we are to do from now on, do you? There's no place to go any more much, and it won't be very pleasant walking the streets this way every night. You don't suppose we could fix it so I could call on you at the Gilpins' once in a while, do you? It isn't the same there now as it was at the Newtons'."

"Oh, I know, but then they use their sitting room every night nearly until ten-thirty or eleven. And besides their two girls are in and out all hours up to twelve, anyhow, and they're in there often. I don't see how I can. Besides, I thought you said you didn't want to have any one see you with me that way, and if you came there I couldn't help introducing you."

"Oh, but I don't mean just that way," replied Clyde audaciously and yet with the feeling that Roberta was much too squeamish and that it was high time she was taking a somewhat more liberal attitude toward him if she cared for him as much as she appeared to: "Why wouldn't it be all right for me to stop in for a little while? They wouldn't need to know, would they?" He took out his watch and discovered with the aid of a match that it was eleven-thirty. He showed the time to her. "There wouldn't be anybody there now, would there?"

She shook her head in opposition. The thought not only terrified but sickened her. Clyde was getting very bold to even suggest anything like that. Besides this suggestion embodied in itself all the secret fears and compelling moods which hitherto, although actual in herself, she was still unwilling to face. There was something sinful, low, dreadful about it. She would not. That was one thing sure. At the same time within her was that overmastering urge of repressed and feared desire now knocking loudly for recognition.

"No, no, I can't let you do that. It wouldn't be right. I don't want to. Some one might see us. Somebody might know you." For the moment the moral repulsion was so great that unconsciously she endeavored to relinquish herself from his embrace.

Clyde sensed how deep was this sudden revolt. All the more was he flagellated by the desire for possession of that which now he half feared to be unobtainable. A dozen seductive excuses sprang to his lips. "Oh, who would be likely to see us anyhow, at this time of night? There isn't any one around. Why shouldn't we go there for a few moments if we want to? No one would be likely to hear us. We needn't talk so loud. There isn't any one on the street, even. Let's walk by the house and see if anybody is up."

Since hitherto she had not permitted him to come within half a block of the house, her protest was not only nervous but vigorous. Nevertheless on this occasion Clyde was proving a little rebellious and Roberta, standing somewhat in awe of him as her superior, as well as her lover, was unable to prevent their walking within a few feet of the house where they stopped. Except for a barking dog there was not a sound to be heard anywhere. And in the house no light was visible.

"See, there's no one up," protested Clyde reassuringly. "Why shouldn't we go in for a little while if we want to? Who will know? We needn't make any noise. Besides, what is wrong with it? Other people do it. It isn't such a terrible thing for a girl to take a fellow to her room if she wants to for a little while."

"Oh, isn't it? Well, maybe not in your set. But I know what's right and I don't think that's right and I won't do it."

At once, as she said this, Roberta's heart gave a pained and weakening throb, for in saying so much she had exhibited more individuality and defiance than ever he had seen or that she fancied herself capable of in connection with him. It terrified her not a little. Perhaps he would not like her so much now if she were going to talk like that.

His mood darkened immediately. Why did she want to act so? She was too cautious, too afraid of anything that spelled a little life or pleasure. Other girls were not like that,—Rita, those girls at the factory. She pretended to love him. She did not object to his holding her in his arms and kissing her under a tree at the end of the street. But when it came to anything slightly more private or intimate, she could not bring herself to agree. What kind of a girl was she, anyhow? What was the use of pursuing her? Was this to be another case of Hortense Briggs with all her wiles and evasions? Of course Roberta was in no wise like her, but still she was so stubborn.

Although she could not see his face she knew he was angry and quite for the first time in this way.

"All right, then, if you don't want to, you don't have to," came his words and with decidedly a cold ring to them. "There are other places I can go. I notice you never want to do anything I want to do, though. I'd like to know how you think we're to do. We can't walk the streets every night." His tone was gloomy and foreboding—more contentious and bitter than at any time ever between them. And his references to other places shocked and frightened Roberta—so much so that instantly almost her own mood changed. Those other girls in his own world that no doubt he saw from time to time! Those other girls at the factory who were always trying to make eyes at him! She had seen them trying, and often. That Ruza Nikoforitch—as coarse as she was, but pretty, too.

And that Flora Brandt! And Martha Bordaloue—ugh! To think that any one as nice as he should be pursued by such wretches as those. However, because of that, she was fearful lest he would think her too difficult—some one without the experience or daring to which he, in his superior world, was accustomed, and so turn to one of those. Then she would lose him. The thought terrified her. Immediately from one of defiance her attitude changed to one of pleading persuasion.

"Oh, please, Clyde, don't be mad with me now, will you? You know that I would if I could. I can't do anything like that here. Can't you see? You know that. Why, they'd be sure to find out. And how would you feel if some one were to see us or recognize you?" In a pleading way she put one hand on his arm, then about his waist and he could feel that in spite of her sharp opposition the moment before, she was very much concerned—painfully so. "Please don't ask me to," she added in a begging tone.

"Well, what did you want to leave the Newtons for then?" he asked sullenly. "I can't see where else we can go now if you won't let me come to see you once in a while. We can't go any place else."

The thought gave Roberta pause. Plainly this relationship was not to be held within conventional lines. At the same time she did not see how she could possibly comply. It was too unconventional—too unmoral—bad.

"I thought we took it," she said weakly and placatively, "just so that we could go places on Saturday and Sunday."

"But where can we go Saturday and Sunday now? Everything's closed."

Again Roberta was checked by these unanswerable complexities which beleaguered them both and she exclaimed futilely, "Oh, I wish I knew what to do."

"Oh, it would be easy enough if you wanted to do it, but that's always the way with you, you don't want to."

She stood there, the night wind shaking the drying whispering leaves. Distinctly the problem in connection with him that she had been fearing this long while was upon her. Could she possibly, with all the right instruction that she had had, now do as he suggested. She was pulled and swayed by contending forces within herself, strong and urgent in either case.

In the one instance, however painful it was to her moral and social mood, she was moved to comply—in another to reject once and for all, any such, as she saw it, bold and unnatural suggestion. Nevertheless, in spite of the latter and because of her compelling affection she could not do other than deal tenderly and pleadingly with him.

"I can't, Clyde, I can't. I would if I could but I can't. It wouldn't be right. I would if I could make myself, but I can't." She looked up into his face, a pale oval in the dark, trying to see if he would not see, sympathize, be moved in her favor. However, irritated by this plainly definite refusal, he was not now to be moved. All this, as he saw it, smacked of that long series of defeats which had accompanied his attentions to Hortense Briggs. He was not going to stand for anything now like that, you bet. If this was the way she was going to act, well, let her act so—but not with him. He could get plenty of girls now—lots of them—who would treat him better than this.

At once, and with an irritated shrug of the shoulders, as she now saw, he turned and started to leave her, saying as he did so, "Oh, that's all right, if that's the way you feel about it." And Roberta dumfounded and terrified, stood there.

"Please don't go, Clyde. Please don't leave me," she exclaimed suddenly and pathetically, her defiance and courage undergoing a deep and sad change. "I don't want you to. I love you so, Clyde. I would if I could. You know that."

"Oh, yes, I know, but you needn't tell me that" (it was his experience with Hortense and Rita that was prompting him to this attitude). With a twist he released his body from her arm and started walking briskly down the street in the dark.

And Roberta, stricken by this sudden development which was so painful to both, called, "Clyde!" And then ran after him a little way, eager that he should pause and let her plead with him more. But he did not return. Instead he went briskly on. And for the moment it was all she could do to keep from following him and by sheer force, if need be, restrain him. Her Clyde! And she started running in his direction a little, but as suddenly stopped, checked for the moment by the begging, pleading, compromising attitude in which she, for the first time, found herself. For on the one hand all her conventional training was now urging her to stand firm—not to belittle herself in this way—whereas on the other, all her desires for love, understanding, companionship, urged her to run after him before it was too late, and he was gone. His beautiful face, his beautiful hands. His eyes. And still the receding echo of his feet. And yet so binding were the conventions which had been urged upon her up to this time that, though suffering horribly, a balance between the two forces was struck, and she paused, feeling that she could neither go forward nor stand still—understand or endure this sudden rift in their wonderful friendship.

Pain constricted her heart and whitened her lips. She stood there numb and silent—unable to voice anything, even the name Clyde which persistently arose as a call in her throat. Instead she was merely thinking, "Oh, Clyde, please don't go, Clyde. Oh, please don't go." And he was already out of hearing, walking briskly and grimly on, the click and echo of his receding steps falling less and less clearly on her suffering ears.

It was the first flashing, blinding, bleeding stab of love for her.

# Chapter XXI

T HE STATE of Roberta's mind for that night is not easily to be described. For here was true and poignant love, and in youth true and poignant love is difficult to withstand. Besides it was coupled with the most stirring and grandiose illusions in regard to Clyde's local material and social condition—illusions which had little to do with anything he had done to build up, but were based rather on conjecture and gossip over which he had no control. And her own home, as well as her personal situation was so unfortunate—no promise of any kind save in his direction. And here she was quarreling with him—sending him away angry. On the other hand was he not beginning to push too ardently toward those troublesome and no doubt dreadful liberties and familiarities which her morally trained conscience would not permit her to look upon as right? How was she to do now? What to say?

Now it was that she said to herself in the dark of her room, after having slowly and thoughtfully undressed and noiselessly crept into the large, old-fashioned bed. "No, I won't do that. I mustn't. I can't. I will be a bad girl if I do. I should not do that for him even though he does want me to, and should threaten to leave me forever in case I refuse. He should be ashamed to ask me." And at the very same moment, or the next, she would be asking herself what else under the circumstances they were to do. For most certainly Clyde was at least partially correct in his contention that they had scarcely anywhere else they could go and not be recognized. How unfair was that rule of the company. And no doubt apart from that rule, the Griffiths would think it beneath him to be troubling with her, as would no doubt the Newtons and the Gilpins for that matter, if they should hear and know who he was. And if this information came to their knowledge it would injure him and her. And she would not do anything that would injure him—never.

One thing that occurred to her at this point was that she should get a place somewhere else so that this problem should be solved—a problem which at the moment seemed to

337

have little to do with the more immediate and intimate one of desiring to enter her room. But that would mean that she would not see him any more all day long—only at night. And then not every night by any means. And that caused her to lay aside this thought of seeking another place.

At the same time as she now meditated the dawn would come to-morrow and there would be Clyde at the factory. And supposing that he should not speak to her nor she to him. Impossible! Ridiculous! Terrible! The mere thought brought her to a sitting posture in bed, where distractedly a vision of Clyde looking indifferently and coldly upon her came to her.

On the instant she was on her feet and had turned on the one incandescent globe which dangled from the center of the room. She went to the mirror hanging above the old walnut dresser in the corner and stared at herself. Already she imagined she could see dark rings under her eyes. She felt numb and cold and now shook her head in a helpless and distracted way. He couldn't be that mean. He couldn't be that cruel to her now—could he? Oh, if he but knew how difficult—how impossible was the thing he was asking of her! Oh, if the day would only come so that she could see his face again! Oh, if it were only another night so that she could take his hands in hers—his arm—feel his arms about her.

"Clyde, Clyde," she exclaimed half aloud, "you wouldn't do that to me, would you—you couldn't."

She crossed to an old, faded and somewhat decrepit over-stuffed chair which stood in the center of the room beside a small table whereon lay some nondescript books and magazines—the *Saturday Evening Post*, *Munsey's*, the *Popular Science Monthly*, *Bebe's Garden Seeds*, and to escape most distracting and searing thoughts, sat down, her chin in her hands, her elbows planted on her knees. But the painful thoughts continuing and a sense of chill overtaking her, she took a comforter off the bed and folded it about her, then opened the seed catalogue—only to throw it down.

"No, no, no, he couldn't do that to me, he wouldn't." She must not let him. Why, he had told her over and over that he was crazy about her—madly in love with her. They had been to all these wonderful places together.

And now, without any real consciousness of her movements, she was moving from the chair to the edge of the bed, sitting with elbows on knees and chin in hands; or she was before the mirror or peering restlessly out into the dark to see if there were any trace of day. And at six, and six-thirty when the light was just breaking and it was nearing time to dress, she was still up—in the chair, on the edge of the bed, in the corner before the mirror.

But she had reached but one definite conclusion and that was that in some way she must arrange not to have Clyde leave her. That must not be. There must be something that she could say or do that would cause him to love her still— even if, even if—well, even if she must let him stop in here or somewhere from time to time—some other room in some other rooming house maybe, where she could arrange in some way beforehand—say that he was her brother or something.

But the mood that dominated Clyde was of a different nature. To have understood it correctly, the full measure and obstinacy and sullen contentiousness that had suddenly generated, one would have had to return to Kansas City and the period in which he had been so futilely dancing attendance upon Hortense Briggs. Also his having been compelled to give up Rita,—yet to no end. For, although the present conditions and situation were different, and he had no moral authority wherewith to charge Roberta with any such unfair treatment as Hortense had meted out to him, still there was this other fact that girls—all of them—were obviously stubborn and self-preservative, always setting themselves apart from and even above the average man and so wishing to compel him to do a lot of things for them without their wishing to do anything in return. And had not Ratterer always told him that in so far as girls were concerned he was more or less of a fool—too easy—too eager to show his hand and let them know that he was struck on them. Whereas, as Ratterer had explained, Clyde possessed the looks—the "goods"—and why should he always be trailing after girls unless they wanted him very much. And this thought and compliment had impressed him very much at that time. Only because of the fiascos in connection with Hortense and Rita he was more earnest now. Yet here he was again in danger of repeating or bringing upon himself what had befallen him in the case of Hortense and Rita.

At the same time he was not without the self-incriminating thought that in seeking this, most distinctly he was driving toward a relationship which was not legitimate and that would prove dangerous in the future. For, as he now darkly and vaguely thought, if he sought a relationship which her prejudices and her training would not permit her to look upon as anything but evil, was he not thereby establishing in some form a claim on her part to some consideration from him in the future which it might not be so easy for him to ignore? For after all he was the aggressor—not she. And because of this, and whatever might follow in connection with it, might not she be in a position to demand more from him than he might be willing to give? For was it his intention to marry her? In the back of his mind there lurked something which even now assured him that he would never desire to marry her—could not in the face of his high family connections here. Therefore should he proceed to demand—or should he not? And if he did, could he avoid that which would preclude any claim in the future?

He did not thus so distinctly voice his inmost feelings to himself, but relatively of such was their nature. Yet so great was the temperamental and physical enticement of Roberta that in spite of a warning nudge or mood that seemed to hint that it was dangerous for him to persist in his demand, he kept saying to himself that unless she would permit him to her room, he would not have anything more to do with her, the desire for her being all but overpowering.

This contest which every primary union between the sexes, whether with or without marriage implies, was fought out the next day in the factory. And yet without a word on either side. For Clyde, although he considered himself to be deeply in love with Roberta, was still not so deeply involved but that a naturally selfish and ambitious and seeking disposition would in this instance stand its ground and master any impulse. And he was determined to take the attitude of one who had been injured and was determined not to be friends any more or yield in any way unless some concession on her part, such as would appease him, was made.

And in consequence he came into the stamping department

that morning with the face and air of one who was vastly pre-occupied with matters which had little, if anything, to do with what had occurred the night before. Yet, being far from certain that this attitude on his part was likely to lead to anything but defeat, he was inwardly depressed and awry. For, after all, the sight of Roberta, freshly arrived, and although pale and distrait, as charming and energetic as ever, was not calculated to assure him of any immediate or even ultimate victory. And knowing her as well as he thought he did, by now, he was but weakly sustained by the thought that she might yield.

He looked at her repeatedly when she was not looking. And when in turn she looked at him repeatedly, but only at first when he was not looking, later when she felt satisfied that his eyes, whether directly bent on her or not, must be encompassing her, still no trace of recognition could she extract. And now to her bitter disappointment, not only did he choose to ignore her, but quite for the first time since they had been so interested in each other, he professed to pay, if not exactly conspicuous at least noticeable and intentional attention to those other girls who were always so interested in him and who always, as she had been constantly imagining, were but waiting for any slight overture on his part, to yield themselves to him in any way that he might dictate.

Now he was looking over the shoulder of Ruza Niko-foritch, her plump face with its snub nose and weak chin turned engagingly toward him, and he commenting on something not particularly connected with the work in hand apparently, for both were idly smiling. Again, in a little while, he was by the side of Martha Bordaloue, her plump French shoulders and arms bare to the pits next to his. And for all her fleshly solidity and decidedly foreign flavor, there was still enough about her which most men would like. And with her Clyde was attempting to jest, too.

And later it was Flora Brandt, the very sensuous and not unpleasing American girl whom Roberta had seen Clyde cultivating from time to time. Yet, even so, she had never been willing to believe that he might become interested in any of these. Not Clyde, surely.

And yet he could not see her at all now—could not find time to say a single word, although all these pleasant words and gay looks for all these others. Oh, how bitter! Oh, how cruel! And how utterly she despised those other girls with their oglings and their open attempts to take him from her. Oh, how terrible. Surely he must be very opposed to her now—otherwise he could not do this, and especially after all that had been between them—the love—the kisses.

The hours dragged for both, and with as much poignance for Clyde as for Roberta. For his was a feverish, urgent disposition where his dreams were concerned, and could ill brook the delay or disappointments that are the chief and outstanding characteristics of the ambitions of men, whatever their nature. He was tortured hourly by the thought that he was to lose Roberta or that to win her back he would have to succumb to her wishes.

And on her part she was torn, not so much by the question as to whether she would have to yield in this matter (for by now that was almost the least of her worries), but whether, once so yielding, Clyde would be satisfied with just some form of guarded social contact in the room—or not. And so continue on the strength of that to be friends with her. For more than this she would not grant—never. And yet—this suspense. The misery of his indifference. She could scarcely endure it from minute to minute, let alone from hour to hour, and finally in an agony of dissatisfaction with herself at having brought all this on herself, she retired to the rest room at about three in the afternoon and there with the aid of a piece of paper found on the floor and a small bit of pencil which she had, she composed a brief note:

"Please, Clyde, don't be mad at me, will you? Please don't. Please look at me and speak to me, won't you? I'm so sorry about last night, really I am—terribly. And I must see you to-night at the end of Elm Street at 8.30 if you can, will you? I have something to tell you. Please do come. And please do look at me and tell me you will, even though you are angry. You won't be sorry. I love you so. You know I do.
                              "Your sorrowful,
                                        "ROBERTA."

And in the spirit of one who is in agonized search for an opiate, she folded up the paper and returning to the room, drew close to Clyde's desk. He was before it at the time, bent over some slips. And quickly as she passed she dropped the paper between his hands. He looked up instantly, his dark eyes still hard at the moment with the mingled pain and unrest and dissatisfaction and determination that had been upon him all day, and noting Roberta's retreating figure as well as the note, he at once relaxed, a wave of puzzled satisfaction as well as delight instantly filling them. He opened it and read. And as instantly his body was suffused with a warm and yet very weakening ray.

And Roberta in turn, having reached her table and paused to note if by any chance any one had observed her, now looked cautiously about, a strained and nervous look in her eyes. But seeing Clyde looking directly at her, his eyes filled with a conquering and yet yielding light and a smile upon his lips, and his head nodding a happy assent, she as suddenly experienced a dizzying sensation, as though her hitherto constricted blood, detained by a constricted heart and constricted nerves, were as suddenly set free. And all the dry marshes and cracked and parched banks of her soul—the dry rivulets and streams and lakes of misery that seemed to dot her being—were as instantly flooded with this rich upwelling force of life and love.

He would meet her. They would meet to-night. He would put his arms around her and kiss her as before. She would be able to look in his eyes. They would not quarrel any more—oh, never if she could help it.

# Chapter XXII

THE WONDER and delight of a new and more intimate form of contact, of protest gainsaid, of scruples overcome! Days, when both, having struggled in vain against the greater intimacy which each knew that the other was desirous of yielding to, and eventually so yielding, looked forward to the approaching night with an eagerness which was as a fever embodying a fear. For with what qualms—what protests on the part of Roberta; what determination, yet not without a sense of evil—seduction—betrayal, on the part of Clyde. Yet the thing once done, a wild convulsive pleasure motivating both. Yet, not without, before all this, an exaction on the part of Roberta to the effect that never—come what might (the natural consequences of so wild an intimacy strong in her thoughts) would he desert her, since without his aid she would be helpless. Yet, with no direct statement as to marriage. And he, so completely overcome and swayed by his desire, thoughtlessly protesting that he never would—never. She might depend on that, at least, although even then there was no thought in his mind of marriage. He would not do that. Yet nights and nights—all scruples for the time being abandoned, and however much by day Roberta might brood and condemn herself—when each yielded to the other completely. And dreamed thereafter, recklessly and wildly, of the joy of it—wishing from day to day for the time being that the long day might end—that the concealing, rewarding feverish night were at hand.

And Clyde feeling, and not unlike Roberta, who was firmly and even painfully convinced of it, that this was sin—deadly, mortal—since both his mother and father had so often emphasized that—the seducer—adulterer—who preys outside the sacred precincts of marriage. And Roberta, peering nervously into the blank future, wondering what—how, in any case, by any chance, Clyde should change, or fail her. Yet the night returning, her mood once more veering, and she as well as he hurrying to meet somewhere—only later, in the silence of the middle night, to slip into this unlighted room which was proving so much more of a Paradise than either might ever know again—so wild and unrecapturable is the fever of youth.

And—at times—and despite all his other doubts and fears, Clyde, because of this sudden abandonment by Roberta of herself to his desires, feeling for the first time, really, in all his feverish years, that at last he was a man of the world—one who was truly beginning to know women. And so taking to himself an air or manner that said as plainly as might have any words—"Behold I am no longer the inexperienced, neglected simpleton of but a few weeks ago, but an individual of import now—some one who knows something about life. What have any of these strutting young men, and gay, coaxing, flirting girls all about me, that I have not? And if I chose—were less loyal that I am—what might I not do?" And this was proving to him that the notion which Hortense Briggs, to say nothing of the more recent fiasco in connection with Rita had tended to build up in his mind, i.e.,—that he was either unsuccessful or ill-fated where girls were concerned was false. He was after all and despite various failures and inhibitions a youth of the Don Juan or Lothario stripe.

And if now Roberta was obviously willing to sacrifice herself for him in this fashion, must there not be others?

And this, in spite of the present indifference of the Griffiths, caused him to walk with even more of an air than had hitherto characterized him. Even though neither they nor any of those connected with them recognized him, still he looked at himself in his mirror from time to time with an assurance and admiration which before this he had never possessed. For now Roberta, feeling that her future was really dependent on his will and whim, had set herself to flatter him almost constantly, to be as obliging and convenient to him as possible. Indeed, according to her notion of the proper order of life, she was now his and his only, as much as any wife is ever to a husband, to do with as he wished.

And for a time therefore, Clyde forgot his rather neglected state here and was content to devote himself to her without thinking much of the future. The one thing that did trouble him at times was the thought that possibly, in connection with the original fear she had expressed to him, something might go wrong, which, considering her exclusive devotion to him, might prove embarrassing. At the same time he did not trouble to speculate too deeply as to that. He had Roberta now. These relations, in so far as either of them could see, or guess, were a dark secret. The pleasures of this left-handed honeymoon were at full tide. And the remaining brisk and often sunshiny and warm November and first December days passed—as in a dream, really—an ecstatic paradise of sorts in the very center of a humdrum conventional and petty and underpaid work-a-day world.

In the meantime the Griffiths had been away from the city since the middle of June and ever since their departure Clyde had been meditating upon them and all they represented in his life and that of the city. Their great house closed and silent, except for gardeners and an occasional chauffeur or servant visible as he walked from time to time past the place, was the same as a shrine to him, nearly—the symbol of that height to which by some turn of fate he might still hope to attain. For he had never quite been able to expel from his mind the thought that his future must in some way be identified with the grandeur that was here laid out before him.

Yet so far as the movements of the Griffiths family and their social peers outside Lycurgus were concerned, he knew little other than that which from time to time he had read in the society columns of the two local papers which almost obsequiously pictured the comings and goings of all those who were connected with the more important families of the city. At times, after reading these accounts he had pictured to himself, even when he was off somewhere with Roberta at some unheralded resort, Gilbert Griffiths racing in his big car, Bella, Bertine and Sondra dancing, canoeing in the moonlight, playing tennis, riding at some of the smart resorts where they were reported to be. The thing had had a bite and ache for him that was almost unendurable and had lit up for him at times and with overwhelming clarity this connection of his with Roberta. For after all, who was she? A factory girl! The daughter of parents who lived and worked on a farm and one who was compelled to work for her own living. Whereas he— he—if fortune would but favor him a little—! Was this to be the end of all his dreams in connection with his perspective superior life here?

So it was that at moments and in his darker moods, and especially after she had abandoned herself to him, his thoughts ran. She was not of his station, really—at least not of that of the Griffiths to which still he most eagerly aspired. Yet at the same time, whatever the mood generated by such items as he read in *The Star*, he would still return to Roberta, picturing her, since the other mood which had drawn him to her had by no means palled as yet, as delightful, precious, exceedingly worth-while from the point of view of beauty, pleasure, sweetness—the attributes and charms which best identify any object of delight.

But the Griffiths and their friends having returned to the city, and Lycurgus once more taken on that brisk, industrial and social mood which invariably characterized it for at least seven months in the year, he was again, and even more vigorously than before, intrigued by it. The beauty of the various houses along Wykeagy Avenue and its immediate tributaries! The unusual and intriguing sense of movement and life there so much in evidence. Oh, if he were but of it!

# Chapter XXIII

AND THEN, one November evening as Clyde was walking along Wykeagy Avenue, just west of Central, a portion of the locally celebrated avenue which, ever since he had moved to Mrs. Peyton's he was accustomed to traverse to and from his work, one thing did occur which in so far as he and the Griffiths were concerned was destined to bring about a chain of events which none of them could possibly have foreseen. At the time there was in his heart and mind that singing which is the inheritance of youth and ambition and which the dying of the old year, instead of depressing, seemed but to emphasize. He had a good position. He was respected here. Over and above his room and board he had not less than fifteen dollars a week to spend on himself and Roberta, an income which, while it did not parallel that which had been derived from the Green-Davidson or the Union League, was still not so involved with family miseries in the one place or personal loneliness in the other. And he had Roberta secretly devoted to him. And the Griffiths, thank goodness, did not and should not know anything of that, though just how in case of a difficulty it was to be avoided, he was not even troubling to think. His was a disposition which did not tend to load itself with more than the most immediate cares.

And although the Griffiths and their friends had not chosen to recognize him socially, still more and more all others who were not connected with local society and who knew of him, did. Only this very day, because the spring before he had been made a room-chief, perhaps, and Samuel Griffiths had recently paused and talked with him, no less an important personage than Mr. Rudolph Smillie, one of the several active vice-presidents, had asked him most cordially and casually whether he played golf, and if so, when spring came again, whether he might not be interested to join the Amoskeag, one of the two really important golf clubs within a half dozen miles of the city. Now, what could that mean, if not that Mr. Smillie was beginning to see him as a social possibility, and that he as well as many others about the factory, were becoming aware of him as some one who was of some importance to the Griffiths, if not the factory.

This thought, together with one other—that once more after dinner he was to see Roberta and in her room as early as eleven o'clock or even earlier—cheered him and caused him to step along most briskly and gayly. For, since having indulged in this secret adventure so many times, both were unconsciously becoming bolder. Not having been detected to date, they were of the notion that it was possible they might not be. Or if they were Clyde might be introduced as her brother or cousin for the moment, anyhow, in order to avoid immediate scandal. Later, to avoid danger of comment or subsequent detection, as both had agreed after some discussion, Roberta might have to move to some other place where the same routine was to be repeated. But that would be easy, or at least better than no freedom of contact. And with that Roberta had been compelled to agree.

However, on this occasion there came a contact and an interruption which set his thoughts careening in an entirely different direction. Reaching the first of the more important houses of Wykeagy Avenue, although he had not the slightest idea who lived there, he was gazing interestedly at the high wrought-iron fence, as well as the kempt lawn within, dimly illuminated by street lamps, and upon the surface of which he could detect many heaps of freshly fallen brown leaves being shaken and rolled by a winnowing and gamboling wind. It was all so starkly severe, placid, reserved, beautiful, as he saw it, that he was quite stirred by the dignity and richness of it. And as he neared the central gate, above which two lights were burning, making a circle of light about it, a closed car of great size and solidity stopped directly in front of it. And the chauffeur stepping down and opening the door, Clyde instantly recognized Sondra Finchley leaning forward in the car.

"Go around to the side entrance, David, and tell Miriam that I can't wait for her because I'm going over to the Trumbulls for dinner, but that I'll be back by nine. If she's not there, leave this note and hurry, will you?" The voice and manner were of that imperious and yet pleasing mode which had so intrigued him the spring before.

At the same time seeing, as she thought, Gilbert Griffiths

approaching along the sidewalk, she called, "Oh, hello. Walking to-night? If you want to wait a minute, you can ride out with me. I've just sent David in with a note. He won't be long."

Now Sondra Finchley, despite the fact that she was interested in Bella and the Griffiths' wealth and prestige in general was by no means as well pleased with Gilbert. He had been indifferent to her in the beginning when she had tried to cultivate him and he had remained so. He had wounded her pride. And to her, who was overflowing with vanity and self-conceit, this was the last offense, and she could not forgive him. She could not and would not brook the slightest trace of ego in another, and most especially the vain, cold, self-centered person of Bella's brother. He had too fine an opinion of himself, as she saw it, was one who was too bursting with vanity to be of service to anyone. "Hmp! That stick." It was so that she invariably thought of him. "Who does he think he is anyhow? He certainly does think he's a lot around here. You'd think he was a Rockefeller or a Morgan. And for my part I can't see where he's a bit interesting—any more. I like Bella. I think she's lovely. But that smarty. I guess he would like to have a girl wait on him. Well, not for me." Such in the main were the comments made by Sondra upon such reported acts and words of Gilbert as were brought to her by others.

And for his part, Gilbert, hearing of the gyrations, airs, and aspirations of Sondra from Bella from time to time, was accustomed to remark: "What, that little snip! Who does she think she is anyhow? If ever there was a conceited little nut! . . ."

However, so tightly were the social lines of Lycurgus drawn, so few the truly eligibles, that it was almost necessary and compulsory upon those "in" to make the best of such others as were "in." And so it was that she now greeted Gilbert as she thought. And as she moved over slightly from the door to make room for him, Clyde almost petrified by this unexpected recognition, and quite shaken out of his pose and self-contemplation, not being sure whether he had heard aright, now approached, his manner the epitome almost of a self-ingratiating and somewhat affectionate and wistful dog of high breeding and fine temperament.

"Oh, good evening," he exclaimed, removing his cap and bowing. "How are you?" while his mind was registering that this truly was the beautiful, the exquisite Sondra whom months before he had met at his uncle's, and concerning whose social activities during the preceding summer he had been reading in the papers. And now here she was as lovely as ever, seated in this beautiful car and addressing him, apparently. However, Sondra on the instant realizing that she had made a mistake and that it was not Gilbert, was quite embarrassed and uncertain for the moment just how to extricate herself from a situation which was a bit ticklish, to say the least.

"Oh, pardon me, you're Mr. Clyde Griffiths, I see now. It's my mistake. I thought you were Gilbert. I couldn't quite make you out in the light." She had for the moment an embarrassed and fidgety and halting manner, which Clyde noticed and which he saw implied that she had made a mistake that was not entirely flattering to him nor satisfactory to her. And this in turn caused him to become confused and anxious to retire.

"Oh, pardon me. But that's all right. I didn't mean to intrude. I thought . . ." He flushed and stepped back really troubled.

But now Sondra, seeing at once that Clyde was if anything much more attractive than his cousin and far more diffident, and obviously greatly impressed by her charms as well as her social state, unbent sufficiently to say with a charming smile: "But that's all right. Won't you get in, please, and let me take you where you are going. Oh, I wish you would. I will be so glad to take you."

For there was that in Clyde's manner the instant he learned that it was due to a mistake that he had been recognized which caused even her to understand that he was hurt, abashed and disappointed. His eyes took on a hurt look and there was a wavering, apologetic, sorrowful smile playing about his lips.

"Why, yes, of course," he said jerkily, "that is, if you want me to. I understand how it was. That's all right. But you needn't mind, if you don't wish to. I thought . . ." He had half turned to go, but was so drawn by her that he could scarcely tear himself away before she repeated: "Oh, do come, get in, Mr. Griffiths. I'll be so glad if you will. It won't take David a moment to take you wherever you are going, I'm sure. And I am sorry about the other, really I am. I didn't mean, you know, that just because you weren't Gilbert Griffiths—"

He paused and in a bewildered manner stepped forward and entering the car, slipped into the seat beside her. And she, interested by his personality, at once began to look at him, feeling glad that it was he now instead of Gilbert. In order the better to see and again reveal her devastating charms, as she saw them, to Clyde, she now switched on the roof light. And the chauffeur returning, she asked Clyde where he wished to go—an address which he gave reluctantly enough, since it was so different from the street in which she resided. As the car sped on, he was animated by a feverish desire to make some use of this brief occasion which might cause her to think favorably of him—perhaps, who knows—lead to some faint desire on her part to contact him again at some time or other. He was so truly eager to be of her world.

"It's certainly nice of you to take me up this way," he now turned to her and observed, smiling. "I didn't think it was my cousin you meant or I wouldn't have come up as I did."

"Oh, that's all right. Don't mention it," replied Sondra archly with a kind of sicky sweetness in her voice. Her original impression of him as she now felt, had been by no means so vivid. "It's my mistake, not yours. But I'm glad I made it now, anyhow," she added most definitely and with an engaging smile. "I think I'd rather pick you up than I would Gil, anyhow. We don't get along any too well, he and I. We quarrel a lot whenever we do meet anywhere." She smiled, having completely recovered from her momentary embarrassment, and now leaned back after the best princess fashion, her glance examining Clyde's very regular features with interest. He had such soft smiling eyes she thought. And after all, as she now reasoned, he was Bella's and Gilbert's cousin, and looked prosperous.

"Well, that's too bad," he said stiffly, and with a very awkward and weak attempt at being self-confident and even high-spirited in her presence.

"Oh, it doesn't amount to anything, really. We just quarrel, that's all, once in a while."

She saw that he was nervous and bashful and decidedly un-resourceful in her presence and it pleased her to think that she could thus befuddle and embarrass him so much. "Are you still working for your uncle?"

"Oh yes," replied Clyde quickly, as though it would make an enormous difference to her if he were not. "I have charge of a department over there now."

"Oh, really, I didn't know. I haven't seen you at all, since that one time, you know. You don't get time to go about much, I suppose." She looked at him wisely, as much as to say, "Your relatives aren't so very much interested in you," but really liking him now, she said instead, "You have been in the city all summer, I suppose?"

"Oh, yes," replied Clyde quite simply and winningly. "I have to be, you know. It's the work that keeps me here. But I've seen your name in the papers often, and read about your riding and tennis contests and I saw you in that flower parade last June, too. I certainly thought you looked beautiful, like an angel almost."

There was an admiring, pleading light in his eyes which now quite charmed her. What a pleasing young man—so different to Gilbert. And to think he should be so plainly and hopelessly smitten, and when she could take no more than a passing interest in him. It made her feel sorry, a little, and hence kindly toward him. Besides what would Gilbert think if only he knew that his cousin was so completely reduced by her—how angry he would be—he, who so plainly thought her a snip? It would serve him just right if Clyde were taken up by some one and made more of than he (Gilbert) ever could hope to be. The thought had a most pleasing tang for her.

However, at this point, unfortunately, the car turned in before Mrs. Peyton's door and stopped. The adventure for Clyde and for her was seemingly over.

"That's awfully nice of you to say that. I won't forget that." She smiled archly as, the chauffeur opening the door, Clyde stepped down, his own nerves taut because of the grandeur and import of this encounter. "So this is where you live. Do you expect to be in Lycurgus all winter?"

"Oh, yes. I'm quite sure of it. I hope to be anyhow," he added, quite yearningly, his eyes expressing his meaning completely.

"Well, perhaps, then I'll see you again somewhere, some time. I hope so, anyhow."

She nodded and gave him her fingers and the most fetching and wreathy of smiles, and he, eager to the point of folly, added: "Oh, so do I."

"Good night! Good night!" she called as the car sprang away, and Clyde, looking after it, wondered if he would ever see her again so closely and intimately as here. To think that he should have met her again in this way! And she had proved so very different from that first time when, as he distinctly recalled, she took no interest in him at all.

He turned hopefully and a little wistfully toward his own door.

And Sondra, . . . why was it, she pondered, as the motor car sped on its way, that the Griffiths were apparently not much interested in him?

# Chapter XXIV

THE EFFECT of this so casual contact was really disrupting in more senses than one. For now in spite of his comfort in and satisfaction with Roberta, once more and in this positive and to him entrancing way, was posed the whole question of his social possibilities here. And that strangely enough by the one girl of this upper level who had most materialized and magnified for him the meaning of that upper level itself. The beautiful Sondra Finchley! Her lovely face, smart clothes, gay and superior demeanor! If only at the time he had first encountered her he had managed to interest her. Or could now.

The fact that his relations with Roberta were what they were now was not of sufficient import or weight to offset the temperamental or imaginative pull of such a girl as Sondra and all that she represented. Just to think the Wimblinger Finchley Electric Sweeper Company was one of the largest manufacturing concerns here. Its tall walls and stacks made a part of the striking sky line across the Mohawk. And the Finchley residence in Wykeagy Avenue, near that of the Griffiths, was one of the most impressive among that distinguished row of houses which had come with the latest and most discriminating architectural taste here—Italian Renaissance—cream hued marble and Dutchess County Sandstone combined. And the Finchleys were among the most discussed of families here.

Ah, to know this perfect girl more intimately! To be looked upon by her with favor,—made, by reason of that favor, a part of that fine world to which she belonged. Was he not a Griffiths—as good looking as Gilbert Griffiths any day? And as attractive if he only had as much money—or a part of it even. To be able to dress in the Gilbert Griffiths' fashion; to ride around in one of the handsome cars he sported! Then, you bet, a girl like this would be delighted to notice him,—mayhap, who knows, even fall in love with him. Analschar and the tray of glasses. But now, as he gloomily thought, he could only hope, hope, hope.

The devil! He would not go around to Roberta's this

evening. He would trump up some excuse—tell her in the morning that he had been called upon by his uncle or cousin to do some work. He could not and would not go, feeling as he did just now.

So much for the effect of wealth, beauty, the peculiar social state to which he most aspired, on a temperament that was as fluid and unstable as water.

On the other hand, later, thinking over her contact with Clyde, Sondra was definitely taken with what may only be described as his charm for her, all the more definite in this case since it represented a direct opposite to all that his cousin offered by way of offense. His clothes and his manner, as well as a remark he had dropped, to the effect that he was connected with the company in some official capacity, seemed to indicate that he might be better placed than she had imagined. Yet she also recalled that although she had been about with Bella all summer and had encountered Gilbert, Myra and their parents from time to time, there had never been a word about Clyde. Indeed all the information she had gathered concerning him was that originally furnished by Mrs. Griffiths, who had said that he was a poor nephew whom her husband had brought on from the west in order to help in some way. Yet now, as she viewed Clyde on this occasion, he did not seem so utterly unimportant or poverty-stricken by any means—quite interesting and rather smart and very attractive, and obviously anxious to be taken seriously by a girl like herself, as she could see. And this coming from Gilbert's cousin—a Griffiths—was flattering.

Arriving at the Trumbulls, a family which centered about one Douglas Trumbull, a prosperous lawyer and widower and speculator of this region, who, by reason of his children as well as his own good manners and legal subtlety, had managed to ingratiate himself into the best circles of Lycurgus society, she suddenly confided to Jill Trumbull, the elder of the lawyer's two daughters: "You know I had a funny experience to-day." And she proceeded to relate all that had occurred in detail. Afterward at dinner, Jill having appeared to find it most fascinating, she again repeated it to Gertrude and Tracy, the younger daughter and only son of the Trumbull family.

"Oh, yes," observed Tracy Trumbull, a law student in his

father's office, "I've seen that fellow, I bet, three of four times on Central Avenue. He looks a lot like Gil, doesn't he? Only not so swagger. I've nodded to him two or three times this summer because I thought he was Gil for the moment."

"Oh, I've seen him, too," commented Gertrude Trumbull. "He wears a cap and a belted coat like Gilbert Griffiths, sometimes, doesn't he? Arabella Stark pointed him out to me once and then Jill and I saw him passing Stark's once on a Saturday afternoon. He is better looking than Gil, any day, I think."

This confirmed Sondra in her own thoughts in regard to Clyde and now she added: "Bertine Cranston and I met him one evening last spring at the Griffiths. We thought he was too bashful, then. But I wish you could see him now—he's positively handsome, with the softest eyes and the nicest smile."

"Oh, now, Sondra," commented Jill Trumbull, who, apart from Bertine and Bella, was as close to Sondra as any girl here, having been one of her classmates at the Snedeker School, "I know some one who would be jealous if he could hear you say that."

"And wouldn't Gil Griffiths like to hear that his cousin's better looking than he is?" chimed in Tracy Trumbull. "Oh, say—"

"Oh, he," sniffed Sondra irritably. "He thinks he's so much, I'll bet anything it's because of him that the Griffiths won't have anything to do with their cousin. I'm sure of it, now that I think of it. Bella would, of course, because I heard her say last spring that she thought he was good-looking. And Myra wouldn't do anything to hurt anybody. What a lark if some of us were to take him up some time and begin inviting him here and there—once in a while, you know—just for fun, to see how he would do. And how the Griffiths would take it. I know well enough it would be all right with Mr. Griffiths and Myra and Bella, but Gil I'll bet would be as peeved as anything. I couldn't do it myself very well, because I'm so close to Bella, but I know who could and they couldn't say a thing." She paused, thinking of Bertine Cranston and how she disliked Gil and Mrs. Griffiths. "I wonder if he dances or rides or plays tennis or anything like that?" She stopped and meditated amusedly, the while the others studied her. And Jill Trumbull, a restless, eager girl like herself, without so much of her looks or flare, however, observed: "It would be a prank, wouldn't it? Do you suppose the Griffiths really would dislike it very much?"

"What's the difference if they did?" went on Sondra. "They couldn't do anything more than ignore him, could they? And who would care about that, I'd like to know. Not the people who invited him."

"Go on, you fellows, stir up a local scrap, will you?" put in Tracy Trumbull. "I'll bet anything that's what comes of it in the end. Gil Griffiths won't like it, you can gamble on that. I wouldn't if I were in his position. If you want to stir up a lot of feeling here, go to it, but I'll lay a bet that's what it comes to."

Now Sondra Finchley's nature was of just such a turn that a thought of this kind was most appealing to her. However, as interesting as the idea was to her at the time, nothing definite might have come of it, had it not been that subsequent to this conversation and several others held with Bertine Cranston, Jill Trumbull, Patricia Anthony, and Arabella Stark, the news of this adventure, together with some comments as to himself, finally came to the ears of Gilbert Griffiths, yet only via Constance Wynant to whom, as local gossips would have it, he was prospectively engaged. And Constance, hoping that Gilbert would marry her eventually, was herself irritated by the report that Sondra had chosen to interest herself in Clyde, and then, for no sane reason, as she saw it, proclaim that he was more attractive than Gilbert. So, as much to relieve herself as to lay some plan of avenging herself upon Sondra, if possible, she conveyed the whole matter in turn to Gilbert, who at once proceeded to make various cutting references to Clyde and Sondra. And these carried back to Sondra, along with certain embellishments by Constance, had the desired effect. It served to awaken in her the keenest desire for retaliation. For if she chose she certainly could be nice to Clyde, and have others be nice to him, too. And that would mean perhaps that Gilbert would find himself faced by a social rival of sorts—his own cousin, too, who, even though he was poor, might come to be liked better. What a lark! At the very same

time there came to her a way by which she might most easily
introduce Clyde, and yet without seeming so to do, and without any great harm to herself, if it did not terminate as she
wished.

For in Lycurgus among the younger members of those
smarter families whose children had been to the Snedeker
School, existed a rather illusory and casual dinner and dance
club called the "Now and Then." It had no definite organization, officers or abode. Any one, who, because of class and
social connections was eligible and chose to belong, could call
a meeting of other members to give a dinner or dance or tea
in their homes.

And how simple, thought Sondra in browsing around for a
suitable vehicle by which to introduce Clyde, if some one
other than herself who belonged could be induced to get up
something and then at her suggestion invite Clyde. How easy,
say, for Jill Trumbull to give a dinner and dance to the "Now
and Thens," to which Clyde might be invited. And by this
ruse she would thus be able to see him again and find out just
how much he did interest her and what he was like.

Accordingly a small dinner for this club and its friends was
announced for the first Thursday in December, Jill Trumbull
to be the hostess. To it were to be invited Sondra and her
brother, Stuart, Tracy and Gertrude Trumbull, Arabella Stark,
Bertine and her brother, and some others from Utica and
Gloversville as well. And Clyde. But in order to safeguard
Clyde against any chance of failure or even invidious comment of any kind, not only she but Bertine and Jill and
Gertrude were to be attentive to and considerate of him.
They were to see that his dance program was complete and
that neither at dinner nor on the dance floor was he to be left
to himself, but was to be passed on most artfully from one to
the other until the evening should be over. For, by reason of
that, others might come to be interested in him, which would
not only take the thorn from the thought that Sondra alone,
of all the better people of Lycurgus, had been friendly to him,
but would sharpen the point of this development for Gilbert,
if not for Bella and the other members of the Griffiths family.

And in accordance with this plan, so it was done.

And so it was that Clyde, returning from the factory one

early December evening about two weeks after his encounter with Sondra, was surprised by the sight of a cream-colored note leaning against the mirror of his dresser. It was addressed in a large, scrawly and unfamiliar hand. He picked it up and turned it over without being able in any way to fix upon the source. On the back were the initials B. T. or J. T., he could not decide which, so elaborately intertwined was the engraved penmanship. He tore it open and drew out a card which read:

*The Now and Then Club*
*Will Hold Its First*
*Winter Dinner Dance*
*At the Home of*
*Douglas Trumbull*
*135 Wykeagy Ave.*
*On Thursday, December 4*
*You Are Cordially Invited*
*Will You Kindly Reply to Miss Jill Trumbull?*

On the back of this, though, in the same scrawly hand that graced the envelope was written: "Dear Mr. Griffiths: Thought you might like to come. It will be quite informal. And I'm sure you'll like it. If so, will you let Jill Trumbull know? Sondra Finchley."

Quite amazed and thrilled, Clyde stood and stared. For ever since that second contact with her, he had been more definitely fascinated than at any time before by the dream that somehow, in some way, he was to be lifted from the lowly state in which he now dwelt. He was, as he now saw it, really too good for the commonplace world by which he was environed. And now here was this—a social invitation issued by the "Now and Then Club," of which, even though he had never heard of it, must be something, since it was sponsored by such exceptional people. And on the back of it, was there not the writing of Sondra herself? How marvelous, really!

So astonished was he that he could scarcely contain himself for joy, but now on the instant must walk to and fro, looking at himself in the mirror, washing his hands and face, then deciding that his tie was not just right, perhaps, and changing to another—thinking forward to what he should wear and back upon how Sondra had looked at him on that last occasion.

And how she had smiled. At the same time he could not help wondering even at this moment of what Roberta would think, if now, by some extra optical power of observation she could note his present joy in connection with this note. For plainly, and because he was no longer governed by the conventional notions of his parents, he had been allowing himself to drift into a position in regard to her which would certainly spell torture to her in case she should discover the nature of his present mood, a thought which puzzled him not a little, but did not serve to modify his thoughts in regard to Sondra in the least.

That wonderful girl!

That beauty!

That world of wealth and social position she lived in!

At the same time so innately pagan and unconventional were his thoughts in regard to all this that he could now ask himself, and that seriously enough, why should he not be allowed to direct his thoughts toward her and away from Roberta, since at the moment Sondra supplied the keener thought of delight. Roberta could not know about this. She could not see into his mind, could she—become aware of any such extra experience as this unless he told her. And most assuredly he did not intend to tell her. And what harm, he now asked himself, was there in a poor youth like himself aspiring to such heights? Other youths as poor as himself had married girls as rich as Sondra.

For in spite of all that had occurred between him and Roberta he had not, as he now clearly recalled, given her his word that he would marry her except under one condition. And such a condition, especially with the knowledge that he had all too clearly acquired in Kansas City, was not likely to happen as he thought.

And Sondra, now that she had thus suddenly burst upon him again in this way was the same as a fever to his fancy. This goddess in her shrine of gilt and tinsel so utterly enticing to him, had deigned to remember him in this open and direct way and to suggest that he be invited. And no doubt she, herself, was going to be there, a thought which thrilled him beyond measure.

And what would not Gilbert and the Griffiths think if they

were to hear of his going to this affair now, as they surely would? Or meet him later at some other party to which Sondra might invite him? Think of that! Would it irritate or please them? Make them think less or more of him? For, after all, this certainly was not of his doing. Was he not properly invited by people of their own station here in Lycurgus whom most certainly they were compelled to respect? And by no device of his, either—sheer accident—the facts concerning which would most certainly not reflect on him as pushing. As lacking as he was in some of the finer shades of mental discrimination, a sly and ironic pleasure lay in the thought that now Gilbert and the Griffiths might be compelled to countenance him whether they would or not—invite him to their home, even. For, if these others did, how could they avoid it, really? Oh, joy! And that in the face of Gilbert's high contempt for him. He fairly chuckled as he thought of it, feeling that however much Gilbert might resent it, neither his uncle nor Myra were likely to, and that hence he would be fairly safe from any secret desire on the part of Gilbert to revenge himself on him for this.

But how wonderful this invitation! Why that intriguing scribble of Sondra's unless she was interested in him some? Why? The thought was so thrilling that Clyde could scarcely eat his dinner that night. He took up the card and kissed the handwriting. And instead of going to see Roberta as usual, he decided as before on first reëncountering her, to walk a bit, then return to his room, and retire early. And on the morrow as before he could make some excuse—say that he had been over to the Griffiths' home, or some one of the heads of the factory, in order to listen to an explanation in regard to something in connection with the work, since there were often such conferences. For, in the face of this, he did not care to see or talk to Roberta this night. He could not. The other thought—that of Sondra and her interest in him—was too enticing.

# Chapter XXV

B UT in the interim, in connection with his relations with Roberta no least reference to Sondra, although, even when near her in the factory or her room, he could not keep his thoughts from wandering away to where Sondra in her imaginary high social world might be. The while Roberta, at moments only sensing a drift and remoteness in his thought and attitude which had nothing to do with her, was wondering what it was that of late was beginning to occupy him so completely. And he, in his turn, when she was not looking was thinking—supposing?—supposing—(since she had troubled to recall herself to him), that he could interest a girl like Sondra in him? What then of Roberta? What? And in the face of this intimate relation that had now been established between them? (Goodness! The deuce!) And that he did care for her (yes, he did), although now—basking in the direct rays of this newer luminary—he could scarcely see Roberta any longer, so strong were the actinic rays of this other. Was he all wrong? Was it evil to be like this? His mother would say so! And his father too—and perhaps everybody who thought right about life—Sondra Finchley, maybe—the Griffiths—all.

And yet! And yet! It was snowing the first light snow of the year as Clyde, arrayed in a new collapsible silk hat and white silk muffler, both suggested by a friendly haberdasher—Orrin Short, with whom recently he had come in contact here—and a new silk umbrella wherewith to protect himself from the snow, made his way toward the very interesting, if not so very imposing residence of the Trumbulls on Wykeagy Avenue. It was quaint, low and rambling, and the lights beaming from within upon the many drawn blinds gave it a Christmas-card effect. And before it, even at the prompt hour at which he arrived, were ranged a half dozen handsome cars of various builds and colors. The sight of them, sprinkled on tops, running boards and fenders with the fresh, flaky snow, gave him a keen sense of a deficiency that was not likely soon to be remedied in his case—the want of ample means wherewith to equip himself with such a necessity as that. And inside as he approached the door he could hear voices, laughter and conversation commingled.

A tall, thin servant relieved him of his hat, coat and umbrella and he found himself face to face with Jill Trumbull, who apparently was on the look-out for him—a smooth, curly-haired blonde girl, not too thrillingly pretty, but brisk and smart, in white satin with arms and shoulders bare and rhinestones banded around her forehead.

"No trouble to tell who you are," she said gayly, approaching and giving Clyde her hand. "I'm Jill Trumbull. Miss Finchley hasn't come yet. But I can do the honors just as well, I guess. Come right in where the rest of us are."

She led the way into a series of connecting rooms that seemed to join each other at right angles, adding as she went, "You do look an awful lot like Gil Griffiths, don't you?"

"Do I?" smiled Clyde simply and courageously and very much flattered by the comparison.

The ceilings were low. Pretty lamps behind painted shades hugged dark walls. Open fires in two connecting rooms cast a rosy glow upon cushioned and comfortable furniture. There were pictures, books, objects of art.

"Here, Tracy, you do the announcing, will you?" she called. "My brother, Tracy Trumbull, Mr. Griffiths. Mr. Clyde Griffiths, everybody," she added, surveying the company in general which in turn fixed varying eyes upon him, while Tracy Trumbull took him by the hand. Clyde, suffering from a sense of being studied, nevertheless achieved a warm smile. At the same time he realized that for the moment at least conversation had stopped. "Don't all stop talking on my account," he ventured, with a smile, which caused most of those present to conceive of him as at his ease and resourceful. At the same time Tracy added: "I'm not going to do any man-to-man introduction stuff. We'll stand right here and point 'em out. That's my sister, Gertrude, over there talking to Scott Nicholson." Clyde noted that a small, dark girl dressed in pink with a pretty and yet saucy and piquant face, nodded to him. And beside her a very de rigueur youth of fine physique and pink complexion nodded jerkily. "Howja do." And a few feet from them near a deep window stood a tall and yet graceful girl of dark and by no means ravishing features talking to a broad-shouldered and deep-chested youth of less than her height, who were proclaimed to be Arabella Stark and Frank Harriet. "They're arguing over a recent Cornell-Syracuse foot-ball game . . . Burchard Taylor and Miss Phant of Utica," he went on almost too swiftly for Clyde to assemble any mental notes. "Perley Haynes and Miss Vanda Steele . . . well, I guess that's all as yet. Oh, no, here come Grant and Nina Temple." Clyde paused and gazed as a tall and somewhat dandified-looking youth, sharp of face and with murky gray eyes, steered a trim, young, plump girl in fawn gray and with a light chestnut braid of hair laid carefully above her forehead, into the middle of the room.

"Hello, Jill. Hello, Vanda. Hello, Wynette." In the midst of these greetings on his part, Clyde was presented to these two, neither of whom seemed to pay much attention to him. "Didn't think we'd make it," went on young Cranston speaking to all at once. "Nina didn't want to come, but I promised Bertine and Jill or I wouldn't have, either. We were up at the Bagley's. Guess who's up there, Scott. Van Peterson and Rhoda Hull. They're just over for the day."

"You don't say," called Scott Nicholson, a determined and self-centered looking individual. Clyde was arrested by the very definite sense of social security and ease that seemed to reside in everybody. "Why didn't you bring 'em along? I'd like to see Rhoda again and Van, too."

"Couldn't. They have to go back early, they say. They may stop in later for a minute. Gee, isn't dinner served yet? I expected to sit right down."

"These lawyers! Don't you know they don't eat often?" commented Frank Harriet, who was a short, but broad-chested and smiling youth, very agreeable, very good-looking and with even, white teeth. Clyde liked him.

"Well, whether they do or not, we do, or out I go. Did you hear who is being touted for stroke next year over at Cornell?" This college chatter relating to Cornell and shared by Harriet, Cranston and others, Clyde could not understand. He had scarcely heard of the various colleges with which this group was all too familiar. At the same time he was wise enough to sense the defect and steer clear of any questions or conversations which might relate to them. However, because of this, he at once felt out of it. These people were better informed than he was—had been to colleges. Perhaps he had better claim that he had been to some school. In Kansas City he had heard of the State University of Kansas—not so very far from there. Also the University of Missouri. And in Chicago of the University of Chicago. Could he say that he had been to one of those—that Kansas one, for a little while, anyway? On the instant he proposed to claim it, if asked, and then look up afterwards what, if anything, he was supposed to know about it—what, for instance, he might have studied. He had heard of mathematics somewhere. Why not that?

But these people, as he could see, were too much interested in themselves to pay much attention to him now. He might be a Griffiths and important to some outside, but here not so much—a matter of course, as it were. And because Tracy Trumbull for the moment had turned to say something to Wynette Phant, he felt quite alone, beached and helpless and with no one to talk to. But just then the small, dark girl, Gertrude, came over to him.

"The crowd's a little late in getting together. It always is. If we said eight, they'd come at eight-thirty or nine. Isn't that always the way?"

"It certainly is," replied Clyde gratefully, endeavoring to appear as brisk and as much at ease as possible.

"I'm Gertrude Trumbull," she repeated. "The sister of the good-looking Jill," a cynical and yet amused smile played about her mouth and eyes. "You nodded to me, but you don't know me. Just the same we've been hearing a lot about you." She teased in an attempt to trouble Clyde a little, if possible. "A mysterious Griffiths here in Lycurgus whom no one seems to have met. I saw you once in Central Avenue, though. You were going into Rich's candy store. You didn't know that, though. Do you like candy?"

"Oh, yes, I like candy. Why?" asked Clyde on the instant feeling teased and disturbed, since the girl for whom he was buying the candy was Roberta. At the same time he could not help feeling slightly more at ease with this girl than with some others, for although cynical and not so attractive, her manner was genial and she now spelled escape from isolation and hence diffidence.

"You're probably just saying that," she laughed, a bantering look in her eyes. "More likely you were buying it for some girl. You have a girl, haven't you?"

"Why—" Clyde paused for the fraction of a second because as she asked this Roberta came into his mind and the query, "Had any one ever seen him with Roberta?" flitted through his brain. Also thinking at the same time, what a bold, teasing, intelligent girl this was, different from any that thus far he had known. Yet quite without more pause he added: "No, I haven't. What makes you ask that?"

As he said this there came to him the thought of what Roberta would think if she could hear him. "But what a question," he continued a little nervously now. "You like to tease, don't you?"

"Who, me? Oh, no. I wouldn't do anything like that. But I'm sure you have just the same. I like to ask questions sometimes, just to see what people will say when they don't want you to know what they really think." She beamed into Clyde's eyes amusedly and defiantly. "But I know you have a girl just the same. All good-looking fellows have."

"Oh, am I good-looking?" he beamed nervously, amused and yet pleased. "Who said so?"

"As though you didn't know. Well, different people. I for one. And Sondra Finchley thinks you're good-looking, too. She's only interested in men who are. So does my sister Jill, for that matter. And she only likes men who are good-looking. I'm different because I'm not so good-looking myself." She blinked cynically and teasingly into his eyes, which caused him to feel oddly out of place, not able to cope with such a girl at all, at the same time very much flattered and amused. "But don't you think you're better looking than your cousin," she went on sharply and even commandingly. "Some people think you are."

Although a little staggered and yet flattered by this question which propounded what he might have liked to believe, and although intrigued by this girl's interest in him, still Clyde would not have dreamed of venturing any such assertion even though he had believed it. Too vividly it brought the aggressive and determined and even at times revengeful-looking features of Gilbert before him, who, stirred by such a report as this, would not hesitate to pay him out.

"Why I don't think anything of the kind," he laughed. "Honest, I don't. Of course I don't."

"Oh, well, then maybe you don't, but you are just the same. But that won't help you much either, unless you have money—that is, if you want to run with people who have." She looked up at him and added quite blandly. "People like money even more than they do looks."

What a sharp girl this was, he thought, and what a hard, cold statement. It cut him not a little, even though she had not intended that it should.

But just then Sondra herself entered with some youth whom Clyde did not know—a tall, gangling, but very smartly-dressed individual. And after them, along with others, Bertine and Stuart Finchley.

"Here she is now," added Gertrude a little spitefully, for she resented the fact that Sondra was so much better-looking than either she or her sister, and that she had expressed an interest in Clyde. "She'll be looking to see if you notice how pretty she looks, so don't disappoint her."

The impact of this remark, a reflection of the exact truth, was not necessary to cause Clyde to gaze attentively, and even eagerly. For apart from her local position and means and taste in dress and manners, Sondra was of the exact order and spirit that most intrigued him—a somewhat refined (and because of means and position showered upon her) less savage, although scarcely less self-centered, Hortense Briggs. She was, in her small, intense way, a seeking Aphrodite, eager to prove to any who were sufficiently attractive the destroying power of her charm, while at the same time retaining her own personality and individuality free of any entangling alliance or compromise. However, for varying reasons which she could not quite explain to herself, Clyde appealed to her. He might not be anything socially or financially, but he was interesting to her.

Hence she was now keen, first to see if he were present, next to be sure that he gained no hint that she had seen him first, and lastly to act as grandly as possible for his benefit—a Hortensian procedure and type of thought that was exactly the thing best calculated to impress him. He gazed and there she was—tripping here and there in a filmy chiffon dance frock, shaded from palest yellow to deepest orange, which most enhanced her dark eyes and hair. And having exchanged a dozen or more "Oh, Hellos," and references with one and another to this, that and the other local event, she at last condescended to evince awareness of his proximity.

"Oh, here you are. You decided to come after all. I wasn't sure whether you would think it worth while. You've been introduced to everybody, of course?" She looked around as much as to say, that if he had not been she would proceed to serve him in this way. The others, not so very much impressed by Clyde, were still not a little interested by the fact that she seemed so interested in him.

"Yes, I met nearly everybody, I think."

"Except Freddie Sells. He came in with me just now. Here you are, Freddie," she called to a tall and slender youth, smooth of cheek and obviously becurled as to hair, who now came over and in his closely-fitting dress coat looked down on Clyde about as a spring rooster might look down on a sparrow.

"This is Clyde Griffiths, I was telling you about, Fred," she began briskly. "Doesn't he look a lot like Gilbert?"

"Why, you do at that," exclaimed this amiable person, who seemed to be slightly troubled with weak eyes since he bent close. "I hear you're a cousin of Gil's. I know him well. We went through Princeton together. I used to be over here before I joined the General Electric over at Schenectady. But I'm around a good bit yet. You're connected with the factory, I suppose."

"Yes, I am," said Clyde, who, before a youth of obviously so much more training and schooling than he possessed, felt not a little reduced. He began to fear that this individual would try to talk to him about things which he could not understand, things concerning which, having had no consecutive training of any kind, he had never been technically informed.

"In charge of some department, I suppose?"

"Yes, I am," said Clyde, cautiously and nervously.

"You know," went on Mr. Sells, briskly and interestingly,

being of a commercial as well as technical turn, "I've always wondered just what, outside of money, there is to the collar business. Gil and I used to argue about that when we were down at college. He used to try to tell me that there was some social importance to making and distributing collars, giving polish and manner to people who wouldn't otherwise have them, if it weren't for cheap collars. I think he musta read that in a book somewhere. I always laughed at him."

Clyde was about to attempt an answer, although already beyond his depth in regard to this. "Social importance." Just what did he mean by that—some deep, scientific information that he had acquired at college. He was saved a non-committal or totally uninformed answer by Sondra who, without thought or knowledge of the difficulty which was then and there before him, exclaimed: "Oh, no arguments, Freddie. That's not interesting. Besides I want him to meet my brother and Bertine. You remember Miss Cranston. She was with me at your uncle's last spring."

Clyde turned, while Fred made the best of the rebuff by merely looking at Sondra, whom he admired so very much.

"Yes, of course," Clyde began, for he had been studying these two along with others. To him, apart from Sondra, Bertine seemed exceedingly attractive, though quite beyond his understanding also. Being involved, insincere and sly, she merely evoked in him a troubled sense of ineffectiveness, and hence uncertainty, in so far as her particular world was concerned—no more.

"Oh, how do you do? It's nice to see you again," she drawled, the while her greenish-gray eyes went over him in a smiling and yet indifferent and quizzical way. She thought him attractive, but not nearly as shrewd and hard as she would have preferred him to be. "You've been terribly busy with your work, I suppose. But now that you've come out once, I suppose we'll see more of you here and there."

"Well, I hope so," he replied, showing his even teeth.

Her eyes seemed to be saying that she did not believe what she was saying and that he did not either, but that it was necessary, possibly amusing, to say something of the sort.

And a related, though somewhat modified, version of this

same type of treatment was accorded him by Stuart, Sondra's brother.

"Oh, how do you do. Glad to know you. My sister has just been telling me about you. Going to stay in Lycurgus long? Hope you do. We'll run into one another once in a while then, I suppose."

Clyde was by no means so sure, but he admired the easy, shallow way in which Stuart laughed and showed his even white teeth—a quick, genial, indifferent laugh. Also the way in which he turned and laid hold of Wynette Phant's white arm as she passed. "Wait a minute, Wyn. I want to ask you something." He was gone—into another room—bending close to her and talking fast. And Clyde had noticed that his clothes were perfectly cut.

What a gay world, he thought. What a brisk world. And just then Jill Trumbull began calling, "Come on, people. It's not my fault. The cook's mad about something and you're all late anyhow. We'll get it over with and then dance, eh?"

"You can sit between me and Miss Trumbull when she gets the rest of us seated," assured Sondra. "Won't that be nice? And now you may take me in."

She slipped a white arm under Clyde's and he felt as though he were slowly but surely being transported to paradise.

## Chapter XXVI

THE DINNER itself was chatter about a jumble of places, personalities, plans, most of which had nothing to do with anything that Clyde had personally contacted here. However, by reason of his own charm, he soon managed to overcome the sense of strangeness and hence indifference in some quarters, more particularly the young women of the group who were interested by the fact that Sondra Finchley liked him. And Jill Trumbull, sitting beside him, wanted to know where he came from, what his own home life and connections were like, why he had decided to come to Lycurgus, questions which, interjected as they were between silly banter concerning different girls and their beaus, gave Clyde pause. He did not feel that he could admit the truth in connection with his family at all. So he announced that his father conducted a hotel in Denver—not so very large, but still a hotel. Also that he had come to Lycurgus because his uncle had suggested to him in Chicago that he come to learn the collar business. He was not sure that he was wholly interested in it or that he would continue indefinitely unless it proved worth while; rather he was trying to find out what it might mean to his future, a remark which caused Sondra, who was also listening, as well as Jill, to whom it was addressed, to consider that in spite of all rumors attributed to Gilbert, Clyde must possess some means and position to which, in case he did not do so well here, he could return.

This in itself was important, not only to Sondra and Jill, but to all the others. For, despite his looks and charm and family connections here, the thought that he was a mere nobody, seeking, as Constance Wynant had reported, to attach himself to his cousin's family, was disquieting. One couldn't ever be anything much more than friendly with a moneyless clerk or pensioner, whatever his family connections, whereas if he had a little money and some local station elsewhere, the situation was entirely different.

And now Sondra, relieved by this and the fact that he was proving more acceptable than she had imagined he would, was inclined to make more of him than she otherwise would have done.

"Are you going to let me dance with you after dinner?" was one of the first things he said to her, infringing on a genial smile given him in the midst of clatter concerning an approaching dance somewhere.

"Why, yes, of course, if you want me to," she replied, coquettishly, seeking to intrigue him into further romanticisms in regard to her.

"Just one?"

"How many do you want? There are a dozen boys here, you know. Did you get a program when you came in?"

"I didn't see any."

"Never mind. After dinner you can get one. And you may put me down for three and eight. That will leave you room for others." She smiled bewitchingly. "You have to be nice to everybody, you know."

"Yes, I know." He was still looking at her. "But ever since I saw you at my uncle's last April, I've been wishing I might see you again. I always look for your name in the papers."

He looked at her seekingly and questioningly and in spite of herself, Sondra was captivated by this naïve confession. Plainly he could not afford to go where or do what she did, but still he would trouble to follow her name and movements in print. She could not resist the desire to make something more of this.

"Oh, do you?" she added. "Isn't that nice? But what do you read about me?"

"That you were at Twelfth and Greenwood Lakes and up at Sharon for the swimming contests. I saw where you went up to Paul Smith's, too. The papers here seemed to think you were interested in some one from Schroon Lake and that you might be going to marry him."

"Oh, did they? How silly. The papers here always say such silly things." Her tone implied that he might be intruding. He looked embarrassed. This softened her and after a moment she took up the conversation in the former vein.

"Do you like to ride?" she asked sweetly and placatively.

"I never have. You know I never had much chance at that, but I always thought I could if I tried."

"Of course, it's not hard. If you took a lesson or two you

could, and," she added in a somewhat lower tone, "we might go for a canter sometime. There are lots of horses in our stable that you would like, I'm sure."

Clyde's hair-roots tingled anticipatorily. He was actually being invited by Sondra to ride with her sometime and he could use one of her horses into the bargain.

"Oh, I would love that," he said. "That would be wonderful."

The crowd was getting up from the table. Scarcely any one was interested in the dinner, because a chamber orchestra of four having arrived, the strains of a preliminary fox trot were already issuing from the adjacent living room—a long, wide affair from which all obstructing furniture with the exception of wall chairs had been removed.

"You had better see about your program and your dance before all the others are gone," cautioned Sondra.

"Yes, I will right away," said Clyde, "but is two all I get with you?"

"Well, make it three, five and eight then, in the first half." She waved him gaily away and he hurried for a dance card.

The dances were all of the eager fox-trotting type of the period with interpolations and variations according to the moods and temperaments of the individual dancers. Having danced so much with Roberta during the preceding month, Clyde was in excellent form and keyed to the breaking point by the thought that at last he was in social and even affectional contact with a girl as wonderful as Sondra.

And although wishing to seem courteous and interested in others with whom he was dancing, he was almost dizzied by passing contemplations of Sondra. She swayed so droopily and dreamily in the embrace of Grant Cranston, the while without seeming to, looking in his direction when he was near, permitting him to sense how graceful and romantic and poetic was her attitude toward all things—what a flower of life she really was. And Nina Temple, with whom he was now dancing for his benefit, just then observed: "She is graceful, isn't she?"

"Who?" asked Clyde, pretending an innocence he could not physically verify, for his cheek and forehead flushed. "I don't know who you mean."

"Don't you? Then what are you blushing for?"

He had realized that he was blushing. And that his attempted escape was ridiculous. He turned, but just then the music stopped and the dancers drifted away to their chairs. Sondra moved off with Grant Cranston and Clyde led Nina toward a cushioned seat in a window in the library.

And in connection with Bertine with whom he next danced, he found himself slightly flustered by the cool, cynical aloofness with which she accepted and entertained his attention. Her chief interest in Clyde was the fact that Sondra appeared to find him interesting.

"You do dance well, don't you? I suppose you must have done a lot of dancing before you came here—in Chicago, wasn't it, or where?"

She talked slowly and indifferently.

"I was in Chicago before I came here, but I didn't do so very much dancing. I had to work." He was thinking how such girls as she had everything, as contrasted with girls like Roberta, who had nothing. And yet, as he now felt in this instance, he liked Roberta better. She was sweeter and warmer and kinder—not so cold.

When the music started again with the sonorous melancholy of a single saxophone interjected at times, Sondra came over to him and placed her right hand in his left and allowed him to put his arm about her waist, an easy, genial and unembarrassed approach which, in the midst of Clyde's dream of her, was thrilling.

And then in her coquettish and artful way she smiled up in his eyes, a bland, deceptive and yet seemingly promising smile, which caused his heart to beat faster and his throat to tighten. Some delicate perfume that she was using thrilled in his nostrils as might have the fragrance of spring.

"Having a good time?"

"Yes—looking at you."

"When there are so many other nice girls to look at?"

"Oh, there are no other girls as nice as you."

"And I dance better than any other girl, and I'm much the best-looking of any other girl here. Now—I've said it all for you. Now what are you going to say?"

She looked up at him teasingly, and Clyde realizing that he

had a very different type to Roberta to deal with, was puzzled and flushed.

"I see," he said, seriously. "Every fellow tells you that, so you don't want me to."

"Oh, no, not every fellow." Sondra was at once intrigued and checkmated by the simplicity of his retort. "There are lots of people who don't think I'm very pretty."

"Oh, don't they, though?" he returned quite gayly, for at once he saw that she was not making fun of him. And yet he was almost afraid to venture another compliment. Instead he cast about for something else to say, and going back to the conversation at the table concerning riding and tennis, he now asked: "You like everything out-of-doors and athletic, don't you?"

"Oh, do I?" was her quick and enthusiastic response. "There isn't anything I like as much, really. I'm just crazy about riding, tennis, swimming, motor-boating, aqua-planing. You swim, don't you?"

"Oh, sure," said Clyde, grandly.

"Do you play tennis?"

"Well, I've just taken it up," he said, fearing to admit that he did not play at all.

"Oh, I just love tennis. We might play sometime together."

Clyde's spirits were completely restored by this. And tripping as lightly as dawn to the mournful strains of a popular love song, she went right on. "Bella Griffiths and Stuart and Grant and I play fine doubles. We won nearly all the finals at Greenwood and Twelfth Lake last summer. And when it comes to aqua-planing and high diving you just ought to see me. We have the swiftest motor-boat up at Twelfth Lake now—Stuart has. It can do sixty miles an hour."

At once Clyde realized that he had hit upon the one subject that not only fascinated, but even excited her. For not only did it involve outdoor exercise, in which obviously she reveled, but also the power to triumph and so achieve laurels in such phases of sport as most interested those with whom she was socially connected. And lastly, although this was something which he did not so clearly realize until later, she was fairly dizzied by the opportunity all this provided for frequent changes of costume and hence social show, which was the one thing above all others that did interest her. How she looked in a bathing suit—a riding or tennis or dancing or automobile costume!

They danced on together, thrilled for the moment at least, by this mutual recognition of the identity and reality of this interest each felt for the other—a certain momentary warmth or enthusiasm which took the form of genial and seeking glances into each other's eyes, hints on the part of Sondra that, assuming that Clyde could fit himself athletically, financially and in other ways for such a world as this, it might be possible that he would be invited here and there by her; broad and for the moment self-deluding notions on his part that such could and would be the case, while in reality just below the surface of his outward or seeming conviction and assurance ran a deeper current of self-distrust which showed as a decidedly eager and yet slightly mournful light in his eye, a certain vigor and assurance in his voice, which was nevertheless touched, had she been able to define it, with something that was not assurance by any means.

"Oh, the dance is done," he said sadly.

"Let's try to make them encore," she said, applauding. The orchestra struck up a lively tune and they glided off together once more, dipping and swaying here and there—harmoniously abandoning themselves to the rhythm of the music—like two small chips being tossed about on a rough but friendly sea.

"Oh, I'm so glad to be with you again—to be dancing with you. It's so wonderful . . . Sondra."

"But you mustn't call me that, you know. You don't know me well enough."

"I mean Miss Finchley. But you're not going to be mad at me again, are you?"

His face was very pale and sad again.

She noticed it.

"No. Was I mad at you? I wasn't really. I like you . . . some . . . when you're not sentimental."

The music stopped. The light tripping feet became walking ones.

"I'd like to see if it's still snowing outside, wouldn't you?" It was Sondra asking.

"Oh, yes. Let's go."

Through the moving couples they hurried out a side-door to a world that was covered thick with soft, cottony, silent snow. The air was filled with it silently eddying down.

# Chapter XXVII

THE ENSUING December days brought to Clyde some pleasing and yet complicating and disturbing developments. For Sondra Finchley, having found him so agreeable an admirer of hers, was from the first inclined neither to forget nor neglect him. But, occupying the rather prominent social position which she did, she was at first rather dubious as to how to proceed. For Clyde was too poor and decidedly too much ignored by the Griffiths themselves, even, for her to risk any marked manifestation of interest in him.

And now, in addition to the primary motivating reason for all this—her desire to irritate Gilbert by being friends with his cousin—there was another. She liked him. His charm and his reverence for her and her station flattered and intrigued her. For hers was a temperament which required adulation in about the measure which Clyde provided it—sincere and romantic adulation. And at the very same time he represented physical as well as mental attributes which were agreeable to her—amorousness without the courage at the time, anyhow, to annoy her too much; reverence which yet included her as a very human being; a mental and physical animation which quite matched and companioned her own.

Hence it was decidedly a troublesome thought with Sondra how she was to proceed with Clyde without attracting too much attention and unfavorable comment to herself—a thought which kept her sly little brain going at nights after she had retired. However, those who had met him at the Trumbulls' were so much impressed by her interest in him that evening and the fact that he had proved so pleasing and affable, they in turn, the girls particularly, were satisfied that he was eligible enough.

And in consequence, two weeks later, Clyde, searching for inexpensive Christmas presents in Stark's for his mother, father, sisters, brother and Roberta, and encountering Jill Trumbull doing a little belated shopping herself, was invited by her to attend a pre-Christmas dance that was to be given the next night by Vanda Steele at her home in Gloversville.

Jill herself was going with Frank Harriet and she was not sure but that Sondra Finchley would be there. Another engagement of some kind appeared to be in the way, but still she was intending to come if she could. But her sister Gertrude would be glad to have him escort her—a very polite way of arranging for Gertrude. Besides, as she knew, if Sondra heard that Clyde was to be there, this might induce her to desert her other engagement.

"Tracy will be glad to stop for you in time," she went on, "or—" she hesitated—"perhaps you'd like to come over for dinner with us before we go. It'll be just the family, but we'd be delighted to have you. The dancing doesn't begin till eleven."

The dance was for Friday night, and on that night Clyde had arranged to be with Roberta because on the following day she was leaving for a three-day-over-Christmas holiday visit to her parents—the longest stretch of time thus far she had spent away from him. And because, apart from his knowledge she had arranged to present him with a new fountain pen and eversharp pencil, she had been most anxious that he should spend this last evening with her, a fact which she had impressed upon him. And he, on his part, had intended to make use of this last evening to surprise her with a white-and-black toilet set.

But now, so thrilled was he at the possibility of a reëncounter with Sondra, he decided that he would cancel this last evening engagement with Roberta, although not without some misgivings as to the difficulty as well as the decency of it. For despite the fact that he was now so lured by Sondra, nevertheless he was still deeply interested in Roberta and he did not like to grieve her in this way. She would look so disappointed, as he knew. Yet at the same time so flattered and enthused was he by this sudden, if tardy, social development that he could not now think of refusing Jill. What? Neglect to visit the Steeles in Gloversville and in company with the Trumbulls and without any help from the Griffiths, either? It might be disloyal, cruel, treacherous to Roberta, but was he not likely to meet Sondra?

In consequence he announced that he would go, but immediately afterwards decided that he must go round and explain to Roberta, make some suitable excuse—that the Griffiths, for instance, had invited him for dinner. That would be sufficiently overawing and compelling to her. But upon arriving, and finding her out, he decided to explain the following morning at the factory—by note, if necessary. To make up for it he decided he might promise to accompany her as far as Fonda on Saturday and give her her present then.

But on Friday morning at the factory, instead of explaining to her with the seriousness and even emotional dissatisfaction which would have governed him before, he now whispered: "I have to break that engagement to-night, honey. Been invited to my uncle's, and I have to go. And I'm not sure that I can get around afterwards. I'll try if I get through in time. But I'll see you on the Fonda car to-morrow if I don't. I've got something I want to give you, so don't feel too bad. Just got word this morning or I'd have let you know. You're not going to feel bad, are you?" He looked at her as gloomily as possible in order to express his own sorrow over this.

But Roberta, her presents and her happy last evening with him put aside in this casual way, and for the first time, too, in this fashion, shook her head negatively, as if to say "Oh, no," but her spirits were heavily depressed and she fell to wondering what this sudden desertion of her at this time might portend. For, up to this time, Clyde had been attentiveness itself, concealing his recent contact with Sondra behind a veil of pretended, unmodified affection which had, as yet, been sufficient to deceive her. It might be true, as he said, that an unescapable invitation had come up which necessitated all this. But, oh, the happy evening she had planned! And now they would not be together again for three whole days. She grieved dubiously at the factory and in her room afterwards, thinking that Clyde might at least have suggested coming around to her room late, after his uncle's dinner in order that she might give him the presents. But his eventual excuse made this day was that the dinner was likely to last too late. He could not be sure. They had talked of going somewhere else afterwards.

But meanwhile Clyde, having gone to the Trumbulls', and later to the Steeles', was flattered and reassured by a series of developments such as a month before he would not have dreamed of anticipating. For at the Steeles' he was promptly introduced to a score of personalities there who, finding him chaperoned by the Trumbulls and learning that he was a Griffiths, as promptly invited him to affairs of their own—or hinted at events that were to come to which he might be invited, so that at the close he found himself with cordial invitations to attend a New Year's dance at the Vandams' in Gloversville, as well as a dinner and dance that was to be given Christmas Eve by the Harriets in Lycurgus, an affair to which Gilbert and his sister Bella, as well as Sondra, Bertine and others were invited.

And lastly, there was Sondra herself appearing on the scene at about midnight in company with Scott Nicholson, Freddie Sells and Bertine, at first pretending to be wholly unaware of his presence, yet deigning at last to greet him with an, "Oh, hello, I didn't expect to find you here." She was draped most alluringly in a deep red Spanish shawl. But Clyde could sense from the first that she was quite aware of his presence, and at the first available opportunity he drew near to her and asked yearningly, "Aren't you going to dance with me at all?"

"Why, of course, if you want me to. I thought maybe you had forgotten me by now," she said mockingly.

"As though I'd be likely to forget you. The only reason I'm here to-night is because I thought I might see you again. I haven't thought of any one or anything else since I saw you last."

Indeed so infatuated was he with her ways and airs, that instead of being irritated by her pretended indifference, he was all the more attracted. And he now achieved an intensity which to her was quite compelling. His eyelids narrowed and his eyes lit with a blazing desire which was quite disturbing to see.

"My, but you can say the nicest things in the nicest way when you want to." She was toying with a large Spanish comb in her hair for the moment and smiling. "And you say them just as though you meant them."

"Do you mean to say that you don't believe me, Sondra," he inquired almost feverishly, this second use of her name thrilling her now as much as it did him. Although inclined to frown on so marked a presumption in his case, she let it pass because it was pleasing to her.

"Oh, yes, I do. Of course," she said a little dubiously, and for the first time nervously, where he was concerned. She was beginning to find it a little hard to decipher her proper line of conduct in connection with him, whether to repress him more or less. "But you must say now what dance you want. I see some one coming for me." And she held her small program up to him archly and intriguingly. "You may have the eleventh. That's the next after this."

"Is that all?"

"Well, and the fourteenth, then, greedy," she laughed into Clyde's eyes, a laughing look which quite enslaved him.

Subsequently learning from Frank Harriet in the course of a dance that Clyde had been invited to his house for Christmas Eve, as well as that Jessica Phant had invited him to Utica for New Year's Eve, she at once conceived of him as slated for real success and decided that he was likely to prove less of a social burden than she had feared. He was charming—there was no doubt of it. And he was so devoted to her. In consequence, as she now decided, it might be entirely possible that some of these other girls, seeing him recognized by some of the best people here and elsewhere, would become sufficiently interested, or drawn to him even, to wish to overcome his devotion to her. Being of a vain and presumptuous disposition herself, she decided that that should not be. Hence, in the course of her second dance with Clyde, she said: "You've been invited to the Harriet's for Christmas Eve, haven't you?"

"Yes, and I owe it all to you, too," he exclaimed warmly. "Are you going to be there?"

"Oh, I'm awfully sorry. I am invited and I wish now that I was going. But you know I arranged some time ago to go over to Albany and then up to Saratoga for the holidays. I'm going to-morrow, but I'll be back before New Year's. Some friends of Freddie's are giving a big affair over in Schenectady New Year's Eve, though. And your cousin Bella and my brother Stuart and Grant and Bertine are going. If you'd like to, you might go along with us over there."

She had been about to say "me," but had changed it to "us." She was thinking that this would certainly demonstrate her control over him to all those others, seeing that it nullified Miss Phant's invitation. And at once Clyde accepted, and with delight, since it would bring him in contact with her again.

At the same time he was astonished and almost aghast over

the fact that in this casual and yet very intimate and definite way she was planning for him to reëncounter Bella, who would at once carry the news of his going with her and these others to her family. And what would not that spell, seeing that even as yet the Griffiths had not invited him anywhere—not even for Christmas? For although the fact of Clyde having been picked up by Sondra in her car as well as later, that he had been invited to the Now and Then, had come to their ears, still nothing had been done. Gilbert Griffiths was wroth, his father and mother puzzled as to their proper course but remaining inactive nonetheless.

But the group, according to Sondra, might remain in Schenectady until the following morning, a fact which she did not trouble to explain to Clyde at first. And by now he had forgotten that Roberta, having returned from her long stay at Biltz by then, and having been deserted by him over Christmas, would most assuredly be expecting him to spend New Year's Eve with her. That was a complication which was to dawn later. Now he only saw bliss in Sondra's thought of him and at once eagerly and enthusiastically agreed.

"But you know," she said cautiously, "you mustn't pay so very much attention to me over there or here or anywhere or think anything of it, if I don't to you. I may not be able to see so very much of you if you do. I'll tell you about that sometime. You see my father and mother are funny people. And so are some of my friends here. But if you'll just be nice and sort of indifferent—you know—I may be able to see quite a little of you this winter yet. Do you see?"

Thrilled beyond words by this confession, which came because of his too ardent approaches as he well knew, he looked at her eagerly and searchingly.

"But you care for me a little, then, don't you?" he half-demanded, half-pleaded, his eyes lit with that alluring light which so fascinated her. And cautious and yet attracted, swayed sensually and emotionally and yet dubious as to the wisdom of her course, Sondra replied: "Well, I'll tell you. I do and I don't. That is, I can't tell yet. I like you a lot. Sometimes I think I like you more than others. You see we don't know each other very well yet. But you'll come with me to Schenectady, though, won't you?"

"Oh, will I?"

"I'll write you more about that, or call you up. You have a telephone, haven't you?"

He gave her the number.

"And if by any chance there's any change or I have to break the engagement, don't think anything of it. I'll see you later—somewhere, sure." She smiled and Clyde felt as though he were choking. The mere thought of her being so frank with him, and saying that she cared for him a lot, at times, was sufficient to cause him to almost reel with joy. To think that this beautiful girl was so anxious to include him in her life if she could—this wonderful girl who was surrounded by so many friends and admirers from which she could take her pick.

# Chapter XXVIII

SIX-THIRTY the following morning. And Clyde, after but a single hour's rest after his return from Gloversville, rising, his mind full of mixed and troubled thoughts as to how to readjust his affairs in connection with Roberta. She was going to Biltz to-day. He had promised to go as far as Fonda. But now he did not want to go. Of course he would have to concoct some excuse. But what?

Fortunately the day before he had heard Whiggam tell Liggett there was to be a meeting of department heads after closing hours in Smillie's office to-day, and that he was to be there. Nothing was said to Clyde, since his department was included in Liggett's, but now he decided that he could offer this as a reason and accordingly, about an hour before noon, he dropped a note on her desk which read:

"HONEY: Awfully sorry, but just told that I have to be at a meeting of department heads downstairs at three. That means I can't go to Fonda with you, but will drop around to the room for a few minutes right after closing. Have something I want to give you, so be sure and wait. But don't feel too bad. It can't be helped. See you sure when you come back Wednesday.

"CLYDE."

At first, since she could not read it at once, Roberta was pleased because she imagined it contained some further favorable word about the afternoon. But on opening it in the ladies' rest room a few minutes afterwards, her face fell. Coupled as this was with the disappointment of the preceding evening, when Clyde had failed to appear, together with his manner of the morning which to her had seemed self-absorbed, if not exactly distant, she began to wonder what it was that was bringing about this sudden change. Perhaps he could not avoid attending a meeting any more than he could avoid going to his uncle's when he was asked. But the day before, following his word to her that he could not be with her that evening, his manner was gayer, less sober, than his supposed affection in the face of her departure would warrant.

After all he had known before that she was to be gone for three days. He also knew that nothing weighed on her more than being absent from him any length of time.

At once her mood from one of hopefulness changed to one of deep depression—the blues. Life was always doing things like this to her. Here it was—two days before Christmas, and now she would have to go to Biltz, where there was nothing much but such cheer as she could bring, and all by herself, and after scarcely a moment with him. She returned to her bench, her face showing all the unhappiness that had suddenly overtaken her. Her manner was listless and her movements indifferent—a change which Clyde noticed; but still, because of his sudden and desperate feeling for Sondra, he could not now bring himself to repent.

At one, the giant whistles of some of the neighboring factories sounding the Saturday closing hours, both he and Roberta betook themselves separately to her room. And he was thinking to himself as he went what to say now. What to do? How in the face of this suddenly frosted and blanched affection to pretend an interest he did not feel—how, indeed, continue with a relationship which now, as alive and vigorous as it might have been as little as fifteen days before, appeared exceedingly anemic and colorless. It would not do to say or indicate in any way that he did not care for her any more—for that would be so decidedly cruel and might cause Roberta to say what? Do what? And on the other hand, neither would it do, in the face of his longings and prospects in the direction of Sondra to continue in a type of approach and declaration that was not true or sound and that could only tend to maintain things as they were. Impossible! Besides, at the first hint of reciprocal love on the part of Sondra, would he not be anxious and determined to desert Roberta if he could? And why not? As contrasted with one of Sondra's position and beauty, what had Roberta really to offer him? And would it be fair in one of her station and considering the connections and the possibilities that Sondra offered, for her to demand or assume that he should continue a deep and undivided interest in her as opposed to this other? That would not really be fair, would it?

It was thus that he continued to speculate while Roberta, preceding him to her room, was asking herself what was this now that had so suddenly come upon her—over Clyde—this sudden indifference, this willingness to break a pre-Christmas date, and when she was about to leave for home and not to see him for three days and over Christmas, too, to make him not wish to ride with her even so far as Fonda. He might say that it was that meeting, but was it? She could have waited until four if necessary, but something in his manner had precluded that—something distant and evasive. Oh, what did this all mean? And, so soon after the establishing of this intimacy, which at first and up to now at least had seemed to be drawing them indivisibly together. Did it spell a change— danger to or the end even of their wonderful love dream? Oh, dear! And she had given him so much and now his loyalty meant everything—her future—her life.

She stood in her room pondering this new problem as Clyde arrived, his Christmas package under his arm, but still fixed in his determination to modify his present relationship with Roberta, if he could—yet, at the same time anxious to put as inconsequential a face on the proceeding as possible.

"Gee, I'm awfully sorry about this, Bert," he began briskly, his manner a mixture of attempted gayety, sympathy and uncertainty. "I hadn't an idea until about a couple of hours ago that they were going to have this meeting. But you know how it is. You just can't get out of a thing like this. You're not going to feel too bad, are you?" For already, from her expression at the factory as well as here, he had gathered that her mood was of the darkest. "I'm glad I got the chance to bring this around to you, though," he added, handing the gift to her. "I meant to bring it around last night only that other business came up. Gee, I'm sorry about the whole thing. Really, I am."

Delighted as she might have been the night before if this gift had been given to her, Roberta now put the box on the table, all the zest that might have been joined with it completely banished.

"Did you have a good time last night, dear?" she queried, curious as to the outcome of the event that had robbed her of him.

"Oh, pretty good," returned Clyde, anxious to put as deceptive a face as possible on the night that had meant so much to him and spelled so much danger to her. "I thought

I was just going over to my uncle's for dinner like I told you. But after I got there I found that what they really wanted me for was to escort Bella and Myra over to some doings in Gloversville. There's a rich family over there, the Steeles—big glove people, you know. Well, anyhow, they were giving a dance and they wanted me to take them over because Gil couldn't go. But it wasn't so very interesting. I was glad when it was all over." He used the names Bella, Myra and Gilbert as though they were long and assured intimates of his—an intimacy which invariably impressed Roberta greatly.

"You didn't get through in time then to come around here, did you?"

"No, I didn't 'cause I had to wait for the bunch to come back. I just couldn't get away. But aren't you going to open your present?" he added, anxious to divert her thoughts from this desertion which he knew was preying on her mind.

She began to untie the ribbon that bound his gift, at the same time that her mind was riveted by the possibilities of the party which he had felt called upon to mention. What girls beside Bella and Myra had been there? Was there by any chance any girl outside of herself in whom he might have become recently interested? He was always talking about Sondra Finchley, Bertine Cranston and Jill Trumbull. Were they, by any chance, at this party?

"Who all were over there beside your cousins?" she suddenly asked.

"Oh, a lot of people that you don't know. Twenty or thirty from different places around here."

"Any others from Lycurgus beside your cousins?" she persisted.

"Oh, a few. We picked up Jill Trumbull and her sister, because Bella wanted to. Arabella Stark and Perley Haynes were already over there when we got there." He made no mention of Sondra or any of the others who so interested him.

But because of the manner in saying it—something in the tone of his voice and flick of his eyes, the answer did not satisfy Roberta. She was really intensely troubled by this new development, but did not feel that under the circumstances it was wise to importune Clyde too much. He might resent it. After all he had always been identified with this world since ever she had known him. And she did not want him to feel that she was attempting to assert any claims over him, though such was her true desire.

"I wanted so much to be with you last night to give you your present," she returned instead, as much to divert her own thoughts as to appeal to his regard for her. Clyde sensed the sorrow in her voice and as of old it appealed to him, only now he could not and would not let it take hold of him as much as otherwise it might have.

"But you know how that was, Bert," he replied, with almost an air of bravado. "I just told you."

"I know," she replied sadly and attempting to conceal the true mood that was dominating her. At the same time she was removing the paper and opening the lid to the case that contained her toilet set. And once opened, her mood changed slightly because never before had she possessed anything so valuable or original. "Oh, this is beautiful, isn't it?" she exclaimed, interested for the moment in spite of herself. "I didn't expect anything like this. My two little presents won't seem like very much now."

She crossed over at once to get her gifts. Yet Clyde could see that although his gift was exceptional, still it was not sufficient to overcome the depression which his indifference had brought upon her. His continued love was far more vital than any present.

"You like it, do you?" he asked, eagerly hoping against hope that it would serve to divert her.

"Of course, dear," she replied, looking at it interestedly. "But mine won't seem so much," she added gloomily, and not a little depressed by the general outcome of all her plans. "But they'll be useful to you and you'll always have them near you, next your heart, where I want them to be."

She handed over the small box which contained the metal eversharp pencil and the silver ornamented fountain pen she had chosen for him because she fancied they would be useful to him in his work at the factory. Two weeks before he would have taken her in his arms and sought to console her for the misery he was now causing her. But now he merely stood there wondering how, without seeming too distant, he could assuage her and yet not enter upon the customary demonstrations. And in order so to do he burst into enthusiastic and yet somehow hollow words in regard to her present to him.

"Oh, gee, these are swell, honey, and just what I need. You certainly couldn't have given me anything that would come in handier. I can use them all the time." He appeared to examine them with the utmost pleasure and afterwards fastened them in his pocket ready for use. Also, because for the moment she was before him so downcast and wistful, epitomizing really all the lure of the old relationship, he put his arms around her and kissed her. She was winsome, no doubt of it. And then when she threw her arms around his neck and burst into tears, he held her close, saying that there was no cause for all this and that she would be back Wednesday and all would be as before. At the same time he was thinking that this was not true, and how strange that was—seeing that only so recently he had cared for her so much. It was amazing how another girl could divert him in this way. And yet so it was. And although she might be thinking that he was still caring for her as he did before, he was not and never would again. And because of this he felt really sorry for her.

Something of this latest mood in him reached Roberta now, even as she listened to his words and felt his caresses. They failed to convey sincerity. His manner was too restless, his embraces too apathetic, his tone without real tenderness. Further proof as to this was added when, after a moment or two, he sought to disengage himself and looked at his watch, saying, "I guess I'll have to be going now, honey. It's twenty of three now and that meeting is for three. I wish I could ride over with you, but I'll see you when you get back."

He bent down to kiss her but with Roberta sensing once and for all, this time, that his mood in regard to her was different, colder. He was interested and kind, but his thoughts were elsewhere—and at this particular season of the year, too—of all times. She tried to gather her strength and her self-respect together and did, in part—saying rather coolly, and determinedly toward the last: "Well, I don't want you to be late, Clyde. You better hurry. But I don't want to stay over there either later than Christmas night. Do you suppose if I come back early Christmas afternoon, you will come over here at all? I don't want to be late Wednesday for work."

"Why, sure, of course, honey, I'll be around," replied Clyde genially and even whole-heartedly, seeing that he had nothing else scheduled, that he knew of, for then, and would not so soon and boldly seek to evade her in this fashion. "What time do you expect to get in?"

The hour was to be eight and he decided that for that occasion, anyhow, a reunion would be acceptable. He drew out his watch again and saying, "I'll have to be going now, though," moved toward the door.

Nervous as to the significance of all this and concerned about the future, she now went over to him and seizing his coat lapels and looking into his eyes, half-pleaded and half-demanded: "Now, this is sure for Christmas night, is it, Clyde? You won't make any other engagement this time, will you?"

"Oh, don't worry. You know me. You know I couldn't help that other, honey. But I'll be on hand Tuesday, sure," he returned. And kissing her, he hurried out, feeling, perhaps, that he was not acting as wisely as he should, but not seeing clearly how otherwise he was to do. A man couldn't break off with a girl as he was trying to do, or at least might want to, without exercising some little tact or diplomacy, could he? There was no sense in that nor any real skill, was there? There must be some other and better way than that, surely. At the same time his thoughts were already running forward to Sondra and New Year's Eve. He was going with her to Schenectady to a party and then he would have a chance to judge whether she was caring for him as much as she had seemed to the night before.

After he had gone, Roberta turned in a rather lorn and weary way and looked out the window after him, wondering as to what her future with him was to be, if at all? Supposing now, for any reason, he should cease caring for her. She had given him so much. And her future was now dependent upon him, his continued regard. Was he going to get tired of her now—not want to see her any more? Oh, how terrible that would be. What would she—what could she do then? If only she had not given herself to him, yielded so easily and so soon upon his demand.

She gazed out of her window at the bare snow-powdered branches of the trees outside and sighed. The holidays! And going away like this. Oh! Besides he was so high placed in this local society. And there were so many things brighter and better than she could offer calling him.

She shook her head dubiously, surveyed her face in the mirror, put together the few presents and belongings which she was taking with her to her home, and departed.

# Chapter XXIX

<sub>B</sub> ILTZ and the fungoid farm land after Clyde and Lycurgus was depressing enough to Roberta, for all there was too closely identified with deprivations and repressions which discolor the normal emotions centering about old scenes.

As she stepped down from the train at the drab and aged chalet which did service for a station, she observed her father in the same old winter overcoat he had worn for a dozen years, waiting for her with the old family conveyance, a decrepit but still whole buggy and a horse as bony and weary as himself. He had, as she had always thought, the look of a tired and defeated man. His face brightened when he saw Roberta, for she had always been his favorite child, and he chatted quite cheerfully as she climbed in alongside of him and they turned around and started toward the road that led to the farmhouse, a rough and winding affair of dirt at a time when excellent automobile roads were a commonplace elsewhere.

As they rode along Roberta found herself checking off mentally every tree, curve, landmark with which she had been familiar. But with no happy thoughts. It was all too drab. The farm itself, coupled with the chronic illness and inefficiency of Titus and the inability of the youngest boy Tom or her mother to help much, was as big a burden as ever. A mortgage of $2000 that had been placed on it years before had never been paid off, the north chimney was still impaired, the steps were sagging even more than ever and the walls and fences and outlying buildings were no different—save to be made picturesque now by the snows of winter covering them. Even the furniture remained the same jumble that it had always been. And there were her mother and younger sister and brother, who knew nothing of her true relationship to Clyde—a mere name his here—and assuming that she was wholeheartedly delighted to be back with them once more. Yet because of what she knew of her own life and Clyde's uncertain attitude toward her, she was now, if anything, more depressed than before.

Indeed, the fact that despite her seeming recent success she had really compromised herself in such a way that unless through marriage with Clyde she was able to readjust herself to the moral level which her parents understood and approved, she, instead of being the emissary of a slowly and modestly improving social condition for all, might be looked upon as one who had reduced it to a lower level still—its destroyer—was sufficient to depress and reduce her even more. A very depressing and searing thought.

Worse and more painful still was the thought in connection with all this that, by reason of the illusions which from the first had dominated her in connection with Clyde, she had not been able to make a confidant of her mother or any one else in regard to him. For she was dubious as to whether her mother would not consider that her aspirations were a bit high. And she might ask questions in regard to him and herself which might prove embarrassing. At the same time, unless she had some confidant in whom she could truly trust, all her troublesome doubts in regard to herself and Clyde must remain a secret.

After talking for a few moments with Tom and Emily, she went into the kitchen where her mother was busy with various Christmas preparations. Her thought was to pave the way with some observations of her own in regard to the farm here and her life at Lycurgus, but as she entered, her mother looked up to say: "How does it feel, Bob, to come back to the country? I suppose it all looks rather poor compared to Lycurgus," she added a little wistfully.

Roberta could tell from the tone of her mother's voice and the rather admiring look she cast upon her that she was thinking of her as one who had vastly improved her state. At once she went over to her and, putting her arms about her affectionately, exclaimed: "Oh, mamma, wherever you are is just the nicest place. Don't you know that?"

For answer her mother merely looked at her with affectionate and well-wishing eyes and patted her on the back. "Well, Bobbie," she added, quietly, "you know how you are about me."

Something in her mother's voice which epitomized the long years of affectionate understanding between them—an understanding based, not only on a mutual desire for each other's happiness, but a complete frankness in regard to all emotions and moods which had hitherto dominated both—touched her almost to the point of tears. Her throat tightened and her eyes moistened, although she sought to overcome any show of emotion whatsoever. She longed to tell her everything. At the same time the compelling passion she retained for Clyde, as well as the fact that she had compromised herself as she had, now showed her that she had erected a barrier which could not easily be torn down. The conventions of this local world were much too strong—even where her mother was concerned.

She hesitated a moment, wishing that she could quickly and clearly present to her mother the problem that was weighing upon her and receive her sympathy, if not help. But instead she merely said: "Oh, I wish you could have been with me all the time in Lycurgus, mamma. Maybe—" She paused, realizing that she had been on the verge of speaking without due caution. Her thought was that with her mother near at hand she might have been able to have resisted Clyde's insistent desires.

"Yes, I suppose you do miss me," her mother went on, "but it's better for you, don't you think? You know how it is over here, and you like your work. You do like your work, don't you?"

"Oh, the work is nice enough. I like that part of it. It's been so nice to be able to help here a little, but it's not so nice living all alone."

"Why did you leave the Newtons, Bob? Was Grace so disagreeable? I should have thought she would have been company for you."

"Oh, she was at first," replied Roberta. "Only she didn't have any men friends of her own, and she was awfully jealous of anybody that paid the least attention to me. I couldn't go anywhere but she had to go along, or if it wasn't that then she always wanted me to be with her, so I couldn't go anywhere by myself. You know how it is, mamma. Two girls can't go with one young man."

"Yes, I know how it is, Bob." Her mother laughed a little, then added: "Who is he?"

"It's Mr. Griffiths, mother," she added, after a moment's

hesitation, a sense of the exceptional nature of her contact as contrasted with this very plain world here passing like a light across her eyes. For all her fears, even the bare possibility of joining her life with Clyde's was marvelous. "But I don't want you to mention his name to anybody yet," she added. "He doesn't want me to. His relatives are so very rich, you know. They own the company—that is, his uncle does. But there's a rule there about any one who works for the company—any one in charge of a department. I mean not having anything to do with any of the girls. And he wouldn't with any of the others. But he likes me—and I like him, and it's different with us. Besides I'm going to resign pretty soon and get a place somewhere else, I think, and then it won't make any difference. I can tell anybody, and so can he."

Roberta was thinking now that, in the face of her recent treatment at the hands of Clyde, as well as because of the way in which she had given herself to him without due precaution as to her ultimate rehabilitation via marriage, that perhaps this was not exactly true. He might not—a vague, almost formless, fear this, as yet—want her to tell anybody now—ever. And unless he were going to continue to love her and marry her, she might not want any one to know of it, either. The wretched, shameful, difficult position in which she had placed herself by all this.

On the other hand, Mrs. Alden, learning thus casually of the odd and seemingly clandestine nature of this relationship, was not only troubled but puzzled, so concerned was she for Roberta's happiness. For, although, as she now said to herself, Roberta was such a good, pure and careful girl—the best and most unselfish and wisest of all her children—still might it not be possible—? But, no, no one was likely to either easily or safely compromise or betray Roberta. She was too conservative and good, and so now she added: "A relative of the owner, you say—the Mr. Samuel Griffiths you wrote about?"

"Yes, Mamma. He's his nephew."

"The young man at the factory?" her mother asked, at the same time wondering just how Roberta had come to attract a man of Clyde's position, for, from the very first she had made it plain that he was a member of the family who owned the factory. This in itself was a troublesome fact. The traditional result of such relationships, common the world over, naturally caused her to be intensely fearful of just such an association as Roberta seemed to be making. Nevertheless she was not at all convinced that a girl of Roberta's looks and practicality would not be able to negotiate an association of the sort without harm to herself.

"Yes," Roberta replied simply.

"What's he like, Bob?"

"Oh, awfully nice. So good-looking, and he's been so nice to me. I don't think the place would be as nice as it is except that he is so refined, he keeps those factory girls in their place. He's a nephew of the president of the company, you see, and the girls just naturally have to respect him."

"Well, that *is* nice, isn't it? I think it's so much better to work for refined people than just anybody. I know you didn't think so much of the work over at Trippetts Mills. Does he come to see you often, Bob?"

"Well, yes, pretty often," Roberta replied, flushing slightly, for she realized that she could not be entirely frank with her mother.

Mrs. Alden, looking up at the moment, noticed this, and, mistaking it for embarrassment, asked teasingly: "You like him, don't you?"

"Yes, I do, mother," Roberta replied, simply and honestly.

"What about him? Does he like you?"

Roberta crossed to the kitchen window. Below it at the base of the slope which led to the springhouse, and the one most productive field of the farm, were ranged all the dilapidated buildings which more than anything else about the place bespoke the meager material condition to which the family had fallen. In fact, during the last ten years these things had become symbols of inefficiency and lack. Somehow at this moment, bleak and covered with snow, they identified themselves in her mind as the antithesis of all to which her imagination aspired. And, not strangely either, the last was identified with Clyde. Somberness as opposed to happiness—success in love or failure in love. Assuming that he truly loved her now and would take her away from all this, then possibly the bleakness of it all for her and her mother would be broken. But assuming that he did not, then all the results of her yearning, but possibly mistaken, dreams would be not only upon her own head, but upon those of these others, her mother's first. She troubled what to say, but finally observed: "Well, he says he does."

"Do you think he intends to marry you?" Mrs. Alden asked, timidly and hopefully, because of all her children her heart and hopes rested most with Roberta.

"Well, I'll tell you, Mamma . . ." The sentence was not finished, for just then Emily, hurrying in from the front door, called: "Oh, Gif's here. He came in an automobile. Somebody drove him over, I guess, and he's got four or five big bundles."

And immediately after came Tom with the elder brother, who, in a new overcoat, the first result of his career with the General Electric Company in Schenectady, greeted his mother affectionately, and after her, Roberta.

"Why, Gifford," his mother exclaimed. "We didn't expect you until the nine o'clock. How did you get here so soon?"

"Well, I didn't think I would be. I ran into Mr. Rearick down in Schenectady and he wanted to know if I didn't want to drive back with him. I see old Pop Myers over at Trippetts Mills has got the second story to his house at last, Bob," he turned and added to Roberta: "I suppose it'll be another year before he gets the roof on."

"I suppose so," replied Roberta, who knew the old Trippetts Mills character well. In the meantime she had relieved him of his coat and packages which, piled on the dining-room table, were being curiously eyed by Emily.

"Hands off, Em!" called Gifford to his little sister. "Nothing doing with those until Christmas morning. Has anybody cut a Christmas tree yet? That was my job last year."

"It still is, Gifford," his mother replied. "I told Tom to wait until you came, 'cause you always get such a good one."

And just then through the kitchen door Titus entered, bearing an armload of wood, his gaunt face and angular elbows and knees contributing a sharp contrast to the comparative hopefulness of the younger generation. Roberta noticed it as he stood smiling upon his son, and, because she was so eager for something better than ever had been to come to all, now went over to her father and put her arms around him. "I

know something Santy has brought my Dad that he'll like."
It was a dark red plaid mackinaw that she was sure would
keep him warm while executing his chores about the house,
and she was anxious for Christmas morning to come so that
he could see it.

She then went to get an apron in order to help her mother
with the evening meal. No additional moment for complete
privacy occurring, the opportunity to say more concerning
that which both were so interested in—the subject of Clyde
did not come up again for several hours, after which length of
time she found occasion to say: "Yes, but you mustn't ever say
anything to anybody yet. I told him I wouldn't tell, and you
mustn't."

"No, I won't dear. But I was just wondering. But I suppose
you know what you're doing. You're old enough now to take
care of yourself, Bob, aren't you?"

"Yes, I am, Ma. And you mustn't worry about me, dear,"
she added, seeing a shadow, not of distrust but worry, passing
over her beloved mother's face. How careful she must be not
to cause her to worry when she had so much else to think
about here on the farm.

Sunday morning brought the Gabels with full news of their
social and material progress in Homer. Although her sister
was not as attractive as she, and Fred Gabel was not such a
man as at any stage in her life Roberta could have imagined
herself interested in, still, after her troublesome thoughts in
regard to Clyde, the sight of Agnes emotionally and materially content and at ease in the small security which matrimony
and her none-too-efficient husband provided, was sufficient
to rouse in her that flapping, doubtful mood that had been
assailing her since the previous morning. Was it not better,
she thought, to be married to a man even as inefficient and
unattractive but steadfast as Fred Gabel, than to occupy the
anomalous position in which she now found herself in her relations with Clyde? For here was Gabel now talking briskly of
the improvements that had come to himself and Agnes during the year in which they had been married. In that time he
had been able to resign his position as teacher in Homer and
take over on shares the management of a small book and stationery store whose principal contributory features were a toy

department and soda fountain. They had been doing a good business. Agnes, if all went well, would be able to buy a mission parlor suite by next summer. Fred had already bought her a phonograph for Christmas. In proof of their well-being, they had brought satisfactory remembrances for all of the Aldens.

But Gabel had with him a copy of the Lycurgus *Star*, and at breakfast, which because of the visitors this morning was unusually late, was reading the news of that city, for in Lycurgus was located the wholesale house from which he secured a portion of his stock.

"Well, I see things are going full blast in your town, Bob," he observed. "*The Star* here says the Griffiths Company have got an order for 120,000 collars from the Buffalo trade alone. They must be just coining money over there."

"There's always plenty to do in my department, I know that," replied Roberta, briskly. "We never seem to have any the less to do whether business is good or bad. I guess it must be good all the time."

"Pretty soft for those people. They don't have to worry about anything. Some one was telling me they're going to build a new factory in Ilion to manufacture shirts alone. Heard anything about that down there?"

"Why, no, I haven't. Maybe it's some other company."

"By the way, what's the name of that young man you said was the head of your department? Wasn't he a Griffiths, too?" he asked briskly, turning to the editorial page, which also carried news of local Lycurgus society.

"Yes, his name is Griffiths—Clyde Griffiths. Why?"

"I think I saw his name in here a minute ago. I just wanted to see if it ain't the same fellow. Sure, here you are. Ain't this the one?" He passed the paper to Roberta with his finger on an item which read:

"Miss Vanda Steele, of Gloversville, was hostess at an informal dance held at her home in that city Friday night, at which were present several prominent members of Lycurgus society, among them the Misses Sondra Finchley, Bertine Cranston, Jill and Gertrude Trumbull and Perley Haynes, and Messrs. Clyde Griffiths, Frank Harriet, Tracy Trumbull, Grant Cranston and Scott Nicholson. The party, as is usual whenever the younger group assembles, did not break up until late, the Lycurgus members motoring back just before dawn. It is already rumored that most of this group will gather at the Ellerslies', in Schenectady, New Year's Eve for another event of this same gay nature."

"He seems to be quite a fellow over there," Gabel remarked, even as Roberta was reading.

The first thing that occurred to Roberta on reading this item was that it appeared to have little, if anything, to do with the group which Clyde had said was present. In the first place there was no mention of Myra or Bella Griffiths. On the other hand, all those names with which, because of recent frequent references on the part of Clyde, she was becoming most familiar were recorded as present. Sondra Finchley, Bertine Cranston, the Trumbull girls, Perley Haynes. He had said it had not been very interesting, and here it was spoken of as gay and he himself was listed for another engagement of the same character New Year's Eve, when, as a matter of fact, she had been counting on being with him. He had not even mentioned this New Year's engagement. And perhaps he would now make some last minute excuse for that, as he had for the previous Friday evening. Oh, dear! What did all this mean, anyhow!

Immediately what little romantic glamour this Christmas homecoming had held for her was dissipated. She began to wonder whether Clyde really cared for her as he had pretended. The dark state to which her incurable passion for him had brought her now pained her terribly. For without him and marriage and a home and children, and a reasonable place in such a local world as she was accustomed to, what was there for a girl like her in the world? And apart from his own continuing affection for her—if it was really continuing, what assurance had she, in the face of such incidents as these, that he would not eventually desert her? And if this were true, here was her future, in so far as marriage with any one else was concerned, compromised or made impossible, maybe, and with no reliance to be placed on him.

She fell absolutely silent. And although Gabel inquired: "That's the fellow, isn't it?" she arose without answering and said: "Excuse me, please, a moment. I want to get something out of my bag," and hurried once more to her former room upstairs. Once there she sat down on the bed, and, resting her chin in her hands, a habit when troublesome or necessary thoughts controlled her, gazed at the floor.

Where was Clyde now?

What one, if any, of those girls did he take to the Steele party? Was he very much interested in her? Until this very day, because of Clyde's unbroken devotion to her, she had not even troubled to think there could be any other girl to whom his attentions could mean anything.

But now—now!

She got up and walked to the window and looked out on that same orchard where as a girl so many times she had been thrilled by the beauty of life. The scene was miserably bleak and bare. The thin, icy arms of the trees—the gray, swaying twigs— a lone, rustling leaf somewhere. And snow. And wretched outbuildings in need of repair. And Clyde becoming indifferent to her. And the thought now came to her swiftly and urgently that she must not stay here any longer than she could help—not even this day, if possible. She must return to Lycurgus and be near Clyde, if no more than to persuade him to his old affection for her, or if not that, then by her presence to prevent him from devoting himself too wholly to these others. Decidedly, to go away like this, even for the holidays, was not good. In her absence he might desert her completely for another girl, and if so, then would it not be her fault? At once she pondered as to what excuse she could make in order to return this day. But realizing that in view of all these preliminary preparations this would seem inexplicably unreasonable, to her mother most of all, she decided to endure it as she had planned until Christmas afternoon, then to return, never to leave for so long a period again.

But ad interim, all her thoughts were on how and in what way she could make more sure, if at all, of Clyde's continued interest and social and emotional support, as well as marriage in the future. Supposing he had lied to her, how could she influence him, if at all, not to do so again? How to make him feel that lying between them was not right? How to make herself securely first in his heart against the dreams engendered by the possible charms of another?

How?

# Chapter XXX

B UT Roberta's return to Lycurgus and her room at the
Gilpins' Christmas night brought no sign of Clyde nor
any word of explanation. For in connection with the Griffiths
in the meantime there had been a development relating to all
this which, could she or Clyde have known, would have interested both not a little. For subsequent to the Steele dance
that same item read by Roberta fell under the eyes of Gilbert.
He was seated at the breakfast table the Sunday morning after the party, and was about to sip from a cup of coffee when
he encountered it. On the instant his teeth snapped about as
a man might snap his watch lid, and instead of drinking he
put his cup down and examined the item with more care.
Other than his mother there was no one at the table or in the
room with him, but knowing that she, more than any of
the others, shared his views in regard to Clyde, he now passed
the paper over to her.

"Look at who's breaking into society now, will you?" he
admonished sharply and sarcastically, his eyes radiating the
hard and contemptuous opposition he felt. "We'll be having
him up here next!"

"Who?" inquired Mrs. Griffiths, as she took the paper and
examined the item calmly and judicially, yet not without a
little of outwardly suppressed surprise when she saw the
name. For although the fact of Clyde's having been picked up
by Sondra in her car sometime before and later been invited
to dinner at the Trumbulls', had been conveyed to the family
sometime before, still a society notice in *The Star* was different. "Now I wonder how it was that he came to be invited to
that?" meditated Mrs. Griffiths who was always conscious of
her son's mood in regard to all this.

"Now, who would do it but that little Finchley snip, the
little smart aleck?" snapped Gilbert. "She's got the idea from
somewhere—from Bella for all I know—that we don't care to
have anything to do with him, and she thinks this is a clever
way to hit back at me for some of the things I've done to her,
or that she thinks I've done. At any rate, she thinks I don't

404

like her, and that's right, I don't. And Bella knows it, too. And that goes for that little Cranston show-off, too. They're both always running around with her. They're a set of show-offs and wasters, the whole bunch, and that goes for their brothers, too—Grant Cranston and Stew Finchley—and if something don't go wrong with one or another of that bunch one of these days, I miss my guess. You mark my word! They don't do a thing, the whole lot of them, from one year's end to the other but play around and dance and run here and there, as though there wasn't anything else in the world for them to do. And why you and Dad let Bella run with 'em as much as she does is more than I can see."

To this his mother protested. It was not possible for her to entirely estrange Bella from one portion of this local social group and direct her definitely toward the homes of certain others. They all mingled too freely. And she was getting along in years and had a mind of her own.

Just the same his mother's apology and especially in the face of the publication of this item by no means lessened Gilbert's opposition to Clyde's social ambitions and opportunities. What! That poor little moneyless cousin of his who had committed first the unpardonable offense of looking like him and, second, of coming here to Lycurgus and fixing himself on this very superior family. And after he had shown him all too plainly, and from the first, that he personally did not like him, did not want him, and if left to himself would never for so much as a moment endure him.

"He hasn't any money," he declared finally and very bitterly to his mother, "and he's hanging on here by the skin of his teeth as it is. And what for? If he is taken up by these people, what can he do? He certainly hasn't the money to do as they do, and he can't get it. And if he could, his job here wouldn't let him go anywhere much, unless some one troubled to pay his way. And how he is going to do his work and run with that crowd is more than I know. That bunch is on the go all the time."

Actually he was wondering whether Clyde would be included from now on, and if so, what was to be done about it. If he were to be taken up in this way, how was he, or the family, either, to escape from being civil to him? For obviously, as earlier and subsequent developments proved, his father did not choose to send him away.

Indeed, subsequent to this conversation, Mrs. Griffiths had laid the paper, together with a version of Gilbert's views before her husband at this same breakfast table. But he, true to his previous mood in regard to Clyde, was not inclined to share his son's opinion. On the contrary, he seemed, as Mrs. Griffiths saw it, to look upon the development recorded by the item as a justification in part of his own original estimate of Clyde.

"I must say," he began, after listening to his wife to the end, "I can't see what's wrong with his going to a party now and then, or being invited here and there even if he hasn't any money. It looks more like a compliment to him and to us than anything else. I know how Gil feels about him. But it rather looks to me as though Clyde's just a little better than Gil thinks he is. At any rate, I can't and I wouldn't want to do anything about it. I've asked him to come down here, and the least I can do is to give him an opportunity to better himself. He seems to be doing his work all right. Besides, how would it look if I didn't?"

And later, because of some additional remarks on the part of Gilbert to his mother, he added: "I'd certainly rather have him going with some of the better people than some of the worse ones—that's one thing sure. He's neat and polite and from all I hear at the factory does his work well enough. As a matter of fact, I think it would have been better if we had invited him up to the lake last summer for a few days anyhow, as I suggested. As it is now, if we don't do something pretty soon, it will look as though we think he isn't good enough for us when the other people here seem to think he is. If you'll take my advice, you'll have him up here for Christmas or New Year's, anyhow, just to show that we don't think any less of him than our friends do."

This suggestion, once transferred to Gilbert by his mother, caused him to exclaim: "Well, I'll be hanged! All right, only don't think I'm going to lay myself out to be civil to him. It's a wonder, if father thinks he's so able, that he don't make a real position for him somewhere."

Just the same, nothing might have come of this had it not

been that Bella, returning from Albany this same day, learned via contacts and telephone talks with Sondra and Bertine of the developments in connection with Clyde. Also that he had been invited to accompany them to the New Year's Eve dance at the Ellerslies' in Schenectady, Bella having been previously scheduled to make a part of this group before Clyde was thought of.

This sudden development, reported by Bella to her mother, was of sufficient import to cause Mrs. Griffiths as well as Samuel, if not Gilbert, later to decide to make the best of a situation which obviously was being forced upon them and themselves invite Clyde for dinner—Christmas day—a sedate affair to which many others were bid. For this as they now decided would serve to make plain to all and at once that Clyde was not being as wholly ignored as some might imagine. It was the only reasonable thing to do at this late date. And Gilbert, on hearing this, and realizing that in this instance he was checkmated, exclaimed sourly: "Oh, all right. Invite him if you want to—if that's the way you and Dad feel about it. I don't see any real necessity for it even now. But you fix it to suit yourself. Constance and I are going over to Utica for the afternoon, anyhow, so I couldn't be there even if I wanted to."

He was thinking of what an outrageous thing it was that a girl whom he disliked as much as he did Sondra could thus via her determination and plottings thrust his own cousin on him and he be unable to prevent it. And what a beggar Clyde must be to attempt to attach himself in this way when he knew that he was not wanted! What sort of a youth was he, anyhow?

And so it was that on Monday morning Clyde had received another letter from the Griffiths, this time signed by Myra, asking him to have dinner with them at two o'clock Christmas day. But, since this at that time did not seem to interfere with his meeting Roberta Christmas night at eight, he merely gave himself over to extreme rejoicing in regard to it all now, and at last he was nearly as well placed here, socially, as any one. For although he had no money, see how he was being received—and by the Griffiths, too—among all the others. And Sondra taking so great an interest in him, actually talking and acting as though she might be ready to fall in love. And Gilbert checkmated by his social popularity. What would you say to that? It testified, as he saw it now, that at least his relatives had not forgotten him or that, because of his recent success in other directions, they were finding it necessary to be civil to him—a thought that was the same as the bays of victory to a contestant. He viewed it with as much pleasure almost as though there had never been any hiatus at all.

# Chapter XXXI

UNFORTUNATELY, however, the Christmas dinner at the Griffiths', which included the Starks and their daughter Arabella, Mr. and Mrs. Wynant, who in the absence of their daughter Constance with Gilbert were dining with the Griffiths, the Arnolds, Anthonys, Harriets, Taylors and others of note in Lycurgus, so impressed and even overawed Clyde that although five o'clock came and then six, he was incapable of breaking away or thinking clearly and compellingly of his obligation to Roberta. Even when, slightly before six, the greater portion of those who had been thus cheerfully entertained began rising and making their bows and departing (and when he, too, should have been doing the same and thinking of his appointment with Roberta), being accosted by Violet Taylor, who was part of the younger group, and who now began talking of some additional festivities to be held that same evening at the Anthonys', and who added most urgently, "You're coming with us, aren't you? Sure you are," he at once acquiesced, although his earlier promise to Roberta forced the remembrance that she was probably already back and expecting him. But still he had time even now, didn't he?

Yet, once at the Anthonys', and talking and dancing with various girls, the obligation faded. But at nine he began worrying a little. For by this time she must be in her room and wondering what had become of him and his promise. And on Christmas night, too. And after she had been away three days.

Inwardly he grew more and more restless and troubled, the while outwardly he maintained that same high spirit that characterized him throughout the afternoon. Fortunately for his own mood, this same group, having danced and frolicked every night for the past week until almost nervously exhausted, it now unanimously and unconsciously yielded to weariness and at eleven thirty, broke up. And after having escorted Bella Griffiths to her door, Clyde hurried around to Elm Street to see if by any chance Roberta was still awake.

As he neared the Gilpins' he perceived through the snow-covered bushes and trees the glow of her single lamp. And for the time being, troubled as to what he should say—how excuse himself for this inexplicable lapse—he paused near one of the large trees that bordered the street, debating with himself as to just what he would say. Would he insist that he had again been to the Griffiths', or where? For according to his previous story he had only been there the Friday before. In the months before when he had no social contacts, but was merely romanticizing in regard to them, the untruths he found himself telling her caused him no twinges of any kind. They were not real and took up no actual portion of his time, nor did they interfere with any of his desired contacts with her. But now in the face of the actuality and the fact that these new contacts meant everything to his future, as he saw it, he hesitated. His quick conclusion was to explain his absence this evening by a second invitation which had come later, also by asseverating that the Griffiths being potentially in charge of his material welfare, it was becoming more and more of a duty rather than an idle, evasive pleasure to desert her in this way at their command. Could he help it? And with this half-truth permanently fixed in his mind, he crossed the snow and gently tapped at her window.

At once the light was extinguished and a moment later the curtain lifted. Then Roberta, who had been mournfully brooding, opened the door and admitted him, having previously lit a candle as was her custom in order to avoid detection as much as possible, and at once he began in a whisper:

"Gee, but this society business here is getting to be the dizzy thing, honey. I never saw such a town as this. Once you go with these people one place to do one thing, they always have something else they want you to do. They're on the go all the time. When I went there Friday (he was referring to his lie about having gone to the Griffiths'), I thought that would be the last until after the holidays, but yesterday, and just when I was planning to go somewhere else, I got a note saying they expected me to come there again to-day for dinner sure."

"And to-day when I thought the dinner would begin at two," he continued to explain, "and end in time for me to be around here by eight like I said, it didn't start until three and only broke up a few minutes ago. Isn't that the limit? And I just couldn't get away for the last four hours. How've you been, honey? Did you have a good time? I hope so. Did they like the present I gave you?"

He rattled off these questions, to which she made brief and decidedly terse replies, all the time looking at him as much as to say, "Oh, Clyde, how can you treat me like this?"

But Clyde was so much interested in his own alibi, and how to convince Roberta of the truth of it, that neither before nor after slipping off his coat, muffler and gloves and smoothing back his hair, did he look at her directly, or even tenderly, or indeed do anything to demonstrate to her that he was truly delighted to see her again. On the contrary, he was so fidgety and in part flustered that despite his past professions and actions she could feel that apart from being moderately glad to see her again he was more concerned about himself and his own partially explained defection than he was about her. And although after a few moments he took her in his arms and pressed his lips to hers, still, as on Saturday, she could feel that he was only partially united to her in spirit. Other things—the affairs that had kept him from her on Friday and to-night—were disturbing his thoughts and hers.

She looked at him, not exactly believing and yet not entirely wishing to disbelieve him. He might have been at the Griffiths', as he said, and they might have detained him. And yet he might not have, either. For she could not help recalling that on the previous Saturday he had said he had been there Friday and the paper on the other hand had stated that he was in Gloversville. But if she questioned him in regard to these things now, would he not get angry and lie to her still more? For after all she could not help thinking that apart from his love for her she had no real claim on him. But she could not possibly imagine that he could change so quickly.

"So that was why you didn't come to-night, was it?" she asked, with more spirit and irritation than she had ever used with him before. "I thought you told me sure you wouldn't let anything interfere," she went on, a little heavily.

"Well, so I did," he admitted. "And I wouldn't have either, except for the letter I got. You know I wouldn't let any one but my uncle interfere, but I couldn't turn them down when they asked me to come there on Christmas day. It's too important. It wouldn't look right, would it, especially when you weren't going to be here in the afternoon?"

The manner and tone in which he said this conveyed to Roberta more clearly than anything that he had ever said before how significant he considered this connection with his relatives to be and how unimportant anything she might value in regard to this relationship was to him. It came to her now that in spite of all his enthusiasm and demonstrativeness in the first stages of this affair, possibly she was much more trivial in his estimation than she had seemed to herself. And that meant that her dreams and sacrifices thus far had been in vain. She became frightened.

"Well, anyhow," she went on dubiously in the face of this, "don't you think you might have left a note here, Clyde, so I would have got it when I got in?" She asked this mildly, not wishing to irritate him too much.

"But didn't I just tell you, honey, I didn't expect to be so late. I thought the thing would all be over by six, anyhow."

"Yes—well—anyhow—I know—but still—"

Her face wore a puzzled, troubled, nervous look, in which was mingled fear, sorrow, depression, distrust, a trace of resentment and a trace of despair, all of which, coloring and animating her eyes, which were now fixed on him in round orblike solemnity, caused him to suffer from a sense of having misused and demeaned her not a little. And because her eyes seemed to advertise this, he flushed a dark red flush that colored deeply his naturally very pale cheeks. But without appearing to notice this or lay any stress on it in any way at the time, Roberta added after a moment: "I notice that *The Star* mentioned that Gloversville party Sunday, but it didn't say anything about your cousins being over there. Were they?"

For the first time in all her questioning of him, she asked this as though she might possibly doubt him—a development which Clyde had scarcely anticipated in connection with her up to this time, and more than anything else, it troubled and irritated him.

"Of course they were," he replied falsely. "Why do you want to ask a thing like that when I told you they were?"

"Well, dear, I don't mean anything by it. I only wanted to know. But I did notice that it mentioned all those other people

from Lycurgus that you are always talking about, Sondra
Finchley, Bertine Cranston. You know you never mentioned
anybody but the Trumbulls."

Her tone tended to make him bristle and grow cross, as she
saw.

"Yes, I saw that, too, but it ain't so. If they were there, I
didn't see them. The papers don't always get everything
right." In spite of a certain crossness and irritation at being
trapped in this fashion, his manner did not carry conviction,
and he knew it. And he began to resent the fact that she
should question him so. Why should she? Wasn't he of sufficient importance to move in this new world without her
holding him back in this way?

Instead of denying or reproaching him further, she merely
looked at him, her expression one of injured wistfulness. She
did not believe him now entirely and she did not utterly disbelieve him. A part of what he said was probably true. More
important was it that he should care for her enough not to
want to lie to her or to treat her badly. But how was that to
be effected if he did not want to be kind or truthful? She
moved back from him a few steps and with a gesture of helplessness said: "Oh, Clyde, you don't have to story to me.
Don't you know that? I wouldn't care where you went if you
would just tell me beforehand and not leave me like this all
alone on Christmas night. It's just that that hurts so."

"But I'm not storying to you, Bert," he reiterated crossly.
"I can't help how things look even if the paper did say so.
The Griffiths were over there, and I can prove it. I got around
here as soon as I could to-day. What do you want to get so
mad about all at once? I've told you how things are. I can't
do just as I want to here. They call me up at the last minute
and want me to go. And I just can't get out of it. What's the
use of being so mad about it?"

He stared defiantly while Roberta, checkmated in this general way, was at a loss as to how to proceed. The item about
New Year's Eve was in her mind, but she felt that it might not
be wise to say anything more now. More poignantly than ever
now she was identifying him with that gay life of which he,
but not she, was a part. And yet she hesitated even now to let
him know how sharp were the twinges of jealousy that were

beginning to assail her. They had such a good time in that fine world—he and those he knew—and she had so little. And besides, now he was always talking about that Sondra Finchley and that Bertine Cranston, or the papers were. Was it in either of those that he was most interested?

"Do you like that Miss Finchley very much?" she suddenly asked, looking up at him in the shadow, her desire to obtain some slight satisfaction—some little light on all this trouble— still torturing her.

At once Clyde sensed the importance of the question—a suggestion of partially suppressed interest and jealousy and helplessness, more in her voice even than in the way she looked. There was something so soft, coaxing and sad about her voice at times, especially when she was most depressed. At the same time he was slightly taken back by the shrewd or telepathic way in which she appeared to fix on Sondra. Immediately he felt that she should not know—that it would irritate her. At the same time, vanity in regard to his general position here, which hourly was becoming more secure apparently, caused him to say:

"Oh, I like her some, sure. She's very pretty, and a dandy dancer. And she has lots of money and dresses well." He was about to add that outside of that Sondra appealed to him in no other way, when Roberta, sensing something of the true interest he felt in this girl perhaps and the wide gulf that lay between herself and all his world, suddenly exclaimed: "Yes, and who wouldn't, with all the money she has? If I had as much money as that, I could too."

And to his astonishment and dismay even, at this point her voice grew suddenly vibrant and then broke, as on a sob. And as he could both see and feel, she was deeply hurt—terribly and painfully hurt—heartsore and jealous; and at once, although his first impulse was to grow angry and defiant again, his mood as suddenly softened. For it now pained him not a little to think that some one of whom he had once been so continuously fond up to this time should be made to suffer through jealousy of him, for he himself well knew the pangs of jealousy in connection with Hortense. He could for some reason almost see himself in Roberta's place. And for this reason, if no other, he now said, and quite softly: "Oh, now,

Bert, as though I couldn't tell you about her or any one else
without your getting mad about it! I didn't mean that I was
especially interested in her. I was just telling you what I
thought you wanted to know because you asked me if I liked
her, that's all."

"Oh, yes, I know," replied Roberta, standing tensely and
nervously before him, her face white, her hands suddenly
clenched, and looking up at him dubiously and yet pleadingly.
"But they've got everything. You know they have. And I
haven't got anything, really. And it's so hard for me to keep up
my end and against all of them, too, and with all they have."
Her voice shook, and she ceased talking, her eyes filling and
her lips beginning to quiver. And as swiftly she concealed her
face with her hands and turned away, her shoulders shaking as
she did so. Indeed her body was now torn for the moment by
the most desperate and convulsive sobs, so much so that Clyde,
perplexed and astonished and deeply moved by this sudden
display of a pent-up and powerful emotion, as suddenly was
himself moved deeply. For obviously this was no trick or histrionic bit intended to influence him, but rather a sudden and
overwhelming vision of herself, as he himself could sense, as a
rather lorn and isolated girl without friends or prospects as opposed to those others in whom he was now so interested and
who had so much more—everything in fact. For behind her in
her vision lay all the lorn and detached years that had marred
her youth, now so vivid because of her recent visit. She was
really intensely moved—overwhelmingly and helplessly.

And now from the very bottom of her heart she exclaimed:
"If I'd ever had a chance like some girls—if I'd ever been anywhere or seen anything! But just to be brought up in the
country and without any money or clothes or anything—and
nobody to show you. Oh, oh, oh, oh, oh!"

The moment she said these things she was actually ashamed
of having made so weak and self-condemnatory a confession,
since that was what really was troubling him in connection
with her, no doubt.

"Oh, Roberta, darling," he said instantly and tenderly,
putting his arms around her, genuinely moved by his own
dereliction. "You mustn't cry like that, dearest. You mustn't.
I didn't mean to hurt you, honest I didn't. Truly, I didn't,

dear. I know you've had a hard time, honey. I know how you feel, and how you've been up against things in one way and another. Sure I do, Bert, and you mustn't cry, dearest. I love you just the same. Truly I do, and I always will. I'm sorry if I've hurt you, honest I am. I couldn't help it to-night if I didn't come, honest, or last Friday either. Why, it just wasn't possible. But I won't be so mean like that any more, if I can help it. Honest I won't. You're the sweetest, dearest girl. And you've got such lovely hair and eyes, and such a pretty little figure. Honest you have, Bert. And you can dance too, as pretty as anybody. And you look just as nice, honest you do, dear. Won't you stop now, honey? Please do. I'm so sorry, honey, if I've hurt you in any way."

There was about Clyde at times a certain strain of tenderness, evoked by experiences, disappointments, and hardships in his own life, which came out to one and another, almost any other, under such circumstances as these. At such times he had a soft and melting voice. His manner was as tender and gentle almost as that of a mother with a baby. It drew a girl like Roberta intensely to him. At the same time, such emotion in him, though vivid, was of brief duration. It was like the rush and flutter of a summer storm—soon come and soon gone. Yet in this instance it was sufficient to cause Roberta to feel that he fully understood and sympathized with her and perhaps liked her all the better for it. Things were not so bad for the moment, anyhow. She had him and his love and sympathy to a very marked degree at any rate, and because of this and her very great comfort in it, and his soothing words, she began to dry her eyes, to say that she was sorry to think that she was such a cry-baby and that she hoped he would forgive her, because in crying she had wet the bosom of his spotless white shirt with her tears. And she would not do it any more if Clyde would just forgive her this once—the while, touched by a passion he scarcely believed was buried in her in any such volume, he now continued to kiss her hands, cheeks, and finally her lips.

And between these pettings and coaxings and kissings it was that he reaffirmed to her, most foolishly and falsely in this instance (since he was really caring for Sondra in a way which, while different, was just as vital—perhaps even more so), that he regarded her as first, last and most in his heart, always—a statement which caused her to feel that perhaps after all she might have misjudged him. Also that her position, if anything, was more secure, if not more wonderful than ever it had been before—far superior to that of these other girls who might see him socially perhaps, but who did not have him to love them in this wonderful way.

# Chapter XXXII

CLYDE now was actually part and parcel of this local winter social scene. The Griffiths having introduced him to their friends and connections, it followed as a matter of course that he would be received in most homes here. But in this very limited world, where quite every one who was anything at all knew every one else, the state of one's purse was as much, and in some instances even more, considered than one's social connections. For these local families of distinction were convinced that not only one's family but one's wealth was the be-all and end-all of every happy union meant to include social security. And in consequence, while considering Clyde as one who was unquestionably eligible socially, still, because it had been whispered about that his means were very slender, they were not inclined to look upon him as one who might aspire to marriage with any of their daughters. Hence, while they were to the fore with invitations, still in so far as their own children and connections were concerned they were also to the fore with precautionary hints as to the inadvisability of too numerous contacts with him.

However, the mood of Sondra and her group being friendly toward him, and the observations and comments of their friends and parents not as yet too definite, Clyde continued to receive invitations to the one type of gathering that most interested him—that which began and ended with dancing. And although his purse was short, he got on well enough. For once Sondra had interested herself in him, it was not long before she began to realize what his financial state was and was concerned to make his friendship for her at least as inexpensive as possible. And because of this attitude on her part, which in turn was conveyed to Bertine, Grant Cranston and others, it became possible on most occasions for Clyde, especially when the affair was local, to go here and there without the expenditure of any money. Even when the affair was at any point beyond Lycurgus and he consented to go, the car of another was delegated to pick him up.

Frequently after the New Year's Eve trip to Schenectady, which proved to be an outing of real import to both Clyde and Sondra—seeing that on that occasion she drew nearer to him affectionally than ever before—it was Sondra herself who chose to pick him up in her car. He had actually succeeded in impressing her, and in a way that most flattered her vanity at the same time that it appealed to the finest trait in her—a warm desire to have some one, some youth like Clyde, who was at once attractive and of good social station, dependent upon her. She knew that her parents would not countenance an affair between her and Clyde because of his poverty. She had originally not contemplated any, though now she found herself wishing that something of the kind might be.

However, no opportunity for further intimacies occurred until one night about two weeks after the New Year's Eve party. They were returning from a similar affair at Amsterdam, and after Bella Griffiths and Grant and Bertine Cranston had been driven to their respective homes, Stuart Finchley had called back: "Now we'll take you home, Griffiths." At once Sondra, swayed by the delight of contact with Clyde and not willing to end it so soon, said: "If you want to come over to our place, I'll make some hot chocolate before you go home. Would you like that?"

"Oh, sure I would," Clyde had answered gayly.

"Here goes then," called Stuart, turning the car toward the Finchley home. "But as for me, I'm going to turn in. It's way after three now."

"That's a good brother. Your beauty sleep, you know," replied Sondra.

And having turned the car into the garage, the three made their way through the rear entrance into the kitchen. Her brother having left them, Sondra asked Clyde to be seated at a servants' table while she brought the ingredients. But he, impressed by this culinary equipment, the like of which he had never seen before, gazed about wondering at the wealth and security which could sustain it.

"My, this is a big kitchen, isn't it?" he remarked. "What a lot of things you have here to cook with, haven't you?"

And she, realizing from this that he had not been accustomed to equipment of this order before coming to Lycurgus and hence was all the more easily to be impressed, replied: "Oh, I don't know. Aren't all kitchens as big as this?"

Clyde, thinking of the poverty he knew, and assuming from this that she was scarcely aware of anything less than this, was all the more overawed by the plethora of the world to which she belonged. What means! Only to think of being married to such a girl, when all such as this would become an everyday state. One would have a cook and servants, a great house and car, no one to work for, and only orders to give, a thought which impressed him greatly. It made her various self-conscious gestures and posings all the more entrancing. And she, sensing the import of all this to Clyde, was inclined to exaggerate her own inseparable connection with it. To him, more than any one else, as she now saw, she shone as a star, a paragon of luxury and social supremacy.

Having prepared the chocolate in a commonplace aluminum pan, to further impress him she sought out a heavily chased silver service which was in another room. She poured the chocolate into a highly ornamented urn and then carried it to the table and put it down before him. Then swinging herself up beside him, she said: "Now, isn't this chummy? I just love to get out in the kitchen like this, but I can only do it when the cook's out. He won't let any one near the place when he's here."

"Oh, is that so?" asked Clyde, who was quite unaware of the ways of cooks in connection with private homes—an inquiry which quite convinced Sondra that there must have been little if any real means in the world from which he sprang. Nevertheless, because he had come to mean so much to her, she was by no means inclined to turn back. And so when he finally exclaimed: "Isn't it wonderful to be together like this, Sondra? Just think, I hardly got a chance to say a word to you all evening, alone," she replied, without in any way being irritated by the familiarity, "You think so? I'm glad you do," and smiled in a slightly supercilious though affectionate way.

And at the sight of her now in her white satin and crystal evening gown, her slippered feet swinging so intimately near, a faint perfume radiating to his nostrils, he was stirred. In fact, his imagination in regard to her was really inflamed. Youth, beauty, wealth such as this—what would it not mean? And she, feeling the intensity of his admiration and infected in part at least by the enchantment and fervor that was so definitely dominating him, was swayed to the point where she was seeing him as one for whom she could care—very much. Weren't his eyes bright and dark—very liquid and eager? And his hair! It looked so enticing, lying low upon his white forehead. She wished that she could touch it now—smooth it with her hands and touch his cheeks. And his hands—they were thin and sensitive and graceful. Like Roberta, and Hortense and Rita before her, she noticed them.

But he was silent now with a tightly restrained silence which he was afraid to liberate in words. For he was thinking: "Oh, if only I could say to her how beautiful I really think she is. If I could just put my arms around her and kiss her, and kiss her, and kiss her, and have her kiss me in the same way." And strangely, considering his first approaches toward Roberta, the thought was without lust, just the desire to constrain and fondle a perfect object. Indeed, his eyes fairly radiated this desire and intensity. And while she noted this and was in part made dubious by it, since it was the thing in Clyde she most feared—still she was intrigued by it to the extent of wishing to know its further meaning.

And so she now said, teasingly: "Was there anything very important you wanted to say?"

"I'd like to say a lot of things to you, Sondra, if you would only let me," he returned eagerly. "But you told me not to."

"Oh, so I did. Well, I meant that, too. I'm glad you mind so well." There was a provoking smile upon her lips and she looked at him as much as to say: "But you don't really believe I meant all of that, do you?"

Overcome by the suggestion of her eyes, Clyde got up and, taking both her hands in his and looking directly into her eyes, said: "You didn't mean all of it, then, did you, Sondra? Not all of it, anyhow. Oh, I wish I could tell you all that I am thinking." His eyes spoke, and now sharply conscious again of how easy it was to inflame him, and yet anxious to permit him to proceed as he wished, she leaned back from him and said, "Oh, yes, I'm sure I did. You take almost everything too seriously, don't you?" But at the same time, and in spite of herself, her expression relaxed and she once more smiled.

"I can't help it, Sondra. I can't! I can't!" he began, eagerly and almost vehemently. "You don't know what effect you have on me. You're so beautiful. Oh, you are. You know you are. I think about you all the time. Really I do, Sondra. You've made me just crazy about you, so much so that I can hardly sleep for thinking about you. Gee, I'm wild! I never go anywhere or see you any place but what I think of you all the time afterward. Even to-night when I saw you dancing with all those fellows I could hardly stand it. I just wanted you to be dancing with me—no one else. You've got such beautiful eyes, Sondra, and such a lovely mouth and chin, and such a wonderful smile."

He lifted his hands as though to caress her gently, yet holding them back, and at the same time dreamed into her eyes as might a devotee into those of a saint, then suddenly put his arms about her and drew her close to him. She, thrilled and in part seduced by his words, instead of resisting as definitely as she would have in any other case, now gazed at him, fascinated by his enthusiasms. She was so trapped and entranced by his passion for her that it seemed to her now as though she might care for him as much as he wished. Very, very much, if she only dared. He, too, was beautiful and alluring to her. He, too, was really wonderful, even if he were poor—so much more intense and dynamic than any of these other youths that she knew here. Would it not be wonderful if, her parents and her state permitting, she could share with him completely such a mood as this? Simultaneously the thought came to her that should her parents know of this it might not be possible for her to continue this relationship in any form, let alone to develop it or enjoy it in the future. Yet regardless of this thought now, which arrested and stilled her for a moment, she continued to yearn toward him. Her eyes were warm and tender—her lips wreathed with a gracious smile.

"I'm sure I oughtn't to let you say all these things to me. I know I shouldn't," she protested weakly, yet looking at him affectionately. "It isn't the right thing to do, I know, but still—"

"Why not? Why isn't it right, Sondra? Why mayn't I when I care for you so much?" His eyes became clouded with sadness, and she, noting it, exclaimed: "Oh, well," then paused,

"I—I—" She was about to add, "Don't think they would ever let us go on with it," but instead she only replied, "I guess I don't know you well enough."

"Oh, Sondra, when I love you so much and I'm so crazy about you! Don't you care at all like I care for you?"

Because of the uncertainty expressed by her, his eyes were now seeking, frightened, sad. The combination had an intense appeal for her. She merely looked at him dubiously, wondering what could be the result of such an infatuation as this. And he, noting the wavering something in her own eyes, pulled her closer and kissed her. Instead of resenting it she lay for a moment willingly, joyously, in his arms, then suddenly sat up, the thought of what she was permitting him to do— kiss her in this way—and what it must mean to him, causing her on the instant to recover all her poise. "I think you'd better go now," she said definitely, yet not unkindly. "Don't you?"

And Clyde, who himself had been surprised and afterwards a little startled, and hence reduced by his own boldness, now pleaded rather weakly, and yet submissively. "Angry?"

And she, in turn sensing his submissiveness, that of the slave for the master, and in part liking and in part resenting it, since like Roberta and Hortense, even she preferred to be mastered rather than to master, shook her head negatively and a little sadly.

"It's very late," was all she said, and smiled tenderly.

And Clyde, realizing that for some reason he must not say more, had not the courage or persistence or the background to go further with her now, went for his coat and, looking sadly but obediently back at her, departed.

# Chapter XXXIII

ONE OF the things that Roberta soon found was that her intuitive notions in regard to all this were not without speedy substantiation. For exactly as before, though with the usual insistence afterward that there was no real help for it, there continued to be these same last moment changes of plan and unannounced absences. And although she complained at times, or pleaded, or merely contented herself with quite silent and not always obvious "blues," still these same affected no real modification or improvement. For Clyde was now hopelessly enamored of Sondra and by no means to be changed, or moved even, by anything in connection with Roberta. Sondra was too wonderful!

At the same time because she was there all of the working hours of each day in the same room with him, he could not fail instinctively to feel some of the thoughts that employed her mind—such dark, sad, despairing thoughts. And these seized upon him at times as definitely and poignantly as though they were voices of accusation or complaint—so much so that he could not help but suggest by way of amelioration that he would like to see her and that he was coming around that night if she were going to be home. And so distrait was she, and still so infatuated with him, that she could not resist admitting that she wanted him to come. And once there, the psychic personality of the past as well as of the room itself was not without its persuasion and hence emotional compulsion.

But most foolishly anticipating, as he now did, a future more substantial than the general local circumstances warranted, he was more concerned than ever lest his present relationship to Roberta should in any way prove inimical to all this. Supposing that Sondra at some time, in some way, should find out concerning Roberta? How fatal that would be! Or that Roberta should become aware of his devotion to Sondra and so develop an active resentment which should carry her to the length of denouncing or exposing him. For subsequent to the New Year's Eve engagement, he was all too frequently appearing at the factory of a morning with ex-

planatory statements that because of some invitation from the
Griffiths, Harriets, or others, he would not be able to keep an
engagement with her that night, for instance, that he had
made a day or two before. And later, on three different occasions, because Sondra had called for him in her car, he had
departed without a word, trusting to what might come to
him the next day in the way of an excuse to smooth the matter over.

Yet anomalous, if not exactly unprecedented as it may seem,
this condition of mingled sympathy and opposition gave rise
at last to the feeling in him that come what might he must
find some method of severing this tie, even though it lacer-
ated Roberta to the point of death (Why should he care? He
had never told her that he would marry her.) or endangered
his own position here in case she were not satisfied to release
him as voicelessly as he wished. At other times it caused him
to feel that indeed he was a sly and shameless and cruel person who had taken undue advantage of a girl who, left to herself, would never have troubled with him. And this latter
mood, in spite of slights and lies and thinly excused neglects
and absences at times in the face of the most definite agreements—so strange is the libido of the race—brought about
the reënactment of the infernal or celestial command laid
upon Adam and his breed: "Thy desire shall be to thy mate."

But there was this to be said in connection with the relationship between these two, that at no time, owing to the inexperience of Clyde, as well as Roberta, had there been any
adequate understanding or use of more than the simplest, and
for the most part unsatisfactory, contraceptive devices. About
the middle of February, and, interestingly enough, at about
the time when Clyde, because of the continuing favor of
Sondra, had about reached the point where he was determined once and for all to end, not only this physical, but all
other connection with Roberta, she on her part was beginning
to see clearly that, in spite of his temporizing and her own incurable infatuation for him, pursuit of him by her was futile
and that it would be more to the satisfaction of her pride, if
not to the ease of her heart, if she were to leave here and in
some other place seek some financial help that would permit
her to live and still help her parents and forget him if she

could. Unfortunately for this, she was compelled, to her dismay and terror, to enter the factory one morning, just about this time, her face a symbol of even graver and more terrifying doubts and fears than any that had hitherto assailed her. For now, in addition to her own troubled conclusions in regard to Clyde, there had sprung up over night the dark and constraining fear that even this might not now be possible, for the present at least. For because of her own and Clyde's temporizing over his and her sentimentality and her unconquerable affection for him, she now, at a time when it was most inimical for both, found herself pregnant.

Ever since she had yielded to his blandishments, she had counted the days and always had been able to congratulate herself that all was well. But forty-eight hours since the always exactly calculated time had now passed, and there had been no sign. And for four days preceding this Clyde had not even been near her. And his attitude at the factory was more remote and indifferent than ever.

And now, this!

And she had no one but him to whom she might turn. And he was in this estranged and indifferent mood.

Because of her fright, induced by the fear that with or without Clyde's aid she might not easily be extricated from her threatened predicament, she could see her home, her mother, her relatives, all who knew her, and their thoughts in case anything like this should befall her. For of the opinion of society in general and what other people might say, Roberta stood in extreme terror. The stigma of unsanctioned concupiscence! The shame of illegitimacy for a child! It was bad enough, as she had always thought, listening to girls and women talk of life and marriage and adultery and the miseries that had befallen girls who had yielded to men and subsequently been deserted, for a woman when she was safely married and sustained by the love and strength of a man—such love, for instance, as her brother-in-law Gabel brought to her sister Agnes, and her father to her mother in the first years, no doubt—and Clyde to her when he had so feverishly declared that he loved her.

But now—now!

She could not permit any thoughts in regard to his recent

or present attitude to delay her. Regardless of either, he must help her. She did not know what else to do under such circumstances—which way to turn. And no doubt Clyde did. At any rate he had said once that he would stand by her in case anything happened. And although, because at first, even on the third day on reaching the factory, she imagined that she might be exaggerating the danger and that it was perhaps some physical flaw or lapse that might still overcome itself, still by late afternoon no evidence of any change coming to her, she began to be a prey to the most nameless terrors. What little courage she had mustered up to this time began to waver and break. She was all alone, unless he came to her now. And she was in need of advice and good counsel—loving counsel. Oh, Clyde! Clyde! If he would only not be so indifferent to her! He must not be! Something must be done, and right away—quick—else— Great Heavens, what a terrible thing this could easily come to be!

At once she stopped her work between four and five in the afternoon and hurried to the dressing-room. And there she penned a note—hurried, hysterical—a scrawl.

"CLYDE—I must see you to-night, sure, *sure*. You mustn't fail me. I have something to tell you. Please come as soon after work as possible, or meet me anywhere. I'm not angry or mad about anything. But I must see you to-night, *sure*. Please say right away where. ROBERTA."

And he, sensing a new and strange and quite terrified note in all this the moment he read it, at once looked over his shoulder at her and, seeing her face so white and drawn, signaled that he would meet her. For judging by her face the thing she had to tell must be of the utmost importance to her, else why this tensity and excitement on her part. And although he had another engagement later, as he now troublesomely recalled, at the Starks for dinner, still it was necessary to do this first. Yet, what was it anyhow? Was anybody dead or hurt or what—her mother or father or brother or sister?

At five-thirty, he made his way to the appointed place, wondering what it could be that could make her so pale and concerned. Yet at the same time saying to himself that if this other dream in regard to Sondra were to come true he must

not let himself be reëntangled by any great or moving sympathy—must maintain his new poise and distance so that
Roberta could see that he no longer cared for her as he had.
Reaching the appointed place at six o'clock, he found her
leaning disconsolately against a tree in the shadow. She
looked distraught, despondent.

"Why, what's the matter, Bert? What are you so frightened
about? What's happened?"

Even his obviously dwindling affection was restimulated by
her quite visible need of help.

"Oh, Clyde," she said at last, "I hardly know how to tell
you. It's so terrible for me if it's so." Her voice, tense and yet
low, was in itself a clear proof of her anguish and uncertainty.

"Why, what is it, Bert? Why don't you tell me?" he reiterated,
briskly and yet cautiously, essaying an air of detached assurance
which he could not quite manage in this instance. "What's
wrong? What are you so excited about? You're all trembly."

Because of the fact that never before in all his life had he been
confronted by any such predicament as this, it did not even
now occur to him just what the true difficulty could be. At the
same time, being rather estranged and hence embarrassed by
his recent treatment of her, he was puzzled as to just what attitude to assume in a situation where obviously something was
wrong. Being sensitive to conventional or moral stimuli as he
still was, he could not quite achieve a discreditable thing, even
where his own highest ambitions were involved, without a
measure of regret or at least shame. Also he was so anxious to
keep his dinner engagement and not to be further involved that
his manner was impatient. It did not escape Roberta.

"You know, Clyde," she pleaded, both earnestly and eagerly, the very difficulty of her state encouraging her to be
bold and demanding, "you said if anything went wrong you'd
help me."

At once, because of those recent few and, as he now saw
them, foolish visits to her room, on which occasions because
of some remaining sentiment and desire on the part of both
he had been betrayed into sporadic and decidedly unwise
physical relations with her, he now realized what the difficulty
was. And that it was a severe, compelling, dangerous difficulty, if it were true. Also that he was to blame and that here

was a real predicament that must be overcome, and that quickly, unless a still greater danger was to be faced. Yet, simultaneously, his very recent and yet decidedly compelling indifference dictating, he was almost ready now to assume that this might be little more than a ruse or lovelorn device or bit of strategy intended to retain or reënlist his interest in spite of himself—a thought which he was only in part ready to harbor. Her manner was too dejected and despairing. And with the first dim realization of how disastrous such a complication as this might prove to be in his case, he began to be somewhat more alarmed than irritated. So much so that he exclaimed:

"Yes, but how do you know that there is anything wrong? You can't be sure so soon as all this, can you? How can you? You'll probably be all right to-morrow, won't you?" At the same time his voice was beginning to suggest the uncertainty that he felt.

"Oh, no, I don't think so, Clyde. I wish I did. It's two whole days, and it's never been that way before."

Her manner as she said this was so obviously dejected and self-commiserating that at once he was compelled to dismiss the thought of intrigue. At the same time, unwilling to face so discouraging a fact so soon, he added: "Oh, well, that might not mean anything, either. Girls go longer than two days, don't they?"

The tone, implying as it did uncertainty and non-sophistication even, which previously had not appeared characteristic of him, was sufficient to alarm Roberta to the point where she exclaimed: "Oh, no, I don't think so. Anyhow, it would be terrible, wouldn't it, if something were wrong? What do you suppose I ought to do? Don't you know something I can take?"

At once Clyde, who had been so brisk and urgent in establishing this relationship and had given Roberta the impression that he was a sophisticated and masterful youth who knew much more of life than ever she could hope to know, and to whom all such dangers and difficulties as were implied in the relationship could be left with impunity, was at a loss what to do. Actually, as he himself now realized, he was as sparingly informed in regard to the mysteries of sex and the possible complications attending upon such a situation as any youth of his years could well be. True, before coming here he had browsed about Kansas City and Chicago with such worldly-wise mentors of the hotel bell-boy world as Ratterer, Higby, Hegglund and others and had listened to much of their gossiping and boasting. But their knowledge, for all their boasting, as he now half guessed, must have related to girls who were as careless and uninformed as themselves. And beyond those again, although he was by no means so clearly aware of that fact now, lay little more than those rumored specifics and preventatives of such quack doctors and shady druggists and chemists as dealt with intelligences of the Hegglund and Ratterer order. But even so, where were such things to be obtained in a small city like Lycurgus? Since dropping Dillard he had no intimates let alone trustworthy friends who could be depended on to help in such a crisis.

The best he could think of for the moment was to visit some local or near-by druggist who might, for a price, provide him with some worth-while prescription or information. But for how much? And what were the dangers in connection with such a proceeding? Did they talk? Did they ask questions? Did they tell any one else about such inquiries or needs? He looked so much like Gilbert Griffiths, who was so well known in Lycurgus that any one recognizing him as Gilbert might begin to talk of him in that way and so bring about trouble.

And this terrible situation arising now—when in connection with Sondra, things had advanced to the point where she was now secretly permitting him to kiss her, and, more pleasing still, exhibiting little evidences of her affection and good will in the form of presents of ties, a gold pencil, a box of most attractive handkerchiefs, all delivered to his door in his absence with a little card with her initials, which had caused him to feel sure that his future in connection with her was of greater and greater promise. So much so that even marriage, assuming that her family might not prove too inimical and that her infatuation and diplomacy endured, might not be beyond the bounds of possibility. He could not be sure, of course. Her true intentions and affection so far were veiled behind a tantalizing evasiveness which made her all the more desirable. Yet it was these things that had been causing him to feel that he must now, and speedily, extract himself as gracefully and unirritatingly as possible from his intimacy with Roberta.

For that reason, therefore, he now announced, with pretended assurance: "Well, I wouldn't worry about it any more to-night if I were you. You may be all right yet, you know. You can't be sure. Anyhow, I'll have to have a little time until I can see what I can do. I think I can get something for you. But I wish you wouldn't get so excited."

At the same time he was far from feeling as secure as he sounded. In fact he was very much shaken. His original determination to have as little to do with her as possible, was now complicated by the fact that he was confronted by a predicament that spelled real danger to himself, unless by some argument or assertion he could absolve himself of any responsibility in connection with this—a possibility which, in view of the fact that Roberta still worked for him, that he had written her some notes, and that any least word from her would precipitate an inquiry which would prove fatal to him, was sufficient to cause him to feel that he must assist her speedily and without a breath of information as to all this leaking out in any direction. At the same time it is only fair to say that because of all that had been between them, he did not object to assisting her in any way that he could. But in the event that he could not (it was so that his thoughts raced forward to an entirely possible inimical conclusion to all this) well, then—well, then—might it not be possible at least— some fellows, if not himself would—to deny that he had held any such relationship with her and so escape. That possibly might be one way out—if only he were not as treacherously surrounded as he was here.

But the most troublesome thing in connection with all this was the thought that he knew of nothing that would really avail in such a case, other than a doctor. Also that that probably meant money, time, danger—just what did it mean? He would see her in the morning, and if she weren't all right by then he would act.

And Roberta, for the first time forsaken in this rather casual and indifferent way, and in such a crisis as this, returned to her room with her thoughts and fears, more stricken and agonized than ever before she had been in all her life.

# Chapter XXXIV

B ut the resources of Clyde, in such a situation as this, were
slim. For, apart from Liggett, Whiggam, and a few minor
though decidedly pleasant and yet rather remote department
heads, all of whom were now looking on him as a distinctly
superior person who could scarcely be approached too familiarly in connection with anything, there was no one to whom
he could appeal. In so far as the social group to which he was
now so eagerly attaching himself was concerned, it would have
been absurd for him to attempt, however slyly, to extract any
information there. For while the youths of this world at least
were dashing here and there, and because of their looks, taste
and means indulging themselves in phases of libertinism—the
proper wild oats of youth—such as he and others like himself
could not have dreamed of affording, still so far was he from
any real intimacy with any of these that he would not have
dreamed of approaching them for helpful information.

His sanest thought, which occurred to him almost immediately after leaving Roberta, was that instead of inquiring of
any druggist or doctor or person in Lycurgus—more particularly any doctor, since the entire medical profession here, as
elsewhere, appeared to him as remote, cold, unsympathetic
and likely very expensive and unfriendly to such an immoral
adventure as this—was to go to some near-by city, preferably
Schenectady, since it was larger and as near as any, and there
inquire what, if anything, could be obtained to help in such a
situation as this. For he must find something.

At the same time, the necessity for decision and prompt action was so great that even on his way to the Starks', and
without knowing any drug or prescription to ask for, he resolved to go to Schenectady the next night. Only that meant,
as he later reasoned, that a whole day must elapse before anything could be done for Roberta, and that, in her eyes, as well
as his own, would be leaving her open to the danger that any
delay at all involved. Therefore, he decided to act at once, if
he could; excuse himself to the Starks and then make the trip
to Schenectady on the interurban before the drug-stores over

there should close. But once there—what? How face the local druggist or clerk—and ask for what? His mind was troubled with hard, abrasive thoughts as to what the druggist might think, look or say. If only Ratterer or Hegglund were here! They would know, of course, and be glad to help him. Or Higby, even. But here he was now, all alone, for Roberta knew nothing at all. There must be something though, of course. If not, if he failed there, he would return and write Ratterer in Chicago, only in order to keep himself out of this as much as possible he would say that he was writing for a friend.

Once in Schenectady, since no one knew him there, of course he might say (the thought came to him as an inspiration) that he was a newly married man—why not? He was old enough to be one, and that his wife, and that in the face of inability to care for a child now, was "past her time" (he recalled a phrase that he had once heard Higby use), and that he wanted something that would permit her to escape from that state. What was so wrong with that as an idea? A young married couple might be in just such a predicament. And possibly the druggist would, or should be stirred to a little sympathy by such a state and might be glad to tell him of something. Why not? That would be no real crime. To be sure, one and another might refuse, but a third might not. And then he would be rid of this. And then never again, without knowing a lot more than he did now, would he let himself drift into any such predicament as this. Never! It was too dreadful.

He betook himself to the Stark house very nervous and growing more so every moment. So much so that, the dinner being eaten, he finally declared as early as nine-thirty that at the last moment at the factory a very troublesome report, covering a whole month's activities, had been requested of him. And since it was not anything he could do at the office, he was compelled to return to his room and make it out there—a bit of energetic and ambitious commercialism, as the Starks saw it, worthy of their admiration and sympathy. And in consequence he was excused.

But arrived at Schenectady, he had barely time to look around a little before the last car for Lycurgus should be leaving. His nerve began to fail him. Did he look enough like a young married man to convince any one that he was one? Besides were not such preventatives considered very wrong—even by druggists?

Walking up and down the one very long Main Street still brightly lighted at this hour, looking now in one drug-store window and another, he decided for different reasons that each particular one was not the one. In one, as he saw at a glance, stood a stout, sober, smooth-shaven man of fifty whose bespectacled eyes and iron gray hair seemed to indicate to Clyde's mind that he would be most certain to deny such a youthful applicant as himself—refuse to believe that he was married—or to admit that he had any such remedy, and suspect him of illicit relations with some young, unmarried girl into the bargain. He looked so sober, God-fearing, ultra-respectable and conventional. No, it would not do to apply to him. He had not the courage to enter and face such a person.

In another drug-store he observed a small, shriveled and yet dapper and shrewd-looking man of perhaps thirty-five, who appeared to him at the time as satisfactory enough, only, as he could see from the front, he was being briskly assisted by a young woman of not more than twenty or twenty-five. And assuming that she would approach him instead of the man—an embarrassing and impossible situation—or if the man waited on him, was it not probable that she would hear? In consequence he gave up that place, and a third, a fourth, and a fifth, for varying and yet equally cogent reasons—customers inside, a girl and a boy at a soda fountain in front, an owner posed near the door and surveying Clyde as he looked in and thus disconcerting him before he had time to consider whether he should enter or not.

Finally, however, after having abandoned so many, he decided that he must act or return defeated, his time, and carfare wasted. Returning to one of the lesser stores in a side street, in which a moment before he had observed an undersized chemist idling about, he entered, and summoning all the bravado he could muster, began: "I want to know something. I want to know if you know of anything—well, you see, it's this way—I'm just married and my wife is past her time and I can't afford to have any children now if I can help it. Is there anything a person can get that will get her out of it?"

His manner was brisk and confidential enough, although tinged with nervousness and the inner conviction that the druggist must guess that he was lying. At the same time, although he did not know it, he was talking to a confirmed religionist of the Methodist group who did not believe in interfering with the motives or impulses of nature. Any such trifling was against the laws of God and he carried nothing in stock that would in any way interfere with the ways of the Creator. At the same time he was too good a merchant to wish to alienate a possible future customer, and so he now said: "I'm sorry, young man, but I'm afraid I can't help you in this case. I haven't a thing of that kind in stock here— never handle anything of that kind because I don't believe in 'em. It may be, though, that some of the other stores here in town carry something of the sort. I wouldn't be able to tell you." His manner as he spoke was solemn, the convinced and earnest tone and look of the moralist who knows that he is right.

And at once Clyde gathered, and fairly enough in this instance, that this man was reproachful. It reduced to a much smaller quantity the little confidence with which he had begun his quest. And yet, since the dealer had not directly reproached him and had even said that it might be possible that some of the other druggists carried such a thing, he took heart after a few moments, and after a brief fit of pacing here and there in which he looked through one window and another, he finally espied a seventh dealer alone. He entered, and after repeating his first explanation he was informed, very secretively and yet casually, by the thin, dark, casuistic person who waited on him—not the owner in this instance—that there was such a remedy. Yes. Did he wish a box? That (because Clyde asked the price) would be six dollars—a staggering sum to the salaried inquirer. However, since the expenditure seemed unescapable—to find anything at all a great relief—he at once announced that he would take it, and the clerk, bringing him something which he hinted ought to prove "effectual" and wrapping it up, he paid and went out.

And then actually so relieved was he, so great had been the

strain up to this moment, that he could have danced for joy.
Then there was a cure, and it would work, of course. The excessive and even outrageous price seemed to indicate as
much. And under the circumstances, might he not even consider that sum moderate, seeing that he was being let off so
easily? However, he forgot to inquire as to whether there was
any additional information or special directions that might
prove valuable, and instead, with the package in his pocket,
some central and detached portion of the ego within himself
congratulating him upon his luck and undaunted efficiency in
such a crisis as this, he at once returned to Lycurgus, where
he proceeded to Roberta's room.

And she, like himself, impressed by his success in having secured something which both he and she had feared did not
exist, or if it did, might prove difficult to procure, felt enormously relieved. In fact, she was reimpressed by his ability and
efficiency, qualities with which, up to this time at least, she
had endowed him. Also that he was more generous and considerate than under the circumstances she feared he would be.
At least he was not coldly abandoning her to fate, as previously in her terror she had imagined that he might. And this
fact, even in the face of his previous indifference, was sufficient to soften her mood in regard to him. So with a kind of
ebullience, based on fattened hope resting on the pills, she
undid the package and read the directions, assuring him the
while of her gratitude and that she would not forget how
*good* he had been to her in this instance. At the same time,
even as she untied the package, the thought came to her—
supposing they would not work? Then what? And how would
she go about arranging with Clyde as to that? However, for
the time being, as she now reasoned, she must be satisfied and
grateful for this, and at once took one of the pills.

But once her expressions of gratefulness had been offered
and Clyde sensed that these same might possibly be looked
upon as overtures to a new intimacy between them, he fell
back upon the attitude that for days past had characterized
him at the factory. Under no circumstances must he lend
himself to any additional blandishments or languishments in
this field. And if this drug proved effectual, as he most
earnestly hoped, it must be the last of any save the most acci-

dental and casual contacts. For there was too much danger, as this particular crisis had proved—too much to be lost on his side—everything, in short—nothing but worry and trouble and expense.

In consequence he retreated to his former reserve. "Well, you'll be all right now, eh? Anyhow, let's hope so, huh? It says to take one every two hours for eight or ten hours. And if you're just a little sick, it says it doesn't make any difference. You may have to knock off a day or two at the factory, but you won't mind that, will you, if it gets you out of this? I'll come around to-morrow night and see how you are, if you don't show up any time to-morrow."

He laughed genially, the while Roberta gazed at him, unable to associate his present casual attitude with his former passion and deep solicitude. His former passion! And now this! And yet, under the circumstances, being truly grateful, she now smiled cordially and he the same. Yet, seeing him go out, the door close, and no endearing demonstrations of any kind having been exchanged between them, she returned to her bed, shaking her head dubiously. For, supposing that this remedy did not work after all? And he continued in this same casual and remote attitude toward her? Then what? For unless this remedy proved effectual, he might still be so indifferent that he might not want to help her long—or would he? Could he do that, really? He was the one who had brought her to this difficulty, and against her will, and he had so definitely assured her that nothing would happen. And now she must lie here alone and worry, not a single person to turn to, except him, and he was leaving her for others with the assurance that she would be all right. And he had caused it all! Was that quite right?

"Oh, Clyde! Clyde!"

# Chapter XXXV

**B**UT the remedy he purchased failed to work. And because of nausea and his advice she had not gone to the factory, but lay about worrying. But, no saving result appearing, she began to take two pills every hour instead of one—eager at any cost to escape the fate which seemingly had overtaken her. And this made her exceedingly sick—so much so that when Clyde arrived at six-thirty he was really moved by her deathly white face, drawn cheeks and large and nervous eyes, the pupils of which were unduly dilated. Obviously she was facing a crisis, and because of him, and, while it frightened, at the same time it made him sorry for her. Still, so confused and perplexed was he by the problem which her unchanged state presented to him that his mind now leaped forward to the various phases and eventualities of such a failure as this. The need of additional advice or service of some physician some-where! But where and how and who? And besides, as he now asked himself, where was he to obtain the money in any such event?

Plainly in view of no other inspiration it was necessary for him to return to the druggist at once and there inquire if there was anything else—some other drug or some other thing that one might do. Or if not that, then some low-priced shady doctor somewhere, who, for a small fee, or a promise of payments on time, would help in this case.

Yet even though this other matter was so important—tragic almost—once outside his spirits lifted slightly. For he now re-called that he had an appointment with Sondra at the Cranstons', where at nine he and she, along with a number of others, were to meet and play about as usual—a party. Yet once at the Cranstons', and despite the keen allurement of Sondra, he could not keep his mind off Roberta's state, which rose before him as a specter. Supposing now any one of those whom he found gathered here—Nadine Harriet, Perley Haynes, Violet Taylor, Jill Trumbull, Bella, Bertine, and Sondra, should gain the least inkling of the scene he had just witnessed? In spite of Sondra at the piano throwing him

438

a welcoming smile over her shoulder as he entered, his thoughts were on Roberta. He must go around there again after this was over, to see how she was and so relieve his own mind in case she were better. In case she was not, he must write to Ratterer at once for advice.

In spite of his distress he was trying to appear as gay and unconcerned as ever—dancing first with Perley Haynes and then with Nadine and finally, while waiting for a chance to dance with Sondra, he approached a group who were trying to help Vanda Steele solve a new scenery puzzle and asserted that he could read messages written on paper and sealed in envelopes (the old serial letter trick which he had found explained in an ancient book of parlor tricks discovered on a shelf at the Peytons'). It had been his plan to use it before in order to give himself an air of ease and cleverness, but tonight he was using it to take his mind off the greater problem that was weighing on him. And, although with the aid of Nadine Harriet, whom he took into his confidence, he succeeded in thoroughly mystifying the others, still his mind was not quite on it. Roberta was always there. Supposing something should really be wrong with her and he could not get her out of it. She might even expect him to marry her, so fearful was she of her parents and people. What would he do then? He would lose the beautiful Sondra and she might even come to know how and why he had lost her. But that would be wild of Roberta to expect him to do that. He would not do it. He could not do it.

One thing was certain. He must get her out of this. He must! But how? How?

And although at twelve o'clock Sondra signaled that she was ready to go and that if he chose he might accompany her to her door (and even stop in for a few moments) and although once there, in the shade of a pergola which ornamented the front gate, she had allowed him to kiss her and told him that she was beginning to think he was the nicest ever and that the following spring when the family moved to Twelfth Lake she was going to see if she couldn't think of some way by which she could arrange to have him there over week-ends, still, because of this pressing problem in connection with Roberta, Clyde was so worried that he was not able to completely enjoy this new and to him exquisitely thrilling demonstration of affection on her part—this new and amazing social and emotional victory of his.

He must send that letter to Ratterer to-night. But before that he must return to Roberta as he had promised and find out if she was better. And after that he must go over to Schenectady in the morning, sure, to see the druggist over there. For something must be done about this unless she were better to night.

And so, with Sondra's kisses thrilling on his lips, he left her to go to Roberta, whose white face and troubled eyes told him as he entered her room that no change had taken place. If anything she was worse and more distressed than before, the larger dosage having weakened her to the point of positive illness. However, as she said, nothing mattered if only she could get out of this—that she would almost be willing to die rather than face the consequences. And Clyde, realizing what she meant and being so sincerely concerned for himself, appeared in part distressed for her. However, his previous indifference and the manner in which he had walked off and left her alone this very evening prevented her from feeling that there was any abiding concern in him for her now. And this grieved her terribly. For she sensed now that he did not really care for her any more, even though now he was saying that she mustn't worry and that it was likely that if these didn't work he would get something else that would; that he was going back to the druggist at Schenectady the first thing in the morning to see if there wasn't something else that he could suggest.

But the Gilpins had no telephone, and since he never ventured to call at her room during the day and he never permitted her to call him at Mrs. Peyton's, his plan in this instance was to pass by the following morning before work. If she were all right, the two front shades would be raised to the top; if not, then lowered to the center. In that case he would depart for Schenectady at once, telephoning Mr. Liggett that he had some outside duties to perform.

Just the same, both were terribly depressed and fearful as to what this should mean for each of them. Clyde could not quite assure himself that, in the event that Roberta was not extricated, he would be able to escape without indemnifying her in some form which might not mean just temporary efforts to aid her, but something more—marriage, possibly—since already she had reminded him that he had promised to see her through. But what had he really meant by that at the time that he said it, he now asked himself. Not marriage, most certainly, since his thought was not that he had ever wanted to marry her, but rather just to play with her happily in love, although, as he well knew, she had no such conception of his eager mood at that time. He was compelled to admit to himself that she had probably thought his intentions were more serious or she would not have submitted to him at all.

But reaching home, and after writing and mailing the letter to Ratterer, Clyde passed a troubled night. Next morning he paid a visit to the druggist at Schenectady, the curtains of Roberta's windows having been lowered to the center when he passed. But on this occasion the latter had no additional aid to offer other than the advisability of a hot and hence weakening bath, which he had failed to mention in the first instance. Also some wearying form of physical exercise. But noting Clyde's troubled expression and judging that the situation was causing him great worry, he observed: "Of course, the fact that your wife has skipped a month doesn't mean that there is anything seriously wrong, you know. Women do that sometimes. Anyhow, you can't ever be sure until the second month has passed. Any doctor will tell you that. If she's nervous, let her try something like this. But even if it fails to work, you can't be positive. She might be all right next month just the same."

Thinly cheered by this information, Clyde was about to depart, for Roberta might be wrong. He and she might be worrying needlessly. Still—he was brought up with a round turn as he thought of it—there might be real danger, and waiting until the end of the second period would only mean that a whole month had elapsed and nothing helpful accomplished —a freezing thought. In consequence he now observed: "In case things don't come right, you don't happen to know of a doctor she could go to, do you? This is rather a serious business for both of us, and I'd like to get her out of it if I could."

Something about the way in which Clyde said this—his

extreme nervousness as well as his willingness to indulge in a
form of malpractice which the pharmacist by some logic all
his own considered very different from just swallowing a
preparation intended to achieve the same result—caused him
to look suspiciously at Clyde, the thought stirring in his brain
that very likely after all Clyde was not married, also that this
was one of those youthful affairs which spelled license and future difficulty for some unsophisticated girl. Hence his mood
now changed, and instead of being willing to assist, he now
said coolly: "Well, there may be a doctor around here, but if
so I don't know. And I wouldn't undertake to send any one
to a doctor like that. It's against the law. It would certainly go
hard with any doctor around here who was caught doing that
sort of thing. That's not to say, though, that you aren't at liberty to look around for yourself, if you want to," he added
gravely, giving Clyde a suspicious and examining glance, and
deciding it were best if he had nothing further to do with
such a person.

Clyde therefore returned to Roberta with the same prescription renewed, although she had most decidedly protested
that, since the first box had not worked, it was useless to get
more. But since he insisted, she was willing to try the drug
the new way, although the argument that a cold or nerves was
the possible cause was only sufficient to convince her that
Clyde was at the end of his resources in so far as she was concerned, or if not that, he was far from being alive to the import of this both to herself and to him. And supposing this
new treatment did not work, then what? Was he going to stop
now and let the thing rest there?

Yet so peculiar was Clyde's nature that in the face of his
fears in regard to his future, and because it was far from pleasant to be harried in this way and an infringement on his other
interests, the assurance that the delay of a month might not
prove fatal was sufficient to cause him to be willing to wait,
and that rather indifferently, for that length of time. Roberta
might be wrong. She might be making all this trouble for
nothing. He must see how she felt after she had tried this new
way.

But the treatment failed. Despite the fact that in her distress Roberta returned to the factory in order to weary her-

self, until all the girls in the department assured her that she must be ill—that she should not be working when she looked and plainly felt so bad—still nothing came of it. And the fact that Clyde could dream of falling back on the assurance of the druggist that a first month's lapse was of no import only aggravated and frightened her the more.

The truth was that in this crisis he was as interesting an illustration of the enormous handicaps imposed by ignorance, youth, poverty and fear as one could have found. Technically he did not even know the meaning of the word "midwife," or the nature of the services performed by her. (And there were three here in Lycurgus at this time in the foreign family section.) Again, he had been in Lycurgus so short a time, and apart from the young society men and Dillard whom he had cut, and the various department heads at the factory, he knew no one—an occasional barber, haberdasher, cigar dealer and the like, the majority of whom, as he saw them, were either too dull or too ignorant for his purpose.

One thing, however, which caused him to pause before ever he decided to look up a physician was the problem of who was to approach him and how. To go himself was simply out of the question. In the first place, he looked too much like Gilbert Griffiths, who was decidedly too well-known here and for whom he might be mistaken. Next, it was unquestionable that, being as well-dressed as he was, the physician would want to charge him more, maybe, than he could afford and ask him all sorts of embarrassing questions, whereas if it could be arranged through some one else—the details explained before ever Roberta was sent— Why not Roberta herself! Why not? She looked so simple and innocent and unassuming and appealing at all times. And in such a situation as this, as depressed and downcast as she was, well . . . For after all, as he now casuistically argued with himself, it was she and not he who was facing the immediate problem which had to be solved.

And again, as it now came to him, would she not be able to get it done cheaper? For looking as she did now, so distrait— If only he could get her to say that she had been deserted by some young man, whose name she would refuse to divulge, of course, well, what physician seeing a girl like her alone and in such a state—no one to look after her—would refuse her? It might even be that he would help her out for nothing. Who could tell? And that would leave him clear of it all.

And in consequence he now approached Roberta, intending to prepare her for the suggestion that, assuming that he could provide a physician and the nature of his position being what it was, she must speak for herself. But before he had spoken she at once inquired of him as to what, if anything, more he had heard or done. Wasn't some other remedy sold somewhere? And this giving him the opportunity he desired, he explained: "Well, I've asked around and looked into most of the drug-stores and they tell me if this one won't work that none will. That leaves me sorta stumped now, unless you're willing to go and see a doctor. But the trouble with that is they're hard to find—the ones who'll do anything and keep their mouths shut. I've talked with several fellows without saying who it's for, of course, but it ain't so easy to get one around here, because they are all too much afraid. It's against the law, you see. But what I want to know now is, supposing I find a doctor who would do it, will you have the nerve to go and see him and tell him what the trouble is? That's what I want to know."

She looked at him dazedly, not quite grasping that he was hinting that she was to go entirely alone, but rather assuming that of course he meant to go with her. Then, her mind concentrating nervously upon the necessity of facing a doctor in his company, she first exclaimed: "Oh, dear, isn't it terrible to think of us having to go to a doctor in this way? Then he'll know all about us, won't he? And besides it's dangerous, isn't it, although I don't suppose it could be much worse than those old pills." She went off into more intimate inquiries as to what was done and how, but Clyde could not enlighten her.

"Oh, don't be getting nervous over that now," he said. "It isn't anything that's going to hurt you, I know. Besides we'll be lucky if we find some one to do it. What I want to know is if I do find a doctor, will you be willing to go to him alone?" She started as if struck, but unabashed now he went on, "As things stand with me here, I can't go with you, that's sure. I'm too well known around here, and besides I look too much like Gilbert and he's known to everybody. If I should be mistaken for him, or be taken for his cousin or relative, well, then the jig's up."

His eyes were not only an epitome of how wretched he would feel were he exposed to all Lycurgus for what he was, but also in them lurked a shadow of the shabby rôle he was attempting to play in connection with her—in hiding thus completely behind her necessity. And yet so tortured was he by the fear of what was about to befall him in case he did not succeed in so doing, that he was now prepared, whatever Roberta might think or say, to stand his ground. But Roberta, sensing only the fact that he was thinking of sending her alone, now exclaimed incredulously: "Not alone, Clyde! Oh, no, I couldn't do that! Oh, dear, no! Why, I'd be frightened to death. Oh, dear, no. Why, I'd be so frightened I wouldn't know what to do. Just think how I'd feel, trying to explain to him alone. I just couldn't do that. Besides, how would I know what to say—how to begin? You'll just have to go with me at first, that's all, and explain, or I never can go—I don't care what happens." Her eyes were round and excited and her face, while registering all the depression and fear that had recently been there, was transfigured by definite opposition.

But Clyde was not to be shaken either.

"You know how it is with me here, Bert. I can't go, and that's all there is to it. Why, supposing I were seen—supposing some one should recognize me? What then? You know how much I've been going around here since I've been here. Why, it's crazy to think that I could go. Besides, it will be a lot easier for you than for me. No doctor's going to think anything much of your coming to him, especially if you're alone. He'll just think you're some one who's got in trouble and with no one to help you. But if I go, and it should be any one who knows anything about the Griffiths, there'd be the deuce to pay. Right off he'd think I was stuffed with money. Besides, if I didn't do just what he wanted me to do afterwards, he could go to my uncle, or my cousin, and then, good-night! That would be the end of me. And if I lost my place here now, and with no money and that kind of a scandal connected with me, where do you suppose I would be after that, or you either? I certainly couldn't look after you then. And then what would you do? I should think you'd wake up and see what a tough proposition this is. My name can't be pulled into this without trouble for both of us. It's got to be kept out, that's all, and the only way for me to keep it out is for me to stay away from any doctor. Besides, he'd feel a lot sorrier for you than he would for me. You can't tell me!"

His eyes were distressed and determined, and, as Roberta could gather from his manner, a certain hardness, or at least defiance, the result of fright, showed in every gesture. He was determined to protect his own name, come what might—a fact which, because of her own acquiescence up to this time, still carried great weight with her.

"Oh, dear! dear!" she exclaimed, nervously and sadly now, the growing and drastic terror of the situation dawning upon her, "I don't see how we are to do then. I really don't. For I can't do that and that's all there is to it. It's all so hard—so terrible. I'd feel too much ashamed and frightened to ever go alone."

But even as she said this she began to feel that she might, and even would, go alone, if must be. For what else was there to do? And how was she to compel him, in the face of his own fears and dangers, to jeopardize his position here? He began once more, in self-defense more than from any other motive:

"Besides, unless this thing isn't going to cost very much, I don't see how I'm going to get by with it anyhow, Bert. I really don't. I don't make so very much, you know—only twenty-five dollars up to now." (Necessity was at last compelling him to speak frankly with Roberta.) "And I haven't saved anything—not a cent. And you know why as well as I do. We spent the most of it together. Besides if I go and he thought I had money, he might want to charge me more than I could possibly dig up. But if you go and just tell him how things are—and that you haven't got anything—if you'd only say I'd run away or something, see—"

He paused because, as he said it, he saw a flicker of shame, contempt, despair at being connected with anything so cheap and shabby, pass over Roberta's face. And yet in spite of this sly and yet muddy tergiversation on his part—so great is the compelling and enlightening power of necessity—she could still see that there was some point to his argument. He might be trying to use her as a foil, a mask, behind which he, and she too for that matter, was attempting to hide. But just the same, shameful as it was, here were the stark, bald headlands of fact, and at their base the thrashing, destroying waves of necessity. She heard him say: "You wouldn't have to give your right name, you know, or where you came from. I don't intend to pick out any doctor right around here, see. Then, if you'd tell him you didn't have much money—just your weekly salary—"

She sat down weakly to think, the while this persuasive trickery proceeded from him—the import of most of his argument going straight home. For as false and morally meretricious as this whole plan was, still, as she could see for herself, her own as well as Clyde's situation was desperate. And as honest and punctilious as she might ordinarily be in the matter of truth-telling and honest-dealing, plainly this was one of those whirling tempests of fact and reality in which the ordinary charts and compasses of moral measurement were for the time being of small use.

And so, insisting then that they go to some doctor far away, Utica or Albany, maybe—but still admitting by this that she would go—the conversation was dropped. And he having triumphed in the matter of excepting his own personality from this, took heart to the extent, at least, of thinking that at once now, by some hook or crook, he must find a doctor to whom he could send her. Then his terrible troubles in connection with all this would be over. And after that she could go her way, as surely she must; then, seeing that he would have done all that he could for her he would go his to the glorious dénouement that lay directly before him in case only this were adjusted.

# Chapter XXXVI

NEVERTHELESS hours and even days, and finally a week and then ten days, passed without any word from him as to the whereabouts of a doctor to whom she could go. For although having said so much to her he still did not know to whom to apply. And each hour and day as great a menace to him as to her. And her looks as well as her inquiries registering how intense and vital and even clamorous at moments was her own distress. Also he was harried almost to the point of nervous collapse by his own inability to think of any speedy and sure way by which she might be aided. Where did a physician live to whom he might send her with some assurance of relief for her, and how was he to find out about him?

After a time, however, in running over all the names of those he knew, he finally struck upon a forlorn hope in the guise of Orrin Short, the young man conducting the one small "gents' furnishing store" in Lycurgus which catered more or less exclusively to the rich youths of the city—a youth of about his own years and proclivities, as Clyde had guessed, who ever since he had been here had been useful to him in the matter of tips as to dress and style in general. Indeed, as Clyde had for some time noted, Short was a brisk, inquiring and tactful person, who, in addition to being quite attractive personally to girls, was also always most courteous to his patrons, particularly to those whom he considered above him in the social scale, and among these was Clyde. For having discovered that Clyde was related to the Griffiths, this same Short had sought, as a means for his own general advancement in other directions, to scrape as much of a genial and intimate relationship with him as possible, only, as Clyde saw it, and in view of the general attitude of his very high relatives, it had not, up to this time at least, been possible for him to consider any such intimacy seriously. And yet, finding Short so very affable and helpful in general, he was not above reaching at least an easy and genial surface relationship with him, which Short appeared to accept in good part. Indeed, as at first, his manner remained seeking and not a little syco-

phantic at times. And so it was that among all those with
whom he could be said to be in either intimate or casual contact, Short was about the only one who offered even a chance
for an inquiry which might prove productive of some helpful
information.

In consequence, in passing Short's place each evening and
morning, once he thought of him in this light, he made it a
point to nod and smile in a most friendly manner, until at
least three days had gone by. And then, feeling that he had
paved the way as much as his present predicament would permit, he stopped in, not at all sure that on this first occasion he
would be able to broach the dangerous subject. The tale he
had fixed upon to tell Short was that he had been approached
by a young working-man in the factory, newly-married, who,
threatened with an heir and not being able to afford one as
yet, had appealed to him for information as to where he
might now find a doctor to help him. The only interesting ad-
ditions which Clyde proposed to make to this were that the
young man, being very poor and timid and not so very intelligent, was not able to speak or do much for himself. Also
that he, Clyde, being better informed, although so new locally as not to be able to direct him to any physician (an after-
thought intended to put the idea into Short's mind that he
himself was never helpless and so not likely ever to want such
advice for himself), had already advised the young man of a
temporary remedy. But unfortunately, so his story was to run,
this had already failed to work. Hence something more certain—a physician, no less—was necessary. And Short, having
been here longer, and, as he had heard him explain, hailing
previously from Gloversville, it was quite certain, as Clyde
now argued with himself, that he would know of at least
one—or should. But in order to divert suspicion from himself
he was going to add that of course he probably could get
news of some one in his own set, only, the situation being so
unusual (any reference to any such thing in his own world being likely to set his own group talking), he preferred to ask
some one like Short, who as a favor would keep it quiet.

As it chanced on this occasion, Short himself, owing to his
having done a very fair day's business, was in an exceedingly
jovial frame of mind. And Clyde having entered, to buy a pair

of socks, perhaps, he began: "Well, it's good to see you again, Mr. Griffiths. How are you? I was just thinking it's about time you stopped in and let me show you some of the things I got in since you were here before. How are things with the Griffiths Company anyhow?"

Short's manner, always brisk, was on this occasion doubly reassuring, since he liked Clyde, only now the latter was so intensely keyed up by the daring of his own project that he could scarcely bring himself to carry the thing off with the air he would have liked to have employed.

Nevertheless, being in the store and so, seemingly, committed to the project, he now began: "Oh, pretty fair. Can't kick a bit. I always have all I can do, you know." At the same time he began nervously fingering some ties hung upon movable nickeled rods. But before he had wasted a moment on these, Mr. Short, turning and spreading some boxes of very special ties from a shelf behind him on the glass case, remarked: "Never mind looking at those, Mr. Griffiths. Look at these. These are what I want to show you and they won't cost *you* any more. Just got 'em in from New York this morning." He picked up several bundles of six each, the very latest, as he explained. "See anything else like this anywhere around here yet? I'll say you haven't." He eyed Clyde smilingly, the while he wished sincerely that such a young man, so well connected, yet not rich like the others, would be friends with him. It would place him here.

Clyde, fingering the offerings and guessing that what Short was saying was true, was now so troubled and confused in his own mind that he could scarcely think and speak as planned. "Very nice, sure," he said, turning them over, feeling that at another time he would have been pleased to possess at least two. "I think maybe I'll take this one, anyhow, and this one, too." He drew out two and held them up, while he was thinking how to broach the so much more important matter that had brought him here. For why should he be troubling to buy ties, dilly-dallying in this way, when all he wanted to ask Short about was this other matter? Yet how hard it was now—how very hard. And yet he really must, although perhaps not so abruptly. He would look around a little more at first in order to allay suspicion—ask about some socks. Only why should he be doing that, since he did not need anything, Sondra only recently having presented him with a dozen handkerchiefs, some collars, ties and socks. Nevertheless every time he decided to speak he felt a sort of sinking sensation at the pit of his stomach, a fear that he could not or would not carry the thing off with the necessary ease and conviction. It was all so questionable and treacherous—so likely to lead to exposure and disgrace in some way. He would probably not be able to bring himself to speak to Short to-night. And yet, as he argued with himself, how could the occasion ever be more satisfactory?

Short, in the meantime having gone to the rear of the store and now returning, with a most engaging and even syco-phantic smile on his face, began with: "Saw you last Tuesday evening about nine o'clock going into the Finchleys' place, didn't I? Beautiful house and grounds they have there."

Clyde saw that Short really was impressed by his social sta-tion here. There was a wealth of admiration mingled with a touch of servility. And at once, because of this, he took heart, since he realized that with such an attitude dominating the other, whatever he might say would be colored in part at least by his admirer's awe and respect. And after examining the socks and deciding that one pair at least would soften the dif-ficulty of his demand, he added: "Oh, by the way, before I for-get it. There's something I've been wanting to ask you about. Maybe you can tell me what I want to know. One of the boys at the factory—a young fellow who hasn't been married very long—about four months now, I guess—is in a little trouble on account of his wife." He paused, because of his uncertainty as to whether he could succeed with this now or not, seeing that Short's expression changed ever so slightly. And yet, hav-ing gone so far, he did not know how to recede. So now he laughed nervously and then added: "I don't know why they always come to me with their troubles, but I guess they think I ought to know all about these things." (He laughed again.) "Only I'm about as new and green here as anybody and so I'm kinda stumped. But you've been here longer than I have, I guess, and so I thought I might ask you."

His manner as he said this was as nonchalant as he could make it, the while he decided now that this was a mistake—

that Short would most certainly think him a fool or queer. Yet Short, taken back by the nature of the query, which he sensed as odd coming from Clyde to him (he had noted Clyde's sudden restraint and slight nervousness), was still so pleased to think that even in connection with so ticklish a thing as this, he should be made the recipient of his confidence, that he instantly recovered his former poise and affability, and replied: "Why, sure, if it's anything I can help you with, Mr. Griffiths, I'll be only too glad to. Go ahead, what is it?"

"Well, it's this way," began Clyde, not a little revived by the other's hearty response, yet lowering his voice in order to give the dreadful subject its proper medium of obscurity, as it were. "His wife's already two months gone and he can't afford a kid yet and he doesn't know how to get rid of it. I told him last month when he first came to me to try a certain medicine that usually works"—this to impress Short with his own personal wisdom and resourcefulness in such situations and hence by implication to clear his own skirts, as it were—"But I guess he didn't handle it right. Anyhow he's all worked up about it now and wants to see some doctor who could do something for her, you see. Only I don't know anybody here myself. Haven't been here long enough. If it were Kansas City or Chicago now," he interpolated securely, "I'd know what to do. I know three or four doctors out there." (To impress Short he attempted a wise smile.) "But down here it's different. And if I started asking around in my crowd and it ever got back to my relatives, they wouldn't understand. But I thought if you knew of any one you wouldn't mind telling me. I wouldn't really bother myself, only I'm sorry for this fellow."

He paused, his face, largely because of the helpful and interested expression on Short's, expressing more confidence than when he had begun. And although Short was still surprised he was more than pleased to be as helpful as he could.

"You say it's been two months now."

"Yes."

"And the stuff you suggested didn't work, eh?"

"No."

"She's tried it again this month, has she?"

"Yes."

"Well, that is bad, sure enough. I guess she's in bad all right. The trouble with this place is that I haven't been here so very long either, Mr. Griffiths. I only bought this place about a year and a half ago. Now, if I were over in Gloversville—" He paused for a moment, as though, like Clyde, he too were dubious of the wisdom of entering upon details of this kind, but after a few seconds continued: "You see a thing like that's not so easy, wherever you are. Doctors are always afraid of getting in trouble. I did hear once of a case over there, though, where a girl went to a doctor—a fellow who lived a couple miles out. But she was of pretty good family too, and the fellow who took her to him was pretty well-known about there. So I don't know whether this doctor would do anything for a stranger, although he might at that. But I know that sort of thing is going on all the time, so you might try. If you wanta send this fellow to him, tell him not to mention me or let on who sent him, 'cause I'm pretty well-known around there and I wouldn't want to be mixed up in it in case anything went wrong, you see. You know how it is."

And Clyde, in turn, replied gratefully: "Oh, sure, he'll understand all right. I'll tell him not to mention any names." And getting the doctor's name, he extracted a pencil and notebook from his pocket in order to be sure that the important information should not escape him.

Short, sensing his relief, was inclined to wonder whether there was a working-man, or whether it was not Clyde himself who was in this scrape. Why should he be speaking for a young working-man at the factory? Just the same, he was glad to be of service, though at the same time he was thinking what a bit of local news this would be, assuming that any time in the future he should choose to retail it. Also that Clyde, unless he was truly playing about with some girl here who was in trouble, was foolish to be helping anybody else in this way—particularly a working-man. You bet he wouldn't.

Nevertheless he repeated the name, with the initials, and the exact neighborhood, as near as he could remember, giving the car stop and a description of the house. Clyde, having obtained what he desired, now thanked him, and then went out while the haberdasher looked after him genially and a little suspiciously. These rich young bloods, he thought. That's a funny request for a fellow like that to make of me. You'd think with all the people he knows and runs with here he'd know some one who would tip him off quicker than I could. Still, maybe, it's just because of them that he is afraid to ask around here. You don't know who he might have got in trouble—that young Finchley girl herself, even. You never can tell. I see him around with her occasionally, and she's gay enough. But, gee, wouldn't that be the . . .

# Chapter XXXVII

THE INFORMATION thus gained was a relief, but only partially so. For both Clyde and Roberta there was no real relief now until this problem should be definitely solved. And although within a few moments after he had obtained it, he appeared and explained that at last he had secured the name of some one who might help her, still there was yet the serious business of heartening her for the task of seeing the doctor alone, also for the story that was to exculpate him and at the same time win for her sufficient sympathy to cause the doctor to make the charge for his service merely nominal.

But now, instead of protesting as at first he feared that she might, Roberta was moved to acquiesce. So many things in Clyde's attitude since Christmas had so shocked her that she was bewildered and without a plan other than to extricate herself as best she might without any scandal attaching to her or him and then going her own way—pathetic and abrasive though it might be. For since he did not appear to care for her any more and plainly desired to be rid of her, she was in no mood to compel him to do other than he wished. Let him go. She could make her own way. She had, and she could too, without him, if only she could get out of this. Yet, as she said this to herself, however, and a sense of the full significance of it all came to her, the happy days that would never be again, she put her hands to her eyes and brushed away uncontrollable tears. To think that all that was should come to this.

Yet when he called the same evening after visiting Short, his manner redolent of a fairly worth-while achievement, she merely said, after listening to his explanation in as receptive a manner as she could: "Do you know just where this is, Clyde? Can we get there on the car without much trouble, or will we have to walk a long way?" And after he had explained that it was but a little way out of Gloversville, in the suburbs really, an interurban stop being but a quarter of a mile from the house, she had added: "Is he home at night, or will we have to go in the daytime? It would be so much better if we could go at night. There'd be so much less danger of any one see-ing us." And being assured that he was, as Clyde had learned from Short, she went on: "But do you know is he old or young? I'd feel so much easier and safer if he were old. I don't like young doctors. We've always had an old doctor up home and I feel so much easier talking to some one like him."

Clyde did not know. He had not thought to inquire, but to reassure her he ventured that he was middle-aged—which chanced to be the fact

The following evening the two of them departed, but sepa-rately as usual, for Fonda, where it was necessary to change cars. And once within the approximate precincts of the physi-cian's residence, they stepped down and made their way along a road, which in this mid-state winter weather was still covered with old and dry-packed snow. It offered a comparatively smooth floor for their quick steps. For in these days there was no longer that lingering intimacy which formerly would have characterized both. In those other and so recent days, as Roberta was constantly thinking, he would have been only too glad in such a place as this, if not on such an occasion, to drag his steps, put an arm about her waist, and talk about nothing at all—the night, the work at the factory, Mr. Liggett, his uncle, the current movies, some place they were planning to go, something they would love to do together if they could. But now . . . And on this particular occasion, when most of all, and if ever, she needed the full strength of his devotion and support! Yet now, as she could see, he was most nervously con-cerned as to whether, going alone in this way, she was going to get scared and "back out"; whether she was going to think to say the right thing at the right time and convince the doctor that he must do something for her, and for a nominal fee.

"Well, Bert, how about you? All right? You're not going to get cold feet now, are you? Gee, I hope not because this is going to be a good chance to get this thing done and over with. And it isn't like you were going to some one who hadn't done anything like this before, you know, because this fellow has. I got that straight. All you have to do now, is to say, well, you know, that you're in trouble, see, and that you don't know how you're going to get out of it unless he'll help you in some way, because you haven't any friends here you can go to. And besides, as things are, you couldn't go to 'em if you wanted to. They'd tell on you, see. Then if he asks where I am or who I am, you just say that I was a fellow here—but that I've gone—give any name you want to, but that I've gone, and you don't know where I've gone to—run away, see. Then you'd better say, too, that you wouldn't have come to him only that you heard of another case in which he helped some one else—that a girl told you, see. Only you don't want to let on that you're paid much, I mean,—because if you do he may want to make the bill more than I can pay, see, unless he'll give us a few months in which to do it, or something like that, you see."

Clyde was so nervous and so full of the necessity of charging Roberta with sufficient energy and courage to go through with this and succeed, now that he had brought her this far along with it, that he scarcely realized how inadequate and trivial, even, in so far as her predicament and the doctor's mood and temperament were concerned, his various instructions and bits of inexperienced advice were. And she on her part was not only thinking how easy it was for him to stand back and make suggestions, while she was confronted with the necessity of going forward, and that alone, but also that he was really thinking more of himself than he was of her—some way to make her get herself out of it inexpensively and without any real trouble to him.

At the same time, even here and now, in spite of all this, she was still decidedly drawn to him—his white face, his thin hands, nervous manner. And although she knew he talked to encourage her to do what he had not the courage or skill to do himself, she was not angry. Rather, she was merely saying to herself in this crisis that although he advised so freely she was not going to pay attention to him—much. What she was going to say was not that she was deserted, for that seemed too much of a disagreeable and self-incriminating remark for her to make concerning herself, but rather that she was married and that she and her young husband were too poor to have a baby as yet—the same story Clyde had told the druggist in Schenectady, as she recalled. For after all, what did he know about how she felt? And he was not going with her to make it easier for her.

Yet dominated by the purely feminine instinct to cling to some one for support, she now turned to Clyde, taking hold of his hands and standing quite still, wishing that he would hold and pet her and tell her that it was all right and that she must not be afraid. And although he no longer cared for her, now in the face of this involuntary evidence of her former trust in him, he released both hands and putting his arms about her, the more to encourage her than anything else, observed: "Come on now, Bert. Gee, you can't act like this, you know. You don't want to lose your nerve now that we're here, do you? It won't be so hard once you get there. I know it won't. All you got to do is to go up and ring the bell, see, and when he comes, or whoever comes, just say you want to see the doctor alone, see. Then he'll understand it's something private and it'll be easier."

He went on with more advice of the same kind, and she, realizing from his lack of spontaneous enthusiasm for her at this moment how desperate was her state, drew herself together as vigorously as she could, and saying: "Well, wait here, then, will you? Don't go very far away, will you? I may be right back," hurried along in the shadow through the gate and up a walk which led to the front door.

In answer to her ring the door was opened by one of those exteriorly as well as mentally sober, small-town practitioners who, Clyde's and Short's notion to the contrary notwithstanding, was the typical and fairly conservative physician of the countryside—solemn, cautious, moral, semi-religious to a degree, holding some views which he considered liberal and others which a fairly liberal person would have considered narrow and stubborn into the bargain. Yet because of the ignorance and stupidity of so many of those about him, he was able to consider himself at least fairly learned. In constant touch with all phases of ignorance and dereliction as well as sobriety, energy, conservatism, success and the like, he was more inclined, where fact appeared to nullify his early conclusions in regard to many things, to suspend judgment between the alleged claims of heaven and hell and leave it there suspended and undisturbed. Physically he was short, stocky, bullet-headed and yet interestingly-featured, with quick gray eyes and a pleasant mouth and smile. His short iron-gray hair was worn "bangs" fashion, a bit of rural vanity. And his arms and hands, the latter fat and pudgy, yet sensitive, hung limply at his sides. He was fifty-eight, married, the father of three children, one of them a son already studying medicine in order to succeed to his father's practice.

After showing Roberta into a littered and commonplace waiting room and asking her to remain until he had finished his dinner, he presently appeared in the door of an equally commonplace inner room, or office, where were his desk, two chairs, some medical instruments, books and apparently an ante-chamber containing other medical things, and motioned her to a chair. And because of his grayness, solidity, stolidity, as well as an odd habit he had of blinking his eyes, Roberta was not a little overawed, though by no means so unfavorably impressed as she had feared she might be. At least he was old and he seemed intelligent and conservative, if not exactly sympathetic or warm in his manner! And after looking at her curiously a moment, as though seeking to recognize some one of the immediate vicinity, he began: "Well, now who is this, please? And what can I do for you?" His voice was low and quite reassuring—a fact for which Roberta was deeply grateful.

At the same time, startled by the fact that at last she had reached the place and the moment when, if ever, she must say the degrading truth about herself, she merely sat there, her eyes first upon him, then upon the floor, her fingers beginning to toy with the handle of the small bag she carried.

"You see, well," she began, earnestly and nervously, her whole manner suddenly betraying the terrific strain under which she was laboring. "I came . . . I came . . . that is . . . I don't know whether I can tell you about myself or not. I thought I could just before I came in, but now that I am here and I see you . . ." She paused and moved back in her chair as though to rise, at the same time that she added: "Oh, dear, how very dreadful it all is. I'm so nervous and . . ."

"Well, now, my dear," he resumed, pleasantly and reassuringly, impressed by her attractive and yet sober appearance and wondering for the moment what could have upset so clean, modest and sedate-looking a girl, and hence not a little amused by her "now that I see you,"—"Just what is there

about me 'now that you see me,'" he repeated after her, "that
so frightens you? I am only a country doctor, you know, and
I hope I'm not as dreadful as you seem to think. You can be
sure that you can tell me anything you wish—anything at all
about yourself—and you needn't be afraid. If there's anything
I can do for you, I'll do it."

He was decidedly pleasant, as she now thought, and yet so
sober and reserved and probably conventional withal that
what she was holding in mind to tell him would probably
shock him not a little—and then what? Would he do anything
for her? And if he would, how was she to arrange about
money, for that certainly would be a point in connection with
all this? If only Clyde or some one were here to speak for her.
And yet she must speak now that she was here. She could not
leave without. Once more she moved and twisted, seizing
nervously on a large button of her coat to turn between her
thumb and forefinger, and then went on chokingly.

"But this is . . . this is . . . well, something different, you
know, maybe not what you think. . . . I . . . I . . . well . . ."

Again she paused, unable to proceed, shading from white
to red and back as she spoke. And because of the troubled
modesty of her approach, as well as a certain clarity of eye,
whiteness of forehead, sobriety of manner and dress, the doctor could scarcely bring himself to think for a moment that
this was anything other than one of those morbid exhibitions
of innocence, or rather inexperience, in connection with
everything relating to the human body—so characteristic of
the young and unsophisticated in some instances. And so he
was about to repeat his customary formula in such cases that
all could be told to him without fear or hesitation, whatever
it might be, when a secondary thought, based on Roberta's
charm and vigor, as well as her own thought waves attacking
his cerebral receptive centers, caused him to decide that he
might be wrong. After all, why might not this be another of
those troublesome youthful cases in which possibly immorality and illegitimacy was involved. She was so young, healthy
and attractive, besides, they were always cropping up, these
cases,—in connection with the most respectable-looking girls
at times. And invariably they spelled trouble and distress for
doctors. And, for various reasons connected with his own

temperament, which was retiring and recessive, as well as the nature of this local social world, he disliked and hesitated to even trifle with them. They were illegal, dangerous, involved little or no pay as a rule, and the sentiment of this local world was all against them as he knew. Besides he personally was more or less irritated by these young scamps of boys and girls who were so free to exercise the normal functions of their natures in the first instance, but so ready to refuse the social obligations which went with them—marriage afterwards. And so, although in several cases in the past ten years where family and other neighborhood and religious considerations had made it seem quite advisable, he had assisted in extricating from the consequences of their folly several young girls of good family who had fallen from grace and could not otherwise be rescued, still he was opposed to aiding, either by his own countenance or skill, any lapses or tangles not heavily sponsored by others. It was too dangerous. Ordinarily it was his custom to advise immediate and unconditional marriage. Or, where that was not possible, the perpetrator of the infamy having decamped, it was his general and self-consciously sanctioned practice to have nothing at all to do with the matter. It was too dangerous and ethically and socially wrong and criminal into the bargain.

In consequence he now looked at Roberta in an extremely sober manner. By no means, he now said to himself, must he allow himself to become emotionally or otherwise involved here. And so in order to help himself as well as her to attain and maintain a balance which would permit of both extricating themselves without too much trouble, he drew toward him his black leather case record book and, opening it, said: "Now, let's see if we can't find out what the trouble is here. What is your name?"

"Ruth Howard. Mrs. Howard," replied Roberta nervously and tensely, at once fixing upon a name which Clyde had suggested for her use. And now, interestingly enough, at mention of the fact that she was married, he breathed easier. But why the tears then? What reason could a young married woman have for being so intensely shy and nervous?

"And your husband's first name?" he went on.

As simple as the question was, and as easy as it should have been to answer, Roberta nevertheless hesitated before she could bring herself to say: "Gifford," her older brother's name.

"You live around here, I presume?"

"In Fonda."

"Yes. And how old are you?"

"Twenty-two."

"How long have you been married?"

This inquiry being so intimately connected with the problem before her, she again hesitated before saying, "Let me see—three months."

At once Dr. Glenn became dubious again, though he gave her no sign. Her hesitancy arrested him. Why the uncertainty? He was wondering now again whether he was dealing with a truthful girl or whether his first suspicions were being substantiated. In consequence he now asked: "Well, now what seems to be the trouble, Mrs. Howard? You need have no hesitancy in telling me—none whatsoever. I am used to such things year in and out, whatever they are. That is my business, listening to the troubles of people."

"Well," began Roberta, nervously once more, this terrible confession drying her throat and thickening her tongue almost, while once more she turned the same button of her coat and gazed at the floor. "It's like this . . . You see . . . my husband hasn't much money . . . and I have to work to help out with expenses and neither of us make so very much." (She was astonishing herself with her own shameful power to lie in this instance—she, who had always hated to lie.) "So . . . of course . . . we can't afford to . . . to have . . . well, any . . . children, you see, so soon, anyhow, and . . ."

She paused, her breath catching, and really unable to proceed further with this wholesale lying.

The doctor realizing from this, as he thought, what the true problem was—that she was a newly-married girl who was probably faced by just such a problem as she was attempting to outline—yet not wishing to enter upon any form of malpractice and at the same time not wishing to appear too discouraging to a young couple just starting out in life, gazed at her somewhat more sympathetically, the decidedly unfortunate predicament of these young people, as well as her appropriate modesty in the face of such a conventionally delicate situation, appealing to him. It was too bad. Young people these days did have a rather hard time of it, getting started in some cases, anyhow. And they were no doubt faced by some pressing financial situations. Nearly all young people were. Nevertheless, this business of a contraceptal operation or interference with the normal or God-arranged life processes, well, that was a ticklish and unnatural business at best which he wanted as little as possible to do with. Besides, young, healthy people, even though poor, when they undertook marriage, knew what they were about. And it was not impossible for them to work, the husband anyhow, and hence manage in some way.

And now straightening himself around in his chair very soberly and authoritatively, he began: "I think I understand what you want to say to me, Mrs. Howard. But I'm also wondering if you have considered what a very serious and dangerous thing it is you have in mind. But," he added, suddenly, another thought as to whether his own reputation in this community was in any way being tarnished by rumor of anything he had done in the past coming to him, "just how did you happen to come to me, anyhow?"

Something about the tone of his voice, the manner in which he asked the question—the caution of it as well as the possibly impending resentment in case it should turn out that any one suspected him of a practice of this sort—caused Roberta to hesitate and to feel that any statement to the effect that she had heard of or been sent by any one else— Clyde to the contrary notwithstanding—might be dangerous. Perhaps she had better not say that she had been sent by any one. He might resent it as an insult to his character as a reputable physician. A budding instinct for diplomacy helped her in this instance, and she replied: "I've noticed your sign in passing several times and I've heard different people say you were a good doctor."

His uncertainty allayed, he now continued: "In the first place, the thing you want done is something my conscience would not permit me to advise. I understand, of course, that you consider it necessary. You and your husband are both young and you probably haven't very much money to go on, and you both feel that an interruption of this kind will be a great strain in every way. And no doubt it will be. Still, as I see it, marriage is a very sacred thing, and children are a blessing—not a curse. And when you went to the altar three months ago you were probably not unaware that you might have to face just such a situation as this. All young married people are, I think." ("The altar," thought Roberta sadly. If only it were so.) "Now I know that the tendency of the day in some quarters is very much in this direction, I am sorry to say. There are those who feel it quite all right if they can shirk the normal responsibilities in such cases as to perform these operations, but it's very dangerous, Mrs. Howard, very dangerous legally and ethically as well as medically very wrong. Many women who seek to escape childbirth die in this way. Besides it is a prison offense for any doctor to assist them, whether there are bad consequences or not. You know that, I suppose. At any rate, I, for one, am heartily opposed to this sort of thing from every point of view. The only excuse I have ever been able to see for it is when the life of the mother, for instance, depends upon such an operation. Not otherwise. And in such cases the medical profession is in accord. But in this instance I'm sure the situation isn't one which warrants anything like that. You seem to me to be a strong, healthy girl. Motherhood should hold no serious consequences for you. And as for money reasons, don't you really think now that if you just go ahead and have this baby, you and your husband would find means of getting along? You say your husband is an electrician?"

"Yes," replied Roberta, nervously, not a little overawed and subdued by his solemn moralizing.

"Well, now, there you are," he went on. "That's not such an unprofitable profession. At least all electricians charge enough. And when you consider, as you must, how serious a thing you are thinking of doing, that you are actually planning to destroy a young life that has as good a right to its existence as you have to yours . . ." he paused in order to let the substance of what he was saying sink in—"well, then, I think you might feel called upon to stop and consider—both you and your husband. Besides," he added, in a diplomatic and more fatherly and even intriguing tone of voice, "I think

that once you have it it will more than make up to you both
for whatever little hardship its coming will bring you. Tell
me," he added curiously at this point, "does your husband
know of this? Or is this just some plan of yours to save him
and yourself from too much hardship?" He almost beamed
cheerfully as, fancying he had captured Roberta in some
purely nervous and feminine economy as well as dread, he decided that if so he could easily extract her from her present
mood. And she, sensing his present drift and feeling that one
lie more or less could neither help nor harm her, replied
quickly: "He knows."

"Well, then," he went on, slightly reduced by the fact that
his surmise was incorrect, but none the less resolved to dissuade her and him, too: "I think you two should really consider very seriously before you go any further in this matter. I
know when young people first face a situation like this they always look on the darkest side of it, but it doesn't always work
out that way. I know my wife and I did with our first child.
But we got along. And if you will only stop now and talk it
over, you'll see it in a different light, I'm sure. And then you
won't have your conscience to deal with afterwards, either."
He ceased, feeling reasonably sure that he had dispelled the
fear, as well as the determination that had brought Roberta to
him—that, being a sensible, ordinary wife, she would now desist of course—think nothing more of her plan and leave.

But instead of either acquiescing cheerfully or rising to go,
as he thought she might, she gave him a wide-eyed terrified
look and then as instantly burst into tears. For the total effect
of his address had been to first revive more clearly than ever
the normal social or conventional aspect of the situation
which all along she was attempting to shut out from her
thoughts and which, under ordinary circumstances, assuming
that she was really married, was exactly the attitude she would
have taken. But now the realization that her problem was not
to be solved at all, by this man at least, caused her to be
seized with what might best be described as morbid panic.

Suddenly beginning to open and shut her fingers and at the
same time beating her knees, while her face contorted itself
with pain and terror, she exclaimed: "But you don't understand, doctor, you don't understand! I *have* to get out of this

in some way! I have to. It isn't like I told you at all. I'm not married. I haven't any husband at all. But, oh, you don't know what this means to me. My family! My father! My mother! I can't tell you. But I must get out of it. I must! I must! Oh, you don't know, you don't know! I must! I must!" She began to rock backward and forward, at the same time swaying from side to side as in a trance.

And Glenn, surprised and startled by this sudden demonstration as well as emotionally affected, and yet at the same time advised thereby that his original surmise had been correct, and hence that Roberta had been lying, as well as that if he wished to keep himself out of this he must now assume a firm and even heartless attitude, asked solemnly: "You are not married, you say?"

For answer now Roberta merely shook her head negatively and continued to cry. And at last gathering the full import of her situation, Dr. Glenn got up, his face a study of troubled and yet conservative caution and sympathy. But without saying anything at first he merely looked at her as she wept. Later he added: "Well, well, this is too bad. I'm sorry." But fearing to commit himself in any way, he merely paused, adding after a time soothingly and dubiously: "You mustn't cry. That won't help you any." He then paused again, still determined not to have anything to do with this case. Yet a bit curious as to the true nature of the story he finally asked: "Well, then where is the young man who is the cause of your trouble? Is he here?"

Still too overcome by shame and despair to speak, Roberta merely shook her head negatively.

"But he knows that you're in trouble, doesn't he?"

"Yes," replied Roberta faintly.

"And he won't marry you?"

"He's gone away."

"Oh, I see. The young scamp! And don't you know where he's gone?"

"No," lied Roberta, weakly.

"How long has it been since he left you?"

"About a week now." Once more she lied.

"And you don't know where he is?"

"No."

"How long has it been since you were sick?"

"Over two weeks now," sobbed Roberta.

"And before that you have always been regular?"

"Yes."

"Well, in the first place," his tone was more comfortable and pleasant than before—he seemed to be snatching at a plausible excuse for extricating himself from a case which promised little other than danger and difficulty, "this may not be as serious as you think. I know you're probably very much frightened, but it's not unusual for women to miss a period. At any rate, without an examination it wouldn't be possible to be sure, and even if you were, the most advisable thing would be to wait another two weeks. You may find then that there is nothing wrong. I wouldn't be surprised if you did. You seem to be oversensitive and nervous and that sometimes brings about delays of this kind—mere nervousness. At any rate, if you'll take my advice, whatever you do, you'll not do anything now but just go home and wait until you're really sure. For even if anything were to be done, it wouldn't be advisable for you to do anything before then."

"But I've already taken some pills and they haven't helped me," pleaded Roberta.

"What were they?" asked Glenn interestedly, and, after he had learned, merely commented: "Oh, those. Well, they wouldn't be likely to be of any real service to you, if you were pregnant. But I still suggest that you wait, and if you find you pass your second period, then it will be time enough to act, although I earnestly advise you, even then, to do nothing if you can help it, because I consider it wrong to interfere with nature in this way. It would be much better, if you would arrange to have the child and take care of it. Then you wouldn't have the additional sin of destroying a life upon your conscience."

He was very grave and felt very righteous as he said this. But Roberta, faced by terrors which he did not appear to be able to grasp, merely exclaimed, and as dramatically as before: "But I can't do that, doctor, I tell you! I can't. I can't! You don't understand. Oh, I don't know what I shall do unless I find some way out of this. I don't! I don't! I don't!"

She shook her head and clenched her fingers and rocked to and fro while Glenn, impressed by her own terrors, the pity of the folly which, as he saw it, had led her to this dreadful pass, yet professionally alienated by a type of case that spelled nothing but difficulty for him stood determinedly before her and added: "As I told you before, Miss—" (he paused) "Howard, if that is your name, I am seriously opposed to operations of this kind, just as I am to the folly that brings girls and young men to the point where they seem to think they are necessary. A physician may not interfere in a case of this kind unless he is willing to spend ten years in prison, and I think that law is fair enough. Not that I don't realize how painful your present situation appears to you. But there are always those who are willing to help a girl in your state, providing she doesn't wish to do something which is morally and legally wrong. And so the very best advice I can give you now is that you do nothing at all now or at any time. Better go home and see your parents and confess. It will be much better—much better, I assure you. Not nearly as hard as you think or as wicked as this other way. Don't forget there is a life there—a human— if it is really as you think. A human life which you are seeking to end and that I cannot help you to do. I really cannot. There may be doctors—I know there are—men here and there who take their professional ethics a little less seriously than I do; but I cannot let myself become one of them. I am sorry—very.

"So now the best I can say is—go home to your parents and tell them. It may look hard now but you are going to feel better about it in the long run. If it will make you or them feel any better about it, let them come and talk to me. I will try and make them see that this is not the worst thing in the world, either. But as for doing what you want—I am very, very sorry, but I cannot. My conscience will not permit me."

He paused and gazed at her sympathetically, yet with a determined and concluded look in his eye. And Roberta, dumbfounded by this sudden termination of all her hopes in connection with him and realizing at last that not only had she been misled by Clyde's information in regard to this doctor, but that her technical as well as emotional plea had failed, now walked unsteadily to the door, the terrors of the future crowding thick upon her. And once outside in the dark, after the doctor had most courteously and ruefully closed the door

behind her, she paused to lean against a tree that was there—
her nervous and physical strength all but failing her. He had
refused to help her. He had refused to help her. And now
what?

# Chapter XXXVIII

THE FIRST EFFECT of the doctor's decision was to shock and terrify them both—Roberta and Clyde—beyond measure. For apparently now here was illegitimacy and disgrace for Roberta. Exposure and destruction for Clyde. And this had been their one solution seemingly. Then, by degrees, for Clyde at least, there was a slight lifting of the heavy pall. Perhaps, after all, as the doctor had suggested—and once she had recovered her senses sufficiently to talk, she had told him—the end had not been reached. There was the bare possibility, as suggested by the druggist, Short and the doctor, that she might be mistaken. And this, while not producing a happy reaction in her, had the unsatisfactory result of inducing in Clyde a lethargy based more than anything else on the ever-haunting fear of inability to cope with this situation as well as the certainty of social exposure in case he did not which caused him, instead of struggling all the more desperately, to defer further immediate action. For, such was his nature that, although he realized clearly the probable tragic consequences if he did not act, still it was so hard to think to whom else to apply to without danger to himself. To think that the doctor had "turned her down," as he phrased it, and that Short's advice should have been worth as little as that!

But apart from nervous thoughts as to whom to turn to next, no particular individual occurred to him before the two weeks were gone, or after. It was so hard to just ask anywhere. One just couldn't do it. Besides, of whom could he ask now? Of whom? These things took time, didn't they? Yet in the meantime, the days going by, both he and Roberta had ample time to consider what, if any, steps they must take—the one in regard to the other—in case no medical or surgical solution was found. For Roberta, while urging and urging, if not so much by words as by expression and mood at her work, was determined that she must not be left to fight this out alone—she could not be. On the other hand, as she could see, Clyde did nothing. For apart from what he had already attempted to do, he was absolutely at a loss how to proceed. He had no in-

timates and in consequence he could only think of presenting
the problem as an imaginary one to one individual and another here or there in the hope of extracting some helpful information. At the same time, and as impractical and evasive as
it may seem, there was the call of that diverting world of
which Sondra was a part, evenings and Sundays, when, in
spite of Roberta's wretched state and mood, he was called to
go here and there, and did, because in so doing he was actually relieving his own mind of the dread specter of disaster
that was almost constantly before it. If only he could get her
out of this! If only he could. But how, without money, intimates, a more familiar understanding of the medical or if not
that exactly, then the sub rosa world of sexual free-masonry
which some at times—the bell-hops of the Green-Davidson,
for instance, seemed to understand. He had written to Ratterer, of course, but there had been no answer, since Ratterer
had removed to Florida and as yet Clyde's letter had not
reached him. And locally all those he knew best were either
connected with the factory or society—individuals on the one
hand too inexperienced or dangerous, or on the other hand,
too remote and dangerous, since he was not sufficiently intimate with any of them as yet to command their true confidence and secrecy.

At the same time he must do something—he could not just
rest and drift. Assuredly Roberta could not long permit him
to do that—faced as she was by exposure. And so from time
to time he actually racked himself—seized upon straws and
what would have been looked upon by most as forlorn
chances. Thus, for instance, an associate foreman, chancing to
reminisce one day concerning a certain girl in his department
who had "gotten in trouble" and had been compelled to
leave, he had been given the opportunity to inquire what he
thought such a girl did in case she could not afford or did not
want to have a child. But this particular foreman, being as uninformed as himself, merely observed that she probably had
to see a doctor if she knew one or "go through with it"—
which left Clyde exactly where he was. On another occasion,
in connection with a conversation in a barber shop relating to
a local case reported in *The Star* where a girl was suing a local ne'er-do-well for breach of promise, the remark was made

that she would "never have sued that guy, you bet, unless she had to." Whereupon Clyde seized the opportunity to remark hopefully, "But wouldn't you think that she could find some way of getting out of trouble without marrying a fellow she didn't like?"

"Well, that's not so easy as you may think, particularly around here," elucidated the wiseacre who was trimming his hair. "In the first place it's agin' the law. And next it takes a lotta money. An' in case you ain't got it, well, money makes the mare go, you know." He snip-snipped with his scissors while Clyde, confronted by his own problem, meditated on how true it was. If he had a lot of money—even a few hundred dollars—he might take it now and possibly persuade her—who could tell— to go somewhere by herself and have an operation performed.

Yet each day, as on the one before, he was saying to himself that he must find some one. And Roberta was saying to herself that she too must act—must not really depend on Clyde any longer if he were going to act so. One could not trifle or compromise with a terror of this kind. It was a cruel imposition on her. It must be that Clyde did not realize how terribly this affected her and even him. For certainly, if he were not going to help her out of it, as he had distinctly said he would do at first, then decidedly she could not be expected to weather the subsequent storm alone. Never, never, never! For, after all, as Roberta saw it, Clyde was a man—he had a good position—it was not he, but she, who was in this treacherous position and unable to extricate herself alone.

And beginning with the second day after the second period, when she discovered for once and all that her worst suspicions were true, she not only emphasized the fact in every way that she could that she was distressed beyond all words, but on the third day announced to him in a note that she was again going to see the doctor near Gloversville that evening, regardless of his previous refusal—so great was her need—and also asking Clyde whether he would accompany her—a request which, since he had not succeeded in doing anything, and although he had an engagement with Sondra, he instantly acceded to—feeling it to be of greater importance than anything else. He must excuse himself to Sondra on the ground of work.

And accordingly this second trip was made, a long and nervous conversation between himself and Roberta on the way resulting in nothing more than some explanations as to why thus far he had not been able to achieve anything, plus certain encomiums addressed to her concerning her courage in acting for herself in this way.

Yet the doctor again would not and did not act. After waiting nearly an hour for his return from somewhere, she was merely permitted to tell him of her unchanged state and her destroying fears in regard to herself, but with no hint from him that he could be induced to act as indeed he could act. It was against his prejudices and ethics.

And so once more Roberta returned, this time not crying, actually too sad to cry, choked with the weight of her impending danger and the anticipatory fears and miseries that attended it.

And Clyde, hearing of this defeat, was at last reduced to a nervous, gloomy silence, absolutely devoid of a helpful suggestion. He could not think what to say and was chiefly fearful lest Roberta now make some demand with which socially or economically he could not comply. However, in regard to this she said little on the way home. Instead she sat and stared out of the window—thinking of her defenseless predicament that was becoming more real and terrible to her hourly. By way of excuse she pleaded that she had a headache. She wanted to be alone—only to think more—to try to work out a solution. She must work out some way. That she knew. But what? How? What could she do? How could she possibly escape? She felt like a cornered animal fighting for its life with all odds against it, and she thought of a thousand remote and entirely impossible avenues of escape, only to return to the one and only safe and sound solution that she really felt should be possible—and that was marriage. And why not? Hadn't she given him all, and that against her better judgment? Hadn't he overpersuaded her? Who was he anyway to so cast her aside? For decidedly at times, and especially since this latest crisis had developed, his manner, because of Sondra and the Griffiths and what he felt to be the fatal effect of all this on his dreams here, was sufficient to make plain that love was decidedly dead, and that he was not thinking nearly so much of the meaning of her state to her, as he was of its import, the injury that was most certain to accrue to him. And when this did not completely terrify her, as mostly it did, it served to irritate and slowly develop the conclusion that in such a desperate state as this, she was justified in asking more than ordinarily she would have dreamed of asking, marriage itself, since there was no other door. And why not? Wasn't her life as good as his? And hadn't he joined his to hers, voluntarily? Then, why shouldn't he strive to help her now—or, failing that, make this final sacrifice which was the only one by which she could be rescued apparently. For who were all the society people with whom he was concerned anyhow? And why should he ask her in such a crisis to sacrifice herself, her future and good name, just because of his interest in them? They had never done anything very much for him, certainly not as much as had she. And, just because he was wearying now, after persuading her to do his bidding—was that any reason why now, in this crisis, he should be permitted to desert her? After all, wouldn't all of these society people in whom he was so much interested feel that whatever his relationship to them, she would be justified in taking the course which she might be compelled to take?

She brooded on this much, more especially on the return from this second attempt to induce Dr. Glenn to help her. In fact, at moments, her face took on a defiant, determined look which was seemingly new to her, but which only developed suddenly under such pressure. Her jaw became a trifle set. She had made a decision. He would have to marry her. She must make him if there were no other way out of this. She must— she must. Think of her home, her mother, Grace Marr, the Newtons, all who knew her in fact—the terror and pain and shame with which this would sear all those in any way identified with her—her father, brothers, sisters. Impossible! Impossible! It must not and could not be! Impossible. It might seem a little severe to her, even now, to have to insist on this, considering all the emphasis Clyde had hitherto laid upon his prospects here. But how, how else was she to do?

Accordingly the next day, and not a little to his surprise, since for so many hours the night before they had been together, Clyde received another note telling him that he must come again that night. She had something to say to him, and there was something in the tone of the note that seemed to indicate or suggest a kind of defiance of a refusal of any kind, hitherto absent in any of her communications to him. And at once the thought that this situation, unless cleared away, was certain to prove disastrous, so weighed upon him that he could not but put the best face possible on it and consent to go and hear what it was that she had to offer in the way of a solution— or—on the other hand, of what she had to complain.

Going to her room at a late hour, he found her in what seemed to him a more composed frame of mind than at any time since this difficulty had appeared, a state which surprised him a little, since he had expected to find her in tears. But now, if anything, she appeared more complacent, her nervous thoughts as to how to bring about a satisfactory conclusion for herself having called into play a native shrewdness which was now seeking to exercise itself.

And so directly before announcing what was in her mind, she began by asking: "You haven't found out about another doctor, have you, Clyde, or thought of anything?"

"No, I haven't, Bert," he replied most dismally and wearisomely, his own mental tether-length having been strained to the breaking point. "I've been trying to, as you know, but it's so darn hard to find any one who isn't afraid to monkey with a case like this. Honest, to tell the truth, Bert, I'm about stumped. I don't know what we are going to do unless you can think of something. You haven't thought or heard of any one else you could go to, have you?" For, during the conversation that had immediately followed her first visit to the doctor, he had hinted to her that by striking up a fairly intimate relationship with one of the foreign family girls, she might by degrees extract some information there which would be of use to both. But Roberta was not of a temperament that permitted of any such facile friendships, and nothing had come of it.

However, his stating that he was "stumped" now gave her the opportunity she was really desiring, to present the proposition which she felt to be unavoidable and not longer to be delayed. Yet being fearful of how Clyde would react, she hesitated as to the form in which she would present it, and, after shaking her head and manifesting a nervousness which was real enough, she finally said: "Well, I'll tell you, Clyde. I've been thinking about it and I don't see any way out of it unless—unless you, well, marry me. It's two months now, you know, and unless we get married right away, everybody'll know, won't they?"

Her manner as she said this was a mixture of outward courage born out of her conviction that she was in the right and an inward uncertainty about Clyde's attitude, which was all the more fused by a sudden look of surprise, resentment, uncertainty and fear that now transformation-wise played over his countenance; a variation and play which, if it indicated anything definite, indicated that she was seeking to inflict an unwarranted injury on him. For since he had been drawing closer and closer to Sondra, his hopes had heightened so intensely that, hearkening to this demand on the part of Roberta now, his brow wrinkled and his manner changed from one of comparatively affable, if nervous, consideration to that of mingled fear, opposition as well as determination to evade drastic consequence. For this would spell complete ruin for him, the loss of Sondra, his job, his social hopes and ambitions in connection with the Griffiths—all—a thought which sickened and at the same time caused him to hesitate about how to proceed. But he would not! he would not! He would not do this! Never! Never!! Never!!!

Yet after a moment he exclaimed equivocally: "Well, gee, that's all right, too, Bert, for you, because that fixes everything without any trouble at all. But what about me? You don't want to forget that that isn't going to be easy for me, the way things are now. You know I haven't any money. All I have is my job. And besides, the family don't know anything about you yet—not a thing. And if it should suddenly come out now that we've been going together all this time, and that this has happened, and that I was going to have to get married right away, well, gee, they'll know I've been fooling 'em and they're sure to get sore. And then what? They might even fire me."

He paused to see what effect this explanation would have, but noting the somewhat dubious expression which of late characterized Roberta's face whenever he began excusing himself, he added hopefully and evasively, seeking by any trick that he could to delay this sudden issue: "Besides, I'm not so sure that I can't find a doctor yet, either. I haven't had much luck so far, but that's not saying that I won't. And there's a little time yet, isn't there? Sure there is. It's all right up to three months anyway." (He had since had a letter from Ratterer who had commented on this fact.) "And I did hear something the other day of a doctor over in Albany who might do it. Anyway, I thought I'd go over and see before I said anything about him."

His manner, when he said this, was so equivocal that Roberta could tell he was merely lying to gain time. There was no doctor in Albany. Besides it was so plain that he resented her suggestion and was only thinking of some way of escaping it. And she knew well enough that at no time had he said directly that he would marry her. And while she might urge, in the last analysis she could not force him to do anything. He might just go away alone, as he had once said in connection with inadvertently losing his job because of her. And how much greater might not his impulse in that direction now be, if this world here in which he was so much interested were taken away from him, and he were to face the necessity of taking her and a child, too. It made her more cautious and caused her to modify her first impulse to speak out definitely and forcefully, however great her necessity might be. And so disturbed was he by the panorama of the bright world of which Sondra was the center and which was now at stake, that he could scarcely think clearly. Should he lose all this for such a world as he and Roberta could provide for themselves—a small home—a baby, such a routine work-a-day life as taking care of her and a baby on such a salary as he could earn, and from which most likely he would never again be freed! God! A sense of nausea seized him. He could not and would not do this. And yet, as he now saw, all his dreams could be so easily tumbled about his ears by her and because of one false step on his part. It made him cautious and for the first time in his life caused tact and cunning to visualize itself as a profound necessity.

And at the same time, Clyde was sensing inwardly and somewhat shamefacedly all of this profound change in himself.

But Roberta was saying: "Oh, I know, Clyde, but you yourself said just now that you were stumped, didn't you? And every day that goes by just makes it so much the worse for me, if we're not going to be able to get a doctor. You can't get married and have a child born within a few months—you know that. Every one in the world would know. Besides I have myself to consider as well as you, you know. And the baby, too." (At the mere mention of a coming child Clyde winced and recoiled as though he had been slapped. She noted it.) "I just must do one of two things right away, Clyde—get married or get out of this and you don't seem to be able to get me out of it, do you? If you're so afraid of what your uncle might think or do in case we get married," she added nervously and yet suavely, "why couldn't we get married right away and then keep it a secret for a while—as long as we could, or as long as you thought we ought to," she added shrewdly. "Meanwhile I could go home and tell my parents about it—that I am married, but that it must be kept a secret for a while. Then when the time came, when things got so bad that we couldn't stay here any longer without telling, why we could either go away somewhere, if we wanted to—that is, if you didn't want your uncle to know, or we could just announce that we were married some time ago. Lots of young couples do that nowadays. And as for getting along," she went on, noting a sudden dour shadow that passed over Clyde's face like a cloud, "why we could always find something to do—I know I could, anyhow, once the baby is born."

When first she began to speak, Clyde had seated himself on the edge of the bed, listening nervously and dubiously to all she had to offer. However, when she came to that part which related to marriage and going away, he got up—an irresistible impulse to move overcoming him. And when she concluded with the commonplace suggestion of going to work as soon as the baby was born, he looked at her with little less than panic in his eyes. To think of marrying and being in a position where it would be necessary to do that, when with a little luck and without interference from her, he might marry Sondra.

"Oh, yes, that's all right for you, Bert. That fixes everything up for you, but how about me? Why, gee whiz, I've

only got started here now as it is, and if I have to pack up and
get out, and I would have to, if ever they found out about
this, why I don't know what I'd do. I haven't any business or
trade that I could turn my hand to. It might go hard with
both of us. Besides my uncle gave me this chance because I
begged him to, and if I walked off now he never would do
anything for me."

In his excitement he was forgetting that at one time and
another in the past he had indicated to Roberta that the state
of his own parents was not wholly unprosperous and that if
things did not go just to his liking here, he could return west
and perhaps find something to do out there. And it was some
general recollection of this that now caused her to ask:
"Couldn't we go out to Denver or something like that?
Wouldn't your father be willing to help you get something for
a time, anyhow?"

Her tone was very soft and pleading, an attempt to make
Clyde feel that things could not be as bad as he was imagining. But the mere mention of his father in connection with all
this—the assumption that he, of all people, might prove an
escape from drudgery for them both, was a little too much. It
showed how dreadfully incomplete was her understanding of
his true position in this world. Worse, she was looking for
help from that quarter. And, not finding it, later might possibly reproach him for that—who could tell—for his lies in connection with it. It made so very clear now the necessity for
frustrating, if possible, and that at once, any tendency toward
this idea of marriage. It could not be—ever.

And yet how was he to oppose this idea with safety, since
she felt that she had this claim on him—how say to her
openly and coldly that he could not and would not marry
her? And unless he did so now she might think it would be
fair and legitimate enough for her to compel him to do so.
She might even feel privileged to go to his uncle—his cousin
(he could see Gilbert's cold eyes) and expose him! And then
destruction! Ruin! The end of all his dreams in connection
with Sondra and everything else here. But all he could think
of saying now was: "But I can't do this, Bert, not now, anyway," a remark which at once caused Roberta to assume that
the idea of marriage, as she had interjected it here, was not

one which, under the circumstances, he had the courage to oppose—his saying, "not now, anyway." Yet even as she was thinking this, he went swiftly on with: "Besides I don't want to get married so soon. It means too much to me at this time. In the first place I'm not old enough and I haven't got anything to get married on. And I can't leave here. I couldn't do half as well anywhere else. You don't realize what this chance means to me. My father's all right, but he couldn't do what my uncle could and he wouldn't. You don't know or you wouldn't ask me to do this."

He paused, his face a picture of puzzled fear and opposition. He was not unlike a harried animal, deftly pursued by hunter and hound. But Roberta, imagining that his total defection had been caused by the social side of Lycurgus as opposed to her own low state and not because of the superior lure of any particular girl, now retorted resentfully, although she desired not to appear so: "Oh, yes, I know well enough why you can't leave. It isn't your position here, though, half as much as it is those society people you are always running around with. I know. You don't care for me any more, Clyde, that's it, and you don't want to give these other people up for me. I know that's it and nothing else. But just the same it wasn't so very long ago that you did, although you don't seem to remember it now." Her cheeks burned and her eyes flamed as she said this. She paused a moment while he gazed at her wondering about the outcome of all this. "But you can't leave me to make out any way I can, just the same, because I won't be left this way, Clyde. I can't! I can't! I tell you." She grew tense and staccato, "It means too much to me. I don't know how to do alone and I, besides, have no one to turn to but you and you must help me. I've got to get out of this, that's all, Clyde, I've got to. I'm not going to be left to face my people and everybody without any help or marriage or anything." As she said this, her eyes turned appealingly and yet savagely toward him and she emphasized it all with her hands, which she clinched and unclinched in a dramatic way. "And if you can't help me out in the way you thought," she went on most agonizedly as Clyde could see, "then you've got to help me out in this other, that's all. At least until I can do for myself. I just won't be left. I don't ask you to marry me forever," she now added, the thought that if by presenting this demand in some modified form, she could induce Clyde to marry her, it might be possible afterwards that his feeling toward her would change to a much more kindly one. "You can leave me after a while if you want to. After I'm out of this. I can't prevent you from doing that and I wouldn't want to if I could. But you can't leave me now. You can't. You can't! Besides," she added, "I didn't want to get myself in this position and I wouldn't have, but for you. But you made me and made me let you come in here. And now you want to leave me to shift for myself, just because you think you won't be able to go in society any more, if they find out about me."

She paused, the strain of this contest proving almost too much for her tired nerves. At the same time she began to sob nervously and yet not violently—a marked effort at self-restraint and recovery marking her every gesture. And after a moment or two in which both stood there, he gazing dumbly and wondering what else he was to say in answer to all this, she struggling and finally managing to recover her poise, she added: "Oh, what is it about me that's so different to what I was a couple of months ago, Clyde? Will you tell me that? I'd like to know. What is it that has caused you to change so? Up to Christmas, almost, you were as nice to me as any human being could be. You were with me nearly all the time you had, and since then I've scarcely had an evening that I didn't beg for. Who is it? What is it? Some other girl, or what, I'd like to know—that Sondra Finchley or Bertine Cranston, or who?"

Her eyes as she said this were a study. For even to this hour, as Clyde could now see to his satisfaction, since he feared the effect on Roberta of definite and absolute knowledge concerning Sondra, she had no specific suspicion, let alone positive knowledge concerning any girl. And coward-wise, in the face of her present predicament and her assumed and threatened claims on him, he was afraid to say what or who the real cause of this change was. Instead he merely replied and almost unmoved by her sorrow, since he no longer really cared for her: "Oh, you're all wrong, Bert. You don't see what the trouble is. It's my future here—if I leave here I certainly will never find such an opportunity. And if I have to marry in this way or leave here it will all go flooey. I want to wait and get some place first before I marry, see—save some money and if I do this I won't have a chance and you won't either," he added feebly, forgetting for the moment that up to this time he had been indicating rather clearly that he did not want to have anything more to do with her in any way.

"Besides," he continued, "if you could only find some one, or if you would go away by yourself somewhere for a while, Bert, and go through with this alone, I could send you the money to do it on, I know. I could have it between now and the time you had to go."

His face, as he said this, and as Roberta clearly saw, mirrored the complete and resourceless collapse of all his recent plans in regard to her. And she, realizing that his indifference to her had reached the point where he could thus dispose of her and their prospective baby in this casual and really heartless manner, was not only angered in part, but at the same time frightened by the meaning of it all.

"Oh, Clyde," she now exclaimed boldly and with more courage and defiance than at any time since she had known him, "how you have changed! And how hard you can be. To want me to go off all by myself and just to save you—so you can stay here and get along and marry some one here when I am out of the way and you don't have to bother about me any more. Well, I won't do it. It's not fair. And I won't, that's all. I won't. And that's all there is to it. You can get some one to get me out of this or you can marry me and come away with me, at least long enough for me to have the baby and place myself right before my people and every one else that knows me. I don't care if you leave me afterwards, because I see now that you really don't care for me any more, and if that's the way you feel, I don't want you any more than you want me. But just the same, you must help me now—you must. But, oh, dear," she began whimpering again, and yet only slightly and bitterly. "To think that all our love for each other should have come to this—that I am asked to go away by myself—all alone—with no one—while you stay here, oh, dear! oh, dear! And with a baby on my hands afterwards. And no husband."

She clinched her hands and shook her head bleakly. Clyde,

realizing well enough that his proposition certainly was cold and indifferent but, in the face of his intense desire for Sondra, the best or at least safest that he could devise, now stood there unable for the moment to think of anything more to say.

And although there was some other discussion to the same effect, the conclusion of this very difficult hour was that Clyde had another week or two at best in which to see if he could find a physician or any one who would assist him. After that—well after that the implied, if not openly expressed, threat which lay at the bottom of this was, unless so extricated and speedily, that he would have to marry her, if not permanently, then at least temporarily, but legally just the same, until once again she was able to look after herself—a threat which was as crushing and humiliating to Roberta as it was torturing to him.

# Chapter XXXIX

OPPOSING VIEWS such as these, especially where no real skill to meet such a situation existed, could only spell greater difficulty and even eventual disaster unless chance in some form should aid. And chance did not aid. And the presence of Roberta in the factory was something that would not permit him to dismiss it from his mind. If only he could persuade her to leave and go somewhere else to live and work so that he should not always see her, he might then think more calmly. For with her asking continuously, by her presence if no more, what he intended to do, it was impossible for him to think. And the fact that he no longer cared for her as he had, tended to reduce his normal consideration of what was her due. He was too infatuated with, and hence disarranged by his thoughts of Sondra.

For in the very teeth of this grave dilemma he continued to pursue the enticing dream in connection with Sondra—the dark situation in connection with Roberta seeming no more at moments than a dark cloud which shadowed this other. And hence nightly, or as often as the exigencies of his still unbroken connection with Roberta would permit, he was availing himself of such opportunities as his flourishing connections now afforded. Now, and to his great pride and satisfaction, it was a dinner at the Harriets' or Taylors' to which he was invited; or a party at the Finchleys' or the Cranstons', to which he would either escort Sondra or be animated by the hope of encountering her. And now, also without so many of the former phases or attempts at subterfuge, which had previously characterized her curiosity in regard to him, she was at times openly seeking him out and making opportunities for social contact. And, of course, these contacts being identical with this typical kind of group gathering, they seemed to have no special significance with the more conservative elders.

For although Mrs. Finchley, who was of an especially shrewd and discerning turn socially, had at first been dubious over the attentions being showered upon Clyde by her daughter and others, still observing that Clyde was more and more being entertained, not only in her own home by the group of which her daughter was a part, but elsewhere, everywhere, was at last inclined to imagine that he must be more solidly placed in this world than she had heard, and later to ask her son and even Sondra concerning him. But receiving from Sondra only the equivocal information that, since he was Gil and Bella Griffiths' cousin, and was being taken up by everybody because he was so charming—even if he didn't have any money—she couldn't see why she and Stuart should not be allowed to entertain him also, her mother rested on that for the time being—only cautioning her daughter under no circumstances to become too friendly. And Sondra, realizing that in part her mother was right, yet being so drawn to Clyde was now determined to deceive her, at least to the extent of being as clandestinely free with Clyde as she could contrive. And was, so much so that every one who was privy to the intimate contacts between Clyde and Sondra might have reported that the actual understanding between them was assuming an intensity which most certainly would have shocked the elder Finchleys, could they have known. For apart from what Clyde had been, and still was dreaming in regard to her, Sondra was truly being taken with thoughts and moods in regard to him which were fast verging upon the most destroying aspects of the very profound chemistry of love. Indeed, in addition to handclasps, kisses and looks of intense admiration always bestowed when presumably no one was looking, there were those nebulous and yet strengthening and lengthening fantasies concerning a future which in some way or other, not clear to either as yet, was still always to include each other.

Summer days perhaps, and that soon, in which he and she would be in a canoe at Twelfth Lake, the long shadows of the trees on the bank lengthening over the silvery water, the wind rippling the surface while he paddled and she idled and tortured him with hints of the future; a certain forest path, grass-sodden and sun-mottled to the south and west of the Cranston and Phant estates, near theirs, through which they might canter in June and July to a wonderful view known as Inspiration Point some seven miles west; the country fair at

Sharon, at which, in a gypsy costume, the essence of romance itself, she would superintend a booth, or, in her smartest riding habit, give an exhibition of her horsemanship—teas, dances in the afternoon and in the moonlight at which, languishing in his arms, their eyes would speak.

None of the compulsion of the practical. None of the inhibitions which the dominance and possible future opposition of her parents might imply. Just love and summer, and idyllic and happy progress toward an eventual secure and unopposed union which should give him to her forever.

And in the meantime, in so far as Roberta was concerned, two more long, dreary, terrifying months going by without that meditated action on her part which must result once it was taken in Clyde's undoing. For, as convinced as she was that apart from meditating and thinking of some way to escape his responsibility, Clyde had no real intention of marrying her, still, like Clyde, she drifted, fearing to act really. For in several conferences following that in which she had indicated that she expected him to marry her, he had reiterated, if vaguely, a veiled threat that in case she appealed to his uncle he would not be compelled to marry her, after all, for he could go elsewhere.

The way he put it was that unless left undisturbed in his present situation he would be in no position to marry her and furthermore could not possibly do anything to aid her at the coming time when most of all she would stand in need of aid—a hint which caused Roberta to reflect on a hitherto not fully developed vein of hardness in Clyde, although had she but sufficiently reflected, it had shown itself at the time that he compelled her to admit him to her room.

In addition and because she was doing nothing and yet he feared that at any moment she might, he shifted in part at least from the attitude of complete indifference, which had availed him up to the time that she had threatened him, to one of at least simulated interest and good-will and friendship. For the very precarious condition in which he found himself was sufficiently terrifying to evoke more diplomacy than ever before had characterized him. Besides he was foolish enough to hope, if not exactly believe, that by once more conducting himself as though he still entertained a lively sense of the problem that afflicted her and that he was willing, in case no other way was found, to eventually marry her (though he could never definitely be persuaded to commit himself as to this), he could reduce her determination to compel him to act soon at least to a minimum, and so leave him more time in which to exhaust every possibility of escape without marriage, and without being compelled to run away.

And although Roberta sensed the basis of this sudden shift, still she was so utterly alone and distrait that she was willing to give ear to Clyde's mock genial, if not exactly affectionate observations and suggestions. It caused her, at his behest, to wait a while longer, the while, as he now explained, he would not only have saved up some money, but devised some plan in connection with his work which would permit him to leave for a time anyhow, marry her somewhere and then establish her and the baby as a lawful married woman somewhere else, while, although he did not explain this just now, he returned to Lycurgus and sent her such aid as he could. But on condition, of course, that never anywhere, unless he gave her permission, must she assert that he had married her, or point to him in any way as the father of her child. Also it was understood that she, as she herself had asserted over and over that she would, if only he would do this—marry her—take steps to free herself on the ground of desertion, or something, in some place sufficiently removed from Lycurgus for no one to hear. And that within a reasonable time after her marriage to him, although he was not at all satisfied that, assuming that he did marry her, she would.

But Clyde, of course, was insincere in regard to all his overtures at this time, and really not concerned as to her sincerity or insincerity. Nor did he have any intention of leaving Lycurgus even for the moderate length of time that her present extrication would require unless he had to. For that meant that he would be separated from Sondra, and such absence, for whatever period, would most definitely interfere with his plans. And so, on the contrary, he drifted—thinking most idly at times of some possible fake or mock marriage such as he had seen in some melodramatic movie—a fake minister and witnesses combining to deceive some simple country girl such as Roberta was not, but at such expense of time, resources, courage and subtlety as Clyde himself, after a little reflection, was wise enough to see was beyond him.

Again, knowing that, unless some hitherto unforeseen aid should eventuate, he was heading straight toward a disaster which could not much longer be obviated, he even allowed himself to dream that, once the fatal hour was at hand and Roberta, no longer to be put off by any form of subterfuge, was about to expose him, he might even flatly deny that he had ever held any such relationship with her as then she would be charging—rather that at all times his relationship with her had been that of a department manager to employee—no more. Terror—no less!

But at the same time, early in May, when Roberta, because of various gestative signs and ailments, was beginning to explain, as well as insist, to Clyde that by no stretch of the imagination or courage could she be expected to retain her position at the factory or work later than June first, because by then the likelihood of the girls there beginning to notice something, would be too great for her to endure, Sondra was beginning to explain that not so much later than the fourth or fifth of June she and her mother and Stuart, together with some servants, would be going to their new lodge at Twelfth Lake in order to supervise certain installations then being made before the regular season should begin. And after that, not later than the eighteenth, at which time the Cranstons, Harriets, and some others would have arrived, including very likely visits from Bella and Myra, he might expect a week-end invitation from the Cranstons, with whom, through Bertine, she would arrange as to this. And after that, the general circumstances proving fairly propitious, there would be, of course, other week-end invitations to the Harriets', Phants' and some others who dwelt there, as well as to the Griffiths' at Greenwood, to which place, on account of Bella, he could easily come. And during his two weeks' vacation in July, he could either stop at the Casino, which was at Pine Point, or perhaps the Cranstons or Harriets, at her suggestion, might choose to invite him. At any rate, as Clyde could see, and with no more than such expenditures as, with a little scrimping during his ordinary working days here, he could provide for, he might see not a little of that lake life of which he had read so much in the local papers, to say nothing of Sondra at one and another of the lodges, the masters of which were not so inimical to his presence and overtures as were Sondra's parents.

For now it was, and for the first time, as she proceeded to explain to him that her mother and father, because of his continued and reported attentions to her, were already beginning to talk of an extended European tour which might keep her and Stuart and her mother abroad for at least the next two years. But since, at news of this, Clyde's face as well as his spirits darkened, and she herself was sufficiently enmeshed to suffer because of this, she at once added that he must not feel so bad—he must not; things would work out well enough, she knew. For at the proper time, and unless between then and now, something—her own subtle attack if not her at present feverish interest in Clyde—should have worked to alter her mother's viewpoint in regard to him—she might be compelled to take some steps of her own in order to frustrate her mother. Just what, she was not willing to say at this time, although to Clyde's overheated imagination it took the form of an elopement and marriage, which could not then be gainsaid by her parents whatever they might think. And it was true that in a vague and as yet repressed way some such thought was beginning to form in Sondra's mind. For, as she now proceeded to explain to Clyde, it was so plain that her mother was attempting to steer her in the direction of a purely social match—the one with the youth who had been paying her such marked attention the year before. But because of her present passion for Clyde, as she now gayly declared, it was not easy to see how she was to be made to comply. "The only trouble with me is that I'm not of age yet," she here added briskly and slangily. "They've got me there, of course. But I will be by next October and they can't do very much with me after that, I want to let you know. I can marry the person I want, I guess. And if I can't do it here, well, there are more ways than one to kill a cat."

The thought was like some sweet, disarranging poison to Clyde. It fevered and all but betrayed him mentally. If only—if only—it were not for Roberta now. That terrifying and all but insoluble problem. But for that, and the opposition of Sondra's parents which she was thinking she would be able to overcome, did not heaven itself await him? Sondra, Twelfth Lake, society, wealth, her love and beauty. He grew not a little wild in thinking of it all. Once he and she were married, what could Sondra's relatives do? What, but acquiesce and take them into the glorious bosom of their resplendent home at Lycurgus or provide for them in some other way—he to no doubt eventually take some place in connection with the Finchley Electric Sweeper Company. And then would he not be the equal, if not the superior, of Gilbert Griffiths himself and all those others who originally had ignored him here— joint heir with Stuart to all the Finchley means. And with Sondra as the central or crowning jewel to so much sudden and such Aladdin-like splendor.

No thought as to how he was to overcome the time between now and October. No serious consideration of the fact that Roberta then and there was demanding that he marry her. He could put her off, he thought. And yet, at the same time, he was painfully and nervously conscious of the fact that at no period in his life before had he been so treacherously poised at the very brink of disaster. It might be his duty as the world would see it—his mother would say so—to at least extricate Roberta. But in the case of Esta, who had come to her rescue? Her lover? He had walked off from her without a qualm and she had not died. And why, when Roberta was no worse off than his sister had been, why should she seek to destroy him in this way? Force him to do something which would be little less than social, artistic, passional or emotional assassination? And when later, if she would but spare him for this, he could do so much more for her—with Sondra's money of course. He could not and would not let her do this to him. His life would be ruined!

# Chapter XL

Two incidents which occurred at this time tended still more to sharpen the contrary points of view holding between Clyde and Roberta. One of these was no more than a glimpse which Roberta had one evening of Clyde pausing at the Central Avenue curb in front of the post-office to say a few words to Arabella Stark, who in a large and impressive-looking car, was waiting for her father who was still in the Stark Building opposite. And Miss Stark, fashionably outfitted according to the season, her world and her own pretentious taste, was affectedly posed at the wheel, not only for the benefit of Clyde but the public in general. And to Roberta, who by now was reduced to the verge of distraction between Clyde's delay and her determination to compel him to act in her behalf, she appeared to be little less than an epitome of all the security, luxury and freedom from responsibility which so enticed and hence caused Clyde to delay and be as indifferent as possible to the dire state which confronted her. For, alas, apart from this claim of her condition, what had she to offer him comparable to all he would be giving up in case he acceded to her request? Nothing—a thought which was far from encouraging.

Yet, at this moment contrasting her own wretched and neglected state with that of this Miss Stark, for example, she found herself a prey to an even more complaining and antagonistic mood than had hitherto characterized her. It was not right. It was not fair. For during the several weeks that had passed since last they had discussed this matter, Clyde had scarcely said a word to her at the factory or elsewhere, let alone called upon her at her room, fearing as he did the customary inquiry which he could not satisfy. And this caused her to feel that not only was he neglecting but resenting her most sharply.

And yet as she walked home from this trivial and fairly representative scene, her heart was not nearly so angry as it was sad and sore because of the love and comfort that had vanished and was not likely ever to come again . . . ever . . . ever . . . ever. Oh, how terrible, . . . how terrible!

On the other hand, Clyde, and at approximately this same time, was called upon to witness a scene identified with Roberta, which, as some might think, only an ironic and even malicious fate could have intended or permitted to come to pass. For motoring north the following Sunday to Arrow Lake to the lodge of the Trumbulls' to take advantage of an early spring week-end planned by Sondra, the party on nearing Biltz, which was in the direct line of the trip, was compelled to detour east in the direction of Roberta's home. And coming finally to a north and south road which ran directly from Trippettsville past the Alden farm, they turned north into that. And a few minutes later, came directly to the corner adjoining the Alden farm, where an east and west road led to Biltz. Here Tracy Trumbull, driving at the time, requested that some one should get out and inquire at the adjacent farm-house as to whether this road did lead to Biltz. And Clyde, being nearest to one door, jumped out. And then, glancing at the name on the mail-box which stood at the junction and evidently belonged to the extremely dilapidated old farm-house on the rise above, he was not a little astonished to note that the name was that of Titus Alden— Roberta's father. Also, as it instantly came to him, since she had described her parents as being near Biltz, this must be her home. It gave him pause, caused him for the moment to hesitate as to whether to go on or not, for once he had given Roberta a small picture of himself, and she might have shown it up here. Again the mere identification of this lorn, dilapidated realm with Roberta and hence himself, was sufficient to cause him to wish to turn and run.

But Sondra, who was sitting next him in the car and now noting his hesitation, called: "What's the matter, Clyde? Afraid of the bow-wow?" And he, realizing instantly that they would comment further on his actions if he did not proceed at once, started up the path. But the effect of this house, once he contemplated it thoroughly, was sufficient to arouse in his brain the most troubled and miserable of thoughts. For what a house, to be sure! So lonely and bare, even in this bright, spring weather! The decayed and sagging roof. The broken chimney to the north—rough lumps of cemented field stones lying at its base; the sagging and semi-toppling chimney to the south, sustained in place by a log chain. The unkempt path from the road below, which slowly he ascended! He was not a little dejected by the broken and displaced stones which served as steps before the front door. And the unpainted dilapidated out-buildings, all the more dreary because of these others.

"Gee!" To think that this was Roberta's home. And to think, in the face of all that he now aspired to in connection with Sondra and this social group at Lycurgus, she should be demanding that he marry her! And Sondra in the car with him here to see—if not know. The poverty! The reduced grimness of it all. How far he had traveled away from just such a beginning as this!

With a weakening and sickening sensation at the pit of his stomach, as of some blow administered there, he now approached the door. And then, as if to further distress him, if that were possible, the door was opened by Titus Alden, who, in an old, thread-bare and out-at-elbows coat, as well as baggy, worn, jean trousers and rough, shineless, ill-fitting country shoes, desired by his look to know what he wanted. And Clyde, being taken aback by the clothes, as well as a marked resemblance to Roberta about the eyes and mouth, now as swiftly as possible asked if the east and west road below ran through Biltz and joined the main highway north. And although he would have preferred a quick "yes" so that he might have turned and gone, Titus preferred to step down into the yard and then, with a gesture of the arm, indicate that if they wanted to strike a really good part of the road, they had better follow this Trippettsville north and south road for at least two more miles, and then turn west. Clyde thanked him briefly and turned almost before he had finished and hurried away.

For, as he now recalled, and with an enormous sense of depression, Roberta was thinking and at this very time, that soon now, and in the face of all Lycurgus had to offer him— Sondra—the coming spring and summer—the love and romance, gayety, position, power—he was going to give all that up and go away with and marry her. Sneak away to some out-of-the-way place! Oh, how horrible! And with a child at his age! Oh, why had he ever been so foolish and weak as to identify himself with her in this intimate way? Just because of a few lonely evenings! Oh, why, why couldn't he have waited and then this other world would have opened up to him just the same? If only he could have waited!

And now unquestionably, unless he could speedily and easily disengage himself from her, all this other splendid recognition would be destined to be withdrawn from him, and this other world from which he sprang might extend its gloomy, poverty-stricken arms to him and envelop him once more, just as the poverty of his family had enveloped and almost strangled him from the first. And it even occurred to him, in a vague way for the first time, how strange it was that this girl and he, whose origin had been strikingly similar, should have been so drawn to each other in the beginning. Why should it have been? How strange life was, anyway? But even more harrowing than this, was the problem of a way out that was before him. And his mind from now on, on this trip, was once more searching for some solution. A word of complaint from Roberta or her parents to his uncle or Gilbert, and assuredly he would be done for.

The thought so troubled him that once in the car, and although previously he had been chattering along with the others about what might be in store ahead in the way of divertissement, he now sat silent. And Sondra, who sat next to him and who previously had been whispering at intervals of her plans for the summer, now, instead of resuming the patter, whispered: "What come over de sweet phing?" (When Clyde appeared to be the least reduced in mind she most affected this patter with him, since it had an almost electric, if sweetly tormenting effect on him. "His baby-talking girl," he sometimes called her.) "Facey all dark now. Little while ago facey all smiles. Come make facey all nice again. Smile at Sondra. Squeeze Sondra's arm like good boy, Clyde."

She turned and looked up into his eyes to see what if any effect this baby-worded cajolery was having, and Clyde did his best to brighten, of course. But even so, and in the face of all this amazingly wonderful love on her part for him, the specter of Roberta and all that she represented now in connection with all this, was ever before him—her state, her very recent edict in regard to it, the obvious impossibility of doing anything now but go away with her.

Why—rather than let himself in for a thing like that—would it not be better, and even though he lost Sondra once and for all, for him to decamp as in the instance of the slain child in Kansas City—and be heard of nevermore here. But then he would lose Sondra, his connections here, and his uncle—this world! The loss! The loss! The misery of once more drifting about here and there; of being compelled to write his mother once more concerning certain things about his flight, which some one writing from here might explain to her afterwards—and so much more damagingly. And the thoughts concerning him on the part of his relatives! And of late he had been writing his mother that he was doing so well. What was it about his life that made things like this happen to him? Was this what his life was to be like? Running away from one situation and another just to start all over somewhere else—perhaps only to be compelled to flee from something worse. No, he could not run away again. He must face it and solve it in some way. He must!

God!

# Chapter XLI

THE FIFTH of June arriving, the Finchleys departed as Sondra had indicated, but not without a most urgent request from her that he be prepared to come to the Cranstons' either the second or third week-end following—she to advise him definitely later—a departure which so affected Clyde that he could scarcely think what to do with himself in her absence, depressed as he was by the tangle which Roberta's condition presented. And exactly at this time also, Roberta's fears and demands had become so urgent that it was really no longer possible for him to assure her that if she would but wait a little while longer, he would be prepared to act in her behalf. Plead as he might, her case, as she saw it, was at last critical and no longer to be trifled with in any way. Her figure, as she insisted (although this was largely imaginative on her part), had altered to such an extent that it would not be possible for her longer to conceal it, and all those who worked with her at the factory were soon bound to know. She could no longer work or sleep with any comfort—she must not stay here any more. She was having preliminary pains—purely imaginary ones in her case. He must marry her now, as he had indicated he would, and leave with her at once—for some place—any place, really—near or far—so long as she was extricated from this present terrible danger. And she would agree, as she now all but pleaded, to let him go his way again as soon as their child was born—truly—and would not ask any more of him ever—ever. But now, this very week—not later than the fifteenth at the latest—he must arrange to see her through with this as he had promised.

But this meant that he would be leaving with her before ever he should have visited Sondra at Twelfth Lake at all, and without ever seeing her any more really. And, besides, as he so well knew, he had not saved the sum necessary to make possible the new venture on which she was insisting. In vain it was that Roberta now explained that she had saved over a hundred, and they could make use of that once they were married or to help in connection with whatever expenses might be incurred in getting to wherever he should decide they were going. All that he would see or feel was that this meant the loss of everything to him, and that he would have to go away with her to some relatively near-by place and get work at anything he could, in order to support her as best he might. But the misery of such a change! The loss of all his splendid dreams. And yet, racking his brains, he could think of nothing better than that she should quit and go home for the time being, since as he now argued, and most shrewdly, as he thought, he needed a few more weeks to prepare for the change which was upon them both. For, in spite of all his ef-forts, as he now falsely asserted, he had not been able to save as much as he had hoped. He needed at least three or four more weeks in which to complete the sum, which he had been looking upon as advisable in the face of this meditated change. Was not she herself guessing, as he knew, that it could not be less than a hundred and fifty or two hundred dollars—quite large sums in her eyes—whereas, above his cur-rent salary, Clyde had no more than forty dollars and was dreaming of using that and whatever else he might secure in the interim to meet such expenses as might be incurred in the anticipated visit to Twelfth Lake.

But to further support his evasive suggestion that she now return to her home for a short period, he added that she would want to fix herself up a little, wouldn't she? She couldn't go away on a trip like this, which involved marriage and a change of social contacts in every way, without some improvements in her wardrobe. Why not take her hundred dollars or a part of it anyhow and use it for that? So desper-ate was his state that he even suggested that. And Roberta, who, in the face of her own uncertainty up to this time as to what was to become of her had not ventured to prepare or purchase anything relating either to a trousseau or layette, now began to think that whatever the ulterior purpose of his suggestion, which like all the others was connected with delay, it might not be unwise even now if she did take a fortnight or three weeks, and with the assistance of an inexpensive and yet tolerable dressmaker, who had aided her sister at times, make at least one or two suitable dresses—a flowered gray taffeta afternoon dress, such as she had once seen in a movie, in which, should Clyde keep his word, she could be married. To match this pleasing little costume, she planned to add a chic little gray silk hat—poke-shaped, with pink or scarlet cherries nestled up under the rim, together with a neat little blue serge traveling suit, which, with brown shoes and a brown hat, would make her as smart as any bride. The fact that such preparations as these meant additional delay and expense, or that Clyde might not marry her after all, or that this proposed marriage from the point of view of both was the tarnished and discolored thing that it was, was still not sufficient to take from the thought of marriage as an event, or sacrament even, that proper color and romance with which it was invested in her eyes and from which, even under such an unsatisfactory set of circumstances as these, it could not be divorced. And, strangely enough, in spite of all the troubled and strained relations that had developed between them, she still saw Clyde in much the same light in which she had seen him at first. He was a Griffiths, a youth of genuine social, if not financial distinction, one whom all the girls in her position, as well as many of those far above her, would be delighted to be connected with in this way—that is, via marriage. He might be objecting to marrying her, but he was a person of consequence, just the same. And one with whom, if he would but trouble to care for her a little, she could be perfectly happy. And at any rate, once he had loved her. And it was said of men—some men, anyway (so she had heard her mother and others say) that once a child was presented to them, it made a great difference in their attitude toward the mother, sometimes. They came to like the mother, too. Anyhow for a little while—a very little while—if what she had agreed to were strictly observed, she would have him with her to assist her through this great crisis—to give his name to her child—to aid her until she could once more establish herself in some way.

For the time being, therefore, and with no more plan than this, although with great misgivings and nervous qualms, since, as she could see, Clyde was decidedly indifferent, she rested on this. And it was in this mood that five days later, and after Roberta had written to her parents that she was coming home for two weeks at least, to get a dress or two made and to rest a little, because she was not feeling very well, that Clyde saw her off for her home in Biltz, riding with her as far as Fonda. But in so far as he was concerned, and since he had really no definite or workable idea, it seemed important to him that only silence, *silence* was the great and all essential thing now, so that, even under the impending edge of the knife of disaster, he might be able to think more, and more, and more, without being compelled to do anything, and without momentarily being tortured by the thought that Roberta, in some nervous or moody or frantic state, would say or do something which, assuming that he should hit upon some helpful thought or plan in connection with Sondra, would prevent him from executing it.

And about the same time, Sondra was writing him gay notes from Twelfth Lake as to what he might expect upon his arrival a little later. Blue water—white sails—tennis—golf—horseback riding—driving. She had it all arranged with Bertine, as she said. And kisses—kisses—kisses!

# Chapter XLII

Two letters, which arrived at this time and simultaneously, but accentuated the difficulty of all this.

Pine Point Landing, June 10th.

CLYDE MYDIE:

How is my pheet phing? All wytie? It's just glorious up here. Lots of people already here and more coming every day. The Casino and golf course over at Pine Point are open and lots of people about. I can hear Stuart and Grant with their launches going up toward Gray's Inlet now. You must hurry and come up, dear. It's too nice for words. Green roads to gallop through, and swimming and dancing at the Casino every afternoon at four. Just back from a wonderful gallop on Dickey and going again after luncheon to mail these letters. Bertine says she'll write you a letter to-day or to-morrow good for any week-end or any old time, so when Sonda says come, you come, you hear, else Sonda whip hard. You baddie, good boy.

Is he working hard in the baddie old factory? Sonda wisses he was here wiss her instead. We'd ride and drive and swim and dance. Don't forget your tennis racquet and golf clubs. There's a dandy course on the Casino grounds.

This morning when I was riding a bird flew right up under Dickey's heels. It scared him so that he bolted and Sonda got all switched and scwatched. Isn't Clydie sorry for his Sonda?

She is writing lots of notes to-day. After lunch and the ride to catch the down mail, Sonda and Bertine and Nina going to the Casino. Don't you wish you were going to be there? We could dance to "Taudy." Sonda just loves that song. But she has to dress now. More to-morrow, baddie boy. And when Bertine writes, answer right away. See all 'ose dots? Kisses. Big and little ones. All for baddie boy. And wite Sonda every day and she'll write 'oo.

More kisses.

To which Clyde responded eagerly and in kind in the same hour. But almost the same mail, at least the same day, brought the following letter from Roberta.

Biltz, June 10th.

DEAR CLYDE:

I am nearly ready for bed, but I will write you a few lines. I had such a tiresome journey coming up that I was nearly sick. In the first

500

place I didn't want to come much (alone) as you know. I feel too upset and uncertain about everything, although I try not to feel so now
that we have our plan and you are going to come for me as you said.

(At this point, while nearly sickened by the thought of the
wretched country world in which she lived, still, because of
Roberta's unfortunate and unavoidable relation to it, he now
experienced one of his old time twinges of remorse and pity in
regard to her. For after all, this was not her fault. She had so
little to look forward to—nothing but her work or a commonplace marriage. For the first time in many days, really, and in the
absence of both, he was able to think clearly—and to sympathize deeply, if gloomily. For the remainder of the letter read:)

But it's very nice here now. The trees are so beautifully green and
the flowers in bloom. I can hear the bees in the orchard whenever I go
near the south windows. On the way up instead of coming straight
home I decided to stop at Homer to see my sister and brother-in-law,
since I am not so sure now when I shall see them again, if ever, for I
am resolved that they shall see me respectable, or never at all any more.
You mustn't think I mean anything hard or mean by this. I am just sad.
They have such a cute little home there, Clyde—pretty furniture, a
victrola and all, and Agnes is so very happy with Fred. I hope she always will be. I couldn't help thinking of what a dear place we might
have had, if only my dreams had come true. And nearly all the time I
was there Fred kept teasing me as to why I don't get married, until I
said, "Oh, well, Fred, you mustn't be too sure that I won't one of
these days. All good things come to him who waits, you know." "Yes,
unless you just turn out to be a waiter," was the way he hit me back.

But I was truly glad to see mother again, Clyde. She's so loving
and patient and helpful. The sweetest, dearest mother that ever, ever
was. And I just hate to hurt her in any way. And Tom and Emily,
too. They have had friends here every evening since I've been here—
and they want me to join in, but I hardly feel well enough now to
do all the things they want me to do—play cards and games—dance.

(At this point Clyde could not help emphasizing in his own
mind the shabby home world of which she was a part and
which so recently he had seen—that rickety house! those toppling chimneys! Her uncouth father. And that in contrast to
such a letter as this other from Sondra.)

Father and mother and Tom and Emily just seem to hang around
and try to do things for me. And I feel remorseful when I think how

they would feel if they knew, for, of course, I have to pretend that it is work that makes me feel so tired and depressed as I am sometimes. Mother keeps saying that I must stay a long time or quit entirely and rest and get well again, but she just don't know of course—poor dear. If she did! I can't tell you how that makes me feel sometimes, Clyde. Oh, dear!

But there, I mustn't put my sad feelings over on you either. I don't want to, as I told you, if you will only come and get me as we've agreed. And I won't be like that either, Clyde. I'm not that way all the time now. I've started to get ready and do all the things it'll take to do in three weeks and that's enough to keep my mind off everything but work. But you will come for me, won't you, dear? You won't disappoint me any more and make me suffer this time like you have so far, for, oh, how long it has been now—ever since I was here before at Christmas time, really. But you were truly nice to me. I promise not to be a burden on you, for I know you don't really care for me any more and so I don't care much what happens now, so long as I get out of this. But I truly promise not to be a burden on you.

Oh, dear, don't mind this blot. I just don't seem to be able to control myself these days like I once could.

But as for what I came for. The family think they are clothes for a party down in Lycurgus and that I must be having a wonderful time. Well, it's better that way than the other. I may have to come as far as Fonda to get some things, if I don't send Mrs. Anse, the dressmaker, and if so, and if you wanted to see me again before you come, although I don't suppose you do, you could. I'd like to see you and talk to you again if you care to, before we start. It all seems so funny to me, Clyde, having these clothes made and wishing to see you so much and yet knowing that you would rather not do this. And yet I hope you are satisfied now that you have succeeded in making me leave Lycurgus and come up here and are having what you call a good time. Are they so very much better than the ones we used to have last summer, when we went about to the lakes and everywhere? But whatever they are, Clyde, surely you can afford to do this for me without feeling too bad. I know it seems hard to you now, but you don't want to forget either that if I was like some that I know, I might and would ask more. But as I told you I'm not like that and never could be. If you don't really want me after you have helped me out like I said, you can go.

Please write me, Clyde, a long, cheery letter, even though you don't want to, and tell me all about how you have not thought of me once since I've been away or missed me at all—you used to, you know, and how you don't want me to come back and you can't possibly come up before two weeks from Saturday if then.

Oh, dear, I don't mean the horrid things I write, but I'm so blue and tired and lonely that I can't help it at times. I need some one to talk to—not just any one here, because they don't understand, and I can't tell anybody.

But there, I said I wouldn't be blue or gloomy or cross and yet I haven't done so very well this time, have I? But I promise to do better next time—to-morrow or next day, because it relieves me to write to you, Clyde. And won't you please write me just a few words to cheer me up while I'm waiting, whether you mean it or not, I need it so. And you will come, of course. I'll be so happy and grateful and try not to bother you too much in any way.

Your lonely<br>BERT.

And it was the contrast presented by these two scenes which finally determined for him the fact that he would never marry Roberta—never—nor even go to her at Biltz, or let her come back to him here, if he could avoid that. For would not his going, or her return, put a period to all the joys that so recently in connection with Sondra had come to him here— make it impossible for him to be with Sondra at Twelfth Lake this summer—make it impossible for him to run away with and marry her? In God's name was there no way? No outlet from this horrible difficulty which now confronted him?

And in a fit of despair, having found the letters in his room on his return from work one warm evening in June, he now threw himself upon his bed and fairly groaned. The misery of this! The horror of his almost insoluble problem! Was there no way by which she could be persuaded to go away—and stay—remain at home, maybe for a while longer, while he sent her ten dollars a week, or twelve, even—a full half of all his salary? Or could she go to some neighboring town— Fonda, Gloversville, Schenectady—she was not so far gone but what she could take care of herself well enough as yet, and rent a room and remain there quietly until the fatal time, when she could go to some doctor or nurse? He might help her to find some one like that when the time came, if only she would be willing not to mention his name.

But this business of making him come to Biltz, or meeting her somewhere, and that within two weeks or less. He would not, he would not. He would do something desperate if she

tried to make him do that—run away—or—maybe go up to
Twelfth Lake before it should be time for him to go to Biltz,
or before she would think it was time, and then persuade
Sondra if he could—but oh, what a wild, wild chance was
that—to run away with and marry him, even if she wasn't
quite eighteen—and then—and then—being married, and her
family not being able to divorce them, and Roberta not being
able to find him, either, but only to complain—well, couldn't
he deny it—say that it was not so—that he had never had any
relationship, other than that which any department head
might have with any girl working for him. He had not been
introduced to the Gilpins, nor had he gone with Roberta to
see that Dr. Glenn near Gloversville, and she had told him at
the time, she had not mentioned his name.

But the nerve of trying to deny it!

The courage it would take.

The courage to try to face Roberta when, as he knew, her
steady, accusing, horrified, innocent blue eyes would be about
as difficult to face as anything in all the world. And could he
do that? Had he the courage? And would it all work out satisfactorily if he did? Would Sondra believe him—once she
heard?

But just the same in pursuance of this idea, whether finally
he executed it or not, even though he went to Twelfth Lake,
he must write Sondra a letter saying that he was coming. And
this he did at once, writing her passionately and yearningly. At
the same time he decided not to write Roberta at all. Maybe
call her on long distance, since she had recently told him that
there was a neighbor near-by who had a telephone, and if for
any reason he needed to reach her, he could use that. For
writing her in regard to all this, even in the most guarded
way, would place in her hands, and at this time, exactly the
type of evidence in regard to this relationship which she
would most need, and especially when he was so determined
not to marry her. The trickery of all this! It was low and
shabby, no doubt. Yet if only Roberta had agreed to be a little
reasonable with him, he would never have dreamed of indulging in any such low and tricky plan as this. But, oh,
Sondra! Sondra! And the great estate that she had described,
lying along the west shore of Twelfth Lake. How beautiful

that must be! He could not help it! He must act and plan as he was doing! He must!

And forthwith he arose and went to mail the letter to Sondra. And then while out, having purchased an evening paper and hoping via the local news of all whom he knew, to divert his mind for the time being, there, upon the first page of the *Times-Union* of Albany, was an item which read:

ACCIDENTAL DOUBLE TRAGEDY AT PASS LAKE—UPTURNED
CANOE AND FLOATING HATS REVEAL PROBABLE LOSS OF TWO
LIVES AT RESORT NEAR PITTSFIELD—UNIDENTIFIED BODY OF GIRL
RECOVERED—THAT OF COMPANION STILL MISSING

Because of his own great interest in canoeing, and indeed in any form of water life, as well as his own particular skill when it came to rowing, swimming, diving, he now read with interest:

Pancoast, Mass., June 7th. . . . What proved to be a fatal boat ride for two, apparently, was taken here day before yesterday by an unidentified man and girl who came presumably from Pittsfield to spend the day at Pass Lake, which is fourteen miles north of this place.

Tuesday morning a man and a girl, who said to Thomas Lucas, who conducts the Casino Lunch and Boat House there, that they were from Pittsfield, rented a small row-boat about ten o'clock in the morning and with a basket, presumably containing lunch, departed for the northern end of the lake. At seven o'clock last evening, when they did not return, Mr. Lucas, in company with his son Jeffrey, made a tour of the lake in his motor boat and discovered the row-boat upside down in the shallows near the north shore, but no trace of the occupants. Thinking at the time that it might be another instance of renters having decamped in order to avoid payment, he returned the boat to his own dock.

But this morning, doubtful as to whether or not an accident had occurred, he and his assistant, Fred Walsh, together with his son, made a second tour of the north shore and finally came upon the hats of both the girl and the man floating among some rushes near the shore. At once a dredging party was organized, and by three o'clock to-day the body of the girl, concerning whom nothing is known here, other than that she came here with her companion, was brought up and turned over to the authorities. That of the man has not yet been found. The water in the immediate vicinity of the accident in some places being over thirty feet deep, it is not certain whether the trolling and dredging will yield the other body or not.

In the case of a similar accident which took place here some fifteen years ago, neither body was ever recovered.

To the lining of the small jacket which the girl wore was sewed the tag of a Pittsfield dealer. Also in her shoe lining was stamped the name of Jacobs of this same city. But other than these there was no evidence as to her identity. It is assumed by the authorities here that if she carried a bag of any kind it lies at the bottom of the lake.

The man is recalled as being tall, dark, about thirty-five years of age, and wore a light green suit and straw hat with a white and blue band. The girl appears to be not more than twenty-five, five feet five inches tall, and weighs 130 pounds. She wore her hair, which was long and dark brown, in braids about her forehead. On her left middle finger is a small gold ring with an amethyst setting. The police of Pittsfield and other cities in this vicinity have been notified, but as yet no word as to her identity has been received.

This item, commonplace enough in the usual grist of summer accidents, interested Clyde only slightly. It seemed odd, of course, that a girl and a man should arrive at a small lake anywhere, and setting forth in a small boat in broad daylight thus lose their lives. Also it was odd that afterwards no one should be able to identify either of them. And yet here it was. The man had disappeared for good. He threw the paper down, little concerned at first, and turned to other things— the problem that was confronting him really—how he was to do. But later—and because of that, and as he was putting out the light before getting into bed, and still thinking of the complicated problem which his own life here presented, he was struck by the thought (what devil's whisper?—what evil hint of an evil spirit?)—supposing that he and Roberta—no, say he and Sondra—(no, Sondra could swim so well, and so could he)—he and Roberta were in a small boat somewhere and it should capsize at the very time, say, of this dreadful complication which was so harassing him? What an escape? What a relief from a gigantic and by now really destroying problem! On the other hand—hold—not so fast!—for could a man even think of such a solution in connection with so difficult a problem as his without committing a crime in his heart, really—a horrible, terrible crime? He must not even think of such a thing. It was wrong—wrong—terribly wrong. And yet, supposing,—by accident, of course—such a thing as this did occur? That would be the end, then, wouldn't it, of all his troubles in connection with Roberta? No more terror as to her—no more fear and heartache even as to Sondra. A noiseless, pathless, quarrelless solution of all his present difficulties, and only joy before him forever. Just an accidental, unpremeditated drowning—and then the glorious future which would be his!

But the mere thinking of such a thing in connection with Roberta at this time—(why was it that his mind persisted in identifying her with it?) was terrible, and he must not, he must not, allow such a though to enter his mind. Never, never, never! He must not. It was horrible! Terrible! A thought of murder, no less! Murder?!!! Yet so wrought up had he been, and still was, by the letter which Roberta had written him, as contrasted with the one from Sondra—so delightful and enticing was picture of her life and his as she now described it, that he could not for the life of him quite expel that other and seemingly easy and so natural a solution of all his problem—if only such an accident could occur to him and Roberta. For after all he was not planning any crime, was he? Was he not merely thinking of an accident that, had it occurred or could it but occur in his case. . . . Ah—but that "*could it but occur.*" There was the dark and evil thought about which he must not, *he must not think.* He MUST NOT. And yet—and yet, . . . He was an excellent swimmer and could swim ashore, no doubt—whatever the distance. Whereas Roberta, as he knew from swimming with her at one beach and another the previous summer, could not swim. And then—and then—well and then, unless he chose to help her, of course. . . .

As he thought, and for the time, sitting in the lamplight of his own room between nine-thirty and ten at night, a strange and disturbing creepiness as to flesh and hair and finger-tips assailed him. The wonder and the horror of such a thought! And presented to him by this paper in this way. Wasn't that strange? Besides, up in that lake country to which he was now going to Sondra, were many, many lakes about everywhere— were there not? Scores up there where Sondra was. Or so she had said. And Roberta loved the out-of-doors and the water so—although she could not swim—could not swim—could not swim. And they or at least he was going where lakes were, or they might, might they not—and if not, why not? since both had talked of some Fourth of July resort in their planning, their final departure—he and Roberta.

But, no! no! The mere thought of an accident such as that in connection with her, however much he might wish to be rid of her—was sinful, dark and terrible! He must not let his mind run on any such things for even a moment. It was too wrong—too vile—too terrible! Oh, dreadful thought! To think it should have come to him! And at this time of all times—when she was demanding that he go away with her!

Death!

Murder!

The murder of Roberta!

But to escape her of course—this unreasonable, unshakable, unchangeable demand of hers! Already he was quite cold, quite damp—with the mere thought of it. And now—when—when——! But he must not think of that! The death of that unborn child, too!!

But how could any one even think of doing any such thing with calculation—deliberately? And yet—many people were drowned like that—boys and girls—men and women—here and there—everywhere the world over in the summer time. To be sure, he would not want anything like that to happen to Roberta. And especially at this time. He was not that kind of a person, whatever else he was. He was not. He was not. He was not. The mere thought now caused a damp perspiration to form on his hands and face. He was not that kind of a person. Decent, sane people did not think of such things. And so he would not either—from this hour on.

In a tremulous state of dissatisfaction with himself—that any such grisly thought should have dared to obtrude itself upon him in this way—he got up and lit the lamp—re-read this disconcerting item in as cold and reprobative way as he could achieve, feeling that in so doing he was putting anything at which it hinted far from him once and for all. Then, having done so, he dressed and went out of the house for a walk—up Wykeagy Avenue, along Central Avenue, out Oak, and then back on Spruce and to Central again—feeling that he was walking away from the insinuating thought or suggestion that had so troubled him up to now. And after a time, feeling better, freer, more natural, more human, as he so much wished to feel—he returned to his room, once more to sleep, with the feeling that he had actually succeeded in eliminating completely a most insidious and horrible visitation. He must never think of it again! He must never think of it again. He must never, never, never think of it—never.

And then falling into a nervous, feverish doze soon thereafter, he found himself dreaming of a savage black dog that was trying to bite him. Having escaped from the fangs of the creature by waking in terror, he once more fell asleep. But now he was in some very strange and gloomy place, a wood or a cave or narrow canyon between deep hills, from which a path, fairly promising at first, seemed to lead. But soon the path, as he progressed along it, became narrower and narrower and darker, an finally disappeared entirely. And then, turning to see if he could not get back as he had come, there directly behind him were arrayed an entangled mass of snakes that at first looked more like a pile of brush. But above it waved the menacing heads of at least a score of reptiles, forked tongues and agate eyes. And in front now, as he turned swiftly, a horned and savage animal—huge, it was—its heavy tread crushing the brush—blocked the path in that direction. And then, horrified and crying out in hopeless desperation, once more he awoke—not to sleep again that night.

# Chapter XLIII

YET a thought such as that of the lake, connected as it was with the predicament by which he was being faced, and shrink from it though he might, was not to be dismissed as easily as he desired. Born as it was of its accidental relation to this personal problem that was shaking and troubling and all but disarranging his own none-too-forceful mind, this smooth, seemingly blameless, if dreadful, blotting out of two lives at Pass Lake, had its weight. That girl's body—as some peculiar force in his own brain now still compelled him to think—being found, but the man's not. In that interesting fact—and this quite in spite of himself—lurked a suggestion that insisted upon obtruding itself on his mind—to wit, that it might be possible that the man's body was not in that lake at all. For, since evil-minded people did occasionally desire to get rid of other people, might it not be possible that that man had gone there with that girl in order to get rid of her? A very smooth and devilish trick, of course, but one which, in this instance at least, seemed to have succeeded admirably.

But as for him accepting such an evil suggestion and acting upon it . . . never! Yet here was his own problem growing hourly more desperate, since every day, or at least every other day, brought him either letters from Roberta or a note from Sondra—their respective missives maintaining the same relative contrast between ease and misery, gayety of mood and the somberness of defeat and uncertainty.

To Roberta, since he would not write her, he was telephoning briefly and in as non-committal a manner as possible. How was she? He was so glad to hear from her and to know that she was out in the country and at home, where it must be much nicer than in the factory here in this weather. Everything was going smoothly, of course, and except for a sudden rush of orders which made it rather hard these last two days, all was as before. He was doing his best to save a certain amount of money for a certain project about which she knew, but otherwise he was not worrying about anything—and she must not. He had not written before because of the work, and could not write much—there were so many things to do—but he missed seeing her in her old place, and was looking forward to seeing her again soon. If she were coming down toward Lycurgus as she said, and really thought it important to see him, well, that could be arranged, maybe—but was it necessary right now? He was so very busy and expected to see her later, of course.

But at the same time he was writing Sondra that assuredly on the eighteenth, and the week-end following, if possible, he would be with her.

So, by virtue of such mental prestidigitation and tergiversation, inspired and animated as it was by his desire for Sondra, his inability to face the facts in connection with Roberta, he achieved the much-coveted privilege of again seeing her, over one week-end at least, and in such a setting as never before in his life had he been privileged to witness.

For as he came down to the public dock at Sharon, adjoining the veranda of the inn at the foot of Twelfth Lake, he was met by Bertine and her brother as well as Sondra, who, in Grant's launch, had motored down the Chain to pick him up. The bright blue waters of the Indian Chain. The tall, dark, spear pines that sentineled the shores on either side and gave to the waters at the west a band of black shadow where the trees were mirrored so clearly. The small and large, white and pink and green and brown lodges on every hand, with their boathouses. Pavilions by the shore. An occasional slender pier reaching out from some spacious and at times stately summer lodge, such as those now owned by the Cranstons, Finchleys and others. The green and blue canoes and launches. The gay hotel and pavilion at Pine Point already smartly attended by the early arrivals here! And then the pier and boathouse of the Cranston Lodge itself, with two Russian wolfhounds recently acquired by Bertine lying on the grass near the shore, apparently awaiting her return, and a servant John, one of a half dozen who attended the family here, waiting to take the single bag of Clyde, his tennis racquet and golf sticks. But most of all he was impressed by the large rambling and yet smartly-designed house, with its bright geranium-bordered walks, its wide, brown, wicker-studded veranda commanding a beautiful view of the lake; the cars and personalities of the various guests, who in golf, tennis or lounging clothes were to be seen idling here and there.

At Bertine's request, John at once showed him to a spacious room overlooking the lake, where it was his privilege now to bathe and change for tennis with Sondra, Bertine and Grant. After dinner, as explained by Sondra, who was over at Bertine's for the occasion, he was to come over with Bertine and Grant to the Casino, where he would be introduced to such as all here knew. There was to be dancing. To-morrow, in the morning early, before breakfast, if he chose—he should ride with her and Bertine and Stuart along a wonderful woodland trail through the forests to the west which led to Inspiration Point and a more distant view of the lake. And, as he now learned, except for a few such paths as this, the forest was trackless for forty miles. Without a compass or guide, as he was told, one might wander to one's death even—so evasive were directions to those who did not know. And after breakfast and a swim she and Bertine and Nina Temple would demonstrate their new skill with Sondra's aquaplane. After that, lunch, tennis, or golf, a trip to the Casino for tea. After dinner at the lodge of the Brookshaws of Utica across the lake, there was to be dancing.

Within an hour after his arrival, as Clyde could see, the program for the week-end was already full. But that he and Sondra would contrive not only moments but possibly hours together he well knew. And then he would see what new delight, in connection with her many-faceted temperament, the wonderful occasion would provide. To him, in spite of the dour burden of Roberta, which for this one week-end at least he could lay aside, it was as though he were in Paradise.

And on the tennis grounds of the Cranstons, it seemed as though never before had Sondra, attired in a short, severe white tennis skirt and blouse, with a yellow-and-green dotted handkerchief tied about her hair, seemed so gay, graceful and happy. The smile that was upon her lips! The gay, laughing light of promise that was in her eyes whenever she glanced at him! And now and then, in running to serve him, it was as though she were poised bird-like in flight—her racquet arm high, a single toe seeming barely to touch the ground, her head thrown back, her lips parted and smiling always. And in calling twenty love, thirty love, forty love, it was always with a laughing accent on the word love, which at once thrilled and saddened him, as he saw, and rejoiced in from one point of view, she was his to take, if only he were free to take her now. But this other black barrier which he himself had built!

And then this scene, where a bright sun poured a flood of crystal light upon a greensward that stretched from tall pines to the silver rippling waters of a lake. And off shore in a half dozen different directions the bright white sails of small boats—the white and green and yellow splashes of color, where canoes paddled by idling lovers were passing in the sun! Summertime—leisure—warmth—color—ease—beauty—love—all that he had dreamed of the summer before, when he was so very much alone.

At moments it seemed to Clyde that he would reel from very joy of the certain fulfillment of a great desire, that was all but immediately within his control; at other times (the thought of Roberta sweeping down upon him as an icy wind), as though nothing could be more sad, terrible, numbing to the dreams of beauty, love and happiness than this which now threatened him. That terrible item about the lake and those two people drowned! The probability that in spite of his wild plan within a week, or two or three at most, he would have to leave all this forever. And then of a sudden he would wake to realize that he was fumbling or playing badly—that Bertine or Sondra or Grant was calling: "Oh, Clyde, what are you thinking of, anyhow?" And from the darkest depths of his heart he would have answered, had he spoken, "Roberta."

At the Brookshaws', again, that evening, a smart company of friends of Sondra's, Bertine's and others. On the dance floor a reëncounter with Sondra, all smiles, for she was pretending for the benefit of others here—her mother and father in particular—that she had not seen Clyde before—did not even know that he was here.

"You up here? That's great. Over at the Cranstons'? Oh, isn't that dandy? Right next door to us. Well, we'll see a lot of each other, what? How about a canter to-morrow before seven? Bertine and I go nearly every day. And we'll have a picnic to-morrow, if nothing interferes, canoeing and motoring.

Don't worry about not riding well. I'll get Bertine to let you have Jerry—he's just a sheep. And you don't need to worry about togs, either. Grant has scads of things. I'll dance the next two dances with others, but you sit out the third one with me, will you? I know a peach of a place outside on the balcony."

She was off with fingers extended but with a "we-understand-each-other" look in her eye. And outside in the shadow later she pulled his face to hers when no one was looking and kissed him eagerly, and, before the evening was over, they had managed, by strolling along a path which led away from the house along the lake shore, to embrace under the moon.

"Sondra so glad Clydie here. Misses him so much." She smoothed his hair as he kissed her, and Clyde, bethinking him of the shadow which lay so darkly between them, crushed her feverishly, desperately. "Oh, my darling baby girl," he exclaimed. "My beautiful, beautiful Sondra! If you only knew how much I love you! If you only knew! I wish I could tell you *all*. I wish I could."

But he could not now—or ever. He would never dare to speak to her of even so much as a phase of the black barrier that now lay between them. For, with her training, the standards of love and marriage that had been set for her, she would never understand, never be willing to make so great a sacrifice for love, as much as she loved him. And he would be left, abandoned on the instant, and with what horror in her eyes!

Yet looking into his eyes, his face white and tense, and the glow of the moon above making small white electric sparks in his eyes, she exclaimed as he gripped her tightly: "Does he love Sondra so much? Oh, sweetie boy! Sondra loves him, too." She seized his head between her hands and held it tight, kissing him swiftly and ardently a dozen times. "And Sondra won't give her Clydie up either. She won't. You just wait and see! It doesn't matter what happens now. It may not be so very easy, but she won't." Then as suddenly and practically, as so often was her way, she exclaimed: "But we must go now, right away. No, not another kiss now. No, no, Sondra says no, now. They'll be missing us." And straightening up and pulling him by the arm she hurried him back to the house in time to meet Palmer Thurston, who was looking for her.

The next morning, true to her promise, there was the canter to Inspiration Point, and that before seven—Bertine and Sondra in bright red riding coats and white breeches and black boots, their hair unbound and loose to the wind, and riding briskly on before for the most part, then racing back to where he was. Or Sondra halloing gaily for him to come on, or the two of them laughing and chatting a hundred yards ahead in some concealed chapel of the aisled trees where he could not see them. And because of the interest which Sondra was so obviously manifesting in him these days—an interest which Bertine herself had begun to feel might end in marriage, if no family complications arose to interfere—she, Bertine, was all smiles, the very soul of cordiality, winsomely insisting that he should come up and stay for the summer and she would chaperon them both so that no one would have a chance to complain. And Clyde thrilling, and yet brooding too—by turns—occasionally—and in spite of himself drifting back to the thought that the item in the paper had inspired— and yet fighting it—trying to shut it out entirely.

And then at one point, Sondra, turning down a steep path which led to a stony and moss-lipped spring between the dark trees, called to Clyde to "Come on down. Jerry knows the way. He won't slip. Come and get a drink. If you do, you'll come back again soon—so they say."

And once he was down and had dismounted to drink, she exclaimed: "I've been wanting to tell you something. You should have seen Mamma's face last night when she heard you were up here. She can't be sure that I had anything to do with it, of course, because she thinks that Bertine likes you, too. I made her think that. But just the same she suspects that I had a hand in it, I guess, and she doesn't quite like it. But she can't say anything more than she has before. And I had a talk with Bertine just now and she's agreed to stick by me and help me all she can. But we'll have to be even more careful than ever now, because I think if Mamma got too suspicious I don't know what she might do—want us to leave here, even now maybe, just so I couldn't see you. You know she feels that I shouldn't be interested in any one yet except some one she likes. You know how it is. She's that way with Stuart, too. But if you'll take care not to show that you care for me so much whenever we're around any one of our crowd, I don't think she'll do anything—not now, anyhow. Later on, in the fall, when we're back in Lycurgus, things will be different. I'll be of age then, and I'm going to see what I can do. I never loved any one before, but I do love you, and, well, I won't give you up, that's all. I won't. And they can't make me, either!"

She stamped her foot and struck her boot, the while the two horses looked idly and vacantly about. And Clyde, enthused and astonished by this second definite declaration in his behalf, as well as fired by the thought that now, if ever, he might suggest the elopement and marriage and so rid himself of the sword that hung so threateningly above him, now gazed at Sondra, his eyes filled with a nervous hope and a nervous fear. For she might refuse, and change, too, shocked by the suddenness of his suggestion. And he had no money and no place in mind where they might go either, in case she accepted his proposal. But she had, perhaps, or she might have. And having once consented, might she not help him? Of course. At any rate, he felt that he must speak, leaving luck or ill luck to the future.

And so he said: "Why couldn't you run away with me now, Sondra, darling? It's so long until fall and I want you so much. Why couldn't we? Your mother's not likely to want to let you marry me then, anyhow. But if we went away now, she couldn't help herself, could she? And afterwards, in a few months or so, you could write her and then she wouldn't mind. Why couldn't we, Sondra?" His voice was very pleading, his eyes full of a sad dread of refusal—and of the future that lay unprotected behind that.

And by now so caught was she by the tremor with which his mood invested him, that she paused—not really shocked by the suggestion at all—but decidedly moved, as well as flattered by the thought that she was able to evoke in Clyde so eager and headlong a passion. He was so impetuous—so blazing now with a flame of her own creating, as she felt, yet which she was incapable of feeling as much as he, as she knew—such a flame as she had never seen in him or any one else before. And would it not be wonderful if she could run away with him now—secretly—to Canada or New York or Boston, or anywhere? The excitement her elopement would

create here and elsewhere—in Lycurgus, Albany, Utica! The
talk and feeling in her own family as well as elsewhere! And
Gilbert would be related to her in spite of him—and the Griffiths, too, whom her mother and father so much admired.

For a moment there was written in her eyes the desire and
the determination almost, to do as he suggested—run away—
make a great lark of this, her intense and true love. For, once
married, what could her parents do? And was not Clyde worthy of her and them, too? Of course—even though nearly all
in her set fancied that he was not quite all he should be, just
because he didn't have as much money as they had. But he
would have—would he not—after he was married to her—
and get as good a place in her father's business as Gil Griffiths
had in his father's?

Yet a moment later, thinking of her life here and what her
going off in such a way would mean to her father and mother
just then—in the very beginning of the summer season—as
well as how it would disrupt her own plans and cause her
mother to feel especially angry, and perhaps even to bring
about the dissolution of the marriage on the ground that she
was not of age, she paused—that gay light of adventure replaced by a marked trace of the practical and the material that
so persistently characterized her. What difference would a few
months make, anyhow? It might, and no doubt would, save
Clyde from being separated from her forever, whereas their
present course might insure their separation.

Accordingly she now shook her head in a certain, positive
and yet affectionate way, which by now Clyde had come to
know spelled defeat—the most painful and irremediable defeat that had yet come to him in connection with all this. She
would not go! Then he was lost—lost—and she to him forever maybe. Oh, God! For while her face softened with a tenderness which was not usually there—even when she was
most moved emotionally—she said: "I would, honey, if I did
not think it best not to, now. It's too soon. Mamma isn't
going to do anything right now. I know she isn't. Besides she
has made all her plans to do a lot of entertaining here this
summer, and for my particular benefit. She wants me to be
nice to—well, you know who I mean. And I can be, without
doing anything to interfere with us in any way, I'm sure—so

long as I don't do anything to really frighten her." She paused
to smile a reassuring smile. "But you can come up here as often as you choose, don't you see, and she and these others
won't think anything of it, because you won't be our guest,
don't you see? I've fixed all that with Bertine. And that means
that we can see each other all summer long up here, just
about as much as we want to, don't you see? Then in the fall,
when I come back, and if I find that I can't make her be nice
to you at all, or consider our being engaged, why, I will run
away with you. Yes, I will, darling—really and truly."

Darling! The fall!

She stopped, her eyes showing a very shrewd conception of
all the practical difficulties before them, while she took both
of his hands in hers and looked up into his face. Then, im-
pulsively and conclusively, she threw both arms about his neck
and, pulling his head down, kissed him.

"Can't you see, dearie? Please don't look so sad, darling.
Sondra loves her Clyde so much. And she'll do anything and
everything to make things come out right. Yes, she will. And
they will, too. Now you wait and see. She won't give him up
ever—ever!"

And Clyde, realizing that he had not one moving argument
wherewith to confront her, really—not one that might not
cause her to think strangely and suspiciously of his intense
anxiety, and that this, because of Roberta's demand, and unless—unless—well—, unless Roberta let him go it all spelled
defeat for him, now looked gloomily and even desperately
upon her face. The beauty of her! The completeness of this
world! And yet not to be allowed to possess her or it, ever.
And Roberta with her demand and his promise in the immediate background! And no way of escape save by flight! God!

At this point it was that a nervous and almost deranged
look—never so definite or powerful at any time before in his
life—the border-line look between reason and unreason, no
less—so powerful that the quality of it was even noticeable to
Sondra—came into his eyes. He looked sick, broken, unbelievably despairing. So much so that she exclaimed, "Why,
what is it, Clyde, dearie—you look so—oh, I can't say just
how—forlorn or— Does he love me so much? And can't he
wait just three or four months? But, oh, yes he can, too. It

isn't as bad as he thinks. He'll be with me most of the time—the lovekins will. And when he isn't, Sondra'll write him every day—every day."

"But, Sondra! Sondra! If I could just tell you. If you knew how much it were going to mean to me——"

He paused here, for as he could see at this point, into the expression of Sondra came a practical inquiry as to what it was that made it so urgent for her to leave with him at once. And immediately, on his part, Clyde sensing how enormous was the hold of this world on her—how integral a part of it she was—and how, by merely too much insistence here and now, he might so easily cause her to doubt the wisdom of her primary craze for him, was moved to desist, sure that if he spoke it would lead her to questioning him in such a way as might cause her to change—or at least to modify her enthusiasm to the point where even the dream of the fall might vanish.

And so, instead of explaining further why he needed a decision on her part, he merely desisted, saying: "It's because I need you so much now, dear—all of the time. That's it, just that. It seems at times as though I could never be away from you another minute any more. Oh, I'm so hungry for you all of the time."

And yet Sondra, flattered as she was by this hunger, and reciprocating it in part at least, merely repeated the various things she had said before. They must wait. All would come out all right in the fall. And Clyde, quite numb because of his defeat, yet unable to forego or deny the delight of being with her now, did his best to recover his mood—and think, think, think that in some way—somehow—maybe via that plan of that boat or in some other way!

But what other way?

But no, no, no—not that. He was not a murderer and never could be. He was not a murderer—never—never—never.

And yet this loss.

This impending disaster.

This impending disaster.

How to avoid that and to win Sondra after all.

How, how, how?

# Chapter XLIV

A<small>ND THEN</small> on his return to Lycurgus early Monday morning, the following letter from Roberta,

D<small>EAR</small> C<small>LYDE</small>:

My dear, I have often heard the saying, "it never rains but it pours," but I never knew what it meant until to-day. About the first person I saw this morning was Mr. Wilcox, a neighbor of ours, who came to say that Mrs. Anse would not be out to-day on account of some work she had to do for Mrs. Dinwiddie in Biltz, although when she left yesterday everything had been prepared for her so that I could help her a little with the sewing and so hurry things up a bit. And now she won't be here until to-morrow. Next word came that Mother's sister, Mrs. Nichols, is very ill and Mother had to go over to her house at Baker's Pond, which is about twelve miles east of here, Tom driving her, although he ought to be here to help father with all the work that there is to do about the farm. And I don't know if Mother will be able to get back before Sunday. If I were better and didn't have all this work of my own on my hands I would have to go too, I suppose, although Mother insists not.

Next, Emily and Tom, thinking all is going so well with me and that I might enjoy it, were having four girls and four boys come here to-night for a sort of June moon-party, with ice cream and cake to be made by Emily and Mother and myself. But now, poor dear, she has to do a lot of telephoning over Mr. Wilcox's phone, which we share, in order to put it off until some day next week, if possible. And she's just heartsick and gloomy, of course.

As for myself, I'm trying to keep a stiff upper lip, as the saying is. But it's pretty hard, dear, I'll tell you. For so far I have only had three small telephone talks with you, saying that you didn't think you would have the necessary money before July fifth. And to put the finishing touches on it, as I only learned to-day, Mamma and Papa have about decided to go to my Uncle Charlie's in Hamilton for over the fourth (from the fourth to the fifteenth) and take me with them, unless I decide to return to Lycurgus, while Tom and Emily visit with my sister at Homer. But, dear, I can't do that, as you know. I'm too sick and worried. Last night I vomited dreadful and have been half dead on my feet all day, and I am just about crazy to-night.

Dear, what can we do? Can't you come for me before July third, which will be the time they will be going? You will have to come for

me before then, really, because I just can't go up there with them.
It's fifty miles from here. I could say I would go up there with them
if only you would be sure to come for me before they start. But I
must be absolutely sure that you are coming—absolutely.

Clyde, I have done nothing but cry since I got here. If you were
only here I wouldn't feel so badly. I do try to be brave, dear, but
how can I help thinking at times that you will never come for me
when you haven't written me one single note and have only talked
to me three times since I've been up here. But then I say to myself
you couldn't be so mean as that, and especially since you have
promised. Oh, you will come, won't you? Everything worries me so
now, Clyde, for some reason and I'm so frightened, dear. I think of
last summer and then this one, and all my dreams. It won't make any
real difference to you about your coming a few days sooner than you
intended, will it, dear? Even if we have to get along on a little less. I
know that we can. I can be very saving and economical. I will try to
have my dresses made by then. If not, I will do with what I have and
finish them later. And I will try and be very brave, dear, and not annoy you much, if only you will come. You must, you know, Clyde.
It can't be any other way, although for your sake now I wish it could.

Please, please, Clyde, write and tell me that you will be here at the
end of the time that you said. I worry so and get so lonesome off
here all by myself. I will come straight back to see you if you don't
come by the time you said. I know you will not like me to say this,
but, Clyde, I can't stay here and that's all there is to it. And I can't
go away with Mamma and Papa either, so there is only one way out.
I don't believe I will sleep a wink to-night, so please write me and in
your letter tell me over and over not to worry about your not coming for me. If you could only come to-day, dear, or this week-end, I
wouldn't feel so blue. But nearly two weeks more! Every one is in
bed and the house is still, so I will stop.

But please write me, dear, right away, or if you won't do that call
me up sure to-morrow, because I just can't rest one single minute
until I do hear from you.

                                        Your miserable ROBERTA.
P. S.: This is a horrid letter, but I just can't write a better one. I'm
so blue.

But the day this letter arrived in Lycurgus Clyde was not
there to answer it at once. And because of that, Roberta being
in the darkest and most hysterical mood and thought, sat down
on Saturday afternoon and, half-convinced as she was that he
might already have departed for some distant point without

any word to her, almost shrieked or screamed, if one were to properly characterize the mood that animated the following:

Biltz, Saturday, June 14th.

MY DEAR CLYDE:

I am writing to tell you that I am coming back to Lycurgus. I simply can't stay here any longer. Mamma worries and wonders why I cry so much, and I am just about sick. I know I promised to stay until the 25th or 26th, but then you said you would write me, but you never have—only an occasional telephone message when I am almost crazy. I woke up this morning and couldn't help crying right away and this afternoon my headache is dreadful.

I'm so afraid you won't come and I'm so frightened, dear. Please come and take me away some place, anywhere, so I can get out of here and not worry like I do. I'm so afraid in the state that I'm in that Papa and Mamma may make me tell the whole affair or that they will find it out for themselves.

Oh, Clyde, you will never know. You have said you would come, and sometimes I just know you will. But at other times I get to thinking about other things and I'm just as certain you won't, especially when you don't write or telephone. I wish you would write and say that you will come just so I can stand to stay here. Just as soon as you get this, I wish you would write me and tell me the exact day you can come—not later than the first, really, because I know I cannot stand to stay here any longer than then. Clyde, there isn't a girl in the whole world as miserable as I am, and you have made me so. But I don't mean that, either, dear. You were good to me once, and you are now, offering to come for me. And if you will come right away I will be so grateful. And when you read this, if you think I am unreasonable, please do not mind it, Clyde, but just think I am crazy with grief and worry and that I just don't know what to do. Please write me, Clyde. If you only knew how I need a word.

ROBERTA.

This letter, coupled as it was with a threat to come to Lycurgus, was sufficient to induce in Clyde a state not unlike Roberta's. To think that he had no additional, let alone plausible, excuse to offer Roberta whereby she could be induced to delay her final and imperative demand. He racked his brains. He must not write her any long and self-incriminating letters. That would be foolish in the face of his determination not to marry her. Besides his mood at the moment, so fresh from the arms and kisses of Sondra, was not for anything like that. He could not, even if he would.

At the same time, something must be done at once, as he could see, in order to allay her apparently desperate mood. And ten minutes after he had finished reading the last of these two letters, he was attempting to reach Roberta over the telephone. And finally getting her after a troublesome and impatient half-hour, he heard her voice, thin and rather querulous as it seemed to him at first, but really only because of a poor connection, saying: "Hello, Clyde, hello. Oh, I'm so glad you called. I've been terribly nervous. Did you get my two letters? I was just about to leave here in the morning if I didn't hear from you by then. I just couldn't stand not to hear anything. Where have you been, dear? Did you read what I said about my parents going away? That's true. Why don't you write, Clyde, or call me up anyhow? What about what I said in my letter about the third? Will you be sure and come then? Or shall I meet you somewhere? I've been so nervous the last three or four days, but now that I hear you again, maybe I'll be able to quiet down some. But I do wish you would write me a note every few days anyhow. Why won't you, Clyde? You haven't even written me one since I've been here. I can't tell you what a state I'm in and how hard it is to keep calm now."

Plainly Roberta was very nervous and fearsome as she talked. As a matter of fact, except that the home in which she was telephoning was deserted at the moment she was talking very indiscreetly, it seemed to Clyde. And it aided but little in his judgment for her to explain that she was all alone and that no one could hear her. He did not want her to use his name or refer to letters written to him.

Without talking too plainly, he now tried to make it clear that he was very busy and that it was hard for him to write as much as she might think necessary. Had he not said that he was coming on the 28th or thereabouts if he could? Well, he would if he could, only it looked now as though it might be necessary for him to postpone it for another week or so, until the seventh or eighth of July—long enough for him to get together an extra fifty for which he had a plan, and which would be necessary for him to have. But really, which was the thought behind this other, long enough for him to pay one

more visit to Sondra as he was yearning to do, over the next
week-end. But this demand of hers, now! Couldn't she go
with her parents for a week or so and then let him come for
her there or she come to him? It would give him more
needed time, and——

But at this Roberta, bursting forth in a storm of nervous
disapproval—saying that most certainly if that were the case
she was going back to her room at the Gilpins', if she could
get it, and not waste her time up there getting ready and
waiting for him when he was not coming—he suddenly decided that he might as well say that he was coming on the
third, or that if he did not, that at least by then he would have
arranged with her where to meet him. For even by now, he
had not made up his mind as to how he was to do. He must
have a little more time to think—more time to think.

And so now he altered his tone greatly and said: "But listen, Bert. Please don't be angry with me. You talk as though
I didn't have any troubles in connection with all this, either.
You don't know what this may be going to cost me before
I'm through with it, and you don't seem to care much. I
know you're worried and all that, but what about me? I'm
doing the very best I can now, Bert, with all I have to think
about. And won't you just be patient now until the third,
anyhow? Please do. I promise to write you and if I don't, I'll
call you up every other day. Will that be all right? But I certainly don't want you to be using my name like you did a
while ago. That will lead to trouble, sure. Please don't. And
when I call again, I'll just say it's Mr. Baker asking, see, and
you can say it's any one you like afterwards. And then, if by
any chance anything should come up that would stop our
starting exactly on the third, why you can come back here if
you want to, see, or somewhere near here, and then we can
start as soon as possible after that."

His tone was so pleading and soothing, infused as it was—
but because of his present necessity only with a trace of that
old tenderness and seeming helplessness which, at times, had
quite captivated Roberta, that even now it served to win her
to a bizarre and groundless gratitude. So much so that at
once she had replied, warmly and emotionally, even: "Oh, no,
dear. I don't want to do anything like that. You know I don't.

It's just because things are so bad as they are with me and I can't help myself now. You know that, Clyde, don't you? I can't help loving you. I always will, I suppose. And I don't want to do anything to hurt you, dear, really I don't if I can help it."

And Clyde, hearing the ring of genuine affection, and sensing anew his old-time power over her, was disposed to reënact the rôle of lover again, if only in order to dissuade Roberta from being too harsh and driving with him now. For while he could not like her now, he told himself, and could not think of marrying her, still in view of this other dream he could at least be gracious to her—could he not?—Pretend! And so this conversation ended with a new peace based on this agreement.

The preceding day—a day of somewhat reduced activities on the lakes from which he had just returned—he and Sondra and Stuart and Bertine, together with Nina Temple and a youth named Harley Baggott, then visiting the Thurstons, had motored first from Twelfth Lake to Three Mile Bay, a small lakeside resort some twenty-five miles north, and from thence, between towering walls of pines, to Big Bittern and some other smaller lakes lost in the recesses of the tall pines of the region to the north of Trine Lake. And en route, Clyde, as he now recalled, had been most strangely impressed at moments and in spots by the desolate and for the most part lonely character of the region. The narrow and rain-washed and even rutted nature of the dirt roads that wound between tall, silent and darksome trees—forests in the largest sense of the word—that extended for miles and miles apparently on either hand. The decadent and weird nature of some of the bogs and tarns on either side of the only comparatively passable dirt roads which here and there were festooned with funereal or viperous vines, and strewn like deserted battlefields with soggy and decayed piles of fallen and criss-crossed logs—in places as many as four deep—one above the other—in the green slime that an undrained depression in the earth had accumulated. The eyes and backs of occasional frogs that, upon lichen or vine or moss-covered stumps and rotting logs in this warm June weather, there sunned themselves apparently undisturbed; the spirals of gnats, the solitary flick of a snake's tail as disturbed by the sudden approach of the machine, one made off into the muck and the poisonous grasses and water-plants which were thickly imbedded in it.

And in seeing one of these Clyde, for some reason, had thought of the accident at Pass Lake. He did not realize it, but at the moment his own subconscious need was contemplating the loneliness and the usefulness at times of such a lone spot as this. And at one point it was that a weir-weir, one of the solitary water-birds of this region, uttered its ouphe and barghest cry, flying from somewhere near into some darker recess within the woods. And at this sound it was that Clyde had stirred nervously and then sat up in the car. It was so very different to any bird-cry he had ever heard anywhere.

"What was that?" he asked of Harley Baggott, who sat next him.

"What?"

"Why, that bird or something that just flew away back there just now?"

"I didn't hear any bird."

"Gee! That was a queer sound. It makes me feel creepy."

As interesting and impressive as anything else to him in this almost tenantless region had been the fact that there were so many lonesome lakes, not one of which he had ever heard of before. The territory through which they were speeding as fast as the dirt roads would permit, was dotted with them in these deep forests of pine. And only occasionally in passing near one, were there any signs indicating a camp or lodge, and those to be reached only by some half-blazed trail or rutty or sandy road disappearing through darker trees. In the main, the shores of the more remote lakes passed, were all but untenanted, or so sparsely that a cabin or a distant lodge to be seen across the smooth waters of some pine-encircled gem was an object of interest to all.

Why must he think of that other lake in Massachusetts! That boat! The body of that girl found—but not that of the man who accompanied her! How terrible, really!

He recalled afterwards,—here in his room, after this last conversation with Roberta—that the car, after a few more miles, had finally swung into an open space at the north end of a long narrow lake—the south prospect of which appeared to be divided by a point or an island suggesting a greater length and further windings or curves than were visible from where the car had stopped. And except for the small lodge and boathouse at this upper end it had appeared so very lonesome—not a launch or canoe on it at the time their party arrived. And as in the case of all the other lakes seen this day, the banks to the very shore line were sentineled with those same green pines—tall, spear-shaped—their arms widespread like one outside his window here in Lycurgus. And beyond them in the distance, to the south and west, rose the humped and still smooth and green backs of the nearer Adirondacks. And the water before them, now ruffled by a light wind and glowing in the afternoon sun, was of an intense Prussian blue, almost black, which suggested, as was afterwards confirmed by a guide who was lounging upon the low veranda of the small inn—that it was very deep—"all of seventy feet not more than a hundred feet out from that boathouse."

And at this point Harley Baggott, who was interested to learn more about the fishing possibilities of this lake in behalf of his father, who contemplated coming to this region in a few days, had inquired of the guide who appeared not to look at the others in the car: "How long is this lake, anyhow?"

"Oh, about seven miles." "Any fish in it?" "Throw a line in and see. The best place for black bass and the like of that almost anywhere around here. Off the island down yonder, or just to the south of it round on the other side there, there's a little bay that's said to be one of the best fishin' holes in any of the lakes up this way. I've seen a coupla men bring back as many as seventy-five fish in two hours. That oughta satisfy anybody that ain't tryin' to ruin the place for the rest of us."

The guide, a thinnish, tall and wizened type, with a long, narrow head and small, keen, bright blue eyes laughed a yokelish laugh as he studied the group. "Not thinkin' of tryin' your luck to-day?"

"No, just inquiring for my dad. He's coming up here next week, maybe. I want to see about accommodations."

"Well, they ain't what they are down to Raquette, of course, but then the fish down there ain't what they are up here, either." He visited all with a sly and wry and knowing smile.

Clyde had never seen the type before. He was interested by all the anomalies and contrarities of this lonesome world as contrasted with cities he had known almost exclusively, as well as the decidedly exotic and material life and equipment with which, at the Cranstons' and elsewhere, he was then surrounded. The strange and comparatively deserted nature of this region as contrasted with the brisk and vigorous life of Lycurgus, less than a hundred miles to the south.

"The country up here kills me," commented Stuart Finchley at this point. "It's so near the Chain and yet it's so different, scarcely any one living up here at all, it seems."

"Well, except for the camps in summer and the fellows that come up to hunt moose and deer in the fall, there ain't much of anybody or anything around here after September first," commented the guide. "I've been guidin' and trappin' for nigh onto seventeen years now around here and 'cept for more and more people around some of the lakes below here—the Chain principally in summer—I ain't see much change. You need to know this country purty well if yer goin't strike out anywhere away from the main roads, though o' course about five miles to the west o' here is the railroad. Gun Lodge is the station. We bring 'em by bus from there in the summer. And from the south end down there is a sorta road leadin' down to Greys Lake and Three Mile Bay. You musta come along a part of it, since it's the only road up into this country as yet. They're talkin' of cuttin' one through to Long Lake sometime, but so far it's mostly talk. But from most of these other lakes around here, there's no road at all, not that an automobile could make. Just trails and there's not even a decent camp on some o' 'em. You have to bring your own outfit. Bud Ellis and me was over to Gun Lake last summer—that's thirty miles west o' here and we had to walk every inch of the way and carry our packs. But, oh, say, the fishin' and moose and deer come right down to the shore in places to drink. See 'em as plain as that stump across the lake."

And Clyde remembered that, along with the others, he had carried away the impression that for solitude and charm—or at least mystery—this region could scarcely be matched. And to think it was all so comparatively near Lycurgus—not more than a hundred miles by road; not more than seventy by rail, as he eventually came to know.

But now once more in Lycurgus and back in his room after just explaining to Roberta, as he had, he once more encountered on his writing desk, the identical paper containing the item concerning the tragedy at Pass Lake. And in spite of himself, his eye once more followed nervously and yet unwaveringly to the last word all the suggestive and provocative details. The uncomplicated and apparently easy way in which the lost couple had first arrived at the boathouse; the commonplace and entirely unsuspicious way in which they had hired a boat and set forth for a row; the manner in which they had disappeared to the north end; and then the upturned boat, the floating oars and hats near the shore. He stood reading in the still strong evening light. Outside the windows were the dark boughs of the fir tree of which he had thought the preceding day and which now suggested all those firs and pines about the shores of Big Bittern.

But, good God! What was he thinking of anyhow? He, Clyde Griffiths! The nephew of Samuel Griffiths! What was "getting into" him? Murder! That's what it was. This terrible item—this devil's accident or machination that was constantly putting it before him! A most horrible crime, and one for which they electrocuted people if they were caught. Besides, he could not murder anybody—not Roberta, anyhow. Oh, no! Surely not after all that had been between them. And yet—this other world!—Sondra—which he was certain to lose now unless he acted in some way——

His hands shook, his eyelids twitched—then his hair at the roots tingled and over his body ran chill nervous titillations in waves. Murder! Or upsetting a boat at any rate in deep water, which of course might happen anywhere, and by accident, as at Pass Lake. And Roberta could not swim. He knew that. But she might save herself at that—scream—cling to the boat—and then—if there were any to hear—and she told afterwards! An icy perspiration now sprang to his forehead; his lips trembled and suddenly his throat felt parched and dry. To prevent a thing like that he would have to—to—but no—he was not like that. He could not do a thing like that—hit any

one—a girl—Roberta—and when drowning or struggling.
Oh, no, no—no such thing as that! Impossible.

He took his straw hat and went out, almost before any one
heard him *think*, as he would have phrased it to himself, such
horrible, terrible thoughts. He could not and would not think
them from now on. He was no such person. And yet—and
yet—these thoughts. The solution—if he wanted one. The
way to stay here—not leave—marry Sondra—be rid of
Roberta and all—all—for the price of a little courage or daring. But no!

He walked and walked—away from Lycurgus—out on a
road to the southeast which passed through a poor and decidedly unfrequented rural section, and so left him alone to
think—or, as he felt, not to be heard in his thinking.

Day was fading into dark. Lamps were beginning to glow
in the cottages here and there. Trees in groups in fields or
along the road were beginning to blur or smokily blend. And
although it was warm—the air lifeless and lethargic—he
walked fast, thinking, and perspiring as he did so, as though
he were seeking to outwalk and outthink or divert some inner
self that preferred to be still and think.

That gloomy, lonely lake up there!

That island to the south!

Who would see?

Who could hear?

That station at Gun Lodge with a bus running to it at this
season of the year. (Ah, he remembered that, did he? The
deuce!) A terrible thing, to remember a thing like that in connection with such a thought as this! But if he were going to
think of such a thing as this at all, he had better think well—
he could tell himself that—or stop thinking about it now—
once and forever—forever. But Sondra! Roberta! If ever he
were caught—electrocuted! And yet the actual misery of his
present state. The difficulty! The danger of losing Sondra.
And yet, murder—

He wiped his hot and wet face, and paused and gazed at a
group of trees across a field which somehow reminded him of
the trees of . . . well . . . he didn't like this road. It was getting too dark out here. He had better turn and go back. But
that road at the south and leading to Three Mile Bay and

Greys Lake—if one chose to go that way—to Sharon and the Cranston Lodge—whither he would be going afterwards if he did go that way. God! Big Bittern—the trees along there after dark would be like that—blurred and gloomy. It would have to be toward evening, of course. No one would think of trying to . . . well . . . in the morning, when there was so much light. Only a fool would do that. But at night, toward dusk, as it was now, or a little later. But, damn it, he would not listen to such thoughts. Yet no one would be likely to see him or Roberta either—would they—there? It would be so easy to go to a place like Big Bittern—for an alleged wedding trip—would it not—over the Fourth, say—or after the fourth or fifth, when there would be fewer people. And to register as some one else—not himself—so that he could never be traced that way. And then, again, it would be so easy to get back to Sharon and the Cranstons' by midnight, or the morning of the next day, maybe, and then, once there he could pretend also that he had come north on that early morning train that arrived about ten o'clock. And then . . .

Confound it—why should his mind keep dwelling on this idea? Was he actually planning to do a thing like this? But he was not! He could not be! He, Clyde Griffiths, could not be serious about a thing like this. That was not possible. He could not be. Of course! It was all too impossible, too wicked, to imagine that he, Clyde Griffiths, could bring himself to execute a deed like that. And yet . . .

And forthwith an uncanny feeling of wretchedness and insufficiency for so dark a crime insisted on thrusting itself forward. He decided to retrace his steps toward Lycurgus, where at least he could be among people.

# Chapter XLV

THERE ARE moments when in connection with the sensitively imaginative or morbidly anachronistic—the mentality assailed and the same not of any great strength and the problem confronting it of sufficient force and complexity— the reason not actually toppling from its throne, still totters or is warped or shaken—the mind befuddled to the extent that for the time being, at least, unreason or disorder and mistaken or erroneous counsel would appear to hold against all else. In such instances the will and the courage confronted by some great difficulty which it can neither master nor endure, appears in some to recede in precipitate flight, leaving only panic and temporary unreason in its wake.

And in this instance, the mind of Clyde might well have been compared to a small and routed army in full flight before a major one, yet at various times in its precipitate departure, pausing for a moment to meditate on some way of escaping complete destruction and in the coincident panic of such a state, resorting to the weirdest and most haphazard of schemes of escaping from an impending and yet wholly unescapable fate. The strained and bedeviled look in his eyes at moments—the manner in which, from moment to moment and hour to hour, he went over and over his hitherto poorly balanced actions and thoughts but with no smallest door of escape anywhere. And yet again at moments the solution suggested by the item in *The Times-Union* again thrusting itself forward, psychogenetically, born of his own turbulent, eager and disappointed seeking. And hence persisting.

Indeed, it was now as though from the depths of some lower or higher world never before guessed or plumbed by him . . . a region otherwhere than in life or death and peopled by creatures otherwise than himself . . . there had now suddenly appeared, as the genii at the accidental rubbing of Aladdin's lamp—as the efrit emerging as smoke from the mystic jar in the net of the fisherman—the very substance of some leering and diabolic wish or wisdom concealed in his own nature, and that now abhorrent and yet compelling, leering and

yet intriguing, friendly and yet cruel, offered him a choice between an evil which threatened to destroy him (and against
his deepest opposition) and a second evil which, however it
might disgust or sear or terrify, still provided for freedom and
success and love.

Indeed the center or mentating section of his brain at this
time might well have been compared to a sealed and silent
hall in which alone and undisturbed, and that in spite of himself, he now sat thinking on the mystic or evil and terrifying
desires or advice of some darker or primordial and unregenerate nature of his own, and without the power to drive the
same forth or himself to decamp, and yet also without the
courage to act upon anything.

For now the genii of his darkest and weakest side was
speaking. And it said: "And would you escape from the demands of Roberta that but now and unto this hour have appeared unescapable to you? Behold! I bring you a way. It is
the way of the lake—Pass Lake. This item that you have
read—do you think it was placed in your hands for nothing?
Remember Big Bittern, the deep, blue-black water, the island
to the south, the lone road to Three Mile Bay? How suitable
to your needs! A rowboat or a canoe upset in such a lake and
Roberta would pass forever from your life. She cannot swim!
The lake—the lake—that you have seen—that I have shown
you—is it not ideal for the purpose? So removed and so little
frequented and yet comparatively near—but a hundred miles
from here. And how easy for you and Roberta to go there—
not directly but indirectly—on this purely imaginative marriage-trip that you have already agreed to. And all that you
need do now is to change your name—and hers—or let her
keep her own and you use yours. You have never permitted
her to speak of you and this relationship, and she never has.
You have written her but formal notes. And now if you
should meet her somewhere as you have already agreed to,
and without any one seeing you, you might travel with her, as
in the past to Fonda, to Big Bittern—or some point near
there."

"But there is no hotel at Big Bittern," at once corrected
Clyde. "A mere shack that entertains but few people and that
not very well."

"All the better. The less people are likely to be there."

"But we might be seen on the train going up together. I would be identified as having been with her."

"Were you seen at Fonda, Gloversville, Little Falls? Have you not ridden in separate cars or seats before and could you not do so now? Is it not presumably to be a secret marriage? Then why not a secret honeymoon?"

"True enough—true enough."

"And once you have arranged for that and arrive at Big Bittern or some lake like it—there are so many there—how easy to row out on such a lake? No questions. No registry under your own name or hers. A boat rented for an hour or half-day or day. You saw the island far to the south on that lone lake. Is it not beautiful? It is well worth seeing. Why should you not go there on such a pleasure trip before marriage? Would she not be happy so to do—as weary and distressed as she is now—an outing—a rest before the ordeal of the new life? Is not that sensible—plausible? And neither of you will ever return presumably. You will both be drowned, will you not? Who is to see? A guide or two—the man who rents you the boat—the innkeeper once, as you go. But how are they to know who you are? Or who she is? And you heard the depth of the water."

"But I do not want to kill her. I do not want to kill her. I do not want to injure her in any way. If she will but let me go and she go her own way, I will be so glad and so happy never to see her more."

"But she will not let you go or go her way unless you accompany her. And if you go yours, it will be without Sondra and all that she represents, as well as all this pleasant life here—your standing with your uncle, his friends, their cars, the dances, visits to the lodges on the lakes. And what then? A small job! Small pay! Another such period of wandering as followed that accident at Kansas City. Never another chance like this anywhere. Do you prefer that?"

"But might there not be some accident here, destroying all my dreams—my future—as there was in Kansas City?"

"An accident, to be sure—but not the same. In this instance the plan is in your hands. You can arrange it all as you will. And how easy! So many boats upsetting every summer—the occupants of them drowning, because in most cases they cannot swim. And will it ever be known whether the man who was with Roberta Alden on Big Bittern could swim? And of all deaths, drowning is the easiest—no noise—no outcry— perhaps the accidental blow of an oar—the side of a boat. And then silence! Freedom—a body that no one may ever find. Or if found and identified, will it not be easy, if you but trouble to plan, to make it appear that you were elsewhere, visiting at one of the other lakes before you decided to go to Twelfth Lake. What is wrong with it? Where is the flaw?"

"But assuming that I should upset the boat and that she should not drown, then what? Should cling to it, cry out, be saved and relate afterward that . . . But no, I cannot do that—will not do it. I will not hit her. That would be too terrible . . . too vile."

"But a little blow—any little blow under such circumstances would be sufficient to confuse and complete her undoing. Sad, yes, but she has an opportunity to go her own way, has she not? And she will not, nor let you go yours. Well, then, is this so terribly unfair? And do not forget that afterwards there is Sondra—the beautiful—a home with her in Lycurgus—wealth, a high position such as elsewhere you may never obtain again—never—never. Love and happiness—the equal of any one here—superior even to your cousin Gilbert."

The voice ceased temporarily, trailing off into shadow,— silence, dreams.

And Clyde, contemplating all that had been said, was still unconvinced. Darker fears or better impulses supplanted the counsel of the voice in the great hall. But presently thinking of Sondra and all that she represented, and then of Roberta, the dark personality would as suddenly and swiftly return and with amplified suavity and subtlety.

"Ah, still thinking on the matter. And you have not found a way out and you will not. I have truly pointed out to you and in all helpfulness the only way—the only way—It is a long lake. And would it not be easy in rowing about to eventually find some secluded spot—some invisible nook near that south shore where the water is deep? And from there how easy to walk through the woods to Three Mile Bay and Upper Greys Lake? And from there to the Cranstons'? There is a boat from there, as you know. Pah—how cowardly—how lacking in

courage to win the thing that above all things you desire—
beauty—wealth—position—the solution of your every material and spiritual desire. And with poverty, commonplace, hard
and poor work as the alternative to all this."

"But you must choose—choose! And then act. You must!
You must! You must!"

Thus the voice in parting, echoing from some remote part
of the enormous chamber.

And Clyde, listening at first with horror and in terror, later
with a detached and philosophic calm as one who, entirely
apart from what he may think or do, is still entitled to consider
even the wildest and most desperate proposals for his release,
at last, because of his own mental and material weakness before
pleasures and dreams which he could not bring himself to
forego, psychically intrigued to the point where he was beginning to think that it might be possible. Why not? Was it not
even as the voice said—a possible and plausible way—all his desires and dreams to be made real by this one evil thing? Yet in
his case, because of flaws and weaknesses in his own unstable
and highly variable will, the problem was not to be solved by
thinking thus—then—nor for the next ten days for that matter.

He could not really act on such a matter for himself and
would not. It remained as usual for him to be forced either to
act or to abandon this most *wild* and terrible thought. Yet
during this time a series of letters—seven from Roberta, five
from Sondra—in which in somber tones in so far as Roberta
was concerned—in gay and colorful ones in those which came
from Sondra—was painted the now so sharply contrasting
phases of the black rebus which lay before him. To Roberta's
pleadings, argumentative and threatening as they were, Clyde
did not trust himself to reply, not even by telephone. For now
he reasoned that to answer would be only to lure Roberta to
her doom—or to the attempted drastic conclusion of his difficulties as outlined by the tragedy at Pass Lake.

At the same time, in several notes addressed to Sondra, he
gave vent to the most impassioned declarations of love—his
darling—his wonder girl—how eager he was to be at Twelfth
Lake by the morning of the Fourth, if he could, and so
thrilled to see her there again. Yet, alas, as he also wrote now,
so uncertain was he, even now, as to how he was to do, there

were certain details in connection with his work here that might delay him a day or two or three—he could not tell as yet—but would write her by the second at the latest, when he would know positively. Yet saying to himself as he wrote this, if she but knew what those details were—if she but knew. Yet in penning this, and without having as yet answered the last importunate letter from Roberta, he was also saying to himself that this did not mean that he was planning to go to Roberta at all, or that if he did, it did not mean that he was going to attempt to kill her. Never once did he honestly, or to put it more accurately, forthrightly and courageously or coldly face the thought of committing so grim a crime. On the contrary, the nearer he approached a final resolution or the need for one in connection with all this, the more hideous and terrible seemed the idea—hideous and difficult, and hence the more improbable it seemed that he should ever commit it. It was true that from moment to moment—arguing with himself as he constantly was—sweating mental sweats and fleeing from moral and social terrors in connection with it all, he was thinking from time to time that he might go to Big Bittern in order to quiet her in connection with these present importunities and threats and hence (once more evasion—tergiversation with himself) give himself more time in which to conclude what his true course must be.

The way of the Lake.

The way of the Lake.

But once there—whether it would then be advisable so to do—or not—well who could tell. He might even yet be able to convert Roberta to some other point of view. For, say what you would, she was certainly acting very unfairly and captiously in all this. She was, as he saw it in connection with his very vital dream of Sondra, making a mountain—an immense terror—out of a state that when all was said and done, was not so different from Esta's. And Esta had not compelled any one to marry her. And how much better were the Aldens to his own parents—poor farmers as compared to poor preachers. And why should he be so concerned as to what they would think when Esta had not troubled to think what her parents would feel?

In spite of all that Roberta had said about blame, was she

so entirely lacking in blame herself? To be sure, he had sought to entice or seduce her, as you will, but even so, could she be held entirely blameless? Could she not have refused, if she was so positive at the time that she was so very moral? But she had not. And as to all this, all that he had done, had he not done all he could to help her out of it? And he had so little money too. And was placed in such a difficult position. She was just as much to blame as he was. And yet now she was so determined to drive him this way. To insist on his marrying her, whereas if she would only go her own way—as she could with his help—she might still save both of them all this trouble.

But no, she would not, and he would not marry her and that was all there was to it. She need not think that she could make him. No, no, no! At times, when in such moods, he felt that he could do anything—drown her easily enough, and she would only have herself to blame.

Then again his more cowering sense of what society would think and do, if it knew, what he himself would be compelled to think of himself afterwards, fairly well satisfied him that as much as he desired to stay, he was not the one to do anything at all and in consequence must flee.

And so it was that Tuesday, Wednesday and Thursday following Roberta's letter received on Monday, had passed. And then, on Thursday night, following a most torturesome mental day on his and Roberta's part for that matter, this is what he received:

Biltz, Wednesday, June 30th.

DEAR CLYDE:
    This is to tell you that unless I hear from you either by telephone or letter before noon, Friday, I shall be in Lycurgus that same night, and the world will know how you have treated me. I cannot and will not wait and suffer one more hour. I regret to be compelled to take this step, but you have allowed all this time to go in silence really, and Saturday is the third, and without any plans of any kind. My whole life is ruined and so will yours be in a measure, but I cannot feel that I am entirely to blame. I have done all I possibly could to make this burden as easy for you as possible and I certainly regret all the misery it will cause my parents and friends and all whom you know and hold dear. But I will not wait and suffer one hour more.
                                                            ROBERTA.

And with this in his hands, he was finally all but numbed by the fact that now decidedly he must act. She was actually coming! Unless he could soothe or restrain her in some manner she would be here to-morrow—the second. And yet the second, or the third, or any time until after the Fourth, was no time to leave with her. The holiday crowds would be too great. There would be too many people to see—to encounter. There must be more secrecy. He must have at least a little more time in which to get ready. He must think now quickly and then act. Great God! Get ready. Could he not telephone her and say that he had been sick or so worried on account of the necessary money or something that he could not write— and that besides his uncle had sent for him to come to Greenwood Lake over the Fourth. His uncle! His uncle! No, that would not do. He had used his name too much. What difference should it make to him or her now, whether he saw his uncle once more or not? He was leaving once and for all, or so he had been telling her, on her account, was he not? And so he had better say that he was going to his uncle, in order to give a reason why he was going away so that, possibly, he might be able to return in a year or so. She might believe that. At any rate he must tell her something that would quiet her until after the Fourth—make her stay up there until at least he could perfect some plan—bring himself to the place where he could do one thing or the other. One thing or the other.

Without pausing to plan anything more than just this at this time, he hurried to the nearest telephone where he was least likely to be overheard. And, getting her once more, began one of those long and evasive and, in this instance, ingratiating explanations which eventually, after he had insisted that he had actually been sick—confined to his room with a fever and hence not able to get to a telephone—and because, as he now said, he had finally decided that it would be best if he were to make some explanation to his uncle, so that he might return some time in the future, if necessary—he, by using the most pleading, if not actually affectionate, tones and asking her to consider what a state he had been in, too, was able not only to make her believe that there was some excuse for his delay and silence, but also to introduce the plan that he now had in mind; which was if only she could wait until the sixth, then assuredly, without fail as to any particular, he would meet her at any place she would choose to come—Homer, Fonda, Lycurgus, Little Falls—only since they were trying to keep everything so secret, he would suggest that she come to Fonda on the morning of the sixth in order to make the noon train for Utica. There they could spend the night since they could not very well discuss and decide on their plans over the telephone, now, and then they could act upon whatever they had decided. Besides he could tell her better then just how he thought they ought to do. He had an idea—a little trip maybe, somewhere before they got married or after, just as she wished, but—something nice anyhow—(his voice grew husky and his knees and hands shook slightly as he said this, only Roberta could not detect the sudden perturbation within him). But she must not ask him now. He could not tell her over the phone. But as sure as anything, at noon on the sixth, he would be on the station platform at Fonda. All she had to do after seeing him was to buy her ticket to Utica and get in one coach, and he would buy his separately and get in another—the one just ahead or behind hers. On the way down, if she didn't see him at the station beforehand, he would pass through her car for a drink so that she could see that he was there—no more than that—but she mustn't speak to him. Then once in Utica, she should check her bag and he would follow her out to the nearest quiet corner. After that he would go and get her bag, and then they could go to some little hotel and he would take care of all the rest.

But she must do this. Would she have that much faith in him? If so, he would call her up on the third—the very next day—and on the morning of the sixth—sure, so that both he and she would know that everything was all right—that she was starting and that he would be there. What was that? Her trunk? The little one? Sure. If she needed it, certainly bring it. Only, if he were she, he would not trouble to try to bring too much now, because once she was settled somewhere, it would be easy enough to send for anything else that she really needed.

As Clyde stood at the telephone in a small outlying drug store and talked—the lonely proprietor buried in a silly romance among his pots and phials at the back—it seemed as though the Giant Efrit that had previously materialized in the silent halls of his brain, was once more here at his elbow—that he himself, cold and numb and fearsome, was being talked through—not actually talking himself.

Go to the lake which you visited with Sondra!

Get travel folders of the region there from either the Lycurgus House here or the depot.

Go to the south end of it and from there walk south, afterwards.

Pick a boat that will upset easily—one with a round bottom, such as those you have seen here at Crum Lake and up there.

Buy a new and different hat and leave that on the water—one that cannot be traced to you. You might even tear the lining out of it so that it cannot be traced.

Pack all of your things in your trunk here, but leave it, so that swiftly, in the event that anything goes wrong, you can return here and get it and depart.

And take only such things with you as will make it seem as though you were going for an outing to Twelfth Lake—not away, so that should you be sought at Twelfth Lake, it will look as though you had gone only there, not elsewhere.

Tell her that you intend to marry her, but *after* you return from this outing, not before.

And if necessary strike a light blow, so as to stun her—no more—so that falling in the water, she will drown the more easily.

Do not fear!

Do not be weak!

Walk through the woods by night, not by day—so that when seen again you will be in Three Mile Bay or Sharon—and can say that you came from Raquette or Long Lake south, or from Lycurgus north.

Use a false name and alter your handwriting as much as possible.

Assume that you will be successful.

And whisper, whisper—let your language be soft, your tone tender, loving, even. It must be, if you are to win her to your will now.

So the Efrit of his own darker self.

# Chapter XLVI

$A$ ND THEN at noon on Tuesday, July sixth, the station platform of the railroad running from Fonda to Utica, with
Roberta stepping down from the train which came south
from Biltz to await Clyde, for the train that was to take them
to Utica was not due for another half hour. And fifteen minutes later Clyde himself coming from a side street and approaching the station from the south, from which position
Roberta could not see him but from where, after turning the
west corner of the depot and stationing himself behind a pile
of crates, he could see her. How thin and pale indeed! By
contrast with Sondra, how illy-dressed in the blue traveling
suit and small brown hat with which she had equipped herself
for this occasion—the promise of a restricted and difficult life
as contrasted with that offered by Sondra. And she was thinking of compelling him to give up Sondra in order to marry
her, and from which union he might never be able to extricate himself until such time as would make Sondra and all she
represented a mere recollection. The difference between the
attitudes of these two girls—Sondra with everything offering
all—asking nothing of him; Roberta, with nothing, asking all.

A feeling of dark and bitter resentment swept over him and
he could not help but feel sympathetic toward that unknown
man at Pass Lake and secretly wish that he had been successful. Perhaps he, too, had been confronted by a situation just
like this. And perhaps he had done right, too, after all, and
that was why it had not been found out. His nerves twitched.
His eyes were somber, resentful and yet nervous. Could it not
happen again successfully in this case?

But here he was now upon the same platform with her as
the result of her persistent and illogical demands, and he must
be thinking how, and boldly, he must carry out the plans
which, for four days, or ever since he had telephoned her, and
in a dimmer way for the ten preceding those, he had been
planning. This settled course must not be interfered with
now. He must act! He must not let fear influence him to anything less than he had now planned.

And so it was that he now stepped forth in order that she might see him, at the same time giving her a wise and seemingly friendly and informative look as if to say, "You see I am here." But behind the look! If only she could have pierced beneath the surface and sensed that dark and tortured mood, how speedily she would have fled. But now seeing him actually present, a heavy shadow that was lurking in her eyes lifted, the somewhat down-turned corners of her mouth reversed themselves, and without appearing to recognize him, she nevertheless brightened and at once proceeded to the window to purchase her ticket to Utica, as he had instructed her to do.

And she was now thinking that at last, at last he had come. And he was going to take her away. And hence a kind of gratefulness for this welling up in her. For they were to be together for seven or eight months at the least. And while it might take tact and patience to adjust things, still it might and probably could be done. From now on she must be the very soul of caution—not do or say anything that would irritate him in any way, since naturally he would not be in the best mood because of this. But he must have changed some—perhaps he was seeing her in a more kindly light—sympathizing with her a little, since he now appeared at last to have most gracefully and genially succumbed to the unavoidable. And at the same time noting his light gray suit, his new straw hat, his brightly polished shoes and the dark tan suitcase and (strange, equivocal, frivolous erraticism of his in this instance) the tripod of a recently purchased camera together with his tennis racquet in its canvas case strapped to the side—more than anything to conceal the initials C.G.—she was seized with much of her old-time mood and desire in regard to his looks and temperament. He was still, and despite his present indifference to her, her Clyde.

Having seen her secure her ticket, he now went to get his own, and then, with another knowing look in her direction, which said that everything was now all right, he returned to the eastern end of the platform, while she returned to her position at the forward end.

(*Why was that old man in that old brown winter suit and hat and carrying that bird cage in a brown paper looking at him so? Could he sense anything? Did he know him? Had he ever worked in Lycurgus or seen him before?*)

He was going to buy a second straw hat in Utica to-day—he must remember that—a straw hat with a Utica label, which he would wear instead of his present one. Then, when she was not looking, he would put the old one in his bag with his other things. That was why he would have to leave her for a little while after they reached Utica—at the depot or library or somewhere—perhaps as was his first plan, take her to some small hotel somewhere and register as Mr. and Mrs. Carl Graham or Clifford Golden or Gehring (there was a girl in the factory by that name) so if they were ever traced in any way, it would be assumed that she had gone away with some man of that name.

(*That whistle of a train afar off. It must be coming now. His watch said twelve-twenty-seven.*)

And again he must decide what his manner toward her in Utica must be—whether very cordial or the opposite. For over the telephone, of course, he had talked very soft and genial-like because he had to. Perhaps it would be best to keep that up, otherwise she might become angry or suspicious or stubborn and that would make it hard.

(*Would that train never get here?*)

At the same time it was going to be very hard on him to be so very pleasant when, after all, she was driving him as she was—expecting him to do all that she was asking him to do and yet be nice to her. Damn! And yet if he weren't?—Supposing she should sense something of his thoughts in connection with this—really refuse to go through with it this way and spoil his plans.

(*If only his knees and hands wouldn't tremble so at times.*)

But no, how was she to be able to detect anything of that kind, when he himself had not quite made up his mind as to whether he would be able to go through with it or not? He only knew he was not going away with her, and that was all there was to that. He might not upset the boat, as he had decided on the day before, but just the same he was not going away with her.

But here now was the train. And there was Roberta lifting her bag. Was it too heavy for her in her present state? It probably was. Well, too bad. It was very hot to-day, too. At any rate he would help her with it later, when they were where no one could see them. She was looking toward him to be sure he was getting on—so like her these days, in her suspicious, doubtful mood in regard to him. But here was a seat in the rear of the car on the shady side, too. That was not so bad. He would settle himself comfortably and look out. For just outside Fonda, a mile or two beyond, was that same Mohawk that ran through Lycurgus and past the factory, and along the banks of which the year before, he and Roberta had walked about this time. But the memory of that being far from pleasant now, he turned his eyes to a paper he had bought, and behind which he could shield himself as much as possible, while he once more began to observe the details of the more inward scene which now so much more concerned him—the nature of the lake country around Big Bittern, which ever since that final important conversation with Roberta over the telephone, had been interesting him more than any other geography of the world.

For on Friday, after the conversation, he had stopped in at the Lycurgus House and secured three different folders relating to hotels, lodges, inns and other camps in the more remote region beyond Big Bittern and Long Lake. (If only there were some way to get to one of those completely deserted lakes described by that guide at Big Bittern—only, perhaps, there might not be any rowboats on any of these lakes at all! And again on Saturday, had he not secured four more circulars from the rack at the depot (they were in his pocket now)? Had they not proved how many small lakes and inns there were along this same railroad, which ran north to Big Bittern, to which he and Roberta might resort for a day or two if she would—a night, anyhow, before going to Big Bittern and Grass Lake—had he not noted that in particular—a beautiful lake it had said—near the station, and with at least three attractive lodges or country home inns where two could stay for as low as twenty dollars a week. That meant that two could stay for one night surely for as little as five dollars. It must be so surely—and so he was going to say to her, as he had already planned these several days, that she needed a little rest before going away to a strange place. That it would not cost very much—about fifteen dollars for fares and all, so the circulars said—if they went to Grass Lake for a night—this same night after reaching Utica—or on the morrow, anyhow. And he would have to picture it all to her as a sort of honeymoon journey—a little pleasant outing—before getting married. And it would not do to succumb to any plan of hers to get married before they did this—that would never do.

(*Those five birds winging toward that patch of trees over there—below that hill.*)

It certainly would not do to go direct to Big Bittern from Utica for a boat ride—just one day—seventy miles. That would not sound right to her, or to any one. It would make her suspicious, maybe. It might be better, since he would have to get away from her to buy a hat in Utica, to spend this first night there at some inexpensive, inconspicuous hotel, and once there, suggest going up to Grass Lake. And from there they could go to Big Bittern in the morning. He could say that Big Bittern was nicer—or that they would go down to Three Mile Bay—a hamlet really as he knew—where they could be married, but en route stop at Big Bittern as a sort of lark. He would say that he wanted to show her the lake—take some pictures of her and himself. He had brought his camera for that and for other pictures of Sondra later.

The blackness of this plot of his!

(*Those nine black and white cows on that green hillside.*)

But again, strapping that tripod along with his tennis racquet to the side of his suitcase, might not that cause people to imagine that they were passing tourists from some distant point, maybe, and if they both disappeared, well, then, they were not people from anywhere around here, were they? Didn't the guide say that the water in the lake was all of seventy-five feet deep—like that water at Pass Lake? And as for Roberta's grip—oh, yes, what about that? He hadn't even thought about that as yet, really.

(*Those three automobiles out there running almost as fast as this train.*)

Well, in coming down from Grass Lake after one night there (he could say that he was going to marry her at Three Mile Bay at the north end of Greys Lake, where a minister lived whom he had met), he would induce her to leave her

bag at that Gun Lodge station, where they took the bus over
to Big Bittern, while he took his with him. He could just say
to some one—the boatman, maybe, or the driver, that he was
taking his camera in his bag, and ask where the best views
were. Or maybe a lunch. Was that not a better idea—to take
a lunch and so deceive Roberta, too, perhaps? And that would
tend to mislead the driver, also, would it not? People did
carry cameras in bags, when they went out on lakes, at times.
At any rate it was most necessary for him to carry his bag in
this instance. Else why the plan to go south to that island and
from thence through the woods?

( *Oh, the grimness and the terror of this plan! Could he really
execute it?* )

But that strange cry of that bird at Big Bittern. He had not
liked that, or seeing that guide up there who might remember him now. He had not talked to him at all—had not even
gotten out of the car, but had only looked out at him through
the window; and in so far as he could recall the guide had not
even once looked at him—had merely talked to Grant
Cranston and Harley Baggott, who had gotten out and had
done all the talking. But supposing this guide should be there
and remember him? But how could that be when he really
had not seen him? This guide would probably not remember
him at all—might not even be there. But why should his
hands and face be damp all the time now—wet almost, and
cold—his knees shaky?

( *This train was following the exact curve of this stream—and
last summer he and Roberta. But no—* )

As soon as they reached Utica now this was the way he would
do—and must keep it well in mind and not get rattled in any
way. He must not—he must not. He must let her walk up the
street before him, say a hundred feet or so between them, so
that no one would think he was following her, of course. And
then when they were quite alone somewhere he would catch up
with her and explain all about this—be very nice as though he
cared for her as much as ever now—he would have to—if he
were to get her to do as he wanted. And then—and then, oh,
yes, have her wait while he went for that extra straw hat that he
was going to—well, leave on the water, maybe. And the oars,
too, of course. And her hat—and—well—

(*The long, sad sounding whistle of this train. Damn. He was getting nervous already.*)

But before going to the hotel, he must go back to the depot and put his new hat in the bag, or better yet, carry it while he looked for the sort of hotel he wanted, and then, before going to Roberta, take the hat and put it in his bag. Then he would go and find her and have her come to the entrance of the hotel he had found and wait for him, while he got the bags. And, of course, if there was no one around or very few, they would enter together, only she could wait in the ladies' parlor somewhere, while he went and registered as Charles Golden, maybe, this time. And then, well, in the morning, if she agreed, or to-night, for that matter, if there were any trains—he would have to find out about that—they could go up to Grass Lake in separate cars until they were past Twelfth Lake and Sharon, at any rate.

(*The beautiful Cranston Lodge there and Sondra.*)

And then—and then—

(*That big red barn and that small white house near it. And that wind-mill. So like those houses and barns that he had seen out there in Illinois and Missouri. And Chicago, too.*)

And at the same time Roberta in her car forward thinking that Clyde had not appeared so very unfriendly to her. To be sure, it was hard on him, making him leave Lycurgus in this way, and when he might be enjoying himself as he wished to. But on the other hand, here was she—and there was no other way for her to be. She must be very genial and yet not put herself forward too much or in his way. And yet she must not be too receding or weak, either, for, after all, Clyde was the one who had placed her in this position. And it was only fair, and little enough for him to do. She would have a baby to look after in the future, and all that trouble to go through with from now on. And later, she would have to explain to her parents this whole mysterious proceeding, which covered her present disappearance and marriage, if Clyde really did marry her now. But she must insist upon that—and soon—in Utica, perhaps—certainly at the very next place they went to —and get a copy of her marriage certificate, too, and keep it for her own as well as the baby's sake. He could get a divorce as he pleased after that. She would still be Mrs. Griffiths.

And Clyde's baby and hers would be a Griffiths, too. That was something.

(*How beautiful the little river was. It reminded her of the Mohawk and the walks she and he had taken last summer when they first met. Oh, last summer! And now this!*)

And they would settle somewhere—in one or two rooms, no doubt. Where, she wondered—in what town or city? How far away from Lycurgus or Biltz—the farther from Biltz the better, although she would like to see her mother and father again, and soon—as soon as she safely could. But what matter, as long as they were going away together and she was to be married?

Had he noticed her blue suit and little brown hat? And had he thought she looked at all attractive compared to those rich girls with whom he was always running? She must be very tactful—not irritate him in any way. But—oh, the happy life they could have if only—if only he cared for her a little—just a little . . .

And then Utica, and on a quiet street Clyde catching up with Roberta, his expression a mixture of innocent geniality and good-will, tempered by worry and opposition, which was really a mask for the fear of the deed that he himself was contemplating—his power to execute it—the consequences in case he failed.

# Chapter XLVII

A ND THEN, as planned that night between them—a trip to
Grass Lake the next morning in separate cars, but
which, upon their arrival and to his surprise, proved to be so
much more briskly tenanted than he anticipated. He was very
much disturbed and frightened by the evidence of so much
active life up here. For he had fancied this, as well as Big Bittern, would be all but deserted. Yet here now, as both could
see, it was the summer seat and gathering place of some small
religious organization or group—the Winebrennarians of
Pennsylvania—as it proved, with a tabernacle and numerous
cottages across the lake from the station. And Roberta at once
exclaiming:

"Now, there, isn't that cute? Why couldn't we be married
over there by the minister of that church?"

And Clyde, puzzled and shaken by this sudden and highly
unsatisfactory development, at once announced: "Why,
sure—I'll go over after a bit and see," yet his mind busy with
schemes for circumventing her. He would take her out in a
boat after registering and getting settled and remain too long.
Or should a peculiarly remote and unobserved spot be found
. . . but no, there were too many people here. The lake was
not large enough, and probably not very deep. It was black or
dark like tar, and sentineled to the east and north by tall, dark
pines—the serried spears of armed and watchful giants, as
they now seemed to him—ogres almost—so gloomy, suspicious and fantastically erratic was his own mood in regard to
all this. But still there were too many people—as many as ten
on the lake.

The weirdness of it.

The difficulty.

But whisper:—one could not walk from here through any
woods to Three Mile Bay. Oh, no. That was all of thirty miles
to the south now. And besides this lake was less lonely—probably continually observed by members of this religious group.
Oh, no—he must say—he must say—but what—could he say?
That he had inquired, and that no license could be procured

here? Or that the minister was away, or that he required certain identifications which he did not have—or—or, well, well—anything that would serve to still Roberta until such hour tomorrow, as the train south from here left for Big Bittern and Sharon, where, of course, they would surely be married.

Why should she be so insistent? And why, anyhow, and except for her crass determination to force him in this way, should he be compelled to track here and there with her—every hour—every minute of which was torture—an unending mental crucifixion really, when, if he were but rid of her! Oh, Sondra, Sondra, if but now from your high estate, you might bend down and aid me. No more lies! No more suffering! No more misery of any kind!

But instead, more lies. A long and aimless and pestilential search for water-lilies, which because of his own restless mood, bored Roberta as much as it did him. For why, she was now thinking to herself as they rowed about, this indifference to this marriage possibility, which could have been arranged before now and given this outing the dream quality it would and should have had, if only—if only he had arranged for everything in Utica, even as she had wanted. But this waiting—evasion—and so like Clyde, his vacillating, indefinite, uncertain mood, always. She was beginning to wonder now as to his intentions again—whether really and truly he did intend to marry her as he had promised. To-morrow, or the next day at most, would show. So why worry now?

And then the next day at noon, Gun Lodge and Big Bittern itself and Clyde climbing down from the train at Gun Lodge and escorting Roberta to the waiting bus, the while he assured her that since they were coming back this way, it would be best if she were to leave her bag here, while he, because of his camera as well as the lunch done up at Grass Lake and crowded into his suitcase, would take his own with him, because they would lunch on the lake. But on reaching the bus, he was dismayed by the fact that the driver was the same guide whom he had heard talk at Big Bittern. What if it should prove now that this guide had seen and remembered him! Would he not at least recall the handsome Finchley car—Bertine and Stuart on the front seat—himself and Sondra at the back—Grant and that Harley Baggott talking to him outside?

At once that cold perspiration that had marked his more nervous and terrified moods for weeks past, now burst forth on his face and hands. Of what had he been thinking, anyhow? How planning? In God's name, how expect to carry a thing like this through, if he were going to think so poorly? It was like his failing to wear his cap from Lycurgus to Utica, or at least getting it out of his bag before he tried to buy that straw hat; it was like not buying the straw hat before he went to Utica at all.

Yet the guide did not remember him, thank God! On the contrary he inquired rather curiously, and as of a total stranger: "Goin' over to the lodge at Big Bittern? First time up here?" And Clyde, enormously relieved and yet really tremulous, replied: "Yes," and then in his nervous excitement asked: "Many people over there to-day?" a question which the moment he had propounded it, seemed almost insane. Why, why, of all questions, should he ask that? Oh, God, would his silly, self-destructive mistakes never cease?

So troubled was he indeed, now, that he scarcely heard the guide's reply, or, if at all, as a voice speaking from a long way off. "Not so many. About seven or eight, I guess. We did have about thirty over the Fourth, but the most o' them went down yesterday."

The stillness of these pines lining this damp yellow road along which they were traveling; the cool and the silence; the dark shadows and purple and gray depths and nooks in them, even at high noon. If one were slipping away at night or by day, who would encounter one here? A blue-jay far in the depths somewhere uttered its metallic shriek; a field sparrow, tremulous upon some distant twig, filled the silver shadows with its perfect song. And Roberta, as this heavy, covered bus crossed rill and thin stream, and then rough wooden bridges here and there, commented on the clarity and sparkle of the water: "Isn't that wonderful in there? Do you hear the tinkling of that water, Clyde? Oh, the freshness of this air!"

And yet she was going to die so soon!

God!

But supposing now, at Big Bittern—the lodge and boathouse there—there were many people. Or that the lake, peradventure, was literally dotted with those that were there

—all fishermen and all fishing here and there, each one separate and alone—no privacy or a deserted spot anywhere. And
how strange he had not thought of that. This lake was probably not nearly as deserted as he had imagined, or would not
be to-day, any more than Grass Lake had proved. And then
what?

Well, flight then—flight—and let it go at that. This strain
was too much—hell—he would die, thinking thoughts like
these. How could he have dreamed to better his fortunes by
any so wild and brutal a scheme as this anyhow—to kill and
then run away—or rather to kill and pretend that he and she
had drowned—while he—the real murderer—slipped away to
life and happiness. What a horrible plan! And yet how else?
How? Had he not come all this way to do this? And was he
going to turn back now?

And all this time Roberta at his side was imagining that
she was not going to anything but marriage—to-morrow
morning sure; and now only to the passing pleasure of seeing this beautiful lake of which he had been talking—talking, as though it were something more important and
delectable than any that had as yet been in her or his life for
that matter.

But now the guide was speaking again, and to him: "You're
not mindin' to stay over, I suppose. I see you left the young
lady's bag over there." He nodded in the direction of Gun
Lodge.

"No, we're going on down to-night—on that 8:10. You
take people over to that?"

"Oh, sure."

"They said you did—at Grass Lake."

But now why should he have added that reference to Grass
Lake, for that showed that he and Roberta had been there before coming here. But this fool with his reference to "the
young lady's bag!" And leaving it at Gun Lodge. The Devil!
Why shouldn't he mind his own business? Or why should he
have decided that he and Roberta were not married? Or had
he so decided? At any rate, why such a question when they
were carrying two bags and he had brought one? Strange!
The effrontery! How should he know or guess or what? But
what harm could it do—married or unmarried? If she were

not found—"married or unmarried" would make no difference, would it? And if she were, and it was discovered that she
was not married, would that not prove that she was off with
some one else? Of course! So why worry over that now?

And Roberta asking: "Are there any hotels or boarding
houses on the lake besides this one we're going to?"

"Not a one, miss, outside o' the inn that we're goin' to.
There was a crowd of young fellers and girls campin' over on
the east shore, yisterday, I believe, about a mile from the
inn—but whether they're there now or not, I dunno. Ain't
seen none of 'em to-day."

A crowd of young fellows and girls! For God's sake! And
might not they now be out on the water—all of them—
rowing—or sailing—or what? And he here with her! Maybe
some of them from Twelfth Lake! Just as he and Sondra and
Harriet and Stuart and Bertine had come up two weeks before—some of them friends of the Cranstons, Harriets, Finchleys or others who had come up here to play and who would
remember him, of course. And again, then, there must be a
road to the east of this lake. And all this knowledge and their
presence there now might make this trip of his useless. Such
silly plotting! Such pointless planning as this—when at least
he might have taken more time—chosen a lake still farther
away and should have—only so tortured had he been for
these last many days, that he could scarcely think how to
think. Well, all he could do now was to go and see. If there
were many he must think of some way to row to some real
lonely spot or maybe turn and return to Grass Lake—or
where? Oh, what could or would he do—if there were many
over here?

But just then a long aisle of green trees giving out at the far
end as he now recalled upon a square of lawn, and the lake itself, the little inn with its pillared verandah, facing the dark
blue waters of Big Bittern. And that low, small red-roofed
boathouse to the right on the water that he had seen before
when he was here. And Roberta exclaiming on sight, "Oh, it is
pretty, isn't it—just beautiful." And Clyde surveying that dark,
low island in the distance, to the south, and seeing but few
people about—none on the lake itself—exclaiming nervously,
"Yes, it is, you bet." But feeling half choked as he said it.

And now the host of the inn himself appearing and approaching—a medium-sized, red-faced, broad-shouldered man who was saying most intriguingly, "Staying over for a few days?"

But Clyde, irritated by this new development and after paying the guide a dollar, replying crustily and irritably, "No, no—just came over for the afternoon. We're going on down to-night."

"You'll be staying over for dinner then, I suppose? The train doesn't leave till eight fifteen."

"Oh, yes—that's so. Sure. Yes, well, in that case, we will." . . . For, of course, Roberta on her honeymoon—the day before her wedding and on a trip like this, would be expecting her dinner. Damn this stocky, red-faced fool, anyway.

"Well, then, I'll just take your bag and you can register. Your wife'll probably be wanting to freshen up a bit anyway."

He led the way, bag in hand, although Clyde's greatest desire was to snatch it from him. For he had not expected to register here—nor leave his bag either. And would not. He would recapture it and hire a boat. But on top of that, being compelled "for the register's sake," as Boniface phrased it, to sign Clifford Golden and wife—before he could take his bag again.

And then to add to the nervousness and confusion engendered by all this, thoughts as to what additional developments or persons, even, he might encounter before leaving on his climacteric errand—Roberta announcing that because of the heat and the fact that they were coming back to dinner, she would leave her hat and coat—a hat in which he had already seen the label of Braunstein in Lycurgus—and which at the time caused him to meditate as to the wisdom of leaving or extracting it. But he had decided that perhaps afterwards—afterwards—if he should really do this—it might not make any difference whether it was there or not. Was she not likely to be identified anyhow, if found, and if not found, who was to know who she was?

In a confused and turbulent state mentally, scarcely realizing the clarity or import of any particular thought or movement or act now, he took up his bag and led the way to the boathouse platform. And then, after dropping the bag into the boat, asking of the boathouse keeper if he knew where the best views were, that he wanted to photograph them. And this done—the meaningless explanation over, assisting Roberta (an almost nebulous figure, she now seemed, stepping down into an insubstantial rowboat upon a purely ideational lake), he now stepped in after her, seating himself in the center and taking the oars.

The quiet, glassy, iridescent surface of this lake that now to both seemed, not so much like water as oil—like molten glass that, of enormous bulk and weight, resting upon the substantial earth so very far below. And the lightness and freshness and intoxication of the gentle air blowing here and there, yet scarcely rippling the surface of the lake. And the softness and furry thickness of the tall pines about the shore. Everywhere pines—tall and spearlike. And above them the humped backs of the dark and distant Adirondacks beyond. Not a rower to be seen. Not a house or cabin. He sought to distinguish the camp of which the guide had spoken. He could not. He sought to distinguish the voices of those who might be there—or any voices. Yet, except for the lock-lock of his own oars as he rowed and the voice of the boathouse keeper and, the guide in converse two hundred, three hundred, five hundred, a thousand feet behind, there was no sound.

"Isn't it still and peaceful?" It was Roberta talking. "It seems to be so restful here. I think it's beautiful, truly, so much more beautiful than that other lake. These trees are so tall, aren't they? And those mountains. I was thinking all the way over how cool and silent that road was, even if it was a little rough."

"Did you talk to any one in the inn there just now?"

"Why, no; what makes you ask?"

"Oh, I thought you might have run into some one. There don't seem to be very many people up here to-day, though, does there?"

"No, I don't see any one on the lake. I saw two men in that billiard room at the back there, and there was a girl in the ladies' room, that was all. Isn't this water cold?" She had put her hand over the side and was trailing it in the blue-black ripples made by his oars.

"Is it? I haven't felt it yet."

He paused in his rowing and put out his hand, then resumed. He would not row directly to that island to the south.
It was—too far—too early. She might think it odd. Better a
little delay. A little time in which to think—a little while in
which to reconnoiter. Roberta would be wanting to eat her
lunch (her lunch!) and there was a charming looking point of
land there to the west about a mile further on. They could go
there and eat first—or she could—for he would not be eating
to-day. And then—and then——

She was looking at the very same point of land that he
was—a curved horn of land that bent to the south and yet
reached quite far out into the water and combed with tall
pines. And now she added:

"Have you any spot in mind, dear, where we could stop
and eat? I'm getting a little hungry, aren't you?" (If she
would only not call him *dear*, here and now!)

The little inn and the boathouse to the north were growing momentarily smaller,—looking now, like that other
boathouse and pavilion on Crum Lake the day he had first
rowed there, and when he had been wishing that he might
come to such a lake as this in the Adirondacks, dreaming of
such a lake—and wishing to meet such a girl as Roberta—
then—— And overhead was one of those identical woolly
clouds that had sailed above him at Crum Lake on that fate-
ful day.

The horror of this effort!

They might look for water-lilies here to-day to kill time a
little, before—to kill time . . . to kill, (God)—he must quit
thinking of that, if he were going to do it at all. He needn't
be thinking of it now, at any rate.

At the point of land favored by Roberta, into a minute protected bay with a small, curved, honey-colored beach, and
safe from all prying eyes north or east. And then he and she
stepping out normally enough. And Roberta, after Clyde had
extracted the lunch most cautiously from his bag, spreading it
on a newspaper on the shore, while he walked here and there,
making strained and yet admiring comments on the beauty of
the scene—the pines and the curve of this small bay, yet
thinking—thinking, thinking of the island farther on and the
bay below that again somewhere, where somehow, and in the

face of a weakening courage for it, he must still execute this grim and terrible business before him—not allow this carefully planned opportunity to go for nothing—if—if—he were to not really run away and leave all that he most desired to keep.

And yet the horror of this business and the danger, now that it was so close at hand—the danger of making a mistake of some kind—if nothing more, of not upsetting the boat right—of not being able to—to—oh, God! And subsequently, maybe, to be proved to be what he would be—then—a murderer. Arrested! Tried. (He could not, he would not, go through with it. No, no, no!)

And yet Roberta, sitting here with him now on the sand, feeling quite at peace with all the world as he could see. And she was beginning to hum a little, and then to make advisory and practical references to the nature of their coming adventure together—their material and financial state from now on—how and where they would go from here—Syracuse, most likely—since Clyde seemed to have no objection to that—and what, once there, they would do. For Roberta had heard from her brother-in-law, Fred Gabel, of a new collar and shirt factory that was just starting up in Syracuse. Might it not be possible for Clyde, for the time being at least, to get himself a position with that firm at once? And then later, when her own worst trouble was over, might not she connect herself with the same company, or some other? And temporarily, since they had so little money, could they not take a small room together somewhere in some family home, or if he did not like that, since they were by no means so close temperamentally as they once had been, then two small adjoining rooms, maybe. She could still feel his unrelenting opposition under all this present show of courtesy and consideration.

And he thinking, Oh, well, what difference such talk now? And whether he agreed or whether he did not. What difference since he was not going—or she either—that way. Great God! But here he was talking as though to-morrow she would be here still. And she would not be.

If only his knees would not tremble so; his hands and face and body continue so damp.

And after that, farther on down the west shore of this small lake in this little boat, to that island, with Clyde looking nervously and wearily here and there to see that there was no one—no one—not anywhere in sight on land or water—no one. It was so still and deserted here, thank God. Here—or anywhere near here might do, really,—if only he had the courage so to do now, which he had not,—yet. Roberta trailing her hand in the water, asking him if he thought they might find some water-lilies or wild flowers somewhere on shore. Water-lilies! Wild flowers! And he convincing himself as he went that there were no roads, cabins, tents, paths, anything in the form of a habitation among these tall, close, ranking pines—no trace of any little boat on the widespread surface of this beautiful lake on this beautiful day. Yet might there not be some lone, solitary hunter and trapper or guide or fisherman in these woods or along these banks? Might there not be? And supposing there were one here now somewhere? And watching!

Fate!

Destruction!

Death! Yet no sound and no smoke. Only—only—these tall, dark, green pines—spear-shaped and still, with here and there a dead one—ashen pale in the hard afternoon sun, its gaunt, sapless arms almost menacingly outstretched.

Death!

And the sharp metallic cry of a blue-jay speeding in the depths of these woods. Or the lone and ghostly tap-tap-tap of some solitary woodpecker, with now and then the red line of a flying tanager, the yellow and black of a yellow-shouldered blackbird.

"Oh, the sun shines bright in my old Kentucky home."

It was Roberta singing cheerfully, one hand in the deep blue water.

And then a little later—"I'll be there Sunday if you will," one of the popular dance pieces of the day.

And then at last, after fully an hour of rowing, brooding, singing, stopping to look at some charming point of land, reconnoitering some receding inlet which promised water-lilies, and with Roberta already saying that they must watch the time and not stay out too long,—the bay, south of the island itself—a beautiful and yet most funereally pine-encircled and land delimited bit of water—more like a smaller lake, connected by an inlet or passage to the larger one, and yet itself a respectable body of water of perhaps twenty acres of surface and almost circular in form. The manner in which to the east, the north, the south, the west, even, except for the passage by which the island to the north of it was separated from the mainland, this pool or tarn was encircled by trees! And cat-tails and water-lilies here and there—a few along its shores. And somehow suggesting an especially arranged pool or tarn to which one who was weary of life and cares—anxious to be away from the strife and contentions of the world, might most wisely and yet gloomily repair.

And as they glided into this, this still dark water seemed to grip Clyde as nothing here or anywhere before this ever had—to change his mood. For once here he seemed to be fairly pulled or lured along into it, and having encircled its quiet banks, to be drifting, drifting—in endless space where was no end of anything—no plots—no plans—no practical problems to be solved—nothing. The insidious beauty of this place! Truly, it seemed to mock him—this strangeness—this dark pool, surrounded on all sides by those wonderful, soft, fir trees. And the water itself looking like a huge, black pearl cast by some mighty hand, in anger possibly, in sport or phantasy maybe, into the bosom of this valley of dark, green plush—and which seemed bottomless as he gazed into it.

And yet, what did it all suggest so strongly? Death! Death! More definitely than anything he had ever seen before. Death! But also a still, quiet, unprotesting type of death into which one, by reason of choice or hypnosis or unutterable weariness, might joyfully and gratefully sink. So quiet—so shaded—so serene. Even Roberta exclaimed over this. And he now felt for the first time the grip of some seemingly strong, and yet friendly sympathetic, hands laid firmly on his shoulders. The comfort of them! The warmth! The strength! For now they seemed to have a steadying effect on him and he liked them—their reassurance—their support. If only they would not be removed! If only they would remain always—the hands of this friend! For where had he ever known this comforting and almost tender sensation before in all his life?

Not anywhere—and somehow this calmed him and he seemed to slip away from the reality of all things.

To be sure, there was Roberta over there, but by now she had faded to a shadow or thought really, a form of illusion more vaporous than real. And while there was something about her in color, form that suggested reality—still she was very insubstantial—so very—and once more now he felt strangely alone. For the hands of the friend of firm grip had vanished also. And Clyde was alone, so very much alone and forlorn, in this somber, beautiful realm to which apparently he had been led, and then deserted. Also he felt strangely cold— the spell of this strange beauty overwhelming him with a kind of chill.

He had come here for what?

And he must do what?

Kill Roberta? Oh, no.

And again he lowered his head and gazed into the fascinating and yet treacherous depths of that magnetic, bluish, purple pool, which, as he continued to gaze, seemed to change its form kaleidoscopically to a large, crystalline ball. But what was that moving about in this crystal? A form! It came nearer—clearer—and as it did so, he recognized Roberta struggling and waving her thin white arms out of the water and reaching toward him! God! How terrible! The expression on her face! What in God's name was he thinking of anyway? Death! Murder!

And suddenly becoming conscious that his courage, on which he had counted so much this long while to sustain him here, was leaving him, and he instantly and consciously plumbing the depths of his being in a vain search to recapture it.

> Kit, kit, kit, Ca-a-a-ah!
> Kit, kit, kit, Ca-a-a-ah!
> Kit, kit, kit, Ca-a-a-ah!

(The weird, haunting cry of that unearthly bird again. So cold, so harsh! Here it was once more to startle him out of his soul flight into a realization of the real or unreal immediate problem with all of its torturesome angles that lay before him.)

He must face this thing! He must!

Kit, kit, kit, Ca-a-a-ah!
Kit, kit, kit, Ca-a-a-ah!

What was it sounding—a warning—a protest—condemnation? The same bird that had marked the very birth of this
miserable plan. For there it was now upon that dead tree—
that wretched bird. And now it was flying to another one—as
dead—a little farther inland and crying as it did so. God!

And then to the shore again in spite of himself. For Clyde,
in order to justify his having brought his bag, now must suggest that pictures of this be taken—and of Roberta—and of
himself, possibly—on land and water. For that would bring
her into the boat again, without his bag, which would be safe
and dry on land. And once on shore, actually pretending to be
seeking out various special views here and there, while he fixed
in his mind the exact tree at the base of which he might leave
his bag against his return—which must be soon now—must
be soon. They would not come on shore again together.
Never! Never! And that in spite of Roberta protesting that she
was getting tired; and did he not think they ought to be starting back pretty soon? It must be after five, surely. And Clyde,
assuring her that presently they would—after he had made one
or two more pictures of her in the boat with those wonderful
trees—that island and this dark water around and beneath her.

His wet, damp, nervous hands!
And his dark, liquid, nervous eyes, looking anywhere but at
her.

And then once more on the water again—about five hundred feet from shore, the while he fumbled aimlessly with the
hard and heavy and yet small camera that he now held, as the
boat floated out nearer the center. And then, at this point and
time looking fearfully about. For now—now—in spite of himself, the long evaded and yet commanding moment. And no
voice or figure or sound on shore. No road or cabin or
smoke! And the moment which he or something had planned
for him, and which was now to decide his fate at hand! The
moment of action—of crisis! All that he needed to do now
was to turn swiftly and savagely to one side or the other—leap

up—upon the left wale or right and upset the boat; or, failing
that, rock it swiftly, and if Roberta protested too much, strike
her with the camera in his hand, or one of the oars free at his
right. It could be done—it could be done—swiftly and simply, were he now of the mind and heart, or lack of it—with
him swimming swiftly away thereafter to freedom—to success—of course—to Sondra and happiness—a new and greater
and sweeter life than any he had ever known.

Yet why was he waiting now?

What was the matter with him, anyhow?

Why was he waiting?

At this cataclysmic moment, and in the face of the utmost,
the most urgent need of action, a sudden palsy of the will—
of courage—of hate or rage sufficient; and with Roberta from
her seat in the stern of the boat gazing at his troubled and
then suddenly distorted and fulgurous, yet weak and even unbalanced face—a face of a sudden, instead of angry, ferocious,
demoniac—confused and all but meaningless in its registration of a balanced combat between fear (a chemic revulsion
against death or murderous brutality that would bring death)
and a harried and restless and yet self-repressed desire to
do—to do—to do—yet temporarily unbreakable here and
now—a static between a powerful compulsion to do and yet
not to do.

And in the meantime his eyes—the pupils of the same
growing momentarily larger and more lurid; his face and body
and hands tense and contracted—the stillness of his position,
the balanced immobility of the mood more and more ominous, yet in truth not suggesting a brutal, courageous power
to destroy, but the imminence of trance or spasm.

And Roberta, suddenly noticing the strangeness of it all—
the something of eerie unreason or physical and mental inde-
termination so strangely and painfully contrasting with this
scene, exclaiming: "Why, Clyde! Clyde! What is it? Whatever
is the matter with you anyhow? You look so—so strange—
so—so— Why, I never saw you look like this before. What is
it?" And suddenly rising, or rather leaning forward, and by
crawling along the even keel, attempting to approach him,
since he looked as though he was about to fall forward into
the boat—or to one side and out into the water. And Clyde,

as instantly sensing the profoundness of his own failure, his own cowardice or inadequateness for such an occasion, as instantly yielding to a tide of submerged hate, not only for himself, but Roberta—her power—or that of life to restrain him in this way. And yet fearing to act in any way—being unwilling to—being willing only to say that never, never would he marry her—that never, even should she expose him, would he leave here with her to marry her—that he was in love with Sondra and would cling only to her—and yet not being able to say that even. But angry and confused and glowering. And then, as she drew near him, seeking to take his hand in hers and the camera from him in order to put it in the boat, he flinging out at her, but not even then with any intention to do other than free himself of her—her touch—her pleading—consoling sympathy—her presence forever—God!

Yet (the camera still unconsciously held tight) pushing at her with so much vehemence as not only to strike her lips and nose and chin with it, but to throw her back sidewise toward the left wale which caused the boat to careen to the very water's edge. And then he, stirred by her sharp scream, (as much due to the lurch of the boat, as the cut on her nose and lip), rising and reaching half to assist or recapture her and half to apologize for the unintended blow—yet in so doing completely capsizing the boat—himself and Roberta being as instantly thrown into the water. And the left wale of the boat as it turned, striking Roberta on the head as she sank and then rose for the first time, her frantic, contorted face turned to Clyde, who by now had righted himself. For she was stunned, horror-struck, unintelligible with pain and fear—her lifelong fear of water and drowning and the blow he had so accidentally and all but unconsciously administered.

"Help! Help!

"Oh, my God, I'm drowning, I'm drowning. Help! Oh, my God!

"Clyde, Clyde!"

And then the voice at his ear!

"But this—this—is not this that which you have been

thinking and wishing for this while—you in your great need? And behold! For despite your fear, your cowardice, this—this—has been done for you. An accident—an accident—an unintentional blow on your part is now saving you the labor of what you sought, and yet did not have the courage to do! But will you now, and when you need not, since it is an accident, by going to her rescue, once more plunge yourself in the horror of that defeat and failure which has so tortured you and from which this now releases you? You might save her. But again you might not! For see how she strikes about. She is stunned. She herself is unable to save herself and by her erratic terror, if you draw near her now, may bring about your own death also. But you desire to live! And her living will make your life not worth while from now on. Rest but a moment—a fraction of a minute! Wait—wait—ignore the pity of that appeal. And then—then— But there! Behold. It is over. She is sinking now. You will never, never see her alive any more—ever. And there is your own hat upon the water—as you wished. And upon the boat, clinging to that rowlock a veil belonging to her. Leave it. Will it not show that this was an accident?"

And apart from that, nothing—a few ripples—the peace and solemnity of this wondrous scene. And then once more the voice of that weird, contemptuous, mocking, lonely bird.

Kit, kit, kit, Ca-a-a-ah!
Kit, kit, kit, Ca-a-a-ah!
Kit, kit, kit, Ca-a-a-ah!

The cry of that devilish bird upon that dead limb—the weir-weir.

And then Clyde, with the sound of Roberta's cries still in his ears, that last frantic, white, appealing look in her eyes, swimming heavily, gloomily and darkly to shore. And the thought that, after all, he had not really killed her. No, no. Thank God for that. He had not. And yet (stepping up on the near-by bank and shaking the water from his clothes) had he? Or, had he not? For had he not refused to go to her rescue, and when he might have saved her, and when the fault for casting her in the water, however accidentally, was so truly his? And yet—and yet—

The dusk and silence of a closing day. A concealed spot in the depths of the same sheltering woods where alone and dripping, his dry bag near, Clyde stood, and by waiting, sought to dry himself. But in the interim, removing from the side of the bag the unused tripod of his camera and seeking an obscure, dead log farther in the woods, hiding it. Had any one seen? Was any one looking? Then returning and wondering as to the direction! He must go west and then south. He must not get turned about! But the repeated cry of that bird,—harsh, nerve shaking. And then the gloom, in spite of the summer stars. And a youth making his way through a dark, uninhabited wood, a dry straw hat upon his head, a bag in his hand, walking briskly and yet warily—south—south.

# BOOK THREE

# *Chapter I*

CATARAQUI COUNTY extending from the northernmost line of the village known as Three Mile Bay on the south to the Canadian border, on the north a distance of fifty miles. And from Senaschet and Indian Lakes on the east to the Rock and Scarf Rivers on the west—a width of thirty miles. Its greater portion covered by uninhabited forests and lakes, yet dotted here and there with such villages and hamlets as Koontz, Grass Lake, North Wallace, Brown Lake, with Bridgeburg, the county seat, numbering no less than two thousand souls of the fifteen thousand in the entire county. And the central square of the town occupied by the old and yet not ungraceful county courthouse, a cupola with a clock and some pigeons surmounting it, the four principal business streets of the small town facing it.

In the office of the County Coroner in the northeast corner of the building on Friday, July ninth, one Fred Heit, coroner, a large and broad-shouldered individual with a set of gray-brown whiskers such as might have graced a Mormon elder. His face was large and his hands and his feet also. And his girth was proportionate.

At the time that this presentation begins, about two-thirty in the afternoon, he was lethargically turning the leaves of a mail-order catalogue for which his wife had asked him to write. And while deciphering from its pages the price of shoes, jackets, hats, and caps for his five omnivorous children, a greatcoat for himself of soothing proportions, high collar, broad belt, large, impressive buttons chancing to take his eye, he had paused to consider regretfully that the family budget of three thousand dollars a year would never permit of so great luxury this coming winter, particularly since his wife, Ella, had had her mind upon a fur coat for at least three winters past.

However his thoughts might have eventuated on this occasion, they were interrupted by the whirr of a telephone bell.

"Yes, this is Mr. Heit speaking—Wallace Upham of Big

Bittern. Why, yes, go on, Wallace—young couple drowned—all right, just wait a minute——"

He turned to the politically active youth who drew a salary from the county under the listing of "secretary to the coroner"—"Get these points, Earl." Then into the telephone: "All right, Wallace, now give me all the facts—everything—yes. The body of the wife found but not that of the husband—yes—a boat upset on the south shore—yes—straw hat without any lining—yes—some marks about her mouth and eye—her coat and hat at the inn—yes—a letter in one of the pockets of the coat—addressed to who?—Mrs. Titus Alden, Biltz, Mimico County—yes—still dragging for the man's body, are they?—yes—no trace of him yet—I see. All right, Wallace—— Well—I'll tell you, Wallace, have them leave the coat and the hat just where they are. Let me see—it's two-thirty now. I'll be up on the four o'clock. The bus from the inn there meets that, doesn't it? Well, I'll be over on that, sure—— And, Wallace, I wish you'd write down the names of all present who saw the body brought up. What was that?—eighteen feet of water at least?—yes—a veil caught in one of the row-locks—yes—a brown veil—yes—sure, that's all—— Well, then have them leave everything just as found, Wallace, and I'll be right up. Yes. Wallace, thank you—Good-by."

Slowly Mr. Heit restored the receiver to the hook and as slowly arose from the capacious walnut-hued chair in which he sat, stroking his heavy whiskers, while he eyed Earl Newcomb, combination typist, record clerk, and what not.

"You got all that down, did you, Earl?"

"Yes, sir."

"Well, you better get your hat and coat and come along with me. We'll have to catch that 3:10. You can fill in a few subpœnas on the train. I should say you better take fifteen or twenty—to be on the safe side, and take the names of such witnesses as we can find on the spot. And you better call up Mrs. Heit and say 'taint likely I'll be home for dinner to-night or much before the down train. We may have to stay up there until to-morrow. You never can tell in these cases how they're going to turn out and it's best to be on the safe side."

Heit turned to a coat-room in one corner of the musty old room and extracted a large, soft-brimmed, straw hat, the downward curving edges of which seemed to heighten the really bland and yet ogreish effect of his protruding eyes and voluminous whiskers, and having thus equipped himself, said: "I'm just going in the sheriff's office a minute, Earl. You'd better call up the *Republican* and the *Democrat* and tell 'em about this, so they won't think we're slightin' 'em. Then I'll meet you down at the station." And he lumbered out.

And Earl Newcomb, a tall, slender, shock-headed young man of perhaps nineteen, and of a very serious, if at times be-fuddled, manner, at once seized a sheaf of subpœnas, and while stuffing these in his pocket, sought to get Mrs. Heit on the telephone. And then, after explaining to the newspapers about a reported double drowning at Big Bittern, he seized his own blue-banded straw hat, some two sizes too large for him, and hurried down the hall, only to encounter, opposite the wide-open office door of the district attorney, Zillah Saunders, spinster and solitary stenographer to the locally somewhat famous and mercurial Orville W. Mason, district at-torney. She was on her way to the auditor's office, but being struck by the preoccupation and haste of Mr. Newcomb, usu-ally so much more deliberate, she now called: "Hello, Earl. What's the rush? Where you going so fast?"

"Double drowning up at Big Bittern, we hear. Maybe something worse. Mr. Heit's going up and I'm going along. We have to make that 3:10."

"Who said so? Is it any one from here?"

"Don't know yet, but don't think so. There was a letter in the girl's pocket addressed to some one in Biltz, Mimico County, a Mrs. Alden. I'll tell you when we get back or I'll telephone you."

"My goodness, if it's a crime, Mr. Mason'll be interested, won't he?"

"Sure, I'll telephone him, or Mr. Heit will. If you see Bud Parker or Karel Badnell, tell 'em I had to go out of town, and call up my mother for me, will you, Zillah, and tell her, too. I'm afraid I won't have time."

"Sure I will, Earl."

"Thanks."

And, highly interested by this latest development in the or-dinary humdrum life of his chief, he skipped gayly and even eagerly down the south steps of the Cataraqui County Court-house, while Miss Saunders, knowing that her own chief was off on some business connected with the approaching County Republican Convention, and there being no one else in his office with whom she could communicate at this time, went on to the auditor's office, where it was possible to retail to any who might be assembled there, all that she had gathered concerning this seemingly important lake tragedy.

# Chapter II

THE INFORMATION obtained by Coroner Heit and his assistant was of a singular and disturbing character. In the
first instance, because of the disappearance of a boat and an
apparently happy and attractive couple bent on sight-seeing,
an early morning search, instigated by the inn-keeper of this
region, had revealed, in Moon Cove, the presence of the
overturned canoe, also the hat and veil. And immediately
such available employees, as well as guides and guests of the
Inn, as could be impressed, had begun diving into the waters
or by means of long poles equipped with hooks attempting to
bring one or both bodies to the surface. The fact, as reported
by Sim Shoop, the guide, as well as the innkeeper and the
boat-house lessee, that the lost girl was both young and attractive and her companion seemingly a youth of some
means, was sufficient to whet the interest of this lake group of
woodsmen and inn employees to a point which verged on
sorrow. And in addition, there was intense curiosity as to
how, on so fair and windless a day, so strange an accident
could have occurred.

But what created far more excitement after a very little time
was the fact that at high noon one of the men who trolled—
John Pole—a woodsman, was at last successful in bringing to
the surface Roberta herself, drawn upward by the skirt of her
dress, obviously bruised about the face—the lips and nose and
above and below the right eye—a fact which to those who
were assisting at once seemed to be suspicious. Indeed, John
Pole, who with Joe Rainer at the oars was the one who had
succeeded in bringing her to the surface, had exclaimed at
once on seeing her: "Why, the pore little thing! She don't
seem to weigh more'n nothin' at all. It's a wonder tuh me she
coulda sunk." And then reaching over and gathering her in
his strong arms, he drew her in, dripping and lifeless, while
his companions signaled to the other searchers, who came
swiftly. And putting back from her face the long, brown, thick
hair which the action of the water had swirled concealingly
across it, he had added: "I do declare, Joe! Looka here. It

does look like the child mighta been hit by somethin'! Looka here, Joe!" And soon the group of woodsmen and inn guests in their boats alongside were looking at the brownish-blue marks on Roberta's face.

And forthwith, even while the body of Roberta was being taken north to the boat-house, and the dragging for the body of the lost man was resumed, suspicions were being voiced in such phrases as: "Well, it looks kinda queer—them marks—an' all,—don't it? It's curious a boat like that coulda upset on a day like yesterday." "We'll soon know if he's down there or not!"; the feeling, following failure after hours of fruitless search for him, definitely coalescing at last into the conclusion that more than likely he was not down there at all—a hard and stirring thought to all.

Subsequent to this, the guide who had brought Clyde and Roberta from Gun Lodge conferring with the inn-keepers at Big Bittern and Grass Lake, it was factually determined: (1) that the drowned girl had left her bag at Gun Lodge whereas Clifford Golden had taken his with him; (2) that there was a disturbing discrepancy between the registration at Grass Lake and that at Big Bittern, the names Carl Graham and Clifford Golden being carefully discussed by the two inn-keepers and the identity of the bearer as to looks established; and (3) that the said Clifford Golden or Carl Graham had asked of the guide who had driven him over to Big Bittern whether there were many people on the lake that day. And thereafter the suspicions thus far engendered further coalescing into the certainty that there had been foul play. There was scarcely any doubt of it.

Immediately upon his arrival Coroner Heit was made to understand that these men of the north woods were deeply moved and in addition determined in their suspicions. They did not believe that the body of Clifford Golden or Carl Graham had ever sunk to the bottom of the lake. With the result that Heit on viewing the body of the unknown girl laid carefully on a cot in the boat-house, and finding her young and attractive, was strangely affected, not only by her looks but this circumambient atmosphere of suspicion. Worse yet, on retiring to the office of the manager of the inn, and being handed the letter found in the pocket of Roberta's coat, he

was definitely swayed in the direction of a somber and unshakable suspicion. For he read:

Grass Lake, N.Y., July 8th.
DEAREST MAMMA:
We're up here and we're going to be married, but this is for your
eyes alone. Please don't show it to papa or any one, for it mustn't
become known yet. I told you why at Christmas. And you're not to
worry or ask any questions or tell any one except just that you've
heard from me and know where I am—not anybody. And you
mustn't think I won't be getting along all right because I will be.
Here's a big hug and kiss for each cheek, mamma. Be sure and make
father understand that it's all right without telling him anything, or
Emily or Tom or Gifford, either, do you hear? I'm sending you nice,
big kisses.

Lovingly,
BERT.
P.S. This must be your secret and mine until I write you different
a little later on.

And in the upper right-hand corner of the paper, as well as on
the envelope, were printed the words: "Grass Lake Inn, Grass
Lake, N.Y., Jack Evans, Prop." And the letter had evidently
been written the morning after the night they had spent at
Grass Lake as Mr. and Mrs. Carl Graham.

The waywardness of young girls!

For plainly, as this letter indicated, these two had stayed together as man and wife at that inn when they were not as yet
married. He winced as he read, for he had daughters of his
own of whom he was exceedingly fond. But at this point he
had a thought. A quadrennial county election was impending,
the voting to take place the following November, at which
were to be chosen for three years more the entire roster of
county offices, his own included, and in addition this year a
county judge whose term was for six years. In August, some
six weeks further on, were to be held the county Republican
and Democratic conventions at which were to be chosen the
regular party nominees for these respective offices. Yet for no
one of these places, thus far, other than that of the county
judgeship, could the present incumbent of the office of district attorney possibly look forward with any hope, since already he had held the position of district attorney for two

consecutive terms, a length of office due to the fact that not only was he a good orator of the inland political stripe but also, as the chief legal official of the county, he was in a position to do one and another of his friends a favor. But now, unless he were so fortunate as to be nominated and subsequently elected to this county judgeship, defeat and political doldrums loomed ahead. For during all his term of office thus far, there had been no really important case in connection with which he had been able to distinguish himself and so rightfully and hopefully demand further recognition from the people. But this . . .

But now, as the Coroner shrewdly foresaw, might not this case prove the very thing to fix the attention and favor of the people upon one man—the incumbent district attorney—a close and helpful friend of his, thus far—and so sufficiently redound to his credit and strength, and through him to the party ticket itself, so that at the coming election all might be elected—the reigning district attorney thus winning for himself not only the nomination for but his election to the six-year term judgeship. Stranger things than this had happened in the political world.

Immediately he decided not to answer any questions in regard to this letter, since it promised a quick solution of the mystery of the perpetrator of the crime, if there had been one, plus exceptional credit in the present political situation to whosoever should appear to be instrumental in the same. At the same time he at once ordered Earl Newcomb, as well as the guide who had brought Roberta and Clyde to Big Bittern, to return to Gun Lodge station from where the couple had come and say that under no circumstances was the bag held there to be surrendered to any one save himself or a representative of the district attorney. Then, when he was about to telephone to Biltz to ascertain whether there was such a family as Alden possessing a daughter by the name of Bert, or possibly Alberta, he was most providentially, as it seemed to him, interrupted by two men and a boy, trappers and hunters of this region, who, accompanied by a crowd of those now familiar with the tragedy, were almost tumultuously ushered into his presence. For they had news—news of the utmost importance! As they now related, with many interruptions and corrections, at about five o'clock of the afternoon of the day on which Roberta was drowned, they were setting out from Three Mile Bay, some twelve miles south of Big Bittern, to hunt and fish in and near this lake. And, as they now unanimously testified, on the night in question, at about nine o'clock, as they were nearing the south shore of Big Bittern— perhaps three miles to the south of it—they had encountered a young man, whom they took to be some stranger making his way from the inn at Big Bittern south to the village at Three Mile Bay. He was a smartishly and decidedly well dressed youth for these parts, as they now said—wearing a straw hat and carrying a bag, and at the time they wondered why such a trip on foot and at such an hour since there was a train south early next morning which reached Three Mile Bay in an hour's time. And why, too, should he have been so startled at meeting them? For as they described it, on his encountering them in the woods thus, he had jumped back as though startled and worse—terrified—as though about to run. To be sure, the lantern one of them was carrying was turned exceedingly low, the moon being still bright, and they had walked quietly, as became men who were listening for wild life of any kind. At the same time, surely this was a perfectly safe part of the country, traversed for the most part by honest citizens such as themselves, and there was no need for a young man to jump as though he were seeking to hide in the brush. However, when the youth, Bud Brunig, who carried the light, turned it up the stranger seemed to recover his poise and after a moment in response to their "Howdy" had replied: "How do you do? How far is it to Three Mile Bay?" and they had replied, "About seven mile." And then he had gone on and they also, discussing the encounter.

And now, since the description of this youth tallied almost exactly with that given by the guide who had driven Clyde over from Gun Lodge, as well as that furnished by the innkeepers at Big Bittern and Grass Lake, it seemed all too plain that he must be the same youth who had been in that boat with the mysterious dead girl.

At once Earl Newcomb suggested to his chief that he be permitted to telephone to the one inn-keeper at Three Mile Bay to see if by any chance this mysterious stranger had been seen or had registered there. He had not. Nor apparently at that time had he been seen by any other than the three men. In fact, he had vanished as though into air, although by nightfall of this same day it was established that on the morning following the chance meeting of the men with the stranger, a youth of somewhat the same description and carrying a bag, but wearing a cap—not a straw hat—had taken passage for Sharon on the small lake steamer "Cygnus" plying between that place and Three Mile Bay. But again, beyond that point, the trail appeared to be lost. No one at Sharon, at least up to this time, seemed to recall either the arrival or departure of any such person. Even the captain himself, as he later testified, had not particularly noted his debarkation— there were some fourteen others going down the lake that day and he could not be sure of any one person.

But in so far as the group at Big Bittern was concerned, the conclusion slowly but definitely impressed itself upon all those present that whoever this individual was, he was an unmitigated villain—a reptilian villain! And forthwith there was doubled and trebled in the minds of all a most urgent desire that he be overtaken and captured. The scoundrel! The murderer! And at once there was broadcast throughout this region by word of mouth, telephone, telegraph, to such papers as *The Argus* and *Times-Union* of Albany, and *The Star* of Lycurgus, the news of this pathetic tragedy with the added hint that it might conceal a crime of the gravest character.

# Chapter III

CORONER HEIT, his official duties completed for the time being, found himself pondering, as he traveled south on the lake train, how he was to proceed farther. What was the next step he should take in this pathetic affair? For the coroner, as he had looked at Roberta before he left, was really deeply moved. She seemed so young and innocent-looking and pretty. The little blue serge dress lying heavily and clinging tightly to her, her very small hands folded across her breast, her warm, brown hair still damp from its twenty-four hours in the water, yet somehow suggesting some of the vivacity and passion that had invested her in life—all seemed to indicate a sweetness which had nothing to do with crime.

But deplorable as it might be, and undoubtedly was, there was another aspect of the case that more vitally concerned himself. Should he go to Biltz and convey to the Mrs. Alden of the letter the dreadful intelligence of her daughter's death, at the same time inquiring about the character and whereabouts of the man who had been with her, or should he proceed first to District Attorney Mason's office in Bridgeburg and having imparted to him all of the details of the case, allow that gentleman to assume the painful responsibility of devastating a probably utterly respectable home? For there was the political situation to be considered. And while he himself might act and so take personal credit, still there was this general party situation to be thought of. A strong man should undoubtedly head and so strengthen the party ticket this fall and here was the golden opportunity. The latter course seemed wiser. It would provide his friend, the district attorney, with his great chance. Arriving in Bridgeburg in this mood, he ponderously invaded the office of Orville W. Mason, the district attorney, who immediately sat up, all attention, sensing something of import in the coroner's manner.

Mason was a short, broad-chested, broad-backed and vigorous individual physically, but in his late youth had been so unfortunate as to have an otherwise pleasant and even arresting face marred by a broken nose, which gave to him a most unprepossessing, almost sinister, look. Yet he was far from sinister. Rather, romantic and emotional. His boyhood had been one of poverty and neglect, causing him in his later and somewhat more successful years to look on those with whom life had dealt more kindly as too favorably treated. The son of a poor farmer's widow, he had seen his mother put to such straits to make ends meet that by the time he reached the age of twelve he had surrendered nearly all of the pleasures of youth in order to assist her. And then, at fourteen, while skating, he had fallen and broken his nose in such a way as to forever disfigure his face. Thereafter, feeling himself handicapped in the youthful sorting contests which gave to other boys the female companions he most craved, he had grown exceedingly sensitive to the fact of his facial handicap. And this had eventually resulted in what the Freudians are accustomed to describe as a psychic sex scar.

At the age of seventeen, however, he had succeeded in interesting the publisher and editor of the Bridgeburg *Republican* to the extent that he was eventually installed as official local news-gatherer of the town. Later he came to be the Cataraqui County correspondent of such papers as the Albany *Times-Union* and the Utica *Star*, ending eventually at the age of nineteen with the privilege of studying law in the office of one ex-Judge Davis Richofer, of Bridgeburg. And a few years later, after having been admitted to the bar, he had been taken up by several county politicians and merchants who saw to it that he was sent to the lower house of the state legislature for some six consecutive years, where, by reason of a modest and at the same time shrewd and ambitious willingness to do as he was instructed, he attained favor with those at the capital while at the same time retaining the good will of his home-town sponsors. Later, returning to Bridgeburg and possessing some gifts of oratory, he was given, first, the position of assistant district attorney for four years, and following that elected auditor, and subsequently district attorney for two terms of four years each. Having acquired so high a position locally, he was able to marry the daughter of a local druggist of some means, and two children had been born to them.

In regard to this particular case he had already heard from

Miss Saunders all she knew of the drowning, and, like the coroner, had been immediately impressed with the fact that the probable publicity attendant on such a case as this appeared to be might be just what he needed to revive a wavering political prestige and might perhaps solve the problem of his future. At any rate he was most intensely interested. So that now, upon sight of Heit, he showed plainly the keen interest he felt in the case.

"Well, Colonel Heit?"

"Well, Orville, I'm just back from Big Bittern. It looks to me as though I've got a case for you now that's going to take quite a little of your time."

Heit's large eyes bulged and conveyed hints of much more than was implied by his non-committal opening remark.

"You mean that drowning up there?" returned the district attorney.

"Yes, sir. Just that," replied the coroner.

"You've some reason for thinking there's something wrong up there?"

"Well, the truth is, Orville, I think there's hardly a doubt that this is a case of murder." Heit's heavy eyes glowed somberly. "Of course, it's best to be on the safe side, and I'm only telling you this in confidence, because even yet I'm not absolutely positive that that young man's body may not be in the lake. But it looks mighty suspicious to me, Orville. There's been at least fifteen men up there in rowboats all day yesterday and to-day, dragging the south part of that lake. I had a number of the boys take soundings here and there, and the water ain't more than twenty-five feet deep at any point. But so far they haven't found any trace of him. They brought her up about one o'clock yesterday, after they'd been only dragging a few hours, and a mighty pretty girl she is too, Orville—quite young—not more than eighteen or twenty, I should say. But there are some very suspicious circumstances about it all that make me think that he ain't in there. In fact, I never saw a case that I thought looked more like a devilish crime than this."

As he said this, he began to search in the right-hand pocket of his well-worn and baggy linen suit and finally extracted Roberta's letter, which he handed his friend, drawing up a

chair and seating himself while the district attorney proceeded
to read.

"Well, this does look rather suspicious, don't it?" he announced, as he finished. "You say they haven't found him yet.
Well, have you communicated with this woman to see what
she knows about it?"

"No, Orville, I haven't," replied Heit, slowly and meditatively. "And I'll tell you why. The fact is, I decided up there
last night that this was something I had better talk over with
you before I did anything at all. You know what the political
situation here is just now. And how the proper handling of a
case like this is likely to affect public opinion this fall. And
while I certainly don't think we ought to mix politics in with
crime there certainly is no reason why we shouldn't handle
this in such a way as to make it count in our favor. And so I
thought I had better come and see you first. Of course, if you
want me to, Orville, I'll go over there. Only I was thinking
that perhaps it would be better for you to go, and find out
just who this fellow is and all about him. You know what a
case like this might mean from a political point of view, if only
we clean it up, and I know you're the one to do it, Orville."

"Thanks, Fred, thanks," replied Mason, solemnly, tapping
his desk with the letter and squinting at his friend. "I'm grateful to you for your opinion and you've outlined the very best
way to go about it, I think. You're sure no one outside yourself has seen this letter?"

"Only the envelope. And no one but Mr. Hubbard, the
proprietor of the inn up there, has seen that, and he told me
that he found it in her pocket and took charge of it for fear it
might disappear or be opened before I got there. He said he
had a feeling there might be something wrong the moment
he heard of the drowning. The young man had acted so nervous—strange-like, he said."

"Very good, Fred. Then don't say anything more about it
to any one for the present, will you? I'll go right over there,
of course. But what else did you find, anything?" Mr. Mason
was quite alive now, interrogative, dynamic, and a bit dictatorial in his manner, even to his old friend.

"Plenty, plenty," replied the coroner, most sagely and
solemnly. "There were some suspicious cuts or marks under

the girl's right eye and above the left temple, Orville, and
across the lip and nose, as though the poor little thing mighta
been hit by something—a stone or a stick or one of those oars
that they found floating up there. She's just a child yet,
Orville, in looks and size, anyhow—a very pretty girl—but
not as good as she might have been, as I'll show you
presently." At this point the coroner paused to extract a large
handkerchief and blow into it a very loud blast, brushing his
beard afterward in a most orderly way. "I didn't have time to
get a doctor up there and besides I'm going to hold the inquest down here Monday, if I can. I've ordered the Lutz boys
to go up there to-day and bring her body down. But the most
suspicious of all the evidence that has come to light so far,
Orville, is the testimony of two men and a boy who live up at
Three Mile Bay and who were walking up to Big Bittern on
Thursday night to hunt and fish. I had Earl take down their
names and subpœna 'em for the inquest next Monday."

And the coroner proceeded to detail their testimony about
their accidental meeting of Clyde.

"Well, well!" interjected the district attorney, thoroughly
interested.

"Then, another thing, Orville," continued the coroner, "I
had Earl telephone the Three Mile Bay people, the owner of
the hotel there as well as the postmaster and the town mar-
shal, but the only person who appears to have seen the young
man is the captain of that little steamboat that runs from
Three Mile Bay to Sharon. You know the man, I guess, Captain Mooney. I left word with Earl to subpœna him too. According to him, about eight-thirty Friday morning, or just
before his boat started for Sharon on its first trip, this same
young man, or some one very much like the description furnished, carrying a suitcase and wearing a cap—he had on a
straw hat when those three men met him—came on board
and paid his way to Sharon and got off there. Good-looking
young chap, the captain says. Very spry and well-dressed,
more like a young society man than anything else, and very
stand-offish."

"Yes, yes," commented Mason.

"I also had Earl telephone the people at Sharon—whoever
he could reach—to see if he had been seen there getting off,

but up to the time I left last night no one seemed to remember him. But I left word for Earl to telegraph a description of him to all the resort hotels and stations hereabouts so that if he's anywhere around, they'll be on the lookout for him. I thought you'd want me to do that. But I think you'd better give me a writ for that bag at Gun Lodge Station. That may contain something we ought to know. I'll go up and get it myself. Then I want to go to Grass Lake and Three Mile Bay and Sharon yet to-day, if I can, and see what else I can find. But I'm afraid, Orville, it's a plain case of murder. The way he took that young girl to that hotel up there at Grass Lake and then registered under another name at Big Bittern, and the way he had her leave her bag and took his own with him!" He shook his head most solemnly. "Those are not the actions of an honest young man, Orville, and you know it. What I can't understand is how her parents could let her go off like that anywhere with a man without knowing about him in the first place."

"That's true," replied Mason, tactfully, but made intensely curious by the fact that it had at least been partially established that the girl in the case was not as good as she should have been. Adultery! And with some youth of means, no doubt, from some one of the big cities to the south. The prominence and publicity with which his own activities in connection with this were likely to be laden! At once he got up, energetically stirred. If he could only catch such a reptilian criminal, and that in the face of all the sentiment that such a brutal murder was likely to inspire! The August convention and nominations. The fall election.

"Well, I'll be switched," he exclaimed, the presence of Heit, a religious and conservative man, suppressing anything more emphatic. "I do believe we're on the trail of something important, Fred. I really think so. It looks very black to me— a most damnable outrage. I suppose the first thing to do, really, is to telephone over there and see if there is such a family as Alden and exactly where they live. It's not more than fifty miles direct by car, if that much. Poor roads, though," he added. Then: "That poor woman. I dread that scene. It will be a painful one, I know."

Then he called Zillah and asked her to ascertain if there was such a person as Titus Alden living near Biltz. Also, exactly how to get there. Next he added: "The first thing to do will be to get Burton back here" (Burton being Burton Burleigh, his legal assistant, who had gone away for a week-end vacation) "and put him in charge so as to furnish you whatever you need in the way of writs and so on, Fred, while I go right over to see this poor woman. And then, if you'll have Earl go back up there and get that suitcase, I'll be most obliged to you. I'll bring the father back with me, too, to identify the body. But don't say anything at all about this letter now or my going over there until I see you later, see." He grasped the hand of his friend. "In the meantime," he went on, a little grandiosely, now feeling the tang of great affairs upon him, "I want to thank you, Fred. I certainly do, and I won't forget it, either. You know that, don't you?" He looked his old friend squarely in the eye. "This may turn out better than we think. It looks to be the biggest and most important case in all my term of office, and if we can only clean it up satisfactorily and quickly, before things break here this fall, it may do us all some good, eh?"

"Quite so, Orville, quite so," commented Fred Heit. "Not, as I said before, that I think we ought to mix politics in with a thing like this, but since it has come about so——" he paused, meditatively.

"And in the meantime," continued the district attorney, "if you'll have Earl have some pictures made of the exact position where the boat, oars, and hat were found, as well as mark the spot where the body was found, and subpœna as many witnesses as you can, I'll have vouchers for it all put through with the auditor. And to-morrow or Monday I'll pitch in and help myself."

And here he gripped Heit's right hand—then patted him on the shoulder. And Heit, much gratified by his various moves so far—and in consequence hopeful for the future—now took up his weird straw hat and buttoning his thin, loose coat, returned to his office to get his faithful Earl on the long distance telephone to instruct him and to say that he was returning to the scene of the crime himself.

# Chapter IV

ORVILLE MASON could readily sympathize with a family which on sight struck him as having, perhaps, like himself endured the whips, the scorns and the contumelies of life. As he drove up in his official car from Bridgeburg at about four o'clock that Saturday afternoon, there was the old tatter demalion farmhouse and Titus Alden himself in his shirt-sleeves and overalls coming up from a pig-pen at the foot of the hill, his face and body suggesting a man who is constantly conscious of the fact that he has made out so poorly. And now Mason regretted that he had not telephoned before leaving Bridgeburg, for he could see that the news of his daughter's death would shock such a man as this most terribly. At the same time, Titus, noting his approach and assuming that it might be some one who was seeking a direction, civilly approached him.

"Is this Mr. Titus Alden?"

"Yes, sir, that's my name."

"Mr. Alden, my name is Mason. I am from Bridgeburg, district attorney of Cataraqui County."

"Yes, sir," replied Titus, wondering by what strange chance the district attorney of so distant a county should be approaching and inquiring of him. And Mason now looked at Titus, not knowing just how to begin. The bitterness of the news he had to impart—the crumpling power of it upon such an obviously feeble and inadequate soul. They had paused under one of the large, dark fir trees that stood in front of the house. The wind in its needles was whispering its world-old murmur.

"Mr. Alden," began Mason, with more solemnity and delicacy than ordinarily characterized him, "you are the father of a girl by the name of Bert, or possibly Alberta, are you not? I'm not sure that I have the name right."

"Roberta," corrected Titus Alden, a titillating sense of something untoward affecting his nerves as he said it.

And Mason, before making it impossible, probably, for this man to connectedly inform him concerning all that he wished to know, now proceeded to inquire: "By the way, do you happen to know a young man around here by the name of Clifford Golden?"

"I don't recall that I ever heard of any such person," replied Titus, slowly.

"Or Carl Graham?"

"No, sir. No one by that name either that I recall now."

"I thought so," exclaimed Mason, more to himself than to Titus. "By the way," this shrewdly and commandingly, "where is your daughter now?"

"Why, she's in Lycurgus at present. She works there. But why do you ask? Has she done anything she shouldn't—been to see you about anything?" He achieved a wry smile while his gray-blue eyes were by now perturbed by puzzled inquiry.

"One moment, Mr. Alden," proceeded Mason, tenderly and yet most firmly and effectively. "I will explain everything to you in a moment. Just now I want to ask you a few necessary questions." And he gazed at Titus earnestly and sympathetically. "How long has it been since you last saw your daughter?"

"Why, she left here last Tuesday morning to go back to Lycurgus. She works down there for the Griffiths Collar & Shirt Company. But——?"

"Now, one moment," insisted the district attorney determinedly, "I'll explain all in a moment. She was up here over the week-end, possibly. Is that it?"

"She was up here on a vacation for about a month," explained Titus, slowly and meticulously. "She wasn't feeling so very good and she came home to rest up a bit. But she was all right when she left. You don't mean to tell me, Mr. Mason, that anything has gone wrong with her, do you?" He lifted one long, brown hand to his chin and cheek in a gesture of nervous inquiry. "If I thought there was anything like that——?" He ran his hand through his thinning gray hair.

"Have you had any word from her since she left here?" Mason went on quietly, determined to extract as much practical information as possible before the great blow fell. "Any information that she was going anywhere but back there?"

"No, sir, we haven't. She's not hurt in any way, is she? She's not done anything that's got her into trouble? But, no, that couldn't be. But your questions! The way you talk." He was now trembling slightly, the hand that sought his thin, pale lips, visibly and aimlessly playing about his mouth. But instead of answering, the district attorney drew from his pocket the letter of Roberta to her mother, and displaying only the handwriting on the envelope, asked: "Is that the handwriting of your daughter?"

"Yes, sir, that's her handwriting," replied Titus, his voice rising slightly. "But what is this, Mr. District Attorney? How do you come to have that? What's in there?" He clinched his hands in a nervous way, for in Mason's eyes he now clearly foresaw tragedy in some form. "What is this—this—what has she written in that letter? You must tell me—if anything has happened to my girl!" He began to look excitedly about as though it were his intention to return to the house for aid— to communicate to his wife the dread that was coming upon him—while Mason, seeing the agony into which he had plunged him, at once seized him firmly and yet kindly by the arms and began:

"Mr. Alden, this is one of those dark times in the lives of some of us when all the courage we have is most needed. I hesitate to tell you because I am a man who has seen something of life and I know how you will suffer."

"She is hurt. She is dead, maybe," exclaimed Titus, almost shrilly, the pupils of his eyes dilating.

Orville Mason nodded.

"Roberta! My first born! My God! Our Heavenly Father!" His body crumpled as though from a blow and he leaned to steady himself against an adjacent tree. "But how? Where? In the factory by a machine? Oh, dear God!" He turned as though to go to his wife, while the strong, scar-nosed district attorney sought to detain him.

"One moment, Mr. Alden, one moment. You must not go to your wife yet. I know this is very hard, terrible, but let me explain. Not in Lycurgus. Not by any machine. No! No— drowned! In Big Bittern. She was up there on an outing on Thursday, do you understand? Do you hear? Thursday. She was drowned in Big Bittern on Thursday in a boat. It over-turned."

The excited gestures and words of Titus at this point so disturbed the district attorney that he found himself unable to explain as calmly as he would have liked the process by which even an assumed accidental drowning had come about. From the moment the word death in connection with Roberta had been used by Mason, the mental state of Alden was that of one not a little demented. After his first demands he now began to vent a series of animal-like groans as though the breath had been knocked from his body. At the same time, he bent over, crumpled up as from pain—then struck his hands together and threw them to his temples.

"My Roberta dead! My daughter! Oh, no, no, Roberta! Oh, my God! Not drowned! It can't be. And her mother speaking of her only an hour ago. This will be the death of her when she hears it. It will kill me, too. Yes, it will. Oh, my poor, dear, dear girl! My darling! I'm not strong enough to stand anything like this, Mr. District Attorney."

He leaned heavily and wearily upon Mason's arms while the latter sustained him as best he could. Then, after a moment, he turned questioningly and erratically toward the front door of the house at which he gazed as one might who was wholly demented. "Who's to tell her?" he demanded. "How is any one to tell her?"

"But, Mr. Alden," consoled Mason, "for your own sake, for your wife's sake, I must ask you now to calm yourself and help me consider this matter as seriously as you would if it were not your daughter. There is much more to this than I have been able to tell you. But you must be calm. You must allow me to explain. This is all very terrible and I sympathize with you wholly. I know what it means. But there are some dreadful and painful facts that you will have to know about. Listen. Listen."

And then, still holding Titus by the arm he proceeded to explain as swiftly and forcefully as possible, the various additional facts and suspicions in connection with the death of Roberta, finally giving him her letter to read, and winding up with: "A crime! A crime, Mr. Alden! That's what we think over in Bridgeburg, or at least that's what we're afraid of—plain murder, Mr. Alden, to use a hard, cold word in connection with it." He paused while Alden, struck by this—the element of crime—gazed as one not quite able to comprehend. And, as he gazed, Mason went on: "And as much as I respect your feelings, still as the chief representative of the law in my county, I felt it to be my personal duty to come here to-day in order to find out whether there is anything that you or your wife or any of your family know about this Clifford Golden, or Carl Graham, or whoever he is who lured your daughter to that lonely lake up there. And while I know that the blackest of suffering is yours right now, Mr. Alden, I maintain that it should be your wish, as well as your duty, to do whatever you can to help us clear up this matter. This letter here seems to indicate that your wife at least knows something concerning this individual—his name, anyhow." And he tapped the letter significantly and urgently.

The moment the suggested element of violence and wrong against his daughter had been injected into this bitter loss, there was sufficient animal instinct, as well as curiosity, resentment and love of the chase inherent in Titus to cause him to recover his balance sufficiently to give silent and solemn ear to what the district attorney was saying. His daughter not only drowned, but murdered, and that by some youth who according to this letter she was intending to marry! And he, her father, not even aware of his existence! Strange that his wife should know and he not. And that Roberta should not want him to know.

And at once, born for the most part of religion, convention and a general rural suspicion of all urban life and the mystery and involuteness of its ungodly ways, there sprang into his mind the thought of a city seducer and betrayer—some youth of means, probably, whom Roberta had met since going to Lycurgus and who had been able to seduce her by a promise of marriage which he was not willing to fulfill. And forthwith there flared up in his mind a terrible and quite uncontrollable desire for revenge upon any one who could plot so horrible a crime as this against his daughter. The scoundrel! The raper! The murderer!

Here he and his wife had been thinking that Roberta was quietly and earnestly and happily pursuing her hard, honest way in Lycurgus in order to help them and herself. And from Thursday afternoon until Friday her body had lain beneath the waters of that lake. And they asleep in their comfortable beds, or walking about, totally unaware of her dread state.

And now her body in a strange room or morgue somewhere, unseen and unattended by any of all those who loved her so— and to-morrow to be removed by cold, indifferent public officials to Bridgeburg.

"If there is a God," he exclaimed excitedly, "He will not let such a scoundrel as this go unpunished! Oh, no, He will not! 'I have yet to see,'" he suddenly quoted, "'the children of the righteous forsaken or their seed begging for bread.'" At the same time, a quivering compulsion for action dominating him, he added: "I must talk to my wife about this right away. Oh, yes, I must. No, no, you wait here. I must tell her first, and alone. I'll be back. I'll be back. You just wait here. I know it will kill her. But she must know about this. Maybe she can tell us who this is and then we can catch him before he manages to get too far away. But, oh, my poor girl! My poor, dear Roberta! My good, kind, faithful daughter!"

And so, talking in a maundering manner, his eyes and face betraying an only half-sane misery, he turned, the shambling, automaton-like motions of his angular figure now directing him to a lean-to, where, as he knew, Mrs. Alden was preparing some extra dishes for the next day, which was Sunday. But once there he paused in the doorway without the courage to approach further, a man expressing in himself all the pathos of helpless humanity in the face of the relentless and inexplicable and indifferent forces of Life!

Mrs. Alden turned, and at the sight of his strained expression, dropped her own hands lifelessly, the message of his eyes as instantly putting to flight the simple, weary and yet peaceful contemplation in her own.

"Titus! For goodness' sake! Whatever *is* the matter?"

Lifted hands, half-open mouth, an eerie, eccentric and uncalculated tensing and then widening of the eyelids, and then the word: "Roberta!"

"What about her? What about her? Titus—what about her?"

Silence. More of those nervous twitchings of the mouth, eyes, hands. Then . . . "Dead! She's been—been drowned!" followed by his complete collapse on a bench that stood just inside the door. And Mrs. Alden, staring for a moment, at first not quite comprehending, then fully realizing, sinking heavily and without a word to the floor. And Titus, looking at her and nodding his head as if to say: "Quite right. So should it be. Momentary escape for her from the contemplation of this horrible fact." And then slowly rising, going to her and kneeling beside her, straightening her out. Then as slowly going out of the door and around to the front of the house where Orville Mason was seated on the broken front steps, contemplating speculatively along with the afternoon sun in the west the misery that this lorn and incompetent farmer was conveying to his wife. And wishing for the moment that it might be otherwise—that no such case, however profitable to himself, had arisen.

But now, at sight of Titus Alden, he jumped up and preceded the skeleton-like figure into the lean-to. And finding Mrs. Alden, as small as her daughter nearly, and limp and still, he gathered her into his strong arms and carried her through the dining-room into the living-room, where stood an antiquated lounge, on which he laid her. And there, feeling for her pulse, and then hurrying for some water, while he looked for some one—a son, daughter, neighbor, any one. But not seeing any one, hurrying back with the water to dash a little of it on her face and hands.

"Is there a doctor anywhere near here?" He was addressing Titus, who was now kneeling by his wife.

"In Biltz—yes—Dr. Crane."

"Have you—has any one around here a telephone?"

"Mr. Wilcox." He pointed in the direction of the Wilcox's, whose telephone Roberta had so recently used.

"Just watch her. I'll be back."

Forthwith he was out of the house and away to call Crane or any other doctor, and then as swiftly returning with Mrs. Wilcox and her daughter. And then waiting, waiting, until first neighbors arrived and then eventually Dr. Crane, with whom he consulted as to the advisability of discussing with Mrs. Alden yet this day the unescapable mystery which had brought him here. And Dr. Crane, very much impressed by Mr. Mason's solemn, legal manner, admitting that it might even be best.

And at last Mrs. Alden treated with heroin and crooned and mourned over by all present, being brought to the stage where it was possible, slowly and with much encouragement, to hear in the first place what the extenuating circumstances were; next being questioned concerning the identity of the cryptic individual referred to in Roberta's letter. The only person whom Mrs. Alden could recall as ever having been mentioned by Roberta as paying particular attention to her, and that but once the Christmas before, was Clyde Griffiths, the nephew of the wealthy Samuel Griffiths, of Lycurgus, and the manager of the department in which Roberta worked.

But this in itself, as Mason and the Aldens themselves at once felt, was something which assuredly could not be taken to mean that the nephew of so great a man could be accused of the murder of Roberta. Wealth! Position! Indeed, in the face of such an accusation Mason was inclined to pause and consider. For the social difference between this man and this girl from his point of view seemed great. At that, it might be so. Why not? Was it not likely that a youth of such a secure position would possibly more than another, since she was so attractive as Heit had said, be the one to be paying casual and secret attention to a girl like Roberta? Did she not work in his uncle's factory? And was she not poor? Besides, as Fred Heit had already explained, whoever it was that this girl was with at the time of her death, she had not hesitated to cohabit with him before marriage. And was that not part and parcel of a rich and sophisticated youth's attitude toward a poor girl? By reason of his own early buffetings at the mood of chance and established prosperity the idea appealed to him intensely. The wretched rich! The indifferent rich! And here were her mother and father obviously believing most firmly in her innocence and virtue.

Further questioning of Mrs. Alden only brought out the fact that she had never seen this particular youth, and had never even heard of any other. The only additional data that either she or her husband could furnish was that during her last home-coming of a month Roberta had not been feeling at all well—drooped about the house and rested a good deal. Also that she had written a number of letters which she had given to the postman or placed in the delivery box at the road-crossing below. Neither Mr. nor Mrs. Alden knew to whom they were addressed, although the postman would be likely to know, as Mason quickly thought. Also, during this period, she had been busy making some dresses, at least four. And during the latter part of her stay, she had been the recipient of a number of telephone calls—from a certain Mr. Baker, as Titus had heard Mr. Wilcox say. Also, on departing, she had taken only such baggage as she had brought with her—her small trunk and her bag. The trunk she had checked herself at the station, but just where, other than Lycurgus, Titus could not say.

But now, suddenly, since he was attaching considerable importance to the name Baker, there popped into Mason's mind: "Clifford Golden! Carl Graham! Clyde Griffiths!" and at once the identity of the initials as well as the related euphony of the names gave him pause. An astounding coincidence truly, if this same Clyde Griffiths had nothing to do with this crime! Immediately he was anxious to go direct to the mailman and question him.

But since Titus Alden was important not only as a witness in identifying Roberta's body and the contents of the suitcase left by her at Gun Lodge but also to persuade the postman to talk freely, he now asked him to dress and accompany him, assuring him that he would allow him to return to-morrow.

After cautioning Mrs. Alden to talk to no one in regard to this, he now proceeded to the post office to question the mailman. That individual when found, recalled, upon inquiry, and in the presence of Titus who stood like a galvanized corpse by the side of the district attorney, that not only had there been a few letters—no less than twelve or fifteen even—handed him by Roberta during her recent stay here, but that all of them had been addressed to some one in Lycurgus by the name of—let him see—Clyde Griffiths—no less—care of General Delivery there. Forthwith, the district attorney proceeded with him to a local notary's office where a deposition was made, after which he called his office, and learning that Roberta's body had been brought to Bridgeburg, he drove there with as much speed as he could attain. And once there and in the presence of the body along with Titus, Burton Burleigh, Heit and Earl Newcomb, he was able to decide for himself, even while Titus, half demented, gazed upon the features of his child, first that she truly was Roberta Alden and next as to whether he considered her of the type who would wantonly yield herself to such a liaison as the registration at Grass Lake seemed to indicate. He decided he did not. This was a case of sly, evil seduction as well as murder. Oh, the scoundrel! And still at large. Almost the political value of all this was obscured by an angry social resentfulness against men of means in general.

But this particular contact with the dead, made at ten o'clock at night in the receiving parlors of the Lutz Brothers, Undertakers, and with Titus Alden falling on his knees by the side of his daughter and emotionally carrying her small, cold hands to his lips while he gazed feverishly and protestingly upon her waxy face, framed by her long brown hair, was scarcely such as to promise an unbiased or even legal opinion. The eyes of all those present were wet with tears.

And now Titus Alden injected a new and most dramatic note into the situation. For while the Lutz Brothers, with three of their friends who kept an automobile shop next door, Everett Beeker, the present representative of the Bridgeburg *Republican*, and Sam Tacksun, the editor and publisher of the *Democrat*, awesomely gazed over or between the heads of each other from without a side door which gave into the Lutzs' garage, he suddenly rose and moving wildly toward Mason, exclaimed: "I want you to find the scoundrel who did this, Mr. District Attorney. I want him to be made to suffer as this pure, good girl has been made to suffer. She's been murdered—that's all. No one but a murderer would take a girl out on a lake like that and strike her as any one can see she has been struck." He gestured toward his dead child. "I have no money to help prosecute a scoundrel like that. But I will work. I will sell my farm."

His voice broke and seemingly he was in danger of falling as he turned toward Roberta again. And now, Orville Mason, swept into this father's stricken and yet retaliatory mood, pressed forward to exclaim: "Come away, Mr. Alden. We know this is your daughter. I swear all you gentlemen as witnesses to this identification. And if it shall be proved that this little girl of yours was murdered, as it now seems, I promise you, Mr. Alden, faithfully and dutifully as the district attorney of this county, that no time or money or energy on my part will be spared to track down this scoundrel and hale him before the proper authorities! And if the justice of Cataraqui County is what I think it is, you can leave him to any jury which our local court will summon. And you won't need to sell your farm, either."

Mr. Mason, because of his deep, if easily aroused, emotion, as well as the presence of the thrilled audience, was in his most forceful as well as his very best oratorical mood.

And one of the Lutz Brothers—Ed—the recipient of all of the county coroner's business—was moved to exclaim: "That's the ticket, Orville. You're the kind of a district attorney we like." And Everett Beeker now called out: "Go to it, Mr. Mason. We're with you to a man when it comes to that." And Fred Heit, as well as his assistant, touched by Mason's dramatic stand, his very picturesque and even heroic appearance at the moment, now crowded closer, Heit to take his friend by the hand, Earl to exclaim: "More power to you, Mr. Mason. We'll do all we can, you bet. And don't forget that bag that she left at Gun Lodge is over at your office. I gave it to Burton two hours ago."

"That's right, too. I was almost forgetting that," exclaimed Mason, most calmly and practically at the moment, the previous burst of oratory and emotion having by now been somehow merged in his own mind with the exceptional burst of approval which up to this hour he had never experienced in any case with which previously he had been identified.

# Chapter V

As HE proceeded to his office, accompanied by Alden and the officials in this case, his thought was running on the motive of this heinous crime—the motive. And because of his youthful sexual deprivations, his mind now tended continually to dwell on that. And meditating on the beauty and charm of Roberta, contrasted with her poverty and her strictly moral and religious upbringing, he was convinced that in all likelihood this man or boy, whoever he was, had seduced her and then later, finding himself growing tired of her, had finally chosen this way to get rid of her—this deceitful, alleged marriage trip to the lake. And at once he conceived an enormous personal hate for the man. The wretched rich! The idle rich! The wastrel and evil rich—a scion or representative of whom this young Clyde Griffiths was. If he could but catch him.

At the same time it now suddenly occurred to him that because of the peculiar circumstances attending this case—this girl cohabiting with this man in this way—she might be pregnant. And at once this suspicion was sufficient, not only to make him sexually curious in regard to all the details of the life and courtship that had led to this—but also very anxious to substantiate for himself whether his suspicions were true. Immediately he began to think of a suitable doctor to perform an autopsy—if not here, then in Utica or Albany—also of communicating to Heit his suspicions in the connection, and of having this, as well as the import of the blows upon her face, determined.

But in regard to the bag and its contents, which was the immediate matter before him, he was fortunate in finding one additional bit of evidence of the greatest importance. For, apart from the dresses and hats made by Roberta, her lingerie, a pair of red silk garters purchased at Braunstein's in Lycurgus and still in their original box, there was the toilet set presented by Clyde to her the Christmas before. And with it the small, plain white card, held in place by a portion of the gray silk lining of the case, on which Clyde had written: "For Bert from Clyde—Merry Xmas." But no family name. And the writing a hurried scrawl, since it had been written at a time when Clyde was most anxious to be elsewhere than with her.

At once it occurred to Mason—how odd that the presence of this toilet set in this bag, together with the card, should not have been known to the slayer. But if it were, and he had not removed the card, could it be possible that this same Clyde was the slayer? Would a man contemplating murder fail to see a card such as this, with his own handwriting on it? What sort of a plotter and killer would that be? Immediately afterward he thought: Supposing the presence of this card could be concealed until the day of the trial and then suddenly produced, assuming the criminal denied any intimacy with the girl, or having given her any toilet set? And for the present he took the card and put it in his pocket, but not before Earl Newcomb, looking at it carefully, had observed: "I'm not positive, Mr. Mason, but that looks to me like the writing on the register up at Big Bittern." And at once Mason replied: "Well, it won't take long to establish the fact."

He then signaled Heit to follow him into an adjoining chamber, where once alone with him, free from the observation and hearing of the others, he began: "Well, Fred, you see it was just as you thought. She did know who she was going with." (He was referring to his own advice over the telephone from Biltz that Mrs. Alden had provided him with definite information as to the criminal.) "But you couldn't guess in a thousand years unless I told you." He leaned over and looked at Heit shrewdly.

"I don't doubt it, Orville. I haven't the slightest idea."

"Well, you know of Griffiths & Company, of Lycurgus?"

"Not the collar people?"

"Yes, the collar people."

"Not the son." Fred Heit's eyes opened wider than they had in years. His wide, brown hand grasped the end of his beard.

"No, not the son. A nephew!"

"Nephew! Of Samuel Griffiths? Not truly!" The old, moral-religious-politic-commercial coroner stroked his beard again and stared.

"The fact seems to point that way, Fred, now at least. I'm going down there yet to-night, though, and I hope to know a lot more to-morrow. But this Alden girl—they're the poorest kind of farm people, you know—worked for Griffiths & Company in Lycurgus and this nephew, Clyde Griffiths, as I understand it, is in charge of the department in which she worked."

"Tst! Tst! Tst!" interjected the coroner

"She was home for a month—*sick*" (he emphasized the word) "just before she went on this trip last Tuesday. And during that time she wrote him at least ten letters, and maybe more. I got that from the rural delivery man. I have his affidavit here." He tapped his coat. "All addressed to Clyde Griffiths in Lycurgus. I even have his house number. And the name of the family with whom she lived. I telephoned down there from Biltz. I'm going to take the old man with me to-night in case anything comes up that he might know about."

"Yes, yes, Orville. I understand. I see. But a Griffiths!" And once more he clucked with his tongue.

"But what I want to talk to you about is the inquest," now went on Mason quickly and sharply. "You know I've been thinking that it couldn't have been just because he didn't want to marry her that he wanted to kill her. That doesn't seem reasonable to me," and he added the majority of the thoughts that had caused him to conclude that Roberta was pregnant. And at once Heit agreed with him.

"Well, then that means an autopsy," Mason resumed. "As well as medical opinion as to the nature of those wounds. We'll have to know beyond a shadow of a doubt, Fred, and before that body is taken away from here, whether that girl was killed before she was thrown out of that boat, or just stunned and then thrown out, or the boat upset. That's very vital to the case, as you know. We'll never be able to do anything unless we're positive about those things. But what about the medical men around here? Do you think any of them will be able to do all these things in a shipshape way so that what they say will hold water in court?"

Mason was dubious. Already he was building his case.

"Well, as to that, Orville," Heit replied slowly, "I can't say exactly. You'd be a better judge, maybe, than I would. I've already asked Dr. Mitchell to step over to-morrow and take a look at her. Also Betts. But if there's any other doctor you'd rather have—Bavo or Lincoln of Coldwater—how about Bavo?"

"I'd rather have Webster, of Utica," went on Mason, "or Beemis, or both. Four or five opinions in a case like this won't be any too many."

And Heit, sensing the importance of the great responsibility now resting on him, added: "Well, I guess you're right, Orville. Maybe four or five would be better than one or two. That means, though, that the inquest will have to be postponed for a day or two more, till we get these men here."

"Quite right! Quite right," went on Mason, "but that will be a good thing, too, as long as I'm going down to Lycurgus to-night to see what I can find out. You never can tell. I may catch up with him. I hope so, anyhow, or if not that, then I may come upon something that'll throw some extra light on this. For this is going to be a big thing, Fred. I can see that— the most difficult case that ever came my way, or yours, either,—and we can't be too careful as to how we move from now on. He's likely to be rich, you see, and if he is he'll fight. Besides there's that family down there to back him up."

He ran a nervous hand through his shock of hair, then added: "Well, that's all right too. The next thing to do is to get Beemis and Webster of Utica—better wire them to-night, eh, or call them up. And Sprull of Albany, and then, to keep peace in the family around here, perhaps we'd better have Lincoln and Betts over here. And maybe Bavo." He permitted himself the faintest shadow of a smile. "In the meantime, I'll be going along, Fred. Arrange to have them come up Monday or Tuesday, instead of to-morrow. I expect to be back by then and if so I can be with you. If you can, better get 'em up here, Monday—see—the quicker the better—and we'll see what we know by then."

He went to a drawer to secure some extra writs. And then into the outer room to explain to Alden the trip that was before him. And to have Burleigh call up his wife, to whom he explained the nature of his work and haste and that he might not be back before Monday.

And all the way down to Utica, which took three hours, as well as a wait of one hour before a train for Lycurgus could be secured, and an additional hour and twenty minutes on that train, which set them down at about seven, Orville Mason was busy extracting from the broken and gloomy Titus, as best he could, excerpts from his own as well as Roberta's humble past—her generosity, loyalty, virtue, sweetness of heart, and the places and conditions under which previously she had worked, and what she had received, and what she had done with the money—a humble story which he was quite able to appreciate.

Arriving at Lycurgus with Titus by his side, he made his way as quickly as possible to the Lycurgus House, where he took a room for the father in order that he might rest. And after that to the office of the local district attorney, from whom he must obtain authority to proceed, as well as an officer who would execute his will for him here. And then being supplied with a stalwart detective in plain clothes, he proceeded to Clyde's room in Taylor Street, hoping against hope that he might find him there. But Mrs. Peyton appearing and announcing that Clyde lived there but that at present he was absent (having gone the Tuesday before to visit friends at Twelfth Lake, she believed), he was rather painfully compelled to announce, first, that he was the district attorney of Cataraqui County, and, next, that because of certain suspicious circumstances in connection with the drowning of a girl in Big Bittern, with whom they had reason to believe that Clyde was at the time, they would now be compelled to have access to his room, a statement which so astonished Mrs. Peyton that she fell back, an expression of mixed amazement, horror, and unbelief overspreading her features.

"Not Mr. Clyde Griffiths! Oh, how ridiculous! Why, he's the nephew of Mr. Samuel Griffiths and very well known here. I'm sure they can tell you all about him at their residence, if you must know. But anything like—oh, impossible!" And she looked at both Mason and the local detective who was already displaying his official badge, as though she doubted both their honesty and authority.

At the same time, the detective, being all too familiar with such circumstances, had already placed himself beyond Mrs. Peyton at the foot of the stairs leading to the floor above. And Mason now drew from his pocket a writ of search, which he had been careful to secure.

"I am sorry, Madam, but I am compelled to ask you to show us his room. This is a search warrant and this officer is here at my direction." And at once struck by the futility of contending with the law, she now nervously indicated Clyde's room, feeling still that some insane and most unfair and insulting mistake was being made.

But the two having proceeded to Clyde's room, they began to look here and there. At once both noted one small and not very strong trunk, locked and standing in one corner, which Mr. Faunce, the detective, immediately began to lift to decide upon its weight and strength, while Mason began to examine each particular thing in the room—the contents of all drawers and boxes, as well as the pockets of all clothes. And in the chiffonier drawers, along with some discarded underwear and shirts and a few old invitations from the Trumbulls, Starks, Griffiths, and Harriets, he now found a memorandum sheet which Clyde had carried home from his desk and on which he had written: "Wednesday, Feb. 20th, dinner at Starks"—and below that, "Friday, 22nd, Trumbulls"—and this handwriting Mason at once compared with that on the card in his pocket, and being convinced by the similarity that he was in the room of the right man, he took the invitations and then looked toward the trunk which the detective was now contemplating.

"What about this, chief? Will you take it away or open it here?"

"I think," said Mason solemnly, "we'd better open that right here, Faunce. I'll send for it afterwards, but I want to see what's in it now." And at once the detective extracted from his pocket a heavy chisel, while he began looking around for a hammer.

"It isn't very strong," he said, "I think I can kick it open if you say so."

At this point, Mrs. Peyton, most astounded by these developments, and anxious to avoid any such rough procedure, exclaimed: "You can have a hammer if you wish, but why not wait and send for a key man? Why, I never heard of such a thing in all my life."

However, the detective having secured the hammer and jarred the lock loose, there lay revealed in a small top crate various unimportant odds and ends of Clyde's wardrobe—

socks, collars, ties, a muffler, suspenders, a discarded sweater, a pair of not too good high-top winter shoes, a cigarette holder, a red lacquer ash tray, and a pair of skates. But in addition among these, in the corner in one compact bundle, the final fifteen letters of Roberta, written him from Biltz, together with a small picture of herself given him the year before, as well as another small bundle consisting of all the notes and invitations written him by Sondra up to the time she had departed for Pine Point. The letters written from there Clyde had taken with him—laid next his heart. And, even more incriminating, a third bundle, consisting of eleven letters from his mother, the first two addressed to Harry Tenet, care of general delivery, Chicago—a most suspicious circumstance on the surface—whereas the others of the bundle were addressed to Clyde Griffiths, not only care of the Union League, Chicago, but to Lycurgus.

Without waiting further to see what else the trunk might contain, the district attorney began opening these and reading—first three from Roberta, after which the reason she had gone to Biltz was made perfectly plain—then the three first letters from his mother, on most pathetically commonplace stationery, as he could see, hinting at the folly of the life as well as the nature of the accident that had driven him from Kansas City, and at the same time advising him most solicitously and tenderly as to the proper path for his feet in the future, the general effect of which was to convey to a man of Mason's repressed temperament and limited social experience the impression that from the very beginning this individual had been of a loose, wayward and errant character.

At the same time, and to his surprise, he now learned that except for what his rich uncle might have done for him here, Clyde was obviously of a poor, as well as highly religious, branch of the Griffiths family, and while ordinarily this might have influenced him in Clyde's favor a little, still now, in view of the notes of Sondra, as well as the pathetic letters of Roberta and his mother's reference to some earlier crime in Kansas City, he was convinced that not only was Clyde of such a disposition as could plot such a crime but also one who could execute it in cold blood. That crime in Kansas City. He must wire the district attorney there for particulars.

And with this thought in mind, he now scanned more briefly but none the less sharply and critically the various notes or invitations or love messages from Sondra, all on heavily perfumed and monogrammed stationery, which grew more and more friendly and intimate as the correspondence progressed, until toward the last they invariably began: "Clydie-Mydie," or "Sweetest Black Eyes," or "My sweetest boy," and were signed "Sonda," or "Your own Sondra." And some of them dated so recently as May 10th, May 15th, May 26th, or up to the very time at which, as he instantly noted, Roberta's most doleful letters began to arrive.

It was all so plain, now. One secretly betrayed girl in the background while he had the effrontery to ingratiate himself into the affections of another, this time obviously one of much higher social position here.

Although fascinated and staggered by this interesting development, he at the same time realized that this was no hour in which to sit meditating. Far from it. This trunk must be transferred at once to his hotel. Later he must go forth to find out, if he could, exactly where this individual was, and arrange for his capture. And while he ordered the detective to call up the police department and arrange for the transfer of the trunk to his room at the Lycurgus House, he hurried next to the residence of Samuel Griffiths, only to learn that no member of the family was then in the city. They were all at Greenwood Lake. But a telephone message to that place brought the information that in so far as they knew, this same Clyde Griffiths, their nephew, was at the Cranston lodge on Twelfth Lake, near Sharon, adjoining the Finchley lodge. The name Finchley, together with the town of Sharon, being already identified in Mason's mind with Clyde, he at once decided that if he were still anywhere in this region, he would be there—at the summer home perhaps of this girl who had written him the various notes and invitations he had seen— this Sondra Finchley. Also had not the captain of the "Cygnus" declared that he had seen the youth who had come down from Three Mile Bay debark there? Eureka! He had him!

And at once, after meditating sharply on the wisdom of his course, he decided to proceed to Sharon and Pine Point himself. But in the meantime being furnished with an accurate description of Clyde, he now furnished this as well as the fact that he was wanted for murder, not only to the district attorney and the chief of police of Lycurgus, but to Newton Slack, the sheriff at Bridgeburg, as well as to Heit and his own assistant, urging all three to proceed at once to Sharon, where he would meet them.

At the same time, speaking as though for Mrs. Peyton, he now called upon the long distance telephone the Cranston lodge at Pine Point, and getting the butler on the wire, inquired whether Mr. Clyde Griffiths chanced to be there. "Yes, sir, he is, sir, but he's not here now, sir. I think he's on a camping party farther up the lake, sir. Any message, sir?" And in response to further inquiries, he replied that he could not say exactly—a party had gone, presumably, to Bear Lake some thirty miles farther up, but when it would return he could not say—not likely before a day or two. But distinctly this same Clyde was with that party.

And at once Mason recalled the sheriff at Bridgeburg, instructing him to take four or five deputies with him so that the searching party might divide at Sharon and seize this same Clyde wherever he chanced to be. And throw him in jail at Bridgeburg, where he could explain, with all due process of law, the startling circumstances that thus far seemed to unescapably point to him as the murderer of Roberta Alden.

# Chapter VI

IN THE INTERIM the mental state of Clyde since that hour
when, the water closing over Roberta, he had made his
way to the shore, and then, after changing his clothes, had
subsequently arrived at Sharon and the lakeside lodge of the
Cranstons, was almost one of complete mental derangement,
mainly caused by fear and confusion in his own mind as to
whether he did or did not bring about her untimely end. At
the same time at the lakeside the realization that if by any
chance he were then and there found, skulking south rather
than returning north to the inn at Big Bittern to report this
seeming accident, there would be sufficient hardness and
cruelty to the look of it all to convince any one that a charge
of murder should be made against him, had fiercely tortured
him. For, as he now saw it, he really was not guilty—was he,
since at the last moment he had experienced that change of
heart?

But who was going to believe that now, since he did not go
back to explain? And it would never do to go back now! For
if Sondra should hear that he had been on this lake with this
factory girl—that he had registered with her as husband and
wife . . . God!

And then trying to explain to his uncle afterwards, or his
cold, hard cousin—or all those smart, cynical Lycurgus people! No! No! Having gone so far he must go on. Disaster—if
not death—lay in the opposite direction. He would have to
make the best of this terrible situation—make the best of this
plan that had ended so strangely and somewhat exculpatorily
for him.

And yet these woods! This approaching night. The eerie
loneliness and danger of it all now. How now to do, what to
say, if met by any one. He was so confused—mentally and
nervously sick. The crackle of a twig and he leaped forward as
a hare.

And in this state, it was that after having recovered his bag
and changed his clothes, wringing out his wet suit and attempting to dry it, then packing it in his bag under some dry

twigs and pine-needles and burying the tripod beneath a rotting log, that he plunged into the woods after night had fallen. Yet meditating more and more on his very strange and perilous position. For supposing, just as he had unintentionally struck at her, and they had fallen into the water and she uttered those piercing and appealing cries, there had been some one on the shore—some one watching—one of those strong, hardy men whom he had seen loitering about during the day and who might even at this moment be sounding a local alarm that would bring a score of such men to the work of hunting for him this very night! A man hunt! And they would take him back and no one would ever believe that he had not intentionally struck her! They might even lynch him before he could so much as secure a fair trial. It was possible. It had been done. A rope around his neck. Or shot down in these woods, maybe. And without an opportunity to explain how it had all come about—how harried and tortured he had been by her for so long. They would never understand that.

And so thinking he hurried faster and faster—as fast as strong and serried and brambly young firs and dead branches that cracked most ominously at times would permit, thinking always as he went that the road to Three Mile Bay must be to his right hand, the moon to his left when it should rise.

But, God, what was that?

Oh, that terrible sound!

Like a whimpering, screeching spirit in this dark!

There!

What was it?

He dropped his bag and in a cold sweat sunk down, crouching behind a tall, thick tree, rigid and motionless with fear.

That sound!

But only a screech-owl! He had heard it several weeks before at the Cranston lodge. But here! In this wood! This dark! He must be getting on and out of here. There was no doubt of that. He must not be thinking such horrible, fearful thoughts, or he would not be able to keep up his strength or courage at all.

But that look in the eyes of Roberta! That last appealing

look! God! He could not keep from seeing it! Her mournful,
terrible screams! Could he not cease from hearing them—until he got out of here anyhow?

Had she understood, when he struck her, that it was not
intentional—a mere gesture of anger and protest? Did she
know that *now*, wherever she was—in the bottom of the
lake—or here in the dark of these woods beside him, mayhap?
Ghosts! Hers. But he must get out of this—out of this! He
must—and yet the safety of these woods, too. He must not be
too brash in stepping out into any road, either. Pedestrians!
People in search of him, maybe! But did people really live
after death? Were there ghosts? And did they know the truth?
Then she must know—but how he plotted before that, too.
And what would she think of that! And was she here now reproachfully and gloomily pursuing him with mistaken accusa-
tions, as true as it might be that he had intended to kill her at
first? He had! He had! And that was the great sin, of course.
Even though he had not killed her, yet something had done
it for him! That was true.

But ghosts—God—spirits that might pursue you after they
were dead, seeking to expose and punish you—seeking to set
people on your track, maybe! Who could tell? His mother had
confessed to him and Frank and Esta and Julia that she believed in ghosts.

And then at last the moon, after three such hours of stumbling, listening, waiting, perspiring, trembling. No one in
sight now, thank God! And the stars overhead—bright and
yet soft, as at Pine Point where Sondra was. If she could see
him now, slipping away from Roberta dead in that lake, his
own hat upon the waters there! If she could have heard
Roberta's cries! How strange that never, never, never would
he be able to tell her that because of her, her beauty, his passion for her and all that she had come to mean to him, he had
been able to . . . to . . . to . . . well, *attempt* this terrible
thing—kill a girl whom once he had loved. And all his life he
would have this with him, now,—this thought! He would
never be able to shake it off—never, never, never. And he had
not thought of that, before. It was a terrible thing in its way,
just that, wasn't it?

But then suddenly there in the dark, at about eleven

o'clock, as he afterwards guessed, the water having stopped his watch, and after he had reached the highroad to the west—and walked a mile or two,—those three men, quick, like ghosts coming out of the shadow of the woods. He thought at first that having seen him at the moment he had struck Roberta or the moment afterward, they had now come to take him. The sweating horror of that moment! And that boy who had held up the light the better to see his face. And no doubt he had evinced most suspicious fear and perturbation, since at the moment he was most deeply brooding on all that had happened, terrorized really by the thought that somehow, in some way, he had left some clue that might lead directly to him. And he did jump back, feeling that these were men sent to seize him. But at that moment, the foremost, a tall, bony man, without appearing to be more than amused at his obvious cowardice, had called, "Howdy, stranger!" while the youngest, without appearing to be suspicious at all, had stepped forward and then turned up the light. And it was then that he had begun to understand that they were just countrymen or guides—not a posse in pursuit of him—and that if he were calm and civil they would have no least suspicion that he was the murderer that he was.

But afterward he had said to himself—"But they will remember me, walking along this lonely road at this hour with this bag, won't they?" And so at once he had decided that he must hurry—hurry—and not be seen by any others anywhere there.

Then, hours later and just as the moon was lowering toward the west, a sickly yellow pallor overspreading the woods and making the night even more wretched and wearisome, he had come to Three Mile Bay itself—a small collection of native and summer cottages nestling at the northernmost end of what was known as the Indian Chain. And in it, as he could see from a bend in the road, a few pale lights still twinkling. Stores. Houses. Street lamps. But all dim in the pale light—so dim and eerie to him. One thing was plain—at this hour and dressed as he was and with his bag in hand, he could not enter there. That would be to fix curiosity as well as suspicion on him, assuredly, if any one was still about. And as the launch that ran between this place and Sharon, from whence he would proceed to Pine Point, did not leave until eight-thirty, he must hide away in the meantime and make himself as presentable as possible.

And accordingly re-entering a thicket of pines that descended to the very borders of the town, there to wait until morning, being able to tell by a small clock-face which showed upon the sides of a small church tower, when the hour for emerging had arrived. But, in the interim debating,—"Was it wise so to do?" For who might not be here to wait for him? Those three men—or some one else who might have seen?—Or an officer, notified from somewhere else. Yet deciding after a time that it was best to go just the same. For to stalk along in the woods west of this lake—and by night rather than day—seeing that by day he might be seen, and when by taking this boat he could reach in an hour and a half—or two hours at the most—the Cranston lodge at Sharon, whereas by walking he would not arrive until to-morrow,—was not that unwise, more dangerous? Besides, he had promised Sondra and Bertine that he would be there Tuesday. And here it was Friday! Again, by to-morrow, might not a hue and cry be on—his description sent here and there—whereas this morning—well, how could Roberta have been found as yet? No, no. Better this way. For who knew him here—or could identify him as yet with either Carl Graham or Clifford Golden. Best go this way,—speedily, before anything else in connection with her developed. Yes, yes. And finally, the clock-hands pointing to eight-ten, making his way out, his heart beating heavily as he did so.

At the foot of this street was the launch which steamed from here to Sharon. And as he loitered he observed the bus from Raquette Lake approaching. It now occurred to him, if he encountered any one he knew on the steamer dock or boat, could he not say that he was fresh from Raquette Lake, where Sondra, as well as Bertine, had many friends, or in case they themselves came down on the boat, that he had been there the day before. What matter whose name or lodge he mentioned—an invented one, if need be.

And so, at last, making his way to the boat and boarding it. And later at Sharon, leaving it again and without, as he thought, appearing to attract any particular attention at either end. For, although there were some eleven passengers, all strangers to him, still no one other than a young country girl in a blue dress and a white straw hat, whom he guessed to be from this vicinity, appeared to pay any particular attention to him. And her glances were admiring rather than otherwise, although sufficient, because of his keen desire for secrecy, to cause him to retire to the rear of the boat, whereas the others appeared to prefer the forward deck. And once at Sharon, knowing that the majority were making for the railway station to catch the first morning train down, he followed briskly in their wake, only to turn into the nearest lunch-room in order to break the trail, as he hoped. For although he had walked the long distance from Big Bittern to Three Mile Bay, and previously had rowed all afternoon, and merely made a pretense of eating the lunch which Roberta had prepared at Grass Lake, still even now he was not hungry. Then seeing a few passengers approaching from the station, yet none whom he knew, he joined these again as though just coming to the inn and launch from the train.

For at this time there had come to him the thought that this south train from Albany, as well as Utica being due here at this hour, it was only natural that he should seem to come on that. Pretending first, therefore, to be going to the station, yet stopping en route to telephone Bertine and Sondra that he was here, and being assured that a car rather than a launch would be sent for him, he explained that he would be waiting on the west veranda of the inn. En route also he stopped at a news stand for a morning paper, although he knew there could be nothing in it as yet. And he had barely crossed to the veranda of the inn and seated himself before the Cranston car approached.

And in response to the greeting of the Cranston family chauffeur, whom he knew well, and who smiled most welcomingly, he was now able to achieve a seemingly easy and genial smile, though still inwardly troubled by his great dread. For no doubt by now, as he persistently argued with himself, the three men whom he had met had reached Big Bittern. And by now both Roberta and he must assuredly have been missed, and maybe, who knows, the upturned boat with his hat and her veil discovered! If so, might they not have already reported that they had seen such a man as himself, carrying a bag, and making his way to the south in the night? And, if so, would not that, regardless of whether the body was found or not, cause them to become dubious as to whether a double drowning had occurred? And supposing by some strange chance her body should come to the surface? Then what? And might there not be a mark left by that hard blow he had given her? If so, would they not suspect murder, and his body not coming up and those men describing the man they had seen, would not Clifford Golden or Carl Graham be suspected of murder?

But neither Clifford Golden nor Carl Graham were Clyde Griffiths by any means. And they could not possibly identify Clyde Griffiths—with either Clifford Golden or Carl Graham. For had he not taken every precaution, even searching through Roberta's bag and purse there at Grass Lake while at his request after breakfast she had gone back to see about the lunch? Had he not? True, he had found those two letters from that girl, Theresa Bouser, addressed to Roberta at Biltz, and he had destroyed them before ever leaving for Gun Lodge. And as for that toilet set in its original case, with the label "Whitely-Lycurgus" on it, while it was true that he had been compelled to leave that, still might not any one—Mrs. Clifford Golden, or Mrs. Carl Graham—have bought that in Whitely's, and so without the possibility of its being traced to him? Assuredly. And as for her clothes, even assuming that they did go to prove her identity, would it not be assumed, by her parents as well as others, that she had gone on this trip with a strange man by the name of Golden or Graham, and would they not want that hushed up without further ado? At any rate, he would hope for the best—keep up his nerve, put on a strong, pleasant, cheerful front here, so that no one would think of him as the one, since he had not actually killed her, anyhow.

Here he was in this fine car. And Sondra, as well as Bertine, waiting for him. He would have to say that he was just up from Albany—had been on some errand over there for his uncle which had taken all of his time since Tuesday. And while he should be blissfully happy with Sondra, still here were all of those dreadful things of which now all of the time he

would be compelled to think. The danger that in some inad-
vertent way he had not quite covered all the tracks that might
lead to him. And if he had not! Exposure! Arrest! Perhaps a
hasty and unjust conviction—punishment, even! Unless he
was able to explain about that accidental blow. The end of all
his dreams in connection with Sondra—Lycurgus—the great
life that he had hoped for himself. But could he explain as to
that? Could he? God!

# Chapter VII

ROM Friday morning until the following Tuesday noon, moving amid such scenes as previously had so exhilarated and enthralled him, Clyde was now compelled to suffer the most frightful fears and dreads. For, although met by Sondra, as well as Bertine, at the door of the Cranston lodge, and shown by them to the room he was to occupy, he could not help but contrast every present delight here with the danger of his immediate and complete destruction.

As he had entered, Sondra had poutingly whispered, so that Bertine might not hear: "Baddie! Staying down there a whole week when you might have been up here. And Sondra planning everything for you! You ought to have a good spanking. I was going to call up to-day to see where you were." Yet at the same time her eyes conveying the infatuation that now dominated her.

And he, in spite of his troubled thoughts achieving a gay smile,—for once in her presence even the terror of Roberta's death, his own present danger appeared to dwindle. If only all went well, now,—nothing were traced to him! A clear path! A marvelous future! Her beauty! Her love! Her wealth. And yet, after being ushered to his room, his bag having been carried in before him, at once becoming nervous as to the suit. It was damp and wrinkled. He must hide it on one of the upper shelves of a closet, maybe. And the moment he was alone and the door locked, taking it out, wet and wrinkled, the mud of the shores of Big Bittern still about the legs—yet deciding perhaps not—perhaps he had better keep it locked in his bag until night when he could better decide what to do. Yet trying up in a single bundle, in order to have them laundered, other odds and ends he had worn that day. And, as he did so, terribly, sickeningly conscious of the mystery and drama as well as the pathos of his life—all he had contacted since his arrival in the east, how little he had in his youth. How little he had now, really. The spaciousness and grandeur of this room as contrasted with the one he occupied in Lycurgus. The strangeness of his being here at all after yesterday. The blue waters of this bright lake without as contrasted with the darker ones of Big Bittern. And on the green-sward that reached from this bright, strong, rambling house, with its wide veranda and striped awnings to the shore of the lake itself, Stuart Finchley and Violet Taylor, together with Frank Harriet and Wynette Phant, in the smartest of sport clothes, playing tennis, while Bertine and Harley Baggott lolled in the shade of a striped marquee swing.

And, he himself, after bathing and dressing, assuming a jocular air although his nerves remained tense and his mood apprehensive. And then descending to where Sondra and Burchard Taylor and Jill Trumbull were laughing over some amusing experiences in connection with motor-boating the day before. Jill Trumbull called to him as he came out: "Hello, Clyde! Been playing hookey or what? I haven't seen you in I don't know when." And he, after smiling wistfully at Sondra, craving as never before her sympathy as well as her affection, drawing himself up on the railing of the veranda and replying, as smoothly as he could: "Been working over at Albany since Tuesday. Hot down there. It's certainly fine to be up here to-day. Who's all up?" And Jill Trumbull, smiling: "Oh, nearly every one, I guess. I saw Vanda over at the Randalls' yesterday. And Scott wrote Bertine he was coming to the Point next Tuesday. It looks to me as though no one was going over to Greenwood much this year." And then a long and intense discussion as to why Greenwood was no longer what it had been. And then Sondra exclaiming: "That reminds me! I have to phone Bella to-day. She promised to come up to that horse show over at Bristol week after next, sure." And then more talk of horses and dogs. And Clyde, listening intently in his anxiety to seem an integral part of it all, yet brooding on all that so desperately concerned him. Those three men. Roberta. Maybe they had found her body by now—who could tell, yet saying to himself—why so fearsome? Was it likely that in that depth of water—fifty feet maybe, for all he knew—that they would find her? Or that they could ever identify him with Clifford Golden or Carl Graham? How could they? Hadn't he really and truly covered his tracks except for those three men? *Those three men!* He shivered, as with cold, in spite of himself.

And then Sondra, sensing a note of depression about him. (She had determined from his obvious lack of equipment on his first visit that perhaps the want of money was at the bottom of his present mood, and so proposed later this day to extract seventy-five dollars from her purse and force that upon him in order that at no point where petty expenditures should be required, should he feel the least bit embarrassed during his stay this time.) And after a few moments, thinking of the short golf course, with its variety of concealing hazards for unseen kisses and embraces, she now jumped up with: "Who's for a mixed foursome? Come on, Jill, Clyde, Burch! I'll bet Clyde and I can turn in a lower card than you two can!"

"I'll take that!" exclaimed Burchard Taylor, rising and straightening his yellow and blue striped sweater, "even if I didn't get in until four this morning. How about you, Jilly? If you want to make that for the lunches, Sonny, I'll take it."

And at once Clyde wincing and chilling, for he was thinking of the miserable twenty-five dollars left him from all his recent ghastly adventures. And a lunch for four here would cost not less than eight or ten dollars! Perhaps more. At the same time, Sondra, noting his expression, exclaimed: "That's a go!" and drawing near to Clyde tapped him gently with her toe, exclaiming: "But I have to change. I'll be right down. In the meantime, Clyde, I'll tell you what you do—go and find Andrew and tell him to get the clubs, will you? We can go over in your boat, can't we, Burchy?" And Clyde, hurrying to find Andrew, and thinking of the probable cost of the lunch if he and Sondra were defeated, but being caught up with by Sondra and seized by the arm. "Wait a minute, honey, I'll be right back." Then dashing up the steps to her room, and in a moment down again, a handful of bills she had reserved shut tightly in her little fist: "Here, darling, quick!" she whispered, taking hold of one of Clyde's coat pockets and putting the money into it. "Ssh! Not a word, now! Hurry! It's to pay for the lunch in case we lose, and some other things. I'll tell you afterwards. Oh, but I do love you, baby boy!" And then, her warm, brown eyes fixed on him for a moment in profound admiration, dashing up the stairs again, from where she called: "Don't stand there, silly! Get the golf clubs! The golf clubs!" And she was gone.

And Clyde, feeling his pocket and realizing that she had given him much—plenty, no doubt, for all of his needs while here, as well as to escape if need be. And exclaiming to himself: "Darling!" "Baby girl!" His beautiful, warm, generous Sondra! She loved him so—truly loved him. But if ever she should find out! Oh, God! And yet all for her, if she only knew. All for her! And then finding Andrew and returning with him carrying the bags.

And here was Sondra again, dancing down in a smart green knitted sports costume. And Jill in a new cap and blouse which made her look like a jockey, laughing at Burchard who was at the wheel of the boat. And Sondra calling back to Bertine and Harley Baggott in the swing as she was passing: "Hey, fellows! You won't come, eh?"

"Where?"

"Casino Golf Club."

"Oh, too far. See you after lunch on the beach, though."

And then Burchard shooting the boat out in the lake with a whir that set it bounding like a porpoise—and Clyde gazing half in a dream, half delight and hope and the other half a cloud of shadow and terror, with arrest and death, maybe, stalking close behind. For in spite of all his preliminary planning, he was beginning to feel that he had made a mistake in openly coming out of the wood this morning. And yet had it not been best, since the only alternative was that of remaining there by day and coming out at night and following the shore road on foot to Sharon? That would have required two or three days. And Sondra, anxious as well as curious about the delay, might have telephoned to Lycurgus, thereby raising some question in regard to him which might have proved dangerous later might it not?

But here now, this bright day, with seemingly no cares of any kind, for these others at least, however dark and bleak his own background might be. And Sondra, all gayety because of his presence, now jumping up, her bright scarf held aloft in one hand like a pennant, and exclaiming foolishly and gayly: "Cleopatra sailing to meet—to meet—who was it she was sailing to meet, anyhow?"

"Charlie Chaplin," volunteered Taylor, at the same time proceeding to ricochet the boat as roughly and erratically as possible in order to make her lose her balance.

"Oh, you silly!" returned Sondra, spreading her feet sufficiently apart to maintain her equilibrium, and adding for the benefit of Burchard: "No, you don't either, Burchy," then continuing: "Cleopatra sailing, a-a-oh, I know, aquaplaning," and throwing her head back and her arms wide, while the boat continued to jump and lurch like a frightened horse.

"See if you can upset me now, Burchy," she called.

And Buchard, throwing the boat from side to side as swiftly as he dared, with Jill Trumbull, anxious for her own safety, calling: "Oh, say, what do you want to do? Drown us all?" at which Clyde winced and blanched as though struck.

At once he felt sick, weak. He had never imagined that it was going to be like this; that he was going to suffer so. He had imagined that it was all going to be different. And yet here he was, blanching at every accidental and unintended word! Why, if he were put to any real test—an officer descending on him unexpectedly and asking him where he had been yesterday and what he knew of Roberta's death—why, he would mumble, shiver, not be able to talk, maybe—and so give his whole case away wouldn't he! He must brace up, try to look natural, happy—mustn't he—for this first day at least.

Fortunately in the speed and excitement of the play, the others seemed not to notice the startling effect of the remark upon him, and he managed by degrees to recover his outward composure. Then the launch approached the Casino and Sondra, wishing to execute some last showy stunt, jumped up and catching the rail pulled herself up, while the boat rolled past only to reverse later. And Clyde, because of a happy smile in his direction, was seized by an uncontrollable desire for her—her love, sympathy, generosity, courage. And so now, to match her smiles, he jumped up and after assisting Jill to the steps, quickly climbed up after her, pretending a gayety and enthusiasm that was as hollow inwardly as outwardly it was accurate.

"Gee! Some athlete you are!"

And then on the links a little later with her, and under her guidance and direction, playing as successful a game as it was possible with his little experience and as troubled as he was. And she, because of the great delight of having him all to herself in shadowy hazards where they might kiss and embrace, beginning to tell him of a proposed camping trip which she, Frank Harriet, Wynette Phant, Burchard Taylor, her brother Stuart, Grant Cranston and Bertine, as well as Harley Baggott, Perly Hayes, Jill Trumbull and Violet Taylor, had been organizing for a week, and which was to begin on the morrow afternoon, with a motor trip thirty miles up the lake and then forty miles east to a lake known as Bear, along which, with tents and equipment, they were to canoe to certain beaches and scenes known only to Harley and Frank. Different days, different points. The boys would kill squirrels and catch fish for food. Also there would be moonlight trips to an inn that could be reached by boat, so they said. A servant or two or three from different homes was to accompany them, as well as a chaperon or two. But, oh, the walks in the woods! The opportunities for love—canoe trips on the lake—hours of uninterrupted love-making for at least a week!

In spite of all that had occurred thus far to give him pause, he could not help thinking that whatever happened, was it not best to go? How wonderful to have her love him so! And what else here could he do? It would take him out of this, would it not—farther and farther from the scene of the—of the—accident and in case any one were looking for any one who looked like him, for instance—well, he would not be around where he could be seen and commented upon. *Those three men.*

Yet, as it now instantly occurred to him, under no circumstances must he leave here without first finding out as definitely as possible whether any one was as yet suspected. And once at the Casino, and for the moment left alone, he learned on inquiring at the news stand that there would be no Albany, Utica, or any local afternoon paper here until seven or seven-thirty. He must wait until then to know.

And so although after the lunch there was swimming and dancing, then a return to the Cranstons with Harley Baggott and Bertine—Sondra going to Pine Point, with an agreement to meet him afterwards at the Harriets for dinner—still his mind was on the business of getting these papers at the first possible opportunity. Yet unless, as he now saw, he was so fortunate as to be able to stop on his way from the Cranstons' to the Harriets' and so obtain one or all, he must manage to come over to this Casino in the morning before leaving for Bear Lake. He must have them. He must know what, if anything, was either being said or done so far in regard to that drowned couple.

But on his way to the Harriets' he was not able to get the papers. They had not come. And none at the Harriets' either, when he first arrived. Yet sitting on the veranda about a half hour later, talking with the others although brooding as to all this, Sondra herself appeared and said: "Oh, say, people! I've got something to tell you. Two people were drowned this morning or yesterday up at Big Bittern, so Blanche Locke was telling me just now over the phone. She's up at Three Mile Bay to-day and she says they've found the body of the girl but not the man yet. They were drowned in the south part of the lake somewhere, she said."

At once Clyde sat up, rigid and white, his lips a bloodless line, his eyes fixed not on anything here but rather the distant scene at Big Bittern—the tall pines, the dark water closing over Roberta. Then they had found her body. And now would they believe that his body was down there, too, as he had planned? But, listen! He must hear in spite of his dizziness.

"Gee, that's tough!" observed Burchard Taylor, stopping his strumming on a mandolin. "Anybody we know?"

"She says she didn't hear yet."

"I never did like that lake," put in Frank Harriet. "It's too lonely. Dad and I and Mr. Randall were up there fishing last summer, but we didn't stay long. It's too gloomy."

"We were up there three weeks ago—don't you remember, Sondra?" added Harley Baggott. "You didn't care for it."

"Yes, I remember," replied Sondra. "A dreadfully lonely place. I can't imagine any one wanting to go up there for anything."

"Well, I only hope it isn't any one we know from around here," added Burchard, thoughtfully. "It would put a crimp in the fun around here for a while, anyhow."

And Clyde unconsciously wet his dry lips with his tongue and swallowed to moisten his already dry throat.

"I don't suppose any of to-day's papers would have anything about it yet. Has any one looked?" inquired Wynette Phant, who had not heard Sondra's opening remark.

"There ain't no papers," commented Burchard Taylor. "Besides, it's not likely yet, didn't Sondra say she just heard it from Blanche Locke over the phone? She's up near there."

"Oh, yes, that's right."

And yet might not that small local afternoon paper of Sharon—*The Banner*, wasn't it—have something as to this? If only he could see it yet to-night!

But another thought! For Heaven's sake! It came to him now for the first time. His footprints! Were there any in the mud of that shore? He had not even stopped to look, climbing out so hastily as he did. And might there not have been? And then would they not know and proceed to follow him— the man those three men saw? Clifford Golden! That ride down this morning. His going out to the Cranstons' in their car. That wet suit over in the room at the Cranstons'! Had any one in his absence been in his room as yet to look, examine, inquire—open his bag, maybe? An officer? God! It was there in his bag. But why in his bag or anywhere else near him now? Why had he not hidden it before this—thrown it in the lake here, maybe, with a stone in it? That would keep it down. God! What was he thinking in the face of such a desperate situation as this? Supposing he did need the suit!

He was now up, standing—mentally and physically frozen really—his eyes touched with a stony glaze for the moment. He must get out of here. He must go back there, at once, and dispose of that suit—drop it in the lake—hide it somewhere in those woods beyond the house! And yet—he could not do that so swiftly, either—leave so instantly after this light conversation about the drowning of those two people. How would that look?

And as instantly there came the thought—no—be calm— show no trace of excitement of any kind, if you can manage it—appear cool—make some unimportant remark, if you can.

And so now, mustering what nervous strength he had, and drawing near to Sondra, he said: "Too bad, eh?" Yet in a

voice that for all its thinly-achieved normality was on the bor-
derline of shaking and trembling. His knees and his hands,
also.

"Yes, it certainly is," replied Sondra, turning to him alone
now. "I always hate to hear of anything like that, don't you?
Mother worries so about Stuart and me fooling around these
lakes as it is."

"Yes, I know." His voice was thick and heavy. He could
scarcely form the words. They were smothered, choked. His
lips tightened to a thinner white line than before. His face
grew paler still.

"Why, what's the matter, Clydie?" Sondra asked, of a sudden, looking at him more closely. "You look so pale! Your
eyes. Anything wrong? Aren't you feeling well to-night, or is
it this light out here?"

She turned to look at some of the others in order to make
sure, then back at him. And he, feeling the extreme importance of looking anything but the way she was describing
him, now drew himself up as best he could, and replied: "Oh,
no. It must be the light, I guess. Sure, it's the light. I had a—
a—hard day yesterday, that's all. I shouldn't have come over
to-night, I suppose." And then achieving the weirdest and
most impossible of smiles. And Sondra, gazing most sympathetically, adding: "Was he so tired? My Clydie-mydie boy,
after his work yesterday. Why didn't my baby boy tell me that
this morning instead of doing all that we did to-day? Want me
to get Frank to run you down to the Cranstons' now? Or
maybe you'd like to go up in his room and lie down? He
won't mind, I know. Shall I ask him?"

She turned as if to speak to Frank, but Clyde, all but panic-
stricken by this latest suggestion, and yet angling for an excuse to leave, exclaimed earnestly and yet shakily: "Please,
please don't, darling. I—I—don't want you to. I'll be all
right. I'll go up after a bit if I want to, or maybe home a little
early, if you're going after a while, but not now. I'm not feeling as good as I should, but I'll be all right."

Sondra, because of his strained and as she now fancied almost peevish tone, desisted with: "All right, honey. All right.
But if you don't feel well, I wish you would let me get Frank
to take you down or go upstairs. He won't mind. And then

after a while—about ten-thirty—I'll excuse myself and you can go down with me to your place. I'll take you there before I go home and whoever else wants to go. Won't my baby boy do something like that?"

And Clyde saying: "Well, I think I'll go up and get a drink, anyhow." And disappearing in one of the spacious baths of the Harriet home, locking the door and sitting down and thinking, thinking—of Roberta's body recovered, of the possibilities of a bruise of some kind, of the possibility of the print of his own feet in the mud and sandy loam of the shore; of that suit over at the Cranstons', the men in the wood, Roberta's bag, hat and coat, his own liningless hat left on the water—and wondering what next to do. How to act! How to talk! Whether to go downstairs to Sondra now and persuade her to go, or whether to stay and suffer and agonize? And what would the morrow's papers reveal? What? What? And was it wise, in case there was any news which would make it look as though eventually he was to be sought after, or in any way connected with this, to go on that proposed camping trip to-morrow! Or, wiser, to run away from here? He had some money now. He could go to New York, Boston, New Orleans where Ratterer was—but oh, no,—not where any one knew him.

Oh, God! The folly of all his planning in connection with all this to date! The flaws! Had he ever really planned it right from the start? Had he ever really imagined, for instance, that Roberta's body would be found in that deep water? And yet, here it was—risen so soon—this first day—to testify against him! And although he had signed as he had on those registers up there, was it not possible now, on account of those three men and that girl on that boat, for him to be traced? He must think, think, think! And get out of here as soon as possible, before anything really fatal in connection with that suit should happen.

Growing momentarily weaker and more terrorized, he now decided to return to Sondra below, and say that he was really feeling quite sick and that if she did not object he would prefer to go home with her, if she could arrange it. And consequently, at ten-thirty, when the evening still had hours to go, Sondra announced to Burchard that she was not feeling well and would he run her and Clyde and Jill down to her place, but that she would see them all on the morrow in time for the proposed departure for Bear Lake.

And Clyde, though brooding as to whether this early leaving on his part was not another of those wretched errors which had seemed to mark every step of this desperate and murderous scheme so far, finally entering the swift launch and being raced to the Cranston lodge in no time. And once there, excusing himself to Burchard and Sondra as nonchalantly and apologetically as might be, and then hurrying to his own room only to find the suit as he had left it—no least evidence that any one had been there to disturb the serenity of his chamber. Just the same, nervously and suspiciously, he now took it out and tied it up, and then waiting and listening for a silent moment in which to slip from the house unobserved—finally ambled out as though going for a short walk. And then, by the shore of the lake—about a quarter of a mile distant from the house—seeking out a heavy stone and tying the suit to that. And then throwing it out into the water, as far as his strength would permit. And then returning, as silently and gloomily and nervously as he had gone, and brooding and brooding as to what the morrow might reveal and what, if any one appeared to question him, he would say.

# Chapter VIII

THE MORROW dawned after an all but sleepless night, harrowed by the most torturesome dreams in regard to Roberta, men who arrived to arrest him, and the like, until at last he arose, his nerves and eyes aching. Then, venturing to come downstairs about an hour later, he saw Frederick, the chauffeur who had driven him out the day before, getting one of the cars out. And thereupon instructing him to bring all the morning Albany and Utica papers. And about nine thirty, when he returned, proceeding to his room with them, where, locking the door and spreading one of the papers before him, he was immediately confronted by the startling headlines:

"MYSTERY IN GIRL'S DEATH
BODY FOUND YESTERDAY IN ADIRONDACK LAKE
MAN COMPANION MISSING"

And at once strained and white he sat down in one of the chairs near the window and began to read:

"Bridgeburg, N.Y., July 9.—The body of an unknown girl, presumably the wife of a young man who registered first on Wednesday morning at Grass Lake Inn, Grass Lake, N.Y., as Carl Graham and wife, and later, Thursday noon, at Big Bittern Lodge, Big Bittern, as Clifford Golden and wife was taken from the waters of the south end of Big Bittern just before noon yesterday. Because of an upturned boat, as well as a man's straw hat found floating on the water in Moon Cove, dredging with hooks and lines had been going on all morning. . . . Up to seven o'clock last evening, however, the body of the man had not as yet been recovered, and according to Coroner Heit of Bridgeburg, who by two o'clock had been summoned to the scene of the tragedy, it was not considered at all likely that it would be. Several marks and abrasions found upon the dead girl's head and face, as well as the testimony of three men who arrived on the scene while the search was still on and testified to having met a young man who answered to the description of Golden or Graham in the woods to the south of the lake the night before, caused many to conclude that a murder had been committed and that the murderer was seeking to make his escape.

The girl's brown leather traveling bag, as well as a hat and coat

623

belonging to her, were left, the bag in the ticket agent's room at Gun Lodge, which is the railway station five miles east of Big Bittern, and the hat and coat in the coatroom of the inn at the Lake, whereas Graham or Golden is said to have taken his suitcase with him into the boat.

According to the innkeeper at Big Bittern, the couple on their arrival registered as Clifford Golden and wife of Albany. They remained in the inn but a few minutes before Golden walked to the boat-landing just outside and procured a light boat, in which, accompanied by the girl and his suitcase, he went out on the lake. They did not return, and yesterday morning the boat was found bottomside up in what is known as Moon Cove, a small bay or extension at the extreme south end of the lake, from the waters of which soon afterwards the body of the young woman was recovered. As there are no known rocks in the lake at that point, and the wounds upon the face are quite marked, suspicion was at once aroused that the girl might have been unfairly dealt with. This, together with the testimony of the three men, as well as the fact that a man's straw hat found nearby contained no lining or other method of identification, has caused Coroner Heit to assert that unless the body of the man is found he will assume that murder has been committed.

Golden or Graham, as described by innkeepers and guests and guides at Grass Lake and Big Bittern, is not more than twenty-four or twenty-five years of age, slender, dark, and not more than five feet eight or nine inches tall. At the time he arrived he was dressed in a light gray suit, tan shoes, and a straw hat and carried a brown suitcase to which was attached an umbrella and some other object, presumably a cane.

The hat and coat left by the girl at the inn were of dark and light tan respectively, her dress a dark blue.

Notice has been sent to all railroad stations in this vicinity to be on the lookout for Golden, or Graham, in order that he may be arrested if he is alive and attempts to make his escape. The body of the drowned girl is to be removed to Bridgeburg, the county seat of this county, where an inquest is later to be held."

In frozen silence he sat and pondered. For would not the news of such a dastardly murder as this now appeared to be, together with the fact that it had been committed in this immediate vicinity, stir up such marked excitement as to cause many—perhaps all—to scan all goers and comers everywhere in the hope of detecting the one who had thus been described? Might it not be better, therefore, since they were so

close on his trail already, if he were to go to the authorities at
Big Bittern or here and make a clean breast of all that had
thus far occurred, the original plot and the reasons therefor,
only explaining how at the very last he had not really killed
her—had experienced a change of heart and had not been
able to do as he had planned? But, no. That would be to give
away to Sondra and the Griffiths all that had been going on
between him and Roberta—and before it was absolutely certain that all was ended for him here. And besides, would they
believe him now, after that flight—those reported wounds?
Did it not really look as though he had killed her, regardless
of how he might try to explain that he had not?

It was not unlikely also that at least some among all those
who had seen him would be able to detect him from this
printed description, even though he no longer wore the gray
suit or the straw hat. God! They were looking for him, or
rather for that Clifford Golden or Carl Graham who looked
like him, in order to charge him with murder! But if he
looked exactly like Clifford Golden and those three men
came! He began to shiver. And worst yet. A new and horrible
thought, this—and at this instant, and for the first time flashing upon his mind—the similarity of those initials to his own!
He had never thought of them in an unfavorable light before,
but now he could see that they were detrimental. Why was it
that he had never thought of that before? Why was it? Why
was it? Oh, God!

Just then a telephone call for him came from Sondra. It was
announced as from her. Yet even so he was compelled to
brace himself in order to make even an acceptable showing,
vocally. How was her sick boy this morning? Any better? How
dreadful that illness last night to come on him so suddenly.
Was he really all right now? And was he going to be able to
go on the trip all right? That was fine. She had been so frightened and so worried all night for fear he might be too sick to
want to go. But he was going, so everything was all right
again now. Darling! Precious baby! Did her baby boy love her
so? She was just sure that the trip would do him a lot of good.
But until noon, now, dear, she would be using all her spare
time getting ready, but at one, or one-thirty, everybody
would be at the Casino pier. And then—oh, my! Ho! for a

great old time up there! He was to come with Bertine and Grant and whoever else was coming from there, and then at the pier he could change to Stuart's launch. They were certain to have so much fun—just loads of it—but just now she would have to go. Bye-bye!

And once more like a bright-colored bird she was gone.

But three hours to wait before he could leave here and so avoid the danger of encountering any one who might be looking for Clifford Golden or Carl Graham! Still until then he could walk up the lake shore into the woods, couldn't he?—or sit below, his bag all packed, and watch who, if anybody, might approach along the long-winding path from the road or by launch across the lake. And if he saw any one who looked at all suspicious, he could take flight, could he not? And afterwards doing just that—first walking away into the woods and looking back, as might a hunted animal. Then later returning and sitting or walking, but always watching, watching. (What man was that? What boat was that? Where was it going? Was it coming here, by any chance? Who was in it? Supposing an officer—a detective? Then flight, of course—if there was still time.)

But, at last one o'clock, and the Cranston launch, with Bertine and Harley and Wynette, as well as Grant and himself, setting out for the pier. And once there, joined by all who were going, together with the servants. And at Little Fish Inlet, thirty miles north, on the eastern shore, they were met by the cars of the Baggotts, Harriets and others, from where, with their goods and canoes, they were portaged forty miles east to Bear Lake, as lonely and as arresting almost as Big Bittern itself.

The joy of this trip if only that other thing were not hanging over him now. This exquisite pleasure of being near Sondra, her eyes constantly telling him how much she cared. And her spirit's flame so high because of his presence here with her now. And yet Roberta's body up! That search for Clifford Golden—Carl Graham. His identical description wired as well as published everywhere. These others—all of them in their boats and cars had probably read it. And yet, because of their familiarity with him and his connections— Sondra, the Griffiths—not suspecting him—not thinking of the description even. But if they should! If they should guess! The horror! The flight! The exposure! The police! The first to desert him—these—all save Sondra perhaps. And even she, too. Yes, she, of course. The horror in her eyes.

And then that evening at sundown, on the west shore of this same lake, on an open sward that was as smooth as any well-kept lawn, the entire company settled, in five different colored tents ranged about a fire like an Indian village, with cooks' and servants' tents in the distance. And the half dozen canoes beached like bright fish along the grassy shore of the lake. And then supper around an open fire. And Baggott and Harriet and Stuart and Grant, after furnishing music for the others to dance by, organizing, by the flare of a large gasoline lamp, a poker game. And the others joining in singing ribald camping and college songs, no one of which Clyde knew, yet in which he tried to join. And shouts of laughter. And bets as to who would be the first to catch the first fish, to shoot the first squirrel or partridge, to win the first race. And lastly, solemn plans for moving the camp at least ten miles farther east, after breakfast, on the morrow where was an ideal beach, and where they would be within five miles of the Wetissic Inn, and where they could dine and dance to their heart's content.

And then the silence and the beauty of this camp at night, after all had presumably gone to bed. The stars! The mystic, shadowy water, faintly rippling in a light wind, the mystic, shadowy pines conferring in the light breezes, the cries of night birds and owls—too disturbing to Clyde to be listened to with anything but inward distress. The wonder and glory of all this—if only—if only he were not stalked after, as by a skeleton, by the horror not only of what he had done in connection with Roberta but the danger and the power of the law that deemed him a murderer! And then Sondra, the others having gone to bed—or off into the shadow,—stealing out for a few last words and kisses under the stars. And he whispering to her how happy he was, how grateful for all her love and faith, and at one point almost tempted to ask whether in case it should ever appear that he was not as good as she now seemed to imagine him, she would still love him a little—not hate him entirely—yet refraining for fear that after that exhibition of terror the preceding night she might connect his present mood with that, or somehow with the horrible, destructive secret that was gnawing at his vitals.

And then afterwards, lying in the four-cot tent with Baggott, Harriet and Grant, listening nervously for hours for any prowling steps that might mean—that might mean—God—what might they not mean even up here?—the law! arrest! exposure! Death. And waking twice in the night out of dread, destructive dreams,—and feeling as though—and fearing—that he had cried out in his sleep.

But then the glory of the morning once more—with its rotund and yellow sun rising over the waters of the lake—and in a cove across the lake wild ducks paddling about. And after a time Grant and Stuart and Harley, half-clad and with guns and a great show of fowling skill, foolishly setting forth in canoes in the hope of bagging some of the game with long distance shots, yet getting nothing, to the merriment of all the others. And the boys and girls, stealing out in bright-colored bathing suits and silken beach robes to the water, there to plunge gayly in and shout and clatter concerning the joy of it all. And breakfast at nine, with afterwards the gayety and beauty of the bright flotilla of canoes making eastward along the southern lake shore, banjos, guitars and mandolins strumming and voices raised in song, jest, laughter.

"Whatever matter wissum sweet to-day? Face all dark. Cantum be happy out here wis Sonda and all these nicey good-baddies?"

And Clyde as instantly realizing that he must pretend to be gay and care-free.

And then Harley Baggott and Grant and Harriet at about noon announcing that there—just ahead—was the fine beach they had in mind—the Ramshorn, a spit of land commanding from its highest point all the length and breadth of the lake. And with room on the shore below for all the tents and paraphernalia of the company. And then, throughout this warm, pleasant Sunday afternoon, the usual program of activities—lunching, swimming, dancing, walking, card-playing, music. And Clyde and Sondra, like other couples, stealing off—Sondra with a mandolin—to a concealed rock far to the east of the camp, where in the shade of the pines they could lie—Sondra in Clyde's arms—and talk of the things they were certain to do later, even though, as she now announced, Mrs. Finchley was declaring that after this particular visit of Clyde's her daughter was to have nothing more to do with him in any such intimate social way as this particular trip gave opportunity for. He was too poor—too nondescript a relative of the Griffiths. (It was so that Sondra, yet in a more veiled way, described her mother as talking.) Yet adding: "How ridiculous, sweetum! But don't you mind. I just laughed and agreed because I don't want to aggravate her just now. But I did ask her how I was to avoid meeting you here or anywhere now since you are as popular as you are. My sweetum is so goodlooking. Everybody thinks so—even the boys."

At this very hour, on the veranda of the Silver Inn at Sharon, District Attorney Mason, with his assistant Burton Burleigh, Coroner Heit and Earl Newcomb, and the redoubtable Sheriff Slack, paunched and scowling, yet genial enough in ordinary social intercourse, together with three assistants—first, second and third deputies Kraut, Sissel and Swenk—conferring as to the best and most certain methods of immediate capture.

"He has gone to Bear Lake. We must follow and trap him before news reaches him in any way that he is wanted."

And so they set forth—this group—Burleigh and Earl Newcomb about Sharon itself in order to gather such additional data as they might in connection with Clyde's arrival and departure from here for the Cranstons' on Friday, talking with and subpoenaing any such individuals as might throw any light on his movements; Heit to Three Mile Bay on much the same errand, to see Captain Mooney of the "Cygnus" and the three men and Mason, together with the sheriff and his deputies, in a high-powered launch chartered for the occasion, to follow the now known course of the only recently-departed camping party, first to Little Fish Inlet and from there, in case the trail proved sound, to Bear Lake.

And on Monday morning, while those at Ramshorn Point after breaking camp were already moving on toward Shelter Beach fourteen miles east, Mason, together with Slack and his three deputies, arriving at the camp deserted the morning before. And there, the Sheriff and Mason taking counsel with each other and then dividing their forces so that in canoes commandeered from lone residents of the region they now proceeded, Mason and First Deputy Kraut along the south shore, Slack and Second Deputy Sissel along the north shore, while young Swenk, blazing with a desire to arrest and hand-cuff some one, yet posing for the occasion as a lone young hunter or woodsman, paddled directly east along the center of the lake in search of any informing smoke or fires or tents or individuals idling along the shores. And with great dreams of being the one to capture the murderer—I arrest you, Clyde Griffiths, in the name of the law!—yet because of instructions from Mason, as well as Slack, grieving that instead, should he detect any signs, being the furthermost outpost, he must, in order to avoid frightening the prey or losing him, turn on his track and from some point not so likely to be heard by the criminal fire one single shot from his eight-chambered re-peater, whereupon whichever party chanced to be nearest would fire one shot in reply and then proceed as swiftly as possible in his direction. But under no circumstances was he to attempt to take the criminal alone, unless noting the de-parture by boat or on foot of a suspicious person who an-swered the description of Clyde.

At this very hour, Clyde, with Harley Baggott, Bertine and Sondra, in one of the canoes, paddling eastward along with the remainder of the flotilla, looking back and wondering. Supposing by now, some officer or some one had arrived at Sharon and was following him up here? For would it be hard to find where he had gone, supposing only that they knew his name?

But they did not know his name. Had not the items in the papers proved that? Why worry so always, especially on this utterly wonderful trip and when at last he and Sondra could be together again? And besides, was it not now possible for him to wander off by himself into these thinly populated woods along the shore to the eastward, toward that inn at the other end of the lake—and not return? Had he not inquired most casually on Saturday afternoon of Harley Baggott as well as others as to whether there was a road south or east from the east end of the lake? And had he not learned there was?

And at last, at noon, Monday, reaching Shelter Beach, the

third spot of beauty contemplated by the planners of this outing, where he helped to pitch the tents again while the girls
played about.

Yet at the same hour, at the Ramshorn site, because of the
ashes from their fires left upon the shore, young Swenk, most
eagerly and enthusiastically, like some seeking animal, approaching and examining the same and then going on—
swiftly. And but one hour later, Mason and Kraut, reconnoitering the same spot, but without either devoting more
than a cursory glance, since it was obvious that the prey had
moved farther on.

But then greater speed in paddling on the part of Swenk,
until by four he arrived at Shelter Beach. And then, descrying
as many as a half dozen people in the water in the distance, at
once turning and retreating in the direction of the others in
order to give the necessary signal. And some two miles back
firing one shot, which in its turn was responded to by Mason
as well as Sheriff Slack. Both parties had heard and were now
paddling swiftly east.

At once Clyde in the water—near Sondra—hearing this was
made to wonder. The ominous quality of that first shot! Followed by those two additional signals—farther away, yet
seemingly in answer to the first! And then the ominous silence thereafter! What was that? And with Harley Baggott
jesting: "Listen to the guys shooting game out of season, will
you? It's against the law, isn't it?"

"Hey, you!" Grant Cranston shouted. "Those are my ducks
down there! Let 'em alone."

"If they can't shoot any better than you, Granty, they will
let 'em alone." This from Bertine.

Clyde, while attempting to smile, looked in the direction of
the sound and listened like a hunted animal.

What was it now that urged him to get out of the water
and dress and run? Hurry! Hurry! To your tent! To the
woods, quick! Until at last heeding this, and while most of
the others were not looking, hurrying to his tent, changing to
the one plain blue business suit and cap that he still possessed,
then slipping into the woods back of the camp—out of sight
and hearing of all present until he should be able to think and
determine, but keeping always safely inland out of the direct

view of the water, for fear—for fear—who could tell exactly what those shots meant?

Yet Sondra! And her words of Saturday and yesterday and to-day. Could he leave her in this way, without being sure? Could he? Her kisses! Her dear assurances as to the future! What would she think now—and those others—in case he did not go back? The comment which was certain to be made in the Sharon and other papers in regard to this disappearance of his, and which was certain to identify him with this same Clifford Golden or Carl Graham! was it not?

Then reflecting also—the possible groundlessness of these fears, based on nothing more, maybe, than the chance shots of passing hunters on the lake or in these woods. And then pausing and debating with himself whether to go on or not. Yet, oh, the comfort of these tall, pillared trees—the softness and silence of these brown, carpeting needles on the ground—the clumps and thickets of underbrush under which one could lie and hide until night should fall again. And then on—and on. But turning, none-the-less, with the intention of returning to the camp to see whether any one had come there. (He might say he had taken a walk and got lost in the woods.)

But about this time, behind a protecting group of trees at least two miles west of the camp, a meeting and conference between Mason, Slack and all the others. And later, as a result of this and even as Clyde lingered and returned somewhat nearer the camp, Mason, Swenk paddling the canoe, arriving and inquiring of those who were now on shore if a Mr. Clyde Griffiths was present and might he see him. And Harley Baggott, being nearest, replying: "Why, yes, sure. He's around here somewhere." And Stuart Finchley calling: "Eh-o, Griffiths!" But no reply.

Yet Clyde, not near enough to hear any of this, even now returning toward the camp, very slowly and cautiously. And Mason concluding that possibly he was about somewhere and unaware of anything, of course, deciding to wait a few minutes anyhow—while advising Swenk to fall back into the woods and if by any chance encountering Slack or any other to advise him that one man be sent east along the bank and another west, while he—Swenk—proceeded in a boat eastward as before to the inn at the extreme end, in order that from there word might be given to all as to the presence of the suspect in this region.

In the meanwhile Clyde by now only three-quarters of a mile east, and still whispered to by something which said: Run, run, do not linger! yet lingering, and thinking *Sondra*, this wonderful life! Should he go so? And saying to himself that he might be making a greater mistake by going than by staying. For supposing those shots were nothing—hunters, mere game shots meaning nothing in his case—and yet costing him all? And yet turning at last and saying to himself that perhaps it might be best not to return at present, anyhow at least not until very late—after dark—to see if those strange shots had meant anything.

But then again pausing silently and dubiously, the while vesper sparrows and woodfinches sang. And peering. And peeking nervously.

And then all at once, not more than fifty feet distant, out of the long, tall aisles of the trees before him, a whiskered, woodsman-like type of man approaching swiftly, yet silently —a tall, bony, sharp-eyed man in a brown felt hat and a brownish-gray baggy and faded suit that hung loosely over his spare body. And as suddenly calling as he came—which caused Clyde's blood to run cold with fear and rivet him to the spot.

"Hold on a moment, mister! Don't move. Your name don't happen to be Clyde Griffiths, does it?" And Clyde, noting the sharp inquisitorial look in the eye of this stranger, as well as the fact that he had already drawn a revolver and was lifting it up, now pausing, the definiteness and authority of the man chilling him to the marrow. Was he really being captured? Had the officers of the law truly come for him? God! No hope of flight now! Why had he not gone on? Oh, why not? And at once he was weak and shaking, yet, not wishing to incriminate himself about to reply, "No!" Yet because of a more sensible thought, replying, "Why, yes that's my name."

"You're with this camping party just west of here, aren't you?"

"Yes, sir, I am."

"All right, Mr. Griffiths. Excuse the revolver. I'm told to

get you, whatever happens, that's all. My name is Kraut. Nicholas Kraut. I'm a deputy sheriff of Cataraqui County. And I have a warrant here for your arrest. I suppose you know what for, and that you're prepared to come with me peaceably." And at this Mr. Kraut gripped the heavy, danger-ous-looking weapon more firmly even, and gazed at Clyde in a firm, conclusive way.

"Why—why—no—I don't," replied Clyde, weakly and heavily, his face white and thin. "But if you have a warrant for my arrest, I'll go with you, certainly. But what—what—I don't understand"—his voice began to tremble slightly as he said this—"is—is why you want to arrest me?"

"You don't, eh? You weren't up at either Big Bittern or Grass Lake by any chance on last Wednesday or Thursday, eh?"

"Why, no, sir, I wasn't," replied Clyde, falsely.

"And you don't happen to know anything about the drowning of a girl up there that you were supposed to be with—Roberta Alden, of Biltz, New York, I believe."

"Why, my God, no!" replied Clyde, nervously and staccat-ically, the true name of Roberta and her address being used by this total stranger, and so soon, staggering him. Then they knew! They had obtained a clue. His true name and hers! God! "Am I supposed to have committed a murder?" he added, his voice faint—a mere whisper.

"Then you don't know that she was drowned last Thurs-day? And you weren't with her at that time?" Mr. Kraut fixed a hard, inquisitive, unbelieving eye on him.

"Why, no, of course, I wasn't," replied Clyde, recalling now but one thing—that he must deny all—until he should think or know what else to do or say.

"And you didn't meet three men walking south last Thurs-day night from Big Bittern to Three Mile Bay at about eleven o'clock?"

"Why, no, sir. Of course I didn't. I wasn't up there, I told you."

"Very well, Mr. Griffiths, I haven't anything more to say. All I'm supposed to do is to arrest you, Clyde Griffiths, for the murder of Roberta Alden. You're my prisoner." He drew forth—more by way of a demonstration of force and authority

than anything else—a pair of steel handcuffs, which caused
Clyde to shrink and tremble as though he had been beaten.

"You needn't put those on me, mister," he pleaded. "I wish
you wouldn't. I never had anything like that on before. I'll go
with you without them." He looked longingly and sadly
about at the trees, into the sheltering depths of which so recently he ought to have plunged. To safety.

"Very well, then," replied the redoubtable Kraut. "So long
as you come along peaceful." And he took Clyde by one of
his almost palsied arms.

"Do you mind if I ask you something else," asked Clyde,
weakly and fearsomely, as they now proceeded, the thought of
Sondra and the others shimmering blindingly and reducingly
before his eyes. Sondra! Sondra! To go back there an arrested
murderer! And before her and Bertine! Oh, no! "Are you, are
you intending to take me to that camp back there?"

"Yes, sir, that's where I'm intending to take you now.
Them's my orders. That's where the district attorney and the
sheriff of Cataraqui County are just now."

"Oh, I know, I know," pleaded Clyde, hysterically, for by
now he had lost almost all poise, "but couldn't you—couldn't
you—so long as I go along just as you want—those are all my
friends, you know, back there, and I'd hate . . . couldn't you
just take me around the camp somewhere to wherever you
want to take me? I have a very special reason—that is—I—I,
oh, God, I hope you won't take me back there right now—
will you please, Mr. Kraut?"

He seemed to Kraut very boyish and weak now—clean of
feature, rather innocent as to eye, well-dressed and well-
mannered—not at all the savage and brutal or murderous
type he had expected to find. Indeed quite up to the class
whom he (Kraut) was inclined to respect. And might he not
after all be a youth of very powerful connections? The conversations he had listened to thus far had indicated that this
youth was certainly identified with one of the best families in
Lycurgus. And in consequence he was now moved to a slight
show of courtesy and so added: "Very well, young man, I
don't want to be too hard on you. After all, I'm not the sheriff or the district attorney—just the arresting officer. There are
others down there who are going to be able to say what to do

about you—and when we get down to where they are, you can ask 'em, and it may be that they won't find it necessary to take you back in there. But how about your clothes? They're back there, ain't they?"

"Oh, yes, but that doesn't matter," replied Clyde, nervously and eagerly. "I can get those any time. I just don't want to go back now, if I can help it."

"All right, then, come along," replied Mr. Kraut.

And so it was that they walked on together now in silence, the tall shafts of the trees in the approaching dusk making solemn aisles through which they proceeded as might worshipers along the nave of a cathedral, the eyes of Clyde contemplating nervously and wearily a smear of livid red still visible through the trees to the west.

Charged with murder! Roberta dead! And Sondra dead—to him! And the Griffiths! And his uncle! And his mother! And all those people in that camp!

Oh, oh, God, why was it that he had not run, when that something, whatever it was, had so urged him?

# Chapter IX

IN THE ABSENCE of Clyde, the impressions taken by Mr. Mason of the world in which he moved here, complementing and confirming those of Lycurgus and Sharon, were sufficient to sober him in regard to the ease (possibly) with which previously he had imagined it might be possible to convict him. For about him was such a scene as suggested all the means as well as the impulse to quiet such a scandal as this. Wealth. Luxury. Important names and connections to protect no doubt. Was it not possible that the rich and powerful Griffiths, their nephew seized in this way and whatever his crime, would take steps to secure the best legal talent available, in order to protect their name? Unquestionably— and then with such adjournments as it was possible for such talent to secure, might it not be possible that long before he could hope to convict him, he himself would automatically be disposed of as a prosecutor and without being nominated for and elected to the judgeship he so craved and needed.

Sitting before the circle of attractive tents that faced the lake and putting in order a fishing-pole and reel, was Harley Baggott, in a brightly-colored sweater and flannel trousers. And through the open flies of several tents, glimpses of individuals—Sondra, Bertine, Wynette and others—busy about toilets necessitated by the recent swim. Being dubious because of the smartness of the company as to whether it was politically or socially wise to proclaim openly the import of his errand, he chose to remain silent for a time, reflecting on the difference between the experiences of his early youth and that of Roberta Alden and these others. Naturally as he saw it a man of this Griffiths' connections would seek to use a girl of Roberta's connections thus meanly and brutally and hope to get away with it. Yet, eager to make as much progress as he could against whatever inimical fates might now beset him, he finally approached Baggott, and, most acidly, yet with as much show of genial and appreciative sociability as he could muster, observed:

"A delightful place for a camp, eh?"

"Yeh, we think so."

"Just a group from the estates and hotels about Sharon, I suppose?"

"Yeh. The south and west shore principally."

"Not any of the Griffiths, other than Mr. Clyde, I presume?"

"No, they're still over at Greenwood, I think."

"You know Mr. Clyde Griffiths personally, I suppose?"

"Oh, sure—he's one of the party."

"You don't happen to know how long he's been up here this time, I presume—up with the Cranstons, I mean."

"Since Friday, I think. I saw him Friday morning, anyhow. But he'll be back here soon and you can ask him yourself," concluded Baggott, beginning to sense that Mr. Mason was a little too inquisitive and in addition not of either his or Clyde's world.

And just then, Frank Harriet, with a tennis racquet under his arm, striding across the foreground.

"Where to, Frankie?"

"To try those courts Harrison laid out up here this morning."

"Who with?"

"Violet, Nadine and Stuart."

"Any room for another court?"

"Sure, there's two. Why not get Bert, and Clyde, and Sondra, and come up?"

"Well, maybe, after I get this thing set."

And Mason at once thinking: Clyde and Sondra. Clyde Griffiths and Sondra Finchley—the very girl whose notes and cards were in one of his pockets now. And might he not see her here, along with Clyde—possibly later talk to her about him?

But just then, Sondra and Bertine and Wynette coming out of their respective tents. And Bertine calling: "Oh, say, Harley, seen Nadine anywhere?"

"No, but Frank just went by. He said he was going up to the courts to play with her and Violet and Stew."

"Yes? Well, then, come on, Sondra. You too, Wynette. We'll see how it looks."

Bertine, as she pronounced Sondra's name, turned to take

her arm, which gave Mason the exact information and opportunity he desired—that of seeing and studying for a moment the girl who had so tragically and no doubt all unwittingly replaced Roberta in Clyde's affections. And, as he could see for himself, more beautiful, more richly appareled than ever the other could have hoped to be. And alive, as opposed to the other now dead and in a morgue in Bridgeburg.

But even as he gazed, the three tripping off together arm in arm, Sondra calling back to Harley: "If you see Clyde, tell him to come on up, will you?" And he replying: "Do you think that shadow of yours needs to be told?"

Mason, impressed by the color and the drama, looked intently and even excitedly about. Now it was all so plain why he wanted to get rid of the girl—the true, underlying motive. That beautiful girl there, as well as this luxury to which he aspired. And to think that a young man of his years and opportunities would stoop to such a horrible trick as that! Unbelievable! And only four days after the murder of the other poor girl, playing about with this beautiful girl in this fashion, and hoping to marry her, as Roberta had hoped to marry him. The unbelievable villainies of life!

Now, half-determining since Clyde did not appear, that he would proclaim himself and proceed to search for and seize his belongings here, Ed Swenk re-appearing and with a motion of the head indicating that Mason was to follow him. And once well within the shadow of the surrounding trees, indicating no less an individual than Nicholas Kraut, attended by a slim, neatly-dressed youth of about Clyde's reported years, who, on the instant and because of the waxy paleness of his face, he assumed must be Clyde. And at once he now approached him, as might an angry wasp or hornet, only pausing first to ask of Swenk where he had been captured and by whom—then gazing at Clyde critically and austerely as befitted one who represented the power and majesty of the law.

"So you are Clyde Griffiths, are you?"

"Yes, sir."

"Well, Mr. Griffiths, my name is Orville Mason. I am the district attorney of the county in which Big Bittern and Grass Lake are situated. I suppose you are familiar enough with those two places by now, aren't you?"

He paused to see the effect of this sardonic bit of commentary. Yet although he expected to see him wince and quail, Clyde merely gazed at him, his nervous, dark eyes showing enormous strain. "No, sir, I can't say that I am."

For with each step through the woods thus far back, there had been growing within him the utter and unshakable conviction that in the face of whatever seeming proof or charges might now appear, he dared not tell anything in regard to himself, his connection with Roberta, his visit to Big Bittern or Grass Lake. He dared not. For that would be the same as a confession of guilt in connection with something of which he was not really guilty. And no one must believe— never—Sondra, or the Griffiths, or any of these fine friends of his, that he could ever have been guilty of such a thought, even. And yet here they were, all within call, and at any moment might approach and so learn the meaning of his arrest. And while he felt the necessity for so denying any knowledge in connection with all this, at the same time he stood in absolute terror of this man—the opposition and irritated mood such an attitude might arouse in him. That broken nose. His large, stern eyes.

And then Mason, eyeing him as one might an unheard-of and yet desperate animal and irritated also by his denial, yet assuming from his blanched expression that he might and no doubt would shortly be compelled to confess his guilt, continuing with: "You know what you are charged with, Mr. Griffiths, of course."

"Yes, sir, I just heard it from this man here."

"And you admit it?"

"Why, no, sir, of course I don't admit it," replied Clyde, his thin and now white lips drawn tight over his even teeth, his eyes full of a deep, tremulous yet evasive terror.

"Why, what nonsense! What effrontery! You deny being up to Grass Lake and Big Bittern on last Wednesday and Thursday?"

"Yes, sir."

"Well, then," and now Mason stiffened himself in an angry and at the same time inquisitorial way, "I suppose you are going to deny knowing Roberta Alden—the girl you took to Grass Lake, and then out on Big Bittern in that boat last

Thursday—the girl you knew in Lycurgus all last year, who lived at Mrs. Gilpin's and worked under you in your department at Griffiths & Company—the girl to whom you gave that toilet set last Christmas! I suppose you're going to say that your name isn't Clyde Griffiths and that you haven't been living with Mrs. Peyton in Taylor Street, and that these aren't letters and cards from your trunk there—from Roberta Alden and from Miss Finchley, all these cards and notes." And extracting the letters and cards as he spoke and waving them before Clyde. And at each point in this harangue, thrusting his broad face, with its flat, broken nose and somewhat aggressive chin directly before Clyde's, and blazing at him with sultry, contemptuous eyes, while the latter leaned away from him, wincing almost perceptibly and with icy chills running up and down his spine and affecting his heart and brain. Those letters! All this information concerning him! And back in his bag in the tent there, all those more recent letters of Sondra's in which she dwelt on how they were to elope together this coming fall. If only he had destroyed them! And now this man might find those—would—and question Sondra maybe, and all these others. He shrunk and congealed spiritually, the revealing effects of his so poorly conceived and executed scheme weighing upon him as the world upon the shoulders of an inadequate Atlas.

And yet, feeling that he must say something and yet not admit anything. And finally replying: "My name's Clyde Griffiths all right, but the rest of this isn't true. I don't know anything about the rest of it."

"Oh, come now, Mr. Griffiths! Don't begin by trying to play fast and loose with me. We won't get anywhere that way. You won't help yourself one bit by that with me, and besides I haven't any time for that now. Remember these men here are witnesses to what you say. I've just come from Lycurgus—your room at Mrs. Peyton's—and I have in my possession your trunk and this Miss Alden's letters to you—indisputable proof that you did know this girl, that you courted and seduced her last winter, and that since then—this spring—when she became pregnant on your account, you induced her first to go home and then later to go away with you on this trip in order, as you told her, to marry her. Well, you married her all

right—to the grave—that's how you married her—to the water at the bottom of Big Bittern Lake! And you can actually
stand here before me now, when I tell you that I have all the
evidence I need right on my person, and say that you don't
even know her! Well, I'll be damned!"

And as he spoke his voice grew so loud that Clyde feared
that it could be clearly heard in the camp beyond. And that
Sondra herself might hear it and come over. And although at
the out rush and jab and slash of such dooming facts as Mason so rapidly outlined, his throat tightened and his hands
were with difficulty restrained from closing and clinching vise-
wise, at the conclusion of it all he merely replied: "Yes, sir."

"Well, I'll be damned!" reiterated Mason. "I can well believe now that you would kill a girl and sneak away in just
such a way as you did—and with her in that condition! But
then to try to deny her own letters to you! Why, you might
as well try to deny that you're here and alive. These cards and
notes here—what about them? I suppose they're not from
Miss Finchley? How about those? Do you mean to tell me
these are not from her either?"

He waved them before Clyde's eyes. And Clyde, seeing that
the truth concerning these, Sondra being within call, was capable of being substantiated here and now, replied: "No, I
don't deny that those are from her."

"Very good. But these others from your trunk in the same
room are not from Miss Alden to you?"

"I don't care to say as to that," he replied, blinking feebly
as Mason waved Roberta's letters before him.

"Tst! Tst! Tst! Of all things," clicked Mason in high dud-
geon. "Such nonsense! Such effrontery! Oh, very well, we
won't worry about all that now. I can easily prove it all when
the time comes. But how you can stand there and deny it,
knowing that I have the evidence, is beyond me! A card in
your own handwriting which you forgot to take out of the
bag you had her leave at Gun Lodge while you took yours
with you. Mr. Carl Graham, Mr. Clifford Golden, Mr. Clyde
Griffiths,—a card on which you wrote 'From Clyde to Bert,
Merry Xmas.' Do you remember that? Well, here it is." And
here he reached into his pocket and drew forth the small card
taken from the toilet set and waved it under Clyde's nose.

"Have you forgotten that, too? Your own handwriting!" And then pausing and getting no reply, finally adding: "Why, what a dunce you are!—what a poor plotter, without even the brains not to use your own initials in getting up those fake names you had hoped to masquerade under—Mr. Carl Graham—Mr. Clifford Golden!"

At the same time, fully realizing the importance of a confession and wondering how it was to be brought about here and now, Mason suddenly—Clyde's expression, his frozen-faced terror, suggesting the thought that perhaps he was too frightened to talk at once changed his tactics—at least to the extent of lowering his voice, smoothing the formidable wrinkles from his forehead and about his mouth.

"You see, it's this way, Griffiths," he now began, much more calmly and simply. "Lying or just foolish thoughtless denial under such circumstances as these can't help you in the least. It can only harm you, and that's the truth. You may think I've been a little rough so far, but it was only because I've been under a great strain myself in connection with this case, trying to catch up with some one I thought would be a very different type from yourself. But now that I see you and see how you feel about it all—how really frightened you are by what has happened—it just occurs to me that there may be something in connection with this case, some extenuating circumstances, which, if they were related by you now, might throw a slightly different light on all this. Of course, I don't know. You yourself ought to be the best judge, but I'm laying the thought before you for what it's worth. For, of course, here are these letters. Besides, when we get to Three Mile Bay to-morrow, as we will, I hope, there will be those three men who met you the other night walking south from Big Bittern. And not only those, but the innkeeper from Grass Lake, the innkeeper from Big Bittern, the boatkeeper up there who rented that boat, and the driver who drove you and Roberta Alden over from Gun Lodge. They will identify you. Do you think they won't know you—not any of them—not be able to say whether you were up there with her or not, or that a jury when the time comes won't believe them?"

And all this Clyde registered mentally like a machine clicking to a coin, yet said nothing,—merely staring, frozen.

"And not only that," went on Mason, very softly and most ingratiatingly, "but there's Mrs. Peyton. She saw me take these letters and cards out of that trunk of yours in your room and from the top drawer of your chiffonier. Next, there are all those girls in that factory where you and Miss Alden worked. Do you suppose they're not going to remember all about you and her when they learn that she is dead? Oh, what nonsense! You ought to be able to see that for yourself, whatever you think. You certainly can't expect to get away with that. It makes a sort of a fool out of you. You can see that for yourself."

He paused again, hoping for a confession. But Clyde still convinced that any admission in connection with Roberta or Big Bittern spelled ruin, merely stared while Mason proceeded to add:

"All right, Griffiths, I'm now going to tell you one more thing, and I couldn't give you better advice if you were my own son or brother and I were trying to get you out of this instead of merely trying to get you to tell the truth. If you hope to do anything at all for yourself now, it's not going to help you to deny everything in the way you are doing. You are simply making trouble and condemning yourself in other people's eyes. Why not say that you did know her and that you were up there with her and that she wrote you those letters, and be done with it? You can't get out of that, whatever else you may hope to get out of. Any sane person—your own mother, if she were here—would tell you the same thing. It's too ridiculous and indicates guilt rather than innocence. Why not come clean here and now as to those facts, anyhow, before it's too late to take advantage of any mitigating circumstances in connection with all this—if there are any? And if you do *now*, and I can help you in any way, I promise you here and now that I'll be only too glad to do so. For, after all, I'm not out here just to hound a man to death or make him confess to something that he hasn't done, but merely to get at the truth in the case. But if you're going to deny that you even knew this girl when I tell you I have all the evidence and can prove it, why then——" and here the district attorney lifted his hands aloft most wearily and disgustedly.

But now as before Clyde remained silent and pale. In spite

of all Mason had revealed, and all that this seemingly friendly, intimate advice seemed to imply, still he could not conceive that it would be anything less than disastrous for him to admit that he even knew Roberta. The fatality of such a confession in the eyes of these others here. The conclusion of all his dreams in connection with Sondra and this life. And so, in the face of this—silence, still. And at this, Mason, irritated beyond measure, finally exclaiming: "Oh, very well, then. So you've finally decided not to talk, have you?" And Clyde, blue and weak, replied: "I had nothing to do with her death. That's all I can say now," yet even as he said it thinking that perhaps he had better not say that—that perhaps he had better say—well, what? That he knew Roberta, of course, had been up there with her, for that matter—but that he had never intended to kill her—that her drowning was an accident. For he had not struck her at all, except by accident, had he? Only it was best not to confess to having struck her at all, wasn't it? For who under such circumstances would believe that he had struck her with a camera by accident. Best not to mention the camera, since there was no mention anywhere in the papers that he had had one with him.

And he was still cogitating while Mason was exclaiming: "Then you admit that you knew her?"

"No, sir."

"Very well, then," he now added, turning to the others, "I suppose there's nothing for it but to take him back there and see what they know about him. Perhaps that will get something out of this fine bird—to confront him with his friends. His bag and things are still back there in one of those tents, I believe. Suppose we take him down there, gentlemen, and see what these other people know about him."

And now, swiftly and coldly he turned, while Clyde, already shrinking at the horror of what was coming, exclaimed: "Oh, please, no! You don't mean to do that, do you? Oh, you won't do that! Oh, please, no!"

And at this point Kraut speaking up and saying: "He asked me back there in the woods if I wouldn't ask you not to take him in there." "Oh, so that's the way the wind blows, is it?" exclaimed Mason at this. "Too thin-skinned to be shown up before ladies and gentlemen of the Twelfth Lake colony, but not even willing to admit that you knew the poor little work-ing-girl who worked for you. Very good. Well, then, my fine friend, suppose you come through with what you really do know now, or down there you go." And he paused a moment to see what effect that would have. "We'll call all those peo-ple together and explain just how things are, and then see if you will be willing to stand there and deny everything!" But noting still a touch of hesitation in Clyde he now added: "Bring him along, boys." And turning toward the camp he proceeded to walk in that direction a few paces while Kraut taking one arm, and Swenk another, and beginning to move Clyde he ended by exclaiming:

"Oh, please, no! Oh, I hope you won't do anything like that, will you, Mr. Mason? Oh, I don't want to go back there if you don't mind. It isn't that I'm guilty, but you can get all my things without my going back there. And besides it will mean so much to me just now." Beads of perspiration once more burst forth on his pale face and hands and he was deadly cold.

"Don't want to go, eh?" exclaimed Mason, pausing as he heard this. "It would hurt your pride, would it, to have 'em know? Well, then, supposing you just answer some of the things I want to know—and come clean and quick, or off we go—and that without one more moment's delay! Now, will you answer or won't you?" And again he turned to confront Clyde, who, with lips trembling and eyes confused and wa-vering, nervously and emphatically announced:

"Of course I knew her. Of course I did. Sure! Those letters show that. But what of it? I didn't kill her. And I didn't go up there with her with any intention of killing her, either. I didn't. I didn't, I tell you! It was all an accident. I didn't even want to take her up there. She wanted me to go—to go away with her somewhere, because—because, well you know—her letters show. And I was only trying to get her to go off some-where by herself, so she would let me alone, because I didn't want to marry her. That's all. And I took her out there, not to kill her at all, but to try to persuade her, that's all. And I didn't upset the boat—at least, I didn't mean to. The wind blew my hat off, and we—she and I—got up at the same time to reach for it and the boat upset—that's all. And the side of it hit her on the head. I saw it, only I was too frightened the way she was struggling about in the water to go near her, because I was afraid that if I did she might drag me down. And then she went down. And I swam ashore. And that's the God's truth!"

His face, as he talked, had suddenly become all flushed, and his hands also. Yet his eyes were tortured, terrified pools of misery. He was thinking—but maybe there wasn't any wind that afternoon and maybe they would find that out. Or the tripod hidden under a log. If they found that, wouldn't they think he hit her with that? He was wet and trembling.

But already Mason was beginning to question him again.

"Now, let's see as to this a minute. You say you didn't take her up there with any intention of killing her?"

"No, sir, I didn't."

"Well, then, how was it that you decided to write your name two different ways on those registers up there at Big Bittern and Grass Lake?"

"Because I didn't want any one to know that I was up there with her."

"Oh, I see. Didn't want any scandal in connection with the condition she was in?"

"No, sir. Yes, sir, that is."

"But you didn't mind if her name was scandalized in case she was found afterwards?"

"But I didn't know she was going to be drowned," replied Clyde, slyly and shrewdly, sensing the trap in time.

"But you did know that you yourself weren't coming back, of course. You knew that, didn't you?"

"Why, no, sir, I didn't know that I wasn't coming back. I thought I was."

"Pretty clever. Pretty clever," thought Mason to himself, but not saying so, and then, rapidly: "And so in order to make everything easy and natural as possible for you to come back, you took your own bag with you and left hers up there. Is that the way? How about that?"

"But I didn't take it because I was going away. We decided to put our lunch in it."

"We, or you?"

"We."

"And so you had to carry that big bag in order to take a little lunch along, eh? Couldn't you have taken it in a paper, or in her bag?"

"Well, her bag was full, and I didn't like to carry anything in a paper."

"Oh, I see. Too proud and sensitive, eh? But not too proud to carry a heavy bag all the way, say twelve miles, in the night to Three Mile Bay, and not ashamed to be seen doing it, either, were you?"

"Well, after she was drowned and I didn't want to be known as having been up there with her, and had to go along——"

He paused while Mason merely looked at him, thinking of the many, many questions he wanted to ask him—so many, many more, and which, as he knew or guessed, would be impossible for him to explain. Yet it was getting late, and back in the camp were Clyde's as yet unclaimed belongings—his bag and possibly that suit he had worn that day at Big Bittern—a gray one as he had heard—not this one. And to catechize him here this way in the dusk, while it might be productive of much if only he could continue it long enough, still there was the trip back, and en route he would have ample time to continue his questionings.

And so, although he disliked much so to do at the moment, he now concluded with: "Oh, well, I tell you, Griffiths, we'll let you rest here for the present. It may be that what you are saying is so—I don't know. I most certainly hope it is, for your sake. At any rate, you go along there with Mr. Kraut. He'll show you where to go."

And then turning to Swenk and Kraut, he exclaimed: "All right, boys. I'll tell you how we'll do. It's getting late and we'll have to hurry a little if we expect to get anywhere yet tonight. Mr. Kraut, suppose you take this young man down where those other two boats are and wait there. Just halloo a little as you go along to notify the sheriff and Sissell that we're ready. And then Swenk and I'll be along in the other boat as soon as we can."

And so saying and Kraut obeying, he and Swenk proceeded inward through the gathering dusk to the camp, while Kraut with Clyde went west, hallooing for the sheriff and his deputy until a response was had.

# Chapter X

THE EFFECT of Mason's re-appearance in the camp with the news, announced first to Frank Harriet, next to Harley Baggott and Grant Cranston, that Clyde was under arrest—that he actually had confessed to having been with Roberta at Big Bittern, if not to having killed her, and that he, Mason, was there with Swenk to take possession of his property—was sufficient to destroy this pretty outing as by a breath. For although amazement and disbelief and astounded confusion were characteristic of the words of all, nevertheless here was Mason demanding to know where were Clyde's things, and asserting that it was at Clyde's request only that he was not brought here to identify his own possessions.

Frank Harriet, the most practical of the group, sensing the truth and authority of this, at once led the way to Clyde's tent, where Mason began an examination of the contents of the bag and clothes, while Grant Cranston, as well as Baggott, aware of Sondra's intense interest in Clyde, departed first to call Stuart, then Bertine, and finally Sondra—moving apart from the rest the more secretly to inform her as to what was then occurring. And she, following the first clear understanding as to this, turning white and fainting at the news, falling back in Grant's arms and being carried to her tent, where, after being restored to consciousness, she exclaimed: "I don't believe a word of it! It's not true! Why, it couldn't be! That poor boy! Oh, Clyde! Where is he? Where have they taken him?" But Stuart and Grant, by no means as emotionally moved as herself, cautioning her to be silent. It might be true at that. Supposing it were! The others would hear, wouldn't they? And supposing it weren't—he could soon prove his innocence and be released, couldn't he? There was no use in carrying on like this now.

But then, Sondra in her thoughts going over the bare possibility of such a thing—a girl killed by Clyde at Big Bittern— himself arrested and being taken off in this way—and she thus publicly—or at least by this group—known to be so interested in him,—her parents to know, the public itself to know— maybe——

But Clyde must be innocent. It must be all a mistake. And then her mind turning back and thinking of that news of the drowned girl she had first heard over the telephone there at the Harriets'. And then Clyde's whiteness—his illness—his all but complete collapse. Oh, no!—not that! Yet his delay in coming from Lycurgus until the Friday before. His failure to write from there. And then, the full horror of the charge returning, as suddenly collapsing again, lying perfectly still and white while Grant and the others agreed among themselves that the best thing to be done was to break up the camp, either now or early in the morning, and depart for Sharon.

And Sondra returning to consciousness after a time tearfully announcing that she must get out of here at once, that she couldn't "endure this place," and begging Bertine and all the others to stay close to her and say nothing about her having fainted and cried, since it would only create talk. And thinking all the time of how, if this were all true, she could secure those letters she had written him! Oh, heavens! For supposing now at this time they should fall into the hands of the police or the newspapers, and be published? And yet moved by her love for him and for the first time in her young life shaken to the point where the grim and stern realities of life were thrust upon her gay and vain notice.

And so it was immediately arranged that she leave with Stuart, Bertine and Grant for the Metissic Inn at the eastern end of the Lake, since from there, at dawn, according to Baggott, they might leave for Albany—and so, in a roundabout way for Sharon.

In the meantime, Mason, after obtaining possession of all Clyde's belongings here, quickly making his way west to Little Fish Inlet and Three Mile Bay, stopping only for the first night at a farmhouse and arriving at Three Mile Bay late on Tuesday night. Yet not without, en route, catechizing Clyde as he had planned, the more particularly since in going through his effects in the tent at the camp he had not found the gray suit said to have been worn by Clyde at Big Bittern.

And Clyde, troubled by this new development, denying that he had worn a gray suit and insisting that the suit he had on was the one he had worn.

"But wasn't it thoroughly soaked?"

"Yes."

"Well, then, where was it cleaned and pressed afterward?"

"In Sharon."

"In Sharon?"

"Yes, sir."

"By a tailor there?"

"Yes, sir."

"What tailor?"

Alas, Clyde could not remember.

"Then you wore it crumpled and wet, did you, from Big Bittern to Sharon?"

"Yes, sir."

"And no one noticed it, of course."

"Not that I remember—no."

"Not that you remember, eh? Well, we'll see about that later," and deciding that unquestionably Clyde was a plotter and a murderer. Also that eventually he could make Clyde show where he had hidden the suit or had had it cleaned.

Next there was the straw hat found on the lake. What about that? By admitting that the wind had blown his hat off, Clyde had intimated that he had worn a hat on the lake, but not necessarily the straw hat found on the water. But now Mason was intent on establishing within hearing of these witnesses, the ownership of the hat found on the water as well as the existence of a second hat worn later.

"That straw hat of yours that you say the wind blew in the water? You didn't try to get that either at the time, did you?"

"No, sir."

"Didn't think of it, I suppose, in the excitement?"

"No, sir."

"But just the same, you had another straw hat when you went down through the woods there. Where did you get that one?"

And Clyde, trapped and puzzled by this, pausing for the fraction of a second, frightened and wondering whether or not it could be proved that this second straw hat he was wearing was the one he had worn through the woods. Also whether the one on the water had been purchased in Utica, as it had. And then deciding to lie. "But I didn't have another straw hat." Without paying any attention to that, Mason

reached over and took the straw hat on Clyde's head and proceeded to examine the lining with its imprint—Stark & Company, Lycurgus.

"This one has a lining, I see. Bought this in Lycurgus, eh?"

"Yes, sir."

"When?"

"Oh, back in June."

"But still you're sure now it's not the one you wore down
through the woods that night?"

"No, sir."

"Well, where was it then?"

And Clyde once more pausing like one in a trap and thinking: My God! How am I to explain this now? Why did I admit that the one on the lake was mine? Yet, as instantly
recalling that whether he had denied it or not, there were
those at Grass Lake and Big Bittern who would remember
that he had worn a straw hat on the lake, of course.

"Where was it then?" insisted Mason.

And Clyde at last saying: "Oh, I was up here once before
and wore it then. I forgot it when I went down the last time
but I found it again the other day."

"Oh, I see. Very convenient, I must say." He was beginning to believe that he had a very slippery person to deal
with indeed—that he must think of his traps more shrewdly,
and at the same time determining to summon the Cranstons
and every member of the Bear Lake party in order to discover whether any recalled Clyde not wearing a straw hat on
his arrival this time, also whether he had left a straw hat the
time before. He was lying, of course, and he would catch
him.

And so no real peace for Clyde at any time between there
and Bridgeburg and the county jail. For however much he
might refuse to answer, still Mason was forever jumping at
him with such questions as: Why was it if all you wanted to
do was to eat lunch on shore that you had to row all the way
down to that extreme south end of the lake when it isn't
nearly so attractive there as it is at other points? And: Where
was it that you spent the rest of that afternoon—surely not
just there? And then, jumping back to Sondra's letters discovered in his bag. How long had he known her? Was he as

much in love with her as she appeared to be with him? Wasn't it because of her promise to marry him in the fall that he had decided to kill Miss Alden?

But while Clyde vehemently troubled to deny this last charge, still for the most part he gazed silently and miserably before him with his tortured and miserable eyes.

And then a most wretched night spent in the garret of a farm-house at the west end of the lake, and on a pallet on the floor, while Sissel, Swenk and Kraut, gun in hand, in turn kept watch over him, and Mason and the sheriff and the others slept below stairs. And some natives, because of information distributed somehow, coming toward morning to inquire: "We hear the feller that killed the girl over to Big Bittern is here—is that right?" And then waiting to see them off at dawn in the Fords secured by Mason.

And again at Little Fish Inlet as well as Three Mile Bay, actual crowds—farmers, store-keepers, summer residents, woodsmen, children—all gathered because of word telephoned on ahead apparently. And at the latter place, Burleigh, Heit and Newcomb, who, because of previously telephoned information, had brought before one Gabriel Gregg, a most lanky and crusty and meticulous justice of the peace, all of the individuals from Big Bittern necessary to identify him fully. And now Mason, before this local justice, charging Clyde with the death of Roberta and having him properly and legally held as a material witness to be lodged in the county jail at Bridgeburg. And then taking him, along with Burton, the sheriff and his deputies, to Bridgeburg, where he was promptly locked up.

And once there, Clyde throwing himself on the iron cot and holding his head in a kind of agony of despair. It was three o'clock in the morning, and just outside the jail as they approached he had seen a crowd of at least five hundred— noisy, jeering, threatening. For had not the news been forwarded that because of his desire to marry a rich girl he had most brutally assaulted and murdered a young and charming working-girl whose only fault had been that she loved him too well. There had been hard and threatening cries of "There he is, the dirty bastard! You'll swing for this yet, you young devil, wait and see!" This from a young woodsman not unlike Swenk in type—a hard, destroying look in his fierce young eyes, leaning out from the crowd. And worse, a waspish type of small-town slum girl, dressed in a gingham dress, who in the dim light of the arcs, had leaned forward to cry: "Lookit, the dirty little sneak—the murderer! You thought you'd get away with it, didnja?"

And Clyde, crowding closer to Sheriff Slack, and thinking: Why, they actually think I did kill her! And they may even lynch me! But so weary and confused and debased and miserable that at the sight of the outer steel jail door swinging open to receive him, he actually gave vent to a sigh of relief because of the protection it afforded.

But once in his cell, suffering none the less without cessation the long night through, from thoughts—thoughts concerning all that had just gone. Sondra! the Griffiths! Bertine. All those people in Lycurgus when they should hear in the morning. His mother eventually, everybody. Where was Sondra now? For Mason had told her, of course, and all those others, when he had gone back to secure his things. And they knew him now for what he was—a plotter of murder! Only, only, if somebody could only know how it had all come about! If Sondra, his mother, any one, could truly see!

Perhaps if he were to explain all to this man Mason now, before it all went any further, exactly how it all had happened. But that meant a true explanation as to his plot, his real original intent, that camera, his swimming away. That unintended blow—(and who was going to believe him as to that)—his hiding the tripod afterwards. Besides once all that was known would he not be done for just the same in connection with Sondra, the Griffiths—everybody. And very likely prosecuted and executed for murder just the same. Oh, heavens—murder. And to be tried for that now; this terrible crime against her proved. They would electrocute him just the same— wouldn't they? And then the full horror of that coming upon him,—death, possibly—and for murder—he sat there quite still. Death! God! If only he had not left those letters written him by Roberta and his mother in his room there at Mrs. Peyton's. If only he had removed his trunk to another room, say, before he left. Why hadn't he thought of that? Yet as in-

stantly thinking, might not that have been a mistake, too, being seemingly a suspicious thing to have done then? But how
came they to know where he was from and what his name
was? Then, as instantly returning in mind to the letters in the
trunk. For, as he now recalled, in one of those letters from his
mother she had mentioned that affair in Kansas City, and Mason would come to know of that. If only he had destroyed
them. Roberta's, his mother's, all! Why hadn't he? But not
being able to answer why—just an insane desire to keep
things maybe—anything that related to him—a kindness, a
tenderness toward him. If only he had not worn that second
straw hat—had not met those three men in the woods! God!
He might have known they would be able to trace him in
some way. If only he had gone on in that wood at Bear Lake,
taking his suit case and Sondra's letters with him. Perhaps,
perhaps, who knows, in Boston, or New York, or somewhere
he might have hidden away.

Unstrung and agonized, he was unable to sleep at all, but
walked back and forth, or sat on the side of the hard and
strange cot, thinking, thinking. And at dawn, a bony, aged,
rheumy jailer, in a baggy, worn, blue uniform, bearing a
black, iron tray, on which was a tinful of coffee, some bread
and a piece of ham with one egg. And looking curiously and
yet somehow indifferently at Clyde, while he forced it
through an aperture only wide and high enough for its admission, though Clyde wanted nothing at all.

And then later Kraut and Sissell and Swenk, and eventually
the sheriff himself, each coming separately, to look in and say:
"Well, Griffiths, how are you this morning?" or, "Hello, anything we can do for you?", while their eyes showed the astonishment, disgust, suspicion or horror with which his
assumed crime had filled them. Yet, even in the face of that,
having one type of interest and even sycophantic pride in his
presence here. For was he not a Griffiths—a member of the
well-known social group of the big central cities to the south
of here. Also the same to them, as well as to the enormously
fascinated public outside, as a trapped and captured animal,
taken in their legal net by their own superlative skill and now
held as witness to it? And with the newspapers and people
certain to talk, enormous publicity for them—their pictures in

the papers as well as his, their names persistently linked with his.

And Clyde, looking at them between the bars, attempted to be civil, since he was now in their hands and they could do with him as they would.

# Chapter XI

IN CONNECTION with the autopsy and its results there was a decided set-back. For while the joint report of the five doctors showed: "An injury to the mouth and nose; the tip of the nose appears to have been slightly flattened, the lips swollen, one front tooth slightly loosened, and an abrasion of the mucous membrane within the lips"—all agreed that these injuries were by no means fatal. The chief injury was to the skull (the very thing which Clyde in his first confession had maintained), which appeared to have been severely bruised by a blow of "some sharp instrument," unfortunately in this instance, because of the heaviness of the blow of the boat, "signs of fracture and internal hæmorrhage which might have produced death."

But—the lungs when placed in water, sinking—an absolute proof that Roberta could not have been dead when thrown into the water, but alive and drowning, as Clyde had maintained. And no other signs of violence or struggle, although her arms and fingers appeared to be set in such a way as to indicate that she might have been reaching or seeking to grasp something. The wale of the boat? Could that be? Might Clyde's story, after all, conceal a trace of truth? Certainly these circumstances seemed to favor him a little. Yet as Mason and the others agreed, all these circumstances most distinctly seemed to prove that although he might not have slain her outright before throwing her into the water, none the less he had struck her and then had thrown her, perhaps unconscious, into the water.

But with what? If he could but make Clyde say that!

And then an inspiration! He would take Clyde and, although the law specifically guaranteed accused persons against compulsions, compel him to retrace the scenes of his crime. And although he might not be able to make him commit himself in any way, still, once on the ground and facing the exact scene of his crime, his actions might reveal something of the whereabouts of the suit, perhaps, or possibly some instrument with which he had struck her.

And in consequence, on the third day following Clyde's incarceration, a second visit to Big Bittern, with Kraut, Heit, Mason, Burton, Burleigh, Earl Newcomb and Sheriff Slack as his companions, and a slow re-canvassing of all the ground he had first traveled on that dreadful day. And with Kraut, following instructions from Mason, "playing up" to him, in order to ingratiate himself into his good graces, and possibly cause him to make a clean breast of it. For Kraut was to argue that the evidence, so far was so convincing that you "never would get a jury to believe that you didn't do it," but that, "if you would talk right out to Mason, he could do more for you with the judge and the governor than any one could—get you off, maybe, with life or twenty years, while this way you're likely to get the chair, sure."

Yet Clyde, because of that same fear that had guided him at Bear Lake, maintaining a profound silence. For why should he say that he had struck her, when he had not—intentionally at least? Or with what, since no thought of the camera had come up as yet.

At the lake, after definite measurements by the county surveyor as to the distance from the spot where Roberta had drowned to the spot where Clyde had landed, Earl Newcomb suddenly returning to Mason with an important discovery. For under a log not so far from the spot at which Clyde had stood to remove his wet clothes, the tripod he had hidden, a little rusty and damp, but of sufficient weight, as Mason and all these others were now ready to believe, to have delivered the blow upon Roberta's skull which had felled her and so make it possible for him to carry her to the boat and later drown her. Yet, confronted with this and turning paler than before, Clyde denying that he had a camera or a tripod with him, although Mason was instantly deciding that he would re-question all witnesses to find out whether any recalled seeing a tripod or camera in Clyde's possession.

And before the close of this same day learning from the guide who had driven Clyde and Roberta over, as well as the boatman who had seen Clyde drop his bag into the boat, and a young waitress at Grass Lake who had seen Clyde and Roberta going out from the inn to the station on the morning of their departure from Grass Lake, that all now recalled a "yellow bundle of sticks," fastened to his bag which must have been the very tripod.

And then Burton Burleigh deciding that it might not really have been the tripod, after all, with which he had struck her but possibly and even probably the somewhat heavier body of the camera itself, since an edge of it would explain the wound on the top of the head and the flat surface would well explain the general wounds on her face. And because of this conclusion, without any knowledge on the part of Clyde, however, Mason securing divers from among the woodsmen of the region and setting them to diving in the immediate vicinity of the spot where Roberta's body had been found, with the result that after an entire day's diving on the part of six—and because of a promised and substantial reward, one Jack Bogart arose with the very camera which Clyde, as the boat had turned over, had let fall. Worse, after examination it proved to contain a roll of films, which upon being submitted to an expert chemist for development, showed finally to be a series of pictures of Roberta, made on shore—one sitting on a log, a second posed by the side of the boat on shore, a third reaching up toward the branches of a tree—all very dim and water-soaked but still decipherable. And the exact measurements of the broadest side of the camera corresponding in a general way to the length and breadth of the wounds upon Roberta's face, which caused it now to seem positive that they had discovered the implement wherewith Clyde had delivered the blows.

Yet no trace of blood upon the camera itself. And none upon the side or bottom of the boat, which had been brought to Bridgeburg for examination. And none upon the rug which had lain in the bottom of the boat.

In Burton Burleigh there existed as sly a person as might have been found in a score of such backwoods counties as this, and soon he found himself meditating on how easy it would be, supposing irrefragable evidence were necessary, for him or any one to cut a finger and let it bleed on the rug or the side of the boat or the edge of the camera. Also, how easy to take from the head of Roberta two or three hairs and thread them between the sides of the camera, or about the row-lock to which her veil had been attached. And after due and secret meditation, he actually deciding to visit the Lutz Brothers morgue and secure a few threads of Roberta's hair. For he himself was convinced that Clyde had murdered the girl in cold blood. And for want of a bit of incriminating proof, was such a young, silent, vain crook as this to be allowed to escape? Not if he himself had to twine the hairs about the rowlock or inside the lid of the camera, and then call Mason's attention to them as something overlooked!

And in consequence, upon the same day that Heit and Mason were personally re-measuring the wounds upon Roberta's face and head, Burleigh slyly threading two of Roberta's hairs in between the door and the lens of the camera, so that Mason and Heit a little while later unexpectedly coming upon them, and wondering why they had not seen them before—nevertheless accepting them immediately as conclusive evidence of Clyde's guilt. Indeed, Mason thereupon announcing that in so far as he was concerned, his case was complete. He had truly traced out every step in this crime and if need be was prepared to go to trial on the morrow.

Yet, because of the very completeness of the testimony, deciding for the present, at least, not to say anything in connection with the camera—to seal, if possible, the mouth of every one who knew. For, assuming that Clyde persisted in denying that he had carried a camera, or that his own lawyer should be unaware of the existence of such evidence, then how damning in court, and out of a clear sky, to produce this camera, these photographs of Roberta made by him, and the proof that the very measurements of one side of the camera coincided with the size of the wounds upon her face! How complete! How incriminating!

Also since he personally having gathered the testimony was the one best fitted to present it, he decided to communicate with the governor of the state for the purpose of obtaining a special term of the Supreme Court for this district, with its accompanying special session of the local grand jury, which would then be subject to his call at any time. For with this granted, he would be able to impanel a grand jury and in the event of a true bill being returned against Clyde, then within a month or six weeks, proceed to trial. Strictly to himself, however, he kept the fact that in view of his own approaching nomination in the ensuing November election this should all prove most opportune, since in the absence of any such special term the case could not possibly be tried before the succeeding regular January term of the Supreme Court, by which time he would be out of office and although possibly elected to the local judgeship still not able to try the case in person. And in view of the state of public opinion, which was most bitterly and vigorously anti-Clyde, a quick trial would seem fair and logical to every one in this local world. For why delay? Why permit such a criminal to sit about and speculate on some plan of escape? And especially when his trial by him, Mason, was certain to rebound to his legal and political and social fame the country over.

# Chapter XII

A<small>ND THEN</small> out of the north woods a crime sensation of the first magnitude, with all of those intriguingly colorful, and yet morally and spiritually atrocious, elements—love, romance, wealth, poverty, death. And at once picturesque accounts of where and how Clyde had lived in Lycurgus, with whom he had been connected, how he had managed to conceal his relations with one girl while obviously planning to elope with another—being wired for and published by that type of editor so quick to sense the national news value of crimes such as this. And telegrams of inquiry pouring in from New York, Chicago, Boston, Philadelphia, San Francisco and other large American cities east and west, either to Mason direct or the representatives of the Associated or United Press in this area, asking for further and more complete details of the crime. Who was this beautiful wealthy girl with whom it was said this Griffiths was in love? Where did she live? What were Clyde's exact relations with her? Yet Mason, over-awed by the wealth of the Finchleys and the Griffiths, loath to part with Sondra's name, simply asserting for the present that she was the daughter of a very wealthy manufacturer in Lycurgus, whose name he did not care to furnish—yet not hesitating to show the bundle of letters carefully tied with a ribbon by Clyde.

But Roberta's letters on the other hand being described in detail,—even excerpts of some of them—the more poetic and gloomy being furnished the Press for use, for who was there to protect her. And on their publication a wave of hatred for Clyde as well as a wave of pity for her—the poor, lonely, country girl who had had no one but him—and he cruel, faithless,—a murderer even. Was not hanging too good for him? For enroute to and from Bear Lake, as well as since, Mason had pored over these letters. And because of certain intensely moving passages relating to her home life, her gloomy distress as to her future, her evident loneliness and weariness of heart, he had been greatly moved, and later had been able to convey this feeling to others—his wife and Heit and the local newspapermen. So much so that the latter in particular were sending from Bridgeburg vivid, if somewhat distorted, descriptions of Clyde, his silence, his moodiness, and his hard-heartedness.

And then a particularly romantic young reporter from *The Star*, of Utica arriving at the home of the Aldens, there was immediately given to the world a fairly accurate picture of the weary and defeated Mrs. Alden, who, too exhausted to protest or complain, merely contented herself with a sincere and graphic picture of Roberta's devotion to her parents, her simple ways of living, her modesty, morality, religious devotion—how once the local pastor of the Methodist Church had said that she was the brightest and prettiest and kindest girl he had ever known, and how for years before leaving home she had been as her mother's own right hand. And that undoubtedly because of her poverty and loneliness in Lycurgus, she had been led to listen to the honeyed words of this scoundrel, who, coming to her with promises of marriage, had lured her into this unhallowed and, in her case, all but unbelievable relationship which had led to her death. For she was good and pure and sweet and kind always. "And to think that she is dead. I can't believe it."

It was so that her mother was quoted.

"Only Monday a week ago she was about—a little depressed, I thought, but smiling, and for some reason which I thought odd at the time went all over the place Monday afternoon and evening, looking at things and gathering some flowers. And then she came over and put her arms around me and said: 'I wish I were a little girl again, mamma, and that you would take me in your arms and rock me like you used to.' And I said, 'Why, Roberta, what makes you so sad tonight, anyhow?' And she said, 'Oh, nothing. You know I'm going back in the morning. And somehow I feel a little foolish about it to-night.' And to think that it was this trip that was in her mind. I suppose she had a premonition that all would not work out as she had planned. And to think he struck my little girl, she who never could harm anything, not even a fly." And here, in spite of herself, and with the saddened Titus in the background, she began to cry silently.

But from the Griffiths and other members of this local

social world, complete and almost unbreakable silence. For in so far as Samuel Griffiths was concerned, it was impossible for him at first either to grasp or believe that Clyde could be capable of such a deed. What! That bland and rather timid and decidedly gentlemanly youth, as he saw him, charged with murder? Being rather far from Lycurgus at the time—Upper Saranac—where he was reached with difficulty by Gilbert,—he was almost unprepared to think, let alone act. Why, how impossible! There must be some mistake here. They must have confused Clyde with some one else.

Nevertheless, Gilbert proceeding to explain that it was unquestionably true, since the girl had worked in the factory under Clyde, and the district attorney at Bridgeburg with whom he had already been in communication had assured him that he was in possession of letters which the dead girl had written to Clyde and that Clyde did not attempt to deny them.

"Very well, then," countered Samuel. "Don't act hastily, and above all, don't talk to any one outside of Smillie or Gotboy until I see you. Where's Brookhart?"—referring to Darrah Brookhart, of counsel for Griffiths & Company.

"He's in Boston to-day," returned his son. "I think he told me last Friday that he wouldn't be back here until Monday or Tuesday."

"Well, wire him that I want him to return at once. Incidentally, have Smillie see if he can arrange with the editors of *The Star* and *Beacon* down there to suspend any comment until I get back. I'll be down in the morning. Also tell him to get in the car and run up there" (Bridgeburg) "to-day if he can. I must know from first hand all there is to know. Have him see Clyde if he can, also this district attorney, and bring down any news that he can get. And all the newspapers. I want to see for myself what has been published."

And at approximately the same time, in the home of the Finchleys on Fourth Lake, Sondra herself, after forty-eight hours of most macerating thoughts spent brooding on the astounding climax which had put a period to all her girlish fancies in regard to Clyde, deciding at last to confess all to her father, to whom she was more drawn than to her mother. And accordingly approaching him in the library, where usually he sat after dinner, reading or considering his various affairs. But having come within earshot of him, beginning to sob, for truly she was stricken in the matter of her love for Clyde, as well as her various vanities and illusions in regard to her own high position, the scandal that was about to fall on her and her family. Oh, what would her mother say now, after all her warnings? And her father? And Gilbert Griffiths and his affianced bride? And the Cranstons, who except for her influence over Bertine, would never have been drawn into this intimacy with Clyde?

Her sobs arresting her father's attention, he at once paused to look up, the meaning of this quite beyond him. Yet instantly sensing something very dreadful, gathering her up in his arms, and consolingly murmuring: "There, there! For heaven's sake, what's happened to my little girl now? Who's done what and why?" And then, with a decidedly amazed and shaken expression, listening to a complete confession of all that had occurred thus far—the first meeting with Clyde, her interest in him, the attitude of the Griffiths, her letters, her love, and then this—this awful accusation and arrest. And if it were true! And her name were used, and her daddy's! And once more she fell to weeping as though her heart would break, yet knowing full well that in the end she would have her father's sympathy and forgiveness, whatever his subsequent suffering and mood.

And at once Finchley, accustomed to peace and order and tact and sense in his own home, looking at his daughter in an astounded and critical and yet not uncharitable way, and exclaiming: "Well, well, of all things! Well, I'll be damned! I am amazed, my dear! I am astounded! This is a little too much, I must say. Accused of murder! And with letters of yours in your own handwriting, you say, in his possession, or in the hands of this district attorney, for all we know by now. Tst! Tst! Tst! Damned foolish, Sondra, damned foolish! Your mother has been talking to me for months about this, and you know I was taking your word for it against hers. And now see what's happened! Why couldn't you have told me or listened to her? Why couldn't you have talked all this over with me before going so far? I thought we understood each other, you and I. Your mother and I have always acted for your own good, haven't we? You know that. Besides, I certainly thought you had better sense. Really, I did. But a murder case, and you connected with it! My God!"

He got up, a handsome blond man in carefully made clothes, and paced the floor, snapping his fingers irritably, while Sondra continued to weep. Suddenly, ceasing his walking, he turned again toward her and resumed with: "But, there, there! There's no use crying over it. Crying isn't going to fix it. Of course, we may be able to live it down in some way. I don't know. I don't know. I can't guess what effect this is likely to have on you personally. But one thing is sure. We do want to know something about those letters."

And forthwith, and while Sondra wept on, he proceeded first to call his wife in order to explain the nature of the blow—a social blow that was to lurk in her memory as a shadow for the rest of her years—and next to call up Legare Atterbury, lawyer, state senator, chairman of the Republican State Central Committee and his own private counsel for years past, to whom he explained the amazing difficulty in which his daughter now found herself. Also to inquire what was the most advisable thing to be done.

"Well, let me see," came from Atterbury, "I wouldn't worry very much if I were you, Mr. Finchley. I think I can do something to straighten this out for you before any real public damage is done. Now, let me see. Who is the district attorney of Cataraqui County, anyhow? I'll have to look that up and get in touch with him and call you back. But never mind, I promise you I'll be able to do something—keep the letters out of the papers, anyhow. Maybe out of the trial—I'm not sure—but I am sure I can fix it so that her name will not be mentioned, so don't worry."

And then Atterbury in turn calling up Mason, whose name he found in his lawyers' directory, and at once arranging for a conference with him, since Mason seemed to think that the letters were most vital to his case, although he was so much over-awed by Atterbury's voice that he was quick to explain that by no means had he planned as yet to use publicly the name of Sondra or the letters either, but rather to reserve their actuality for the private inspection of the grand jury, unless Clyde should choose to confess and avoid a trial.

But Atterbury, after referring back to Finchley and finding

him opposed to any use of the letters whatsoever, or Sondra's name either, assuring him that on the morrow or the day after he would himself proceed to Bridgeburg with some plans and political information which might cause Mason to think twice before he so much as considered referring to Sondra in any public way.

And then after due consideration by the Finchley family, it was decided that at once, and without explanation or apology to any one, Mrs. Finchley, Stuart and Sondra should leave for the Maine coast or any place satisfactory to them. Finchley himself proposed to return to Lycurgus and Albany. It was not wise for any of them to be about where they could be reached by reporters or questioned by friends. And forthwith, a hegira of the Finchleys to Narragansett, where under the name of Wilson they secluded themselves for the next six weeks. Also, and because of the same cause the immediate removal of the Cranstons to one of the Thousand Islands, where there was a summer colony not entirely unsatisfactory to their fancy. But on the part of the Baggots and the Harriets, the contention that they were not sufficiently incriminated to bother and so remaining exactly where they were at Twelfth Lake. But all talking of Clyde and Sondra—this horrible crime and the probable social destruction of all those who had in any way been thus innocently defiled by it.

And in the interim, Smillie, as directed by Griffiths, proceeding to Bridgeburg, and after two long hours with Mason, calling at the jail to see Clyde. And because of authorization from Mason being permitted to see him quite alone in his cell. Smillie having explained that it was not the intention of the Griffiths to try to set up any defense for Clyde, but rather to discover whether under the circumstances there was a possibility for a defense, Mason had urged upon him the wisdom of persuading Clyde to confess, since, as he insisted, there was not the slightest doubt as to his guilt, and a trial would but cost the county money without result to Clyde—whereas if he chose to confess, there might be some undeveloped reasons for clemency—at any rate, a great social scandal prevented from being aired in the papers.

And thereupon Smillie proceeding to Clyde in his cell where brooding most darkly and hopelessly he was wondering how to do. Yet at the mere mention of Smillie's name shrinking as though struck. The Griffiths—Samuel Griffiths and Gilbert! Their personal representative. And now what would he say? For no doubt, as he now argued with himself, Smillie, having talked with Mason, would think him guilty. And what was he to say now? What sort of a story tell—the truth or what? But without much time to think, for even while he was trying to do so Smillie had been ushered into his presence. And then moistening his dry lips with his tongue, he could only achieve, "Why, how do you do, Mr. Smillie?" to which the latter replied, with a mock geniality, "Why, hello, Clyde, certainly sorry to see you tied up in a place like this." And then continuing: "The papers and the district attorney over here are full of a lot of stuff about some trouble you're in, but I suppose there can't be much to it—there must be some mistake, of course. And that's what I'm up here to find out. Your uncle telephoned me this morning that I was to come up and see you to find out how they come to be holding you. Of course, you can understand how they feel down there. So they wanted me to come up and get the straight of it so as to get the charge dismissed, if possible—so now if you'll just let me know the ins and outs of this—you know—that is——"

He paused there, confident because of what the district attorney had just told him, as well as Clyde's peculiarly nervous and recessive manner, that he would not have very much that was exculpatory to reveal.

And Clyde, after moistening his lips once more, beginning with: "I suppose things do look pretty bad for me, Mr. Smillie. I didn't think at the time that I met Miss Alden that I would ever get into such a scrape as this. But I didn't kill her, and that's the God's truth. I never even wanted to kill her or take her up to that lake in the first place. And that's the truth, and that's what I told the district attorney. I know he has some letters from her to me, but they only show that she wanted me to go away with her—not that I wanted to go with her at all——"

He paused, hoping that Smillie would stamp this with his approval of faith. And Smillie, noting the agreement between his and Mason's assertions, yet anxious to placate him, returned: "Yes, I know. He was just showing them to me."

"I knew he would," continued Clyde, weakly. "But you know how it is sometimes, Mr. Smillie," his voice, because of his fears that the sheriff or Kraut were listening, pitched very low. "A man can get in a jam with a girl when he never even intended to at first. You know that yourself. I did like Roberta at first, and that's the truth, and I did get in with her just as those letters show. But you know that rule they have down there, that no one in charge of a department can have anything to do with any of the women under him. Well, that's what started all the trouble for me, I guess. I was afraid to let any one know about it in the first place, you see."

"Oh, I see."

And so by degrees, and growing less and less tense as he proceeded, since Smillie appeared to be listening with sympathy, he now outlined most of the steps of his early intimacy with Roberta, together with his present defense. But with no word as to the camera, or the two hats or the lost suit, which things were constantly and enormously troubling him. How could he ever explain these, really? And with Smillie at the conclusion of this and because of what Mason had told him, asking: "But what about those two hats, Clyde? This man over here was telling me that you admit to having two straw hats—the one found on the lake and the one you wore away from there."

And Clyde, forced to say something, yet not knowing what, replying: "But they're wrong as to my wearing a straw hat away from there, Mr. Smillie, it was a cap."

"I see. But still you did have a straw hat up at Bear Lake, he tells me."

"Yes, I had one there, but as I told him, that was the one I had with me when I went up to the Cranstons' the first time. I told him that. I forgot it and left it there."

"Oh, I see. But now there was something about a suit—a gray one, I believe—that he says you were seen wearing up there but that he can't find now? Were you wearing one?"

"No. I was wearing the blue suit I had on when I came down here. They've taken that away now and given me this one."

"But he says that you say you had it dry-cleaned at Sharon, but that he can't find any one there who knows anything about it. How about that? Did you have it dry-cleaned there?"

"Yes, sir."

"By whom?"

"Well, I can't just remember now. But I think I can find the man if I were to go up there again—he's near the depot," but at the same time looking down and away from Smillie.

And then Smillie, like Mason before him, proceeding to ask about the bag in the boat, and whether it had not been possible, if he could swim to shore with his shoes and suit on, for him to have swam to Roberta and assisted her to cling to the overturned boat. And Clyde explaining, as before, that he was afraid of being dragged down, but adding now, for the first time, that he had called to her to hang on to the boat, whereas previously he had said that the boat had drifted away from them. And Smillie recalled that Mason had told him this. Also, in connection with Clyde's story of the wind blowing his hat off, Mason had said he could prove by witnesses, as well as the U.S. Government reports, that there was not a breath of air stirring on that most halcyon day. And so, plainly, Clyde was lying. His story was too thin. Yet Smillie, not wishing to embarrass him, kept saying: "Oh, I see," or, "To be sure," or "That's the way it was, was it?"

And then finally asking about the marks on Roberta's face and head. For Mason had called his attention to them and insisted that no one blow from a boat would make both abrasions. But Clyde sure that the boat had only struck her once and that all the bruises had come from that or else he could not guess from what they had come. But then beginning to see how hopeless was all this explanation. For it was so plain from his restless, troubled manner that Smillie did not believe him. Quite obviously he considered his not having aided Roberta as dastardly—a thin excuse for letting her die.

And so, too weary and disheartened to lie more, finally ceasing. And Smillie, too sorry and disturbed to wish to catechize or confuse him further, fidgeting and fumbling and finally declaring: "Well, I'm afraid I'll have to be going now, Clyde. The roads are pretty bad between here and Sharon. But I've been mighty glad to hear your side of it. And I'll present it to your uncle just as you have told it to me. But in the meantime, if I were you, I wouldn't do any more talking than I could help—not until you hear further from me. I was instructed to find an attorney up here to handle this case for you, if I could, but since it's late and Mr. Brookhart, our chief counsel, will be back to-morrow, I think I'll just wait until I can talk to him. So if you'll take my advice, you'll just not say anything until you hear from him or me. Either he'll come or he'll send some one—he'll bring a letter from me, whoever he is, and then he'll advise you."

And with this parting admonition, leaving Clyde to his thoughts and himself feeling no least doubt of his guilt and that nothing less than the Griffiths' millions, if so they chose to spend them, could save him from a fate which was no doubt due him.

# Chapter XIII

A ND then on the following morning Samuel Griffiths, with his own son Gilbert standing by, in the large drawing room of their Wykeagy Avenue mansion, listening to Smillie's report of his conference with Clyde and Mason. And Smillie reporting all he had heard and seen. And with Gilbert Griffiths, unbelievably shaken and infuriated by all this, exclaiming at one point:

"Why, the little devil! The little beast! But what did I tell you, dad? Didn't I warn you against bringing him on?"

And Samuel Griffiths after meditating on this reference to his earlier sympathetic folly now giving Gilbert a most suggestive and intensely troubled look, which said: Are we here to discuss the folly of my original, if foolish, good intentions, or the present crisis? And Gilbert thinking: The murderer! And that wretched little show-off, Sondra Finchley, trying to make something of him in order to spite me, Gilbert, principally, and so getting herself smirched. The little fool! But it served her right. She would get her share of this now. Only it would cause him and his father and all of them infinite trouble also. For was this not an ineradicable stain which was likely to defile all—himself, his fiancée, Bella, Myra, his parents—and perhaps cost them their position here in Lycurgus society? The tragedy! Maybe an execution! And in this family!

Yet Samuel Griffiths, on his part, going back in his mind to all that had occurred since Clyde had arrived in Lycurgus.

His being left to work in that basement at first and ignored by the family. Left to his own devices for fully eight months. Might not that have been at least a contributing cause to all this horror? And then being put over all those girls! Was not that a mistake? He could see all this now clearly, although by no means condoning Clyde's deed in any way—far from it. The wretchedness of such a mind as that—the ungoverned and carnal desires! The uncontrollable brutality of seducing that girl and then because of Sondra—the pleasant, agreeable little Sondra—plotting to get rid of her! And now in jail, and offering no better explanation of all the amazing circum-

672

stances, as reported by Smillie, than that he had not intended
to kill her at all—had not even plotted to do so—that the
wind had blown his hat off! How impossibly weak! And with
no suitable explanation for the two hats, or the missing suit,
or of not going to the aid of the drowning girl. And those un-
explained marks on her face. How strongly all these things
pointed to his guilt.

"For God's sake," exclaimed Gilbert, "hasn't he anything
better than that to offer, the little fool!" And Smillie replied
that that was all he could get him to say, and that Mr. Mason
was absolutely and quite dispassionately convinced of his
guilt. "Dreadful! Dreadful!" put in Samuel. "I really can't
grasp it yet. I can't! It doesn't seem possible that any one of
my blood could be guilty of such a thing!" And then getting
up and walking the floor in real and crushing distress and fear.
His family! Gilbert and his future! Bella, with all her ambitions and dreams! And Sondra! And Finchley!

He clinched his hands. He knitted his brows and tightened
his lips. He looked at Smillie, who, immaculate and sleek,
showed nevertheless the immense strain that was on him,
shaking his head dismally whenever Griffiths looked at him.

And then after nearly an hour and a half more of such questioning and requestioning as to the possibility of some other
interpretation than the data furnished by Smillie would permit, Griffiths, senior, pausing and declaring: "Well, it does
look bad, I must say. Still, in the face of what you tell me, I
can't find it in me to condemn completely without more
knowledge than we have here. There may be some other facts
not as yet come to light—he won't talk, you say, about most
things—some little details we don't know about—some slight
excuse of some kind—for without that this does appear to be
a most atrocious crime. Has Mr. Brookhart got in from
Boston?"

"Yes, sir, he's here," replied Gilbert. "He telephoned Mr.
Smillie."

"Well, have him come out here at two this afternoon to see
me. I'm too tired to talk more about this right now. Tell him
all that you have told me, Smillie. And then come back here
with him at two. It may be that he will have some suggestion
to make that will be of value to us, although just what I can't

see. Only one thing I want to say—I hope he isn't guilty. And I want every proper step taken to discover whether he is or not, and if not, to defend him to the limit of the law. But no more than that. No trying to save anybody who is guilty of such a thing as this—no, no, no!—not even if he is my nephew! Not me! I'm not that kind of a man! Trouble or no trouble—disgrace or no disgrace—I'll do what I can to help him if he's innocent—if there's even the faintest reason for believing so. But guilty? No! Never! If this boy is really guilty, he'll have to take the consequences. Not a dollar—not a penny—of my money will I devote to any one who could be guilty of such a crime, even if he is my nephew!"

And turning and slowly and heavily moving toward the rear staircase, while Smillie, wide-eyed, gazed after him in awe. The power of him! The decision of him! The fairness of him in such a deadly crisis! And Gilbert equally impressed, also sitting and staring. His father was a man, really. He might be cruelly wounded and distressed, but, unlike himself, he was neither petty nor revengeful.

And next Mr. Darrah Brookhart, a large, well-dressed, well-fed, ponderous and cautious corporation lawyer, with one eye half concealed by a drooping lid and his stomach rather protuberant, giving one the impression of being mentally if not exactly physically suspended, balloon-wise, in some highly rarefied atmosphere where he was moved easily hither and yon by the lightest breath of previous legal interpretations or decisions of any kind. In the absence of additional facts, the guilt of Clyde (to him) seemed obvious. Or, waiving that, as he saw it after carefully listening to Smillie's recounting of all the suspicious and incriminating circumstances, he would think it very difficult to construct an even partially satisfactory defense, unless there were some facts favoring Clyde which had not thus far appeared. Those two hats, that bag—his slipping away like that. Those letters. But he would prefer to read them. For upon the face of the data so far, unquestionably public sentiment would be all against Clyde and in favor of the dead girl and her poverty and her class, a situation which made a favorable verdict in such a backwoods county seat as Bridgeburg almost impossible. For Clyde, although himself poor, was the nephew of a rich man and hitherto in good

standing in Lycurgus society. That would most certainly tend
to prejudice country-born people against him. It would probably be better to ask for a change of venue so as to nullify the
force of such a prejudice.

On the other hand, without first sending a trained cross-
examiner to Clyde—one, who being about to undertake the
defense should be able to extract the facts from him on the
plea that on his truthful answers depended his life—he would
not be able to say whether there was any hope or not. In his
office was a certain Mr. Catchuman, a very able man, who
might be sent on such a mission and on whose final report
one could base a reasonable opinion. However, there were
now various other aspects of such a case as this which, in his
estimation, needed to be carefully looked into and decided
upon. For, of course, as Mr. Griffiths and his son so well
knew, in Utica, New York City, Albany (and now that he
came to think of it, more particularly in Albany, where were
two brothers, Canavan & Canavan, most able if dubious individuals), there were criminal lawyers deeply versed in the ab-
strusities and tricks of the criminal law. And any of them—no
doubt—for a sufficient retainer, and irrespective of the primary look of a situation of this kind, might be induced to undertake such a defense. And, no doubt, via change of venue,
motions, appeals, etc., they might and no doubt would be
able to delay and eventually effect an ultimate verdict of
something less than death, if such were the wish of the head
of this very important family. On the other hand, there was
the undeniable fact that such a hotly contested trial as this
would most assuredly prove to be would result in an enormous amount of publicity, and did Mr. Samuel Griffiths want
that? For again, under such circumstances, was it not likely to
be said, if most unjustly, of course, that he was using his great
wealth to frustrate justice? The public was so prejudiced
against wealth in such cases. Yet, some sort of a defense on
the part of the Griffiths would certainly be expected by the
public, whether subsequently the same necessity for such defense was criticized by them or not.

And in consequence, it was now necessary for Mr. Griffiths
and his son to decide how they would prefer to proceed—
whether with very distinguished criminal lawyers such as the

two he had just named, or with less forceful counsel, or none. For, of course, it would be possible, and that quite inconspicuously, to supply Clyde with a capable and yet thoroughly conservative trial lawyer—some one residing and practising in Bridgeburg possibly—whose duty it would be to see that all blatant and unjustified reference to the family on the part of the newspapers was minimized.

And so, after three more hours of conference, it was finally decided by Samuel himself that at once Mr. Brookhart was to despatch his Mr. Catchuman to Bridgeburg to interview Clyde, and thereafter, whatever his conclusions as to his guilt or innocence, he was to select from the local array of legal talent—for the present, anyhow—such a lawyer as would best represent Clyde fairly. Yet with no assurances of means or encouragement to do more than extract from Clyde the true details of his relationship to this charge. And those once ascertained to center upon such a defense as would most honestly tend to establish only such facts as were honestly favorable to Clyde—in short, in no way, either by legal chicane or casuistry or trickery of any kind, to seek to establish a false innocence and so defeat the ends of justice.

# Chapter XIV

M R. CATCHUMAN did not prove by any means to be the one to extract from Clyde anything more than had either Mason or Smillie. Although shrewd to a degree in piecing together out of the muddled statements of another such data as seemed most probable, still he was not so successful in the realm of the emotions, as was necessary in the case of Clyde. He was too legal, chilling—unemotional. And in consequence, after grilling Clyde for four long hours one hot July afternoon, he was eventually compelled to desist with the feeling that as a plotter of crime Clyde was probably the most arresting example of feeble and blundering incapacity he had ever met.

For since Smillie's departure Mason had proceeded to the shores of Big Bittern with Clyde. And there discovered the tripod and camera. Also listened to more of Clyde's lies. And as he now explained to Catchuman that, while Clyde denied owning a camera, nevertheless he had proof that he did own one and had taken it with him when he left Lycurgus. Yet when confronted with this fact by Catchuman, as the latter now noticed, Clyde had nothing to say other than that he had not taken a camera with him and that the tripod found was not the one belonging to any camera of his—a lie which so irritated Catchuman that he decided not to argue with him further.

At the same time, however, Brookhart having instructed him that, whatever his personal conclusions in regard to Clyde, a lawyer of sorts was indispensable—the charity, if not the honor, of the Griffiths being this much involved, the western Griffiths, as Brookhart had already explained to him, having nothing and not being wanted in the case anyhow—be decided that he must find one before leaving. In consequence, and without any knowledge of the local political situation, he proceeded to the office of Ira Kellogg, president of the Cataraqui County National Bank, who, although Catchuman did not know it, was high in the councils of the Democratic organization. And because of his religious and moral

views, this same Kellogg was already highly incensed and irritated by the crime of which Clyde was accused. On the other
hand, however, because as he well knew this case was likely to
pave the way for an additional Republican sweep at the approaching primaries, he was not blind to the fact that some
reducing opposition to Mason might not be amiss. Fate
seemed too obviously to be favoring the Republican machine
in the person of and crime committed by Clyde.

For since the discovery of this murder, Mason had been
basking in such publicity and even nation-wide notoriety as
had not befallen any district attorney of this region in years and
years. Newspaper correspondents and reporters and illustrators
from such distant cities as Buffalo, Rochester, Chicago, New
York and Boston, were already arriving as everybody knew or
saw, to either interview or make sketches or take photos of
Clyde, Mason, the surviving members of the Alden family, et
cetera, while locally Mason was the recipient of undiluted
praise, even the Democratic voters in the county joining with
the Republicans in assuring each other that Mason was all
right, that he was handling this young murderer in the way that
he deserved to be handled, and that neither the wealth of the
Griffiths nor of the family of that rich girl whom he appeared
to have been trying to capture, was influencing this young tri-
bune of the people in the least. He was a real attorney. He had
not "allowed any grass to grow under his feet, you bet."

Indeed previous to Catchuman's visit, a coroner's jury had
been called, with Mason attending and directing even, the
verdict being that the dead girl had come to her death
through a plot devised and executed by one Clyde Griffiths
who was then and there in the county jail of Bridgeburg and
that he be held to await the verdict of the County Grand Jury
to whom his crime was soon to be presented. And Mason,
through an appeal to the Governor, as all now knew was planning to secure a special sitting of the Supreme Court, which
would naturally involve an immediate session of the County
Grand Jury in order to hear the evidence and either indict or
discharge Clyde. And now, Catchuman arriving to inquire
where he was likely to find a local lawyer of real ability who
could be trusted to erect some sort of a defense for Clyde.
And immediately as an offset to all this there popped into

Kellogg's mind the name and reputation of one Hon. Alvin Belknap, of Belknap and Jephson, of this same city—an individual who had been twice state senator, three times Democratic assemblyman from this region, and more recently looked upon by various Democratic politicians as one who would be favored with higher honors as soon as it was possible to arrange an issue which would permit the Democrats to enter into local office. In fact, only three years before, in a contest with Mason for the district attorneyship, this same Belknap had run closer to victory than any other candidate on the Democratic ticket. Indeed, so rounded a man was he politically that this year he had been slated for that very county judgeship nomination which Mason had in view. And but for this sudden and most amazing development in connection with Clyde, it had been quite generally assumed that Belknap, once nominated, would be elected. And although Mr. Kellogg did not quite trouble to explain to Catchuman all the complicated details of this very interesting political situation, he did explain that Mr. Belknap was a very exceptional man, almost the ideal one, if one were looking for an opponent to Mason.

And with this slight introduction, Kellogg now offered personally to conduct Catchuman to Belknap and Jephson's office, just across the way in the Bowers Block.

And then knocking at Belknap's door, they were admitted by a brisk, medium-sized and most engaging-looking man of about forty-eight, whose gray-blue eyes at once fixed themselves in the mind of Catchuman as the psychic windows of a decidedly shrewd if not altogether masterful and broad-gauge man. For Belknap was inclined to carry himself with an air which all were inclined to respect. He was a college graduate, and in his youth because of his looks, his means, and his local social position (his father had been a judge as well as a national senator from here), he had seen so much of what might be called near-city life that all those gaucheries as well as sex-inhibitions and sex-longings which still so greatly troubled and motivated and even marked a man like Mason had long since been covered with an easy manner and social understanding which made him fairly capable of grasping any reasonable moral or social complication which life was prepared to offer.

Indeed he was one who naturally would approach a case such as Clyde's with less vehemence and fever than did Mason. For once, in his twentieth year, he himself had been trapped between two girls, with one of whom he was merely playing while being seriously in love with the other. And having seduced the first and being confronted with an engagement or flight, he had chosen flight. But not before laying the matter before his father, by whom he was advised to take a vacation, during which time the services of the family doctor were engaged with the result that for a thousand dollars and expenses necessary to house the pregnant girl in Utica, the father had finally extricated his son and made possible his return, and eventual marriage to the other girl.

And therefore, while by no means sympathizing with the more cruel and drastic phases of Clyde's attempt at escape—as so far charged (never in all the years of his law practice had he been able to grasp the psychology of a murderer) still because of the rumored existence and love influence of a rich girl whose name had not as yet been divulged he was inclined to suspect that Clyde had been emotionally betrayed or bewitched. Was he not poor and vain and ambitious? He had heard so: had even been thinking that he—the local political situation being what it was might advantageously to himself—and perhaps most disruptingly to the dreams of Mr. Mason be able to construct a defense—or at least a series of legal contentions and delays which might make it not so easy for Mr. Mason to walk away with the county judgeship as he imagined. Might it not, by brisk, legal moves now—and even in the face of this rising public sentiment, or because of it,—be possible to ask for a change of venue—or time to develop new evidence in which case a trial might not occur before Mr. Mason was out of office. He and his young and somewhat new associate, Mr. Reuben Jephson, of quite recently the state of Vermont, had been thinking of it.

And now Mr. Catchuman accompanied by Mr. Kellogg. And thereupon a conference with Mr. Catchuman and Mr. Kellogg, with the latter arguing quite politically the wisdom of his undertaking such a defense. And his own interest in the case being what it was, he was not long in deciding, after a conference with his younger associate, that he would. In the long run it could not possibly injure him politically, however the public might feel about it now.

And then Catchuman having handed over a retainer to Belknap as well as a letter introducing him to Clyde, Belknap had Jephson call up Mason to inform him that Belknap & Jephson, as counsel for Samuel Griffiths on behalf of his nephew, would require of him a detailed written report of all the charges as well as all the evidence thus far accumulated, the minutes of the autopsy and the report of the coroner's inquest. Also information as to whether any appeal for a special term of the Supreme Court had as yet been acted upon, and if so what judge had been named to sit, and when and where the Grand Jury would be gathered. Incidentally, he said, Messrs. Belknap and Jephson, having heard that Miss Alden's body had been sent to her home for burial, would request at once a counsel's agreement whereby it might be exhumed in order that other doctors now to be called by the defense might be permitted to examine it—a proposition which Mason at once sought to oppose but finally agreed to rather than submit to an order from a Supreme Court judge.

These details having been settled, Belknap announced that he was going over to the jail to see Clyde. It was late and he had had no dinner, and might get none now, but he wanted to have a "heart to heart" with this youth, whom Catchuman informed him he would find very difficult. But Belknap, buoyed up as he was by his opposition to Mason, his conviction that he was in a good mental state to understand Clyde, was in a high degree of legal curiosity. The romance and drama of this crime! What sort of a girl was this Sondra Finchley, of whom he had already heard through secret channels? And could she by any chance be brought to Clyde's defense? He had already understood that her name was not to be mentioned—high politics demanding this. He was really most eager to talk to this sly and ambitious and futile youth.

However, on reaching the jail, and after showing Sheriff Slack a letter from Catchuman and asking as a special favor to himself that he be taken upstairs to some place near Clyde's cell in order that, unannounced, he might first observe Clyde, he was quietly led to the second floor and, the outside door leading to the corridor which faced Clyde's cell being opened for him, allowed to enter there alone. And then walking to within a few feet of Clyde's cell he was able to view him—at the moment lying face down on his iron cot, his arms above his head, a tray of untouched food standing in the aperture, his body sprawled and limp. For, since Catchuman's departure, and his second failure to convince any one of his futile and meaningless lies, he was more despondent than ever. In fact, so low was his condition that he was actually crying, his shoulders heaving above his silent emotion. At sight of this, and remembering his own youthful escapades, Belknap now felt intensely sorry for him. No soulless murderer, as he saw it, would cry.

Approaching Clyde's cell door, after a pause, he began with: "Come, come, Clyde! This will never do. You mustn't give up like this. Your case mayn't be as hopeless as you think. Wouldn't you like to sit up and talk to a lawyer fellow who thinks he might be able to do something for you? Belknap is my name—Alvin Belknap. I live right here in Bridgeburg and I have been sent over by that other fellow who was here a while ago—Catchuman, wasn't that his name? You didn't get along with him so very well, did you? Well, I didn't either. He's not our kind, I guess. But here's a letter from him authorizing me to represent you. Want to see it?"

He poked it genially and authoritatively through the narrow bars toward which Clyde, now curious and dubious, approached. For there was something so whole-hearted and unusual and seemingly sympathetic and understanding in this man's voice that Clyde took courage. And without hesitancy, therefore, he took the letter and looked at it, then returned it with a smile.

"There, I thought so," went on Belknap, most convincingly and pleased with his effect, which he credited entirely to his own magnetism and charm. "That's better. I know we're going to get along. I can feel it. You are going to be able to talk to me as easily and truthfully as you would to your mother. And without any fear that any word of anything you ever tell me is going to reach another ear, unless you want it to, see? For I'm going to be your lawyer, Clyde, if you'll let me, and you're going to be my client, and we're going to sit down together to-morrow, or whenever you say so, and you're going to tell me all you think I ought to know, and I'm going to tell you what I think I ought to know, and whether I'm going to be able to help you. And I'm going to prove to you that in every way that you help me, you're only helping yourself, see? And I'm going to do my damnedest to get you out of this. Now, how's that, Clyde?"

He smiled most encouragingly and sympathetically—even affectionately. And Clyde, feeling for the first time since his arrival here that he had found some one in whom he could possibly confide without danger, was already thinking it might be best if he should tell this man all—everything—he could not have said why, quite, but he liked him. In a quick, if dim way he felt that this man understood and might even sympathize with him, if he knew all or nearly all. And after Belknap had detailed how eager this enemy of his—Mason—was to convict him, and how, if he could but devise a reasonable defense, he was sure he could delay the case until this man was out of office, Clyde announced that if he would give him the night to think it all out, to-morrow or any time he chose to come back, he would tell him all.

And then, the next day Belknap sitting on a stool and munching chocolate bars, listened while Clyde before him on his iron cot, poured forth his story—all the details of his life since arriving at Lycurgus—how and why he had come there, the incident of the slain child in Kansas City, without, however, mention of the clipping which he himself had preserved and then forgotten; his meeting with Roberta, and his desire for her; her pregnancy and how he had sought to get her out of it—on and on until, she having threatened to expose him, he had at last, and in great distress and fright, found the item in *The Times-Union* and had sought to emulate that in action. But he had never plotted it personally, as Belknap was to understand. Nor had he intentionally killed her at the last. No, he had not. Mr. Belknap must believe that, whatever else he thought. He had never deliberately struck her. No, no, no! It had been an accident. There had been a camera, and the tripod reported to have been found by Mason was unquestionably his tripod. Also, he had hidden it under a log, after accidentally striking Roberta with the camera and then seeing that sink under the waters, where no doubt it still was, and with pictures of himself and Roberta on the film it contained, if they were not dissolved by the water. But he had not struck her intentionally. No—he had not. She had approached and he had struck, but not intentionally. The boat had upset. And then as nearly as he could, he described how before that he had seemed to be in a trance almost, because having gone so far he could go no farther.

But in the meantime, Belknap, himself finally wearied and confused by this strange story, the impossibility as he now saw it of submitting to, let alone convincing, any ordinary backwoods jury of this region, of the innocence of these dark and bitter plans and deeds, finally in great weariness and uncertainty and mental confusion, even, getting up and placing his hands on Clyde's shoulders, saying: "Well, that'll be enough of this for to-day, Clyde, I think. I see how you felt and how it all came about—also I see how tired you are, and I'm mighty glad you've been able to give me the straight of this, because I know how hard it's been for you to do it. But I don't want you to talk any more now. There are going to be other days, and I have a few things I want to attend to before I take up some of the minor phases of this with you to-morrow or next day. Just you sleep and rest for the present. You'll need all you can get for the work both of us will have to do a little later. But just now, you're not to worry, because there's no need of it, do you see? I'll get you out of this—or we will—my partner and I. I have a partner that I'm going to bring around here presently. You'll like him, too. But there are one or two things that I want you to think about and stick to—and one of these is that you're not to let anybody frighten you into anything, because either myself or my partner will be around here once a day anyhow, and anything you have to say or want to know you can say or find out from us. Next you're not to talk to anybody—Mason, the sheriff, these jailers, no one—unless I tell you to. No one, do you hear! And above all things, don't cry any more. For if you are as innocent as an angel, or as black as the devil himself, the worst thing you can do is to cry before any one. The public and these jail officers don't understand that—they invariably look upon it as weakness or a confession of guilt. And I don't want them to feel any such thing about you now, and especially when I know that you're really not guilty. I know that now. I believe it. See! So keep a stiff upper lip before Mason and everybody.

"In fact, from now on I want you to try and laugh a little— or at any rate, smile and pass the time of day with these fellows around here. There's an old saying in law, you know, that the consciousness of innocence makes any man calm. Think and look innocent. Don't sit and brood and look as though you had lost your last friend, because you haven't. I'm here, and so is my partner, Mr. Jephson. I'll bring him around here in a day or two, and you're to look and act toward him exactly as you have toward me. Trust him, because in legal matters he's even smarter than I am in some ways. And to-morrow I'm going to bring you a couple of books and some magazines and papers, and I want you to read them or look at the pictures. They'll help keep your mind off your troubles."

Clyde achieved a rather feeble smile and nodded his head.

"From now on, too,—I don't know whether you're at all religious—but whether you are or not, they hold services here in the jail on Sundays, and I want you to attend 'em regularly—that is, if they ask you to. For this is a religious community and I want you to make as good an impression as you can. Never mind what people say or how they look—you do as I tell you. And if this fellow Mason or any of those fellows around here get to pestering you any more, send me a note.

"And now I'll be going along, so give me a cheerful smile as I go out—and another one as I come in. And don't talk, see?"

Then shaking Clyde briskly by the shoulders and slapping him on the back, he strode out, actually thinking to himself: "But do I really believe that this fellow is as innocent as he says? Would it be possible for a fellow to strike a girl like that and not know that he was doing it intentionally? And then swimming away afterwards, because, as he says, if he went near her he thought he might drown too. Bad. Bad! What twelve men are going to believe that? And that bag, those two hats, that missing suit! And yet he swears he didn't intentionally strike her. But what about all that planning—the intent— which is just as bad in the eyes of the law. Is he telling the truth or is he lying even now—perhaps trying to deceive himself as well as me? And that camera—we ought to get hold of that before Mason finds it and introduces it. And that suit. I ought to find that and mention it, maybe, so as to offset the look of its being hidden—say that we had it all the time—send it to Lycurgus to be cleaned. But no, no—wait a minute—I must think about that."

And so on, point by point, while deciding wearily that perhaps it would be better not to attempt to use Clyde's story at all, but rather to concoct some other story—this one changed or modified in some way which would make it appear less cruel or legally murderous.

# Chapter XV

M R. REUBEN JEPHSON was decidedly different from Belknap, Catchuman, Mason, Smillie—in fact any one, thus far, who had seen Clyde or become legally interested in this case. He was young, tall, thin, rugged, brown, cool but not cold spiritually, and with a will and a determination of the tensile strength of steel. And with a mental and legal equipment which for shrewdness and self-interest was not unlike that of a lynx or a ferret. Those shrewd, steel, very light blue eyes in his brown face. The force and curiosity of the long nose. The strength of the hands and the body. He had lost no time, as soon as he discovered there was a possibility of their (Belknap & Jephson) taking over the defense of Clyde, in going over the minutes of the coroner's inquest as well as the doctors' reports and the letters of Roberta and Sondra. And now being faced by Belknap who was explaining that Clyde did now actually admit to having plotted to kill Roberta, although not to having actually done so, since at the fatal moment, some cataleptic state of mind or remorse had intervened and caused him to unintentionally strike her—he merely stared without the shadow of a smile or comment of any kind.

"But he wasn't in such a state when he went out there with her, though?"

"No."

"Nor when he swam away afterwards?"

"No."

"Nor when he went through those woods, or changed to another suit and hat, or hid that tripod?"

"No."

"Of course you know, constructively, in the eyes of the law, if we use his own story, he's just as guilty as though he had struck her, and the judge would have to so instruct."

"Yes, I know. I've thought of all that."

"Well, then——"

"Well, I'll tell you, Jephson, it's a tough case and no mistake. It looks to me now as though Mason has all the cards.

687

If we can get this chap off, we can get anybody off. But as I see it, I'm not so sure that we want to mention that cataleptic business yet—at least not unless we want to enter a plea of insanity or emotional insanity, or something like that—about like that Harry Thaw case, for instance." He paused and scratched his slightly graying temple dubiously.

"You think he's guilty, of course?" interpolated Jephson, drily.

"Well, now, as astonishing as it may seem to you, no. At least, I'm not positive that I do. To tell you the truth, this is one of the most puzzling cases I have ever run up against. This fellow is by no means as hard as you think, or as cold—quite a simple, affectionate chap, in a way, as you'll see for yourself—his manner, I mean. He's only twenty-one or two. And for all his connections with these Griffiths, he's very poor—just a clerk, really. And he tells me that his parents are poor, too. They run a mission of some kind out west—Denver, I believe—and before that in Kansas City. He hasn't been home in four years. In fact, he got into some crazy boy scrape out there in Kansas City when he was working for one of the hotels as a bellboy, and had to run away. That's something we've got to look out for in connection with Mason—whether he knows about that or not. It seems he and a bunch of other bell-hops took some rich fellow's car without his knowing it, and then because they were afraid of being late, they ran over and killed a little girl. We've got to find out about that and prepare for it, for if Mason does know about it, he'll spring it at the trial, and just when he thinks we're least expecting it."

"Well, he won't pull that one," replied Jephson, his hard, electric, blue eyes gleaming, "not if I have to go to Kansas City to find out."

And Belknap went on to tell Jephson all that he knew about Clyde's life up to the present time—how he had worked at dish-washing, waiting on table, soda-clerking, driving a wagon, anything and everything, before he had arrived in Lycurgus—how he had always been fascinated by girls—how he had first met Roberta and later Sondra. Finally how he found himself trapped by one and desperately in love with the other, whom he could not have unless he got rid of the first one.

"And notwithstanding all that, you feel a doubt as to whether he did kill her?" asked Jephson, at the conclusion of all this.

"Yes, as I say, I'm not at all sure that he did. But I do know that he is still hipped over this second girl. His manner changed whenever he or I happened to mention her. Once, for instance, I asked him about his relations with her—and in spite of the fact that he's accused of seducing and killing this other girl, he looked at me as though I had said something I shouldn't have—insulted him or her." And here Belknap smiled a wry smile, while Jephson, his long, bony legs propped against the walnut desk before him, merely stared at him.

"You don't say," he finally observed.

"And not only that," went on Belknap, "but he said, 'Why, no, of course not. She wouldn't allow anything like that, and besides,' and then he stopped. 'And besides what, Clyde,' I asked. 'Well, you don't want to forget who she is.' 'Oh, I see,' I said. And then, will you believe it, he wanted to know if there wasn't some way by which her name and those letters she wrote him couldn't be kept out of the papers and this case—her family prevented from knowing so that she and they wouldn't be hurt too much."

"Not really? But what about the other girl?"

"That's just the point I'm trying to make. He could plot to kill one girl and maybe even did kill her, for all I know, after seducing her, but because he was being so sculled around by his grand ideas of this other girl, he didn't quite know what he was doing, really. Don't you see? You know how it is with some of these young fellows of his age, and especially when they've never had anything much to do with girls or money, and want to be something grand."

"You think that made him a little crazy, maybe?" put in Jephson.

"Well, it's possible—confused, hypnotized, loony—you know—a brain storm as they say down in New York. But he certainly is still cracked over that other girl. In fact, I think most of his crying in jail is over her. He was crying, you know, when I went in to see him, sobbing as if his heart would break."

Meditatively Belknap scratched his right ear. "But just the same, there certainly is something to this other idea—that his mind was turned by all this—that Alden girl forcing him on the one hand to marry her while the other girl was offering to marry him. I know. I was once in such a scrape myself." And here he paused to relate that to Jephson. "By the way," he went on, "he says we can find that item about that other couple drowning in *The Times-Union* of about June 18th or 19th."

"All right," replied Jephson, "I'll get it."

"What I want you to do to-morrow," continued Belknap, "is to go over there with me and see what impression you get of him. I'll be there to see if he tells it all to you in the same way. I want your own individual viewpoint of him."

"You most certainly will get it," snapped Jephson.

Belknap and Jephson proceeded the next day to visit Clyde in jail. And Jephson, after interviewing him and meditating once more on his strange story, was even then not quite able to make up his mind whether Clyde was as innocent of intending to strike Roberta as he said, or not. For if he were, how could he have swum away afterward, leaving her to drown? Decidedly it would be more difficult for a jury than for himself, even, to be convinced.

At the same time, there was that contention of Belknap's as to the possibility of Clyde's having been mentally upset or unbalanced at the time that he accepted *The Times-Union* plot and proceeded to act on it. That might be true, of course, yet personally, to Jephson at least, Clyde appeared to be wise and sane enough now. As Jephson saw him, he was harder and more cunning than Belknap was willing to believe—a cunning, modified of course, by certain soft and winning social graces for which one could hardly help liking him. However, Clyde was by no means as willing to confide in Jephson as he had been in Belknap—an attitude which did little to attract Jephson to him at first. At the same time, there was about Jephson a hard, integrated earnestness which soon convinced Clyde of his technical, if not his emotional interest. And after a while he began looking toward this younger man, even more than toward Belknap as the one who might do most for him.

"Of course, you know that those letters which Miss Alden wrote you are very strong?" began Jephson, after hearing Clyde restate his story.

"Yes, sir."

"They're very sad to anyone who doesn't know all of the facts, and on that account they are likely to prejudice any jury against you, especially when they're put alongside Miss Finchley's letters."

"Yes, I suppose they might," replied Clyde, "but then, she wasn't always like that, either. It was only after she got in trouble and I wanted her to let me go that she wrote like that."

"I know. I know. And that's a point we want to think about and maybe bring out, if we can. If only there were some way to keep those letters out," he now turned to Belknap to say. Then, to Clyde, "but what I want to ask you now is this—you were close to her for something like a year, weren't you?"

"Yes."

"In all of that time that you were with her, or before, was she ever friendly, or maybe intimate, with any other young man anywhere—that is, that you know of?"

As Clyde could see, Jephson was not afraid, or perhaps not sufficiently sensitive, to refrain from presenting any thought or trick that seemed to him likely to provide a loophole for escape. But, far from being cheered by this suggestion, he was really shocked. What a shameful thing in connection with Roberta and her character it would be to attempt to introduce any such lie as this. He could not and would not hint at any such falsehood, and so he replied:

"No, sir. I never heard of her going with any one else. In fact, I know she didn't."

"Very good! That settles that," snapped Jephson. "I judged from her letters that what you say is true. At the same time, we must know all the facts. It might make a very great difference if there were some one else."

And at this point Clyde could not quite make sure whether he was attempting to impress upon him the value of this as an idea or not, but just the same he decided it was not right even to consider it. And yet he was thinking: If only this man could think of a real defense for me! He looks so shrewd.

"Well, then," went on Jephson, in the same hard, searching tone, devoid, as Clyde saw it, of sentiment or pity of any kind, "here's something else I want to ask you. In all the time that you knew her, either before you were intimate with her or afterwards, did she ever write you a mean or sarcastic or demanding or threatening letter of any kind?"

"No, sir, I can't say that she ever did," replied Clyde, "in fact, I know she didn't. No, sir. Except for those few last ones, maybe—the very last one."

"And you never wrote her any, I suppose?"

"No, sir, I never wrote her any letters."

"Why?"

"Well, she was right there in the factory with me, you see. Besides at the last there, after she went home, I was afraid to."

"I see."

At the same time, as Clyde now proceeded to point out, and that quite honestly, Roberta could be far from sweet-tempered at times—could in fact be quite determined and even stubborn. And she had paid no least attention to his plea that her forcing him to marry her now would ruin him socially as well as in every other way, and that even in the face of his willingness to work along and pay for her support—an attitude which, as he now described it, was what had caused all the trouble—whereas Miss Finchley (and here he introduced an element of reverence and enthusiasm which Jephson was quick to note) was willing to do everything for him.

"So you really loved that Miss Finchley very much then, did you?"

"Yes, sir."

"And you couldn't care for Roberta any more after you met her?"

"No, no. I just couldn't."

"I see," observed Jephson, solemnly nodding his head, and at the same time meditating on how futile and dangerous, even, it might be to let the jury know that. And then thinking that possibly it were best to follow the previous suggestion of Belknap's, based on the customary legal proceeding of the time, and claim insanity, or a brain storm, brought about by the terrifying position in which he imagined himself to be. But apart from that he now proceeded:

"You say something came over you when you were in the boat out there with her on that last day—that you really didn't know what you were doing at the time that you struck her?"

"Yes, sir, that's the truth." And here Clyde went on to explain once more just what his state was at that time.

"All right, all right, I believe you," replied Jephson, seemingly believing what Clyde said but not actually able to conceive it at that. "But you know, of course, that no jury, in the face of all these other circumstances, is going to believe that," he now announced. "There are too many things that'll have to be explained and that we can't very well explain as things now stand. I don't know about that idea." He now turned and was addressing Belknap. "Those two hats, that bag—unless we're going to plead insanity or something like that. I'm not so sure about all this. Was there ever any insanity in your family that you know of?" he now added, turning to Clyde once more.

"No, sir, not that I know of."

"No uncle or cousin or grandfather who had fits or strange ideas or anything like that?"

"Not that I ever heard of, no, sir."

"And your rich relatives down there in Lycurgus—I suppose they'd not like it very much if I were to step up and try to prove anything like that?"

"I'm afraid they wouldn't, no, sir," replied Clyde, thinking of Gilbert.

"Well, let me see," went on Jephson after a time. "That makes it rather hard. I don't see, though, that anything else would be as safe." And here he turned once more to Belknap and began to inquire as to what he thought of suicide as a theory, since Roberta's letters themselves showed a melancholy trend which might easily have led to thoughts of suicide. And could they not say that once out on the lake with Clyde and pleading with him to marry her, and he refusing to do so, she had jumped overboard. And he was too astounded and mentally upset to try to save her.

"But what about his own story that the wind had blown his hat off, and in trying to save that he upset the boat?" interjected Belknap, and exactly as though Clyde were not present.

"Well, that's true enough, too, but couldn't we say that perhaps, since he was morally responsible for her condition, which in turn had caused her to take her life, he did not want to confess to the truth of her suicide?"

At this Clyde winced, but neither now troubled to notice him. They talked as though he was not present or could have no opinion in the matter, a procedure which astonished but by no means moved him to object, since he was feeling so helpless.

"But the false registrations! The two hats—the suit—his bag!" insisted Belknap staccatically, a tone which showed Clyde how serious Belknap considered his predicament to be.

"Well, whatever theory we advance, those things will have to be accounted for in some way," replied Jephson, dubiously. "We can't admit the true story of his plotting without an insanity plea, not as I see it—at any rate. And unless we use that, we've got that evidence to deal with whatever we do." He threw up his hands wearily and as if to say: I swear I don't know what to do about this.

"But," persisted Belknap, "in the face of all that, and his refusal to marry her, after his promises referred to in her letters—why, it would only react against him, so that public opinion would be more prejudiced against him than ever. No, that won't do," he concluded. "We'll have to think of something which will create some sort of sympathy for him."

And then once more turning to Clyde as though there had been no such discussion. And looking at him as much as to say: "You are a problem indeed." And then Jephson, observing: "And, oh, yes, that suit you dropped in that lake up there near the Cranstons—describe the spot to me as near as you can where you threw it—how far from the house was it?" He waited until Clyde haltingly attempted to recapture the various details of the hour and the scene as he could recall it.

"If I could go up there, I could find it quick enough."

"Yes, I know, but they won't let you go up there without Mason being along," he returned. "And maybe not even then. You're in prison now, and you can't be taken out without the state's consent, you see. But we must get that suit." Then turning to Belknap and lowering his voice, he added:

"We want to get it and have it cleaned and submit it as having been sent away to be cleaned by him—not hidden, you see."

"Yes, that's so," commented Belknap idly while Clyde stood listening curiously and a little amazed by this frank program of trickery and deception on his behalf.

"And now in regard to that camera that fell in the lake—we have to try and find that, too. I think maybe Mason may know about it or suspect that it's there. At any rate it's very important that we should find it before he does. You think that about where that pole was that day you were up there is where the boat was when it overturned?"

"Yes, sir."

"Well, we must see if we can get that," he continued, turning to Belknap. "We don't want that turning up in the trial, if we can help it. For without that, they'll have to be swearing that he struck her with that tripod or something that he didn't, and that's where we may trip 'em up."

"Yes, that's true, too," replied Belknap.

"And now in regard to the bag that Mason has. That's another thing I haven't seen yet, but I will see it to-morrow. Did you put that suit, as wet as it was, in the bag when you came out of the water?"

"No, sir, I wrung it out first. And then I dried it as much as I could. And then I wrapped it up in the paper that we had the lunch in and then put some dry pine needles underneath it in the bag and on top of it."

"So there weren't any wet marks in the bag after you took it out, as far as you know?"

"No, sir, I don't think so."

"But you're not sure?"

"Not exactly sure now that you ask me—no, sir."

"Well, I'll see for myself to-morrow. And now as to those marks on her face, you have never admitted to any one around here or anywhere that you struck her in any way?"

"No, sir."

"And the mark on the top of her head was made by the boat, just as you said?"

"Yes, sir."

"But the others you think you might have made with the camera?"

"Yes, sir. I suppose they were."

"Well, then, this is the way it looks to me," said Jephson, again turning to Belknap. "I think we can safely say when the time comes that those marks were never made by him at all, see?—but by the hooks and the poles with which they were scraping around up there when they were trying to find her. We can try it, anyhow. And if the hooks and poles didn't do it," he added, a little grimly and dryly, "certainly hauling her body from that lake to that railroad station and from there to here on the train might have."

"Yes, I think Mason would have a hard time proving that they weren't made that way," replied Belknap.

"And as for that tripod, well, we'd better exhume the body and make our own measurements, and measure the thickness of the edge of that boat, so that it may not be so easy for Mason to make any use of the tripod now that he has it, after all."

Mr. Jephson's eyes were very small and very clear and very blue, as he said this. His head, as well as his body, had a thin, ferrety look. And it seemed to Clyde, who had been observing and listening to all this with awe, that this younger man might be the one to aid him. He was so shrewd and practical, so very direct and chill and indifferent, and yet confidence-inspiring, quite like an uncontrollable machine of a kind which generates power.

And when at last these two were ready to go, he was sorry. For with them near him, planning and plotting in regard to himself, he felt so much safer, stronger, more hopeful, more certain of being free, maybe, at some future date.

# Chapter XVI

THE RESULT of all this, however, was that it was finally decided that perhaps the easiest and safest defense that could be made, assuming that the Griffiths family of Lycurgus would submit to it, would be that of insanity or "brain storm"—a temporary aberration due to love and an illusion of grandeur aroused in Clyde by Sondra Finchley and the threatened disruption by Roberta of all his dreams and plans. But after consultation with Catchuman and Darrah Brookhart at Lycurgus, and these in turn conferring with Samuel and Gilbert Griffiths, it was determined that this would not do. For to establish insanity or "brain storm" would require previous evidence or testimony to the effect that Clyde was of none too sound mind, erratic his whole life long, and with certain specific instances tending to demonstrate how really peculiar he was—relatives (among them the Griffiths of Lycurgus themselves, perhaps), coming on to swear to it—a line of evidence, which, requiring as it would, outright lying and perjury on the part of many as well as reflecting on the Griffiths' blood and brain, was sufficient to alienate both Samuel and Gilbert to the extent that they would have none of it. And so Brookhart was compelled to assure Belknap that this line of defense would have to be abandoned.

Such being the case, both Belknap and Jephson were once more compelled to sit down and consider. For any other defense which either could think of now seemed positively hopeless.

"I want to tell you one thing!" observed the sturdy Jephson, after thumbing through the letters of both Roberta and Sondra again. "These letters of this Alden girl are the toughest things we're going to have to face. They're likely to make any jury cry if they're read right, and then to introduce those letters from that other girl on top of these would be fatal. It will be better, I think, if we do not mention hers at all, unless he does. It will only make it look as though he had killed that Alden girl to get rid of her. Mason couldn't want anything better, as I see it." And with this Belknap agreed most heartily.

At the same time, some plan must be devised immediately. And so, out of these various conferences, it was finally deduced by Jephson, who saw a great opportunity for himself in this matter, that the safest possible defense that could be made, and one to which Clyde's own suspicions and most peculiar actions would most exactly fit, would be that he had never contemplated murder. On the contrary, being a moral if not a physical coward, as his own story seemed to suggest, and in terror of being exposed and driven out of Lycurgus and of the heart of Sondra, and never as yet having told Roberta of Sondra and thinking that knowledge of this great love for her (Sondra) might influence Roberta to wish to be rid of him, he had hastily and without any worse plan in mind, decided to persuade Roberta to accompany him to any near-by resort but not especially Grass Lake or Big Bittern, in order to tell her all this and so win his freedom—yet not without offering to pay her expenses as nearly as he could during her very trying period.

"All well and good," commented Belknap. "But that involves his refusing to marry her, doesn't it? And what jury is going to sympathize with him for that or believe that he didn't want to kill her?"

"Wait a minute, wait a minute," replied Jephson, a little testily. "So far it does. Sure. But you haven't heard me to the end yet. I said I had a plan."

"All right, then what is it?" replied Belknap most interested.

"Well, I'll tell you—my plan's this—to leave all the facts just as they are, and just as he tells them, and just as Mason has discussed them so far, except, of course, his striking her—and then explain them—the letters, the wounds, the bag, the two hats, everything—not deny them in any way."

And here he paused and ran his long, thin, freckled hands eagerly through his light hair and looked across the grass of the public square to the jail where Clyde was, then toward Belknap again.

"All very good, but how?" queried Belknap.

"There's no other way, I tell you," went on Jephson quite

to himself, and ignoring his senior, "and I think this will do it." He turned to look out the window again, and began as though talking to some one outside: "He goes up there, you see, because he's frightened and because he has to do something or be exposed. And he signs those registers just as he did because he's afraid to have it known by anybody down there in Lycurgus that he is up there. And he has this plan about confessing to her about this other girl. *BUT*," and now he paused and looked fixedly at Belknap, "and this is the keystone of the whole thing—if this won't hold water, then down we go! Listen! He goes up there with her, frightened, and not to marry her or to kill her but to argue with her to go away. But once up there and he sees how sick she is, and tired, and sad—well, you know how much she still loves him, and he spends two nights with her, see?"

"Yes, I see," interrupted Belknap, curiously, but not quite so dubiously now. "And that might explain those nights."

"MIGHT? Would!" replied Jephson, slyly and calmly, his harebell eyes showing only cold, eager, practical logic, no trace of emotion or even sympathy of any kind, really. "Well, while he's up there with her under those conditions—so close to her again, you see" (and his facial expression never altered so much as by a line) "he experiences a change of heart. You get me? He's sorry for her. He's ashamed of himself—his sin against her. That ought to appeal to these fellows around here, these religious and moral people, oughtn't it?"

"It might," quietly interpolated Belknap, who by now was very much interested and a little hopeful.

"He sees that he's done her a wrong," continued Jephson, intent, like a spider spinning a web, on his own plan, "and in spite of all his affection for this other girl, he's now ready to do the right thing by this Alden girl, do you see, because he's sorry and ashamed of himself. That takes the black look off his plotting to kill her while spending those two nights in Utica and Grass Lake with her."

"He still loves the other girl, though?" interjected Belknap.

"Well, sure. He likes her at any rate, has been fascinated by that life down there and sort of taken out of himself, made over into a different person, but now he's ready to marry

Roberta, in case, after telling her all about this other girl and his love for her, she still wants him to."

"I see. But how about the boat now and that bag and his going up to this Finchley girl's place afterwards?"

"Just a minute! Just a minute! I'll tell you about that," continued Jephson, his blue eyes boring into space like a powerful electric ray. "Of course, he goes out in the boat with her, and of course he takes that bag, and of course he signs those registers falsely, and walks away through those woods to that other girl, after Roberta is drowned. But why? Why? Do you want to know why? I'll tell you! He felt sorry for her, see, and he wanted to marry her, or at least he wanted to do the right thing by her at the very last there. Not before, not before, remember, but *after* he had spent a night with her in Utica and another one in Grass Lake. But once she was drowned—and accidentally, of course, as he says, there was his love for that other girl. He hadn't ceased loving her even though he was willing to sacrifice her in order to do the right thing by Roberta. See?"

"I see."

"And how are they going to prove that he didn't experience a change of heart if he says he did and sticks to it?"

"I see, but he'll have to tell a mighty convincing story," added Belknap, a little heavily. "And how about those two hats? They're going to have to be explained."

"Well, I'm coming to those now. The one he had was a little soiled. And so he decided to buy another. As for that story he told Mason about wearing a cap, well, he was frightened and lied because he thought he would have to get out of it. Now, of course, before he goes to that other girl afterwards—while Roberta is still alive, I mean, there's his relationship with the other girl, what he intends to do about her. He's talking to Roberta, now you see," he continued, "and that has to be disposed of in some way. But, as I see it, that's easy, for of course after he experiences a change of heart and wants to do the right thing by Roberta, all he has to do is to write that other girl or go to her and tell her—about the wrong he has done Roberta."

"Yes."

"For, as I see it now, she can't be kept out of the case entirely, after all. We'll have to ring her in, I'm afraid."

"All right; then we have to," said Belknap.

"Because you see, if Roberta still feels that he ought to marry her—he'll go first and tell that Finchley girl that he can't marry her—that he's going away—that is, if Roberta doesn't object to his leaving her that long, don't you see?"

"Yes."

"If she does, he'll marry her, either at Three Mile Bay or some other place."

"Yes."

"But you don't want to forget that while she's still alive he's puzzled and distressed. And it's only after that second night, at Grass Lake, that he begins to see how wrong all his actions have been, you understand. Something happens. Maybe she cries or talks about wanting to die, like she does in those letters."

"Yes."

"And so he wants a quiet place where they can sit down in peace and talk, where no one else will see or hear them."

"Yes, yes—go on."

"Well, he thinks of Big Bittern. He's been up there once before or they're near there, then, and just below there, twelve miles, is Three Mile Bay, where, if they decide to marry, they can."

"I see."

"If not, if she doesn't want to marry him after his full confession, he can row her back to the inn, can't he, and he or she can stay there or go on."

"Yes, yes."

"In the meantime, not to have any delay or be compelled to hang about that inn—it's rather expensive, you know, and he hasn't any too much money—he takes that lunch in his bag. Also his camera, because he wants to take some pictures. For if Mason should turn up with that camera, it's got to be explained, and it will be better explained by us than it will be by him, won't it?"

"I see, I see," exclaimed Belknap, intensely interested by now and actually smiling and beginning to rub his hands.

"So they go out on the lake."

"Yes."

"And they row around."

"Yes."

"And finally after lunch on shore, some pictures taken——"

"Yes."

"He decides to tell her just how things stand with him. He's ready, willing——"

"I get you."

"Only just before doing that, he wants to take one or two more pictures of her there in the boat, just off shore."

"Yes."

"And then he'll tell her, see?"

"Yes."

"And so they go out in the boat again for a little row, just as he did, see?"

"Yes."

"But because they intend to go ashore again for some flowers, he's left the bag there, see? That explains the bag."

"Yes."

"But before taking any more pictures there, in the boat on the water, he begins to tell her about his love for this other girl—that if she wants him to, now he'll marry her and then write this Sondra a letter. Or, if she feels she doesn't want to marry him with him loving this other girl . . ."

"Yes, go on!" interrupted Belknap, eagerly.

"Well," continued Jephson, "he'll do his best to take care of her and support her out of the money he'll have after he marries the rich girl."

"Yes."

"Well, she wants him to marry her and drop this Miss Finchley!"

"I see."

"And he agrees?"

"Sure."

"Also she's so grateful that in her excitement, or gratitude, she jumps up to come toward him, you see?"

"Yes."

"And the boat rocks a little, and he jumps up to help her because he's afraid she's going to fall, see?"

"Yes, I see."

"Well, now if we wanted to we could have him have that camera of his in his hand or not, just as you think fit."

"Yes, I see what you're driving at."

"Well, whether he keeps it in his hand or doesn't there's some misstep on his part or hers, just as he says, or just the motion of the two bodies, causes the boat to go over, and he strikes her, or not, just as you think fit, but accidentally, of course."

"Yes, I see, and I'll be damned!" exclaimed Belknap. "Fine, Reuben! Excellent! Wonderful, really!"

"And the boat strikes her too, as well as him, a little, see?" went on Jephson, paying no attention to this outburst, so interested was he in his own plot, "and makes him a little dizzy, too."

"I see."

"And he hears her cries and sees her, but he's a little stunned himself, see? And by the time he's ready to do something——"

"She's gone," concluded Belknap, quietly. "Drowned. I get you."

"And then, because of all those other suspicious circumstances and false registrations—and because now she's gone and he can't do anything more for her, anyhow—her relatives might not want to know her condition, you know——"

"I see."

"He slips away, frightened, a moral coward, just as we'll have to contend from the first, anxious to stand well with his uncle and not lose his place in this world. Doesn't that explain it?"

"About as well as anything could explain it, Reuben, I think. In fact, I think it's a plausible explanation and I congratulate you. I don't see how any one could hope to find a better. If that doesn't get him off, or bring about a disagreement, at least we might get him off with, well, say, twenty years, don't you think?" And very much cheered, he got up, and after eyeing his long, thin associate admiringly, added: "Fine!" while Jephson, his blue eyes for all the world like windless, still pools, looked steadily back.

"But of course you know what that means?" Jephson now added, calmly and softly.

"That we have to put him on the witness stand? Surely, surely. I see that well enough. But it's his only chance."

"And he won't strike people as a very steady or convincing fellow, I'm afraid—too nervous and emotional."

"Yes, I know all that," replied Belknap, quickly. "He's easily rattled. And Mason will go after him like a wild bull. But we'll have to coach him as to all this—drill him. Make him understand that it's his only chance—that his very life depends on it. Drill him for months."

"If he fails, then he's gone. If only we could do something to give him courage—teach him to act it out." Jephson's eyes seemed to be gazing directly before him at the very courtroom scene in which Clyde on the stand would have Mason before him. And then picking up Roberta's letters (copies of them furnished by Mason) and looking at them, he concluded: "If it only weren't for these—here." He weighed them up and down in his hand. "Christ!" he finally concluded, darkly. "What a case! But we're not licked yet, not by a darn sight! Why, we haven't begun to fight yet. And we'll get a lot of publicity, anyhow. By the way," he added, "I'm having a fellow I know down near Big Bittern dredge for that camera to-night. Wish me luck."

"Do I?" was all Belknap replied.

## Chapter XVII

THE STRUGGLE and excitement of a great murder trial! Belknap and Jephson, after consulting with Brookhart and Catchuman, learning that they considered Jephson's plan "perhaps the only way," but with as little reference to the Griffiths as possible.

And then at once, Messrs. Belknap and Jephson issuing preliminary statements framed in such a manner as to show their faith in Clyde, presenting him as being, in reality, a much maligned and entirely misunderstood youth, whose intentions and actions toward Miss Alden were as different from those set forth by Mason as white from black. And intimating that the undue haste of the district attorney in seeking a special term of the Supreme Court might possibly have a political rather than a purely legal meaning. Else why the hurry, especially in the face of an approaching county election? Could there be any plan to use the results of such a trial as this to further any particular person's, or group of persons', political ambitions? Messrs. Belknap and Jephson begged to hope not.

But regardless of such plans or the prejudices or the political aspirations of any particular person or group, the defense in this instance did not propose to permit a boy as innocent as Clyde, trapped by circumstances—as counsel for the defense would be prepared to show—to be railroaded to the electric chair merely to achieve a victory for the Republican party in November. Furthermore, to combat these strange and yet false circumstances, the defense would require a considerable period of time to prepare its case. Therefore, it would be necessary for them to file a formal protest at Albany against the district attorney's request to the governor for a special term of the Supreme Court. There was no need for the same, since the regular term for the trial of such cases would fall in January, and the preparation of their case would require that much time.

But while this strong, if rather belated, reply was listened to with proper gravity by the representatives of the various

newspapers, Mason vigorously pooh-poohed this "windy" assertion of political plotting, as well as the talk of Clyde's innocence. "What reason have I, a representative of all the
people of this county, to railroad this man anywhere or make
one single charge against him unless the charges make themselves? Doesn't the evidence itself show that he did kill this
girl? And has he ever said or done one thing to clear up any
of the suspicious circumstances? No! Silence or lies. And until these circumstances are disproved by these very able gentlemen, I am going right ahead. I have all the evidence
necessary to convict this young criminal now. And to delay it
until January, when I shall be out of office, as they know, and
when a new man will have to go over all this evidence with
which I have familiarized myself, is to entail great expense to
the county. For all the witnesses I have gotten together are
right here now, easy to bring into Bridgeburg without any
great expense to the county. But where will they be next January or February, especially after the defense has done its best
to scatter them? No, sir! I will not agree to it. But, if within
ten days or two weeks from now even, they can bring me
something that will so much as make it look as though even
some of the charges I have made are not true, I'll be perfectly
willing to go before the presiding judge with them, and if
they can show him any evidence they have or hope to have,
or that there are any distant known witnesses to be secured
who can help prove this fellow's innocence, why, then, well
and good. I'll be willing to ask the judge to grant them as
much time as he may see fit, even if it throws the trial over
until I am out of office. But if the trial comes up while I'm
here, as I honestly hope it will, I'll prosecute it to the best of
my ability, not because I'm looking for an office of any kind
but because I am now the district attorney and it is my duty
to do so. And as for my being in politics, well, Mr. Belknap is
in politics, isn't he? He ran against me the last time, and I
hear he desires to run again."

Accordingly he proceeded to Albany further to impress
upon the Governor the very great need of an immediate special term of the Court so that Clyde might be indicted. And
the Governor, hearing the personal arguments of both Mason
and Belknap, decided in favor of Mason, on the ground that

the granting of a special term did not militate against any necessary delay of the trial of the case, since nothing which the defense as yet had to offer seemed to indicate that the calling of a special term was likely in any way to prevent it from obtaining as much time wherein to try the case as needed. Besides, it would be the business of the Supreme Court justice appointed to consider such arguments—not himself. And accordingly, a special term of the Supreme Court was ordered, with one Justice Frederick Oberwaltzer of the eleventh judicial district designated to preside. And when Mason appeared before him with the request that he fix the date of the Special Grand Jury by which Clyde might be indicted, this was set for August fifth.

And then that body sitting, it was no least trouble for Mason to have Clyde indicted.

And thereafter the best that Belknap and Jephson could do was to appear before Oberwaltzer, a Democrat, who owed his appointment to a previous governor, to argue for a change of venue, on the ground that by no possible stretch of the imagination could any twelve men residing in Cataraqui County be found who, owing to the public and private statements of Mason, were not already vitally opposed to Clyde and so convinced of his guilt that before ever such a jury could be addressed by a defense, he would be convicted.

"But where are you going then?" injuired Justice Oberwaltzer, who was impartial enough. "This same material has been published everywhere"

"But, your Honor, this crime which the district attorney here has been so busy in magnifying—" (a long and heated objection on the part of Mason).

"But we contend just the same," continued Belknap, "that the public has been unduly stirred and deluded. You can't get twelve men now who will try this man fairly."

"What nonsense!" exclaimed Mason, angrily. "Mere twaddle! Why, the newspapers themselves have gathered and published more evidence than I have. It's the publicly discovered facts in this case that have aroused prejudice, if any has been aroused. But no more than would be aroused anywhere, I maintain. Besides, if this case is to be transferred to a distant county when the majority of the witnesses are right here, this county is going to be saddled with an enormous expense, which it cannot afford and which the facts do not warrant."

Justice Oberwaltzer, who was of a sober and moral turn, a slow and meticulous man inclined to favor conservative procedure in all things, was inclined to agree. And after five days, in which he did no more than muse idly upon the matter, he decided to deny the motion. If he were wrong, there was the Appellate Division to which the defense could resort. As for stays, having fixed the date of the trial for October fifteenth (ample time, as he judged, for the defense to prepare its case), he adjourned for the remainder of the summer to his cottage on Blue Mountain Lake, where both the prosecution and the defense, should any knotty or locally insoluble legal complication arise, would be able to find him and have his personal attention.

But with the entry of the Messrs. Belknap and Jephson into the case, Mason found it advisable to redouble his efforts to make positive, in so far as it was possible, the conviction of Clyde. He feared the young Jephson as much as he did Belknap. And for that reason, taking with him Burton Burleigh and Earl Newcomb, he now revisited Lycurgus, where among other things he was able to discover (1) where Clyde had purchased the camera; (2) that three days before his departure for Big Bittern he had said to Mrs. Peyton that he was thinking of taking his camera with him and that he must get some films for it; (3) that there was a haberdasher by the name of Orrin Short who had known Clyde well and that but four months before Clyde had applied to him for advice in connection with a factory hand's pregnant wife—also (and this in great confidence to Burton Burleigh, who had unearthed him) that he had recommended to Clyde a certain Dr. Glenn, near Gloversville; (4) Dr. Glenn himself being sought and pictures of Clyde and Roberta being submitted, he was able to identify Roberta, although not Clyde, and to describe the state of mind in which she had approached him, as well as the story she had told—a story which in no way incriminated Clyde or herself, and which, therefore, Mason decided might best be ignored, for the present, anyhow.

And (5), via these same enthusiastic efforts, there rose to the surface the particular hat salesman in Utica who had sold

Clyde the hat. For Burton Burleigh being interviewed while in Utica, and his picture published along with one of Clyde, this salesman chanced to see it and recalling him at once made haste to communicate with Mason, with the result that his testimony, properly typewritten and sworn to, was carried away by Mason.

And, in addition, the country girl who had been on the steamer "Cygnus" and who had noticed Clyde, wrote Mason that she remembered him wearing a straw hat, also his leaving the boat at Sharon, a bit of evidence which most fully confirmed that of the captain of the boat and caused Mason to feel that Providence or Fate was working with him. And last, but most important of all to him, there came a communication from a woman residing in Bedford, Pennsylvania, who announced that during the week of July third to tenth, she and her husband had been camping on the east shore of Big Bittern, near the southern end of the lake. And while rowing on the lake on the afternoon of July eighth, at about six o'clock, she had heard a cry which sounded like that of a woman or girl in distress—a plaintive, mournful cry. It was very faint and had seemed to come from beyond the island which was to the south and west of the bay in which they were fishing.

Mason now proposed to remain absolutely silent regarding this information, and that about the camera and films and the data regarding Clyde's offense in Kansas City, until nearer the day of trial, or during the trial itself, when it would be impossible for the defense to attempt either to refute or ameliorate it in any way.

As for Belknap and Jephson, apart from drilling Clyde in the matter of his general denial based on his change of heart once he had arrived at Grass Lake, and the explanation of the two hats and the bag, they could not see that there was much to do. True, there was the suit thrown in Fourth Lake near the Cranstons, but after much trolling on the part of a seemingly casual fisherman, that was brought up, cleaned and pressed, and now hung in a locked closet in the Belknap and Jephson office. Also, there was the camera at Big Bittern, dived for but never found by them—a circumstance which led Jephson to conclude that Mason must have it, and so caused him to decide that he would refer to it at the earliest possible opportunity at the trial. But as for Clyde striking her with it, even accidentally, well, it was decided at that time at least, to contend that he had not—although after exhuming Roberta's body at Biltz it had been found that the marks on her face, even at this date, did correspond in some degree to the size and shape of the camera.

For, in the first place, they were exceedingly dubious of Clyde as a witness. Would he or would he not, in telling of how it all happened, be sufficiently direct or forceful and sincere to convince any jury that he had so struck her without intending to strike her? For on that, marks or no marks, would depend whether the jury was going to believe him. And if it did not believe that he struck her accidentally, then a verdict of guilty, of course.

And so they prepared to await the coming of the trial, only working betimes and in so far as they dared, to obtain testimony or evidence as to Clyde's previous good character, but being blocked to a degree by the fact that in Lycurgus, while pretending to be a model youth outwardly, he had privately been conducting himself otherwise, and that in Kansas City his first commercial efforts had resulted in such a scandal.

However, one of the most difficult matters in connection with Clyde and his incarceration here, as Belknap and Jephson as well as the prosecution saw it, was the fact that thus far not one single member of his own or his uncle's family had come forward to champion him. And to no one save Belknap and Jephson had he admitted where his parents were. Yet would it not be necessary, as both Belknap and Jephson argued from time to time, if any case at all were to be made out for him, to have his mother or father, or at least a sister or a brother, come forward to say a good word for him? Otherwise, Clyde might appear to be a pariah, one who had been from the first a drifter and a waster and was now purposely being avoided by all who knew him.

For this reason, at their conference with Darrah Brookhart they had inquired after Clyde's parents and had learned that in so far as the Griffiths of Lycurgus were concerned, there lay a deep objection to bringing on any member of this western branch of the family. There was, as he explained, a great

social gap between them, which it would not please the Lycurgus Griffiths to have exploited here. Besides, who could
say but that once Clyde's parents were notified or discovered
by the yellow press, they might not lend themselves to exploitation. Both Samuel and Gilbert Griffiths, as Brookhart
now informed Belknap, had suggested that it was best, if
Clyde did not object, to keeping his immediate relatives in
the background. In fact, on this, in some measure at least, was
likely to depend the extent of their financial aid to Clyde.

Clyde was in accord with this wish of the Griffiths, although no one who talked with him sufficiently or heard him
express how sorry he was on his mother's account that all this
had happened, could doubt the quality of the blood and emotional tie that held him and his mother together. The complete truth was that his present attitude toward her was a
mixture of fear and shame because of the manner in which
she was likely to view his predicament—his moral if not his
social failure. Would she be willing to believe the story prepared by Belknap and Jephson as to his change of heart? But
even apart from that, to have her come here now and look at
him through these bars when he was so disgraced—to be
compelled to face her and talk to her day after day! Her clear,
inquiring, tortured eyes! Her doubt as to his innocence, since
he could feel that even Belknap and Jephson, in spite of all
their plans for him, were still a little dubious as to that unintentional blow of his. They did not really believe it, and they
might tell her that. And would his religious, God-fearing,
crime-abhorring mother be more credulous than they?

Being asked again what he thought ought to be done about
his parents, he replied that he did not believe he could face
his mother yet—it would do no good and would only torture
both.

And fortunately, as he saw it, apparently no word of all that
had befallen him had yet reached his parents in Denver. Because of their peculiar religious and moral beliefs, all copies of
worldly and degenerate daily papers were consistently excluded from their home and Mission. And the Lycurgus Griffiths had had no desire to inform them.

Yet one night, at about the time that Belknap and Jephson
were most seriously debating the absence of his parents and

what, if anything, should be done about it, Esta, who some time after Clyde had arrived in Lycurgus had married and was living in the southeast portion of Denver, chanced to read in *The Rocky Mountain News*—and this just subsequent to Clyde's indictment by the Grand Jury at Bridgeburg:

### "BOY SLAYER OF WORKING GIRL INDICTED"

"Bridgeburg, N.Y., Aug. 6: A special Grand Jury appointed by Governor Stouderback, of this state, to sit in the case of Clyde Griffiths, the nephew of the wealthy collar manufacturer of the same name, of Lycurgus, New York, recently charged with the killing of Miss Roberta Alden, of Biltz, New York, at Big Bittern Lake in the Adirondacks on July 8th last, to-day returned an indictment charging murder in the first degree.

"Subsequent to the indictment, Griffiths, who in spite of almost overwhelming evidence, has persisted in asserting that the alleged crime was an accident, and who, accompanied by his counsel, Alvin Belknap, and Reuben Jephson, of this city, was arraigned before Supreme Court Justice Oberwaltzer, pleaded not guilty. He was remanded for trial, which was set for October 15th.

"Young Griffiths, who is only twenty-two years of age, and up to the day of his arrest a respected member of Lycurgus smart society, is alleged to have stunned and then drowned his working-girl sweetheart, whom he had wronged and then planned to desert in favor of a richer girl. The lawyers in this case have been retained by his wealthy uncle of Lycurgus, who has hitherto remained aloof. But apart from this, it is locally asserted, no relative has come forward to aid in his defense."

Esta forthwith made a hurried departure for her mother's home. Despite the directness and clarity of this she was not willing to believe it was Clyde. Still there was the damning force of geography and names—the rich Lycurgus Griffiths, the absence of his own relatives.

As quickly as the local street car would carry her, she now presented herself at the combined lodging house and mission known as the "Star of Hope," in Bidwell Street, which was scarcely better than that formerly maintained in Kansas City. For while it provided a number of rooms for wayfarers at twenty-five cents a night, and was supposed to be self-supporting, it entailed much work with hardly any more profit. Besides, by now, both Frank and Julia, who long before this had become irked by the drab world in which they found themselves, had earnestly sought to free themselves of it, leaving the burden of the mission work on their father and mother. Julia, now nineteen, was cashiering for a local downtown restaurant, and Frank, nearing seventeen, had but recently found work in a fruit and vegetable commission house. In fact, the only child about the place by day was little Russell, the illegitimate son of Esta—now between three and four years of age, and most reservedly fictionalized by his grandparents as an orphan whom they had adopted in Kansas City. He was a dark-haired child, in some ways resembling Clyde, who, even at this early age, as Clyde had been before him, was being instructed in those fundamental verities which had irritated Clyde in his own childhood.

At the time that Esta, now a decidedly subdued and reserved wife, entered, Mrs. Griffiths was busy sweeping and dusting and making up beds. But on sight of her daughter at this unusual hour approaching, and with blanched cheeks signalling her to come inside the door of a vacant room, Mrs. Griffiths, who, because of years of difficulties of various kinds, was more or less accustomed to scenes such as this, now paused in wonder, the swiftly beclouding mist of apprehension shining in her eyes. What new misery or ill was this? For decidedly Esta's weak gray eyes and manner indicated distress. And in her hand was folded a paper, which she opened and after giving her mother a most solicitous look, pointed to the item, toward which Mrs. Griffiths now directed her look. But what was this?

"BOY SLAYER OF WORKING-GIRL SWEETHEART INDICTED."

"CHARGED WITH THE KILLING OF MISS ROBERTA ALDEN AT BIG BITTERN LAKE IN THE ADIRONDACKS ON JULY 8 LAST."

"RETURNED INDICTMENT CHARGING MURDER IN THE FIRST DEGREE."

"IN SPITE OF ALMOST OVERWHELMING CIRCUMSTANTIAL EVIDENCE."

"PLEADED NOT GUILTY."

"REMANDED FOR TRIAL."

"SET FOR OCTOBER 15."

"STUNNED AND DROWNED HIS WORKING-GIRL
SWEETHEART."

"NO RELATIVE HAS COME FORWARD."

It was thus that her eye and her mind automatically selected the most essential lines. And then as swiftly going over them again.

"CLYDE GRIFFITHS, NEPHEW OF THE WEALTHY
COLLAR MANUFACTURER OF LYCURGUS,
NEW YORK."

Clyde—her son! And only recently—but no, over a month ago—(and they had been worrying a little as to that, she and Asa, because he had not—) July 8th! And it was now August 11th! Then—yes! But not her son! Impossible! Clyde the murderer of a girl who was his sweetheart! But he was not like that! He had written to her how he was getting along—the head of a large department, with a future. But of no girl. But now! And yet that other little girl there in Kansas City. Merciful God! And the Griffiths, of Lycurgus, her husband's brother, knowing of this and not writing! Ashamed, disgusted, no doubt. Indifferent. But no, he had hired two lawyers. Yet the horror! Asa! Her other children! What the papers would say! This mission! They would have to give it up and go somewhere else again. Yet was he guilty or not guilty? She must know that before judging or thinking. This paper said he had pleaded not guilty. Oh, that wretched, worldly, showy hotel in Kansas City! Those other bad boys! Those two years in which he had wandered here and there, not writing, passing as Harry Tenet. Doing what? Learning what?

She paused, full of that intense misery and terror which no faith in the revealed and comforting verities of God and mercy and salvation which she was always proclaiming, could for the moment fend against. Her boy! Her Clyde! In jail, accused of murder! She must wire! She must write! She must go, maybe. But how to get the money! What to do when she got there. How to get the courage—the faith—to endure it. Yet again, neither Asa nor Frank nor Julia must know. Asa, with his protesting and yet somehow careworn faith, his weak eyes and weakening body. And must Frank and Julia, now just starting out in life, be saddled with this? Marked thus?

Merciful God! Would her troubles never end?

She turned, her big, work-worn hands trembling slightly, shaking the paper she held, while Esta, who sympathized greatly with her mother these days because of all she had been compelled to endure, stood by. She looked so tired at times, and now to be racked by this! Yet, as she knew, her mother was the strongest in the family—so erect, so square-shouldered, defiant—a veritable soul pilot in her cross-grained, uniformed way.

"Mamma, I just can't believe it can be Clyde," was all Esta could say now. "It just can't be, can it?"

But Mrs. Griffiths merely continued to stare at that ominous headline, then swiftly ran her gray-blue eyes over the room. Her broad face was blanched and dignified by an enormous strain and an enormous pain. Her erring, misguided, no doubt unfortunate, son, with all his wild dreams of getting on and up, was in danger of death, of being electrocuted for a crime—for murder! He had killed some one—a poor working-girl, the paper said.

"Ssh!" she whispered, putting one finger to her own lips as a sign. "He" (indicating Asa) "must not know yet, anyhow. We must wire first, or write. You can have the answers come to you, maybe. I will give you the money. But I must sit down somewhere now for a minute. I feel a little weak. I'll sit here. Let me have the Bible."

On the small dresser was a Gideon Bible, which, sitting on the edge of the commonplace iron bed, she now opened instinctively at Psalms 3 and 4.

"Lord, how are they increased that trouble."

"Hear me, when I call, O God of my righteousness."

And then reading on silently, even placidly apparently, through 6, 8, 10, 13, 23, 91, while Esta stood by in silent amazement and misery.

"Oh, mamma, I just can't believe it. Oh, this is too terrible!"

But Mrs. Griffiths read on. It was as if, and in spite of all this, she had been able to retreat into some still, silent place, where, for the time being at least, no evil human ill could reach her. Then at last, quite calmly closing the book, and rising, she went on:

"Now, we must think out what to say and who to send that telegram to—I mean to Clyde, of course—at that place, wherever it is—Bridgeburg," she added, looking at the paper, and then interpolating from the Bible—"By terrible things in righteousness wilt thou answer us, O God!" "Or, maybe, those two lawyers—their names are there. I'm afraid to wire Asa's brother for fear he'll wire back to him." (Then: 'Thou art my bulwark and my strength. In Thee will I trust.') "But I suppose they would give it to him if we sent it care of that judge or those lawyers, don't you think? But it would be better if we could send it to him direct, I suppose. ('He leadeth me by the still waters.') Just say that I have read about him and still have faith in and love for him, but he is to tell me the truth and what to do. If he needs money we will have to see what we can do, I suppose. ('He restoreth my soul.')"

And then, despite her sudden peace of the moment, she once more began wringing her large, rough hands. "Oh, it can't be true. Oh, dear, no! After all, he is my son. We all love him and have faith. We must say that. God will deliver him. Watch and pray. Have faith. Under his wings shalt thou trust."

She was so beside herself that she scarcely knew what she was saying. And Esta, at her side, was saying: "Yes, mamma! Oh, of course! Yes, I will! I know he'll get it all right." But she, too, was saying to herself: "My God! My God! What could be worse than this—to be accused of murder! But, of course, it can't be true. It can't be true. If he should hear!" (She was thinking of her husband.) "And after Russell, too. And Clyde's trouble there in Kansas City. Poor mamma. She has so much trouble."

Together, after a time, and avoiding Asa who was in an adjoining room helping with the cleaning, the two made their way to the general mission room below, where was silence and many placards which proclaimed the charity, the wisdom, and the sustaining righteousness of God.

# Chapter XVIII

THE TELEGRAM, worded in the spirit just described, was forthwith despatched care of Belknap and Jephson, who immediately counseled Clyde what to reply—that all was well with him; that he had the best of advice and would need no financial aid. Also that until his lawyers advised it, it would be best if no member of the family troubled to appear, since everything that could possibly be done to aid him was already being done. At the same time they wrote Mrs. Griffiths, assuring her of their interest in Clyde and advising her to let matters rest as they were for the present.

Despite the fact that the Griffiths were thus restrained from appearing in the east, neither Belknap nor Jephson were averse to some news of the existence, whereabouts, faith and sympathy of Clyde's most immediate relatives creeping into the newspapers, since the latter were so persistent in referring to his isolation. And in this connection they were aided by the fact that his mother's telegram on being received in Bridgeburg was at once read by individuals who were particularly interested in the case and by them whispered to the public and the press, with the result that in Denver the family was at once sought out and interviewed. And shortly after, there was circulated in all the papers east and west a more or less complete account of the present state of Clyde's family, the nature of the mission conducted by them, as well as their narrow and highly individualistic religious beliefs and actions, even the statement that often in his early youth Clyde had been taken into the streets to sing and pray—a revelation which shocked Lycurgus and Twelfth Lake society about as much as it did him.

At the same time, Mrs. Griffiths, being an honest woman and whole-heartedly sincere in her faith and in the good of her work, did not hesitate to relate to reporter after reporter who called, all the details of the missionary work of her husband and herself in Denver and elsewhere. Also that neither Clyde nor any of the other children had ever enjoyed the opportunities that come to most. However, her boy, whatever the present charge might be, was not innately bad, and she could not believe that he was guilty of any such crime. It was all an unfortunate and accidental combination of circumstances which he would explain at the trial. However, whatever foolish thing he might have done, it was all to be attributed to an unfortunate accident which broke up the mission work in Kansas City a few years before and compelled the removal of the family from there to Denver, leaving Clyde to make his way alone. And it was because of advice from her that he had written her husband's rich brother in Lycurgus, which led to his going there—a series of statements which caused Clyde in his cell to tingle with a kind of prideful misery and resentment and forced him to write his mother and complain. Why need she always talk so much about the past and the work that she and his father were connected with, when she knew that he had never liked it and resented going on the streets? Many people didn't see it as she and his father did, particularly his uncle and cousin and all those rich people he had come to know, and who were able to make their way in so different and much more brilliant fashion. And now, as he said to himself, Sondra would most certainly read this—all that he had hoped to conceal.

Yet even in the face of all this, because of so much sincerity and force in his mother, he could not help but think of her with affection and respect, and because of her sure and unfailing love for him, with emotion. For in answer to his letter she wrote that she was sorry if she had hurt his feelings or injured him in any way. But must not the truth be shown always? The ways of God were for the best and surely no harm could spring from service in His cause. He must not ask her to lie. But if he said the word, she would so gladly attempt to raise the necessary money and come to his aid—sit in his cell and plan with him—holding his hands—but as Clyde so well knew and thought at this time and which caused him to decide that she must not come yet—demanding of him the truth—with those clear, steady blue eyes of hers looking into his own. He could not stand that now.

For, frowning directly before him, like a huge and basalt headland above a troubled and angry sea, was the trial itself, with all that it implied—the fierce assault of Mason which he

could only confront, for the most part, with the lies framed
for him by Jephson and Belknap. For, although he was constantly seeking to salve his conscience with the thought that
at the last moment he had not had the courage to strike
Roberta, nevertheless this other story was so terribly difficult
for him to present and defend—a fact which both Belknap
and Jephson realized and which caused the latter to appear
most frequently at Clyde's cell door with the greeting: "Well,
how's tricks to-day?"

The peculiarly rusty and disheveled and indifferently tailored
character of Jephson's suits! The worn and disarranged effect
of his dark brown soft hat, pulled low over his eyes! His long,
bony, knotty hands, suggesting somehow an enormous tensile
strength. And the hard, small blue eyes filled with a shrewd,
determined cunning and courage, with which he was seeking
to inoculate Clyde, and which somehow did inoculate him!

"Any more preachers around to-day? Any more country
girls or Mason's boys?" For during this time, because of the
enormous interest aroused by the pitiable death of Roberta,
as well as the evidence of her rich and beautiful rival, Clyde
was being visited by every type of shallow crime-or-sex-
curious country bumpkin lawyer, doctor, merchant, yokel
evangelist or minister, all friends or acquaintances of one or
another of the officials of the city, and who, standing before
his cell door betimes, and at the most unexpected moments,
and after surveying him with curious, or resentful, or horrified
eyes, asked such questions as: "Do you pray, brother? Do you
get right down on your knees and pray?" (Clyde was reminded of his mother and father at such times.) Had he made
his peace with God? Did he actually deny that he had killed
Roberta Alden? In the case of three country girls: "Would
you mind telling us the name of the girl you are supposed to
be in love with, and where she is now? We won't tell any one.
Will she appear at the trial?" Questions which Clyde could do
no more than ignore, or if not, answer as equivocally or evasively or indifferently as possible. For although he was inclined to resent them, still was he not being constantly
instructed by both Belknap and Jephson that for the good of
his own cause he must try to appear genial and civil and optimistic? Then there came also newspaper men, or women, ac-

companied by artists or photographers, to interview and make studies of him. But with these, for the most part and on the advice of Belknap and Jephson he refused to communicate or said only what he was told to say.

"You can talk all you want," suggested Jephson, genially, "so long as you don't say anything. And the stiff upper lip, you know. And the smile that won't come off, see? Not failing to go over that list, are you?" (He had provided Clyde with a long list of possible questions which no doubt would be asked him on the stand and which he was to answer according to answers typewritten beneath them, or to suggest something better. They all related to the trip to Big Bittern, his reason for the extra hat, his change of heart—why, when, where.) "That's your litany, you know." And then he might light a cigarette without ever offering one to Clyde, since for the sake of a reputation for sobriety he was not to smoke here.

And for a time, after each visit, Clyde finding himself believing that he could and would do exactly as Jephson had said—walk briskly and smartly into court—bear up against every one, every eye, even that of Mason himself—forget that he was afraid of him, even when on the witness stand—forget all the terror of those many facts in Mason's possession, which he was to explain with this list of answers—forget Roberta and her last cry, and all the heartache and misery that went with the loss of Sondra and her bright world.

Yet, with the night having once more fallen, or the day dragging on with only the lean and bearded Kraut or the sly and evasive Sissell, or both, hanging about, or coming to the door to say, "Howdy!" or to discuss something that had occurred in town, or to play chess, or checkers, Clyde growing more and more moody and deciding, maybe, that there was no real hope for him after all. For how alone he was, except for his attorneys and mother and brother and sisters! Never a word from Sondra, of course. For along with her recovery to some extent from her original shock and horror, she was now thinking somewhat differently of him—that after all it was for love of her, perhaps, that he had slain Roberta and made himself the pariah and victim that he now was. Yet, because of the immense prejudice and horror expressed by the world, she was by no means able to think of venturing to send him a word. Was he not a murderer? And in addition, that miserable western family of his, pictured as street preachers, and he, too,—or as a singing and praying boy from a mission! Yet occasionally returning in thought, and this quite in spite of herself, to his eager, unreasoning and seemingly consuming enthusiasm for her. (How deeply he must have cared to venture upon so deadly a deed!) And hence wondering whether at some time, once this case was less violently before the public eye, it might not be possible to communicate with him in some guarded and unsigned way, just to let him know, perhaps, that because of his great love for her she desired him to know that he was not entirely forgotten. Yet as instantly deciding, *no*, no—her parents—if they should learn—or guess—or the public, or her one-time associates. Not now, oh, not now at least. Maybe later if he were set free—or—or—convicted—she couldn't tell. Yet suffering heart-aches for the most part—as much as she detested and abhorred the horrible crime by which he had sought to win her.

And in the interim, Clyde in his cell, walking to and fro, or looking out on the dull square through the heavily barred windows, or reading and re-reading the newspapers, or nervously turning the pages of magazines or books furnished by his counsel, or playing chess or checkers, or eating his meals, which, by special arrangement on the part of Belknap and Jephson (made at the request of his uncle), consisted of better dishes than were usually furnished to the ordinary prisoner.

Yet with the iterated and reiterated thought, based on the seemingly irreparable and irreconcilable loss of Sondra, as to whether it was possible for him to go on with this—make this, as he at times saw it, almost useless fight.

At times, in the middle of the night or just before dawn, with all the prison silent—dreams—a ghastly picture of all that he most feared and that dispelled every trace of courage and drove him instantly to his feet, his heart pounding wildly, his eyes strained, a cold damp upon his face and hands. That chair, somewhere in the State penitentiary. He had read of it—how men died in it. And then he would walk up and down, thinking how, how, in case it did not come about as Jephson felt so sure that it would—in case he was convicted and a new trial refused—then, well—then, might one be able to break out of such a jail as this, maybe, and run away? These old brick walls. How thick were they? But was it possible that with a hammer or a stone, or something that some one might bring him—his brother Frank, or his sister Julia, or Ratterer, or Hegglund—if only he could get in communication with some one of them and get him or her to bring him something of the kind——— If only he could get a saw, to saw those bars! And then run, run, as he should have in those woods up there that time! But how? And whither?

# Chapter XIX

OCTOBER 15—with gray clouds and a sharp, almost January wind that herded the fallen leaves into piles and then scurried them in crisp and windy gusts like flying birds here and there. And, in spite of the sense of struggle and tragedy in the minds of many, with an electric chair as the shadowy mental background to it all, a sense of holiday or festival, with hundreds of farmers, woodsmen, traders, entering in Fords and Buicks—farmer wives and husbands—daughters and sons —even infants in arms. And then idling about the public square long before the time for court to convene, or, as the hour neared, congregating before the county jail in the hope of obtaining a glimpse of Clyde, or before the courthouse door nearest the jail, which was to be the one entrance to the courtroom for the public and Clyde, and from which position they could see and assure entrance into the courtroom itself when the time came. And a flock of pigeons parading rather dismally along the cornices and gutters of the upper floor and roof of the ancient court.

And with Mason and his staff—Burton Burleigh, Earl Newcomb, Zillah Saunders, and a young Bridgeburg law graduate by the name of Manigault—helping to arrange the order of evidence as well as direct or instruct the various witnesses and venire-men who were already collecting in the ante-chamber of the now almost nationally known attorney for the people. And with cries outside of: "Peanuts!" "Popcorn!" "Hot dogs!" "Get the story of Clyde Griffiths, with all the letters of Roberta Alden. Only twenty-five cents!" (This being a set of duplicate copies of Roberta's letters which had been stolen from Mason's office by an intimate of Burton Burleigh's and by him sold to a penny-dreadful publisher of Binghamton, who immediately issued them in pamphlet form together with an outline of "the great plot" and Roberta's and Clyde's pictures.)

And in the meantime, over in the reception or conference room of the jail, Alvin Belknap and Reuben Jephson, side by side with Clyde, neatly arrayed in the very suit he had sought

to sink forever in the waters of Lower Twelfth Lake. And with
a new tie and shirt and shoes added in order to present him
in his Lycurgus best. Jephson, long and lean and shabbily
dressed as usual, but with all of that iron and power that so
impressed Clyde in every line of his figure and every movement or gesture of his body. Belknap—looking like an Albany
beau—the one on whom was to fall the burden of the opening presentation of the case as well as the cross-examining,
now saying: "Now you're not going to get frightened or
show any evidence of nervousness at anything that may be
said or done at any time, are you, Clyde? We're to be with
you, you know, all through the trial. You sit right between us.
And you're going to smile and look unconcerned or interested, just as you wish, but never fearful—but not too bold or
gay, you know, so that they'd feel that you're not taking this
thing seriously. You understand—just a pleasant, gentlemanly,
and sympathetic manner all the time. And not frightened. For
that will be certain to do us and you great harm. Since you're
innocent, you have no real reason to be frightened—although
you're sorry, of course. You understand all that, I know, by
now."

"Yes, sir, I understand," replied Clyde. "I will do just as
you say. Besides, I never struck her intentionally, and that's
the truth. So why should I be afraid?" And here he looked at
Jephson, on whom, for psychic reasons, he depended most.
In fact the words he had just spoken were the very words
which Jephson had so drilled into him during the two months
just past. And catching the look, Jephson now drew closer
and fixing Clyde with his gimlet and yet encouraging and sustaining blue eyes, began:

"You're not guilty! You're not guilty, Clyde, see? You understand that fully by now, and you must always believe and
remember that, because it's true. You didn't intend to strike
her, do you hear? You swear to that. You have sworn it to me
and Belknap here, and we believe you. Now, it doesn't make
the least bit of difference that because of the circumstances
surrounding all this we are not going to be able to make the
average jury see this or believe it just as you tell it. That's neither here nor there. I've told you that before. You know what
the truth is—and so do we. *But,* in order to get justice for

you, we've had to get up something else—a dummy or sub-stitute for the real fact, which is that you didn't strike her in-tentionally, but which we cannot hope to make them see without disguising it in some way. You get that, don't you?"

"Yes, sir," replied Clyde, always over-awed and intrigued by this man.

"And for that reason, as I've so often told you, we've in-vented this other story about a change of heart. It's not quite true as to time, but it is true that you did experience a change of heart there in the boat. And that's our justification. But they'd never believe that under all of the peculiar circum-stances, so we're merely going to move that change of heart up a little, see? Make it before you ever went into that boat at all. And while we know it isn't true that way, still neither is the charge that you intentionally struck her true, and they're not going to electrocute you for something that isn't true—not with my consent, at least." He looked into Clyde's eyes for a moment more, and then added: "It's this way, Clyde. It's like having to pay for potatoes, or for suits of clothes, with corn or beans instead of money, when you have money to pay with but when, because of the crazy notions on the part of some one, they won't believe that the money you have is genuine. So you've got to use the potatoes or beans. And beans is what we're going to give 'em. But the justification is that you're not guilty. You're not guilty. You've sworn to me that you didn't intend to strike her there at the last, whatever you might have been provoked to do at first. And that's enough for me. You're not guilty."

And here, firmly and convincingly, which was the illusion in regard to his own attitude which he was determined to con-vey to Clyde, he laid hold of his coat lapels, and after looking fixedly into his somewhat strained and now nervous brown eyes, added: "And now, whenever you get to feeling weak or nervous, or if, when you go on the stand, you think Mason is getting the best of you, I want you to remember this—just say to yourself—'I'm not guilty! I'm not guilty! And they can't fairly convict me unless I really am.' And if that don't pull you together, look at me. I'll be right there. All you have to do, if you feel yourself getting rattled, is to look at me—right into my eyes, just as I'm looking at you now—and then you'll know that I'm wanting you to brace up and do what I'm telling you to do now—swear to the things that we are asking you to swear to, however they may look like lies, and however you may feel about them. I'm not going to have you convicted for something you didn't do, just because you can't be allowed to swear to what is the truth—not if I can help it. And now that's all."

And here he slapped him genially and heartily on the back, while Clyde, strangely heartened, felt, for the time being at least, that certainly he could do as he was told, and would.

And then Jephson, taking out his watch and looking first at Belknap, then out of the nearest window through which were to be seen the already assembled crowds—one about the courthouse steps; a second, including newspapermen and women, newspaper photographers and artists, gathered closely before the jail walk, and eagerly waiting to "snap" Clyde or any one connected with this case—went calmly on with:

"Well, it's about time, I guess. Looks as though all Cataraqui would like to get inside. We're going to have quite an audience." And turning to Clyde once more, he added: "Now, you don't want to let those people disturb you, Clyde. They're nothing but a lot of country people come to town to see a show."

And then the two of them, Belknap and Jephson, going out. And Kraut and Sissell coming in to take personal charge of Clyde, while the two lawyers, passing amid whispers, crossed over to the court building in the square of brown grass beyond.

And after them, and in less than five minutes, and preceded by Slack and Sissell and followed by Kraut and Swenk—yet protected on either side by two extra deputies in case there should be an outbreak or demonstration of any kind—Clyde himself, attempting to look as jaunty and nonchalant as possible, yet because of the many rough and strange faces about him—men in heavy racoon coats and caps, and with thick whiskers, or in worn and faded and nondescript clothes such as characterized many of the farmers of this region, accompanied by their wives and children, and all staring so strangely and curiously—he felt not a little nervous, as though at any moment there might be a revolver shot, or some one might leap at him with a knife—the deputies with their hands on their guns lending not a little to the reality of his mood. Yet only cries of: "Here he comes! Here he comes!" "There he is!" "Would you believe that he could do a thing like that?"

And then the cameras clicking and whirring and his two protectors shouldering closer and closer to him while he shrank down within himself mentally.

And then a flight of five brown stone steps leading up to an old courthouse door. And beyond that, an inner flight of steps to a large, long, brown, high-ceilinged chamber, in which, to the right and left, and in the rear facing east, were tall, thin, round-topped windows, fitted with thin panes, admitting a flood of light. And at the west end, a raised platform, with a highly ornamental, dark brown carved bench upon it. And behind it, a portrait—and on either side, north and south, and at the rear, benches and benches in rows— each tier higher than the other, and all crowded with people, the space behind them packed with standing bodies, and all apparently, as he entered, leaning and craning and examining him with sharp keen eyes, while there went about a conversational buzz or brrh. He could hear a general sssss—pppp—as he approached and passed through a gate to an open space beyond it, wherein, as he could see, were Belknap and Jephson at a table, and between them a vacant chair for him. And he could see and feel the eyes and faces on which he was not quite willing to look.

But directly before him, at another table in the same square, but more directly below the raised platform at the west end, as he could see now, were Mason and several men whom he seemed to recollect—Earl Newcomb and Burton Burleigh and yet another man whom he had never seen before, all four turning and gazing at him as he came.

And about this inner group, an outer circle of men and women writers and sketch artists.

And then, after a time, recalling Belknap's advice, he managed to straighten up and with an air of studied ease and courage—which was belied to a certain extent by his strained, pale face and somewhat hazy stare—look at the writers and artists who were either studying or sketching him, and even to whisper: "Quite a full house, eh?" But just then, and before he could say anything more, a resounding whack, whack, from somewhere. And then a voice: "Order in the Court! His Honor, the Court! Everybody please rise!" And as suddenly the whispering and stirring audience growing completely silent. And then, through a door to the south of the dais, a large, urbane and florid and smooth-faced man, who, in an ample black gown, walked swiftly to the large chair immediately behind the desk, and after looking steadily upon all before him, but without appearing to see any one of them, seated himself. Whereupon every one assembled in the courtroom sat down.

And then to the left, yet below the judge, at a smaller desk, a smaller and older individual standing and calling, "Oyez! Oyez! All persons having business before the honorable, the Supreme Court of the State of New York, County of Cataraqui, draw near and give attention. This court is now in session!"

And after that this same individual again rising and beginning: "The State of New York against Clyde Griffiths." Then Mason, rising and standing before his table, at once announced: "The People are ready." Whereupon Belknap arose, and in a courtly and affable manner, stated: "The defendant is ready."

Then the same clerk reached into a square box that was before him, and drawing forth a piece of paper, called "Simeon Dinsmore," whereupon a little, hunched and brown-suited man, with claw-like hands, and a ferret-like face, immediately scuttled to the jury box and was seated. And once there he was approached by Mason, who, in a brisk manner—his flat-nosed face looking most aggressive and his strong voice reaching to the uttermost corners of the court, began to inquire as to his age, his business, whether he was single or married, how many children he had, whether he believed or did not believe in capital punishment. The latter question as Clyde at once noted seemed to stir in him something akin to resentment or suppressed emotion of some kind, for at once and with emphasis, he answered: "I most certainly do—for some people"—a reply which caused Mason to smile slightly and Jephson to turn and look toward Belknap, who mumbled sarcastically: "And they talk about the possibility of a fair trial here." But at the same time Mason feeling that this very honest, if all too convinced farmer, was a little too emphatic in his beliefs, saying: "With the consent of the Court, the People will excuse the talesman." And Belknap, after an inquiring glance from the Judge, nodding his agreement, at which the prospective juror was excused.

And the clerk, immediately drawing out of the box a second slip of paper, and then calling: "Dudley Sheerline!" Whereupon, a thin, tall man of between thirty-eight and forty, neatly dressed and somewhat meticulous and cautious in his manner, approached and took his place in the box. And Mason once more began to question him as he had the other.

In the meantime, Clyde, in spite of both Belknap's and Jephson's preliminary precautions, was already feeling stiff and chill and bloodless. For, decidedly, as he could feel, this audience was inimical. And amid this closely pressing throng, as he now thought, with an additional chill, there must be the father and mother, perhaps also the sisters and brothers, of Roberta, and all looking at him, and hoping with all their hearts, as the newspapers during the weeks past informed him, that he would be made to suffer for this.

And again, all those people of Lycurgus and Twelfth Lake, no one of whom had troubled to communicate with him in any way, assuming him to be absolutely guilty, of course— were any of those here? Jill or Gertrude or Tracy Trumbull, for instance? Or Wynette Phant or her brother? She had been at that camp at Bear Lake the day he was arrested. His mind ran over all the social personages whom he had encountered during the last year and who would now see him as he was— poor and commonplace and deserted, and on trial for such a crime as this. And after all his bluffing about his rich connections here and in the west. For now, of course, they would believe him as terrible as his original plot, without knowing or caring about his side of the story—his moods and fears—that predicament that he was in with Roberta—his love for Sondra and all that she had meant to him. They wouldn't understand that, and he was not going to be allowed to tell anything in regard to it, even if he were so minded.

And yet, because of the advice of Belknap and Jephson, he

must sit up and smile, or at least look pleasant and meet the gaze of every one boldly and directly. And in consequence, turning, and for the moment feeling absolutely transfixed. For there—God, what a resemblance!—to the left of him on one of those wall benches, was a woman or girl who appeared to be the living image of Roberta! It was that sister of hers— Emily—of whom she had often spoken—but oh, what a shock! His heart almost stopped. It might even be Roberta! And transfixing him with what ghostly, and yet real, and savage and accusing eyes! And next to her another girl, looking something like her, too—and next to her that old man, Roberta's father—that wrinkled old man whom he had encountered that day he had called at his farm door for information, now looking at him almost savagely, a gray and weary look that said so plainly: "Your murderer! Your murderer!" And beside him a mild and small and ill-looking woman of about fifty, veiled and very shrunken and sunken-eyed, who at his glance dropped her own eyes and turned away, as if stricken with a great pain, not hate. Her mother—no doubt of it. Oh, what a situation was this! How unthinkably miserable! His heart fluttered. His hands trembled.

So now to stay himself, he looked down, first at the hands of Belknap and Jephson on the table before him, since each was toying with a pencil poised above the pad of paper before them, as they gazed at Mason and whoever was in the jury box before him—a foolish-looking fat man now. What a difference between Jephson's and Belknap's hands—the latter so short and soft and white, the former's so long and brown and knotty and bony. And Belknap's pleasant and agreeable manner here in court—his voice—"I think I will ask the juror to step down"—as opposed to Mason's revolver-like "Excused!" or Jephson's slow and yet powerful, though whispered, "Better let him go, Alvin. Nothing in him for us." And then all at once Jephson saying to him: "Sit up! Sit up! Look around! Don't sag down like that. Look people in the eye. Smile naturally, Clyde, if you're going to smile at all. Just look 'em in the eye. They're not going to hurt you. They're just a lot of farmers out sight-seeing."

But Clyde, noting at once that several reporters and artists were studying and then sketching or writing of him, now flushed hotly and weakly, for he could feel their eager eyes and their eager words as clearly as he could hear their scratching pens. And all for the papers—his blanching face and trembling hands—they would have that down—and his mother in Denver and everybody else there in Lycurgus would see and read—how he had looked at the Aldens and they had looked at him and then he had looked away again. Still—still—he must get himself better in hand—sit up once more and look about—or Jephson would be disgusted with him. And so once more he did his best to crush down his fear, to raise his eyes and then turn slightly and look about.

But in doing so, there next to the wall, and to one side of that tall window, and just as he had feared, was Tracy Trumbull, who evidently because of the law interest or his curiosity and what not—no pity or sympathy for him, surely—had come up for this day anyhow, and was looking, not at him for the moment, thank goodness, but at Mason, who was asking the fat man some questions. And next to him Eddie Sells, with near-sighted eyes equipped with thick lenses of great distance-power, and looking in Clyde's direction, yet without seeing him apparently, for he gave no sign. Oh, how trying all this!

And five rows from them again, in another direction, Mr. and Mrs. Gilpin, whom Mason had found, of course. And what would they testify to now? His calling on Roberta in her room there? And how secret it had all been? That would be bad, of course. And of all people, Mr. and Mrs. George Newton! What were they going to put them on the stand for? To tell about Roberta's life before she got to going with him, maybe? And that Grace Marr, whom he had seen often but met only once out there on Crum Lake, and whom Roberta had not liked any more. What would she have to say? She could tell how he had met Roberta, of course, but what else? And then—but, no, it could not be—and yet—yet, it was, too—surely—that Orrin Short, of whom he had asked concerning Glenn. Gee!—he was going to tell about that now, maybe—no doubt of it. How people seemed to remember things—more than ever he would have dreamed they would have.

And again, this side of that third window from the front,

but beyond that dreaded group of the Aldens, that very large and whiskered man who looked something like an old-time Quaker turned bandit—Heit was his name. He had met him at Three Mile Bay, and again on that day on which he had been taken up to Big Bittern against his will. Oh, yes, the coroner he was. And beside him, that innkeeper up there who had made him sign the register that day. And next to him the boathouse-keeper who had rented him the boat. And next to him, that tall, lank guide who had driven him and Roberta over from Gun Lodge, a brown and wiry and loutish man who seemed to pierce him now with small, deep-set, animal-like eyes, and who most certainly was going to testify to all the details of that ride from Gun Lodge. Would his nervousness on that day, and his foolish qualms, be as clearly remembered by him as they were now by himself? And if so, how would that affect his plea of a change of heart? Would he not better talk all that over again with Jephson?

But this man Mason! How hard he was! How energetic! And how he must have worked to get all of these people here to testify against him! And now here he was, exclaiming as he chanced to look at him, and as he had in at least the last dozen cases (yet with no perceptible result in so far as the jury box was concerned), "Acceptable to the People!" But, invariably, whenever he had done so, Jepshon had merely turned slightly, but without looking, and had said: "Nothing in him for us, Alvin. As set as a bone." And then Belknap, courteous and bland, had challenged for cause and usually succeeded in having his challenge sustained.

But then at last, and oh, how agreeably, the clerk of the court announcing in a clear, thin, rasping and aged voice, a recess until two P.M. And Jephson smilingly turning to Clyde with: "Well, Clyde, that's the first round—not so very much to it, do you think? And not very hard either, is it? Better go over there and get a good meal, though. It'll be just as long and dull this afternoon."

And in the meantime, Kraut and Sissell, together with the extra deputies, pushing close and surrounding him. And then the crowding and swarming and exclaiming: "There he is! There he is! Here he comes! Herc! Here!" And a large and meaty female pushing as close as possible and staring directly into his face, exclaiming as she did so: "Let me see him! I just want to get a good look at you, young man. I have two daughters of my own." But without one of all those of Lycurgus or Twelfth Lake whom he had recognized in the public benches, coming near him. And no glimpse of Sondra anywhere, of course. For as both Belknap and Jephson had repeatedly assured him, she would not appear. Her name was not even to be mentioned, if possible. The Griffiths, as well as the Finchleys, were opposed.

# Chapter XX

$A$ ND THEN five entire days consumed by Mason and Belknap in selecting a jury. But at last the twelve men who were to try Clyde, sworn and seated. And such men—odd and grizzled, or tanned and wrinkled, farmers and country storekeepers, with here and there a Ford agent, a keeper of an inn at Tom Dixon's Lake, a salesman in Hamburger's dry goods store at Bridgeburg, and a peripatetic insurance agent residing in Purday just north of Grass Lake. And with but one exception, all married. And with but one exception, all religious, if not moral, and all convinced of Clyde's guilt before ever they sat down, but still because of their almost unanimous conception of themselves as fair and open-minded men, and because they were so interested to sit as jurors in this exciting case, convinced that they could pass fairly and impartially on the facts presented to them.

And so, all rising and being sworn in.

And at once Mason rising and beginning: "Gentlemen of the jury."

And Clyde, as well as Belknap and Jephson, now gazing at them and wondering what the impression of Mason's opening charge was likely to be. For a more dynamic and electric prosecutor under these particular circumstances was not to be found. This was his opportunity. Were not the eyes of all the citizens of the United States upon him? He believed so. It was as if some one had suddenly exclaimed: "Lights! Camera!"

"No doubt many of you have been wearied, as well as puzzled, at times during the past week," he began, "by the exceeding care with which the lawyers in this case have passed upon the panels from which you twelve men have been chosen. It has been no light matter to find twelve men to whom all the marshaled facts in this astonishing cause could be submitted and by them weighed with all the fairness and understanding which the law commands. For my part, the care which I have exercised, gentlemen, has been directed by but one motive—that the state shall have justice done. No malice, no pre-conceived notions of any kind. So late as July 9th last

I personally was not even aware of the existence of this defendant, nor of his victim, nor of the crime with which he is now charged. But, gentlemen, as shocked and unbelieving as I was at first upon hearing that a man of the age, training and connections of the defendant here could have placed himself in a position to be accused of such an offense, step by step I was compelled to alter and then dismiss forever from my mind my original doubts and to conclude from the mass of evidence that was literally thrust upon me, that it was my duty to prosecute this action in behalf of the people.

"But, however that may be, let us proceed to the facts. There are two women in this action. One is dead. The other" (and he now turned toward where Clyde sat, and here he pointed a finger in the direction of Belknap and Jephson), "by agreement between the prosecution and the defense is to be nameless here, since no good can come from inflicting unnecessary injury. In fact, the sole purpose which I now announce to you to be behind every word and every fact as it will be presented by the prosecution is that exact justice, according to the laws of this state and the crime with which this defendant is charged, shall be done. *Exact justice*, gentlemen, exact and fair. But if you do not act honestly and render a true verdict according to the evidence, the people of the state of New York and the people of the county of Cataraqui will have a grievance and a serious one. For it is they who are looking to you for a true accounting for your reasoning and your final decision in this case."

And here Mason paused, and then turning dramatically toward Clyde, and with his right index finger pointing toward him at times, continued: "The people of the State of New York *charge*," (and he hung upon this one word as though he desired to give it the value of rolling thunder), "that the crime of murder in the first degree has been committed by the prisoner at the bar—Clyde Griffiths. They *charge* that he willfully, and with malice and cruelty and deception, murdered and then sought to conceal forever from the knowledge and the justice of the world, the body of Roberta Alden, the daughter of a farmer who has for years resided near the village of Biltz, in Mimico County. They *charge*" (and here Clyde, because of whispered advice from Jephson, was leaning back as comfortably as possible and gazing as imperturbably as possible upon the face of Mason, who was looking directly at him) "that this same Clyde Griffiths, before ever this crime was committed by him, plotted for weeks the plan and commission of it, and then, with malice aforethought and in cold blood, executed it.

"And in charging these things, the people of the State of New York expect to, and will, produce before you substantiations of every one of them. You will be given facts, and of these facts you, not I, are to be the sole judge."

And here he paused once more, and shifting to a different physical position while the eager audience crowded and leaned forward, hungry and thirsty for every word he should utter, he now lifted one arm and dramatically pushing back his curly hair, resumed:

"Gentlemen, it will not take me long to picture, nor will you fail to perceive for yourselves as this case proceeds, the type of girl this was whose life was so cruelly blotted out beneath the waters of Big Bittern. All the twenty years of her life" (and Mason knew well that she was twenty-three and two years older than Clyde) "no person who ever knew her ever said one word in criticism of her character. And no evidence to that effect, I am positive, will be introduced in this trial. Somewhat over a year ago—on July 19—she went to the city of Lycurgus, in order that by working with her own hands she might help her family." (And here the sobs of her parents and sisters and brothers were heard throughout the courtroom.)

"Gentlemen," went on Mason, and from this point carrying on the picture of Roberta's life from the time she first left home to join Grace Marr until, having met Clyde on Crum Lake and fallen out with her friend and patrons, the Newtons, because of him, she accepted his dictum that she live alone, amid strange people, concealing the suspicious truth of this from her parents, and then finally succumbing to his wiles— the letters she had written him from Biltz detailing every single progressive step in this story. And from there, by the same meticulous process, he proceeded to Clyde—his interest in the affairs of Lycurgus society and the rich and beautiful Miss X, who because of a purely innocent and kindly, if infatuated, indication on her part that he might hope to aspire to her hand—had unwittingly evoked in him a passion which had been the cause of the sudden change in his attitude and emotions toward Roberta, resulting, as Mason insisted he would show, in the plot that had resulted in Roberta's death.

"But who is the individual," he suddenly and most dramatically exclaimed at this point, "against whom I charge all these things? There he sits! Is he the son of wastrel parents—a product of the slums—one who had been denied every opportunity for a proper or honorable conception of the values and duties of a decent and respectable life? Is he? On the contrary. His father is of the same strain that has given Lycurgus one of its largest and most constructive industries—the Griffiths Collar & Shirt Company. He was poor—yes—no doubt of that. But not more so than Roberta Alden—and her character appears not to have been affected by her poverty. His parents in Kansas City, Denver, and before that Chicago and Grand Rapids, Michigan, appear to have been unordained ministers of the proselytizing and mission-conducting type— people who, from all I can gather, are really, sincerely religious and right-principled in every sense. But this, their oldest son, and the one who might have been expected to be deeply influenced by them, early turned from their world and took to a more garish life. He became a bell-boy in a celebrated Kansas City hotel, the Green-Davidson."

And now he proceeded to explain that Clyde had ever been a rolling stone—one who, by reason of some quirk of temperament, perhaps, perferred to wander here and there. Later, as he now explained, he had been given an important position as head of a department in the well-known factory of his uncle at Lycurgus. And then gradually he was introduced into the circles in which his uncle and his children were familiar. And his salary was such that he could afford to keep a room in one of the better residences of the city, while the girl he had slain lived in a mean room in a back street.

"And yet," he continued, "how much has been made here of the alleged youth of this defendant?" (Here he permitted himself a scornful smile.) "He has been called by his counsel and others in the newspapers a boy, over and over again. He is not a boy. He is a bearded man. He has had more social and educational advantages than any one of you in the jury box. He has traveled. In hotels and clubs and the society with which he was so intimately connected in Lycurgus, he has been in contact with decent, respectable, and even able and distinguished people. Why, as a matter of fact, at the time of his arrest two months ago, he was part of as smart a society and summer resort group as this region boasts. Remember that! His mind is a mature, not an immature one. It is fully developed and balanced perfectly

"Gentlemen, as the state will soon proceed to prove," he went on, "it was no more than four months after his arrival in Lycurgus that this dead girl came to work for this defendant in the department of which he was the head. And it was not more than two months after that before he had induced her to move from the respectable and religious home which she had chosen in Lycurgus, to one concerning which she knew nothing and the principal advantage of which, as he saw it, was that it offered secrecy and seclusion and freedom from observation for that vile purpose which already he entertained in regard to her.

"There was a rule of the Griffiths Company, as we will later show in this trial, which explains much—and that was that no superior officer or head of any department was permitted to have anything to do with any girls working under him, or for the factory, in or out of the factory. It was not conducive to either the morals or the honor of those working for this great company, and they would not allow it. And shortly after coming there, this man had been instructed as to that rule. But did that deter him? Did the so recent and favorable consideration of his uncle in any way deter him? Not in the least. Secrecy! Secrecy! From the very beginning! Seduction! Seduction! The secret and intended and immoral and illegal and socially unwarranted and condemned use of her body outside the regenerative and ennobling pale of matrimony!

"That was his purpose, gentlemen! But was it generally known by any one in Lycurgus or elsewhere that such a relationship as this existed between him and Roberta Alden? Not a soul! *Not a soul!*, as far as I have been able to ascertain, was ever so much as partially aware of this relationship until after this girl was dead. Not a soul! Think of that!

"Gentlemen of the jury," and here his voice took on an almost reverential tone, "Roberta Alden loved this defendant with all the strength of her soul. She loved him with that love which is the crowning mystery of the human brain and the human heart, that transcends in its strength and its weakness all fear of shame or punishment from even the immortal throne above. She was a true and human and decent and kindly girl—a passionate and loving girl. And she loved as only a generous and trusting and self-sacrificing soul can love. And loving so, in the end she gave to him all that any woman can give the man she loves.

"Friends, this thing has happened millions of times in this world of ours, and it will happen millions and millions of times in the days to come. It is not new and it will never be old.

"But in January or February last, this girl, who is now dead in her grave, was compelled to come to this defendant, Clyde Griffiths, and tell him that she was about to become a mother. We shall prove to you that then and later she begged him to go away with her and make her his wife.

"But did he? Would he? Oh, no! For by that time a change had come over the dreams and the affections of Clyde Griffiths. He had had time to discover that the name of Griffiths in Lycurgus was one that would open the doors of Lycurgus exclusive circles—that the man who was no one in Kansas City or Chicago—was very much of a person here, and that it would bring him in contact with girls of education and means, girls who moved far from the sphere to which Roberta Alden belonged. Not only that, but he had found one girl to whom, because of her beauty, wealth, position, he had become enormously attached and beside her the little farm and factory girl in the pathetically shabby and secret room to which he had assigned her, looked poor indeed—good enough to betray but not good enough to marry. And he would not." Here he paused, but only for a moment, then went on:

"But at no point have I been able to find the least modification or cessation of any of these social activities on his part which so entranced him. On the contrary, from January to July fifth last, and after—yes, even after she was finally compelled to say to him that unless he could take her away and marry her, she would have to appeal to the sense of justice in the community in which they moved, and after she was cold and dead under the waters of Big Bittern—dances, lawn fêtes, automobile parties, dinners, gay trips to Twelfth Lake and Bear Lake, and without a thought, seemingly, that her great moral and social need should modify his conduct in any way."

And here he paused and gazed in the direction of Belknap and Jephson, who in turn, were not sufficiently disturbed or concerned to do more than smile, first at him and then at each other, although Clyde, terrorized by the force and the vehemence of it all, was chiefly concerned to note how much of exaggeration and unfairness was in all this.

But even as he was thinking so, Mason was continuing with: "But by this time, gentlemen, as I have indicated, Roberta Alden had become insistent that Griffiths make her his wife. And this he promised to do. Yet, as all the evidence here will show, he never intended to do anything of the kind. On the contrary, when her condition became such that he could no longer endure her pleas or the danger which her presence in Lycurgus unquestionably spelled for him, he induced her to go home to her father's house, with the suggestion, apparently, that she prepare herself by making some necessary clothes, against the day when he would come for her and remove her to some distant city where they would not be known, yet where as his wife she could honorably bring their child into the world. And according to her letters to him, as I will show, that was to have been in three weeks from the time she departed for her home in Biltz. But did he come for her as he had promised? No, he never did.

"Eventually, and solely because there was no other way out, he permitted her to come to him—on July sixth last—exactly two days before her death. But not before—but wait!——In the meantime, or from June fifth to July sixth, he allowed her to brood in that little, lonely farm-house on the outskirts of Biltz in Mimico County, with the neighbors coming in to watch and help her make some clothes, which even then she did not dare announce as her bridal trousseau. And she suspected and feared that this defendant would fail her. For daily, and sometimes twice daily, she wrote him, telling him of her fears and asking him to assure her by letter or word in some form that he would come and take her away.

"But did he even do that? Never by letter! *Never!* Oh, no, gentlemen, oh, no! On the contrary some telephone messages—things that could not be so easily traced or understood. And these so few and brief that she herself complained bitterly of his lack of interest and consideration for her at this time. So much so that at the end of five weeks, growing desperate, she wrote" (and here Mason picked from a collection of letters on the table behind him a particular letter, and read): "'This is to tell you that unless I hear from you either by telephone or letter before noon Friday, I will come to Lycurgus and the world will know how you have treated me.' Those are the words, gentlemen, that this poor girl was at last compelled to write.

"But did Clyde Griffiths want the world to know how he had treated her? Of course not! And there and then began to form in his mind a plan by which he could escape exposure and seal Roberta Alden's lips forever. And, gentlemen, the state will prove that he did so close her mouth."

At this point Mason produced a map of the Adirondacks which he had had made for the purpose, and on which in red ink were traced the movements of Clyde up to and after her death—up to the time of his arrest at Big Bear. Also, in doing this, he paused to tell the jury of Clyde's well-conceived plan of hiding his identity, the various false registrations, the two hats. Here also he explained that on the train between Fonda and Utica, as again between Utica and Grass Lake, he had not ridden in the same car with Roberta. And then he announced:

"Don't forget, gentlemen, that although he had previously indicated to Roberta that this was to be their wedding journey, he did not want anybody to know that he was with his prospective bride—no, not even after they had reached Big Bittern. For he was seeking, not to marry but to find a wilderness in which to snuff out the life of this girl of whom he had tired. But did that prevent him, twenty-four and forty-eight hours before that time, from holding her in his arms and repeating the promises he had no intention of keeping? Did it? I will show you the registers of the two hotels in which they stayed, and where, because of their assumed approaching marriage, they occupied a single room together. Yet the only reason it was forty-eight instead of twenty-four hours was that he had made a mistake in regard to the solitude of Grass Lake. Finding it brisk with life, the center of a summer religious colony, he decided to leave and go to Big Bittern, which was more lonely. And so you have the astounding and bitter spectacle, gentlemen, of a supposedly innocent and highly misunderstood young man dragging this weary and heart-sick girl from place to place, in order to find a lake deserted enough in which to drown her. And with her but four months from motherhood!

"And then, having arrived at last at one lake lonely enough, putting her in a boat and taking her out from the inn where he had again falsely registered as Mr. Clifford Golden and wife, to her death. The poor little thing imagined that she was going for a brief outing before that marriage of which he talked and which was to seal and sanctify it. To seal and sanctify it! To seal and sanctify, as closing waters seal and sanctify, but in no other way—no other way. And with him walking, whole and sly—as a wolf from its kill—to freedom, to marriage, to social and material and affectionate bliss and superiority and ease, while she slept still and nameless in her watery grave.

"But, oh, gentlemen, the ways of nature, or of God, and the Providence that shapes our ends, rough-hew them how we may! It is man who proposes, but God—God—who disposes!

"The defendant is still wondering, I am sure, as to how I know that she thought she was still going to be married after leaving the inn at Big Bittern. And I have no doubt that he still has some comforting thoughts to the effect that I cannot really and truly know it. But how shrewd and deep must be that mind that would foresee and forestall all the accidents and chances of life. For, as he sits there now, secure in the faith that his counsel may be able to extract him safely from this" (and at this Clyde sat bolt upright, his hair tingling, and his hands concealed beneath the table, trembling slightly), "he does not know that that girl, while in her room in the Grass Lake Inn, had written her mother a letter, which she had not had time to mail, and which was in the pocket of her coat left behind because of the heat of the day, and because she imagined she was coming back, of course. And which is here now upon this table."

At this Clyde's teeth fairly chattered. He shook as with a chill. To be sure, she had left her coat behind! And Belknap and Jephson also sat up, wondering what this could be. How fatally, if at all, could it mar or make impossible the plan of defense which they had evolved? They could only wait and see.

"But in that letter," went on Mason, "she tells why she was up there—to be married, no less" (and at this point Jephson and Belknap, as well as Clyde, heaved an enormous sigh of relief—it was directly in the field of their plan) "and within a day or two," continued Mason, thinking still that he was literally riddling Clyde with fear. "But Griffiths, or Graham, of Albany, or Syracuse, or anywhere, knew better. He knew he was not coming back. And he took all of his belongings with him in that boat. And all afternoon long, from noon until evening, he searched for a spot on that lonely lake—a spot not easily observed from any point of the shore, as we will show. And as evening fell, he found it. And walking south through the woods afterwards, with a new straw hat upon his head, a clean, dry bag in his hand, he imagined himself to be secure. Clifford Golden was no more—Carl Graham was no more—drowned—at the bottom of Big Bittern, along with Roberta Alden. But Clyde Griffiths was alive and free, and on his way to Twelfth Lake, to the society he so loved.

"Gentlemen, Clyde Griffiths killed Roberta Alden before he put her in that lake. He beat her on the head and face, and he believed no eye saw him. But, as her last death cry rang out over the water of Big Bittern, there was a witness, and before the prosecution has closed its case, that witness will be here to tell you the story."

Mason had no eye witness, but he could not resist this opportunity to throw so disrupting a thought into the opposition camp.

And decidedly, the result was all that he expected, and more. For Clyde, who up to this time and particularly since the thunderbolt of the letter, had been seeking to face it all with an imperturbable look of patient innocence, now stiffened and then wilted. A witness! And here to testify! God!

Then he, whoever he was, lurking on the lone shore of the lake, had seen the unintended blow, had heard her cries—had seen that he had not sought to aid her! Had seen him swim to shore and steal away—maybe had watched him in the woods as he changed his clothes. God! His hands now gripped the sides of the chair, and his head went back with a jerk as if from a powerful blow, for that meant death—his sure execution. God! No hope now! His head drooped and he looked as though he might lapse into a state of coma.

As to Belknap, Mason's revelation at first caused him to drop the pencil with which he was making notes, then next to stare in a puzzled and dumbfounded way, since they had no evidence wherewith to forefend against such a smash as this— But as instantly recalling how completely off his guard he must look, recovering. Could it be that Clyde might have been lying to them, after all—that he had killed her intentionally, and before this unseen witness? If so it might be necessary for them to withdraw from such a hopeless and unpopular case, after all.

As for Jephson, he was for the moment stunned and flattened. And through his stern and not easily shakable brain raced such thoughts as—was there really a witness?—has Clyde lied?—then the die was cast, for had he not already admitted to them that he had struck Roberta, and the witness must have seen that? And so the end of any plea of a change of heart. Who would believe that, after such testimony as this?

But because of the sheer contentiousness and determination of his nature, he would not permit himself to be completely baffled by this smashing announcement. Instead he turned, and after surveying the flustered and yet self-chastising Belknap and Clyde, commented: "I don't believe it. He's lying, I think, or bluffing. At any rate, we'll wait and see. It's a long time between now and our side of the story. Look at all those witnesses there. And we can cross-question them by the week, if we want to—until he's out of office. Plenty of time to do a lot of things—find out about this witness in the meantime. And besides, there's suicide, or there's the actual thing that happened. We can let Clyde swear to what did happen—a cataleptic trance—no courage to do it.

It's not likely anybody can see that at five hundred feet." And he smiled grimly. At almost the same time he added, but not for Clyde's ears: "We might be able to get him off with twenty years at the worst, don't you think?"

# Chapter XXI

A ND THEN witnesses, witnesses, witnesses—to the number of one hundred and twenty-seven. And their testimony, particularly that of the doctors, three guides, the woman who heard Roberta's last cry, all repeatedly objected to by Jephson and Belknap, for upon such weakness and demonstrable error as they could point out depended the plausibility of Clyde's daring defense. And all of this carrying the case well into November, and after Mason had been overwhelmingly elected to the judgeship which he had so craved. And because of the very vigor and strife of the trial, the general public from coast to coast taking more and more interest. And obviously, as the days passed and the newspaper writers at the trial saw it, Clyde was guilty. Yet he, because of the repeated commands of Jephson, facing each witness who assailed him with calm and even daring.

"Your name?"

"Titus Alden."

"You are the father of Roberta Alden?"

"Yes, sir."

"Now, Mr. Alden, just tell the jury how and under what circumstances it was that your daughter Roberta happened to go to Lycurgus."

"Objected to. Irrelevant, immaterial, incompetent," snapped Belknap.

"I'll connect it up," put in Mason, looking up at the Judge, who ruled that Titus might answer subject to a motion to strike out his testimony if not "connected up."

"She went there to get work," replied Titus.

"And why did she go there to get work?"

Again objection, and the old man allowed to proceed after the legal formalities had again been complied with.

"Well, the farm we have over there near Biltz hasn't ever paid so very well, and it's been necessary for the children to help out and Bobbie being the oldest——"

"Move to strike out!" "Strike it out."

"'Bobbie' was the pet name you gave your daughter Roberta, was it?"

"Objected to," etc., etc. "Exception."

"Yes, sir. 'Bobbie' was what we sometimes called her around there—just Bobbie."

And Clyde listening intently and enduring without flinching the stern and accusing stare of this brooding Priam of the farm, wondering at the revelation of his former sweetheart's pet name. He had nicknamed her "Bert"; she had never told him that at home she was called "Bobbie."

And amid a fusillade of objections and arguments and rulings, Alden continuing, under the leading of Mason, to recite how she had decided to go to Lycurgus, after receipt of a letter from Grace Marr, and stop with Mr. and Mrs. Newton. And after securing work with the Griffiths Company, how little the family had seen of her until June fifth last, when she had returned to the farm for a rest and in order to make some clothes.

"No announcement of any plans for marriage?"

"None."

But she had written a number of long letters—to whom he did not know at the time. And she had been depressed and sick. Twice he had seen her crying, although he said nothing, knowing that she did not want to be noticed. There had been a few telephone calls from Lycurgus, the last on July fourth or fifth, the day before she left, he was quite sure.

"And what did she have with her when she left?"

"Her bag and her little trunk."

"And would you recognize the bag that she carried, if you saw it?"

"Yes, sir."

"Is this the bag?" (A deputy assistant district attorney carrying forward a bag and placing it on a small stand.)

And Alden, after looking at it and wiping his eyes with the back of his hand, announcing: "Yes, sir."

And then most dramatically, as Mason intended in connection with every point in this trial, a deputy assistant carrying in a small trunk, and Titus Alden and his wife and daughters and sons all crying at the sight of it. And after being identified by him as Roberta's, the bag and then the trunk were opened in turn. And the dresses made by Roberta, some underclothing, shoes, hats, the toilet set given her by Clyde, pictures of her mother and father and sister and brothers, an old family cook-book, some spoons and forks and knives and salt and pepper sets—all given her by her grandmother and treasured by her for her married life—held up and identified in turn.

All this over Belknap's objection, and on Mason's promise to "connect it up," which, however, he was unable to do, and the evidence was accordingly ordered "struck out." But its pathetic significance by that time deeply impressed on the minds and hearts of the jurymen. And Belknap's criticism of Mason's tactics merely resulting in that gentleman bellowing, in an infuriated manner: "Who's conducting this prosecution, anyhow?" To which Belknap replied: "The Republican candidate for county judge in this county, I believe!"—thus evoking a wave of laughter which caused Mason to fairly shout: "Your Honor, I protest! This is an unethical and illegal attempt to inject into this case a political issue which has nothing to do with it. It is slyly and maliciously intended to convey to this jury that because I am the Republican nominee for judge of the county, it is impossible for me to properly and fairly conduct the prosecution of this case. And I now demand an apology, and will have it before I proceed one step further in this case."

Whereupon Justice Oberwaltzer, feeling that a very serious breach of court etiquette had occurred, proceeded to summon Belknap and Mason before him, and after listening to placid and polite interpretations of what was meant, and what was not meant, finally ordered, on pain of contempt, that neither of them again refer to the political situation in any way.

Nevertheless, Belknap and Jephson congratulating themselves that in this fashion their mood in regard to Mason's candidacy and his use of this case to further it had effectively gotten before the jury and the court.

But more and more witnesses!

Grace Marr now taking the stand, and in a glib and voluble outpouring describing how and where she had first met Roberta—how pure and clean and religious a girl she was, but, how after meeting Clyde on Crum Lake a great change had come over her. She was more secretive and evasive and given to furnishing all sorts of false excuses for new and strange adventures—as, for instance, going out nights and staying late, and claiming to be places over Saturday and Sunday where she wasn't—until finally, because of criticism which she, Grace Marr, had ventured to make, she had suddenly left, without giving any address. But there was a man, and that man was Clyde Griffiths. For having followed Roberta to her room one evening in September or October of the year before, she had observed her and Clyde in the distance, near the Gilpin home. They were standing under some trees and he had his arm around her.

And thereafter Belknap, at Jephson's suggestion, taking her and by the slyest type of questioning, trying to discover whether, before coming to Lycurgus, Roberta was as religious and conventional as Miss Marr would have it. But Miss Marr, faded and irritable, insisting that up to the day of her meeting with Clyde on Crum Lake, Roberta had been the soul of truth and purity, in so far as she knew.

And next the Newtons swearing to much the same thing.

And then the Gilpins, wife and husband and daughters, each swearing to what she or he alone saw or heard. Mrs. Gilpin as to the approximate day of Roberta's moving into her home with one small trunk and bag—the identical trunk and bag identified by Titus. And thereafter seeming to live very much alone until finally she, feeling sorry for her, had suggested one type of contact and another, but Roberta invariably refusing. But later, along in late November, although she had never had the heart to say anything about it to her because of her sweetness and general sobriety, she and her two daughters had become aware of the fact that occasionally, after eleven o'clock, it had seemed as though Roberta must be entertaining some one in her room, but just whom she could not say. And again at this point, on cross-examination, Belknap trying to extract any admissions or impressions which would tend to make it look as though Roberta was a little less reserved and puritanical than all the witnesses had thus far painted her, but failing. Mrs. Gilpin, as well as her husband, was plainly fond of her and only under pressure from Mason and later Belknap testified to Clyde's late visits.

And then the elder daughter, Stella, testifying that during the latter part of October or the first of November, shortly after Roberta had taken the room, she had passed her and a man, whom she was now able to identify as Clyde, standing less than a hundred feet from the house, and noticing that they were evidently quarreling she had paused to listen. She was not able to distinguish every word of the conversation, but upon leading questions from Mason was able to recall that Roberta had protested that she could not let him come into her room—"it would not look right." And he had finally turned upon his heel, leaving Roberta standing with out-stretched arms as if imploring him to return.

And throughout all this Clyde staring in amazement, for he had in those days—in fact throughout his entire contact with Roberta—imagined himself unobserved. And decidedly this confirmed much of what Mason had charged in his opening address—that he had willfully and with full knowledge of the nature of the offense, persuaded Roberta to do what plainly she had not wanted to do—a form of testimony that was likely to prejudice the judge as well as the jury and all these conventional people of this rural county. And Belknap, realizing this, trying to confuse this Stella in her identification of Clyde. But only succeeding in eliciting information that some time in November or the early part of December, shortly after the above incident, she had seen Clyde arrive, a box of some kind under his arm, and knock at Roberta's door and enter, and was then positive that he was the same young man she had seen that moonlight night quarreling with Roberta.

And next, Whiggam, and after him Liggett, testifying as to the dates of arrival of Clyde at the factory, as well as Roberta, and as to the rule regarding department heads and female help, and, in so far as they could see, the impeccable surface conduct of both Clyde and Roberta, neither seeming to look at the other or at any one else for that matter. (That was Liggett testifying.)

And after them again, others. Mrs. Peyton to testify as to the character of his room and his social activities in so far as she was able to observe them. Mrs. Alden to testify that at Christmas the year before Roberta had confessed to her that her superior at the factory—Clyde Griffiths, the nephew of the owner—was paying attention to her, but that it had to be kept secret for the time being. Frank Harriet, Harley Baggott, Tracy Trumbull and Eddie Sells to testify that during December last Clyde had been invited here and there and had attended various social gatherings in Lycurgus. John Lambert, a druggist of Schenectady, testifying that some time in January he had been applied to by a youth, whom he now identified as the defendant, for some medicine which would bring about a miscarriage. Orrin Short to testify that in late January Clyde had asked him if he knew of a doctor who could aid a young married woman—according to Clyde's story, the wife of an employe of Griffiths & Company—who was too poor to afford a child, and whose husband, according to Clyde, had asked him for this information. And next Dr. Glenn, testifying to Roberta's visit, having previously recalled her from pictures published in the papers, but adding that professionally he had been unwilling to do anything for her.

And then C. B. Wilcox, a farmer neighbor of the Aldens, testifying to having been in the washroom back of the kitchen on or about June twenty-ninth or thirtieth, on which occasion Roberta having been called over the long distance telephone from Lycurgus by a man who gave his name as Baker, he had heard her say to him: "But, Clyde, I can't wait that long. You know I can't. And I won't." And her voice had sounded excited and distressed. Mr. Wilcox was positive as to the name Clyde.

And Ethel Wilcox, a daughter of this same C. B.—short and fat and with a lisp—who swore that on three preceding occasions, having received long distance requests for Roberta, she had proceeded to get her. And each time the call was from Lycurgus from a man named Baker. Also, on one occasion, she had heard her refer to the caller as Clyde. And once she had heard her say that "under no circumstances would she wait that long," although what she meant by that she did not know.

And next Roger Beane, a rural free delivery letter-carrier, who testified that between June seventh or eighth to July fourth or fifth, he had received no less than fifteen letters from Roberta herself or the mail box at the crossroads of the Alden farm, and that he was positive that most of the letters were addressed to Clyde Griffiths, care of General Delivery, Lycurgus.

And next Amos Showalter, general delivery clerk at Lycurgus, who swore that to the best of his recollection, from or between June seventh or eighth and July fourth or fifth, Clyde, whom he knew by name, had inquired for and received not less than fifteen or sixteen letters.

And after him, R. T. Biggen, an oil station manager of Lycurgus, who swore that on the morning of July sixth, at about eight o'clock, having gone to Fielding Avenue, which was on the extreme west of the city, leading on the northern end to a "stop" on the Lycurgus and Fonda electric line, he had seen Clyde, dressed in a gray suit and wearing a straw hat and carrying a brown suit-case, to one side of which was strapped a yellow camera tripod and something else—an umbrella it might have been. And knowing in which direction Clyde lived, he had wondered at his walking, when at Central Avenue, not so far from his home, he could have boarded the Fonda-Lycurgus car. And Belknap in his cross-examination inquiring of this witness how, being one hundred and seventy-five feet distant, he could swear that it was a tripod that he saw, and Biggens insisting that it was—it was bright yellow wood and had brass clops and three legs.

And then after him, John W. Troescher, station master at Fonda, who testified that on the morning of July sixth last (he recalled it clearly because of certain other things which he listed), he had sold Roberta Alden a ticket to Utica. He recalled Miss Alden because of having noted her several times during the preceding winter. She looked quite tired, almost sick, and carried a brown bag, something like the brown bag there and then exhibited to him. Also he recalled the defendant, who also carried a bag. He did not see him notice or talk to the girl.

And next Quincy B. Dale, conductor of the particular train that ran from Fonda to Utica. He had noticed, and now recalled, Clyde in one car toward the rear. He also noticed, and from photographs later published, had recalled Roberta. She gave him a friendly smile and he had said that such a bag as she was carrying seemed rather heavy for her and that he would have one of the brakemen carry it out for her at Utica, for which she thanked him. He had seen her descend at Utica and disappear into the depot. He had not noticed Clyde there.

And then the identification of Roberta's trunk as having been left in the baggage room at the station at Utica for a number of days. And after that the guest page of the Renfrew House, of Utica, for July sixth last, identified by Jerry K. Kernocian, general manager of said hotel, which showed an entry—"Clifford Golden and wife." And the same then and there compared by handwriting experts with two other registration pages from the Grass Lake and Big Bittern Inns and sworn to as being identically the same handwriting. And these compared with the card in Roberta's suit-case, and all received in evidence and carefully examined by each juror in turn and by Belknap and Jephson, who, however, had seen all but the card before. And once more a protest on the part of Belknap as to the unwarranted and illegal and shameful withholding of evidence on the part of the district attorney. And a long and bitter wrangle as to that, serving, in fact, to bring to a close the tenth day of the trial.

# Chapter XXII

A<small>ND THEN</small>, on the eleventh day, Frank W. Schaefer, clerk of the Renfrew House in Utica, recalling the actual arrival of Clyde and Roberta and their actions; also Clyde's registering for both as Mr. and Mrs. Clifford Golden, of Syracuse. And then Wallace Vanderhoff, one of the clerks of the Star Haberdashery in Utica, with a story of Clyde's actions and general appearance at the time of his buying a straw hat. And then the conductor of the train running between Utica and Grass Lake. And the proprietor of the Grass Lake House. And Blanche Pettingill, a waitress, who swore that at dinner she had overheard Clyde arguing with Roberta as to the impossibility of getting a marriage license there—that it would be better to wait until they reached some other place the next day—a bit of particularly damaging testimony, since it predated by a day the proposed confession which Clyde was supposed to have made to Roberta, but which Jephson and Belknap afterward agreed between themselves might easily have had some preliminary phases. And after her the conductor of the train that carried them to Gun Lodge. And after him the guide and the driver of the bus, with his story of Clyde's queer talk about many people being over there and leaving Roberta's bag while he took his own, and saying they would be back.

And then, the proprietor of the Inn at Big Bittern; the boatkeeper; the three men in the woods—their testimony very damaging to Clyde's case, since they pictured his terror on encountering them. And then the story of the finding of the boat and Roberta's body, and the eventual arrival of Heit and his finding of the letter in Roberta's coat. A score of witnesses testifying as to all this. And next the boat captain, the farm girl, the Cranston chauffeur, the arrival of Clyde at the Cranstons', and at last (every step accounted for and sworn to) his arrival at Bear Lake, the pursuit and his capture—to say nothing of the various phases of his arrest—what he said—this being most damaging indeed, since it painted Clyde as false, evasive, and terrified.

But unquestionably, the severest and most damaging testimony related to the camera and the tripod—the circumstances surrounding the finding of them—and on the weight of this Mason was counting for a conviction. His one aim first was to convict Clyde of lying as to his possession of either a tripod or a camera. And in order to do that he first introduced Earl Newcomb, who swore that on a certain day, when he, Mason and Heit and all the others connected with the case were taking Clyde over the area in which the crime had been committed, he and a certain native, one Bill Swarts, who was afterwards put on the stand, while poking about under some fallen logs and bushes, had come across the tripod, hidden under a log. Also (under the leadership of Mason, although over the objections of both Belknap and Jephson, which were invariably overruled), he proceeded to add that Clyde, on being asked whether he had a camera or this tripod, had denied any knowledge of it, on hearing which Belknap and Jephson actually shouted their disapproval.

Immediately following, though eventually ordered stricken from the records by Justice Oberwaltzer, there was introduced a paper signed by Heit, Burleigh, Slack, Kraut, Swenk, Sissell, Bill Swartz, Rufus Forster, county surveyor, and Newcomb, which set forth that Clyde, on being shown the tripod and asked whether he had one, "vehemently and repeatedly denied that he had." But in order to drive the import of this home, Mason immediately adding: "Very well, Your Honor, but I have other witnesses who will swear to everything that is in that paper and more," and at once calling "Joseph Frazer! Joseph Frazer!" and then placing on the stand a dealer in sporting goods, cameras, etc., who proceeded to swear that some time between May fifteenth and June first, the defendant, Clyde Griffiths, whom he knew by sight and name, had applied to him for a camera of a certain size, with tripod attached, and that the defendant had finally selected a Sank, $3\frac{1}{4}$ by $5\frac{1}{2}$, for which he had made arrangements to pay in installments. And after due examination and consulting certain stock numbers with which the camera and the tripod and his own book were marked, Mr. Frazer identifying first the camera now shown him, and immediately after that the yellow tripod as the one he had sold Clyde.

And Clyde sitting up aghast. Then they had found the camera, as well as the tripod, after all. And after he had protested so that he had had no camera with him. What would that jury and the judge and this audience think of his lying about that? Would they be likely to believe his story of a change of heart after this proof that he had lied about a meaningless camera? Better to have confessed in the first place.

But even as he was so thinking Mason calling Simeon Dodge, a young woodsman and driver, who testified that on Saturday, the sixteenth of July, accompanied by John Pole, who had lifted Roberta's body out of the water, he had at the request of the district attorney, repeatedly dived into the exact spot where her body was found, and finally succeeded in bringing up a camera. And then the camera itself identified by Dodge.

Immediately after this all the testimony in regard to the hitherto as yet unmentioned films found in the camera at the time of its recovery, since developed, and now received in evidence, four views which showed a person looking more like Roberta than any one else, together with two, which clearly enough represented Clyde. Belknap was not able to refute or exclude them.

Then Floyd Thurston, one of the guests at the Cranston lodge at Sharon on June eighteenth—the occasion of Clyde's first visit there—placed on the stand to testify that on that occasion Clyde had made a number of pictures with a camera about the size and description of the one shown him, but failing to identify it as the particular one, his testimony being stricken out.

After him again, Edna Patterson, a chambermaid in the Grass Lake Inn, who, as she swore, on entering the room which Clyde and Roberta occupied on the night of July seventh, had seen Clyde with a camera in his hand, which was of the size and color, as far as she could recall, of the one then and there before her. She had also at the same time seen a tripod. And Clyde, in his curious and meditative and half-hypnotized state, recalling well enough the entrance of this girl into that room and marveling and suffering because of the unbreakable chain of facts that could thus be built up by witnesses from such varying and unconnected and unexpected places, and so long after, too.

After her, but on different days, and with Belknap and Jephson contending every inch of the way as to the admissibility of all this, the testimony of the five doctors whom Mason had called in at the time Roberta's body was first brought to Bridgeburg, and who in turn swore that the wounds, both on the face and head, were sufficient, considering Roberta's physical condition, to stun her. And because of the condition of the dead girl's lungs, which had been tested by attempting to float them in water, averring that at the time her body had first entered the water, she must have been still alive, although not necessarily conscious. But as to the nature of the instrument used to make these wounds, they would not venture to guess, other than to say it must have been blunt. And no grilling on the part of either Belknap or Jephson could bring them to admit that the blows could have been of such a light character as not to stun or render unconscious. The chief injury appeared to be on the top of the skull, deep enough to have caused a blood clot, photographs of all of which were put in evidence.

At this psychological point, when both audience and jury were most painfully and effectively stirred, a number of photographs of Roberta's face, made at the time that Heit, the doctors and the Lutz Brothers had her in charge, were introduced. Then the dimensions of the bruises on the right side of her face were shown to correspond exactly in size with two sides of the camera. Immediately after that, Burton Burleigh placed on the stand to swear how he had discovered the two strands of hair which corresponded with the hair on Roberta's head—or so Mason tried to show—caught between the lens and the lid. And then, after hours and hours, Belknap, infuriated and yet made nervous by this type of evidence and seeking to riddle it with sarcasm, finally pulling a light hair out of his head and then asking the jurors and Burleigh if they could venture to tell whether one single hair from any one's head could be an indication of the general color of a person's hair, and if not, whether they were ready to believe that this particular hair was from Roberta's head or not.

Mason then calling a Mrs. Rutger Donahue, who proceeded, in the calmest and most placid fashion, to tell how on the evening of July eighth last, between five-thirty and six, she and her husband immediately after setting up a tent above Moon Cove, had started out to row and fish, when being about a half-mile off shore and perhaps a quarter of a mile above the woods or northern fringe of land which enclosed Moon Cove, she had heard a cry.

"Between half past five and six in the afternoon, you say?"

"Yes, sir."

"And on what date again?"

"July eighth."

"And where were you exactly at that time?"

"We were——"

"Not 'we.' Where were you personally?"

"I was crossing what I have since learned was South Bay in a row boat with my husband."

"Yes. Now tell what happened next."

"When we reached the middle of the bay I heard a cry."

"What was it like?"

"It was penetrating—like the cry of some one in pain—or in danger. It was sharp—a haunting cry."

Here a motion to "strike out," with the result that the last phrase was so ordered stricken out.

"Where did it come from?"

"From a distance. From within or beyond the woods."

"Did you know at the time that there was another bay or cove there—below that strip of woods?"

"No, sir."

"Well, what did you think then—that it might have come from within the woods below where you were?"

(Objected to—and objection sustained.)

"And now tell us, was it a man's or a woman's cry? What kind of a cry was it?"

"It was a woman's cry, and something like 'Oh, oh!' or 'Oh, my!'—very piercing and clear, but distant, of course. A double scream such as one might make when in pain."

"You are sure you could not be mistaken as to the kind of a cry it was—male or female."

"No, sir. I am positive. It was a woman's. It was pitched too high for a man's voice or a boy's. It could not have been anything but a woman's."

"I see. And now tell us, Mrs. Donahue—you see this dot

on the map showing where the body of Roberta Alden was found?"

"Yes, sir."

"And you see this other dot, over those trees, showing approximately where your boat was?"

"Yes, sir."

"Do you think that voice came from where this dot in Moon Cove is?"

(Objected to. Sustained.)

"And was that cry repeated?"

"No, sir. I waited, and I called my husband's attention to it, too, and we waited, but didn't hear it again."

Then Belknap, eager to prove that it might have been a terrified and yet not a pained or injured cry, taking her and going all over the ground again, and finding that neither she nor her husband, who was also put on the stand, could be shaken in any way. Neither, they insisted, could the deep and sad effect of this woman's voice be eradicated from their minds. It had haunted both, and once in their camp again they had talked about it. Because it was dusk he did not wish to go seeking after the spot from which it came; because she felt that some woman or girl might have been slain in those woods, she did not want to stay any longer, and the next morning early they had moved on to another lake.

Thomas Barrett, another Adirondack guide, connected with a camp at Dam's Lake, swore that at the time referred to by Mrs. Donahue, he was walking along the shore toward Big Bittern Inn and had seen not only a man and woman off shore in about the position described, but farther back, toward the south shore of this bay, had noted the tent of these campers. Also that from no point outside Moon Cove, unless near the entrance, could one observe any boat within the cove. The entrance was narrow and any view from the lake proper completely blocked. And there were other witnesses to prove this.

At this psychological moment, as the afternoon sun was already beginning to wane in the tall, narrow court room, and as carefully planned by him beforehand, Mason's reading all of Roberta's letters, one by one, in a most simple and non-declamatory fashion, yet with all the sympathy and emotion which their first perusal had stirred in him. They had made him cry.

He began with letter number one, dated June eighth, only three days after her departure from Lycurgus, and on through them all down to letters fourteen, fifteen, sixteen and seventeen, in which, in piecemeal or by important references here and there, she related her whole contact with Clyde down to his plan to come for her in three weeks, then in a month, then on July eighth or ninth, and then the sudden threat from her which precipitated his sudden decision to meet her at Fonda. And as Mason read them, all most movingly, the moist eyes and the handkerchiefs and the coughs in the audience and among the jurors attested their import:

"You said I was not to worry or think so much about how I feel, and have a good time. That's all right for you to say, when you're in Lycurgus and surrounded by your friends and invited everywhere. It's hard for me to talk over there at Wilcox's with somebody always in earshot and with you constantly reminding me that I mustn't say this or that. But I had so much to ask and no chance there. And all that you would say was that everything was all right. But you didn't say positively that you were coming on the 27th, that because of something I couldn't quite make out—there was so much buzzing on the wire—you might not be able to start until later. But that can't be, Clyde. My parents are leaving for Hamilton where my uncle lives on the third. And Tom and Emily are going to my sister's on the same day. But I can't and won't go there again. I can't stay here all alone. So you must, you really must come, as you agreed. I can't wait any longer than that, Clyde, in the condition that I'm in, and so you just must come and take me away. Oh, please, please, I beg of you, not to torture me with any more delays now."

And again:

"Clyde, I came home because I thought I could trust you. You told me so solemnly before I left that if I would, you would come and get me in three weeks at the most—that it would not take you longer than that to get ready, have enough money for the time we would be together, or until you could get something to do somewhere else. But yesterday, although the third of July will be nearly a month since I left, you were not at all sure at first that you could come by then, and when as I told you my parents are surely leaving for Hamilton to be gone for ten days. Of course, afterwards, you said you would come, but you said it as though you were just trying to quiet me. It has been troubling me awfully ever since.

"For I tell you, Clyde, I am sick, very. I feel faint nearly all the time. And besides, I am so worried as to what I shall do if you don't come that I am nearly out of my mind."

"Clyde, I know that you don't care for me any more like you did and that you are wishing things could be different. And yet, what am I to do? I know you'll say that it has all been as much my fault as yours. And the world, if it knew, might think so, too. But how often did I beg you not to make me do what I did not want to do, and which I was afraid even then I would regret, although I loved you too much to let you go, if you still insisted on having your way."

"Clyde, if I could only die. That would solve all this. And I have prayed and prayed that I would lately, yes I have. For life does not mean as much to me now as when I first met you and you loved me. Oh, those happy days! If only things were different. If only I were out of your way. It would all be so much better for me and for all of us. But I can't now, Clyde, without a penny and no way to save the name of our child, except this. Yet if it weren't for the terrible pain and disgrace it would bring to my mother and father and all my family, I would be willing to end it all in another way. I truly would."

And again:

"Oh, Clyde, Clyde, life is so different to-day to what it was last year. Think—then we were going to Crum and those other lakes over near Fonda and Gloversville and Little Falls, but now—now. Only just now some boy and girl friends of Tom's and Emily came by to get them to go after strawberries, and when I saw them go and knew I couldn't, and that I couldn't be like that any more ever, I cried and cried, ever so long."

And finally:

"I have been bidding good-by to some places to-day. There are so many nooks, dear, and all of them so dear to me. I have lived here all my life, you know. First, there was the springhouse with its great masses of green moss, and in passing it I said good-by to it, for I won't be coming to it soon again—maybe never. And then the old apple tree where we had our playhouse years ago—Emily and Tom and Gifford and I. Then the 'Believe,' a cute little house in the orchard where we sometimes played.

"Oh, Clyde, you can't realize what all this means to me, I feel as though I shall never see my home again after I leave here this time. And mamma, poor dear mamma, how I do love her and how sorry

I am to have deceived her so. She is never cross and she always helps me so much. Sometimes I think if I could tell her, but I can't. She has had trouble enough, and I couldn't break her heart like that. No, if I go away and come back some time, either married or dead—it doesn't make so much difference now—she will never know, and I will not have caused her any pain, and that means so much more than life itself to me. So good-by, Clyde, until I do meet you, as you telephoned. And forgive me all the trouble that I have caused you.

Your sorrowful,<br>ROBERTA."

And at points in the reading, Mason himself crying, and at their conclusion turning, weary and yet triumphant, a most complete and indestructible case, as he saw it, having been presented, and exclaiming: "The People rest." And at that moment, Mrs. Alden, in court with her husband and Emily, and overwrought, not only by the long strain of the trial but this particular evidence, uttering a whimpering yet clear cry and then falling foward in a faint. And Clyde, in his own over-wrought condition, hearing her cry and seeing her fall, jumping up—the restraining hand of Jephson instantly upon him, while bailiffs and others assisted her and Titus who was beside her from the court room. And the audience almost, if not quite, as moved and incensed against Clyde by that develop-ment as though, then and there, he had committed some ad-ditional crime.

But then, that excitement having passed and it being quite dark, and the hands of the court clock pointing to five, and all the court weary, Justice Oberwaltzer signifying his intention of adjourning for the night.

And at once all the newspaper men and feature writers and artists rising and whispering to each other that on the mor-row the defense would start, and wondering as to who and where the witnesses were, also whether Clyde would be per-mitted to go on the stand in his own defense in the face of this amazing mass of evidence against him, or whether his lawyers would content themselves with some specious argu-ment as to mental and moral weakness which might end in prison for life—not less.

And Clyde, hissed and cursed as he left the court, wondering if on the morrow, and as they had planned this long time since, he would have the courage to rise and go on the stand—wondering if there was not some way, in case no one was looking (he was not handcuffed as he went to and from the jail) maybe to-morrow night when all were rising, the crowds moving and these deputies coming toward him—if— well, if he could only run, or walk easily and quietly and yet quickly and seemingly unintentionally, to that stair and then down and out—to—well—to wherever it went—that small side door to the main stairs which before this he had seen from the jail! If he could only get to some woods somewhere, and then walk and walk, or run and run, maybe, without stopping, and without eating, for days maybe, until, well, until he had gotten away—anywhere. It was a chance, of course. He might be shot, or tracked with dogs and men, but still it was a chance, wasn't it?

For this way he had no chance at all. No one anywhere, after all this, was going to believe him not guilty. And he did not want to die that way. No, no, not that way!

And so another miserable, black and weary night. And then another miserable gray and wintry morning.

# Chapter XXIII

B Y EIGHT O'CLOCK the next morning the great city papers were on the stands with the sprawling headlines, which informed every one in no uncertain terms:

"PROSECUTION IN GRIFFITHS' CASE CLOSES WITH IMPRESSIVE DELUGE OF TESTIMONY."

"MOTIVE AS WELL AS METHOD HAMMERED HOME."

"DESTRUCTIVE MARKS ON FACE AND HEAD SHOWN TO CORRESPOND WITH ONE SIDE OF CAMERA."

"MOTHER OF DEAD GIRL FAINTS AT CLOSE OF DRAMATIC READING OF HER LETTERS."

And the architectonic way in which Mason had built his case, together with his striking and dramatic presentation of it, was sufficient to stir in Belknap and Jephson, as well as Clyde, the momentary conviction that they had been completely routed—that by no conceivable device could they possibly convince this jury now that Clyde was not a quadruple-dyed villain.

And all congratulating Mason on the masterly way he had presented his case. And Clyde, greatly reduced and saddened by the realization that his mother would be reading all that had transpired the day before. He must ask Jephson to please wire her so that she would not believe it. And Frank and Julia and Esta. And no doubt Sondra reading all this, too, to-day, yet through all these days, all these black nights, not one word! A reference now and then in the papers to a Miss X but at no time a single correct picture of her. That was what a family with money could do for you. And on this very day his defense would begin and he would have to go forward as the only witness of any import. Yet asking himself, *how could he?* The crowd. Its temper. The nervous strain of its unbelief and hatred by now. And after Belknap was through with him, then Mason. It was all right for Belknap and Jephson. They were in no danger of being tortured, as he was certain of being tortured.

Yet in the face of all this, and after an hour spent with Jephson and Belknap in his cell, finding himself back in the courtroom, under the persistent gaze of this nondescript jury and the tensely interested audience. And now Belknap rising before the jury and after solemnly contemplating each one of them, beginning:

"Gentlemen—somewhat over three weeks ago you were told by the district attorney that because of the evidence he was about to present he would insist that you jurors must find the prisoner at the bar guilty of the crime of which he stands indicted. It has been a long and tedious procedure since then. The foolish and inexperienced, yet in every case innocent and unintentional, acts of a boy of fifteen or sixteen have been gone into before you gentlemen as though they were the deeds of a hardened criminal, and plainly with the intention of prejudicing you against this defendant, who, with the exception of one misinterpreted accident in Kansas City—the most brutally and savagely misinterpreted accident it has ever been my professional misfortune to encounter—can be said to have lived as clean and energetic and blameless and innocent a life as any boy of his years anywhere. You have heard him called a man—a bearded man—a criminal and a crime-soaked product of the darkest vomiting of Hell. And yet he is but twenty-one. And there he sits. And I venture to say that if by some magic of the spoken word I could at this moment strip from your eye the substance of all the cruel thoughts and emotions which have been attributed to him by a clamorous and mistaken and I might say (if I had not been warned not to do so), politically biased prosecution, you could no more see him in the light that you do than you could rise out of that box and fly through those windows.

"Gentlemen of the jury, I have no doubt that you, as well as the district attorney and even the audience, have wondered how under the downpour of such linked and at times almost venomous testimony, I or my colleague or this defendant could have remained as calm and collected as we have." (And here he waved with grave ceremoniousness in the direction of his partner, who was still awaiting his own hour.) "Yet, as you have seen, we have not only maintained but enjoyed the serenity of those who not only feel but *know* that they have the right and just end of any legal contest. You recall, of course, the words of the Avon bard—'Thrice armed is he who hath his quarrel just.'

"In fact, we know, as the prosecution in this case unfortunately does not, the peculiarly strange and unexpected circumstances by which this dramatic and most unfortunate death came about. And before we are through you shall see for yourselves. In the meantime, let me tell you, gentlemen, that since this case opened I have believed that even apart from the light we propose to throw on this disheartening tragedy, you gentlemen are not at all sure that a brutal or bestial crime can be laid upon the shoulders of this defendant. You cannot be! For after all, love is love, and the ways of passion and the destroying emotion of love in either sex are not those of the ordinary criminal. Only remember, we were once all boys. And those of you who are grown women were girls, and know well—oh, how very well—the fevers and aches of youth that have nothing to do with a later practical life. 'Judge not, lest ye be judged and with whatsoever measure ye mete, it will be measured unto ye again.'

"We admit the existence and charm and potent love spell of the mysterious Miss X and her letters, which we have not been able to introduce here, and their effect on this defendant. We admit his love for this Miss X, and we propose to show by witnesses of our own, as well as by analyzing some of the testimony that has been offered here, that perhaps the sly and lecherous overtures with which this defendant is supposed to have lured the lovely soul now so sadly and yet so purely accidentally blotted out, as we shall show, from the straight and narrow path of morality, were perhaps no more sly nor lecherous than the proceedings of any youth who finds the girl of his choice surrounded by those who see life only in the terms of the strictest and narrowest moral régime. And, gentlemen, as your own country district attorney has told you, Roberta Alden loved Clyde Griffiths. At the very opening of this relationship which has since proved to be a tragedy, this dead girl was deeply and irrevocably in love with him, just as at the time he imagined that he was in love with her. And people who are deeply and earnestly in love with each other are not much concerned with the opinions of others in regard to themselves. They are in love—and that is sufficient!

"But, gentlemen, I am not going to dwell on that phase of the question so much as on this explanation which we are about to offer. Why did Clyde Griffiths go to Fonda, or to Utica, or to Grass Lake, or to Big Bittern, at all? Do you think we have any reason for or any desire to deny or discolor in any way the fact of his having done so, or with Roberta Alden either? Or why, after the suddenness and seeming strangeness and mystery of her death, he should have chosen to walk away as he did? If you seriously think so for one fraction of a moment, you are the most hopelessly deluded and mistaken dozen jurymen it has been our privilege to argue before in all our twenty-seven years' contact with juries.

"Gentlemen, I have said to you that Clyde Griffiths is not guilty, and he is not. You may think, perhaps, that we ourselves must be believing in his guilt. But you are wrong. The peculiarity, the strangeness of life, is such that oftentimes a man may be accused of something that he did not do and yet every circumstance surrounding him at the time seems to indicate that he did do it. There have been many very pathetic and very terrible instances of miscarriages of justice through circumstantial evidence alone. Be sure! Oh, be very sure that no such mistaken judgment based on any local or religious or moral theory of conduct or bias, because of presumed irrefutable evidence, is permitted to prejudice you, so that without meaning to, and with the best and highest-minded intentions, you yourselves see a crime, or the intention to commit a crime, when no such crime or any such intention ever truly or legally existed or lodged in the mind or acts of this defendant. Oh, be sure! Be very, very sure!"

And here he paused to rest and seemed to give himself over to deep and even melancholy thought, while Clyde, heartened by this shrewd and defiant beginning was inclined to take more courage. But now Belknap was talking again, and he must listen—not lose a word of all this that was so heartening.

"When Roberta Alden's body was taken out of the water at Big Bittern, gentlemen, it was examined by a physician. He declared at the time that the girl had been drowned. He will be here and testify and the defendant shall have the benefit of that testimony, and you must render it to him.

"You were told by the district attorney that Roberta Alden and Clyde Griffiths were engaged to be married and that she left her home at Biltz and went forth with him on July sixth last on her wedding journey. Now, gentlemen, it is so easy to slightly distort a certain set of circumstances. 'Were engaged to be married' was how the district attorney emphasized the incidents leading up to the departure on July sixth. As a matter of fact, not one iota of any direct evidence exists which shows that Clyde Griffiths was ever formally engaged to Roberta Alden, or that, except for some passages in her letters, he agreed to marry her. And those passages, gentlemen, plainly indicate that it was only under the stress of moral and material worry, due to her condition—for which he was responsible, of course, but which, nevertheless, was with the consent of both—a boy of twenty-one and a girl of twenty-three—that he agreed to marry her. Is that, I ask you, an open and proper engagement—the kind of an engagement you think of when you think of one at all? Mind you, I am not seeking to flout or belittle or reflect in any way on this poor, dead girl. I am simply stating, as a matter of fact and of law, that this boy was not formally engaged to this dead girl. He had not given her his word beforehand that he would marry her . . . Never! There is no proof. You must give him the benefit of that. And only because of her condition, for which we admit he was responsible, he came forward with an agreement to marry her, in case . . . in case" (and here he paused and rested on the phrase), "she was not willing to release him. And since she was not willing to release him, as her various letters read here show, that agreement, on pain of a public exposure in Lycurgus, becomes, in the eyes and words of the district attorney, an engagement, and not only that but a sacred engagement which no one but a scoundrel and a thief and a murderer would attempt to sever! But, getlemen, many engagements, more open and sacred in the eyes of the law and of religion, have been broken. Thousands of men and thousands of women have seen their hearts change, their vows and faith and trust flouted, and have even carried their wounds into the secret places of their souls, or gone forth, and gladly, to death at their own hands because of them. As the district attorney said in his address, it is not new and it will never be old. Never!

"But it is such a case as this last, I warn you, that you are now contemplating and are about to pass upon—a girl who is the victim of such a change of mood. But that is not a legal, however great a moral or social crime it may be. And it is only a curious and almost unbelievably tight and yet utterly misleading set of circumstances in connection with the death of this girl that chances to bring this defendant before you at this time. I swear it. I truly know it to be so. And it can and will be fully explained to your entire satisfaction before this case is closed.

"However, in connection with this statement, there is another which must be made as a preface to all that is to follow.

"Gentlemen of the jury, the individual who is on trial here for his life is a mental as well as a moral coward—no more and no less—not a downright, hardhearted criminal by any means. Not unlike many men in critical situations, he is a victim of a mental and moral fear complex. Why, no one as yet has been quite able to explain. We all have one secret bugbear or fear. And it is these two qualities, and no others, that have placed him in the dangerous position in which he now finds himself. It was cowardice, gentlemen—fear of a rule of the factory of which his uncle is the owner, as well as fear of his own word given to the officials above him, that caused him first to conceal the fact that he was interested in the pretty country girl who had come to work for him. And later, to conceal the fact that he was going with her.

"Yet no statutory crime of any kind there. You could not possibly try a man for that, whatever privately you might think. And it was cowardice, mental and moral, gentlemen, which prevented him, after he became convinced that he could no longer endure a relationship which had once seemed so beautiful, from saying outright that he could not and would not continue with her, let alone marry her. Yet, will you slay a man because he is the victim of fear? And again, after all, if a man has once and truly decided that he cannot and will not endure a given woman, or a woman a man—that to live with her could only prove torturesome—what would you have that person do? Marry her? To what end? That they may hate and despise and torture each other forever after? Can you truly say that you agree with that as a rule, or a method, or a law? Yet, as the defense sees it, a truly intelligent and fair enough thing, under the circumstances, was done in this instance. An offer, but without marriage—and alas, without avail—was made. A suggestion for a separate life, with him working to support her while she dwelt elsewhere. Her own letters, read only yesterday in this court, indicate something of the kind. But the oh, so often tragic insistence upon what in so many cases were best left undone! And then that last, long, argumentative trip to Utica, Grass Lake, and Big Bittern. And all to no purpose. Yet with no intention to kill or betray unto death. Not the slightest. And we will show you why.

"Gentlemen, once more I insist that it was cowardice, mental and moral, and not any plot or plan for any crime of any kind, that made Clyde Griffiths travel with Roberta Alden under various aliases to all the places I have just mentioned—that made him write 'Mr. and Mrs. Carl Graham,' 'Mr. and Mrs. Clifford Golden'—mental and moral fear of the great social mistake as well as sin that he had committed in pursuing and eventually allowing himself to fall into this unhallowed relationship with her—mental and moral fear or cowardice of what was to follow.

"And again, it was mental and moral cowardice that prevented him there at Big Bittern, once the waters of the lake had so accidentally closed over her, from returning to Big Bittern Inn and making public her death. Mental and Moral Cowardice—and nothing more and nothing less. He was thinking of his wealthy relatives in Lycurgus, their rule which his presence here on the lake with this girl would show to have been broken—of the suffering and shame and rage of her parents. And besides, there was Miss X—the brightest star in the brightest constellation of all his dreams.

"We admit all that, and we are completely willing to concede that he was, or must have been, thinking of all these things. The prosecution charges, and we admit that such is the fact, that he had been so completely ensnared by this Miss X, and she by him, that he was willing and eager to forsake

this first love who had given herself to him, for one who, because of her beauty and her wealth, seemed so much more desirable—even as to Roberta Alden he seemed more desirable
than others. And if she erred as to him—as plainly she did—
might not—might not he have erred eventually in his infatuated following of one who in the ultimate—who can
say?—might not have cared so much for him. At any rate, one
of his strongest fear thoughts at this time, as he himself has
confessed to us, his counsel, was that if this Miss X learned
that he had been up there with this other girl of whom she
had not even so much as heard, well then, it would mean the
end of her regard for him.

"I know that as you gentlemen view such things, such conduct has no excuse for being. One may be the victim of an internal conflict between two illicit moods, yet nevertheless, as
the law and the church see it, guilty of sin and crime. But the
truth, none-the-less, is that they do exist in the human heart,
law or no law, religion or no religion, and in scores of cases
they motivated the actions of the victims. And we admit that
they motivated the actions of Clyde Griffiths.

"But did he kill Roberta Alden?

"No!

"And again, no!

"Or did he plot in any way, half-heartedly or otherwise, to
drag her up there under the guise of various aliases and then,
because she would not set him free, drown her? Ridiculous!
Impossible! Insane! His plan was completely and entirely different.

"But, gentlemen," and here he suddenly paused as though
a new or overlooked thought had just come to him, "perhaps
you would be better satisfied with my argument and the final
judgment you are to render if you were to have the testimony
of one eye-witness at least of Roberta Alden's death—one
who, instead of just hearing a voice, was actually present, and
who saw and hence knows how she met her death."

He now looked at Jephson as much as to say: Now,
Reuben, at last, here we are! And Reuben, turning to Clyde,
easily and yet with iron in his every motion, whispered: "Well,
here we are, Clyde, it's up to you now. Only I'm going along
with you, see? I've decided to examine you myself. I've drilled

and drilled you, and I guess you won't have any trouble in telling me, will you?" He beamed on Clyde genially and encouragingly, and Clyde, because of Belknap's strong plea as well as this newest and best development in connection with Jephson, now stood up and with almost a jaunty air, and one out of all proportion to his mood of but four hours before, now whispered: "Gee! I'm glad you're going to do it. I'll be all right now, I think."

But in the meantime the audience, hearing that an actual eye-witness was to be produced, and not by the prosecution but the defense, was at once upon its feet, craning and stirring. And Justice Oberwaltzer, irritated to an exceptional degree by the informality characteristic of this trial, was now rapping with his gavel while his clerk cried loudly: "Order! Order! Unless everybody is seated, all spectators will be dismissed! The deputies will please see that all are seated." And then a hushed and strained silence falling as Belknap called: "Clyde Griffiths, take the witness chair." And the audience— seeing to its astonishment, Clyde, accompanied by Reuben Jephson, making his way forward—straining and whispering in spite of all the gruff commands of the judge and the bailiffs. And even Belknap, as he saw Jephson approaching, being a little astonished, since it was he who according to the original plan was to have led Clyde through his testimony. But now Jephson drawing near to him as Clyde was being seated and sworn, merely whispered: "Leave him to me, Alvin, I think it's best. He looks a little too strained and shaky to suit me, but I feel sure I can pull him through."

And then the audience noting the change and whispering in regard to it. And Clyde, his large nervous eyes turning here and there, thinking: Well, I'm on the witness stand at last. And now everybody's watching me, of course. I must look very calm, like I didn't care so very much, because I didn't really kill her. That's right, I didn't. Yet his skin blue and the lids of his eyes red and puffy and his hands trembling slightly in spite of himself. And Jephson, his long, tensile and dynamic body like that of a swaying birch, turning toward him and looking fixedly into Clyde's brown eyes with his blue ones, beginning:

"Now, Clyde, the first thing we want to do is make sure

that the jury and every one else hears our questions and answers. And next, when you're all set, you're going to begin
with your life as you remember it—where you were born,
where you came from, what your father did and your mother,
too, and finally, what you did and why, from the time you
went to work until now. I may interrupt you with a few questions now and then, but in the main I'm going to let you tell
it, because I know you can tell it better than any one." Yet in
order to reassure Clyde and to make him know each moment
that he was there—a wall, a bulwark, between him and the eager, straining, unbelieving and hating crowd—he now drew
nearer, at times so close as to put one foot on the witness
stand, or if not that to lean forward and lay a hand on the arm
of the chair in which Clyde sat. And all the while saying,
"Yay-uss—Yay-uss." "And then what?" "And then?" And invariably at the strong and tonic or protective sound of his
voice Clyde stirring as with a bolstering force and finding
himself able, and without shaking or quavering, to tell the
short but straitened story of his youth.

"I was born in Grand Rapids, Michigan. My parents were
conducting a mission there at that time and used to hold
open air meetings . . ."

# Chapter XXIV

C LYDE'S testimony proceeded to the point where the family had removed from Quincy, Illinois (a place resorted to on account of some Salvation Army work offered his father and mother), to Kansas City, where from his twelfth to his fifteenth year he had browsed about trying to find something to do while still resenting the combination of school and religious work expected of him.

"Were you up with your classes in the public schools?"

"No, sir. We had moved too much."

"In what grade were you when you were twelve years old?"

"Well, I should have been in the seventh but I was only in the sixth. That's why I didn't like it."

"And how about the religious work of your parents?"

"Well, it was all right—only I never did like going out nights on the street corners."

And so on, through five-and-ten cent store, soda and newspaper carrier jobs, until at last he was a bell-hop at the Green-Davidson, the finest hotel in Kansas City, as he informed them.

"But now, Clyde," proceeded Jephson who, fearful lest Mason on the cross-examination and in connection with Clyde's credibility as a witness should delve into the matter of the wrecked car and the slain child in Kansas City and so mar the effect of the story he was now about to tell, was determined to be beforehand in this. Decidedly, by questioning him properly he could explain and soften all that, whereas if left to Mason it could be tortured into something exceedingly dark indeed. And so now he continued:

"And how long did you work there?"

"A little over a year."

"And why did you leave?"

"Well, it was on account of an accident."

"What kind of an accident?"

And here Clyde, previously prepared and drilled as to all this plunged into the details which led up to and included the death of the little girl and his flight—which Mason, true enough, had been intending to bring up. But, now, as he listened to all this, he merely shook his head and grunted ironically, "He'd better go into all that," he commented. And Jephson, sensing the import of what he was doing—how most likely he was, as he would have phrased it, "spiking" one of Mr. Mason's best guns, continued with:

"How old were you then, Clyde, did you say?"

"Between seventeen and eighteen."

"And do you mean to tell me," he continued, after he had finished with all of the questions he could think of in connection with all this, "that you didn't know that you might have gone back there, since you were not the one who took the car, and after explaining it all, been paroled in the custody of your parents?"

"Object!" shouted Mason. "There's no evidence here to show that he could have returned to Kansas City and been paroled in the custody of his parents."

"Objection sustained!" boomed the judge from his high throne. "The defense will please confine itself a little more closely to the letter of the testimony."

"Exception," noted Belknap, from his seat.

"No, sir. I didn't know that," replied Clyde, just the same.

"Anyhow was that the reason after you got away that you changed your name to Tenet as you told me?" continued Jephson.

"Yes, sir."

"By the way, just where did you get that name of Tenet, Clyde?"

"It was the name of a boy I used to play with in Quincy."

"Was he a good boy?"

"Object!" called Mason, from his chair. "Incompetent, immaterial, irrelevant."

"Oh, he might have associated with a good boy in spite of what you would like to have the jury believe, and in that sense it is very relevant," sneered Jephson.

"Objection sustained!" boomed Justice Oberwaltzer.

"But didn't it occur to you at the time that he might object or that you might be doing him an injustice in using his name to cover the identity of a fellow who was running away?"

"No, sir—I thought there were lots of Tenets."

An indulgent smile might have been expected at this point, but so antagonistic and bitter was the general public toward Clyde that such levity was out of the question in this court-room.

"Now listen, Clyde," continued Jephson, having, as he had just seen, failed to soften the mood of the throng, "you cared for your mother, did you?—or didn't you?"

Objection and argument finally ending in the question being allowed.

"Yes, sir, certainly I cared for her," replied Clyde—but after a slight hesitancy which was noticeable—a tightening of the throat and a swelling and sinking of the chest as he exhaled and inhaled.

"Much?"

"Yes, sir—much." He didn't venture to look at any one now.

"Hadn't she always done as much as she could for you, in her way?"

"Yes, sir."

"Well, then, Clyde, how was it, after all that, and even though that dreadful accident had occurred, you could run away and stay away so long without so much as one word to tell her that you were by no means as guilty as you seemed and that she shouldn't worry because you were working and trying to be a good boy again?"

"But I did write her—only I didn't sign my name."

"I see. Anything else?"

"Yes, sir. I sent her a little money. Ten dollars once."

"But you didn't think of going back at all?"

"No, sir. I was afraid that if I went back they might arrest me."

"In other words," and here Jephson emphasized this with great clearness, "you were a moral and mental coward, as Mr. Belknap, my colleague, said."

"I object to this interpretation of this defendant's testimony for the benefit of the jury!" interrupted Mason.

"This defendant's testimony really needs no interpretation. It is very plain and honest, as any one can see," quickly interjected Jephson.

"Objection sustained!" called the judge. "Proceed. Proceed."

"And it was because you were a moral and mental coward as I see it, Clyde—not that I am condemning you for anything that you cannot help. (After all, you didn't make yourself, did you?)"

But this was too much, and the judge here cautioned him to use more discretion in framing his future questions.

"Then you went about in Alton, Peoria, Bloomington, Milwaukee, and Chicago—hiding away in small rooms in back streets and working as a dishwasher or soda fountain man, or a driver, and changing your name to Tenet when you really might have gone back to Kansas City and resumed your old place?" continued Jephson.

"I object! I object!" yelled Mason. "There is no evidence here to show that he could have gone there and resumed his old place."

"Objection sustained," ruled Oberwaltzer, although at the time in Jephson's pocket was a letter from Francis X. Squires, formerly captain of the bell-boys of the Green-Davidson at the time Clyde was there, in which he explained that apart from the one incident in connection with the purloined automobile, he knew nothing derogatory to Clyde; and that always previously, he had found him prompt, honest, willing, alert and well-mannered. Also that at the time the accident occurred, he himself had been satisfied that Clyde could have been little else than one of those led and that if he had returned and properly explained matters he would have been reinstated. It was irrelevant.

Thereafter followed Clyde's story of how, having fled from the difficulties threatening him in Kansas City and having wandered here and there for two years, he had finally obtained a place in Chicago as a driver and later as a bell-boy at the Union League, and also how while still employed at the first of these places he had written his mother and later at her request was about to write his uncle, when, accidentally meeting him at the Union League, he was invited by him to come to Lycurgus. And thereupon, in their natural order, followed all of the details of how he had gone to work, been promoted and instructed by his cousin and the foreman as to the various rules, and then later how he had met Roberta and still later Miss X. But in between came all the details as to how and why he had courted Roberta Alden, and how and why, having once secured her love he felt and thought himself content—but how the arrival of Miss X, and her overpowering fascination for him, had served completely to change all his notions in regard to Roberta, and although he still admired her, caused him to feel that never again as before could he desire to marry her.

But Jephson, anxious to divert the attention of the jury from the fact that Clyde was so very fickle—a fact too trying to be so speedily introduced into the case—at once interposed with:

"Clyde! You really loved Roberta Alden at first, didn't you?"

"Yes, sir."

"Well, then, you must have known, or at least you gathered from her actions, from the first, didn't you, that she was a perfectly good and innocent and religious girl."

"Yes, sir, that's how I felt about her," replied Clyde, repeating what he had been told to say.

"Well, then, just roughly now, without going into detail, do you suppose you could explain to yourself and this jury how and why and where and when those changes came about which led to that relationship which we all of us" (and here he looked boldly and wisely and coldly out over the audience and then afterwards upon the jurors) "deplore. How was it, if you thought so highly of her at first that you could so soon afterwards descend to this evil relationship? Didn't you know that all men, and all women also, view it as wrong, and outside of marriage unforgivable—a statutory crime?"

The boldness and ironic sting of this was sufficient to cause at first a hush, later a slight nervous tremor on the part of the audience which, Mason as well as Justice Oberwaltzer noting, caused both to frown apprehensively. Why, this brazen young cynic! How dared he, via innuendo and in the guise of serious questioning, intrude such a thought as this, which by implication at least picked at the very foundations of society—religious and moral! At the same time there he was, standing boldly and leoninely, the while Clyde replied:

"Yes, sir, I suppose I did—certainly—but I didn't try to seduce her at first or at any time, really. I was in love with her."

"You were in love with her?"

"Yes, sir."

"Very much?"

"Very much."

"And was she as much in love with you at that time?"

"Yes, sir, she was."

"From the very first?"

"From the very first."

"She told you so?"

"Yes, sir."

"At the time she left the Newtons—you have heard all the testimony here in regard to that—did you induce or seek to induce her in any way, by any trick or agreement, to leave there?"

"No, sir, I didn't. She wanted to leave there of her own accord. She wanted me to help her find a place."

"She wanted you to help her find a place?"

"Yes, sir."

"And just why?"

"Because she didn't know the city very well and she thought maybe I could tell her where there was a nice room she could get—one that she could afford."

"And did you tell her about the room she took at the Gilpins'?"

"No, sir, I didn't. I never told her about any room. She found it herself." (This was the exact answer he had memorized.)

"But why didn't you help her?"

"Because I was busy, days and most evenings. And besides I thought she knew better what she wanted than I did—the kind of people and all."

"Did you personally ever see the Gilpin place before she went there?"

"No, sir."

"Ever have any discussion with her before she moved there as to the kind of a room she was to take—its position as regards to entrance, exit, privacy, or anything of that sort?"

"No, sir, I never did."

"Never insisted, for instance, that she take a certain type of room which you could slip in and out of at night or by day without being seen?"

"I never did. Besides, no one could very well slip in or out of that house without being seen."

"And why not?"

"Because the door to her room was right next to the door to the general front entrance where everybody went in and out and anybody that was around could see." That was another answer he had memorized.

"But you slipped in and out, didn't you?"

"Well, yes, sir—that is, we both decided from the first that the less we were seen together anywhere, the better."

"On account of that factory rule?"

"Yes, sir—on account of that factory rule."

And then the story of his various difficulties with Roberta, due to Miss X coming into his life.

"Now, Clyde, we will have to go into the matter of this Miss X a little. Because of an agreement between the defense and the prosecution which you gentlemen of the jury fully understand, we can only touch on this incidentally, since it all concerns an entirely innocent person whose real name can be of no service here anyhow. But some of the facts must be touched upon, although we will deal with them as light as possible, as much for the sake of the innocent living as the worthy dead. And I am sure Miss Alden would have it so if she were alive. But now in regard to Miss X," he continued, turning to Clyde, "it is already agreed by both sides that you met her in Lycurgus some time in November or December of last year. That is correct, is it not?"

"Yes, sir, that is correct," replied Clyde, sadly.

"And that at once you fell very much in love with her?"

"Yes, sir. That's true."

"She was rich?"

"Yes, sir."

"Beautiful?"

"I believe it is admitted by all that she is," he said to the court in general without requiring or anticipating a reply from Clyde, yet the latter, so thoroughly drilled had he been, now replied: "Yes, sir."

"Had you two—yourself and Miss Alden, I mean—at that time when you first met Miss X already established that illicit relationship referred to?"

"Yes, sir."

"Well, now, in view of all that—but no, one moment, there is something else I want to ask you first—now, let me see—at the time that you first met Miss X you were still in love with Roberta Alden, were you—or were you not?"

"I was still in love with her—yes, sir."

"You had not, up to that time at least, in any way become weary of her? Or had you?"

"No, sir. I had not."

"Her love and her companionship were just as precious and delightful to you as ever?"

"Yes, sir, they were."

And as Clyde said that, he was thinking back and it seemed to him that what he had just said was really true. It was true that just before meeting Sondra he was actually at the zenith of content and delight with Roberta.

"And what, if any, were your plans for your future with Miss Alden—before you met this Miss X? You must have thought at times of that, didn't you?"

"Well, not exactly," (and as he said this he licked his lips in sheer nervousness). "You see, I never had any real plan to do anything—that is, to do anything that wasn't quite right with her. And neither did she, of course. We just drifted kinda, from the first. It was being alone there so much, maybe. She hadn't taken up with anybody yet and I hadn't either. And then there was that rule that kept me from taking her about anywhere, and once we were together, of course we just went on without thinking very much about it, I suppose—either of us."

"You just drifted because nothing had happened as yet and you didn't suppose anything would. Is that the way?"

"No, sir. I mean, yes, sir. That's the way it was." Clyde was very eager to get these much-rehearsed and very important answers, just right.

"But you must have thought of something—one or both of you. You were twenty-one and she was twenty-three."

"Yes, sir. I suppose we did—I suppose I did think of something now and then."

"And what was it that you thought? Can you recollect?"

"Well, yes, sir, I suppose I can. That is, I know that I did think at times that if things went all right and I made a little more money and she got a place somewhere else, that I would begin taking her out openly, and then afterwards maybe, if she and I kept on caring for each other as we did then, marry her, maybe."

"You actually thought of marrying her then, did you?"

"Yes, sir. I know I did in the way that I've said, of course."

"But that was before you met this Miss X?"

"Yes, sir, that was before that."

("Beautifully done!" observed Mason, sarcastically, under his breath to State Senator Redmond. "Excellent stage play," replied Redmond in a stage whisper.)

"But did you ever tell her in so many words?" continued Jephson.

"Well, no, sir. I don't recall that I did—not just in so many words."

"You either told her or you didn't tell her. Now, which was it?"

"Well, neither, quite. I used to tell her that I loved her and that I never wanted her to leave me and that I hoped she never would."

"But not that you wanted to marry her?"

"No, sir. Not that I wanted to marry her."

"Well, well, all right!—and she—what did she say?"

"That she never would leave me," replied Clyde, heavily and fearsomely, thinking, as he did so, of Roberta's last cries and her eyes bent on him. And he took from his pocket a handkerchief and began to wipe his moist, cold face and hands.

("Well staged!" murmured Mason, softly and cynically. "Pretty shrewd—pretty shrewd!" commented Redmond, lightly.)

"But, tell me," went on Jephson, softly and coldly, "feeling as you did about Miss Alden, how was it that upon meeting this Miss X, you could change so quickly? Are you so fickle that you don't know your own mind from day to day?"

"Well, I didn't think so up to that time—no, sir!"

"Had you ever had a strong and binding love affair at any time in your life before you met Miss Alden?"

"No, sir."

"But did you consider this one with Miss Alden strong and binding—a true love affair—up to the time you met this Miss X?"

"Yes, sir, I did."

"And afterwards—then what?"

"Well—afterwards—it wasn't quite like that any more."

"You mean to say that on sight of Miss X, after encountering her once or twice, you ceased to care for Miss Alden entirely?

"Well, no, sir. It wasn't quite like that," volunteered Clyde, swiftly and earnestly. "I did continue to care for her some—quite a lot, really. But before I knew it I had completely lost my head over—over Miss—Miss——"

"Yes, this Miss X. We know. You fell madly and unreasonably in love with her. Was that the way of it?"

"Yes, sir."

"And then?"

"Well—and then—I just couldn't care for Miss Alden so much any more." A thin film of moisture covered Clyde's forehead and cheeks as he spoke.

"I see! I see!" went on Jephson, oratorically and loudly, having the jury and audience in mind. "A case of the Arabian Nights, of the ensorcelled and the ensorcellor."

"I don't think I know what you mean," said Clyde.

"A case of being bewitched, my poor boy—by beauty, love, wealth, by things that we sometimes think we want very, very much, and cannot ever have—that is what I mean, and that is what much of the love in the world amounts to."

"Yes, sir," replied Clyde, quite innocently, concluding rightly that this was a mere show of rhetoric on Jephson's part.

"But what I want to know is—how was it that loving Miss Alden as much as you say you did—and having reached that relationship which should have been sanctioned by marriage—how was it that you could have felt so little bound or obligated to her as to entertain the idea of casting her over for this Miss X? Now just how was that? I would like to know, and so would this jury, I am sure. Where was your sense of gratitude? Your sense of moral obligation? Do you mean to say that you have none? We want to know."

This was really cross-examination—an attack on his own

witness. Yet Jephson was within his rights and Mason did not interfere.

"Well . . ." and here Clyde hesitated and stumbled, quite as if he had not been instructed as to all this beforehand, and seemed to and did truly finger about in his own mind or reason for some thought that would help him to explain all this. For although it was true that he had memorized the answer, now that he was confronted by the actual question here in court, as well as the old problem that had so confused and troubled him in Lycurgus, he could scarcely think clearly of all he had been told to say, but instead twisted and turned, and finally came out with:

"The fact is, I didn't think about those things at all very much. I couldn't after I saw her. I tried to at times, but I couldn't. I only wanted her and I didn't want Miss Alden any more. I knew I wasn't doing right—exactly—and I felt sorry for Roberta—but just the same I didn't seem able to do anything much about it. I could only think of Miss X and I couldn't think of Roberta as I had before no matter how hard I tried."

"Do you mean to say that you didn't suffer in your own conscience on account of this?"

"Yes, sir, I suffered," replied Clyde. "I knew I wasn't doing right, and it made me worry a lot about her and myself, but just the same I didn't seem to be able to do any better." (He was repeating words that Jephson had written out for him, although at the time he first read them he felt them to be fairly true. He had suffered some.)

"And then?"

"Well, then she began to complain because I didn't go round to see her as much as before."

"In other words, you began to neglect her."

"Yes, sir, some—but not entirely—no, sir."

"Well, when you found you were so infatuated with this Miss X, what did you do? Did you go and tell Miss Alden that you were no longer in love with her but in love with some one else?"

"No, I didn't. Not then."

"Why not then? Did you think it fair and honorable to be telling two girls at once that you cared for them?"

"No, sir, but it wasn't quite like that either. You see at that time I was just getting acquainted with Miss X, and I wasn't telling her anything. She wouldn't let me. But I knew then, just the same, that I couldn't care for Miss Alden any more."

"But what about the claim Miss Alden had on you? Didn't you feel that that was enough or should be, to prevent you from running after another girl?"

"Yes, sir."

"Well, why did you then?"

"I couldn't resist her."

"Miss X, you mean?"

"Yes, sir."

"And so you continued to run after her until you had made her care for you?"

"No, sir, that wasn't the way at all."

"Well then, what was the way?"

"I just met her here and there and got crazy about her."

"I see. But still you didn't go and tell Miss Alden that you couldn't care for her any longer?"

"No, sir. Not then."

"And why not?"

"Because I thought it would hurt her, and I didn't want to do that."

"Oh, I see. You didn't have the moral or mental courage to do it then?"

"I don't know about the moral or mental courage," replied Clyde, a little hurt and irritated by this description of himself, "but I felt sorry for her just the same. She used to cry and I didn't have the heart to tell her anything."

"I see. Well, let it stand that way, if you want to. But now answer me one other thing. That relationship between you two—what about that—after you knew that you didn't care for her any more. Did that continue?"

"Well, no, sir, not so very long, anyhow," replied Clyde, most nervously and shamefacedly. He was thinking of all the people before him now—of his mother—Sondra—of all the people throughout the entire United States—who would read and so know. And on first being shown these questions weeks and weeks before he had wanted to know of Jephson what the use of all that was. And Jephson had replied: "Educational effect. The quicker and harder we can shock 'em with some of the real facts of life around here, the easier it is going to be for you to get a little more sane consideration of what your problem was. But don't worry your head over that now. When the time comes, just answer 'em and leave the rest to us. We know what we're doing." And so now Clyde added:

"You see, after meeting Miss X I couldn't care for her so much that way any more, and so I tried not to go around her so much any more. But anyhow, it wasn't so very long after that before she got in trouble and then—well——"

"I see. And when was that—about?"

"Along in the latter part of January last year."

"And once that happened, then what? Did you or did you not feel that it was your duty under the circumstances to marry her?"

"Well, no—not the way things were then—that is, if I could get her out of it, I mean."

"And why not? What do you mean by 'as things were then'?"

"Well, you see, it was just as I told you. I wasn't caring for her any more, and since I hadn't promised to marry her, and she knew it, I thought it would be fair enough if I helped her out of it and then told her that I didn't care for her as I once did."

"But couldn't you help her out of it?"

"No, sir. But I tried."

"You went to that druggist who testified here?"

"Yes, sir."

"To anybody else?"

"Yes, sir—to seven others before I could get anything at all."

"But what you got didn't help?"

"No, sir."

"Did you go to that young haberdasher who testified here as he said?"

"Yes, sir."

"And did he give you the name of any particular doctor?"

"Well—yes—but I wouldn't care to say which one."

"All right, you needn't. But did you send Miss Alden to any doctor?"

"Yes, sir."

"Did she go alone or did you go with her?"

"I went with her—that is, to the door."

"Why only to the door?"

"Well, we talked it over, and she thought just as I did, that it might be better that way. I didn't have any too much money at the time. I thought he might be willing to help her for less if she went by herself than if we both went together."

("I'll be damned if he isn't stealing most of my thunder," thought Mason to himself at this point. "He's forestalling most of the things I intended to riddle him with." And he sat up worried. Burleigh and Redmond and Earl Newcomb—all now saw clearly what Jephson was attempting to do.)

"I see. And it wasn't by any chance because you were afraid that your uncle or Miss X might hear of it?"

"Oh, yes, I . . . that is, we both thought of that and talked of it. She understood how things were with me down there."

"But not about Miss X?"

"No, not about Miss X."

"And why not?"

"Well, because I didn't think I could very well tell her just then. It would have made her feel too bad. I wanted to wait until she was all right again."

"And then tell her and leave her. Is that what you mean?"

"Well, yes, if I still couldn't care for her any more—yes, sir."

"But not if she was in trouble?"

"Well, no, sir, not if she was in trouble. But you see, at that time I was expecting to be able to get her out of that."

"I see. But didn't her condition affect your attitude toward her—cause you to want to straighten the whole thing out by giving up this Miss X and marrying Miss Alden?"

"Well, no, sir—not then exactly—that is, not at that time."

"How do you mean—'not at that time'?"

"Well, I did come to feel that way later, as I told you—but not then—that was afterwards—after we started on our trip to the Adirondacks."

"And why not then?"

"I've said why. I was too crazy about Miss X to think of anything but her."

"You couldn't change even then?"

"No, sir. I felt sorry, but I couldn't."

"I see. But never mind that now. I will come to that later. Just now I want to have you explain to the jury, if you can, just what it was about this Miss X, as contrasted with Miss Alden, that made her seem so very much more desirable in your eyes. Just what characteristics of manner or face or mind or position—or whatever it was that so enticed you? Or do you know?"

This was a question which both Belknap and Jephson in various ways and for various reasons—psychic, legal, personal—had asked Clyde before, and with varying results. At first he could not and would not discuss her at all, fearing that whatever he said would be seized upon and used in his trial and the newspapers along with her name. But later, when because of the silence of the newspapers everywhere in regard to her true name, it became plain that she was not to be featured, he permitted himself to talk more freely about her. But now here on the stand, he grew once more nervous and reticent.

"Well, you see, it's hard to say. She was very beautiful to me. Much more so than Roberta—but not only that, she was different from any one I had ever known—more independent—and everybody paid so much attention to what she did and what she said. She seemed to know more than any one else I ever knew. Then she dressed awfully well, and was very rich and in society and her name and pictures were always in the paper. I used to read about her every day when I didn't see her, and that seemed to keep her before me a lot. She was daring, too—not so simple or trusting as Miss Alden was— and at first it was hard for me to believe that she was becoming so interested in me. It got so that I couldn't think of any one or anything else, and I didn't want Roberta any more. I just couldn't, with Miss X always before me."

"Well, it looks to me as if you might have been in love, or hypnotized at that," insinuated Jephson at the conclusion of this statement, the tail of his right eye upon the jury. "If that isn't a picture of pretty much all gone, I guess I don't know one when I see it." But with the audience and the jury as stony-faced as before, as he could see.

But immediately thereafter the swift and troubled waters of the alleged plot which was the stern trail to which all this was leading.

"Well, now, Clyde, from there on, just what happened? Tell us now, as near as you can recall. Don't shade it or try to make yourself look any better or any worse. She is dead, and you may be, eventually, if these twelve gentlemen here finally so decide." (And at this an icy chill seemed to permeate the entire courtroom as well as Clyde.) "But the truth for the peace of your own soul is the best,"—and here Jephson thought of Mason—let him counteract that if he can.

"Yes, sir," said Clyde, simply.

"Well, then, after she got in trouble and you couldn't help her, then what? What was it you did? How did you act? . . . By the way, one moment—what was your salary at that time?"

"Twenty-five dollars a week," confessed Clyde.

"No other source of income?"

"I didn't quite hear."

"Was there any other source from which you were obtaining any money at that time in any way?"

"No, sir."

"And how much was your room?"

"Seven dollars a week."

"And your board?"

"Oh, from five to six."

"Any other expenses?"

"Yes, sir—my clothes and laundry."

"You had to stand your share of whatever social doings were on foot, didn't you?"

"Objected to as leading!" called Mason.

"Objection sustained," replied Justice Oberwaltzer.

"Any other expenses that you can think of?"

"Well, there were carfares and trainfares. And then I had to share in whatever social expenses there were."

"Exactly!" cried Mason, with great irritation. "I wish you would quit leading this parrot here."

"I wish the honorable district attorney would mind his own business!" snorted Jephson—as much for Clyde's benefit as for his own. He wished to break down his fear of Mason. "I'm examining this defendant, and as for parrots we've seen quite a number of them around here in the last few weeks, and coached to the throat like school-boys."

"That's a malicious lie!" shouted Mason. "I object and demand an apology."

"The apology is to me and to this defendant, if your Honor pleases, and will be exacted quickly if your Honor will only adjourn this court for a few minutes," and then stepping directly in front of Mason, he added: "And I will be able to obtain it without any judicial aid." Whereupon Mason, thinking he was about to be attacked, squared off, the while assistants and deputy sheriffs, and stenographers and writers, and the clerk of the court himself, gathered round and seized the two lawyers while Justice Oberwaltzer pounded violently on his desk with his gavel:

"Gentlemen! Gentlemen! You are both in contempt of court, both of you! You will apologize to the court and to each other, or I'll declare a mis-trial and commit you both for ten days and fine you five hundred dollars each." With this he leaned down and frowned on both. And at once Jephson replied, most suavely and ingratiatingly: "Under the circumstances, your Honor, I apologize to you and to the attorney for the People and to this jury. The attack on this defendant, by the district attorney, seemed too unfair and uncalled for—that was all."

"Never mind that," continued Oberwaltzer.

"Under the circumstances, your Honor, I apologize to you and to the counsel for the defense. I was a little hasty, perhaps. And to this defendant also," sneered Mason, after first looking into Justice Oberwaltzer's angry and uncompromising eyes and then into Clyde's, who instantly recoiled and turned away.

"Proceed," growled Oberwaltzer, sullenly.

"Now, Clyde," resumed Jephson anew, as calm as though he had just lit and thrown away a match. "You say your salary was twenty-five dollars and you had these various expenses. Had you, up to this time, been able to put aside any money for a rainy day?"

"No, sir—not much—not any, really."

"Well, then, supposing some doctor to whom Miss Alden had applied had been willing to assist her and wanted—say a hundred dollars or so—were you ready to furnish that?"

"No, sir—not right off, that is."

"Did she have any money of her own that you know of?"

"None that I know of—no, sir."

"Well, how did you intend to help her then?"

"Well, I thought if either she or I found any one and he would wait and let me pay for it on time, that I could save and pay it that way, maybe."

"I see. You were perfectly willing to do that, were you?"

"Yes, sir, I was."

"You told her so, did you?"

"Yes, sir. She knew that."

"Well, when neither you nor she could find any one to help her, then what? What did you do next?"

"Well, then she wanted me to marry her."

"Right away?"

"Yes, sir. Right away."

"And what did you say to that?"

"I told her I just couldn't then. I didn't have any money to get married on. And besides if I did and didn't go away somewhere, at least until the baby was born, everybody would find out and I couldn't have stayed there anyhow. And she couldn't either."

"And why not?"

"Well, there were my relatives. They wouldn't have wanted to keep me any more, or her either, I guess."

"I see. They wouldn't have considered you fit for the work you were doing, or her either. Is that it?"

"I thought so, anyhow," replied Clyde.

"And then what?"

"Well, even if I had wanted to go away with her and marry her, I didn't have enough money to do that and she didn't either. I would have had to give up my place and gone and found another somewhere before I could let her come. Besides that, I didn't know any place where I could go and earn as much as I did there."

"How about hotel work? Couldn't you have gone back to that?"

"Well, maybe—if I had had an introduction of some kind. But I didn't want to go back to that."

"And why not?"

"Well, I didn't like it so much any more—not that kind of life."

"But you didn't mean that you didn't want to do anything at all, did you? That wasn't your attitude, was it?"

"Oh, no, sir. That wasn't it. I told her right away if she would go away for a while—while she had her baby—and let me stay on there in Lycurgus, that I would try to live on less and give her all I could save until she was all right again."

"But not marry her?"

"No, sir, I didn't feel that I could do that then."

"And what did she say to that?"

"She wouldn't do it. She said she couldn't and wouldn't go through with it unless I would marry her."

"I see. Then and there?"

"Well, yes—pretty soon, anyhow. She was willing to wait a little while, but she wouldn't go away unless I would marry her."

"And did you tell her that you didn't care for her any more?"

"Well, nearly—yes, sir."

"What do you mean by 'nearly'?"

"Well, that I didn't want to. Besides, she knew I didn't care for her any more. She said so herself."

"To you, at that time?"

"Yes, sir. Lots of times."

"Well, yes, that's true—it was in all of those letters of hers that were read here. But when she refused so flatly, what did you then?"

"Well, I didn't know what to do. But I thought maybe if I could get her to go up to her home for a while, while I tried and saved what I could—well . . . maybe . . . once she was up there and saw how much I didn't want to marry her——" (Clyde paused and fumbled at his lips. This lying was hard.)

"Yes, go on. And remember, the truth, however ashamed of it you may be, is better than any lie."

"And maybe when she was a little more frightened and not so determined——"

"Weren't you frightened, too?"

"Yes, sir, I was."

"Well, go on."

"That then—well—maybe if I offered her all that I had been able to save up to then—you see I thought maybe I might be able to borrow some from some one too—that she might be willing to go away and not make me marry her— just live somewhere and let me help her."

"I see. But she wouldn't agree to that?"

"Well, no—not to my not marrying her, no—but to going up there for a month, yes. I couldn't get her to say that she would let me off."

"But did you at that or any other time before or subsequent to that say that you would come up there and marry her?"

"No, sir. I never did."

"Just what did you say then?"

"I said that . . . as soon as I could get the money," stuttered Clyde at this point, so nervous and shamed was he, "I would come for her in about a month and we could go away somewhere until—until—well, until she was out of that."

"But you did not tell her that you would marry her?"

"No, sir. I did not."

"But she wanted you to, of course."

"Yes, sir."

"Had you any notion that she could force you so to do at that time—marry her against your will, I mean?"

"No, sir, I didn't. Not if I could help it. My plan was to wait as long as I could and save all the money I could and then when the time came just refuse and give her all the money that I had and help her all I could from then on."

"But you know," proceeded Jephson, most suavely and diplomatically at this point, "there are various references in these letters here which Miss Alden wrote you"—and he reached over and from the district attorney's table picked up the original letters of Roberta and weighed them solemnly in his hand—"to a *plan* which you two had in connection with this trip—or at least that she seemed to think you had. Now, exactly what was that plan? She distinctly refers to it, if I recall aright, as 'our plan.'"

"I know that," replied Clyde—since for two months now he, along with Belknap and Jephson, had discussed this particular question. "But the only plan I know of"—and here he did his best to look frank and be convincing—"was the one that I offered over and over."

"And what was that?"

"Why, that she go away and take a room somewhere and let me help her and come over and see her once in a while."

"Well, no, you're wrong there," returned Jephson, slyly. "That isn't and couldn't be the plan she had in mind. She says in one of these letters that she knows it will be hard on you to have to go away and stay so long, or until she is out of this thing, but that it can't be helped."

"Yes, I know," replied Clyde, quickly and exactly as he had been told to do, "but that was her plan, not mine. She kept saying to me most of the time that that was what she wanted me to do, and that I would have to do it. She told me that over the telephone several times, and I may have said all right, all right, not meaning that I agreed with her entirely but that I wanted to talk with her about it some more later."

"I see. And so that's what you think—that she meant one thing and you meant another."

"Well, I know I never agreed to her plan—exactly. That is, I never did any more than just to ask her to wait and not do anything until I could get money enough together to come up there and talk to her some more and get her to go away— the way I suggested."

"But if she wouldn't accede to your plan, then what?"

"Well, then I was going to tell her about Miss X, and beg her to let me go."

"And if she still wouldn't?"

"Well, then I thought I might run away, but I didn't like to think about that very much."

"You know, Clyde, of course, that some here are of the opinion that there was a plot on your part which originated in your mind about this time to conceal your identity and hers and lure her up there to one of those lone lakes in the Adirondacks and slay her or drown her in cold blood, in order that you might be free to marry this Miss X. Any truth in that? Tell this jury—yes or no—which is it?"

"No! No! I never did plot to kill her, or any one," protested Clyde, quite dramatically, and clutching at the arms of his chair and seeking to be as emphatic as possible, since he had been instructed so to do. At the same time he arose in his seat and sought to look stern and convincing, although in his heart and mind was the crying knowledge that he had so plotted, and this it was that most weakened him at this moment—most painfully and horribly weakened him. The eyes of all these people. The eyes of the judge and jury and Mason and all the men and women of the press. And once more his brow was wet and cold and he licked his thin lips nervously and swallowed with difficulty because his throat was dry.

And then it was that piecemeal, and beginning with the series of letters written by Roberta to Clyde after she reached her home and ending with the one demanding that he come for her or she would return to Lycurgus and expose him, Jephson took up the various phases of the "alleged" plot and crime, and now did his best to minimize and finally dispel all that had been testified to so far.

Clyde's suspicious actions in not writing Roberta. Well, he was afraid of complications in connection with his relatives, his work, everything. And the same with his arranging to meet her in Fonda. He had no plan as to any trip with her anywhere in particular at the time. He only thought vaguely of meeting her somewhere—anywhere—and possibly persuading her to leave him. But July arriving and his plan still so indefinite, the first thing that occurred to him was that they might go off to some inexpensive resort somewhere. It was Roberta who in Utica had suggested some of the lakes north of there. It was there in the hotel, not at the railway station, that he had secured some maps and folders—a fatal contention in one sense, for Mason had one folder with a Lycurgus House stamp on the cover, which Clyde had not noticed at the time. And as he was so testifying, Mason was thinking of this. In regard to leaving Lycurgus by a back street—well, there had been a desire to conceal his departure with Roberta, of course, but only to protect her name and his from notoriety. And so with the riding in separate cars, registering as Mr. and Mrs. Clifford Golden, and so on indefinitely throughout the entire list of shifty concealments and evasions. In regard to the two hats, well, the one hat was soiled and seeing one that he liked he bought it. Then when he lost the hat in the accident he naturally put on the other. To be sure, he had owned and carried a camera, and it was true that he had it at the Cranstons' on his first visit there on the eighteenth of June. The only reason he denied having it at first was because he was afraid of being identified with this purely accidental death of Roberta in a way that would be difficult to explain. He had been falsely charged with her murder immediately upon his arrest in the woods, and he was fearful of his entire connection with this ill-fated trip, and not having any lawyer or any one to say a word for him, he thought it best to say nothing and so for the time being had denied everything, although at once on being provided counsel he had confided to his attorneys the true facts of the case.

And so, too, with the missing suit, which because it was wet and muddy he had done up in a bundle in the woods and after reaching the Cranstons' had deposited it behind some stones there, intending to return and secure it and have it dry-cleaned. But on being introduced to Mr. Belknap and Mr. Jephson he had at once told both and they had secured it and had it cleaned for him.

"But now, Clyde, in regard to your plans and your being out on that lake in the first place—let's hear about that now."

And then—quite as Jephson had outlined it to Belknap, came the story of how he and Roberta had reached Utica and afterwards Grass Lake. And yet no plan. He intended, if worst came to worst, to tell her of his great love for Miss X and appeal to her sympathy and understanding to set him free at the same time that he offered to do anything that he could for her. If she refused he intended to defy her and leave Lycurgus, if necessary, and give up everything.

"But when I saw her at Fonda, and later in Utica, looking as tired and worried as she was," and here Clyde was endeavoring to give the ring of sincerity to words carefully supplied him, "and sort of helpless, I began to feel sorry for her again."

"Yes, and then what?"

"Well, I wasn't quite so sure whether in case she refused to let me off I could go through with leaving her."

"Well, what did you decide then?"

"Not anything just then. I listened to what she had to say and I tried to tell her how hard it was going to be for me to do anything much, even if I did go away with her. I only had fifty dollars."

"Yes?"

"And then she began to cry, and I decided I couldn't talk to her any more about it there. She was too run-down and nervous. So I asked her if there wasn't any place she would like to go to for a day or two to brace herself up a little," went on to Clyde, only here on account of the blackness of the lie he was telling he twisted and swallowed in the weak, stigmatic way that was his whenever he was attempting something which was beyond him—any untruth or a feat of skill—and then added: "And she said yes, maybe to one of those lakes up in the Adirondacks—it didn't make much difference which one—if we could afford it. And when I told her, mostly because of the way she was feeling, that I thought we could——"

"Then you really only went up there on her account?"

"Yes, sir, only on account of her."

"I see. Go on."

"Well, then she said if I would go downstairs or somewhere and get some folders we might be able to find a place up there somewhere where it wasn't so expensive."

"And did you?"

"Yes, sir."

"Well, and then what?"

"Well, we looked them over and we finally hit on Grass Lake."

"Who did? The two of you—or she?"

"Well, she took one folder and I took another, and in hers she found an ad about an inn up there where two people could stay for twenty-one dollars a week, or five dollars a day for the two. And I thought we couldn't do much better than that for one day."

"Was one day all you intended to stay?"

"No, sir. Not if she wanted to stay longer. My idea at first was that we might stay one or two days or three. I couldn't tell—whatever time it took me to talk things out with her and make her understand and see where I stood."

"I see. And then . . . ?"

"Well, then we went up to Grass Lake the next morning."

"In separate cars still?"

"Yes, sir—in separate cars."

"And when you got there?"

"Why, we registered."

"How?"

"Clifford Graham and wife."

"Still afraid some one would know who you were?"

"Yes, sir."

"Did you try to disguise your handwriting in any way?"

"Yes, sir—a little."

"But just why did you always use your own initials—C. G.?"

"Well, I thought that the initials on my bag should be the same as the initials on the register, and still not be my name either."

"I see. Clever in one sense, not so clever in another—just half clever, which is the worst of all." At this Mason half rose in his seat as though to object, but evidently changing his mind, sank slowly back again. And once more Jephson's right eye swiftly and inquiringly swept the jury to his right. "Well, did you finally explain to her that you wanted to be done with it all as you had planned—or did you not?"

"I wanted to talk to her about it just after we got there if I could—the next morning, anyhow—but just as soon as we got off up there and got settled she kept saying to me that if I would only marry her then—that she would not want to stay married long—that she was so sick and worried and felt so bad—that all she wanted to do was to get through and give the baby a name, and after that she would go away and let me go my way, too."

"And then?"

"Well, and then—then we went out on the lake——"

"Which lake, Clyde?"

"Why, Grass Lake. We went out for a row after we got there."

"Right away? In the afternoon?"

"Yes, sir. She wanted to go. And then while we were out there rowing around——" (He paused.)

"Yes, go on."

"She got to crying again, and she seemed so much up against it and looked so sick and so worried that I decided that after all she was right and I was wrong—that it wouldn't be right, on account of the baby and all, not to marry her, and so I thought I had better do it."

"I see. A change of heart. And did you tell her that then and there?"

"No, sir."

"And why not? Weren't you satisfied with the trouble you had caused her so far?"

"Yes, sir. But you see just as I was going to talk to her at that time I got to thinking of all the things I had been thinking before I came up."

"What, for instance?"

"Why, Miss X and my life in Lycurgus, and what we'd be up against in case we did go away this way."

"Yes."

"And . . . well . . . and then I couldn't just tell her then—not that day, anyhow."

"Well, when did you tell her then?"

"Well, I told her not to cry any more—that I thought maybe it would be all right if she gave me twenty-four hours more to think things all out—that maybe we'd be able to settle on something."

"And then?"

"Well, then she said after a while that she didn't care for Grass Lake. She wished we would go away from there."

"*She* did?"

"Yes. And then we got out the maps again and I asked a fellow at the hotel there if he knew about the lakes up there. And he said of all the lakes around there Big Bittern was the most beautiful. I had seen it once, and I told Roberta about it and what the man said, and then she asked why didn't we go there."

"And is that why you went there?"

"Yes, sir."

"No other reason?"

"No, sir—none—except that it was back, or south, and we were going that way anyhow."

"I see. And that was Thursday, July eighth?"

"Yes, sir."

"Well, now, Clyde, as you have seen, it has been charged

here that you took Miss Alden to and out on that lake with
the sole and premeditated intent of killing her—murdering
her—finding some unobserved and quiet spot and then first
striking her with your camera, or an oar, or club, or stone
maybe, and then drowning her. Now, what have you to say to
that? Is that true, or isn't it?"

"No, sir! It's not true!" returned Clyde, clearly and emphatically. "I never went there of my own accord in the first
place, and I only went there because she didn't like Grass
Lake." And here, because he had been sinking down in his
chair, he pulled himself up and looked at the jury and the
audience with what measure of strength and conviction he
could summon—as previously he had been told to do. At
the same time he added: "And I wanted to please her in any
way that I could so that she might be a little more cheerful."

"Were you still as sorry for her on this Thursday as you had
been the day before?"

"Yes, sir—more, I think."

"And had you definitely made up your mind by then as to
what you wanted to do?"

"Yes, sir."

"Well, and just what was that?"

"Well, I had decided to play as fair as I could. I had been
thinking about it all night, and I realized how badly she
would feel and I too if I didn't do the right thing by her—because she had said three or four times that if I didn't she
would kill herself. And I had made up my mind that morning
that whatever else happened that day, I was going to
straighten the whole thing out."

"This was at Grass Lake. You were still in the hotel on
Thursday morning?"

"Yes, sir."

"And you were going to tell her just what?"

"Well, that I knew that I hadn't treated her quite right and
that I was sorry—besides, that her offer was fair enough, and
that if after what I was going to tell her she still wanted me,
I would go away with her and marry her. But that I had to
tell her first the real reason for my changing as I had—that I
had been and still was in love with another girl and that I

couldn't help it—that probably whether I married her or not——"

"Miss Alden you mean?"

"Yes, sir—that I would always go on loving this other girl, because I just couldn't get her out of my mind. But just the same, if that didn't make any difference to her, that I would marry her even if I couldn't love her any more as I once did. That was all."

"But what about Miss X?"

"Well, I had thought about her too, but I thought she was better off and could stand it easier. Besides, I thought perhaps Roberta would let me go and we could just go on being friends and I would help her all I could."

"Had you decided just where you would marry her?"

"No, sir. But I knew there were plenty of towns below Big Bittern and Grass Lake."

"But were you going to do that without one single word to Miss X beforehand?"

"Well, no, sir—not exactly. I figured that if Roberta wouldn't let me off but didn't mind my leaving her for a few days, I would go down to where Miss X lived and tell her, and then come back. But if she objected to that, why then I was going to write Miss X a letter and explain how it was and then go on and get married to Roberta."

"I see. But, Clyde, among other bits of testimony here, there was that letter found in Miss Alden's coat pocket—the one written on Grass Lake Inn stationery and addressed to her mother, in which she told her that she was about to be married. Had you already told her up there at Grass Lake that morning that you were going to marry her for sure?"

"No, sir. Not exactly, but I did say on getting up that day that it was the deciding day for us and that she was going to be able to decide for herself whether she wanted me to marry her or not."

"Oh, I see. So that's it," smiled Jephson, as though greatly relieved. (And Mason and Newcomb and Burleigh and State Senator Redmond all listening with the profoundest attention, now exclaimed, *sotto voce* and almost in unison: "Of all the bunk!")

"Well, now we come to the trip itself. You have heard the testimony here and the dark motive and plotting that has been attributed to every move in connection with it. Now I want you to tell it in your own way. It has been testified here that you took both bags—yours and hers—up there with you but that you left hers at Gun Lodge when you got there and took your own out on the lake in that boat with you. Now just why did you do that? Please speak so that all of the jurymen can hear you."

"Well, the reason for that was," and here once more his throat became so dry that he could scarcely speak, "we didn't know whether we could get any lunch at Big Bittern, so we decided to take some things along with us from Grass Lake. Her bag was packed full of things, but there was room in mine. Besides, it had my camera with the tripod outside. So I decided to leave hers and take mine."

"*You* decided?"

"Well, I asked her what she thought and she said she thought that was best."

"Where was it you asked her that?"

"On the train coming down."

"And did you know then that you were coming back to Gun Lodge after going out on the lake?"

"Yes, sir, I did. We had to. There was no other road. They told us that at Grass Lake."

"And in riding over to Big Bittern—do you recall the testimony of the driver who drove you over—that you were 'very nervous' and that you asked him whether there were many people over there that day?"

"I recall it, yes, sir, but I wasn't nervous at all. I may have asked about the people, but I can't see anything wrong with that. It seems to me that any one might ask that."

"And so it seems to me," echoed Jephson. "Then what happened after you registered at Big Bittern Inn and got into that boat and went out on the lake with Miss Alden? Were you or she especially preoccupied or nervous or in any state different from that of any ordinary person who goes out on a lake to row? Were you particularly happy or particularly gloomy, or what?"

"Well, I don't think I was especially gloomy—no, sir. I was

thinking of all I was going to tell her, of course, and of what was before me either way she decided. I wasn't exactly gay, I guess, but I thought it would be all right whichever way things went. I had decided that I was willing to marry her."

"And how about her? Was she quite cheerful?"

"Well—yes, sir. She seemed to feel much happier for some reason."

"And what did you talk about?"

"Oh, about the lake first—how beautiful it was and where we would have our lunch when we were ready for it. And then we rowed along the west shore looking for water lilies. She was so happy that I hated to bring up anything just then, and so we just kept on rowing until about two, when we stopped for lunch."

"Just where was that? Just get up and trace on the map with that pointer there just where you did go and how long you stopped and for what."

And so Clyde, pointer in hand and standing before the large map of the lake and region which particularly concerned this tragedy, now tracing in detail the long row along the shore, a group of trees, which, after having lunch, they had rowed to see—a beautiful bed of water lilies which they had lingered over—each point at which they had stopped, until reaching Moon Cove at about five in the afternoon, they had been so entranced by its beauty that they had merely sat and gazed, as he said. Afterwards, in order that he might take some pictures, they had gone ashore in the woods nearby—he all the while preparing himself to tell Roberta of Miss X and ask her for her final decision. And then having left the bag on shore for a few moments while they rowed out and took some snapshots in the boat, they had drifted in the calm of the water and the stillness and beauty until finally he had gathered sufficient courage to tell her what was in his heart. And at first, as he now said, Roberta seemed greatly startled and depressed and began crying a little, saying that perhaps it was best for her not to live any longer—she felt so miserable. But, afterwards, when he had impressed on her the fact that he was really sorry and perfectly willing to make amends, she had suddenly changed and begun to grow more cheerful, and then of a sudden, in a burst of tenderness and gratefulness—

he could not say exactly—she had jumped up and tried to come to him. Her arms were outstretched and she moved as if to throw herself at his feet or into his lap. But just then, her foot, or her dress, had caught and she had stumbled. And he—camera in hand—(a last minute decision or legal precaution on the part of Jephson)—had risen instinctively to try to catch her and stop her fall. Perhaps—he would not be able to say here—her face or hand had struck the camera. At any rate, the next moment, before he quite understood how it all happened, and without time for thought or action on his part or hers, both were in the water and the boat, which had overturned, seemed to have struck Roberta, for she seemed to be stunned.

"I called to her to try to get to the boat—it was moving away—to take hold of it, but she didn't seem to hear me or understand what I meant. I was afraid to go too near her at first because she was striking out in every direction—and before I could swim ten strokes forward her head had gone down once and come up and then gone down again for a second time. By then the boat had floated all of thirty or forty feet away and I knew that I couldn't get her into that. And then I decided that if I wanted to save myself I had better swim ashore."

And once there, as he now narrated, it suddenly occurred to him how peculiar and suspicious were all the circumstances surrounding his present position. He suddenly realized, as he now said, how bad the whole thing looked from the beginning. The false registering. The fact his bag was there—hers not. Besides, to return now meant that he would have to explain and it would become generally known—and everything connected with his life would go—Miss X, his work, his social position—all—whereas, if he said nothing (and here it was, and for the first time, as he now swore, that this thought occurred to him), it might be assumed that he too had drowned. In view of this fact and that any physical help he might now give her would not restore her to life, and that acknowledgment would mean only trouble for him and shame for her, he decided to say nothing. And so, to remove all traces, he had taken off his clothes and wrung them out and wrapped them for packing as best he could. Next, having left the tripod on shore with his bag, he decided to hide that, and did. His first straw hat, the one without the lining (but about which absent lining he now declared he knew nothing), had been lost with the overturning of the boat, and so now he had put on the extra one he had with him, although he also had a cap which he might have worn. (He usually carried an extra hat on a trip because so often, it seemed, something happened to one.) Then he had ventured to walk south through the woods toward a railroad which he thought cut through the woods in that direction. He had not known of any automobile road through there then, and as for making for the Cranstons' so directly, he confessed quite simply that he would naturally have gone there. They were his friends and he wanted to get off somewhere where he could think about this terrible thing that had descended upon him so suddenly out of a clear sky.

And then having testified to so much—and no more appearing to occur either to Jephson or himself—the former after a pause now turned and said, most distinctly and yet somehow quietly:

"Now, Clyde, you have taken a solemn oath before this jury, this judge, all these people here, and above all your God, to tell the truth, the whole truth, and nothing but the truth. You realize what that means, don't you?"

"Yes, sir, I do."

"You swear before God that you did not strike Roberta Alden in that boat?"

"I swear. I did not."

"Or throw her into that lake?"

"I swear it. I did not."

"Or willfully or willingly in any way attempt to upset that boat or in any other fashion bring about the death that she suffered?"

"I swear it!" cried Clyde, emphatically and emotionally.

"You swear that it was an accident—unpremeditated and undesigned by you?"

"I do," lied Clyde, who felt that in fighting for his life he was telling a part of the truth, for that accident was unpremeditated and undesigned. It had not been as he had planned and he could swear to that.

And then Jephson, running one of his large strong hands over his face and looking blandly and nonchalantly around upon the court and jury, the while he compressed his thin lips into a long and meaningful line, announced: "The prosecution may take the witness."

# Chapter XXV

THE MOOD of Mason throughout the entire direct examination was that of a restless harrier anxious to be off at the heels of its prey—of a foxhound within the last leap of its kill. A keen and surging desire to shatter this testimony, to show it to be from start to finish the tissue of lies that in part at least it was, now animated him. And no sooner had Jephson concluded than he leaped up and confronted Clyde, who, seeing him blazing with this desire to undo him, felt as though he was about to be physically attacked.

"Griffiths, you had that camera in your hand at the time she came toward you in the boat?"

"Yes, sir."

"She stumbled and fell and you accidentally struck her with it?"

"Yes."

"I don't suppose in your truthful and honest way you remember telling me there in the woods on the shore of Big Bittern that you never had a camera?"

"Yes, sir—I remember that."

"And that was a lie, of course?"

"Yes, sir."

"And told with all the fervor and force that you are now telling this other lie?"

"I'm not lying. I've explained why I said that."

"You've explained why you said that! You've explained why you said that! And because you lied there you expect to be believed here, do you?"

Belknap rose to object, but Jephson pulled him down.

"Well, this is the truth, just the same."

"And no power under heaven could make you tell another lie here, of course—not a strong desire to save yourself from the electric chair?"

Clyde blanched and quivered slightly; he blinked his red, tired eyelids. "Well, I might, maybe, but not under oath, I don't think."

"You don't think! Oh, I see. Lie all you want wherever you

are—and at any time—and under any circumstances—except when you're on trial for murder!"

"No, sir. It isn't that. But what I just said is so."

"And you swear on the Bible, do you, that you experienced a change of heart?"

"Yes, sir."

"That Miss Alden was very sad and that was what moved you to experience this change of heart?"

"Yes, sir. That's how it was."

"Well, now, Griffiths, when she was up there in the country and waiting for you—she wrote you all those letters there, did she not?"

"Yes, sir."

"You received one on an average of every two days, didn't you?"

"Yes, sir."

"And you knew she was lonely and miserable there, didn't you?"

"Yes, sir—but then I've explained——"

"Oh, you've explained! You mean your lawyers have explained it for you! Didn't they coach you day after day in that jail over there as to how you were to answer when the time came?"

"No, sir, they didn't!" replied Clyde, defiantly, catching Jephson's eye at this moment.

"Well, then when I asked you up there at Bear Lake how it was that this girl met her death—why didn't you tell me then and save all this trouble and suspicion and investigation? Don't you think the public would have listened more kindly and believingly there than it will now after you've taken five long months to think it all out with the help of two lawyers?"

"But I didn't think it out with any lawyers," persisted Clyde, still looking at Jephson, who was supporting him with all his mental strength. "I've just explained why I did that."

"You've explained! You've explained!" roared Mason, almost beside himself with the knowledge that this false explanation was sufficient of a shield or barrier for Clyde to hide behind whenever he found himself being too hard pressed—the little rat! And so now he fairly quivered with baffled rage as he proceeded.

"And before you went up—while she was writing them to you—you considered them sad, didn't you?"

"Why, yes, sir. That is"—he hesitated incautiously—"some parts of them anyhow."

"Oh, I see—only some parts of them now. I thought you just said you considered them sad."

"Well, I do."

"And did."

"Yes, sir—and did." But Clyde's eyes were beginning to wander nervously in the direction of Jephson, who was fixing him as with a beam of light.

"Remember her writing you this?" And here Mason picked up and opened one of the letters and began reading: "Clyde—I shall certainly die, dear, if you don't come. I am so much alone. I am nearly crazy now. I wish I could go away and never return or trouble you any more. But if you would only telephone me, even so much as once every other day, since you won't write. And when I need you and a word of encouragement so." Mason's voice was mellow. It was sad. One could feel, as he spoke, the wave of passing pity that was moving as sound and color not only through him but through every spectator in the high, narrow courtroom. "Does that seem at all sad to you?"

"Yes, sir, it does."

"Did it then?"

"Yes, sir, it did."

"You knew it was sincere, didn't you?" snarled Mason.

"Yes, sir. I did."

"Then why didn't a little of that pity that you claim moved you so deeply out there in the center of Big Bittern move you down there in Lycurgus to pick up the telephone there in Mrs. Peyton's house where you were and reassure that lonely girl by so much as a word that you were coming? Was it because your pity for her then wasn't as great as it was after she wrote you that threatening letter? Or was it because you had a plot and you were afraid that too much telephoning to her might attract attention? How was it that you had so much pity all of a sudden up at Big Bittern, but none at all down there at Lycurgus? Is it something you can turn on and off like a faucet?"

"I never said I had none at all," replied Clyde, defiantly, having just received an eye-flash from Jephson.

"Well, you left her to wait until she had to threaten you because of her own terror and misery."

"Well, I've admitted that I didn't treat her right."

"Ha, ha! Right! *Right!* And because of that admission, and in face of all the other testimony we've had here, your own included, you expect to walk out of here a free man, do you?"

Belknap was not to be restrained any longer. His objection came—and with bitter vehemence he addressed the Judge: "This is infamous, your Honor. Is the district attorney to be allowed to make a speech with every question?"

"I heard no objection," countered the court. "The district attorney will frame his questions properly."

Mason took the rebuke lightly and turned again to Clyde. "In that boat there in the center of Big Bittern you have testified that you had in your hand that camera that you once denied owning?"

"Yes, sir."

"And she was in the stern of the boat?"

"Yes, sir."

"Bring in that boat, will you, Burton?" he called to Burleigh at this point, and forthwith four deputies from the district attorney's office retired through a west door behind the judge's rostrum and soon returned carrying the identical boat in which Clyde and Roberta had sat, and put it down before the jury. And as they did so Clyde chilled and stared. The identical boat! He blinked and quivered as the audience stirred, stared and strained, an audible wave of curiosity and interest passing over the entire room. And then Mason, taking the camera and shaking it up and down, exclaimed: "Well, here you are now, Griffiths! The camera you never owned. Step down here into this boat and take this camera here and show the jury just where you sat, and where Miss Alden sat. And exactly, if you can, how and where it was that you struck Miss Alden and where and about how she fell."

"Object!" declared Belknap.

A long and wearisome legal argument, finally terminating in the judge allowing this type of testimony to be continued for a while at least. And at the conclusion of it, Clyde declaring: "I didn't intentionally strike her with it though"—to which Mason replied: "Yes, we heard you testify that way"—then Clyde stepping down and after being directed here and there finally stepping into the boat at the middle seat and seating himself while three men held it straight.

"And now, Newcomb—I want you to come here and sit wherever Miss Alden was supposed to sit and take any position which he describes as having been taken by her."

"Yes, sir," said Newcomb, coming forward and seating himself while Clyde vainly sought to catch Jephson's eye but could not since his own back was partially turned from him.

"And now, Griffiths," went on Mason, "just you show Mr. Newcomb here how Miss Alden arose and came toward you. Direct him."

And then Clyde, feeling weak and false and hated, arising again and in a nervous and angular way—the eerie strangeness of all this affecting him to the point of unbelievable awkwardness—attempting to show Newcomb just how Roberta had gotten up and half walked and half crawled, then had stumbled and fallen. And after that, with the camera in his hand, attempting to show as nearly as he could recall, how unconsciously his arm had shot out and he had struck Roberta, he scarcely knowing where—on the chin and cheek maybe, he was not sure, but not intentionally, of course, and not with sufficient force really to injure her, he thought at the time. But just here a long wrangle between Belknap and Mason as to the competency of such testimony since Clyde declared that he could not remember clearly—but Oberwaltzer finally allowing the testimony on the ground that it would show, relatively, whether a light or heavy push or blow was required in order to upset any one who might be "lightly" or "loosely" poised.

"But how in Heaven's name are these antics as here demonstrated on a man of Mr. Newcomb's build to show what would follow in the case of a girl of the size and weight of Miss Alden?" persisted Belknap.

"Well, then we'll put a girl of the size and weight of Miss Alden in here." And at once calling for Zillah Saunders and putting her in Newcomb's place. But Belknap none-the-less proceeding with:

"And what of that? The conditions aren't the same. This boat isn't on the water. No two people are going to be alike in their resistance or their physical responses to accidental blows."

"Then you refuse to allow this demonstration to be made?" (This was from Mason, turning and cynically inquiring.)

"Oh, make it if you choose. It doesn't mean anything though, as anybody can see," persisted Belknap, suggestively.

And so Clyde, under directions from Mason, now pushing at Zillah, "about as hard," (he thought) as he had accidentally pushed at Roberta. And she falling back a little—not much— but in so doing being able to lay a hand on each side of the boat and so save herself. And the jury, in spite of Belknap's thought that his contentions would have counteracted all this, gathering the impression that Clyde, on account of his guilt and fear of death, was probably attempting to conjure something that had been much more viciously executed, to be sure. For had not the doctors sworn to the probable force of this and another blow on the top of the head? And had not Burton Burleigh testified to having discovered a hair in the camera? And how about the cry that woman had heard? How about that?

But with that particular incident the court was adjourned for this day.

On the following morning at the sound of the gavel, there was Mason, as fresh and vigorous and vicious as ever. And Clyde, after a miserable night in his cell and much bolstering by Jephson and Belknap, determined to be as cool and insistent and innocent-appearing as he could be, but with no real heart for the job, so convinced was he that local sentiment in its entirety was against him—that he was believed to be guilty. And with Mason beginning most savagely and bitterly:

"You still insist that you experienced a change of heart, do you, Griffiths?"

"Yes, sir, I do."

"Ever hear of people being resuscitated after they have apparently drowned?"

"I don't quite understand."

"You know, of course, that people who are supposed to be drowned, who go down for the last time and don't come up, are occasionally gotten out of the water and revived, brought back to life by first-aid methods—working their arms and rolling them over a log or a barrel. You've heard of that, haven't you?"

"Yes, sir, I think I have. I've heard of people being brought back to life after they're supposed to be drowned, but I don't think I ever heard just how."

"You never did?"

"No, sir."

"Or how long they could stay under water and still be revived?"

"No, sir. I never did."

"Never heard, for instance, that a person who had been in the water as long as fifteen minutes might still be brought to?"

"No, sir."

"So it never occurred to you after you swam to shore yourself that you might still call for aid and so save her life even then?"

"No, sir, it didn't occur to me. I thought she was dead by then."

"I see. But when she was still alive out there in the water—how about that? You're a pretty good swimmer, aren't you?"

"Yes, sir, I swim fairly well."

"Well enough, for instance, to save yourself by swimming over five hundred feet with your shoes and clothes on. Isn't that so?"

"Well, I did swim that distance then—yes, sir."

"Yes, you did indeed—and pretty good for a fellow who couldn't swim thirty-five feet to an overturned boat, I'll say," concluded Mason.

Here Jephson waved aside Belknap's suggestion that he move to have this comment stricken out.

Clyde was now dragged over his various boating and swimming experiences and made to tell how many times he had gone out on lakes in craft as dangerous as canoes and had never had an accident.

"The first time you took Roberta out on Crum Lake was in a canoe, wasn't it?"

"Yes, sir."

"But you had no accident then?"

"No, sir."

"You cared for her then very much, didn't you?"

"Yes, sir."

"But the day she was drowned in Big Bittern, in this solid, round-bottomed row boat, you didn't care for her any more."

"Well, I've said how I felt then."

"And of course there couldn't be any relation between the fact that on Crum Lake you cared for her but on Big Bittern——"

"I said how I felt then."

"But you wanted to get rid of her just the same, didn't you? The moment she was dead to run away to that other girl. You don't deny that, do you?"

"I've explained why I did that," reiterated Clyde.

"Explained! Explained! And you expect any fair-minded, decent, intelligent person to believe that explanation, do you?" Mason was fairly beside himself with rage and Clyde did not venture to comment as to that. The Judge anticipated Jephson's objection to this and bellowed, "Objection sustained." But Mason went right on. "You couldn't have been just a little careless, could you, Griffiths, in the handling of the boat and upset it yourself, say?" He drew near and leered.

"No, sir, I wasn't careless. It was an accident that I couldn't avoid." Clyde was quite cool, though pale and tired.

"An accident. Like that other accident out there in Kansas City, for instance. You're rather familiar with accidents of that kind, aren't you, Griffiths?" queried Mason sneeringly and slowly.

"I've explained how that happened," replied Clyde nervously.

"You're rather familiar with accidents that result in death to girls, aren't you? Do you always run away when one of them dies?"

"Object," yelled Belknap, leaping to his feet.

"Objection sustained," called Oberwaltzer sharply. "There

is nothing before this court concerning any other accident. The prosecution will confine itself more closely to the case in hand."

"Griffiths," went on Mason, pleased with the way he had made a return to Jephson for his apology for the Kansas City accident, "when that boat upset after that accidental blow of yours and you and Miss Alden fell into the water—how far apart were you?"

"Well, I didn't notice just then."

"Pretty close, weren't you? Not much more than a foot or two, surely—the way you stood there in the boat?"

"Well, I didn't notice. Maybe that, yes, sir."

"Close enough to have grabbed her and hung on to her if you had wanted to, weren't you? That's what you jumped up for, wasn't it, when she started to fall out?"

"Yes, that's what I jumped up for," replied Clyde heavily, "but I wasn't close enough to grab her. I know I went right under, and when I came up she was some little distance away."

"Well, how far exactly? As far as from here to this end of the jury box or that end, or half way, or what?"

"Well, I say I didn't notice, quite. About as far from here to that end, I guess," he lied, stretching the distance by at least eight feet.

"Not really!" exclaimed Mason, pretending to evince astonishment. "This boat here turns over, you both fall in the water close together, and when you come up you and she are nearly twenty feet apart. Don't you think your memory is getting a little the best of you there?"

"Well, that's the way it looked to me when I came up."

"Well, now, after that boat turned over and you both came up, where were you in relation to *it*? Here is the boat now and where were you out there in the audience, as to distance, I mean?"

"Well, as I say, I didn't exactly notice when I first came up," returned Clyde, looking nervously and dubiously at the space before him. Most certainly a trap was being prepared for him. "About as far as from here to that railing beyond your table, I guess."

"About thirty to thirty-five feet then," suggested Mason, slyly and hopefully.

"Yes, sir. About that maybe. I couldn't be quite sure."

"And now with you over there and the boat here, where was Miss Alden at that time?"

And Clyde now sensed that Mason must have some geometric or mathematic scheme in mind whereby he proposed to establish his guilt. And at once he was on his guard, and looking in the direction of Jephson. At the same time he could not see how he was to put Roberta too far away either. He had said she couldn't swim. Wouldn't she be nearer the boat than he was? Most certainly. He leaped foolishly— wildly—at the thought that it might be best to say that she was about half that distance—not more, very likely. And said so. And at once Mason proceeded with:

"Well, then she was not more than fifteen feet or so from you or the boat."

"No, sir, maybe not. I guess not."

"Well then, do you mean to say that you couldn't have swum that little distance and buoyed her up until you could reach the boat just fifteen feet beyond her?"

"Well, as I say, I was a little dazed when I came up and she was striking about and screaming so."

"But there was that boat—not more than thirty-five feet away, according to your own story—and a mighty long way for a boat to move in that time, I'll say. And do you mean to say that when you could swim five hundred feet to shore afterwards that you couldn't have swum to that boat and pushed it to her in time for her to save herself? She was struggling to keep herself up, wasn't she?"

"Yes, sir. But I was rattled at first," pleaded Clyde, gloomily, conscious of the eyes of all the jurors and all the spectators fixed upon his face, "and . . . and . . ." (because of the general strain of the suspicion and incredulity now focused as a great force upon him, his nerve was all but failing him, and he was hesitating and stumbling) . . . "I didn't think quite quick enough I guess, what to do. Besides I was afraid if I went near her . . ."

"I know. A mental and moral coward," sneered Mason. "Besides very slow to think when it's to your advantage to be slow and swift when it's to your advantage to be swift. Is that it?"

"No, sir."

"Well, then, if it isn't, just tell me this, Griffiths, why was it, after you got out of the water a few moments later you had sufficient presence of mind to stop and bury that tripod before starting through the woods, whereas, when it came to rescuing her you got rattled and couldn't do a thing? How was it that you could get so calm and calculating the moment you set your foot on land? What can you say to that?"

"Well . . . a . . . I told you that afterwards I realized that there was nothing else to do."

"Yes, we know all about that. But doesn't it occur to you that it takes a pretty cool head after so much panic in the water to stop at a moment like that and take such a precaution as that—burying that tripod? How was it that you could think so well of that and not think anything about the boat a few moments before?"

"Well . . . but . . ."

"You didn't want her to live, in spite of your alleged change of heart! Isn't that it?" yelled Mason. "Isn't that the black, sad truth? She was drowning, as you wanted her to drown, and you just let her drown! Isn't that so?"

He was fairly trembling as he shouted this, and Clyde, the actual boat before him and Roberta's eyes and cries as she sank coming back to him with all their pathetic and horrible force, now shrank and cowered in his seat—the closeness of Mason's interpretation of what had really happened terrifying him. For never, even to Jephson and Belknap, had he admitted that when Roberta was in the water he had not wished to save her. Changelessly and secretively he had insisted he had wanted to but that it had all happened so quickly, and he was so dazed and frightened by her cries and movements, that he had not been able to do anything before she was gone.

"I . . . I wanted to save her," he mumbled, his face quite gray, "but . . . but . . . as I said, I was dazed . . . and . . . and . . ."

"Don't you know that you're lying!" shouted Mason, leaning still closer, his stout arms aloft, his disfigured face glowering and scowling like some avenging nemesis or fury of gargoyle design—"that you deliberately and with cold-hearted cunning allowed that poor, tortured girl to die there when you might have rescued her as easily as you could have swum fifty of those five hundred feet you did swim in order to save yourself?" For by now he was convinced that he knew just how Clyde had actually slain Roberta, something in his manner and mood convincing him, and he was determined to drag it out of him if he could. And although Belknap was instantly on his feet with a protest that his client was being unfairly prejudiced in the eyes of the jury and that he was really entitled to—and now demanded—a mistrial—which complaint Justice Oberwaltzer eventually overruled—still Clyde had time to reply, but most meekly and feebly: "No! No! I didn't. I wanted to save her if I could." Yet his whole manner, as each and every juror noted, was that of one who was not really telling the truth, who was really all of the mental and moral coward that Belknap had insisted he was—but worse yet, really guilty of Roberta's death. For after all, asked each juror of himself as he listened, why couldn't he have saved her if he was strong enough to swim to shore afterwards—or at least have swum to and secured the boat and helped her to take hold of it?

"She only weighed a hundred pounds, didn't she?" went on Mason feverishly.

"Yes, I think so."

"And you—what did you weigh at the time?"

"About a hundred and forty," replied Clyde.

"And a hundred and forty pound man," sneered Mason, turning to the jury, "is afraid to go near a weak, sick, hundred-pound little girl who is drowning, for fear she will cling to him and drag him under! And a perfectly good boat, strong enough to hold three or four up, within fifteen or twenty feet! How's that?"

And to emphasize it and let it sink in, he now paused, and took from his pocket a large white handkerchief, and after wiping his neck and face and wrists—since they were quite damp from his emotional and physical efforts—turned to Burton Burleigh and called: "You might as well have this boat taken out of here, Burton. We're not going to need it for a little while anyhow." And forthwith the four deputies carried it out.

And then, having recovered his poise, he once more turned

to Clyde and began with: "Griffiths, you knew the color and feel of Roberta Alden's hair pretty well, didn't you? You were intimate enough with her, weren't you?"

"I know the color of it or I think I do," replied Clyde wincing—an anguished chill at the thought of it affecting him almost observably.

"And the feel of it, too, didn't you?" persisted Mason. "In those very loving days of yours before Miss X came along—you must have touched it often enough."

"I don't know whether I did or not," replied Clyde, catching a glance from Jephson.

"Well, roughly. You must know whether it was coarse or fine—silky or coarse. You know that, don't you?"

"It was silky, yes."

"Well, here's a lock of it," he now added more to torture Clyde than anything else—to wear him down nervously—and going to his table where was an envelope and from it extracting a long lock of light brown hair. "Don't that look like her hair?" And now he shoved it forward at Clyde who shocked and troubled withdrew from it as from some unclean or dangerous thing—yet a moment after sought to recover himself—the watchful eyes of the jury having noted all. "Oh, don't be afraid," persisted Mason, sardonically. "It's only your dead love's hair."

And shocked by the comment—and noting the curious eyes of the jury, Clyde took it in his hand. "That looks and feels like her hair, doesn't it?" went on Mason.

"Well, it looks like it anyhow," returned Clyde shakily.

"And now here," continued Mason, stepping quickly to the table and returning with the camera in which between the lid and the taking mechanism were caught the two threads of Roberta's hair put there by Burleigh, and then holding it out to him. "Just take this camera. It's yours even though you did swear that it wasn't—and look at those two hairs there. See them?" And he poked the camera at Clyde as though he might strike him with it. "They were caught in there—presumably—at the time you struck her so lightly that it made all those wounds on her face. Can't you tell the jury whether those hairs are hers or not?"

"I can't say," replied Clyde most weakly.

"What's that? Speak up. Don't be so much of a moral and mental coward. Are they or are they not?"

"I can't say," repeated Clyde—but not even looking at them.

"Look at them. Look at them. Compare them with these others. We know these are hers. And you know that these in this camera are, don't you? Don't be so squeamish. You've often touched her hair in real life. She's dead. They won't bite you. Are these two hairs—or are they not—the same as these other hairs here—which we know are hers—the same color—same feel—all? Look! Answer! Are they or are they not?"

But Clyde, under such pressure and in spite of Belknap, being compelled to look and then feel them too. Yet cautiously replying, "I wouldn't be able to say. They look and feel a little alike, but I can't tell."

"Oh, can't you? And even when you know that when you struck her that brutal vicious blow with that camera—these two hairs caught there and held."

"But I didn't strike her any vicious blow," insisted Clyde, now observing Jephson—"and I can't say." He was saying to himself that he would not allow himself to be bullied in this way by this man—yet, at the same time, feeling very weak and sick. And Mason, triumphant because of the psychologic effect, if nothing more, returning the camera and lock to the table and remarking, "Well, it's been amply testified to that those two hairs were in that camera when found in the water. And you yourself swear that it was last in your hand before it reached the water."

He turned to think of something else—some new point with which to rack Clyde and now began once more:

"Griffiths, in regard to that trip south through the woods, what time was it when you got to Three Mile Bay?"

"About four in the morning, I think—just before dawn."

"And what did you do between then and the time that boat down there left?"

"Oh, I walked around."

"In Three Mile Bay?"

"No, sir—just outside of it."

"In the woods, I suppose, waiting for the town to wake up so you wouldn't look so much out of place. Was that it?"

"Well, I waited until after the sun came up. Besides I was tired and I sat down and rested for a while."

"Did you sleep well and did you have pleasant dreams?"

"I was tired and I slept a little—yes."

"And how was it you knew so much about the boat and the time and all about Three Mile Bay? Hadn't you familiarized yourself with this data beforehand?"

"Well, everybody knows about the boat from Sharon to Three Mile Bay around there."

"Oh, do they? Any other reason?"

"Well, in looking for a place to get married, both of us saw it," returned Clyde, shrewdly, "but we didn't see that any train went to it. Only to Sharon."

"But you did notice that it was south of Big Bittern?"

"Why, yes—I guess I did," replied Clyde.

"And that that road west of Gun Lodge led south toward it around the lower edge of Big Bittern?"

"Well, I noticed after I got up there that there was a road of some kind or a trail anyhow—but I didn't think of it as a regular road."

"I see. How was it then that when you met those three men in the woods you were able to ask them how far it was to Three Mile Bay?"

"I didn't ask 'em that," replied Clyde, as he had been instructed by Jephson to say. "I asked 'em if they knew any road to Three Mile Bay, and how far it was. I didn't know whether that was the road or not."

"Well, that wasn't how they testified here."

"Well, I don't care what they testified to, that's what I asked 'em just the same."

"It seems to me that according to you all the witnesses are liars and you are the only truthful one in the bunch. . . . Isn't that it? But, when you reached Three Mile Bay, did you stop to eat? You must have been hungry, weren't you?"

"No, I wasn't hungry," replied Clyde, simply.

"You wanted to get away from that place as quickly as possible, wasn't that it? You were afraid that those three men might go up to Big Bittern and having heard about Miss Alden tell about having seen you—wasn't that it?"

"No, that wasn't it. But I didn't want to stay around there. I've said why."

"I see. But after you got down to Sharon where you felt a little more safe—a little further away, you didn't lose any time in eating, did you? It tasted pretty good all right down there, didn't it?"

"Oh, I don't know about that. I had a cup of coffee and a sandwich."

"And a piece of pie, too, as we've already proved here," added Mason. "And after that you joined the crowd coming up from the depot as though you had just come up from Albany, as you afterwards told everybody. Wasn't that it?"

"Yes, that was it."

"Well, now for a really innocent man who only so recently experienced a kindly change of heart, don't you think you were taking an awful lot of precaution? Hiding away like that and waiting in the dark and pretending that you had just come up from Albany."

"I've explained all that," persisted Clyde.

Mason's next tack was to hold Clyde up to shame for having been willing, in the face of all she had done for him, to register Roberta in three different hotel registers as the unhallowed consort of presumably three different men in three different days.

"Why didn't you take separate rooms?"

"Well, she didn't want it that way. She wanted to be with me. Besides I didn't have any too much money."

"Even so, how could you have so little respect for her there and then be so deeply concerned about her reputation after she was dead that you had to run away and keep the secret of her death all to yourself, in order, as you say, to protect her name and reputation?"

"Your Honor," interjected Belknap, "this isn't a question. It's an oration."

"I withdraw the question," countered Mason, and then went on. "Do you admit, by the way, that you are a mental and moral coward, Griffiths—do you?"

"No, sir. I don't."

"You do not?"

"No, sir."

"Then when you lie, and swear to it, you are just the same as any other person who is not a mental and moral coward, and deserving of all the contempt and punishment due a person who is a perjurer and a false witness. Is that correct?"

"Yes, sir. I suppose so."

"Well, if you are not a mental and moral coward, how can you justify your leaving that girl in that lake—after as you say you accidentally struck her and when you knew how her parents would soon be suffering because of her loss—and not say one word to anybody—just walk off—and hide the tripod and your suit and sneak away like an ordinary murderer? Wouldn't you think that that was the conduct of a man who had plotted and executed murder and was trying to get away with it—if you had heard of it about some one else? Or would you think it was just the sly, crooked trick of a man who was only a mental and moral coward and who was trying to get away from the blame for the accidental death of a girl whom he had seduced and news of which might interfere with his prosperity? Which?"

"Well, I didn't kill her, just the same," insisted Clyde.

"Answer the question!" thundered Mason.

"I ask the court to instruct the witness that he need not answer such a question," put in Jephson, rising and fixing first Clyde and then Oberwaltzer with his eye. "It is purely an argumentative one and has no real bearing on the facts in this case."

"I so instruct," replied Oberwaltzer. "The witness need not answer." Whereupon Clyde merely stared, greatly heartened by this unexpected aid.

"Well, to go on," proceeded Mason, now more nettled and annoyed than ever by this watchful effort on the part of Belknap and Jephson to break the force and significance of his each and every attack, and all the more determined not to be outdone—"you say you didn't intend to marry her if you could help it, before you went up there?"

"Yes, sir."

"That she wanted you to but you hadn't made up your mind?"

"Yes."

"Well, do you recall the cook-book and the salt and pepper

shakers and the spoons and knives and so on that she put in her bag?"

"Yes, sir. I do."

"What do you suppose she had in mind when she left Biltz—with those things in her trunk—that she was going out to live in some hall bedroom somewhere, unmarried, while you came to see her once a week or once a month?"

Before Belknap could object, Clyde shot back the proper answer.

"I can't say what she had in her mind about that."

"You couldn't possibly have told her over the telephone there at Biltz, for instance—after she wrote you that if you didn't come for her she was coming to Lycurgus—that you would marry her?"

"No, sir—I didn't."

"You weren't mental and moral coward enough to be bullied into anything like that, were you?"

"I never said I was a mental and moral coward."

"But you weren't to be bullied by a girl you had seduced?"

"Well, I couldn't feel then that I ought to marry her."

"You didn't think she'd make as good a match as Miss X?"

"I didn't think I ought to marry her if I didn't love her any more."

"Not even to save her honor—and your own decency?"

"Well, I didn't think we could be happy together then."

"That was before your great change of heart, I suppose."

"It was before we went to Utica, yes."

"And while you were still so enraptured with Miss X?"

"I was in love with Miss X—yes."

"Do you recall, in one of those letters to you that you never answered" (and here Mason proceeded to take up and read from one of the first seven letters), "her writing this to you; 'I feel upset and uncertain about everything although I try not to feel so—now that we have our plan and you are going to come for me as you said.' Now just what was she referring to there when she wrote—'now that we have our plan'?"

"I don't know unless it was that I was coming to get her and take her away somewhere temporarily."

"Not to marry her, of course."

"No, I hadn't said so."

"But right after that in this same letter she says: 'On the way up, instead of coming straight home, I decided to stop at Homer to see my sister and brother-in-law, since I am not sure now when I'll see them again, and I want so much that they shall see me respectable or never at all any more.' Now just what do you suppose she meant by that word 're-spectable'? Living somewhere in secret and unmarried and having a child while you sent her a little money, and then coming back maybe and posing as single and innocent or married and her husband dead—or what? Don't you suppose she saw herself married to you, for a time at least, and the child given a name? That 'plan' she mentions couldn't have contemplated anything less than that, could it?"

"Well, maybe as she saw it it couldn't," evaded Clyde. "But I never said I would marry her."

"Well, well—we'll let that rest a minute," went on Mason doggedly. "But now take this," and here he began reading from the tenth letter: "'It won't make any difference to you about your coming a few days sooner than you intended, will it, dear? Even if we have got to get along on a little less, I know we can, for the time I will be with you anyhow, proba-bly no more than six or eight months at the most. I agreed to let you go by then, you know, if you want to. I can be very saving and economical. It can't be any other way now, Clyde, although for your own sake I wish it could.' What do you suppose all that means—'saving and economical'—and not letting you go until after eight months? Living in a hall bed-room and you coming to see her once a week? Or hadn't you really agreed to go away with her and marry her, as she seems to think here?"

"I don't know unless she thought she could make me, maybe," replied Clyde, the while various backwoodsmen and farmers and jurors actually sniffed and sneered, so infuriated were they by the phrase "make me" which Clyde had scarcely noticed. "I never agreed to."

"Unless she could make you. So that was the way you felt about it, was it, Griffiths?"

"Yes, sir."

"You'd swear to that as quick as you would to anything else?"

"Well, I have sworn to it."

And Mason as well as Belknap and Jephson and Clyde himself now felt the strong public contempt and rage that the majority of those present had for him from the start—now surging and shaking all. It filled the room. Yet before him were all the hours Mason needed in which he could pick and choose at random from the mass of testimony as to just what he would quiz and bedevil and torture Clyde with next. And so now, looking over his notes arranged fan wise on the table by Earl Newcomb for his convenience—he now began once more with:

"Griffiths, in your testimony here yesterday, through which you were being led by your counsel, Mr. Jephson" (at this Jephson bowed sardonically). "You talked about that change of heart that you experienced after you encountered Roberta Alden once more at Fonda and Utica back there in July—just as you were starting on this death trip."

Clyde's "yes, sir," came before Belknap could object, but the latter managed to have "death trip" changed to "trip."

"Before going up there with her you hadn't been liking her as much as you might have. Wasn't that the way of it?"

"Not as much as I had at one time—no, sir."

"And just how long—from when to when—was the time in which you really did like her, before you began to dislike her, I mean?"

"Well, from the time I first met her until I met Miss X."

"But not afterwards?"

"Oh, I can't say not entirely afterwards. I cared for her some—a good deal, I guess—but still not as much as I had. I felt more sorry for her than anything else, I suppose."

"And now, let's see—that was between December first last, say, and last April or May—or wasn't it?"

"About that time, I think—yes, sir."

"Well, during that time—December first to April or May first, you were intimate with her, weren't you?"

"Yes, sir."

"Even though you weren't caring for her so much."

"Why—yes, sir," replied Clyde, hesitating slightly, while the rurals jerked and craned at this introduction of the sex crime.

"And yet at nights, and in spite of the fact that she was

alone over there in her little room—as faithful to you, as you yourself have testified, as any one could be—you went off to dances, parties, dinners, and automobile rides, while she sat there."

"Oh, but I wasn't off all the time."

"Oh, weren't you? But you heard the testimony of Tracy and Jill Trumbull, and Frederick Sells, and Frank Harriet, and Burchard Taylor, on this particular point, didn't you?"

"Yes, sir."

"Well, were they all liars, or were they telling the truth?"

"Well, they were telling the truth as near as they could remember, I suppose."

"But they couldn't remember very well—is that it?"

"Well, I wasn't off all the time. Maybe I was gone two or three times a week—maybe four sometimes—not more."

"And the rest you gave to Miss Alden?"

"Yes, sir."

"Is that what she meant in this letter here?" And here he took up another letter from the pile of Roberta's letters, and opening it and holding it before him, read: "'Night after night, almost every night after that dreadful Christmas day when you left me, I was alone nearly always.' Is she lying, or isn't she?" snapped Mason fiercely, and Clyde, sensing the danger of accusing Roberta of lying here, weakly and shamefacedly replied: "No, she isn't lying. But I did spend some evenings with her just the same."

"And yet you heard Mrs. Gilpin and her husband testify here that night after night from December first on Miss Alden was mostly always alone in her room and that they felt sorry for her and thought it so unnatural and tried to get her to join them, but she wouldn't. You heard them testify to that, didn't you?"

"Yes, sir."

"And yet you insist that you were with her some?"

"Yes, sir."

"Yet at the same time loving and seeking the company of Miss X?"

"Yes, sir."

"And trying to get her to marry you?"

"I wanted her to—yes, sir."

"Yet continuing relations with Miss Alden when your other interests left you any time."

"Well . . . yes, sir," once more hesitated Clyde, enormously troubled by the shabby picture of his character which these disclosures seemed to conjure, yet somehow feeling that he was not as bad, or at least had not intended to be, as all this made him appear. Other people did things like that too, didn't they—those young men in Lycurgus society—or they had talked as though they did.

"Well, don't you think your learned counsel found a very mild term for you when they described you as a mental and moral coward?" sneered Mason—and at the same time from the rear of the long narrow courtroom, a profound silence seeming to precede, accompany and follow it,—yet not without an immediate roar of protest from Belknap, came the solemn, vengeful voice of an irate woodsman: "Why don't they kill the God-damned bastard and be done with him?"— And at once Oberwaltzer gaveling for order and ordering the arrest of the offender at the same time that he ordered all those not seated driven from the courtroom—which was done. And then the offender arrested and ordered arraigned on the following morning. And after that, silence, with Mason once more resuming:

"Griffiths, you say when you left Lycurgus you had no intention of marrying Roberta Alden unless you could not arrange it any other way."

"Yes, sir. That was my intention at that time."

"And accordingly you were fairly certain of coming back?"

"Yes, sir—I thought I was."

"Then why did you pack everything in your room in your trunk and lock it?"

"Well . . . well . . . that is," hesitated Clyde, the charge coming so quickly and so entirely apart from what had just been spoken of before that he had scarcely time to collect his wits—"well, you see—I wasn't absolutely sure. I didn't know but what I might have to go whether I wanted to or not."

"I see. And so if you had decided up there unexpectedly— as you did—" (and here Mason smirked on him as much as to say—you think any one believes that?) "you wouldn't have had time to come back and decently pack your things and depart?"

"Well, no, sir—that wasn't the reason either."

"Well then, what was the reason?"

"Well, you see," and here for lack of previous thought on this subject as well as lack of wit to grasp the essentiality of a suitable and plausible answer quickly, Clyde hesitated—as every one—first and foremost Belknap and Jephson—noted—and then went on: "Well, you see—if I had to go away, even for a short time as I thought I might, I decided that I might need whatever I had in a hurry."

"I see. You're quite sure it wasn't that in case the police discovered who Clifford Golden or Carl Graham were, that you might wish to leave quickly?"

"No, sir. It wasn't."

"And so you didn't tell Mrs. Peyton you were giving up the room either, did you?"

"No, sir."

"In your testimony the other day you said something about not having money enough to go up there and take Miss Alden away on any temporary marriage scheme—even one that would last so long as six months."

"Yes, sir."

"When you left Lycurgus to start on the trip, how much did you have?"

"About fifty dollars."

"'About' fifty? Don't you know exactly how much you had?"

"I had fifty dollars—yes, sir."

"And while you were in Utica and Grass Lake and getting down to Sharon afterwards, how much did you spend?"

"I spent about twenty dollars on the trip, I think."

"Don't you know?"

"Not exactly—no, sir—somewhere around twenty dollars, though."

"Well, now let's see about that exactly if we can," went on Mason, and here, once more, Clyde began to sense a trap and grew nervous—for there was all that money given him by Sondra and some of which he had spent, too. "How much was your fare from Fonda to Utica for yourself?"

"A dollar and a quarter."

"And what did you have to pay for your room at the hotel at Utica for you and Roberta?"

"That was four dollars."

"And of course you had dinner that night and breakfast the next morning, which cost you how much?"

"It was about three dollars for both meals."

"Was that all you spent in Utica?" Mason was taking a side glance occasionally at a slip of paper on which he had figures and notes, but which Clyde had not noticed.

"Yes, sir."

"How about the straw hat that it has been proved you purchased while there?"

"Oh, yes, sir, I forgot about that," said Clyde, nervously. "That was two dollars—yes, sir." He realized that he must be more careful.

"And your fares to Grass Lake were, of course, five dollars. Is that right?"

"Yes, sir."

"Then you hired a boat at Grass Lake. How much was that?"

"That was thirty-five cents an hour."

"And you had it how long?"

"Three hours."

"Making one dollar and five cents."

"Yes, sir."

"And then that night at the hotel, they charged you how much? Five dollars, wasn't it?"

"Yes, sir."

"And then didn't you buy that lunch that you carried out in that lake with you up there?"

"Yes, sir. I think that was about sixty cents."

"And how much did it cost you to get to Big Bittern?"

"It was a dollar on the train to Gun Lodge and a dollar on the bus for the two of us to Big Bittern."

"You know these figures pretty well, I see. Naturally, you would. You didn't have much money and it was important. And how much was your fare from Three Mile Bay to Sharon afterwards?"

"My fare was seventy-five cents."

"Did you ever stop to figure this all up exactly?"

"No, sir."

"Well, will you?"

"Well, you know how much it is, don't you?"

"Yes, sir, I do. It is twenty-four dollars and sixty-five cents. You said you spent twenty dollars. But here is a discrepancy of four dollars and sixty-five cents. How do you account for it?"

"Well, I suppose I didn't figure just exactly right," said Clyde, irritated by the accuracy of figures such as these.

But now Mason slyly and softly inquiring: "Oh, yes, Griffiths, I forgot, how much was the boat you hired at Big Bittern?" He was eager to hear what Clyde would have to say as to this, seeing that he had worked hard and long on this pitfall.

"Oh—ah—ah—that is," began Clyde, hesitatingly, for at Big Bittern, as he now recalled, he had not even troubled to inquire the cost of the boat, feeling as he did at the time that neither he nor Roberta were coming back. But now here and in this way it was coming up for the first time. And Mason, realizing that he had caught him here, quickly interpolated a "Yes?" to which Clyde replied, but merely guessing at that: "Why, thirty-five cents an hour—just the same as at Grass Lake—so the boatman said."

But he had spoken too quickly. And he did not know that in reserve was the boatman who was still to testify that he had not stopped to ask the price of the boat. And Mason continued:

"Oh, it was, was it? The boatman told you that, did he?"

"Yes, sir."

"Well now, don't you recall that you never asked the boatman at all? It was not thirty-five cents an hour, but fifty cents. But of course you do not know that because you were in such a hurry to get out on the water and you did not expect to have to come back and pay for it anyway. So you never even asked, you see. Do you see? Do you recall that now?" And here Mason produced a bill that he had gotten from the boatman and waved it in front of Clyde. "It was fifty cents an hour," he repeated. "They charge more than at Grass Lake. But what I want to know is, if you are so familiar with these other figures, as you have just shown that you are, how comes it that you are not familiar with this figure? Didn't you think of the expense of taking her out in a boat and keeping the boat from noon until night?" The attack came so swiftly and bitterly that at once Clyde was confused. He twisted and turned, swallowed and looked nervously at the floor, ashamed to look at Jephson who had somehow failed to coach him as to this.

"Well," bawled Mason, "any explanation to make as to that? Doesn't it strike even you as strange that you can remember every other item of all your expenditures—but not that item?" And now each juror was once more tense and leaning forward. And Clyde noting their interest and curiosity, and most likely suspicion, now returned:

"Well, I don't know just how I came to forget that."

"Oh, no, of course you don't" snorted Mason. "A man who is planning to kill a girl on a lone lake has a lot of things to think of, and it isn't any wonder if you forget a few of them. But you didn't forget to ask the purser the fare to Sharon, once you got to Three Mile Bay, did you?"

"I don't remember if I did or not."

"Well, he remembers. He testified to it here. You bothered to ask the price of the room at Grass Lake. You asked the price of the boat there. You even asked the price of the bus fare to Big Bittern. What a pity you couldn't think to ask the price of the boat at Big Bittern? You wouldn't be so nervous about it now, would you?" and here Mason looked at the jurors as much as to say: You see!

"I just didn't think of it, I guess," repeated Clyde.

"A very satisfactory explanation, I'm sure," went on Mason, sarcastically. And then as swiftly as possible: "I don't suppose you happen to recall an item of thirteen dollars and twenty cents paid for a lunch at the Casino on July ninth—the day after Roberta Alden's death—do you or do you not?" Mason was dramatic, persistent, swift—scarcely giving him time to think or breathe, as he saw it.

At this Clyde almost jumped, so startled was he by this question and charge, for he did not know that they had found out about the lunch. "And do you remember, too," went on Mason, "that over eighty dollars was found on you when you were arrested?"

"Yes, I remember it now," he replied.

As for the eighty dollars he had forgotten. Yet now he said nothing, for he could not think what to say.

"How about that?" went on Mason, doggedly and savagely. "If you only had fifty dollars when you left Lycurgus and over eighty dollars when you were arrested, and you spent twenty-four dollars and sixty-five cents plus thirteen for a lunch, where did you get that extra money from?"

"Well, I can't answer that just now," replied Clyde, sullenly, for he felt cornered and hurt. That was Sondra's money and nothing would drag out of him where he had gotten it.

"Why can't you answer it?" roared Mason. "Where do you think you are, anyhow? And what do you think we are here for? To say what you will or will not answer? You are on trial for your life—don't forget that! You can't play fast and loose with law, however much you may have lied to me. You are here before these twelve men and they are waiting to know. Now, what about it? Where did you get that money?"

"I borrowed it from a friend."

"Well, give his name. What friend?"

"I don't care to."

"Oh, you don't! Well, you're lying about the amount of money you had when you left Lycurgus—that's plain. And under oath, too. Don't forget that! That sacred oath that you respect so much. Isn't that true?"

"No, it isn't," finally observed Clyde, stung to reason by this charge. "I borrowed that money after I got to Twelfth Lake."

"And from whom?"

"Well, I can't say."

"Which makes the statement worthless," retorted Mason.

Clyde was beginning to show a disposition to balk. He had been sinking his voice and each time Mason commanded him to speak up and turn around so the jury could see his face, he had done so, only feeling more and more resentful toward this man who was thus trying to drag out of him every secret he possessed. He had touched on Sondra, and she was still too near his heart to reveal anything that would reflect on her. So now he sat staring down at the jurors somewhat defiantly, when Mason picked up some pictures.

"Remember these?" he now asked Clyde, showing him some of the dim and water-marked reproductions of Roberta besides some views of Clyde and some others—none of them containing the face of Sondra—which were made at the Cranstons' on his first visit, as well as four others made at Bear Lake later, and with one of them showing him holding a banjo, his fingers in position. "Recall where these were made?" asked Mason, showing him the reproduction of Roberta first.

"Yes, I do."

"Where was it?"

"On the south shore of Big Bittern the day we were there." He knew that they were in the camera and had told Belknap and Jephson about them, yet now he was not a little surprised to think that they had been able to develop them.

"Griffiths," went on Mason, "your lawyers didn't tell you that they fished and fished for that camera you swore you didn't have with you before they found that I had it, did they?"

"They never said anything to me about it," replied Clyde.

"Well, that's too bad. I could have saved them a lot of trouble. Well, these were the photos that were found in that camera and that were made just after that change of heart you experienced, you remember?"

"I remember when they were made," replied Clyde, sullenly.

"Well, they were made before you two went out in that boat for the last time—before you finally told her whatever it was you wanted to tell her—before she was murdered out there—at a time when, as you have testified, she was very sad."

"No, that was the day before," defied Clyde.

"Oh, I see. Well, anyhow, these pictures look a little cheerful for one who was as depressed as you say she was."

"Well—but—she wasn't nearly as depressed then as she was the day before," flashed Clyde, for this was the truth and he remembered it.

"I see. But just the same, look at these other pictures. These three here, for instance. Where were they made?"

"At the Cranston Lodge on Twelfth Lake, I think."

"Right. And that was June eighteenth or nineteenth, wasn't it?"

"On the nineteenth, I think."

"Well, now, do you recall a letter Roberta wrote you on the nineteenth?"

"No, sir."

"You don't recall any particular one?"

"No, sir."

"But they were all very sad, you have said."

"Yes, sir—they were."

"Well, this is that letter written at the time these pictures were made." He turned to the jury.

"I would like the jury to look at these pictures and then listen to just one passage from this letter written by Miss Alden to this defendant on the same day. He has admitted that he was refusing to write or telephone her, although he was sorry for her," he said, turning to the jury. And here he opened a letter and read a long sad plea from Roberta. "And now here are four more pictures, Griffiths." And he handed Clyde the four made at Bear Lake. "Very cheerful, don't you think? Not much like pictures of a man who has just experienced a great change of heart after a most terrific period of doubt and worry and evil conduct—and has just seen the woman whom he had most cruelly wronged, but whom he now proposed to do right by, suddenly drowned. They look as though you hadn't a care in the world, don't they?"

"Well, they were just group pictures. I couldn't very well keep out of them."

"But this one in the water here. Didn't it trouble you the least bit to go in the water the second or third day after Roberta Alden had sunk to the bottom of Big Bittern, and especially when you had experienced such an inspiring change of heart in regard to her?"

"I didn't want any one to know I had been up there with her."

"We know all about that. But how about this banjo picture here. Look at this!" And he held it out. "Very gay, isn't it?" he snarled. And now Clyde, dubious and frightened, replied:

"But I wasn't enjoying myself just the same!"

"Not when you were playing the banjo here? Not when you were playing golf and tennis with your friends the very next day after her death? Not when you were buying and eating thirteen-dollar lunches? Not when you were with Miss X again, and where you yourself testified that you preferred to be?"

Mason's manner was snarling, punitive, sinister, bitterly sarcastic.

"Well, not just then, anyhow—no, sir."

"What do you mean—'not just then'? Weren't you where you wanted to be?"

"Well, in one way I was—certainly," replied Clyde, thinking of what Sondra would think when she read this, as unquestionably she would. Quite everything of all this was being published in the papers each day. He could not deny that he was with her and that he wanted to be with her. At the same time he had not been happy. How miserably unhappy he had been, enmeshed in that shameful and brutal plot! But now he must explain in some way so that Sondra, when she should read it, and this jury, would understand. And so now he added, while he swallowed with his dry throat and licked his lips with his dry tongue: "But I was sorry about Miss Alden just the same. I couldn't be happy then—I couldn't be. I was just trying to make people think that I hadn't had anything to do with her going up there—that's all. I couldn't see that there was any better way to do. I didn't want to be arrested for what I hadn't done."

"Don't you know that is false! Don't you know you are lying!" shouted Mason, as though to the whole world, and the fire and the fury of his unbelief and contempt was sufficient to convince the jury, as well as the spectators, that Clyde was the most unmitigated of liars. "You heard the testimony of Rufus Martin, the second cook up there at Bear Lake?"

"Yes, sir."

"You heard him swear that he saw you and Miss X at a certain point overlooking Bear Lake and that she was in your arms and that you were kissing her. Was that true?"

"Yes, sir."

"And that exactly four days after you had left Roberta Alden under the waters of Big Bittern. Were you afraid of being arrested then?"

"Yes, sir."

"Even when you were kissing her and holding her in your arms?"

"Yes, sir," replied Clyde, drearily and hopelessly.

"Well, of all things!" bawled Mason. "Could you imagine such stuff being whimpered before a jury, if you hadn't heard it with your own ears? Do you really sit there and swear to this jury that you could bill and coo with one deceived girl in your arms and a second one in a lake a hundred miles away, and yet be miserable because of what you were doing?"

"Just the same, that's the way it was," replied Clyde.

"Excellent! Incomparable," shouted Mason.

And here he wearily and sighfully drew forth his large white handkerchief once more and surveying the courtroom at large proceeded to mop his face as much as to say: Well, this is a task indeed, then continuing with more force than ever:

"Griffiths, only yesterday on the witness stand you swore that you personally had no plan to go to Big Bittern when you left Lycurgus."

"No, sir, I hadn't."

"But when you two got in that room at the Renfrew House in Utica and you saw how tired she looked, it was you that suggested that a vacation of some kind—a little one—something within the range of your joint purses at the time—would be good for her. Wasn't that the way of it?"

"Yes, sir. That was the way of it," replied Clyde.

"But up to that time you hadn't even thought of the Adirondacks specifically."

"Well, no, sir—no particular lake, that is. I did think we might go to some summer place maybe—they're mostly lakes around here—but not to any particular one that I knew of."

"I see. And after you suggested it, it was she that said that you had better get some folders or maps, wasn't it?"

"Yes, sir."

"And then it was that you went downstairs and got them?"

"Yes, sir."

"At the Renfrew House in Utica?"

"Yes, sir."

"Not anywhere else by any chance?"

"No, sir."

"And afterwards, in looking over those maps, you saw Grass Lake and Big Bittern and decided to go up that way. Was that the way of it?"

"Yes, we did," lied Clyde, most nervously, wishing now that

he had not testified that it was in the Renfrew House that he had secured the folders. There might be some trap here again.

"You and Miss Alden?"

"Yes, sir."

"And you picked on Grass Lake as being the best because it was the cheapest. Wasn't that the way of it?"

"Yes, sir. That was the way."

"I see. And now do you remember these?" he added, reaching over and taking from his table a series of folders all properly identified as part and parcel of the contents of Clyde's bag at Bear Lake at the time he was arrested, and which he now placed in Clyde's hands. "Look them over. Are those the folders I found in your bag at Bear Lake?"

"Well, they look like the ones I had there."

"Are these the ones you found in the rack at the Renfrew House and took upstairs to show Miss Alden?"

Not a little terrified by the care with which this matter of folders was now being gone into by Mason, Clyde opened them and turned them over. Even now, because the label of the Lycurgus House ("Compliments of Lycurgus House, Lycurgus, N.Y.") was stamped in red very much like the printed red lettering on the rest of the folder, he failed to notice it at first. He turned and turned them over, and then having decided that there was no trap here, replied: "Yes, I think these are the ones."

"Well, now," went on Mason, slyly, "in which one of these was it that you found that notice of Grass Lake Inn and the rate they charged up there? Wasn't it in this one?" And here he returned the identical stamped folder, on one page of which—and the same indicated by Mason't left forefinger—was the exact notice to which Clyde had called Roberta's attention. Also in the center was a map showing the Indian Chain together with Twelfth, Big Bittern, and Grass Lakes, as well as many others, and at the bottom of this map a road plainly indicated as leading from Grass Lake and Gun Lodge south past the southern end of Big Bittern to Three Mile Bay. Now seeing this after so long a time again, he suddenly decided that it must be his knowledge of this road that Mason was seeking to establish, and a little quivery and creepy now, he replied: "Yes, it may be the one. It looks like it. I guess it is, maybe."

"Don't you know that it is?" insisted Mason, darkly and dourly. "Can't you tell from reading that item there whether it is or not?"

"Well, it looks like it," replied Clyde, evasively after examining the item which had inclined him toward Grass Lake in the first place. "I suppose maybe it is."

"You suppose! You suppose! Getting a little more cautious now that we're getting down to something practical. Well, just look at that map there again and tell me what you see. Tell me if you don't see a road marked as leading south from Grass Lake."

"Yes," replied Clyde, a little sullenly and bitterly after a time, so flayed and bruised was he by this man who was so determined to harry him to his grave. He fingered the map and pretended to look as directed, but was seeing only all that he had seen long before there in Lycurgus, so shortly before he departed for Fonda to meet Roberta. And now here it was being used against him.

"And where does it run, please? Do you mind telling the jury where it runs—from where to where?"

And Clyde, nervous and fearful and physically very much reduced, now replied: "Well, it runs from Grass Lake to Three Mile Bay."

"And to what or near what other places in between?" continued Mason, looking over his shoulder.

"Gun Lodge. That's all."

"What about Big Bittern? Doesn't it run near that when it gets to the south of it?"

"Yes, sir, it does here."

"Ever notice or study that map before you went to Grass Lake from Utica?" persisted Mason, tensely and forcefully.

"No, sir—I did not."

"Never knew the road was on there?"

"Well, I may have seen it," replied Clyde, "but if so I didn't pay any attention to it."

"And, of course, by no possible chance could you have seen or studied this folder and that road before you left Utica?"

"No, sir. I never saw it before."

"I see. You're absolutely positive as to that?"

"Yes, sir. I am."

"Well then, explain to me, or to this jury, if you can, and under your solemn oath which you respect so much, how it comes that this particular folder chances to be marked, 'Compliments of the Lycurgus House, Lycurgus, N.Y.'" And here he folded the folder and presenting the back, showed Clyde the thin red stamp in between the other red lettering. And Clyde, noting it, gazed as one in a trance. His ultra-pale face now blanched gray again, his long thin fingers opened and shut, the red and swollen and weary lids of his eyes blinked and blinked to break the strain of the damning fact before him.

"I don't know," he said, a little weakly, after a time. "It must have been in the Renfrew House rack."

"Oh, must it? And if I bring two witnesses here to swear that on July third—three days before you left Lycurgus for Fonda—you were seen by them to enter the Lycurgus House and take four or five folders from the rack there, will you still say that it 'musta been in the rack at the Renfrew House' on July sixth?" As he said this, Mason paused and looked triumphantly about as much as to say: There, answer that if you can! and Clyde, shaken and stiff and breathless for the time being, was compelled to wait at least fifteen seconds before he was able sufficiently to control his nerves and voice in order to reply: "Well, it musta been. I didn't get it in Lycurgus."

"Very good. But in the meantime we'll just let these gentlemen here look at this," and he now turned the folder over to the foreman of the jury, who in turn passed it to the juryman next to him, and so on, the while a distinct whisper and buzz passed over the entire courtroom.

And when they had concluded—and much to the surprise of the audience, which was expecting more and more attacks and exposures almost without cessation—Mason turned and explained: "That's all." And at once many of the spectators in the room beginning to whisper: "Trapped! Trapped!" And Justice Oberwaltzer at once announcing that because of the lateness of the hour, and in the face of a number of additional witnesses for the defense, as well as a few in rebuttal for the prosecution, he would prefer it if the work for the day ended here. And both Belknap and Mason gladly agreeing. And Clyde—the doors of the courtroom being stoutly locked until he should be in his cell across the way—being descended upon by Kraut and Sissell and by them led through and down the very door and stairs which for days he had been looking at and pondering about. And once he was gone, Belknap and Jephson looking at each other but not saying anything until once more safely locked in their own office, when Belknap began with: ". . . not carried off with enough of an air. The best possible defense but not enough courage. It just isn't in him, that's all." And Jephson, flinging himself heavily into a chair, his overcoat and hat still on, and saying: "No, that's the real trouble, no doubt. It musta been that he really did kill her. But I suppose we can't give up the ship now. He did almost better than I expected, at that." And Belknap adding: "Well, I'll do my final best and damnedest in my summing up, and that's all I can do." And Jephson replying, a little wearily: "That's right, Alvin, it's mostly up to you now, I'm sorry. But in the meantime, I think I'll go around to the jail and try and hearten 'im up a bit. It won't do to let him look too winged or lame to-morrow. He has to sit up and make the jury feel that he, himself, feels that he isn't guilty whatever they think." And rising he shoved his hands in the side pockets of his long coat and proceeded through the winter's dark and cold of the dreary town to see Clyde.

# Chapter XXVI

THE REMAINDER of the trial consisted of the testimony of eleven witnesses—four for Mason and seven for Clyde. One of the latter—a Dr. A. K. Sword, of Rehobeth—chancing to be at Big Bittern on the day that Roberta's body was returned to the boat-house, now declared that he had seen and examined it there and that the wounds, as they appeared then, did not seem to him as other than such as might have been delivered by such a blow as Clyde admitted to having struck accidentally, and that unquestionably Miss Alden had been drowned while conscious—and not unconscious, as the state would have the jury believe—a result which led Mason into an inquiry concerning the gentleman's medical history, which, alas, was not as impressive as it might have been. He had been graduated from a second-rate medical school in Oklahoma and had practised in a small town ever since. In addition to him—and entirely apart from the crime with which Clyde was charged—there was Samuel Yearsley, one of the farmers from around Gun Lodge, who, driving over the road which Roberta's body had traveled in being removed from Big Bittern to Gun Lodge, now earnestly swore that the road, as he had noticed in driving over it that same morning, was quite rough—making it possible for Belknap, who was examining him, to indicate that this was at least an approximate cause of the extra-severity of the wounds upon Roberta's head and face. This bit of testimony was later contradicted, however, by a rival witness for Mason—the driver for Lutz Brothers, no less, who as earnestly swore that he found no ruts or rough places whatsoever in the road. And again there were Liggett and Whiggam to say that in so far as they had been able to note or determine, Clyde's conduct in connection with his technical efforts for Griffiths & Company had been attentive, faithful and valuable. They had seen no official harm in him. And then several other minor witnesses to say that in so far as they had been able to observe his social comings and goings, Clyde's conduct was most circumspect, ceremonious and guarded. He had done no ill that they knew of.

But, alas, as Mason in cross-examining them was quick to point out, they had never heard of Roberta Alden or her trouble or even of Clyde's social relationship with her.

Finally many small and dangerous and difficult points having been bridged or buttressed or fended against as well as each side could, it became Belknap's duty to say his last word for Clyde. And to this he gave an entire day, most carefully, and in the spirit of his opening address, retracing and emphasizing every point which tended to show how, almost unconsciously, if not quite innocently, Clyde had fallen into the relationship with Roberta which had ended so disastrously for both. Mental and moral cowardice, as he now reiterated, inflamed or at least operated on by various lacks in Clyde's early life, plus new opportunities such as previously had never appeared to be within his grasp, had affected his *"perhaps too pliable and sensual and impractical and dreaming mind."* No doubt he had not been fair to Miss Alden. No question as to that. He had not. But on the other hand—and as had been most clearly shown by the confession which the defense had elicited—he had not proved ultimately so cruel or vile as the prosecution would have the public and this honorable jury believe. Many men were far more cruel in their love life than this young boy had ever dreamed of being, and, of course, they were not necessarily hung for that. And in passing technically on whether this boy had actually committed the crime charged, it was incumbent upon this jury to see that no generous impulse relating to what this poor girl might have suffered in her love-relations with this youth be permitted to sway them to the belief or decision that for that this youth had committed the crime specifically stated in the indictment. Who among both sexes were not cruel at times in their love life, the one to the other?

And then a long and detailed indictment of the purely circumstantial nature of the evidence—no single person having seen or heard anything of the alleged crime itself, whereas Clyde himself had explained most clearly how he came to find himself in the peculiar situation in which he did find himself. And after that, a brushing aside of the incident of the folder, as well as Clyde's not remembering the price of the boat at Big Bittern, his stopping to bury the tripod and his being so near Roberta and not aiding her, as either being mere accidents of chance, or memory, or, in the case of his failing to go to her rescue, of his being dazed, confused, frightened—"hesitating fatally but not criminally at the one time in his life when he should not have hesitated"—a really strong if jesuitical plea which was not without its merits and its weight.

And then Mason, blazing with his conviction that Clyde was a murderer of the coldest and blackest type, and spending an entire day in riddling the "spider's tissue of lies and unsupported statements" with which the defense was hoping to divert the minds of the jury from the unbroken and unbreakable chain of amply substantiated evidence wherewith the prosecution had proved this "bearded man" to be the "redhanded murderer" that he was. And with hours spent in retracing the statements of the various witnesses. And other hours in denouncing Clyde, or re-telling the bitter miseries of Roberta—so much so that the jury, as well as the audience, was once more on the verge of tears. And with Clyde deciding in his own mind, as he sat between Belknap and Jephson, that no jury such as this was likely to acquit him in the face of evidence so artfully and movingly recapitulated.

And then Oberwaltzer from his high seat finally instructing the jury: "Gentlemen—all evidence is, in a strict sense, more or less circumstantial, whether consisting of facts which permit the inference of guilt or whether given by an eyewitness. The testimony of an eyewitness is, of course, based upon circumstances.

"If any of the material facts of the case are at variance with the probability of guilt, it will be the duty of you gentlemen to give the defendant the benefit of the doubt raised.

"And it must be remembered that evidence is not to be discredited or decried because it is circumstantial. It may often be more reliable evidence than direct evidence.

"Much has been said here concerning motive and its importance in this case, but you are to remember that proof of motive is by no means indispensable or essential to conviction. While a motive may be shown as a *circumstance* to aid in *fixing* a crime, yet the people are not required to prove a motive.

"If the jury finds that Roberta Alden accidentally or involuntarily fell out of the boat and that the defendant made no attempt to rescue her, that does not make the defendant guilty and the jury must find the defendant 'not guilty.' On the other hand, if the jury finds that the defendant in any way, intentionally, there and then brought about or contributed to that fatal accident, either by a blow or otherwise, it must find the defendant guilty.

"While I do not say that you must agree upon your verdict, I would suggest that you ought not, any of you, place your minds in a position which will not yield if after careful deliberation you find you are wrong."

So Justice Oberwaltzer—solemnly and didactically from his high seat to the jury.

And then, that point having been reached, the jury rising and filing from the room at five in the afternoon. And Clyde immediately thereafter being removed to his cell before the audience proper was allowed to leave the building. There was constant fear on the part of the sheriff that he might be attacked. And after that five long hours in which he waited, walking to and fro, to and fro, in his cell, or pretending to read or rest, the while Kraut or Sissel, tipped by various representatives of the press for information as to how Clyde "took it" at this time, slyly and silently remained as near as possible to watch.

And in the meantime Justice Oberwaltzer and Mason and Belknap and Jephson, with their attendants and friends, in various rooms of the Bridgeburg Central Hotel, dining and then waiting impatiently, with the aid of a few drinks, for the jury to agree, and wishing and hoping that the verdict would be reached soon, whatever it might be.

And in the meantime the twelve men—farmers, clerks, and storekeepers, re-canvassing for their own mental satisfaction the fine points made by Mason and Belknap and Jephson. Yet out of the whole twelve but one man—Samuel Upham, a druggist—(politically opposed to Mason and taken with the personality of Jephson)—sympathizing with Belknap and Jephson. And so pretending that he had doubts as to the completeness of Mason's proof until at last after five ballots were taken he was threatened with exposure and the public rage and obloquy which was sure to follow in case the jury was hung. "We'll fix you. You won't get by with this without the public knowing exactly where you stand." Whereupon, having a satisfactory drug business in North Mansfield, he at once decided that it was best to pocket this opposition to Mason and agree.

Then four hollow knocks on the door leading from the jury room to the court room. It was the foreman of the jury, Foster Lund, a dealer in cement, lime and stone. His great fist was knocking. And at that the hundreds who had crowded into the hot stuffy court room after dinner—though many had not even left—stirred from the half stupor into which they had fallen. "What's that? What's happened? Is the jury ready to report? What's the verdict?" And men and women and children starting up to draw nearer the excluding rail. And the two deputies on guard before the jury door beginning to call, "All right! All right! As soon as the judge comes." And then other deputies hurrying to the prison over the way in order that the sheriff might be notified and Clyde brought over—and to the Bridgeburg Central Hotel to summon Oberwaltzer and all the others. And then Clyde, in a half stupor or daze from sheer loneliness and killing suspense, being manacled to Kraut and led over between Slack, Sissell and others. And Oberwaltzer, Mason, Belknap and Jephson and the entire company of newspaper writers, artists, photographers and others entering and taking the places that they had occupied all these long weeks. And Clyde winking and blinking as he was seated behind Belknap and Jephson now—not with them, for as stoutly manacled as he was to Kraut, he was compelled to sit by him. And then Oberwaltzer on the bench and the clerk in his place, the jury room door being opened and the twelve men filing solemnly in—quaint and varied figures in angular and for the most part much-worn suits of the ready-made variety. And as they did so, seating themselves in the jury box, only to rise again at the command of the clerk, who began: "Gentlemen of the jury, have you agreed on a verdict?"—yet without one of them glancing in the direction of either Belknap or Jephson or Clyde, which Belknap at once interpreted as fatal.

"It's all off," he whispered to Jephson. "Against us. I can tell." And then Lund announcing: "We have. We find the defendant guilty of murder in the first degree." And Clyde, entirely dazed and yet trying to keep his poise and remain serene, gazing straight before him toward the jury and beyond, and with scarcely a blink of the eye. For had he not, in his cell the night before, been told by Jephson, who had found him deeply depressed, that the verdict in this trial, assuming that it proved to be unfavorable, was of no consequence. The trial from start to finish had been unfair. Prejudice and bias had governed its every step. Such bullying and browbeating and innuendo as Mason had indulged in before the jury would never pass as fair or adequate in any higher court. And a new trial—on appeal—would certainly be granted—although by whom such an appeal was to be conducted he was not now prepared to discuss.

And now, recalling that, Clyde saying to himself that it did not so much matter perhaps, after all. It could not, really—or could it? Yet think what these words meant in case he could not get a new trial! Death! That is what it would mean if this were final—and perhaps it was final. And then to sit in that chair he had seen in his mind's eye for so long—these many days and nights when he could not force his mind to drive it away. Here it was again before him—that dreadful, ghastly chair—only closer and larger than ever before—there in the very center of the space between himself and Justice Oberwaltzer. He could see it plainly now—squarish; heavy-armed, heavy-backed, some straps at the top and sides. God! Supposing no one would help him now! Even the Griffiths might not be willing to pay out any more money! Think of that! The Court of Appeals to which Jephson and Belknap had referred might not be willing to help him either. And then these words would be final. They would! They would! God! His jaws moved slightly, then set—because at the moment he became conscious that they were moving. Besides, at that moment Belknap was rising and asking for an individual poll of the jury, while Jephson leaned over and whispered: "Don't worry about it. It isn't final. We'll get a reversal as sure as anything." Yet as each of the jurors was saying: "Yes"—Clyde was listening to them, not to Jephson. Why should each one say that with so much emphasis? Was there not one who felt that he might not have done as Mason had said—struck her intentionally? Was there not one who even half-believed in that change of heart which Belknap and Jephson had insisted that he had experienced? He looked at them all—little and big. They were like a blackish-brown group of wooden toys with creamish-brown or old ivory faces and hands. Then he thought of his mother. She would hear of this now, for here were all these newspaperwriters and artists and photographers assembled to hear this. And what would the Griffiths—his uncle and Gilbert—think now? And Sondra! Sondra! Not a word from her. And through all this he had been openly testifying, as Belknap and Jephson had agreed that he must do—to the compelling and directing power of his passion for her—the real reason for all this! But not a word. And she would not send him any word now, of course—she who had been going to marry him and give him everything!

But in the meantime the crowd about him silent although—or perhaps because—intensely satisfied. The little devil hadn't "gotten by." He hadn't fooled the twelve sane men of this county with all that bunk about a change of heart. What rot! While Jephson sat and stared, and Belknap, his strong face written all over with contempt and defiance, making his motions. And Mason and Burleigh and Newcomb and Redmond thinly repressing their intense satisfaction behind masks preternaturally severe, the while Belknap continued with a request that the sentence be put off until the following Friday—a week hence, when he could more conveniently attend, but with Justice Oberwaltzer replying that he thought not—unless some good reason could be shown. But on the morrow, if counsel desired, he would listen to an argument. If it were satisfactory he would delay sentence—otherwise, pronounce it the following Monday.

Yet even so, Clyde was not concerned with this argument at the moment. He was thinking of his mother and what she would think—feel. He had been writing her so regularly, insisting always that he was innocent and that she must not believe all, or even a part, of what she read in the newspapers. He was going to be acquitted sure. He was going to go on the stand and testify for himself. But now . . . now . . . oh, he needed her now—so much. Quite every one, as it seemed now, had forsaken him. He was terribly, terribly alone. And he must send her some word quickly. He must. He must. And then asking Jephson for a piece of paper and a pencil, he wrote: "Mrs. Asa Griffiths, care of Star of Hope Mission, Denver, Colorado. Dear mother—I am convicted—Clyde." And then handing that to Jephson, he asked him, nervously and weakly, if he would see that it was sent right away. "Right away, son, sure," replied Jephson, touched by his looks, and waving to a press boy who was near gave it to him together with the money.

And then, while this was going on, all the public exits being locked until Clyde, accompanied by Sissel and Kraut, had been ushered through the familiar side entrance through which he had hoped to escape. And with all the press and the public and the still-remaining jury gazing, for even yet they had not seen enough of Clyde but must stare into his face to see how he was taking it. And because of the local feeling against him, Oberwaltzer, at Slack's request, holding court un-adjourned until word was brought that Clyde was once more locked in his cell, whereupon the doors were re-opened. And then the crowd surging out but only to wait at the court-room door in order to glimpse, as he passed out, Mason, who now, of all the figures in this case, was the true hero—the nemesis of Clyde—the avenger of Roberta. But he not appearing at first but instead Jephson and Belknap together, and not so much depressed as solemn, defiant—Jephson, in particular, looking unconquerably contemptuous. Then some one calling: "Well, you didn't get him off just the same," and Jephson replying, with a shrug of his shoulders, "Not yet, but this county isn't all of the law either." Then Mason, immediately afterward—a heavy, baggy overcoat thrown over his shoulder, his worn soft hat pulled low over his eyes—and followed by Burleigh, Heit, Newcomb and others as a royal train—while he walked in the manner of one entirely oblivious of the meaning or compliment of this waiting throng. For was he not now a victor and an elected judge! And as instantly being set upon by a circling, huzzahing mass—the while a score of those nearest sought to seize him by the hand or place a grateful pat upon his arm or shoulder. "Hurrah for Orville!" "Good for you, judge!" (his new or fast-approaching title). "By God! Orville Mason, you deserve the thanks of this county!" "Hy-oh! Heigh! Heigh!" "Three cheers for Orville

Mason!" And with that the crowd bursting into three resounding huzzahs—which Clyde in his cell could clearly hear
and at the same time sense the meaning of.

They were cheering Mason for convicting him. In that
large crowd out there there was not one who did not believe
him totally and completely guilty. Roberta—her letters—her
determination to make him marry her—her giant fear of exposure—had dragged him down to this. To conviction. To
death, maybe. Away from all he had longed for—away from
all he had dreamed he might possess. And Sondra! Sondra!
Not a word! Not a word! And so now, fearing that Kraut or
Sissell or some one might be watching (ready to report even
now his every gesture), and not willing to show after all how
totally collapsed and despondent he really was, he sat down
and taking up a magazine pretended to read, the while he
looked far, far beyond it to other scenes—his mother—his
brother and sisters—the Griffiths—all he had known. But
finding these unsubstantiated mind visions a little too much,
he finally got up and throwing off his clothes climbed into his
iron cot.

"Convicted! Convicted!" And that meant that he must die!
God! But how blessed to be able to conceal his face upon a
pillow and not let any one see—however accurately they
might guess!

# Chapter XXVII

THE DREARY aftermath of a great contest and a great failure, with the general public from coast to coast—in view
of this stern local interpretation of the tragedy—firmly convinced that Clyde was guilty and, as heralded by the newspapers everywhere, that he had been properly convicted. The
pathos of that poor little murdered country girl! Her sad letters! How she must have suffered! That weak defense! Even
the Griffiths of Denver were so shaken by the evidence as the
trial had progressed that they scarcely dared read the papers
openly—one to the other—but, for the most part, read of it
separately and alone, whispering together afterwards of the
damning, awful deluge of circumstantial evidence. Yet, after
reading Belknap's speech and Clyde's own testimony, this
little family group that had struggled along together for so
long coming to believe in their own son and brother in spite
of all they had previously read against him. And because of
this—during the trial as well as afterwards—writing him
cheerful and hopeful letters, based frequently on letters from
him in which he insisted over and over again that he was not
guilty. Yet once convicted, and out of the depths of his despair wiring his mother as he did—and the papers confirming
it—absolute consternation in the Griffiths family. For was not
this proof? Or, was it? All the papers seemed to think so. And
they rushed reporters to Mrs. Griffiths, who, together with
her little brood, had sought refuge from the unbearable publicity in a remote part of Denver entirely removed from the
mission world. A venal moving-van company had revealed her
address.

And now this American witness to the rule of God upon
earth, sitting in a chair in her shabby, nondescript apartment,
hard-pressed for the very means to sustain herself—degraded
by the milling forces of life and the fell and brutal blows of
chance—yet serene in her trust—and declaring: "I cannot
think this morning. I seem numb and things look strange to
me. My boy found guilty of murder! But I am his mother and
I am not convinced of his guilt by any means! He has written

me that he is not guilty and I believe him. And to whom should he turn with the truth and for trust if not to me? But there is He who sees all things and who knows."

At the same time there was so much in the long stream of evidence, as well as Clyde's first folly in Kansas City, that had caused her to wonder—and fear. Why was he unable to explain that folder? Why couldn't he have gone to the girl's aid when he could swim so well? And why did he proceed so swiftly to the mysterious Miss X—whoever she was? Oh, surely, surely, she was not going to be compelled, in spite of all her faith, to believe that her eldest—the most ambitious and hopeful, if restless, of all of her children, was guilty of such a crime! No! She could not doubt him—even now. Under the merciful direction of a living God, was it not evil in a mother to believe evil of a child, however dread his erring ways might seem? In the silence of the different rooms of the mission, before she had been compelled to remove from there because of curious and troublesome visitors, had she not stood many times in the center of one of those miserable rooms while sweeping and dusting, free from the eye of any observer—her head thrown back, her eyes closed, her strong, brown face molded in homely and yet convinced and earnest lines—a figure out of the early Biblical days of her six thousand-year-old world—and earnestly directing her thoughts to that imaginary throne which she saw as occupied by the living, giant mind and body of the living God—her Creator. And praying by the quarter and the half hour that she be given strength and understanding and guidance to know of her son's innocence or guilt—and if innocent that this searing burden of suffering be lifted from him and her and all those dear to him and her—or if guilty, she be shown how to do—how to endure the while he be shown how to wash from his immortal soul forever the horror of the thing he had done—make himself once more, if possible, white before the Lord.

"Thou art mighty, O God, and there is none beside Thee. Behold, to Thee all things are possible. In Thy favor is Life. Have mercy, O God. Though his sins be as scarlet, make him white as snow. Though they be red like crimson, make them as wool."

Yet in her then—and as she prayed—was the wisdom of Eve

in regard to the daughters of Eve. That girl whom Clyde was alleged to have slain—what about her? Had she not sinned too? And was she not older than Clyde? The papers said so. Examining the letters, line by line, she was moved by their pathos and was intensely and pathetically grieved for the misery that had befallen the Aldens. Nevertheless, as a mother and a woman full of the wisdom of ancient Eve, she saw how Roberta herself must have consented—how the lure of her must have aided in the weakening and the betrayal of her son. A strong, good girl would not have consented—could not have. How many confessions about this same thing had she not heard in the mission and at street meetings? And might it not be said in Clyde's favor—as in the very beginning of life in the Garden of Eden—"the woman tempted me?"

Truly—and because of that——

"His mercy endureth forever," she quoted. And if His mercy endureth—must that of Clyde's mother be less?

"If ye have faith, so much as the grain of a mustard seed," she quoted to herself—and now, in the face of these importuning reporters added: "Did my son kill her? That is the question. Nothing else matters in the eyes of our Maker," and she looked at the sophisticated, callous youths with the look of one who was sure that her God would make them understand. And even so they were impressed by her profound sincerity and faith. "Whether or not the jury has found him guilty or innocent is neither here nor there in the eyes of Him who holds the stars in the hollow of His hand. The jury's finding is of men. It is of the earth's earthy. I have read his lawyer's plea. My son himself has told me in his letters that he is not guilty. I believe my son. I am convinced that he is innocent."

And Asa in another corner of the room, saying little. Because of his lack of comprehension of the actualities as well as his lack of experience of the stern and motivating forces of passion, he was unable to grasp even a tithe of the meaning of this. He had never understood Clyde or his lacks or his feverish imaginings, so he said, and preferred not to discuss him.

"But," continued Mrs. Griffiths, "at no time have I shielded Clyde in his sin against Roberta Alden. He did wrong, but she did wrong too in not resisting him. There can be no compromising with sin in any one. And though my heart goes out in sympathy and love to the bleeding heart of her dear mother and father who have suffered so, still we must not fail to see that this sin was mutual and that the world should know and judge accordingly. Not that I want to shield him," she repeated. "He should have remembered the teachings of his youth." And here her lips compressed in a sad and somewhat critical misery. "But I have read her letters too. And I feel that but for them, the prosecuting attorney would have had no real case against my son. He used them to work on the emotions of the jury." She got up, tried as by fire, and exclaimed, tensely and beautifully: "But he is my son! He has just been convicted. I must think as a mother how to help him, however I feel as to his sin." She gripped her hands together, and even the reporters were touched by her misery. "I must go to him! I should have gone before. I see it now." She paused, discovering herself to be addressing her inmost agony, need, fear, to these public ears and voices, which might in no wise understand or care.

"Some people wonder," now interrupted one of these same—a most practical and emotionally calloused youth of Clyde's own age—"why you weren't there during the trial. Didn't you have the money to go?"

"I had no money," she replied, simply. "Not enough, anyhow. And besides, they advised me not to come—that they did not need me. But now—now I must go—in some way—I must find out how." She went to a small, shabby desk, which was a part of the sparse and colorless equipment of the room. "You boys are going downtown," she said. "Would one of you send a telegram for me if I give you the money?"

"Sure!" exclaimed the one who had asked her the rudest question. "Give it to me. You don't need any money. I'll have the paper send it." Also, as he thought, he would write it up, or in, as a part of his story.

She seated herself at the yellow and scratched desk and after finding a small pad and pen, she wrote: "Clyde—Trust in God. All things are possible to him. Appeal at once. Read Psalms 51. Another trial will prove your innocence. We will come to you soon. Father and Mother."

"Perhaps I had just better give you the money," she added,

nervously, wondering whether it would be well to permit a newspaper to pay for this and wondering at the same time if Clyde's uncle would be willing to pay for an appeal. It might cost a great deal. Then she added: "It's rather long."

"Oh don't bother about that!" exclaimed another of the trio, who was anxious to read the telegram. "Write all you want. We'll see that it goes."

"I want a copy of that," added the third, in a sharp and uncompromising tone, seeing that the first reporter was proceeding to take and pocket the message. "This isn't private. I get it from you or her—now!"

And at this, number one, in order to avoid a scene, which Mrs. Griffiths, in her slow way, was beginning to sense, extracted the slip from his pocket and turned it over to the others, who there and then proceeded to copy it.

At the same time that this was going on, the Griffiths of Lycurgus, having been consulted as to the wisdom and cost of a new trial, disclosed themselves as by no means interested, let alone convinced, that an appeal—at least at their expense—was justified. The torture and socially—if not commercially—destroying force of all this—every hour of it a Golgotha! Bella and her social future, to say nothing of Gilbert and his—completely overcast and charred by this awful public picture of the plot and crime that one of their immediate blood had conceived and executed! Samuel Griffiths himself, as well as his wife, fairly macerated by this blasting flash from his well-intentioned, though seemingly impractical and nonsensical good deed. Had not a long, practical struggle with life taught him that sentiment in business was folly? Up to the hour he had met Clyde he had never allowed it to influence him in any way. But his mistaken notion that his youngest brother had been unfairly dealt with by their father! And now this! This! His wife and daughter compelled to remove from the scene of their happiest years and comforts and live as exiles—perhaps forever—in one of the suburbs of Boston, or elsewhere—or forever endure the eyes and sympathy of their friends! And himself and Gilbert almost steadily conferring ever since as to the wisdom of uniting the business in stock form with some of the others of Lycurgus or elsewhere—or, if not that, of transferring, not by degrees but speedily, to either Rochester or Buffalo or Boston or Brooklyn, where a main plant might be erected. The disgrace of this could only be overcome by absenting themselves from Lycurgus and all that it represented to them. They must begin life all over again—socially at least. That did not mean so much to himself or his wife—their day was about over anyhow. But Bella and Gilbert and Myra—how to rehabilitate them in some way, somewhere?

And so, even before the trial was finished, a decision on the part of Samuel and Gilbert Griffiths to remove the business to South Boston, where they might decently submerge themselves until the misery and shame of this had in part at least been forgotten.

And because of this further aid to Clyde absolutely refused. And Belknap and Jephson then sitting down together to consider. For obviously, their time being as valuable as it was—devoted hitherto to the most successful practice in Bridgeburg—and with many matters waiting on account of the pressure of this particular case—they were by no means persuaded that either their practical self-interest or their charity permitted or demanded their assisting Clyde without further recompense. In fact, the expense of appealing this case was going to be considerable as they saw it. The record was enormous. The briefs would be large and expensive, and the State's allowance for them was pitifully small. At the same time, as Jephson pointed out, it was folly to assume that the western Griffiths might not be able to do anything at all. Had they not been identified with religious and charitable work this long while? And was it not possible, the tragedy of Clyde's present predicament pointed out to them, that they might through appeals of various kinds raise at least sufficient money to defray the actual costs of such an appeal? Of course, they had not aided Clyde up to the present time but that was because his mother had been notified that she was not needed. It was different now.

"Better wire her to come on," suggested Jephson, practically. "We can get Oberwaltzer to set the sentence over until the tenth if we say that she is trying to come on here. Besides, just tell her to do it and if she says she can't we'll see about the money then. But she'll be likely to get it and maybe some towards the appeal too."

And forthwith a telegram and a letter, to Mrs. Griffiths, saying that as yet no word had been said to Clyde but none-the-less his Lycurgus relatives had declined to assist him further in any way. Besides, he was to be sentenced not later than the tenth, and for his own future welfare it was necessary that some one—preferably herself—appear. Also that funds to cover the cost of an appeal be raised, or at least the same guaranteed.

And then Mrs. Griffiths, on her knees praying to her God to help her. Here, *now*, he must show his Almighty hand—his never-failing Mercy. Enlightenment and help must come from somewhere—otherwise how was she to get the fare, let alone raise money for Clyde's appeal?

Yet as she prayed—on her knees—a thought. The newspapers had been hounding her for interviews. They had followed her here and there. Why had she not gone to her son's aid? What did she think of this? What of that? And now she said to herself, why should she not go to the editor of one of the great papers so anxious to question her always and tell him how great was her need? Also, that if he would help her to reach her son in time to be with him on his day of sentence that she, his mother, would report the same for him. These papers were sending their reporters here, there—even to the trial, as she had read. Why not her—his mother? Could she not speak and write too? How many, many tracts had she not composed?

And so now to her feet—only to sink once more on her knees: "Thou hast answered me, oh, my God!" she exclaimed. Then rising, she got out her ancient brown coat, the commonplace brown bonnet with strings—based on some mood in regard to religious livery—and at once proceeded to the largest and most important newspaper. And because of the notoriety of her son's trial she was shown directly to the managing editor, who was as much interested as she was impressed and who listened to her with respect and sympathy. He understood her situation and was under the impression that the paper would be interested in this. He disappeared for a few moments—then returned. She would be employed as a correspondent for a period of three weeks, and after that until further notice. Her expenses to and fro would be covered.

An assistant, into whose hands he would now deliver her would instruct her as to the method of preparing and filing her communications. He would also provide her with some ready cash. She might even leave to-night if she chose—the sooner, the better. The paper would like a photograph or two before she left. But as he talked, and as he noticed, her eyes were closed—her head back. She was offering thanks to the God who had thus directly answered her plea.

# Chapter XXVIII

BRIDGEBURG and a slow train that set down a tired, distrait woman at its depot after midnight on the eighth of December. Bitter cold and bright stars. A lone depot assistant who on inquiry directed her to the Bridgeburg Central House—straight up the street which now faced her, then two blocks to her left after she reached the second street. The sleepy night clerk of the Central House providing her instantly with a room and, once he knew who she was, directing her to the county jail. But she deciding after due rumination that now was not the hour. He might be sleeping. She would go to bed and rise early in the morning. She had sent him various telegrams. He knew that she was coming.

But as early as seven in the morning, rising, and by eight appearing at the jail, letters, telegrams and credentials in hand. And the jail officials, after examining the letters she carried and being convinced of her identity, notifying Clyde of her presence. And he, depressed and forlorn, on hearing this news, welcoming the thought of her as much as at first he had dreaded her coming. For now things were different. All the long grim story had been told. And because of the plausible explanation which Jephson had provided him, he could face her perhaps and say without a quaver that it was true—that he had not plotted to kill Roberta—that he had not willingly left her to die in the water. And then hurrying down to the visitor's room, where, by the courtesy of Slack, he was permitted to talk with his mother alone.

On seeing her rise at his entrance, and hurrying to her, his troubled intricate soul not a little dubious, yet confident also that it was to find sanctuary, sympathy, help, perhaps—and that without criticism—in her heart. And exclaiming with difficulty, as a lump thickened in his throat: "Gee, Ma! I'm glad you've come." But she too moved for words—her condemned boy in her arms—merely drawing his head to her shoulder and then looking up. The Lord God had vouchsafed her this much. Why not more? The ultimate freedom of her son—or if not that, at least a new trial—a fair consideration of the evidence in his favor which had not been had yet, of course. And so they stood for several moments.

Then news of home, the reason for her presence, her duty as a correspondent to interview him—later to appear with him in court at the hour of his sentence—a situation over which Clyde winced. Yet now, as he heard from her, his future was likely to depend on her efforts alone. The Lycurgus Griffiths, for reasons of their own, had decided not to aid him further. But she—if she were but able to face the world with a sound claim—might still aid him. Had not the Lord aided her thus far? Yet to face the world and the Lord with her just plea she must know from him—now—the truth as to whether he had intentionally or unintentionally struck Roberta—whether intentionally or unintentionally he had left her to die. She had read the evidence and his letters and had noted all the defects in his testimony. But were those things as contended by Mason true or false?

Clyde, now as always overawed and thrown back on himself by that uncompromising and shameless honesty which he had never been able quite to comprehend in her, announced, with all the firmness that he could muster—yet with a secret quavering chill in his heart—that he had sworn to the truth. He had not done those things with which he had been charged. He had not. But, alas, as she now said to herself, on observing him, what was that about his eyes—a faint flicker perhaps. He was not so sure—as self-convinced and definite as she had hoped—as she had prayed he would be. No, no, there was something in his manner, his words, as he spoke,—a faint recessive intonation, a sense of something troubled, dubious, perhaps, which quite froze her now.

He was not positive enough. And so he might have plotted, in part at least, as she had feared at first, when she had first heard of this—might have even struck her on that lone, secret lake!—who could tell? (the searing, destroying power of such a thought as that). And that in the face of all his testimony to the contrary.

But "Jehovah, jirah, Thou wilt not require of a mother, in her own and her son's darkest hour, that she doubt him,—make sure his death through her own lack of faith? Oh, no—Thou wilt not. O Lamb of God, Thou wilt not!" She turned;

she bruised under her heel the scaly head of this dark suspicion—as terrifying to her as his guilt was to him. "O Absalom, my Absalom! Come, come, we will not entertain such a thought. God himself would not urge it upon a mother." Was he not here—her son—before her, declaring firmly that he had not done this thing. She must believe—she would believe him utterly. She would—and did—whatever fiend of doubt might still remain locked in the lowest dungeon of her miserable heart. Come, come, the public should know how she felt. She and her son would find a way. He must believe and pray. Did he have a Bible? Did he read it? And Clyde having been long since provided with a Bible by a prison worker, assured her that he had and did read it.

But now she must go first to see his lawyers, next to file her dispatch, after which she would return. But once out on the street being immediately set upon by several reporters and eagerly questioned as to the meaning of her presence here. Did she believe in her son's innocence? Did she or did she not think that he had had a fair trial? Why had she not come on before? And Mrs. Griffiths, in her direct and earnest and motherly way, taking them into her confidence and telling how as well as why she came to be here, also why she had not come before.

But now that she was here she hoped to stay. The Lord would provide the means for the salvation of her son, of whose innocence she was convinced. Would they not ask God to help her? Would they not pray for her success? And with the several reporters not a little moved and impressed, assuring her that they would, of course, and thereafter describing her to the world at large as she was—middle-aged, homely, religious, determined, sincere and earnest and with a moving faith in the innocence of her boy.

But the Griffiths of Lycurgus, on hearing this, resenting her coming as one more blow. And Clyde, in his cell, on reading of it later, somewhat shocked by the gross publicity now attending everything in connection with him, yet, because of his mother's presence, resigned and after a time almost happy. Whatever her faults or defects, after all she was his mother, wasn't she? And she had come to his aid. Let the public think what it would. Was he not in the shadow of death and she at least had not deserted him. And with this, her suddenly manifested skill in connecting herself in this way with a Denver paper, to praise her for.

She had never done anything like this before. And who knew but that possibly, and even in the face of her dire poverty now, she might still be able to solve this matter of a new trial for him and so save his life? Who knew? And yet how much and how indifferently he had sinned against her! Oh, how much. And still here she was—his mother still anxious and tortured and yet loving and seeking to save his life by writing up his own conviction for a western paper. No longer did the shabby coat and the outlandish hat and the broad, immobile face and somewhat stolid and crude gestures seem the racking and disturbing things they had so little time since. She was his mother and she loved him, and believed him and was struggling to save him.

On the other hand Belknap and Jephson on first encountering her were by no means so much impressed. For some reason they had not anticipated so crude and unlettered and yet convinced a figure. The wide, flat shoes. The queer hat. The old brown coat. Yet somehow, after a few moments, arrested by her earnestness and faith and love for her son and her fixed, inquiring, and humanly clean and pure blue eyes in which dwelt immaterial conviction and sacrifice with no shadow of turning.

Did they personally think her son innocent? She must know that first. Or did they secretly believe that he was guilty? She had been so tortured by all the contradictory evidence. God had laid a heavy cross upon her and hers. Nevertheless, Blessed be His name! And both, seeing and feeling her great concern, were quick to assure her that they were convinced of Clyde's innocence. If he were executed for this alleged crime it would be a travesty on justice.

Yet both, now that they saw her, troubled as to the source of any further funds, her method of getting here, which she now explained, indicating that she had nothing. And an appeal sure to cost not less than two thousand. And Mrs. Griffiths, after an hour in their presence, in which they made clear to her the basic cost of an appeal—covering briefs to be prepared, arguments, trips to be made—asserting repeatedly that

she did not quite see how she was to do. Then suddenly, and
to them somewhat inconsequentially, yet movingly and dramatically, exclaiming: "The Lord will not desert me. I know
it. He has declared himself unto me. It was His voice there in
Denver that directed me to that paper. And now that I am
here, I will trust Him and He will guide me."

But Belknap and Jephson merely looking at one another in
unconvinced and pagan astonishment. Such faith! An exhorter! An Evangelist, no less! Yet to Jephson, here was an
idea! There was the religious element to be reckoned with
everywhere—strong in its agreement with just such faith. Assuming the Griffiths of Lycurgus to remain obdurate and unmoved—why then—why then—and now that she was
here—there were the churches and the religious people generally. Might it not be possible, with such a temperament and
such faith as this, to appeal to the very element that had hitherto most condemned Clyde and made his conviction a certainty, for funds wherewith to carry this case to the court of
appeals? This lorn mother. Her faith in her boy.

Presto!

A lecture, at so much for admission, and in which, hard-
pressed as she was and could show, she would set forth the
righteousness of her boy's claim—seek to obtain the sympathy of the prejudiced public and incidentally two thousand
dollars or more with which this appeal could be conducted.

And now Jephson, turning to her and laying the matter before her and offering to prepare a lecture or notes—a con-
densation of his various arguments—in fact, an entire lecture
which she could re-arrange and present as she chose—all the
data which was the ultimate, basic truth in regard to her son.
And she, her brown cheeks flushing and her eyes brightening,
agreeing she would do it. She would try. She could do no less
than try. Verily, verily, was not this the Voice and Hand of
God in the darkest hour of her tribulation?

On the following morning Clyde was arraigned for sentence, with Mrs. Griffiths given a seat near him and seeking,
paper and pencil in hand, to make notes of, for her, an unutterable scene, while a large crowd surveyed her. His own
mother! And acting as a reporter! Something absurd,
grotesque, insensitive, even ludicrous, about such a family and

such a scene. And to think the Griffiths of Lycurgus should be so immediately related to them.

Yet Clyde sustained and heartened by her presence. For had she not returned to the jail the previous afternoon with her plan? And as soon as this was over—whatever the sentence might be—she would begin with her work.

And so, and that almost in spite of himself, in his darkest hour, standing up before Justice Oberwaltzer and listening first to a brief recital of his charge and trial (which was pronounced by Oberwaltzer to have been fair and impartial), then to the customary: "Have you any cause which shows why the judgment of death should not now be pronounced against you according to law?"—to which and to the astonishment of his mother and the auditors (if not Jephson, who had advised and urged him so to do), Clyde now in a clear and firm voice replied:

"I am innocent of the crime as charged in the indictment. I never killed Roberta Alden and therefore I think this sentence should not be passed."

And then staring straight before him conscious only of the look of admiration and love turned on him by his mother. For had not her son now declared himself, here at this fatal moment, before all these people? And his word here, if not in that jail, would be true, would it not? Then her son was not guilty. He was not. He was not. Praised be the name of the Lord in the highest. And deciding to make a great point of this in her dispatch—so as to get it in all the papers, and in her lecture afterwards.

However, Oberwaltzer, without the faintest sign of surprise or perturbation, now continued: "Is there anything else you care to say?"

"No," replied Clyde, after a moment's hesitation.

"Clyde Griffiths," then concluded Oberwaltzer, "the judgment of the Court is that you, Clyde Griffiths, for the murder in the first degree of one, Roberta Alden, whereof you are convicted, be, and you are hereby sentenced to the punishment of death; and it is ordered that, within ten days after this day's session of Court, the Sheriff of this county of Cataraqui deliver you, together with the warrant of this Court, to the Agent and Warden of the State Prison of the State of New

York at Auburn, where you shall be kept in solitary confinement until the week beginning Monday the 28th day of January, 19—, and, upon some day within the week so appointed, the said Agent and Warden of the State Prison of the State of New York at Auburn is commended to do execution upon you, Clyde Griffiths, in the mode and manner prescribed by the laws of the State of New York."

And that done, a smile from Mrs. Griffiths to her boy and an answering smile from Clyde to her. For since he had announced that he was not guilty—*here*—her spirit had risen in the face of this sentence. He was really innocent,—he must be, since he had declared it here. And Clyde because of her smile saying to himself, his mother believed in him now. She had not been swayed by all the evidence against him. And this faith, mistaken or not, was now so sustaining—so needed. What he had just said was true as he now saw it. He had not struck Roberta. That *was* true. And therefore he was not guilty. Yet Kraut and Slack were once more seizing him and escorting him to the cell.

Immediately thereafter his mother seating herself at a press table proceeded to explain to contiguous press representatives now curiously gathering about her: "You mustn't think too badly of me, you gentlemen of the papers. I don't know much about this but it is the only way I could think of to be with my boy. I couldn't have come otherwise." And then one lanky correspondent stepping up to say: "Don't worry, mother. Is there any way I can help you? Want me to straighten out what you want to say? I'll be glad to." And then sitting down beside her and proceeding to help her arrange her impressions in the form in which he assumed her Denver paper might like them. And others as well offering to do anything they could—and all greatly moved.

Two days later, the proper commitment papers having been prepared and his mother notified of the change but not permitted to accompany him, Clyde was removed to Auburn, the western penitentiary of the State of New York, where in the "death house" or "Murderers' Row," as it was called—as gloomy and torturesome an inferno as one could imagine any

human compelled to endure—a combination of some twenty-
two cells on two separate levels—he was to be restrained until ordered re-tried or executed.

Yet as he traveled from Bridgeburg to this place, impressive
crowds at every station—young and old—men, women and
children—all seeking a glimpse of the astonishingly youthly
slayer. And girls and women, under the guise of kindly interest, but which, at best, spelled little more than a desire to
achieve a facile intimacy with this daring and romantic, if unfortunate figure, throwing him a flower here and there and
calling to him gayly and loudly as the train moved out from
one station or another:

"Hello, Clyde! Hope to see you soon again. Don't stay too
long down there." "If you take an appeal, you're sure to be
acquitted. We hope so, anyhow."

And with Clyde not a little astonished and later even heartened by this seemingly favorable discrepancy between the attitude of the crowds in Bridgeburg and this sudden, morbid,
feverish and even hectic curiosity here, bowing and smiling
and even waving with his hand. Yet thinking, none the less, "I
am on the way to the death house and they can be so friendly.
It is a wonder they dare." And with Kraut and Sissell, his
guards, because of the distinction and notoriety of being both
his captors and jailors, as well also because of these unusual attentions from passengers on the train and individuals in these
throngs without being themselves flattered and ennobled.

But after this one brief colorful flight in the open since his
arrest, past these waiting throngs and over winter sun-lit fields
and hills of snow that reminded him of Lycurgus, Sondra,
Roberta, and all that he had so kaleidoscopically and fatally
known in the twenty months just past, the gray and restraining walls of Auburn itself—with, once he was presented to a
clerk in the warden's office and his name and crime entered in
the books—himself assigned to two assistants, who saw to it
that he was given a prison bath and hair cut—all the wavy,
black hair he so much admired cut away—a prison-striped
uniform and hideous cap of the same material, prison underwear and heavy gray felt shoes to quiet the restless prison
tread in which in time he might indulge, together with the
number, 77221.

And so accoutered, immediately transferred to the death house proper, where in a cell on the ground floor he was now locked—a squarish light clean space, eight by ten feet in size and fitted with sanitary plumbing as well as a cot bed, a table, a chair and a small rack for books. And here then, while he barely sensed that there were other cells about him—ranging up and down a wide hall—he first stood—and then seated himself—now no longer buoyed by the more intimate and sociable life of the jail at Bridgeburg—or those strange throngs and scenes that had punctuated his trip here.

The hectic tensity and misery of these hours! That sentence to die; that trip with all those people calling to him; that cutting of his hair downstairs in that prison barber shop—and by a convict; the suit and underwear that was now his and that he now had on. There was no mirror here—or anywhere,—but no matter—he could feel how he looked. This baggy coat and trousers and this striped cap. He threw it hopelessly to the floor. For but an hour before he had been clothed in a decent suit and shirt and tie and shoes, and his appearance had been neat and pleasing as he himself had thought as he left Bridgeburg. But now—how must he look? And to-morrow his mother would be coming—and later Jephson or Belknap, maybe. God!

But worse—there, in that cell directly opposite him, a sallow and emaciated and sinister-looking Chinaman in a suit exactly like his own, who had come to the bars of his door and was looking at him out of inscrutable slant eyes, but as immediately turning and scratching himself—vermin, maybe, as Clyde immediately feared. There had been bedbugs at Bridgeburg.

A Chinese murderer. For was not this the death house? But as good as himself here. And with a garb like his own. Thank God visitors were probably not many. He had heard from his mother that scarcely any were allowed—that only she and Belknap and Jephson and any minister he chose might come once a week. But now these hard, white-painted walls brightly lighted by wide unobstructed skylights by day as he could see—by incandescent lamps in the hall without at night—yet all so different from Bridgeburg,—so much more bright or harsh illuminatively. For there, the jail being old, the walls were a gray-brown, and not very clean—the cells larger, the furnishings more numerous—a table with a cloth on it at times, books, papers, a chess- and checker-board—whereas here—here was nothing, these hard narrow walls—the iron bars rising to a heavy solid ceiling above—and that very, very heavy iron door which yet—like the one at Bridgeburg, had a small hole through which food would be passed, of course.

But just then a voice from somewhere:

"Hey! we got a new one wid us, fellers! Ground tier, second cell, east." And then a second voice: "You don't say. Wot's he like?" And a third: "Wot's yer name, new man? Don't be scared. You ain't no worse off than the rest of us." And then the first voice, answering number two: "Kinda tall and skinny. A kid. Looks a little like mamma's boy, but not bad at dat. Hey, you! Tell us your name!"

And Clyde, amazed and dumb and pondering. For how was one to take such an introduction as this? What to say—what to do? Should he be friendly with these men? Yet, his instinct for tact prompting him even here to reply, most courteously and promptly: "Clyde Griffiths." And one of the first voices continuing: "Oh, sure! We know who you are. Welcome, Griffiths. We ain't as bad as we sound. We been readin' a lot about you, up dere in Bridgeburg. We thought you'd be along pretty soon now." And another voice: "You don't want to be too down. It ain't so worse here. At least de place is all right—a roof over your head, as dey say." And then a laugh from somewhere.

But Clyde, too horrified and sickened for words, was sadly gazing at the walls and door, then over at the Chinaman, who, silent at his door, was once more gazing at him. Horrible! Horrible! And they talked to each other like that, and to a stranger among them so familiarly. No thought for his wretchedness, his strangeness, his timidity—the horror he must be suffering. But why should a murderer seem timid to any one, perhaps, or miserable? Worst of all they had been speculating *here* as to how long it would be before he would be along which meant that everything concerning him was known here. Would they nag—or bully—or make trouble for one unless one did just as they wished? If Sondra, or any one of all the people he had known, should see or even dream of

him as he was here now . . . God!—And his own mother was
coming to-morrow.

And then an hour later, now evening, a tall, cadaverous
guard in a more pleasing uniform, putting an iron tray with
food on it through that hole in the door. Food! And for him
here. And that sallow, rickety Chinaman over the way taking
his. Whom had he murdered? How? And then the savage
scraping of iron trays in the various cells! Sounds that reminded him more of hungry animals being fed than men.
And some of these men were actually talking as they ate and
scraped. It sickened him.

"Gee! It's a wonder them guys in the mush gallery couldn't
think of somepin else besides cold beans and fried potatoes
and coffee."

"The coffee to-night . . . oh, boy! . . . Now in the jail at
Buffalo—though . . ."

"Oh, cut it out," came from another corner. "We've heard
enough about the jail at Buffalo and your swell chow. You
don't show any afternoon tea appetite around here, I notice."

"Just the same," continued the first voice, "as I look back
on't now, it musta been pretty good. Dat's a way it seems,
anyhow, now."

"Oh, Rafferty, do let up," called still another.

And then, presumably "Rafferty" once more, who said:
"Now, I'll just take a little siesta after dis—and den I'll call me
chauffeur and go for a little spin. De air to-night must be
fine."

Then from still another hoarse voice: "Oh, you with your
sick imagination. Say, I'd give me life for a smoker. And den
a good game of cards."

"Do they play cards here?" thought Clyde.

"I suppose since Rosenstein was defeated for mayor here he
won't play."

"Won't he, though?" This presumably from Rosenstein.

To Clyde's left, in the cell next to him, a voice, to a passing
guard, low and yet distinctly audible: "Psst! Any word from
Albany yet?"

"No word, Herman."

"And no letter, I suppose."

"No letter."

The voice was very strained, very tense, very miserable, and after this, silence.

A moment later, from another cell farther off, a voice from the lowest hell to which a soul can descend—complete and unutterable despair—"Oh, my God! Oh, my God! Oh, my God!"

And then from the tier above another voice: "Oh, Jesus! Is that farmer going to begin again? I can't stand it. Guard! Guard! Can't you get some dope for that guy?"

Once more the voice from the lowest: "Oh, my God! Oh, my God! Oh, my God!"

Clyde was up, his fingers clinched. His nerves were as taut as cords about to snap. A murderer! And about to die, perhaps. Or grieving over some terrible thing like his own fate. Moaning—as he in spirit at least had so often moaned there in Bridgeburg. Crying like that! God! And there must be others!

And day after day and night after night more of this, no doubt, until, maybe—who could tell—unless. But, oh, no! Oh, no! Not himself—not that—not his day. Oh, no. A whole year must elapse before that could possibly happen—or so Jephson had said. Maybe two. But, at that—! . . . in two years!!! He found himself stricken with an ague because of the thought that even in so brief a time as two years. . . .

That other room! It was in here somewhere too. This room was connected with it. He knew that. There was a door. It led to that chair. *That chair.*

And then the voice again, as before, "Oh, my God! Oh, my God!"

He sank to his couch and covered his ears with his hands.

# Chapter XXIX

THE "death house" in this particular prison was one of those crass erections and maintenances of human insensitiveness and stupidity principally for which no one primarily was really responsible. Indeed, its total plan and procedure were the results of a series of primary legislative enactments, followed by decisions and compulsions as devised by the temperaments and seeming necessities of various wardens, until at last—by degrees and without anything worthy of the name of thinking on any one's part—there had been gathered and was now being enforced all that could possibly be imagined in the way of unnecessary and really unauthorized cruelty or stupid and destructive torture. And to the end that a man, once condemned by a jury, would be compelled to suffer not alone the death for which his sentence called, but a thousand others before that. For the very room by its arrangement, as well as the rules governing the lives and actions of the inmates, was sufficient to bring about this torture, willy-nilly.

It was a room thirty by forty feet, of stone and concrete and steel, and surmounted some thirty feet from the floor by a skylight. Presumably an improvement over an older and worse death house, with which it was still connected by a door, it was divided lengthwise by a broad passage, along which, on the ground floor, were twelve cells, six on a side and eight by ten each and facing each other. And above again a second tier of what were known as balcony cells—five on a side.

There was, however, at the center of this main passage—and dividing these lower cells equally as to number—a second and narrower passage, which at one end gave into what was now known as the Old Death House (where at present only visitors to the inmates of the new Death House were received), and at the other into the execution room in which stood the electric chair. Two of the cells on the lower passage—those at the junction if the narrower passage—faced the execution-room door. The two opposite these, on the corresponding corners, faced the passage that gave into the old Death House or what now by a large stretch of the imagination, could be called the condemned men's reception room, where twice weekly an immediate relative or a lawyer might be met. But no others.

In the Old Death House (or present reception room), the cells still there, and an integral part of this reception plan, were all in a row and on one side only of a corridor, thus preventing prying inspection by one inmate of another, and with a wire screen in front as well as green shades which might be drawn in front of each cell. For, in an older day, whenever a new convict arrived or departed, or took his daily walk, or went for his bath, or was led eventually through the little iron door to the west where formerly was the execution chamber, these shades were drawn. He was not supposed to be seen by his associates. Yet the old death house, because of this very courtesy and privacy, although intense solitude, was later deemed inhuman and hence this newer and better death house, as the thoughtful and condescending authorities saw it, was devised.

In this, to be sure, were no such small and gloomy cells as those which characterized the old, for there the ceiling was low and the sanitary arrangements wretched, whereas in the new on one the ceiling was high, the rooms and corridors brightly lighted and in every instance no less than eight by ten feet in size. But by contrast with the older room, they had the enormous disadvantage of the unscreened if not uncurtained cell doors.

Besides, by housing all together in two such tiers as were here, it placed upon each convict the compulsion of enduring all the horrors of all the vicious, morbid or completely collapsed and despairing temperaments about him. No true privacy of any kind. By day—a blaze of light pouring through an over-arching skylight high above the walls. By night—glistening incandescents of large size and power which flooded each nook and cranny of the various cells. No privacy, no games other than cards and checkers—the only ones playable without releasing the prisoners from their cells. Books, newspapers, to be sure, for all who could read or enjoy them under the circumstances. And visits—mornings and afternoons, as a rule, from a priest, and less regularly from a rabbi and a

Protestant minister, each offering his sympathies or services to such as would accept them.

But the curse of the place was not because of these advantages, such as they were, but in spite of them—this unremitted contact, as any one could see, with minds now terrorized and discolored by the thought of an approaching death that was so near for many that it was as an icy hand upon brow or shoulder. And none—whatever the bravado—capable of enduring it without mental or physical deterioration in some form. The glooms—the strains—the indefinable terrors and despairs that blew like winds or breaths about this place and depressed or terrorized all by turns! They were manifest at the most unexpected moments, by curses, sighs, tears even, calls for a song—for God's sake!—or the most unintended and unexpected yells or groans.

Worse yet, and productive of perhaps the most grinding and destroying of all the miseries here—the transverse passage leading between the old death house on the one hand and the execution-chamber on the other. For this from time to time—alas, how frequently—was the scene or stage for at least a part of the tragedy that was here so regularly enacted—the final business of execution.

For through this passage, on his last day, a man was transferred from his *better* cell in the new building, where he might have been incarcerated for so much as a year or two, to one of the older ones in the old death house, in order that he might spend his last hours in solitude, although compelled at the final moment, none-the-less (the death march), to retrace his steps along this narrower cross passage—and where all might see—into the execution chamber at the other end of it.

Also at any time, in going to visit a lawyer or relative brought into the old death house for this purpose, it was necessary to pass along the middle passage to this smaller one and so into the old death house, there to be housed in a cell, fronted by a wire screen two feet distant, between which and the cell proper a guard must sit while a prisoner and his guest (wife, son, mother, daughter, brother, lawyer) should converse—the guard hearing all. No handclasps, no kisses, no friendly touches of any kind—not even an intimate word that a listening guard might not hear. And when the fatal hour for

any one had at last arrived, every prisoner—if sinister or simple, sensitive or of rugged texture—was actually if not intentionally compelled to hear if not witness the final
preparations—the removal of the condemned man to one of
the cells of the older death house, the final and perhaps weeping visit of a mother, son, daughter, father.

No thought in either the planning or the practice of all this
of the unnecessary and unfair torture for those who were
brought here, not to be promptly executed, by any means,
but rather to be held until the higher courts should have
passed upon the merits of their cases—an appeal.

At first, of course, Clyde sensed little if anything of all this.
In so far as his first day was concerned, he had but tasted the
veriest spoonful of it all. And to lighten or darken his burden
his mother came at noon the very next day. Not having been
permitted to accompany him, she had waited over for a final
conference with Belknap and Jephson, as well as to write in
full her personal impressions in connection with her son's
departure—(Those nervously searing impressions!) And
although anxious to find a room somewhere near the penitentiary, she hurried first to the office of the penitentiary
immediately upon her arrival at Auburn and, after presenting
an order from Justice Oberwaltzer as well as a solicitous letter from Belknap and Jephson urging the courtesy of a private
interview with Clyde to begin with at least, she was permitted
to see her son in a room entirely apart from the old death
house. For already the warden himself had been reading of
her activities and sacrifices and was interested in seeing not
only her but Clyde also.

But so shaken was she by Clyde's so sudden and amazingly
changed appearance here that she could scarcely speak upon
his entrance, even in recognition of him, so blanched and
gray were his cheeks and so shadowy and strained his eyes.
His head clipped that way! This uniform! And in this dreadful place of iron gates and locks and long passages with uniformed guards at every turn!

For a moment she winced and trembled, quite faint under
the strain, although previous to this she had entered many a
jail and larger prison—in Kansas City, Chicago, Denver—and
delivered tracts and exhortations and proffered her services in

connection with anything she might do. But this—this! Her own son! Her broad, strong bosom began to heave. She looked, and then turned her heavy, broad back to hide her face for the nonce. Her lips and chin quivered. She began to fumble in the small bag she carried for her handkerchief at the same time that she was muttering to herself: "My God—why hast thou forsaken me?" But even as she did so there came the thought—no, no, he must not see her so. What a way was this to do—and by her tears weaken him. And yet despite her great strength she could not now cease at once but cried on.

And Clyde seeing this, and despite his previous determination to bear up and say some comforting and heartening word to his mother, now began:

"But you mustn't, Ma. Gee, you mustn't cry. I know it's hard on you. But I'll be all right. Sure, I will. It isn't as bad as I thought." Yet inwardly saying: "Oh, God, how bad!"

And Mrs. Griffiths adding aloud: "My poor boy! My beloved son! But we mustn't give way. No. No. 'Behold, I will deliver Thee out of the snares of the wicked.' God has not deserted either of us. And He will not—that I know. 'He leadeth me by the still waters.' 'He restoreth my soul.' We must put our trust in Him. Besides," she added, briskly and practically, as much to strengthen herself as Clyde, "haven't I already arranged for an appeal? It is to be made yet this week. They're going to file a notice. And that means that your case can't even be considered under a year. But it is just the shock of seeing you so. You see, I wasn't quite prepared for it." She straightened her shoulders and now looked up and achieved a brave if strained smile. "The warden here seems very kind, but still, somehow, when I saw you just now——"

She dabbed at her eyes which were damp from this sudden and terrific storm, and to divert herself as well as him she talked of the so very necessary work before her. Messrs. Belknap and Jephson had been so encouraging to her just before she left. She had gone to their office and they had urged her and him to be of good cheer. And now she was going to lecture, and at once, and would soon have means to do with that way. Oh, yes. And Mr. Jephson would be down to see him one of these days soon. He was by no means to feel that the legal end of all this had been reached. Far from it. The recent verdict and sentence was sure to be reversed and a new trial ordered. The recent one was a farce, as he knew.

And as for herself—as soon as she found a room near the prison—she was going to the principal ministers of Auburn and see if she could not secure a church, or two, or three, in which to speak and plead his cause. Mr. Jephson was mailing her some information she could use within a day or two. And after that, other churches in Syracuse, Rochester, Albany, Schenectady—in fact many cities in the east—until she had raised the necessary sum. But she would not neglect him. She would see him at least once a week and would write him a letter every other day, or maybe even daily if she could. She would talk to the warden. So he must not despair. She had much hard work ahead of her, of course, but the Lord would guide her in all that she undertook. She knew that. Had He not already shown his gracious and miraculous mercy?

Clyde must pray for her and for himself. Read Isaiah. Read the psalms—the 23rd and the 51st and the 91st daily. Also Habbakuk. "Are there walls against the Hand of the Lord?" And then after more tears, an utterly moving and macerating scene, at last achieving her departure while Clyde, shaken to his soul by so much misery, returned to his cell. His mother. And at her age—and with so little money—she was going out to try to raise the money necessary to save him. And in the past he had treated her so badly—as he now saw.

He sat down on the side of his cot and held his head in his hands the while outside the prison—the iron door of the same closed and only a lonely room and the ordeal of her proposed lecture tour ahead of her—Mrs. Griffiths paused—by no means so assured or convinced of all she had said to Clyde. To be sure God would aid her. He must. Had He ever failed her yet—completely? And now—here—in her darkest hour,— her son's! Would He?

She paused for a moment a little later in a small parking-place, beyond the prison, to stare at the tall, gray walls, the watch towers with armed guards in uniform, the barred windows and doors. A penitentiary. And her son was now within—worse yet, in that confined and narrow death house. And doomed to die in an electric chair. Unless—unless—— But, no, no—that should not be. It could not be. That appeal. The money for it. She must busy herself as to that at once—not think or brood or despair. Oh, no. "My shield and my buckler." "My Light and my Strength." "Oh, Lord, Thou art my strength and my deliverance. In Thee will I trust." And then dabbing at her eyes once more and adding: "Oh, Lord, I believe. Help Thou mine unbelief."

So Mrs. Griffiths, alternately praying and crying as she walked.

# Chapter XXX

B UT AFTER this the long days in prison for Clyde. Except for a weekly visit from his mother, who, once she was entered upon her work, found it difficult to see him more often than that—traveling as she did in the next two months between Albany and Buffalo and even New York City—but without the success she had at first hoped for. For in the matter of her appeal to the churches and the public—as most wearily (and in secret if not to Clyde)—and after three weeks of more or less regional and purely sectarian trying, she was compelled to report the Christians at least were very indifferent—not as Christian as they should be. For as all, but more particularly the ministers of the region, since they most guardedly and reservedly represented their congregations in every instance, unanimously saw it, here was a notorious and, of course, most unsavory trial which had resulted in a conviction with which the more conservative element of the country—if one could judge by the papers at least, were in agreement.

Besides who was this woman—as well as her son? An exhorter—a secret preacher—one, who in defiance of all the tenets and processes of organized and historic, as well as hieratic, religious powers and forms (theological seminaries, organized churches and their affiliations and product—all carefully and advisedly and legitimately because historically and dogmatically interpreting the word of God) choosing to walk forth and without ordination after any fashion conduct an unauthorized and hence nondescript mission. Besides if she had remained at home, as a good mother should, and devoted herself to her son, as well as to her other children—their care and education—would this—have happened?

And not only that—but according to Clyde's own testimony in this trial, had he not been guilty of adultery with this girl—whether he had slain her or not? A sin almost equal to murder in many minds. Had he not confessed it? And was an appeal for a convicted adulterer—if not murderer (who could tell as to that?) to be made in a church? No,—no Christian church was the place to debate, and for a charge, the merits of this case, however much each Christian of each and every church might sympathize with Mrs. Griffiths personally—or resent any legal injustice that might have been done her son. No, no. It was not morally advisable. It might even tend to implant in the minds of the young some of the details of the crime.

Besides, because of what the newspapers had said of her coming east to aid her son and the picture that she herself presented in her homely garb, it was assumed by most ministers that she was one of those erratic persons, not a constituent of any definite sect, or schooled theology, who tended by her very appearance to cast contempt on true and pure religion.

And in consequence, each in turn—not hardening his heart exactly—but thinking twice—and deciding no—there must be some better way—less troublesome to Christians,—a public hall, perhaps, to which Christians, if properly appealed to through the press, might well repair. And so Mrs. Griffiths, in all but one instance, rejected in that fashion and told to go elsewhere—while in regard to the Catholics—instinctively—because of prejudice—as well as a certain dull wisdom not inconsistent with the facts—she failed even to so much as think of them. The mercies of Christ as interpreted by the holder of the sacred keys of St. Peter, as she knew, were not for those who failed to acknowledge the authority of the Vicar of Christ.

And therefore after many days spent in futile knockings here and there she was at last compelled—and in no little depression, to appeal to a Jew who controlled the principal moving picture theater of Utica—a sinful theater. And from him, this she secured free for a morning address on the merits of her son's case—"A mother's appeal for her son," it was entitled—which netted her, at twenty-five cents per person—the amazing sum of two hundred dollars. At first this sum, small as it was, so heartened her that she was now convinced that soon—whatever the attitude of the orthodox Christians—she would earn enough for Clyde's appeal. It might take time—but she would.

Nevertheless, as she soon discovered, there were other factors to be considered—carfare, her own personal expenses in

Utica and elsewhere, to say nothing of certain very necessary sums to be sent to Denver to her husband, who had little or nothing to go on at present, and who, because of this very great tragedy in the family, had been made ill—so ill indeed that the letters from Frank and Julia were becoming very disturbing. It was possible that he might not get well at all. Some help was necessary there.

And in consequence, in addition to paying her own expenses here, Mrs. Griffiths was literally compelled to deduct other reducing sums from this, her present and only source of income. It was terrible—considering Clyde's predicament—but nevertheless must she not sustain herself in every way in order to win to victory? She could not reasonably abandon her husband in order to aid Clyde alone.

Yet in the face of this—as time went on, the audiences growing smaller and smaller until at last they constituted little more than a handful—and barely paying her expenses—although through this process none-the-less she finally managed to put aside—over and above all her expenses—eleven hundred dollars.

Yet, also, just at this time, and in a moment of extreme anxiety, Frank and Julia wiring her that if she desired to see Asa again she had better come home at once. He was exceedingly low and not expected to live. Whereupon, played upon by these several difficulties and there being no single thing other than to visit him once or twice a week—as her engagements permitted—which she could do for Clyde, she now hastily conferred with Belknap and Jephson, setting forth her extreme difficulties.

And these, seeing that eleven hundred dollars of all she had thus far collected was to be turned over to them, now, in a burst of humanity, advised her to return to her husband. Decidedly Clyde would do well enough for the present seeing that there was an entire year—or at least ten months before it was necessary to file the record and the briefs in the case. In addition another year assuredly must elapse before a decision could be reached. And no doubt before that time the additional part of the appeal fee could be raised. Or, if not—well, then—anyhow (seeing how worn and distrait she was at this time) she need not worry. Messrs. Belknap and Jephson would see to it that her son's interests were properly protected. They would file an appeal and make an argument—and do whatever else was necessary to insure her son a fair hearing at the proper time.

And with that great burden off her mind—and two last visits to Clyde in which she assured him of her determination to return as speedily as possible—once Asa was restored to strength again and she could see her way to financing such a return—she now departed only to find that, once she was in Denver once more, it was not so easy to restore him by any means.

And in the meantime Clyde was left to cogitate on and make the best of a world that at its best was a kind of inferno of mental ills—above which—as above Dante's might have been written—"abandon hope—ye who enter here."

The somberness of it. Its slow and yet searing psychic force! The obvious terror and depression—constant and unshakeable of those who, in spite of all their courage or their fears, their bravado or their real indifference (there were even those) were still compelled to think and wait. For, now, in connection with this coldest and bitterest form of prison life he was in constant psychic, if not physical contact, with twenty other convicted characters of varying temperaments and nationalities, each one of whom, like himself, had responded to some heat or lust or misery of his nature or his circumstances. And with murder, a mental as well as physical explosion, as the final outcome or concluding episode which, being detected, and after what horrors and wearinesses of mental as well as legal contest and failure, such as fairly paralleled his own, now found themselves islanded—immured—in one or another of these twenty-two iron cages and awaiting—awaiting what?

How well they knew. And how well he knew. And here with what loud public rages and despairs or prayers—at times. At others—what curses—foul or coarse jests—or tales addressed to all—or ribald laughter—or sighings and groanings in these later hours when the straining spirit having struggled to silence, there was supposedly rest for the body and the spirit.

In an exercise court, beyond the farthermost end of the long corridor, twice daily, for a few minutes each time, between the hours of ten and five—the various inmates in groups of five or six were led forth—to breathe, to walk, to practice calisthenics—or run and leap as they chose. But always under the watchful eyes of sufficient guards to master them in case they attempted rebellion in any form. And to this it was, beginning with the second day, that Clyde himself was led, now with one set of men and now with another. But with the feeling at first strong in him that he could not share in any of these public activities which, nevertheless, these others—and in spite of their impending doom—seemed willing enough to indulge in.

The two dark-eyed sinister-looking Italians, one of whom had slain a girl because she would not marry him; the other who had robbed and then slain and attempted to burn the body of his father-in-law in order to get money for himself and his wife! And big Larry Donahue—square-headed, square-shouldered—big of feet and hands, an overseas soldier, who, being ejected from a job as night watchman in a Brooklyn factory, had lain for the foreman who had discharged him—and then killed him on an open common somewhere at night, but without the skill to keep from losing a service medal which had eventually served to betray and identify him. Clyde had learned all this from the strangely indifferent and non-committal, yet seemingly friendly guards, who were over these cells by night and by day—two and two, turn about—who relieved each other every eight hours. And police officer Riordan of Rochester, who had killed his wife because she was determined to leave him—and now, himself, was to die. And Thomas Mowrer, the young "farmer" or farm hand, as he really was, whom Clyde on his first night had heard moaning—a man who had killed his employer with a pitchfork—and was soon to die now—as Clyde heard, and who walked and walked, keeping close to the wall—his head down, his hands behind his back—a rude, strong, loutish man of about thirty, who looked more beaten and betrayed than as though he had been able to torture or destroy another. Clyde wondered about him—his real guilt.

Again Miller Nicholson, a lawyer of Buffalo of perhaps forty years of age who was tall and slim and decidedly superior looking—a refined, intellectual type, one you would have said was no murderer—any more than Clyde—to look at, who, none-the-less was convicted of poisoning an old man of great wealth and afterwards attempting to convert his fortune to his own use. Yet decidedly with nothing in his look or manner, as Clyde felt, at least, which marked him as one so evil—a polite and courteous man, who, noting Clyde on the very first morning of his arrival here, approached and said: "Scared?" But in the most gentle and solicitous tone, as Clyde could hear and feel, even though he stood blank and icy—afraid almost to move—or think. Yet in this mood—and because he felt so truly done for, replying: "Yes, I guess I am." But once it was out, wondering why he had said it (so weak a confession) and afterwards something in the man heartening him, wishing that he had not.

"Your name's Griffiths, isn't it?"

"Yes."

"Well, my name's Nicholson. Don't be frightened. You'll get used to it." He achieved a cheerful, if wan smile. But his eyes—they did not seem like that—no smile there.

"I don't suppose I'm so scared either," replied Clyde, trying to modify his first, quick and unintended confession.

"Well, that's good. Be game. We all have to be here—or the whole place would go crazy. Better breathe a little. Or walk fast. It'll do you good."

He moved away a few paces and began exercising his arms while Clyde stood there, saying—almost loudly—so shaken was he still: "We all have to be or the whole place would go crazy." That was true, as he could see and feel after that first night. Crazy, indeed. Tortured to death, maybe, by being compelled to witness these terrible and completely destroying—and for each—impending tragedies. But how long would he have to endure this? How long could he?

In the course of a day or two, again he found this death house was not quite like that either—not all terror—on the surface at least. It was in reality—and in spite of impending death in every instance, a place of taunt and jibe and jest—even games, arguments on every conceivable topic from death and women to athletics, the stage—all forms of human contest of skill—or the lack of it, as far at least as the general low intelligence of the group permitted.

For the most part, as soon as breakfast was over—among

those who were not called upon to join the first group for exercise, there were checkers or cards, two games that were played—not with a single set of checkers or a deck of cards between groups released from their cells, but by one of the ever present keepers providing two challenging prisoners (if it were checkers) with one checker-board but no checkers. They were not needed. Thereafter the opening move was called by one. "I move from F2 to E1"—each square being numbered—each side lettered. The moves checked with a pencil.

Thereafter the second party—having recorded this move on his own board and having studied the effect of it on his own general position, would call: "I move from E7 to F5." If more of those present decided to join in this—either on one side or the other, additional boards and pencils were passed to each signifying his desire. Then Shorty Bristol, desiring to aid "Dutch" Swighort, three cells down, might call: "I wouldn't do that, Dutch. Wait a minute, there's a better move than that." And so on with taunts, oaths, laughter, arguments, according to the varying fortunes and difficulties of the game. And so, too, with cards. These were played with each man locked in his cell, yet quite as successfully.

But Clyde did not care for cards—or for these jibing and coarse hours of conversation. There was for him—and with the exception of the speech of one—Nicholson—alone, too much ribald and even brutal talk which he could not appreciate. But he was drawn to Nicholson. He was beginning to think after a time—a few days—that this lawyer—his presence and companionship during the exercise hour—whenever they chanced to be in the same set—could help him to endure this. He was the most intelligent and respectable man here. The others were all so different—taciturn at times—and for the most part so sinister, crude or remote.

But then and that not more than a week after his coming here—and when, because of his interest in Nicholson, he was beginning to feel slightly sustained at least—the execution of Pasquale Cutrone, of Brooklyn, an Italian, convicted of the slaying of his brother for attempting to seduce his wife. He had one of the cells nearest the transverse passage, so Clyde learned after arriving, and had in part lost his mind from worrying. At any rate he was invariably left in his cell when the others—in groups of six—were taken for exercise. But the horror of his emaciated face, as Clyde passed and occasionally looked in—a face divided into three grim panels by two gutters or prison lines of misery that led from the eyes to the corners of the mouth.

Beginning with his, Clyde's, arrival, as he learned, Pasquale had begun to pray night and day. For already, before that, he had been notified of the approximate date of his death which was to be within the week. And after that he was given to crawling up and down his cell on his hands and knees, kissing the floor, licking the feet of a brass Christ on a cross that had been given him. Also he was repeatedly visited by an Italian brother and sister fresh from Italy and for whose benefit at certain hours, he was removed to the old death house. But as all now whispered, Pasquale was mentally beyond any help that might lie in brothers or sisters.

All night long and all day long, when they were not present, he did this crawling to and fro and praying, and those who were awake and trying to read to pass the time, were compelled to listen to his mumbled prayers, the click of the beads of a rosary on which he was numbering numberless Our Fathers and Hail Marys.

And though there were voices which occasionally said: "Oh, for Christ's sake—if he would only sleep a little"—still on, on. And the tap of his forehead on the floor—in prayer, until at last the fatal day preceding the one on which he was to die, when Pasquale was taken from his cell here and escorted to another in the old death house beyond and where, before the following morning, as Clyde later learned, last farewells, if any, were to be said. Also he was to be allowed a few hours in which to prepare his soul for his maker.

But throughout that night what a strange condition was this that settled upon all who were of this fatal room. Few ate any supper as the departing trays showed. There was silence—and after that mumbled prayers on the part of some—not so greatly removed by time from Pasquale's fate, as they knew. One Italian, sentenced for the murder of a bank watchman, became hysterical, screamed, hashed the chair and table of his cell against the bars of his door, tore the sheets of his bed to shreds and even sought to strangle himself before eventually he was overpowered and removed to a cell in a different part of the building to be observed as to his sanity.

As for the others, throughout this excitement, one could hear them walking and mumbling or calling to the guards to do something. And as for Clyde, never having experienced or imagined such a scene, he was literally shivering with fear and horror. All through the last night of this man's life he lay on his pallet, chasing phantoms. So this was what death was like here; men cried, prayed, they lost their minds—yet the deadly process was in no way halted, for all their terror. Instead, at ten o'clock and in order to quiet all those who were left, a cold lunch was brought in and offered—but with none eating save the Chinaman over the way.

And then at four the following morning—the keepers in charge of the deadly work coming silently along the main passage and drawing the heavy green curtains with which the cells were equipped so that none might see the fatal procession which was yet to return along the transverse passage from the old death house to the execution room. And yet with Clyde and all the others waking and sitting up at the sound.

It was here, the execution! The hour of death was at hand. This was the signal. In their separate cells, many of those who through fear or contrition, or because of innate religious convictions, had been recalled to some form of shielding or comforting faith, were upon their knees praying. Among the rest were others who merely walked or muttered. And still others who screamed from time to time in an incontrollable fever of terror.

As for Clyde he was numb and dumb. Almost thoughtless. They were going to kill that man in that other room in there. That chair—that chair that he had so greatly feared this long while was in there—was so close now. Yet his time as Jephson and his mother had told him was so long and distant as yet— if ever—ever it was to be—if ever—ever——

But now other sounds. Certain walkings to and fro. A cell door clanking somewhere. Then plainly the door leading from the old death house into this room opening—for there was a voice—several voices indistinct as yet. Then another voice a little clearer as if some one praying. That tell-tale shuf-

fling of feet as a procession moved across and through that
passage. "Lord have mercy. Christ have mercy."

"Mary, Mother of Grace, Mary, Mother of Mercy, St.
Michael, pray for me; my good Angel, pray for me."

"Holy Mary, pray for me; St. Joseph, pray for me. St.
Ambrose, pray for me; all ye saints and angels, pray for me."

"St. Michael, pray for me; my good Angel, pray for me."

It was the voice of the priest accompanying the doomed
man and reciting a litany. Yet he was no longer in his right
mind they said. And yet was not that his voice mumbling too?
It was. Clyde could tell. He had heard it too much recently.
And now that other door would be opened. He would be
looking through it—this condemned man—so soon to be
dead—at it—seeing it—that cap—those straps. Oh, he knew
all about those by now though they should never come to be
put upon him, maybe.

"Good-by, Cutrone!" It was a hoarse, shaky voice from
some near-by cell—Clyde could not tell which. "Go to a better
world than this." And then other voices: "Good-by, Cutrone.
God keep you—even though you can't talk English."

The procession had passed. That door was shut. He was in
there now. They were strapping him in, no doubt. Asking him
what more he had to say—he who was no longer quite right
in his mind. Now the straps must be fastened on, surely. The
cap pulled down. In a moment, a moment, surely——

And then, although Clyde did not know or notice at the
moment—a sudden dimming of the lights in this room—as
well as over the prison—an idiotic or thoughtless result of
having one electric system to supply the death voltage and the
incandescence of this and all other rooms. And instantly a
voice calling:

"There she goes. That's one. Well, it's all over with him."

And a second voice: "Yes, he's topped off, poor devil."

And then after the lapse of a minute perhaps, a second dimming lasting for thirty seconds—and finally a third dimming.

"There—sure—that's the end now."

"Yes. He knows what's on the other side now."

Thereafter silence—a deadly hush with later some murmured prayers here and there. But with Clyde cold and with
a kind of shaking ague. He dared not think—let alone cry. So

that's how it was. They drew the curtains. And then—and then. He was gone now. Those three dimmings of the lights. Sure, those were the flashes. And after all those nights at prayer. Those moanings! Those beatings of his head! And only a minute ago he had been alive—walking by there. But now dead. And some day he—he!—how could he be sure that he would not? How could he?

He shook and shook, lying on his couch, face down. The keepers came and ran up the curtains—as sure and secure in their lives apparently as though there was no death in the world. And afterwards he could hear them talking—not to him so much—he had proved too reticent thus far—but to some of the others.

Poor Pasquale. This whole business of the death penalty was all wrong. The warden thought so. So did they. He was working to have it abolished.

But that man! His prayers! And now he was gone. His cell over there was empty and another man would be put in it— to go too, later. Some one—many—like Cutrone, like himself—had been in this one—on this pallet. He sat up—moved to the chair. But he—they—had sat on that—too. He stood up—only to sink down on the pallet again. "God! God! God! God!" he now exclaimed to himself—but not aloud—and yet not unlike that other man who had so terrorized him on the night of his arrival here and who was still here. But he would go too. And all of these others—and himself maybe—unless— unless——

He had seen his first man die.

# Chapter XXXI

IN THE MEANTIME, however, Asa's condition had remained serious, and it was four entire months before it was possible for him to sit up again or for Mrs. Griffiths to dream of resuming her lecturing scheme. But by that time, public interest in her and her son's fate was considerably reduced. No Denver paper was interested to finance her return for anything she could do for them. And as for the public in the vicinity of the crime, it remembered Mrs. Griffiths and her son most clearly, and in so far as she was concerned, sympathetically—but only, on the other hand, to think of him as one who probably was guilty and in that case, being properly punished for his crime—that it would be as well if an appeal were not taken—or—if it were—that it be refused. These guilty criminals with their interminable appeals!

And with Clyde where he was, more and more executions—although as he found—and to his invariable horror, no one ever became used to such things there; farmhand Mowrer for the slaying of his former employer; officer Riordan for the slaying of his wife—and a fine upstanding officer too but a minute before his death; and afterwards, within the month, the going of the Chinaman, who seemed, for some reason, to endure a long time (and without a word in parting to any one—although it was well known that he spoke a few words of English). And after him Larry Donahue, the overseas soldier—with a grand call—just before the door closed behind: "Good-by, boys. Good luck."

And after him again—but, oh—that was so hard; so much closer to Clyde—so depleting to his strength to think of bearing this deadly life here without—Miller Nicholson—no less. For after five months in which they had been able to walk and talk and call to each other from time to time from their cells—and Nicholson had begun to advise him as to books to read—as well as one important point in connection with his own case—on appeal—or in the event of any second trial, i.e.,—that the admission of Roberta's letters as evidence, as they stood, at least, be desperately fought on the ground that the emotional force of them was detrimental in the case of any jury anywhere, to a calm unbiased consideration of the material facts presented by them—and that instead of the letters being admitted as they stood they should be digested for the facts alone and that digest—and that only offered to the jury. "If your lawyers can get the Court of Appeals to agree to the soundness of that you will win your case sure."

And Clyde at once, after inducing a personal visit on the part of Jephson, laying this suggestion before him and hearing him say that it was sound and that he and Belknap would assuredly incorporate it in their appeal.

Yet not so long after that the guard, after locking his door on returning from the courtyard whispered, with a nod in the direction of Nicholson's cell, "His next. Did he tell you? Within three days."

And at once Clyde shriveling—the news playing upon him as an icy and congealing breath. For he had just come from the courtyard with him where they had walked and talked of another man who had just been brought in—a Hungarian of Utica who was convicted of burning his paramour—in a furnace—then confessing it—a huge, rough, dark, ignorant man with a face like a gargoyle. And Nicholson saying he was more animal than man, he was sure. Yet no word about himself. And in *three days!* And he could walk and talk as though there was nothing to happen, although, according to the guard, he had been notified the night before.

And the next day the same—walking and talking as though nothing had happened—looking up at the sky and breathing the air. Yet Clyde, his companion, too sick and feverish—too awed and terrified from merely thinking on it all night to be able to say much of anything as he walked but thinking: "And he can walk here. And be so calm. What sort of a man is this?" and feeling enormously overawed and weakened.

The following morning Nicholson did not appear—but remained in his cell destroying many letters he had received from many places. And near noon, calling to Clyde who was two cells removed from him on the other side: "I'm sending you something to remember me by." But not a word as to his going.

And then the guard bringing two books—Robinson Crusoe and the Arabian Nights. That night Nicholson's removal from his cell—and the next morning before dawn the curtains; the same procession passing through, which was by now an old story to Clyde. But somehow this was so different—so intimate—so cruel. And as he passed, calling: "God bless you all. I hope you have good luck and get out." And then that terrible stillness that followed the passing of each man.

And Clyde thereafter—lonely—terribly so. Now there was no one here—no one—in whom he was interested. He could only sit and read—and think—or pretend to be interested in what these others said, for he could not really be interested in what they said. His was a mind that, freed from the miseries that had now befallen him, was naturally more drawn to romance than to reality. Where he read at all he preferred the light, romantic novel that pictured some such world as he would have liked to share, to anything that even approximated the hard reality of the world without, let alone this. Now what was going to become of him eventually? So alone was he! Only letters from his mother, brother and sisters. And Asa getting no better, and his mother not able to return as yet—things were so difficult there in Denver. She was seeking a religious school in which to teach somewhere—while nursing Asa. But she was asking the Rev. Duncan McMillan, a young minister whom she had encountered in Syracuse, in the course of her work there, to come and see him. He was so spiritual and so kindly. And she was sure, if he would but come, that Clyde would find him a helpful and a strong support in these, his dark and weary hours when she could no longer be with him herself.

For while Mrs. Griffiths was first canvassing the churches and ministers of this section for aid for her son, and getting very little from any quarter, she had met the Rev. Duncan McMillan in Syracuse, where he was conducting an independent, non-sectarian church. He was a young, and like herself or Asa, unordained minister or evangelist of, however, far stronger and more effective temperament religiously. At the time Mrs. Griffiths appeared on the scene, he had already read much concerning Clyde and Roberta—and was fairly well satisfied that, by the verdict arrived at, justice had probably been done. However, because of her great sorrow and troubled search for aid he was greatly moved.

He, himself, was a devoted son. And possessing a highly

poetic and emotional though so far repressed or sublimated sex nature, he was one who, out of many in this northern region, had been touched and stirred by the crime of which Clyde was presumed to be guilty. Those highly emotional and tortured letters of Roberta's! Her seemingly sad life at Lycurgus and Biltz! How often he had thought of those before ever he had encountered Mrs. Griffiths. The simple and worthy virtues which Roberta and her family had seemingly represented in that romantic, pretty country world from which they had derived. Unquestionably Clyde was guilty. And yet here, suddenly, Mrs. Griffiths, very lorn and miserable and maintaining her son's innocence. At the same time there was Clyde in his cell doomed to die. Was it possible that by any strange freak or circumstance—a legal mistake had been made and Clyde was not as guilty as he appeared?

The temperament of McMillan was exceptional—tense, exotic. A present hour St. Bernard, Savonarola, St. Simeon, Peter the Hermit. Thinking of life, thought, all forms and social structures as the word, the expression, the breath of God. No less. Yet room for the Devil and his anger—the expelled Lucifer—going to and fro in the earth. Yet, thinking on the Beatitudes, on the Sermon on the Mount, on St. John and his direct seeing and interpretation of Christ and God. "He that is not with me is against me; and he that gathereth not with me, scattereth." A strange, strong, tense, confused, merciful and too, after his fashion beautiful soul; sorrowing with misery yearning toward an impossible justice.

Mrs. Griffiths in her talks with him had maintained that he was to remember that Roberta was not wholly guiltless. Had she not sinned with her son? And how was he to exculpate her entirely? A great legal mistake. Her son was being most unjustly executed—and by the pitiful but none-the-less romantic and poetic letters of this girl which should never have been poured forth upon a jury of men at all. They were, as she now maintained, incapable of judging justly or fairly where anything sad in connection with a romantic and pretty girl was concerned. She had found that to be true in her mission work.

And this idea now appealed to the Rev. Duncan as important and very likely true. And perhaps, as she now contended, if only some powerful and righteous emissary of God would visit Clyde and through the force of his faith and God's word make him see—which she was sure he did not yet, and which she in her troubled state, and because she was his mother, could not make him,—the blackness and terror of his sin with Roberta as it related to his immortal soul here and hereafter,—then in gratitude to, reverence and faith in God, would be washed away, all his iniquity, would it not? For irrespective of whether he had committed the crime now charged against him or not—and she was convinced that he had not—was he not, nevertheless, in the shadow of the electric chair—in danger at any time through death (even before a decision should be reached) of being called before his maker—and with the deadly sin of adultery, to say nothing of all his lies and false conduct, not only in connection with Roberta but that other girl there in Lycurgus, upon him? And by conversion and contrition should he not be purged of this? If only his soul were saved—she and he too would be at peace in this world.

And after a first and later a second pleading letter from Mrs. Griffiths, in which, after she had arrived at Denver, she set forth Clyde's loneliness and need of counsel and aid, the Rev. Duncan setting forth for Auburn. And once there—having made it clear to the warden what his true purpose was—the spiritual salvation of Clyde's soul, for his own, as well as his mother and God's sake, he was at once admitted to the death house and to Clyde's presence—the very door of his cell, where he paused and looked through, observing Clyde lying most wretchedly on his cot trying to read. And then McMillan outlining his tall, thin figure against the bars and without introduction of any kind, beginning, his head bowed in prayer:

"Have mercy upon me, O God, according to thy loving-kindness; according unto the multitude of thy tender mercies, blot out my transgressions."

"Wash me thoroughly from my iniquity and cleanse me from my sin."

"For I acknowledge my transgressions, and my sin is ever before me."

"Against Thee, Thee only have I sinned, and done this evil in thy sight, that Thou mightest be justified when Thou speakest and be clear when Thou judgest."

"Behold, I was shapen in iniquity; and in sin did my mother conceive me."

"Behold, Thou desireth truth in the inward parts; and in the hidden part Thou shalt make me to know wisdom."

"Purge me with hyssop, and I shall be clean; wash me, and I shall be whiter than snow."

"Make me to hear joy and gladness; that the bones which Thou hast broken may rejoice."

"Hide thy face from my sins, and blot out all mine iniquities."

"Create in me a clean heart, O God; and renew a right spirit within me."

"Cast me not away from Thy presence; and take not Thy holy spirit away from me."

"Restore unto me the joy of Thy salvation, and uphold me with Thy free spirit."

"Then will I teach transgressors Thy ways; and sinners will be converted unto Thee."

"Deliver me from blood guiltiness, O God, thou God of my salvation, and my tongue shall sing aloud of Thy righteousness."

"O Lord, open Thou my lips; and my mouth shall show forth Thy praise."

"For Thou desirest not sacrifice; else would I give it; Thou delightest not in burnt offering."

"The sacrifices of God are a broken spirit; a broken and a contrite heart, O God, Thou wilt not despise."

He paused—but only after he had intoned, and in a most sonorous and really beautiful voice the entire 51st Psalm. And then looking up, because Clyde, much astonished, had first sat up and then risen—and curiously enticed by the clean and youthful and vigorous if pale figure had approached nearer the cell door, he now added:

"I bring you, Clyde, the mercy and the salvation of your God. He has called on me and I have come. He has sent me that I may say unto you though your sins be as scarlet, they shall be white—like snow. Though they be red, like crimson, they shall be as wool. Come now, let us reason together with the Lord."

He paused and stared at Clyde tenderly. A warm, youthful, half smile, half romantic, played about his lips. He liked the youth and refinement of Clyde, who, on his part was plainly taken by this exceptional figure. Another religionist, of course. But the Protestant chaplain who was here was nothing like this man—neither so arresting nor attractive.

"Duncan McMillan is my name," he said, "and I come from the work of the Lord in Syracuse. He has sent me—just as he sent your mother to me. She has told me all that she believes. I have read all that you have said. And I know why you are here. But it is to bring you spiritual joy and gladness that I am here."

And he suddenly quoted from Psalms 13:2, "'How shall I take counsel in my soul, having sorrow in my heart, daily.' That is from Psalms 13:2. And here is another thing that now comes to me as something that I should say to you. It is from the Bible, too—the Tenth Psalm: 'He hath said in his heart, I shall not be moved, for I shall never be in adversity.' But you are in adversity, you see. We all are, who live in sin. And here is another thing that comes to me, just now, to say. It is from Psalm 10:11: 'He hath said in his heart, God hath forgotten. He hideth his face.' And I am told to say to you that He does not hide his face. Rather I am told to quote this to you from the Eighteenth Psalm: 'They prevented me in the day of my calamity, but the Lord was my stay. He sent from above, he took me, he drew me out of many waters.'

"'He delivered me from my strong enemy.

"'And from them which hated me, for they were too many for me.

"'He brought me forth also unto a large place.

"'He delivered me because he delighted in me.'

"Clyde, those are all words addressed to you. They come to me here to say to you just as though they were being whispered to me. I am but the mouthpiece for these words spoken direct to you. Take counsel with your own heart. Turn from the shadow to the light. Let us break these bonds of misery and gloom; chase these shadows and this darkness. You have sinned. The Lord can and will forgive. Repent. Join with him who has shaped the world and keeps it. He will not spurn your faith; he will not neglect your prayers. Turn—in yourself—in the confines of this cell—and say: 'Lord, help me. Lord, hear Thou my prayer. Lord, lighten mine eyes!'

"Do you think there is no God—and that He will not answer you? Pray. In your trouble turn to Him—not me—or any other. But to Him. Pray. Speak to Him. Call to Him. Tell Him the truth and ask for help. As surely as you are here before me—and if in your heart you truly repent of any evil you have done—*truly, truly,* you will hear and feel Him. He will take your hand. He will enter this cell and your soul. You will know Him by the peace and the light that will fill your mind and heart. Pray. And if you need me again to help you in any way—to pray with you—or to do you any service of any kind—to cheer you in your loneliness—you have only to send for me; drop me a card. I have promised your mother and I will do what I can. The warden has my address." He paused, serious and conclusive in his tone—because up to this time, Clyde had looked more curious and astonished than anything else.

At the same time because of Clyde's extreme youthfulness and a certain air of lonely dependence which marked him ever since his mother and Nicholson had gone: "I'll always be in easy reach. I have a lot of religious work over in Syracuse but I'll be glad to drop it at any time that I can really do anything more for you." And here he turned as if to go.

But Clyde, now taken by him—his vital, confident and kindly manner—so different to the tense, fearful and yet lonely life here, called after him: "Oh, don't go just yet. Please don't. It's very nice of you to come and see me and I'm obliged to you. My mother wrote me you might. You see, it's very lonely here. I haven't thought much of what you were saying, perhaps, because I haven't felt as guilty as some think I am. But I've been sorry enough. And certainly any one in here pays a good deal." His eyes looked very sad and strained.

And at once, McMillan, now deeply touched for the first time replied: "Clyde, you needn't worry. I'll come to see you again within a week, because now I see you need me. I'm not asking you to pray because I think you are guilty of the death of Roberta Alden. I don't know. You haven't told me. Only you and God know what your sins and your sorrows are. But I do know you need spiritual help and He will give you that—oh, fully. 'The Lord will be a refuge for the oppressed; a refuge in time of trouble.'"

He smiled as though he were now really fond of Clyde. And Clyde feeling this and being intrigued by it, replied that there wasn't anything just then that he wanted to say except to tell his mother that he was all right—and make her feel a little better about him, maybe, if he could. Her letters were very sad, he thought. She worried too much about him. Besides he, himself, wasn't feeling so very good—not a little run down and worried these days. Who wouldn't be in his position? Indeed, if only he could win to spiritual peace through prayer, he would be glad to do it. His mother had always urged him to pray—but up to now he was sorry to say he hadn't followed her advice very much. He looked very distrait and gloomy—the marked prison pallor having long since settled on his face.

And the Reverend Duncan, now very much touched by his state, replied: "Well, don't worry, Clyde. Enlightenment and peace are surely going to come to you. I can see that. You have a Bible there, I see. Open it anywhere in Psalms and read. The 51st, 91st, 23rd. Open to St. John. Read it all—over and over. Think and pray—and think on all the things about you—the moon, the stars, the sun, the trees, the sea—your own beating heart, your body and strength—and ask yourself who made them. How did they come to be? Then, if you can't explain them, ask yourself if the one who made them and you—whoever he is, whatever he is, wherever he is, isn't strong and wise enough and kind enough to help you when you need help—provide you with light and peace and guidance, when you need them. Just ask yourself what of the Maker of all this certain reality. And then ask Him—the Creator of it all—to tell you how and what to do. Don't doubt. Just ask and see. Ask in the night—in the day. Bow your head and pray and see. Verily, He will not fail you. I know because I have that peace."

He stared at Clyde convincingly—then smiled and departed. And Clyde, leaning against his cell door, began to

wonder. The Creator! His Creator! The Creator of the World!
. . . Ask and see——!

And yet—there was still lingering here in him that old contempt of his for religion and its fruits,—the constant and yet
fruitless prayers and exhortations of his father and mother.
Was he going to turn to religion now, solely because he was
in difficulties and frightened like these others? He hoped not.
Not like that, anyway.

Just the same the mood, as well as the temperament of the
Reverend Duncan McMillan—his young, forceful, convinced
and dramatic body, face, eyes, now intrigued and then moved
Clyde as no religionist or minister in all his life before ever
had. He was interested, arrested and charmed by the man's
faith—whether at once or not at all—ever—he could come to
put the reliance in it that plainly this man did.

# Chapter XXXII

THE PERSONAL conviction and force of such an individual as the Reverend McMillan, while in one sense an old story to Clyde and not anything which so late as eighteen months before could have moved him in any way (since all his life he had been accustomed to something like it), still here, under these circumstances, affected him differently. Incarcerated, withdrawn from the world, compelled by the highly circumscribed nature of this death house life to find solace or relief in his own thoughts, Clyde's, like every other temperament similarly limited, was compelled to devote itself either to the past, the present or the future. But the past was so painful to contemplate at any point. It seared and burned. And the present (his immediate surroundings) as well as the future with its deadly fear of what was certain to happen in case his appeal failed, were two phases equally frightful to his waking consciousness.

What followed then was what invariably follows in the wake of every tortured consciousness. From what it dreads or hates, yet knows or feels to be unescapable, it takes refuge in that which may be hoped for—or at least imagined. But what was to be hoped for or imagined? Because of the new suggestion offered by Nicholson, a new trial was all that he had to look forward to, in which case, and assuming himself to be acquitted thereafter, he could go far, far away—to Australia—or Africa—or Mexico—or some such place as that, where, under a different name—his old connections and ambitions relating to that superior social life that had so recently intrigued him, laid aside, he might recover himself in some small way. But directly in the path of that hopeful imagining, of course, stood the death's head figure of a refusal on the part of the Court of Appeals to grant him a new trial. Why not—after that jury at Bridgeburg? And then—as in that dream in which he turned from the tangle of snakes to face the tramping rhinoceros with its two horns—he was confronted by that awful thing in the adjoining room—that chair! That chair! Its straps and its flashes which so regularly dimmed the lights in this room. He could not bear to think of his entering there—ever. And yet supposing his appeal was refused! Away! He would like to think no more about it.

But then, apart from that what was there to think of? It was that very question that up to the time of the arrival of the Rev. Duncan McMillan, with his plea for a direct and certainly (as he insisted) fruitful appeal to the Creator of all things, that had been definitely torturing Clyde. Yet see—how simple was his solution!

"It is given unto you to know the Peace of God," he insisted, quoting Paul and thereafter sentences from Corinthians, Galatians, Ephesians, on how easy it was—if Clyde would but repeat and pray as he had asked him to—for him to know and delight in the "peace that passeth all understanding." It was with him, all around him. He had but to seek; confess the miseries and errors of his heart, and express contrition. "Ask, and ye shall receive; seek, and ye shall find; knock, and it shall be opened unto you. For *every one* that asketh, receiveth; and he that seeketh, findeth; and to him that knocketh it shall be opened. For what man is there of you whom, if his son ask bread, will give him a stone; or, if he ask fish, will give him a serpent?" So he quoted, beautifully and earnestly.

And yet before Clyde always was the example of his father and mother. What had they? It had not availed them much—praying. Neither, as he noticed here, did it appear to avail or aid these other condemned men, the majority of whom lent themselves to the pleas or prayers of either priest or rabbi or minister, one and the other of whom was about daily. Yet were they not led to their death just the same—and complaining or protesting, or mad like Cutrone, or indifferent? As for himself, up to this he had not been interested by any of these. Bunk. Notions. Of what? He could not say. Nevertheless, here was the appealing Rev. Duncan McMillan. His mild, serene eyes. His sweet voice. His faith. It moved and intrigued Clyde deeply. Could there—could there? He was so lonely—so despairing—so very much in need of help.

Was it not also true (the teaching of the Rev. McMillan—influencing him to that extent at least) that if he had led a better life—had paid more attention to what his mother had

said and taught—not gone into that house of prostitution in
Kansas City—or pursued Hortense Briggs in the evil way that
he had—or after her, Roberta—had been content to work
and save, as no doubt most men were—would he not be better off than he now was? But then again, there was the fact or
truth of those very strong impulses and desires within himself
that were so very, very hard to overcome. He had thought of
those, too, and then of the fact that many other people like
his mother, his uncle, his cousin, and this minister here, did
not seem to be troubled by them. And yet also he was given
to imagining at times that perhaps it was because of superior
mental and moral courage in the face of passions and desires,
equivalent to his own, which led these others to do so much
better. He was perhaps just willfully devoting himself to these
other thoughts and ways, as his mother and McMillan and
most every one else whom he had heard talk since his arrest
seemed to think.

What did it all mean? Was there a God? Did He interfere in
the affairs of men as Mr. McMillan was now contending? Was
it possible that one could turn to Him, or at least some cre-
ative power, in some such hour as this and when one had always ignored Him before, and ask for aid? Decidedly one
needed aid under such circumstances—so alone and ordered
and controlled by law—not man—since these, all of them,
were the veriest servants of the law. But would this mysterious
power be likely to grant aid? Did it really exist and hear the
prayers of men? The Rev. McMillan insisted yes. "He hath
said God hath forgotten; He hideth His face. But He has not
forgotten. He has not hidden His face." But was that true?
Was there anything to it? Tortured by the need of some mental if not material support in the face of his great danger,
Clyde was now doing what every other human in related circumstances invariably does—seeking, and yet in the most in-
direct and involute and all but unconscious way, the presence
or existence at least of some superhuman or supernatural personality or power that could and would aid him in some
way—beginning to veer—however slightly or unconsciously
as yet,—toward the personalization and humanization of
forces, of which, except in the guise of religion, he had not
the faintest conception. "The Heavens declare the Glory of

God, and the Firmament sheweth His handiwork." He recalled that as a placard in one of his mother's mission windows. And another which read: "For He is Thy life and Thy
length of Days." Just the same—and far from it as yet, even
in the face of his sudden predisposition toward the Rev.
Duncan McMillan, was he seriously moved to assume that in
religion of any kind was he likely to find surcease from his
present miseries?

And yet the weeks and months going by—the Rev.
McMillan calling regularly thereafter, every two weeks at the
longest, sometimes every week and inquiring after his state,
listening to his wants, advising him as to his health and peace
of mind. And Clyde, anxious to retain his interest and visits,
gradually, more and more, yielding himself to his friendship
and influence. That high spirituality. That beautiful voice.
And quoting always such soothing things. "Brethren *now* are
we the children of God. And it doth not yet appear what we
shall be; but we know that when He shall appear we shall be
like Him, for we shall see Him as He is. And every man that
has this hope in him purifieth himself even as He is pure."

"Hereby know that we dwell in Him and He in us, because
He hath given us of His spirit."

"For ye are bought with a price."

"Of His own will begot He us with the word of truth, and
we should be a kind of first fruits of his creatures. And every
good and every perfect gift is from above and cometh down
from the Father of lights, with whom is no variableness, neither shadow of turning."

"Draw nigh unto God and He will draw nigh unto you."

He was inclined, at times, to feel that there might be peace
and strength—aid, even—who could say, in appealing to this
power. It was the force and the earnestness of the Rev.
McMillan operating upon him.

And yet, the question of repentance—and with it confession. But to whom? The Rev. Duncan McMillan, of course.
He seemed to feel that it was necessary for Clyde to purge his
soul to him—or some one like him—a material and yet spiritual emissary of God. But just there was the trouble. For
there was all of that false testimony he had given in the trial,
yet on which had been based his appeal. To go back on that

now, and when his appeal was pending. Better wait, had he not, until he saw how that appeal had eventuated.

But, ah, how shabby, false, fleeting, insincere. To imagine that any God would bother with a person who sought to dicker in such a way. No, no. That was not right either. What would the Rev. McMillan think of him if he knew what he was thinking?

But again there was the troubling question in his own mind as to his real guilt—the amount of it. True there was no doubt that he had plotted to kill Roberta there at first—a most dreadful thing as he now saw it. For the complications and the fever in connection with his desire for Sondra having subsided somewhat, it was possible on occasion now for him to reason without the desperate sting and tang of the mental state that had characterized him at the time when he was so immediately in touch with her. Those terrible, troubled days when in spite of himself—as he now understood it (Belknap's argument having cleared it up for him) he had burned with that wild fever which was not unakin in its manifestations to a form of insanity. The beautiful Sondra! The glorious Sondra! The witchery and fire of her smile then! Even now that dreadful fever was not entirely out but only smoldering—smothered by all of the dreadful things that had since happened to him.

Also, it must be said on his behalf now, must it not—that never, under any other circumstances, would he have succumbed to any such terrible thought or plot as that—to kill any one—let alone a girl like Roberta—unless he had been so infatuated—lunatic, even. But had not the jury there at Bridgeburg listened to that plea with contempt? And would the Court of Appeals think differently? He feared not. And yet was it not true? Or was he all wrong? Or what? Could the Rev. McMillan or any one else to whom he would explain tell him as to that? He would like to talk to him about it—confess everything perhaps, in order to get himself clear on all this. Further, there was the fact that having plotted for Sondra's sake (and God, if no one else, knew that) he still had not been able to execute it. And that had not been brought out in the trial, because the false form of defense used permitted no explanation of the real truth then—and yet it was a mitigating circumstance, was it not—or would the Rev. McMillan think so? A lie had to be used, as Jephson saw it. But did that make it any the less true?

There were phases of this thing, the tangles and doubts involved in that dark, savage plot of his, as he now saw and brooded on it, which were not so easily to be disposed of. Perhaps the two worst were, first, that in bringing Roberta there to that point on that lake—that lone spot—and then growing so weak and furious with himself because of his own incapacity to do evil, he had frightened her into rising and trying to come to him. And that in the first instance made it possible for her to be thus accidentally struck by him and so made him, in part at least, guilty of that blow—or did it?—a murderous, sinful blow in that sense. Maybe. What would the Rev. McMillan say to that? And since because of that she had fallen into the water, was he not guilty of her falling? It was a thought that troubled him very much now—his constructive share of guilt in all that. Regardless of what Oberwaltzer had said there at the trial in regard to his swimming away from her—that if she had accidentally fallen in the water, it was no crime on his part, supposing he refused to rescue her,—still, as he now saw it, and especially when taken in connection with all that he had thought in regard to Roberta up to that moment, it was a crime just the same, was it not? Wouldn't God—McMillan—think so? And unquestionably, as Mason had so shrewdly pointed out at the trial, he might have saved her. And would have too, no doubt, if she had been Sondra— or even the Roberta of the summer before. Besides, the fear of her dragging him down had been no decent fear. (It was at nights in his bunk at this time that he argued and reasoned with himself, seeing that McMillan was urging him now to repent and make peace with his God.) Yes, he would have to admit that to himself. Decidedly and instantly he would have sought to save her life, if it had been Sondra. And such being the case, he would have to confess that—if he confessed at all to the Rev. McMillan—or to whomever else one told the truth—when one did tell it—the public at large perhaps. But such a confession once made, would it not surely and truly lead to his conviction? And did he want to convict himself now and so die?

No, no, better wait a while perhaps—at least until the

Court of Appeals had passed on his case. Why jeopardize his case when God already knew what the truth was? Truly, truly he was sorry. He could see how terrible all this was now—how much misery and heartache, apart from the death of Roberta, he had caused. But still—still—was not life sweet? Oh, if he could only get out! Oh, if he could only go away from here—never to see or hear or feel anything more of this terrible terror that now hung over him. The slow coming dark—the slow coming dawn. The long night! The sighs—the groans. The tortures by day and by night until it seemed at times as though he should go mad; and would perhaps except for McMillan, who now appeared devoted to him—so kind, appealing and reassuring, too, at times. He would just like to sit down some day—here or somewhere—and tell him all and get him to say how really guilty, if at all, he thought him to be—and if so guilty to get him to pray for him. At times he felt so sure that his mother's and the Rev. Duncan McMillan's prayers would do him so much more good with this God than any prayers of his own would. Somehow he couldn't pray yet. And at times hearing McMillan pray, softly and melodiously, his voice entering through the bars—or, reading from Galatians, Thessalonians, Corinthians, he felt as though he must tell him everything, and soon.

But the days going by until finally one day six weeks after—and when because of his silence in regard to himself, the Rev. Duncan was beginning to despair of ever affecting him in any way toward his proper contrition and salvation—a letter or note from Sondra. It came through the warden's office and by the hand of the Rev. Preston Guilford, the Protestant chaplain of the prison, but was not signed. It was, however, on good paper, and because the rule of the prison so requiring had been opened and read. Nevertheless, on account of the nature of the contents which seemed to both the warden and the Rev. Guilford to be more charitable and punitive than otherwise, and because plainly, if not verifiably, it was from that Miss X of repute or notoriety in connection with his trial, it was decided, after due deliberation, that Clyde should be permitted to read it—even that it was best that he should. Perhaps it would prove of value as a lesson. The way of the transgressor. And so it was handed to him at the close of a late fall day—after a long and dreary summer had passed (soon a year since he had entered here). And he taking it. And although it was typewritten with no date nor place save on the envelope, which was postmarked New York—yet sensing somehow that it might be from her. And growing decidedly nervous—so much so that his hand trembled slightly. And then reading—over and over and over—during many days thereafter: "Clyde—This is so that you will not think that some one once dear to you has utterly forgotten you. She has suffered much, too. And though she can never understand how you could have done as you did, still, even now, although she is never to see you again, she is not without sorrow and sympathy and wishes you freedom and happiness."

But no signature—no trace of her own handwriting. She was afraid to sign her name and she was too remote from him in her mood now to let him know where she was. New York! But it might have been sent there from anywhere to mail. And she would not let him know—would never let him know—even though he died here later, as well he might. His last hope—the last trace of his dream vanished. Forever! It was at that moment, as when night at last falls upon the faintest remaining gleam of dusk in the west. A dim, weakening tinge of pink—and then the dark.

He seated himself on his cot. The wretched stripes of his uniform and his gray felt shoes took his eye. A felon. These stripes. These shoes. This cell. This uncertain, threatening prospect so very terrible to contemplate at any time. And then this letter. So this was the end of all that wonderful dream! And for this he had sought so desperately to disengage himself from Roberta—even to the point of deciding to slay her. This! This! He toyed with the letter, then held it quite still. Where was she now? Who in love with, maybe? She had had time to change perhaps. She had only been captivated by him a little, maybe. And then that terrible revelation in connection with him had destroyed forever, no doubt, all sentiment in connection with him. She was free. She had beauty—wealth. Now some other——

He got up and walked to his cell door to still a great pain. Over the way, in that cell the Chinaman had once occupied, was a negro—Wash Higgins. He had stabbed a waiter in a restaurant, so it was said, who had refused him food and then insulted him. And next to him was a young Jew. He had killed the proprietor of a jewelry store in trying to rob it. But he was very broken and collapsed now that he was here to die—sitting for the most part all day on his cot, his head in his hands. Clyde could see both now from where he stood—the Jew holding his head. But the negro on his cot, one leg above the other, smoking—and singing—

> "Oh, big wheel ro a lin' . . . hmp!
> Oh, big wheel ro-a-lin' . . . hmp!
> Oh, big wheel ro-a-lin' . . . hmp!
> Foh me! Foh me!"

And then Clyde, unable to get away from his own thoughts, turning again.

Condemned to die! He. And this was the end as to Sondra. He could feel it. Farewell. "Although she is never to see you again." He threw himself on his couch—not to weep but to rest—he felt so weary. Lycurgus. Fourth Lake. Bear Lake. Laughter—kisses—smiles. What was to have been in the fall of the preceding year. And now—a year later.

But then,—that young Jew. There was some religious chant into which he fell when his mental tortures would no longer endure silence. And oh, how sad. Many of the prisoners had cried out against it. And yet, oh, how appropriate now, somehow.

"I have been evil. I have been unkind. I have lied. Oh! Oh! Oh! I have been unfaithful. My heart has been wicked. I have joined with those who have done evil things. Oh! Oh! Oh! I have stolen. I have been false. I have been cruel! Oh! Oh! Oh!"

And the voice of Big Tom Rooney sentenced for killing Thomas Tighe, a rival for the hand of an underworld girl. "For Christ's sake! I know you feel bad. But so do I. Oh, for God's sake, don't do that!"

Clyde, on his cot, his thoughts responding rhythmically to the chant of the Jew—and joining with him silently—"I have been evil. I have been unkind. I have lied. Oh! Oh! Oh! I have been unfaithful. My heart has been wicked. I have joined with those who have done evil things. Oh! Oh! Oh! I have been false. I have been cruel. I have sought to murder. Oh! Oh! Oh! And for what? A vain—impossible dream! Oh! Oh! Oh! . . . Oh! Oh! Oh! . . ."

When the guard, an hour later, placed his supper on the shelf in the door, he made no move. Food! And when the guard returned in another thirty minutes, there it was, still untouched, as was the Jew's—and was taken away in silence. Guards knew when blue devils had seized the inmates of these cages. They couldn't eat. And there were times, too, when even guards couldn't eat.

# Chapter XXXIII

THE DEPRESSION resulting even after two days was apparent to the Reverend McMillan, who was concerned to know why. More recently, he had been led to believe by Clyde's manner, his visits, if not the fact that the totality of his preachments, had not been greeted with as much warmth as he would have liked, that by degrees Clyde was being won to his own spiritual viewpoint. With no little success, as it had seemed to him, he had counseled Clyde as to the folly of depression and despair. "What! Was not the peace of God within his grasp and for the asking. To one who sought God and found Him, as he surely would, if he sought, there could be no sorrow, but only joy. 'Hereby know we that we dwell in Him, and He in us, because He hath given us of His spirit.'" So he preached or read,—until finally—two weeks after receiving the letter from Sondra and because of the deep depression into which he had sunk on account of it, Clyde was finally moved to request of him that he try to induce the warden to allow him to be taken to some other cell or room apart from this room or cell which seemed to Clyde to be filled with too many of his tortured thoughts, in order that he might talk with him and get his advice. As he told the Reverend McMillan, he did not appear to be able to solve his true responsibility in connection with all that had so recently occurred in his life, and because of which he seemed not to be able to find that peace of mind of which McMillan talked so much. Perhaps . . . ,—there must be something wrong with his viewpoint. Actually he would like to go over the offense of which he was convicted and see if there was anything wrong in his understanding of it. He was not so sure now. And McMillan, greatly stirred,—an enormous spiritual triumph, this—as he saw it—the true reward of faith and prayer, at once proceeding to the warden, who was glad enough to be of service in such a cause. And he permitted the use of one of the cells in the old death house for as long as he should require, and with no guard between himself and Clyde—one only remaining in the general hall outside.

And there Clyde began the story of his relations with Roberta and Sondra. Yet because of all that had been set forth at the trial, merely referring to most of the evidence—apart from his defense—the change of heart, as so; afterwards dwelling more particularly on the fatal adventure with Roberta in the boat. Did the Reverend McMillan—because of the original plotting—and hence the original intent—think him guilty?—especially in view of his obsession over Sondra—all his dreams in regard to her—did that truly constitute murder? He was asking this because, as he said, it was as he had done—not as his testimony at the trial had indicated that he had done. It was a lie that he had experienced a change of heart. His attorneys had counseled that defense as best, since they did not feel that he was guilty, and had thought that plan the quickest route to liberty. But it was a lie. In connection with his mental state also there in the boat, before and after her rising and attempting to come to him,—and that blow, and after,—he had not told the truth either—quite. That unintentional blow, as he now wished to explain, since it affected his efforts at religious meditation,—a desire to present himself honestly to his Creator, if at all (he did not then explain that as yet he had scarcely attempted to so present himself)—there was more to it than he had been able yet to make clear, even to himself. In fact even now to himself there was much that was evasive and even insoluble about it. He had said that there had been no anger—that there had been a change of heart. But there had been no change of heart. In fact, just before she had risen to come to him, there had been a complex troubled state, bordering, as he now saw it, almost upon trance or palsy, and due—but he could scarcely say to what it was due, exactly. He had thought at first—or afterwards—that it was partly due to pity for Roberta—or, at least the shame of so much cruelty in connection with her—his plan to strike her. At the same time there was anger, too,—hate maybe—because of her determination to force him to do what he did not wish to do. Thirdly—yet he was not so sure as to that—(he had thought about it so long and yet he was not sure even now)—there might have been fear as to the consequences of such an evil deed—although, just at that time, as it seemed to him now, he was not thinking of the consequences—or of anything save his inability to do as he had come to do—and feeling angry as to that.

Yet in the blow—the accidental blow that had followed upon her rising and attempting to come to him, had been some anger against her for wanting to come near him at all. And that it was perhaps—he was truly not sure, even now, that had given that blow its so destructive force. It was so afterward, anyhow, that he was compelled to think of it. And yet there was also the truth that in rising he was seeking to save her—even in spite of his hate. That he was also, for the moment at least, sorry for that blow. Again, though, once the boat had upset and both were in the water—in all that confusion, and when she was drowning, he had been moved by the thought: "Do nothing." For thus he would be rid of her. Yes, he had so thought. But again, there was the fact that all through, as Mr. Belknap and Mr. Jephson had pointed out, he had been swayed by his obsession for Miss X, the super motivating force in connection with all of this. But now, did the Reverend McMillan, considering all that went before and all that came after—the fact that the unintentional blow still had had anger in it—angry dissatisfaction with her—really—and that afterwards he had not gone to her rescue—as now—honestly—and truly as he was trying to show—did he think that that constituted murder—mortal blood guilt for which spiritually, as well as legally, he might be said to deserve death? Did he? He would like to know for his own soul's peace—so that he could pray, maybe.

The Reverend McMillan hearing all this—and never in his life before having heard or having had passed to him so intricate and elusive and strange a problem—and because of Clyde's faith in and regard for him, enormously impressed. And now sitting before him quite still and pondering most deeply, sadly and even nervously—so serious and important was this request for an opinion—something which, as he knew, Clyde was counting on to give him earthly and spiritual peace. But, none-the-less, the Reverend McMillan was himself too puzzled to answer so quickly.

"Up to the time you went in that boat with her, Clyde, you had not changed in your mood toward her—your intention to—to——"

The Reverend McMillan's face was gray and drawn. His

eyes were sad. He had been listening, as he now felt, to a sad and terrible story—an evil and cruel self-torturing and destroying story. This young boy—really——! His hot, restless heart which plainly for the lack of so many things which he, the Reverend McMillan, had never wanted for, had rebelled. And because of that rebellion had sinned mortally and was condemned to die. Indeed his reason was as intensely troubled as his heart was moved.

"No, I had not."

"You were, as you say, angry with yourself for being so weak as not to be able to do what you had planned to do."

"In a way it was like that, yes. But then I was sorry, too, you see. And maybe afraid. I'm not exactly sure now. Maybe not, either."

The Reverend McMillan shook his head. So strange! So evasive! So evil! And yet——

"But at the same time, as you say, you were angry with her for having driven you to that point."

"Yes."

"Where you were compelled to wrestle with so terrible a problem?"

"Yes."

"Tst! Tst! Tst! And so you thought of striking her."

"Yes, I did."

"But you could not."

"No."

"Praised be the mercy of God. Yet in the blow that you did strike—unintentionally—as you say—there was still some anger against her. That was why the blow was so—so severe. You did not want her to come near you."

"No, I didn't. I think I didn't, anyhow. I'm not quite sure. It may be that I wasn't quite right. Anyhow—all worked up, I guess—sick almost. I—I——" In his uniform—his hair cropped so close, Clyde sat there, trying honestly now to think how it really was (exactly) and greatly troubled by his inability to demonstrate to himself even—either his guilt or his lack of guilt. Was he—or was he not? And the Reverend McMillan—himself intensely strained, muttering: "Wide is the gate and broad the way that leadeth to destruction." And yet finally adding: "But you did rise to save her."

"Yes, afterwards, I got up. I meant to catch her after she fell back. That was what upset the boat."

"And you did really want to catch her?"

"I don't know. At the moment I guess I did. Anyhow I felt sorry, I think."

"But can you say now truly and positively, as your Creator sees you, that you were sorry—or that you wanted to save her then?"

"It all happened so quick, you see," began Clyde nervously—hopelessly, almost, "that I'm not just sure. No, I don't know that I was so very sorry. No. I really don't know, you see, now. Sometimes I think maybe I was, a little, sometimes not, maybe. But after she was gone and I was on shore, I felt sorry—a little. But I was sort of glad, too, you know, to be free, and yet frightened, too—— You see——"

"Yes, I know. You were going to that Miss X. But out there, when she was in the water——?"

"No."

"You did not want to go to her rescue?"

"No."

"Tst! Tst! Tst! You felt no sorrow? No shame? Then?"

"Yes, shame, maybe. Maybe sorrow, too, a little. I knew it was terrible. I felt that it was, of course. But still—you see——"

"Yes, I know. That Miss X. You wanted to get away."

"Yes—but mostly I was frightened, and I didn't want to help her."

"Yes! Yes! Tst! Tst! Tst! If she drowned you could go to that Miss X. You thought of that?" The Reverend McMillan's lips were tightly and sadly compressed.

"Yes."

"My son! My son! In your heart was murder then."

"Yes, yes," Clyde said reflectively. "I have thought since it must have been that way."

The Reverend McMillan paused and to hearten himself for this task began to pray—but silently—and to himself: "Our Father who art in Heaven—hallowed be Thy name. Thy Kingdom come, Thy will be done—on earth as it is in Heaven." He stirred again after a time.

"Ah, Clyde. The mercy of God is equal to every sin. I know it. He sent His own son to die for the evil of the world. It must be so—if you will but repent. But that thought! That deed! You have much to pray for, my son—much. Oh, yes. For in the sight of God, I fear,—yes—— And yet—— I must pray for enlightenment. This is a strange and terrible story. There are so many phases. It may be—but pray. Pray with me now that you and I may have light." He bowed his head. He sat for minutes in silence—while Clyde, also, in silence and troubled doubt, sat before him. Then, after a time he began:

"Oh, Lord, rebuke me not in thine anger; neither chasten me in Thy hot displeasure. Have mercy on me, O Lord, for I am weak. Heal me in my shame and sorrow for my soul is wounded and dark in Thy sight. Oh, let the wickedness of my heart pass. Lead me, O God, into Thy righteousness. Let the wickedness of my heart pass and remember it not."

Clyde—his head down—sat still—very still. He, himself, was at last shaken and mournful. No doubt his sin was very great. Very, very terrible! And yet—— But then, the Reverend McMillan ceasing and rising, he, too, rose, the while McMillan added: "But I must go now. I must think—pray. This has troubled and touched me deeply. Oh, very, Lord. And you—my son—you return and pray—alone. Repent. Ask of God on your knees His forgiveness and He will hear you. Yes, He will. And to-morrow—or as soon as I honestly can—I will come again. But do not despair. Pray always—for in prayer alone, prayer and contrition, is salvation. Rest in the strength of Him who holds the world in the hollow of His hand. In His abounding strength and mercy, is peace and forgiveness. Oh, yes."

He struck the iron door with a small key ring that he carried and at once the guard, hearing it, returned.

Then having escorted Clyde to his cell and seen him once more shut within that restraining cage, he took his own departure, heavily and miserably burdened with all that he had heard. And Clyde was left to brood on all he had said—and how it had affected McMillan, as well as himself. His new friend's stricken mood. The obvious pain and horror with which he viewed it all. Was he really and truly guilty? Did he really and truly deserve to die for this? Was that what the Reverend McMillan would decide? And in the face of all his tenderness and mercy?

After another week in which, moved by Clyde's seeming

contrition, and all the confusing and extenuating circumstances of his story, and having wrestled most earnestly with every moral aspect of it, the Reverend McMillan once more before his cell door—but only to say that however liberal or charitable his interpretation of the facts, as at last Clyde had truthfully pictured them, still he could not feel that either primarily or secondarily could he be absolved from guilt for her death. He had plotted—had he not? He had not gone to her rescue when he might have. He had wished her dead and afterwards had not been sorry. In the blow that had brought about the upsetting of the boat had been some anger. Also in the mood that had not permitted him to strike. The facts that he had been influenced by the beauty and position of Miss X to the plotting of this deed, and, after his evil relations with Roberta, that she had been determined he should marry her, far from being points in extenuation of his actions, were really further evidence of his general earthly sin and guilt. Before the Lord then he had sinned in many ways. In those dark days, alas, as Mr. McMillan saw it, he was little more than a compound of selfishness and unhallowed desire and fornication against the evil of which Paul had thundered. It had endured to the end and had not changed—until he had been taken by the law. He had not repented—not even there at Bear Lake where he had time for thought. And besides, had he not, from beginning to end, bolstered it with false and evil pretenses? Verily.

On the other hand, no doubt if he were sent to the chair now in the face of this first—and yet so clear manifestation of contrition—when now, for the first time he was beginning to grasp the enormity of his offense—it would be but to compound crime with crime—the state in this instance being the aggressor. For, like the warden and many others, McMillan was against capital punishment—preferring to compel the wrong-doer to serve the state in some way. But, none-the-less, he felt himself compelled to acknowledge, Clyde was far from innocent. Think as he would—and however much spiritually he desired to absolve him, was he not actually guilty?

In vain it was that McMillan now pointed out to Clyde that his awakened moral and spiritual understanding more perfectly and beautifully fitted him for life and action than ever before. He was alone. He had no one who believed in him. *No one.* He had no one, who, in any of his troubled and tortured actions before that crime saw anything but the darkest guilt apparently. And yet—and yet—(and this despite Sondra and the Reverend McMillan and all the world for that matter, Mason, the jury at Bridgeburg, the Court of Appeals at Albany, if it should decide to confirm the jury at Bridgeburg) he had a feeling in his heart that he was not as guilty as they all seemed to think. After all they had not been tortured as he had by Roberta with her determination that he marry her and thus ruin his whole life. They had not burned with that unquenchable passion for the Sondra of his beautiful dream as he had. They had not been harassed, tortured, mocked by the ill-fate of his early life and training, forced to sing and pray on the streets as he had in such a degrading way, when his whole heart and soul cried out for better things. How could they judge him, these people, all or any one of them, even his own mother, when they did not know what his own mental, physical and spiritual suffering had been? And as he lived through it again in his thoughts at this moment the sting and mental poison of it was as real to him as ever. Even in the face of all the facts and as much as every one felt him to be guilty, there was something so deep within him that seemed to cry out against it that, even now, at times, it startled him. Still—there was the Reverend McMillan—he was a very fair and just and merciful man. Surely he saw all this from a higher light and better viewpoint than his own. While at times he felt strongly that he was innocent, at others he felt that he must be guilty.

Oh, these evasive and tangled and torturesome thoughts!! Would he never be able—quite—to get the whole thing straightened out in his own mind?

So Clyde not being able to take advantage truly of either the tenderness and faith and devotion of so good and pure a soul as the Reverend McMillan or the all merciful and all powerful God of whom here he stood as the ambassador. What was he to do, really? How pray, resignedly, unreservedly, faithfully? And in that mood—and because of the urge of the Reverend Duncan, who was convinced by Clyde's confession that he must have been completely infused with the spirit of God, once more thumbing through the various passages and chapters pointed out to him—reading and re-reading the Psalms most familiar to him, seeking from their inspiration to catch the necessary contrition—which once caught would give him that peace and strength which in these long and dreary hours he so much desired. Yet never quite catching it.

Parallel with all this, four more months passed. And at the end of that time—in January, 19—, the Court of Appeals finding (Fulham, J., reviewing the evidence as offered by Belknap and Jephson)—with Kincaid, Briggs, Truman and Dobshuter concurring, that Clyde was guilty as decided by the Cataraqui County jury and sentencing him to die at some time within the week beginning February 28th or six weeks later—and saying in conclusion:

"We are mindful that this is a case of circumstantial evidence and that the only eyewitness denies that death was the result of crime. But in obedience to the most exacting requirements of that manner of proof, the counsel for the people, with very unusual thoroughness and ability has investigated and presented evidence of a great number of circumstances for the purpose of truly solving the question of the defendant's guilt or innocence.

"We might think that the proof of some of these facts standing by themselves was subject to doubt by reason of unsatisfactory or contradictory evidence, and that other occurrences might be so explained or interpreted as to be reconcilable with innocence. The defense—and very ably—sought to enforce this view.

"But taken all together and considered as a connected whole, they make such convincing proof of guilt that we are not able to escape from its force by any justifiable process of reasoning and we are compelled to say that not only is the verdict not opposed to the weight of evidence, and to the proper inference to be drawn from it, but that it is abundantly justified thereby. Decision of the lower court unanimously confirmed."

On hearing this, McMillan, who was in Syracuse at the time, hurrying to Clyde in the hope that before the news was conveyed officially, he should be there to encourage him spiritually, since, only with the aid of the Lord, as he saw it—the eternal and ever present help in trouble—would Clyde be able to endure so heavy a blow. And finding him—for which he was most deeply grateful—wholly unaware as to what had occurred, since no news of any kind was conveyed to any condemned man until the warrant for his execution had arrived.

After a most tender and spiritual conversation—in which he quoted from Matthew, Paul and John as to the unimportance of this world—the true reality and joy of the next—Clyde was compelled to learn from McMillan that the decision of the court had gone against him. And that—even though McMillan talked of an appeal to the Governor which he—and some others whom he was sure to be able to influence would make—unless the Governor chose to act, within six weeks, as Clyde knew, he would be compelled to die. And then, once the force of that fact had finally burst on him—and while McMillan talked on about faith and the refuge which the mercy and wisdom of God provided—Clyde, standing before him with more courage and character showing in his face and eyes than at any time previously in his brief and eager career.

"So they've decided against me. Now I will have to go through that door after all,—like all those others. They'll draw the curtains for me, too. Into that other room—then back across the passage—saying good-by as I go, like those others. I will not be here any more." He seemed to be going over each step in his mind—each step with which he was so familiar, only now, for the first time, he was living it for himself. Now, in the face of this dread news, which somehow was as fascinating as it was terrible, feeling not as distrait or weak as at first he had imagined he would be. Rather, to his astonishment, considering all his previous terror in regard to this, thinking of what he would do, what he would say, in an outwardly calm way.

Would he repeat prayers read to him by the Reverend McMillan here? No doubt. And maybe gladly, too. And yet—

In his momentary trance he was unconscious of the fact that the Reverend Duncan was whispering:

"But you see we haven't reached the end of this yet. There is a new Governor coming into office in January. He is a very sensible and kindly man, I hear. In fact I know several people who know him—and it is my plan to see him personally—as well as to have some other people whom I know write him on the strength of what I will tell them."

But from Clyde's look at the moment, as well as what he now said, he could tell that he was not listening.

"My mother. I suppose some one ought to telegraph her. She is going to feel very bad." And then: "I don't suppose they believed that those letters shouldn't have been introduced just as they were, did they? I thought maybe they would." He was thinking of Nicholson.

"Don't worry, Clyde," replied the tortured and saddened McMillan, at this point more eager to take him in his arms and comfort him than to say anything at all. "I have already telegraphed your mother. As for that decision—I will see your lawyers right away. Besides—as I say—I propose to see the Governor myself. He is a new man, you see."

Once more he was now repeating all that Clyde had not heard before.

# Chapter XXXIV

THE SCENE was the executive chamber of the newly elected Governor of the State of New York some three weeks after the news conveyed to Clyde by McMillan. After many preliminary and futile efforts on the part of Belknap and Jephson to obtain a commutation of the sentence of Clyde from death to life imprisonment (the customary filing of a plea for clemency, together with such comments as they had to make in regard to the way the evidence had been misinterpreted and the illegality of introducing the letters of Roberta in their original form, to all of which Governor Waltham, an ex-district attorney and judge from the southern part of the state, had been conscientiously compelled to reply that he could see no reason for interfering) there was now before Governor Waltham Mrs. Griffiths together with the Reverend McMillan. For, moved by the widespread interest in the final disposition of Clyde's case, as well as the fact that his mother, because of her unshaken devotion to him, and having learned of the decision of the Court of Appeals, had once more returned to Auburn and since then had been appealing to the newspapers, as well as to himself through letters for a correct understanding of the extenuating circumstances surrounding her son's downfall, and because she herself had repeatedly appealed to him for a personal interview in which she should be allowed to present her deepest convictions in regard to all this, the Governor had at last consented to see her. It could do no harm. Besides it would tend to soothe her. Also variable public sentiment, whatever its convictions in any given case, was usually on the side of the form or gesture of clemency—without, however, any violence to its convictions. And, in this case, if one could judge by the newspapers, the public was convinced that Clyde was guilty. On the other hand, Mrs. Griffiths, owing to her own long meditations in regard to Clyde, Roberta, his sufferings during and since the trial, the fact that according to the Reverend McMillan he had at last been won to a deep contrition and a spiritual union with his Creator whatever his original sin, was now more than

920

ever convinced that humanity and even justice demanded that at least he be allowed to live. And so standing before the Governor, a tall, sober and somewhat somber man who, never in all his life had even so much as sensed the fevers or fires that Clyde had known, yet who, being a decidedly affection- ate father and husband, could very well sense what Mrs. Grif- fiths' present emotions must be. Yet greatly exercised by the compulsion which the facts, as he understood them, as well as a deep-seated and unchangeable submission to law and order, thrust upon him. Like the pardon clerk before him, he had read all the evidence submitted to the Court of Appeals, as well as the latest briefs submitted by Belknap and Jephson. But on what grounds could he—David Waltham, and without any new or varying data of any kind—just a re-interpretation of the evidence as already passed upon—venture to change Clyde's death sentence to life imprisonment? Had not a jury, as well as the Court of Appeals, already said he should die?

In consequence, as Mrs. Griffiths began her plea, her voice shaky—retracing as best she could the story of Clyde's life, his virtues, the fact that at no time ever had he been a bad or cruel boy—that Roberta, if not Miss X, was not entirely guiltless in the matter—he merely gazed at her deeply moved. The love and devotion of such a mother! Her agony in this hour; her faith that her son could not be as evil as the proven facts seemed to indicate to him and every one else. "Oh, my dear Governor, how can the sacrifice of my son's life now, and when spiritually he has purged his soul of sin and is ready to devote himself to the work of God, repay the state for the loss of that poor, dear girl's life, whether it was accidentally or otherwise taken—how can it? Can not the millions of people of the state of New York be merciful? Can- not you as their representative exercise the mercy that they may feel?"

Her voice broke—she could not go on. Instead she turned her back and began to cry silently, while Waltham, shaken by an emotion he could not master, merely stood there. This poor woman! So obviously honest and sincere. Then the Rev- erend McMillan, seeing his opportunity, now entering his plea. Clyde had changed. He could not speak as to his life be- fore—but since his incarceration—or for the last year, at least, he had come into a new understanding of life, duty, his oblig-ations to man and God. If but the death sentence could be commuted to life imprisonment——

And the Governor, who was a very earnest and conscien-tious man, listened with all attention to McMillan, whom, as he saw and concluded was decidedly an intense and vital and highly idealistic person. No question in his own mind but what the words of this man—whatever they were, would be true—in so far as his own understanding would permit the conception of a truth.

"But you, personally, Mr. McMillan," the Governor at last found voice to say, "because of your long contact with him in the prison there—do you know of any material fact not intro-duced at the trial which would in any way tend to invalidate or weaken any phase of the testimony offered at the trial? As you must know this is a legal proceeding. I cannot act upon sentiment alone—and especially in the face of the unanimous decision of two separate courts."

He looked directly at McMillan, who, pale and dumb, now gazed at him in return. For now upon his word—upon his shoulders apparently was being placed the burden of deciding as to Clyde's guilt or innocence. But could he do that? Had he not decided, after due meditation as to Clyde's confes-sions, that he was guilty before God and the law? And could he now—for mercy's sake—and in the face of his deepest spir-itual conviction, alter his report of his conviction? Would that be true—white, valuable before the Lord? And as instantly deciding that he, Clyde's spiritual adviser, must not in any way be invalidated in his spiritual worth to Clyde. "Ye are the salt of the earth; but if the salt have lost his savor, wherewith shall it be salted?" And forthwith he declared: "As his spiritual advisor I have entered only upon the spiritual, not the legal aspect of his life." And thereupon Waltham at once deciding, from something in McMillan's manner that he, like all others, apparently, was satisfied as to Clyde's guilt. And so, finally finding courage to say to Mrs. Griffiths: "Unless some defi-nite evidence such as I have not yet seen and which will affect the legality of these two findings can be brought me, I have no alternative, Mrs. Griffiths, but to allow the verdict as writ-ten to stand. I am very sorry—oh, more than I can tell you.

But if the law is to be respected its decisions can never be altered except for reasons that in themselves are full of legal merit. I wish I could decide differently. I do indeed. My heart and my prayers go with you."

He pressed a button. His secretary entered. It was plain that the interview was ended. Mrs. Griffiths, violently shaken and deeply depressed by the peculiar silence and evasion of McMillan at the crucial moment of this interview when the Governor had asked such an all important and direct question as to the guilt of her son, was still unable to say a word more. But now what? Which way? To whom to turn? God, and God only. She and Clyde must find in their Creator the solace for his failure and death in this world. And as she was thinking and still weeping, the Reverend McMillan approached and gently led her from the room.

When she was gone the Governor finally turned to his secretary:

"Never in my life have I faced a sadder duty. It will always be with me." He turned and gazed out upon a snowy February landscape.

And after this but two more weeks of life for Clyde, during which time, and because of this ultimate decision conveyed to him first by McMillan, but in company with his mother, from whose face Clyde could read all, even before McMillan spoke, and from whom he heard all once more as to his need of refuge and peace in God, his Savior, he now walked up and down his cell, unable to rest for any length of time anywhere. For, because of this final completely convincing sensation, that very soon he was to die, he felt the need, even now of retracing his unhappy life. His youth. Kansas City. Chicago. Lycurgus. Roberta and Sondra. How swiftly they and all that was connected with them passed in review. The few, brief, bright intense moments. His desire for more—more—that intense desire he had felt there in Lycurgus after Sondra came and now this, this! And now even this was ending—this—this—— Why, he had scarcely lived at all as yet—and these last two years so miserably between these crushing walls. And of this life but fourteen, thirteen, twelve, eleven, ten, nine, eight of the filtering and now feverish days left. They were going—going. But life—life—how was one to do without that—the beauty of the days—of the sun and rain—of work, love, energy, desire. Oh, he really did not want to die. He did not. Why say to him so constantly as his mother and the Reverend McMillan now did to resolve all his care in divine mercy and think only of God, when now, now, was all? And yet the Reverend McMillan insisting that only in Christ and the hereafter was real peace. Oh, yes—but just the same, before the Governor might he not have said—might he not have said that he was not guilty—or at least not entirely guilty— if only he had seen it that way—that time—and then— then—why then the Governor might have commuted his sentence to life imprisonment—might he not? For he had asked his mother what the Reverend McMillan had said to the Governor—(yet without saying to her that he had ever confessed all to him), and she had replied that he had told him how sincerely he had humbled himself before the Lord—but not that he was not guilty. And Clyde, feeling how strange it was that the Reverend McMillan could not conscientiously bring himself to do more than that for him. How sad. How hopeless. Would no one ever understand—or give him credit for his human—if all too human and perhaps wrong hungers—yet from which so many others—along with himself suffered?

But worse yet, if anything, Mrs. Griffiths, because of what the Reverend McMillan had said—or failed to say, in answer to the final question asked him by Governor Waltham—and although subsequently in answer to an inquiry of her own, he had repeated the statement, she was staggered by the thought that perhaps, after all, Clyde was as guilty as at first she had feared. And because of that asking at one point:

"Clyde, if there is anything you have not confessed, you must confess it before you go."

"I have confessed everything to God and to Mr. McMillan, mother. Isn't that enough?"

"No, Clyde. You have told the world that you are innocent. But if you are not you must say so."

"But if my conscience tells me that I am right, is not that enough?"

"No, not if God's word says differently, Clyde," replied Mrs. Griffiths nervously—and with great inward spiritual torture. But he chose to say nothing further at that time. How

could he discuss with his mother or the world the strange
shadings which in his confession and subsequent talks with
the Reverend McMillan he had not been able to solve. It was
not to be done.

And because of that refusal on her son's part to confide in
her, Mrs. Griffiths, tortured, not only spiritually but personally. Her own son—and so near death and not willing to say
what already apparently he had said to Mr. McMillan. Would
not God ever be done with this testing her? And yet on account of what McMillan had already said,—that he considered Clyde, whatever his past sins, contrite and clean before
the Lord—a youth truly ready to meet his Maker—she was
prone to rest. The Lord was great! He was merciful. In His
bosom was peace. What was death—what life—to one whose
heart and mind were at peace with Him? It was nothing. A
few years (how very few) and she and Asa and after them, his
brothers and sisters, would come to join him—and all his miseries here would be forgotten. But without peace in the
Lord—the full and beautiful realization of His presence, love,
care and mercy . . . ! She was tremulous at moments now in
her spiritual exaltation—no longer quite normal—as Clyde
could see and feel. But also by her prayers and anxiety as to
his spiritual welfare, he was also able to see how little, really,
she had ever understood of his true mood and aspirations. He
had longed for so much there in Kansas City and he had had
so little. Things—just things—had seemed so very important
to him—and he had so resented being taken out on the street
as he had been, before all the other boys and girls, many of
whom had all the things that he so craved, and when he
would have been glad to have been anywhere else in the
world than out there—on the street! That mission life that to
his mother was so wonderful, yet, to him, so dreary! But was
it wrong for him to feel so? Had it been? Would the Lord resent it now? And, maybe, she was right as to her thoughts
about him. Unquestionably he would have been better off if
he had·followed her advice. But how strange it was, that to
his own mother, and even now in these closing hours, when
above all things he craved sympathy—but more than sympathy, true and deep understanding—even now—and as much
as she loved and sympathized with, and was seeking to aid

him with all her strength in her stern and self-sacrificing way,—still he could not turn to her now and tell her—his own mother, just how it all happened. It was as though there was an unsurmountable wall or impenetrable barrier between them, built by the lack of understanding—for it was just that. She would never understand his craving for ease and luxury, for beauty, for love—his particular kind of love that went with show, pleasure, wealth, position, his eager and immutable aspirations and desires. She could not understand these things. She would look on all of it as sin—evil, selfishness. And in connection with all the fatal steps involving Roberta and Sondra, as adultery—unchastity—murder, even. And she would and did expect him to be terribly sorry and wholly repentant, when, even now, and for all he had said to the Reverend McMillan and to her, he could not feel so—not wholly so—although great was his desire now to take refuge in God, but better yet, if it were only possible, in her own understanding and sympathetic heart. If it were only possible.

Lord, it was all so terrible! He was so alone, even in these last few and elusive hours (the swift passing of the days), with his mother and also the Reverend McMillan here with him, but neither understanding.

But, apart from all this and much worse, he was locked up here and they would not let him go. There was a system—a horrible routine system—as long since he had come to feel it to be so. It was iron. It moved automatically like a machine without the aid or the hearts of men. These guards! They with their letters, their inquiries, their pleasant and yet really hollow words, their trips to do little favors, or to take the men in and out of the yard or to their baths—they were iron, too —mere machines, automatons, pushing and pushing and yet restraining and restraining one—within these walls, as ready to kill as to favor in case of opposition—but pushing, pushing, pushing—always toward that little door over there, from which there was no escape—no escape—just on and on— until at last they would push him through it—never to return! *Never to return!*

Each time he thought of this he arose and walked the floor. Afterwards, usually, he resumed the puzzle of his own guilt. He tried to think of Roberta and the evil he had done her, to read the Bible—even—lying on his face on the iron cot—repeating over and over: "Lord, give me peace. Lord, give me light. Lord, give me strength to resist any evil thoughts that I should not have. I know I am not wholly white. Oh, no. I know I plotted evil. Yes, yes, I know that. I confess. But must I really die now? Is there no help? Will you not help me, Lord? Will you not manifest yourself, as my mother says you will—for me? Will you get the Governor to change my sentence before the final moment to life imprisonment? Will you get the Reverend McMillan to change his views and go to him, and my mother, too? I will drive out all sinful thoughts. I will be different. Oh, yes, I will, if you will only spare me. Do not let me die now—so soon. Do not. I will pray. Yes, I will. Give me the strength to understand and believe—and pray. Oh, do!"

It was like this in those short, horrible days between the return of his mother and the Reverend McMillan from their final visit to the Governor and in his last hour that Clyde thought and prayed—yet finally in a kind of psychic terror, evoked by his uncertainty as to the meaning of the hereafter, his certainty of death, and the faith and emotions of his mother, as well as those of the Reverend McMillan, who was about every day with his interpretations of divine mercy and his exhortations as to the necessity of complete faith and reliance upon it, he, himself coming at last to believe, not only must he have faith but that he had it—and peace—complete and secure. In that state, and at the request of the Reverend McMillan, and his mother, finally composing, with the personal aid and supervision of McMillan, who changed some of the sentences in his presence and with his consent, an address to the world, and more particularly to young men of his own years, which read:

In the shadow of the Valley of Death it is my desire to do everything that would remove any doubt as to my having found Jesus Christ, the personal Savior and unfailing friend. My one regret at this time is that I have not given Him the preëminence in my life while I had the opportunity to work for Him.

If I could only say some one thing that would draw young men to Him I would deem it the greatest privilege ever granted me. But all I can now say is, "I know in whom I have believed, and am persuaded that He is able to keep that which I have committed unto

Him against that day" [a quotation that McMillan had familiarized him with].

If the young men of this country could only know the joy and pleasure of a Christian life, I know they would do all in their power to become earnest, active Christians, and would strive to live as Christ would have them live.

There is not one thing I have left undone which will bar me from facing my God, knowing that my sins are forgiven, for I have been free and frank in my talks with my spiritual adviser, and God knows where I stand.

My task is done, the victory won.

CLYDE GRIFFITHS.

Having written this—a statement so unlike all the previous rebellious moods that had characterized him that even now he was not a little impressed by the difference, handing it to McMillan, who, heartened by this triumph, exclaimed: "And the victory *is* won, Clyde. 'This day shalt thou be with me in Paradise.' You have His word. Your soul and your body belong to Him. Praised, everlastingly, be His name."

And then so wrought up was he by this triumph, taking both Clyde's hands in his and kissing them and then folding him in his arms: "My son, my son, in whom I am well pleased. In you God has truly manifested His truth. His power to save. I see it. I feel it. Your address to the world is really His own voice to the world." And then pocketing the note with the understanding that it was to be issued after Clyde's death—not before. And yet Clyde having written this, still dubious at moments. Was he truly saved? The time was so short. Could he rely on God with that absolute security which he had just announced now characterized him? Could he? Life was so strange. The future so obscure. Was there really a life after death—a God by whom he would be welcomed as the Reverend McMillan and his own mother insisted? Was there?

In the midst of this, two days before his death and in a final burst of panic, Mrs. Griffiths wiring the Hon. David Waltham: "Can you say before your God that you have no doubt of Clyde's guilt? Please wire. If you cannot, then his blood will be upon your head. His mother." And Robert Fessler, the secretary to the Governor replying by wire: "Governor Waltham does not think himself justified in interfering with the decision of the Court of Appeals."

At last the final day—the final hour—Clyde's transfer to a cell in the old death house, where, after a shave and a bath, he was furnished with black trousers, a white shirt without a collar, to be opened at the neck afterwards, new felt slippers and gray socks. So accoutered, he was allowed once more to meet his mother and McMillan, who, from six o'clock in the evening preceding the morning of his death until four of the final morning, were permitted to remain near him to counsel with him as to the love and mercy of God. And then at four the warden appearing to say that it was time, he feared, that Mrs. Griffiths depart leaving Clyde in the care of Mr. McMillan. (The sad compulsion of the law, as he explained.) And then Clyde's final farewell to his mother, before which, and in between the silences and painful twistings of heart strings, he had managed to say:

"Mama, you must believe that I die resigned and content. It won't be hard. God has heard my prayers. He has given me strength and peace." But to himself adding: "Had he?"

And Mrs. Griffiths exclaiming: "My son! My son, I know, I know. I have faith too. I know that my Redeemer liveth and that He is yours. Though we die—yet shall we live!" She was looking heavenward, and seemed transfixed. Yet as suddenly turning to Clyde and gathering him in her arms and holding him long and firmly to her, whispering: "My son— my baby——" and her voice broke and trailed off into breathlessness—and her strength seemed to be going all to him, until she felt she must leave or fall—— And so she turned quickly and unsteadily to the warden, who was waiting for her to lead her to Auburn friends of McMillan's.

And then in the dark of this midwinter morning—the final moment—with the guards coming, first to slit his right trouser leg for the metal plate and then going to draw the curtains before the cells: "It is time, I fear. Courage, my son." It was the Reverend McMillan—now accompanied by the Reverend Gibson, who, seeing the prison guards approaching, was then addressing Clyde.

And Clyde now getting up from his cot, on which, beside the Reverend McMillan, he had been listening to the reading of John, 14, 15, 16: "Let not your heart be troubled. Ye believe in God—believe also in me." And then the final walk with the Reverend McMillan on his right hand and the Reverend Gibson on his left—the guards front and rear. But with, instead of the customary prayers, the Reverend McMillan announcing: "Humble yourselves under the mighty hand of God that He may exalt you in due time. Cast all your care upon Him for He careth for you. Be at peace. Wise and righteous are His ways, who hath called us into His eternal glory by Christ Jesus, after that we have suffered a little. I am the way, the truth and the life—no man cometh unto the Father but by me."

But various voices—as Clyde entered the first door to cross to the chair room, calling: "Good-by, Clyde." And Clyde, with enough earthly thought and strength to reply: "Good-by, all." But his voice sounding so strange and weak, even to himself, so far distant as though it emanated from another being walking alongside of him, and not from himself. And his feet were walking, but automatically, it seemed. And he was conscious of that familiar shuffle—shuffle—as they pushed him on and on toward that door. Now it was here; now it was being opened. There it was—at last—the chair he had so often seen in his dreams—that he so dreaded—to which he was now compelled to go. He was being pushed toward that—into that—on—on—through the door which was now open—to receive him—but which was as quickly closed again on all the earthly life he had ever known.

It was the Reverend McMillan who, gray and weary—a quarter of an hour later, walked desolately—and even a little uncertainly—as one who is physically very weak—through the cold doors of the prison. It was so faint—so weak—so gray as yet—this late winter day—and so like himself now. Dead! He, Clyde, had walked so nervously and yet somehow trustingly beside him but a few minutes before—and now he was dead. The law! Prisons such as this. Strong, evil men who scoffed betimes where Clyde had prayed. That confession! Had he decided truly—with the wisdom of God, as God gave him to see wisdom? Had he? Clyde's eyes! He, himself—the Reverend McMillan had all but fainted beside him as that cap was adjusted to his head—that current turned on—and he had had to be assisted, sick and trembling, from the room—he upon whom Clyde had relied. And he had asked God for strength,—was asking it.

He walked along the silent street—only to be compelled to pause and lean against a tree—leafless in the winter—so bare and bleak. Clyde's eyes! That look as he sank limply into that terrible chair, his eyes fixed nervously and, as he thought, appealingly and dazedly upon him and the group surrounding him.

Had he done right? Had his decision before Governor Waltham been truly sound, fair or merciful? Should he have said to him—that perhaps—perhaps—there had been those other influences playing upon him? . . . Was he never to have mental peace again, perhaps?

"I know my Redeemer liveth and that He will keep him against that day."

And then he walked and walked hours before he could present himself to Clyde's mother, who, on her knees in the home of the Rev. and Mrs. Francis Gault, Salvationists of Auburn, had been, since four-thirty, praying for the soul of her son whom she still tried to visualize as in the arms of his Maker.

"I know in whom I have believed," was a part of her prayer.

## SOUVENIR

Dusk, of a summer night.

And the tall walls of the commercial heart of the city of San Francisco—tall and gray in the evening shade.

And up a broad street from the south of Market—now comparatively hushed after the din of the day, a little band of five—a man of about sixty, short, stout, yet cadaverous as to the flesh of his face—and more especially about the pale, dim eyes—and with bushy white hair protruding from under a worn, round felt hat—a most unimportant and exhausted looking person, who carried a small, portable organ such as is customarily used by street preachers and singers. And by his side, a woman not more than five years his junior—taller, not so broad, but solid of frame and vigorous—with snow white hair and wearing an unrelieved costume of black—dress, bonnet, shoes. And her face broader and more characterful than her husband's, but more definitely seamed with lines of misery and suffering. At her side, again, carrying a Bible and several hymn books—a boy of not more than seven or eight—very round-eyed and alert, who, because of some sympathetic understanding between him and his elderly companion, seemed to desire to walk close to her—a brisk and smart stepping—although none-too-well dressed boy. With these three, again, but walking independently behind, a faded and unattractive woman of twenty-seven or eight and another woman of about fifty—apparently, because of their close resemblance, mother and daughter.

It was hot, with the sweet languor of a Pacific summer about it all. At Market, the great thoroughfare which they had reached—and because of threading throngs of automobiles and various lines of cars passing in opposite directions, they awaited the signal of the traffic officer.

"Russell, stay close now." It was the wife speaking. "Better take hold of my hand."

"It seems to me," commented the husband, very feeble and yet serene, "that the traffic here grows worse all the time."

The cars clanged their bells. The automobiles barked and snorted. But the little group seemed entirely unconscious of anything save a set purpose to make its way across the street.

"Street preachers," observed a passing bank clerk to his cashier girl friend.

"Sure—I see them up here nearly every Wednesday."

"Gee, it's pretty tough on the little kid, I should think. He's pretty small to be dragged around on the streets, don't you think, Ella?"

"We'll, I'll say so. I'd hate to see a brother of mine in on any such game. What kind of a life is that for a kid anyhow?" commented Ella as they passed on.

Having crossed the street and reached the first intersection beyond, they paused and looked around as though they had reached their destination—the man putting down his organ

which he proceeded to open—setting up, as he did so, a small
but adequate music rack. At the same time his wife, taking
from her grandson the several hymnals and the Bible he carried, gave the Bible as well as a hymnal to her husband, put
one on the organ and gave one to each of the remaining
group including one for herself. The husband looked somewhat vacantly about him—yet, none-the-less with a seeming
wide-eyed assurance, and began with:

"We will begin with 276 to-night. 'How firm a foundation.'
All right, Miss Schoof."

At this the younger of the two women—very parched and
spare—angular and homely—to whom life had denied quite
all—seated herself upon the yellow camp chair and after arranging the stops and turning the leaves of the book, began
playing the chosen hymn, to the tune of which they all
joined in.

By this time various homeward bound individuals of diverse
occupations and interests noticing this small group so advantageously disposed near the principal thoroughfare of the city,
hesitated a moment,—either to eye them askance or to ascertain the character of their work. And as they sang, the nondescript and indifferent street audience gazed, held by the
peculiarity of such an unimportant group publicly raising its
voice against the vast skepticism and apathy of life. That gray
and flabby and ineffectual old man, in his worn and baggy
blue suit. This robust and yet uncouth and weary and white-
haired woman; this fresh and unsoiled and unspoiled and un-
comprehending boy. What was he doing here? And again that
neglected and thin spinster and her equally thin and distrait
looking mother. Of the group, the wife stood out in the eyes
of the passers-by as having the force and determination which,
however blind or erroneous, makes for self-preservation, if
not real success in life. She, more than any of the others,
stood up with an ignorant, yet somehow respectable air of
conviction. And as several of the many who chanced to pause,
watched her, her hymn-book dropped to her side, her glance
directed straight before her into space, each said on his way:
"Well, here is one, who, whatever her defects, probably does
what she believes as nearly as possible." A kind of hard, fighting faith in the wisdom and mercy of the definite overruling

and watchful and merciful power which she proclaimed was written in her every feature and gesture.

The song was followed with a long prayer by the wife; then a sermon by the husband, testimonies by the others—all that God had done for them. Then the return march to the hall, the hymnals having been gathered, the organ folded and lifted by a strap over the husband's shoulder. And as they walked—it was the husband that commented: "A fine night. It seemed to me they were a little more attentive than usual."

"Oh, yes," returned the younger woman that had played the organ. "At least eleven took tracts. And one old gentleman asked me where the mission was and when we held services."

"Praise the Lord," commented the man.

And then at last the mission itself—"The Star of Hope. Bethel Independent Mission, Meetings every Wednesday and Saturday night, 8 to 10. Sundays at 11, 3, 8. Everybody welcome." And under this legend in each window—"God is Love." And below that again in smaller type: "How long since you wrote to Mother."

"Kin' I have a dime, grandma? I wana' go up to the corner and git an ice-cream cone." It was the boy asking.

"Yes, I guess so, Russell. But listen to me. You are to come right back."

"Yes, I will, grandma, sure. You know me."

He took the dime that his Grandmother had extracted from a deep pocket in her dress and ran with it to the ice-cream vendor.

Her darling boy. The light and color of her declining years. She must be kind to him, more liberal with him, not restrain him too much, as maybe, maybe, she had—— She looked affectionately and yet a little vacantly after him as he ran. "For *his* sake."

The small company, minus Russell, entered the yellow, unprepossessing door and disappeared.

THE END

CHRONOLOGY

NOTE ON THE TEXTS

NOTES

# Chronology

1871–76    Born August 27 in Terre Haute, Indiana, the twelfth of the thirteen children born to Johann Paul and Sarah Schänäb Dreiser. (His mother, daughter of German Mennonite farmers who moved from Pennsylvania to a small village outside Dayton, Ohio, eloped in 1851 at age 17 with the 29-year-old Dreiser, a devout Roman Catholic who had emigrated from Mayen in the German Rhineland in 1844 to avoid conscription and worked in eastern wool mills before moving to Dayton. Parents lived in Fort Wayne, Terre Haute, and Sullivan, Indiana, where father was proprietor of a wool mill until a fire and a disabling accident caused him to lose his job.) Baptized Herman Theodore (called Theo, Thee, Dorsch, and Dorse) at Church of St. Benedict, September 10. Brothers and sisters are Johann Paul (John Paul Jr., Paul), b. 1858; Markus Romanus (Rome), b. 1860; Maria Franziska (Mary Frances, Mame), b. 1861; Emma Wilhelmina (Em), b. 1863; Mary Theresa (Theresa, Tres), b. 1865; Cacilia (Zwillig, Sylvia), b. 1866; Alphons Joachim (Al), b. 1867; Clara Clothilde (Claire, Tillie), b. 1869. (The three oldest children—Jacob, George, and Xavier—died in early childhood.) Shortly after Dreiser's birth, family purchases home for $1,200 at 12th Street and Walnut in Terre Haute. Another brother, Eduard Minerod (Ed), born 1873. Father works sporadically. Paul Jr. arrested for stealing (Feb. 1876) and father pays $300 bond.

1877–78    Enters St. Benedict's Catholic School; classes are conducted in German. Attends German Mass daily and hears German at home. Does poorly in sports, develops stutter, is bullied by other boys, and becomes an avid reader. Gathers coal from railroad tracks; sometimes has only potatoes and fried mush to eat. May 1878, father sells home for $1,400 and moves family to smaller house at 2533 North 7th Street. Hears parents fight over "what should be done for the children." (Remembers Terre Haute years as "a dour and despondent period which seems to have colored my life forever.")

937

1879–81     Father, now employed as a foreman at a carpet factory, finds jobs there and in domestic service for Mame, Emma, Sylvia, and Theresa, and they help support family. Al works on relative's farm. Rome runs away and works as vendor on railroad. With mother, Ed, and Claire, Dreiser moves in spring to Vincennes, Indiana; they occupy small, rent-free room in firehouse at invitation of young woman mother had once befriended. Enjoys the firehouse and winding streets of Vincennes and sees first telephone. After five weeks, mother discovers that friend procures sexual favors for the firemen and moves with children back to Sullivan, Indiana. Older sisters quarrel with father and wish to join mother in Sullivan. Rome visits, penniless and alcoholic, but full of tales of adventure in the West. Along with Sullivan's handful of Catholic children, Dreiser receives parochial education in the homes of church members. Picks coal with Ed and, with Claire, teaches mother to write English. Fall 1880, mother opens boarding house, but coal mines close in fall 1881, and some boarders leave without paying. Winter is severe and food scarce.

1882–84     Family fears eviction. February, Paul, absent for years, arrives, bringing gifts and money; has played in minstrel shows, changed his name to "Paul Dresser" and published *The Paul Dresser Songster*. In May, Dreiser, Ed, and Claire move with mother to Evansville, Indiana, and occupy a furnished brick cottage at 1415 East Franklin Street that Paul has rented for them. Groceries and secondhand clothes are sent regularly by Sallie Walker (real name Annie Brace), prosperous madam of Evansville brothel with whom Paul now lives. Reads Ouida's *Wanda*, Bulwer's *Ernest Maltravers*, Horatio Alger's stories, as well as *The Family Story Paper*, *The Fireside Companion*, and *The New York Weekly*. Father visits from Terre Haute and enrolls children in *Heilige Dreifaltighet Kirchet* (Holy Trinity Parochial School). Brother Al comes from Chicago and sisters Emma and Sylvia return. Dreiser works in five-and-dime store on Saturdays, earning pocket money and free ice cream. Rome visits, drinks heavily, is arrested and bailed out by Paul.

1884–85     Summer, Paul breaks up with Sallie Walker and is no longer able to provide sufficient support. Mother moves family to apartment found by Theresa in Chicago at West Madison and Throop Street. Dreiser sells newspapers with Ed. Father, unemployed, arrives. Sisters Mame, Emma, and Theresa date older men. By fall, Chicago proves too expensive and Dreiser, Ed, and Claire move with mother to Warsaw, Indiana. Father (now working again in Terre Haute), older sisters, and Paul send money for support. Enters seventh grade in West Ward, his first public school experience; is delighted by coeducational classes and attractive 21-year-old teacher, May Calvert. Feels self-conscious because of cast in right eye and buck teeth. Does well in all subjects and pleases father, who approves purchase of sets of works by Irving, Dickens, and Scott. Reads Kingsley's *Water Babies*, Hawthorne's *The House of the Seven Gables* and *The Scarlet Letter*, Lew Wallace's *Ben Hur*, Samuel Smiles' *Self-help*, and works by Cooper, Bryant, Whittier, Poe, and Longfellow. Late spring, Rome arrives drunk and troublesome. Summer, Sylvia loses her job in Chicago and comes to stay; Emma, who has broken up with her architect lover, visits. Dreiser embarrassed by ostentatious dress and free behavior of sisters and violent quarrels between them and father. Emma returns to Chicago.

1885–86 Enters eighth grade of Central High School where teacher Mildred Fielding tells him he has mental potential to overcome socially inferior family life. Fall, family moves to 14-room "Thrall's House" on three acres with grove of pine trees ("of all the places we lived this was the most charming"). Theresa, deserted by Chicago manufacturer, comes to Warsaw to recuperate from severe illness. Detectives come in search of Emma, and family learns she has run off with L. A. Hopkins, a married saloon clerk who has stolen $3,500 from employer. Reads Thackeray, Bunyan, Dryden, Pope, Emerson, Thoreau, and Mark Twain, as well as *Tom Jones*, *Moll Flanders*, and pamphlets on sex circulating among his friends. Suffers dizzy spells and ringing in ears. April, has first sexual experience with 15-year-old baker's daughter. Takes course in German literature at urging of ninth-grade teacher, Alvira Skarr. ("At once my estimate of my father's native land [hitherto, because of his financial failure and religiosity, exceedingly low] rose.") Sylvia reveals she is carrying the child of son of wealthy Warsaw family; she joins Emma and Hopkins in New York to have baby. Dreiser, Ed, and Claire feel socially ostracized. Spring, Sylvia brings baby boy, Carl, to mother in Warsaw and returns to New York. With advice from superintendent of schools, who praises his academic abilities, Dreiser reads Shakespeare and studies German history; also reads Carlyle, Macaulay's *History of England*, Guizot's *History of France*, and Taine's *History of English Literature*.

1887–88    Summer, after a brief attempt at farm and railroad work moves to Chicago and takes cheap room on West Madison Street. Gets job as dishwasher in Paradiso Restaurant for $5/week plus meals; tells sisters that he is haberdashery clerk for $7. Mother, Claire, Ed, and Sylvia's child, Carl, arrive in September, and family, joined by Theresa and Al, moves to apartment on Ogden Avenue. Quits restaurant and is out of work for a month. Family moves to cheaper apartment at 61 Flourney Street in October. Works as stock boy at wholesale hardware firm for $5/week; gives mother $3/week. Dislikes job but forms friendship with 45-year-old intellectual and alcoholic Danish immigrant, Christian Aaberg, who talks to him about Voltaire, Ibsen, Goethe, Wagner, Schopenhauer, ancient Greece, Peter the Great, and Napoleon. Fired, but rehired after appeal to company director. Develops stomach problems, chronic cough, and fears consumption.

1889       Summer, former teacher Mildred Fielding, now principal of suburban Chicago high school, arranges for his admission as special student to Indiana University at Bloomington, and pays living expenses ($300) for year. Resents not being invited to join fraternity. Elected secretary of Philomathean, school literary society. Shyness with girls is painful; finds concentration on studies difficult.

1890       Takes final exams and passes all classes. In June, returns to Chicago. Paul has written hit song "I Believe It for My Mother Told Me So," and now travels as the leading comedian in *The Tin Soldier*. Dreiser's health is improved, stomach troubles and cough are gone. Finds job selling real estate at $3/week plus commission; though boss is unable to pay his wages, enjoys free use of buggy and takes ailing mother for rides. Mother dies November 14 in Dreiser's arms. (Later writes, "Our youth and home were over . . . now I was I. And alone. Her part—her strength and living sustaining love—had gone from me.") Owed $21 for seven weeks' back pay, uses employer's credit to buy clothes. Finds work as driver with laundry company at $8/week.

1891    Family quarrels, and he takes small apartment on Taylor Street with Claire and Ed. Gets better-paying job collecting installments on cheap household goods sold to the poor. Writes pieces about Chicago influenced by Eugene Field's *Daily News* column "Sharps and Flats"; sends them to Field, but receives no response. November, uses $25 of company's money to buy new overcoat, gloves, and cane, intending to pay it back a little each week, but is discovered and fired. Wishes to become a newspaperman, but can only get job with *Chicago Herald* giving away toys for its Christmas promotion.

1892    Stands 6 feet 1 1/2 inches tall, weighs 137 pounds. Gets job with another collection firm. Quarrels with Claire and moves with Ed to room of their own. June, becomes reporter for Chicago *Daily Globe* for $15/week. Learns how to write news stories from copy editor John Milo Maxwell. Covers Democratic National Convention and by luck scoops other reporters with news of Grover Cleveland's nomination. Takes room alone on Ogden Place. Publishes first fiction, "The Return of Genius," in the *Globe* under the name Carl Dreiser. Moves to St. Louis when city editor helps him get job with respected St. Louis *Globe-Democrat* in November at $20/week; covers night beat at North 7th Street police station. Depressed and lonely at first, then meets bohemian staff artists Peter B. McCord and Richard Wood.

1893    Interviews celebrities passing through town, including former boxing champion John L. Sullivan and theosophist Annie Besant. January, eyewitness account of railroad disaster in Alton, Illinois, earns a bonus and a raise in pay. Becomes drama critic and plans play, *Jeremiah I*, with McCord to design costumes and sets. Favorable review of black singer Sissieretta Jones is criticized as "black Republicanism" by rival newspapers. April, unable to attend three plays because of crime assignment, writes reviews from advance clippings. Next day, discovers none of the touring companies had reached town because of floods. Humiliated, resigns from job. Becomes reporter for the St. Louis *Republic* at $18/week. Accompanies 20 Missouri schoolteachers (including 24-year-old Sara Osborne "Jug" White), winners of *Republic*-sponsored popularity contest, to Chicago World's Fair. Visits 72-year-old father, and brothers Al, now an electrician, and Ed, who drives a delivery wagon, in Chicago. Courts Sara White, who teaches in a suburb of St. Louis, and they become engaged.

1894    January, covers story of lynching of black youth. Feeling restless, decides to leave St. Louis in spite of the *Republic*'s offer of an editorial post and more money. With fellow reporter J. T. Hutchinson, considers buying small country weekly in Ohio, but is disappointed by its condition. Goes to Toledo, where he becomes close friend of Toledo *Blade* city editor Arthur Henry, who gives him temporary job covering streetcar strike. Then goes to Cleveland and Buffalo, and finally to Pittsburgh in April; impressed by the city, decides to stay. Receives wire from Henry offering job at $18/week at the *Blade*; changes figure to $25 and uses it to negotiate successfully with city editor of Pittsburgh *Dispatch*. Assigned to cover police and court news. Spends free time in nearby Carnegie Library; reads Balzac, beginning with *The Wild Ass's Skin* and *Lost Illusions* ("For a period of four or five months I ate, slept, dreamed, lived him and his characters and his views and his city"). Discovers Herbert Spencer's *First Principles*, which becomes lifelong philosophical influence. July, makes brief visit to Montgomery City, Missouri, to see Sara White and to meet her parents. Goes to New York to visit brother Paul, now successful and living with sister Emma and Hopkins and their two children. Feels both strongly attracted to and overwhelmed by New York ("here were huge dreams and lusts and vanities being gratified hourly"). In November moves to New York. Works briefly as space-rate reporter for the New York *World* at $7.50 for 21-inch-column.

1895    February, helps Emma leave Hopkins (now unemployed and alcoholic). Disillusioned, he abandons newspaper work and unsuccessfully tries to write articles and stories. Paul's business partners hire him to edit magazine to sell

their music. October, large-format magazine *Ev'ry Month*
appears, containing four songs per issue. Selects fiction,
poetry, and pictures, gives household hints, writes cap-
tions, book reviews, and editorial column, "Reflections,"
signed "The Prophet." Salary is $10/week during sum-
mer and $15 when magazine appears. Becomes friend of
the painters and illustrators William Louis Sonntag Jr.,
J. Francis Murphy, Bruce Crane, and others while residing at the artists' Salmagundi Club.

1896      April, visits Sara White, now teaching in Danville, Mis-
          souri. *Ev'ry Month* becomes modest success (circulation
          65,000), publishing syndicated stories by Bret Harte and
          Stephen Crane. Goes to theater regularly and reads
          Darwin. Ed comes to New York determined to be an ac-
          tor. Sylvia moves to New York to become a songwriter.
          Mame and husband, Austin Brennan, arrive for Christmas
          from Chicago with Claire, who is ill.

1897      At Paul's urging, writes words to first verse of "On the
          Banks of the Wabash." Increasingly resents publishing
          second-rate material. Quarrels with Paul and his partners
          over magazine's contents and leaves *Ev'ry Month* in
          August. Writes articles and occasional verse for *Munsey's*,
          *Ainslee's*, *Metropolitan*, and *Cosmopolitan*. Receives news
          that sister Theresa has been killed by train in Chicago.

1898      Lives at 232 West 15th Street. For Orison Swett Marden's
          magazine *Success*, writes series of "inspirational" pieces
          about famous people for $100 each. Series impresses
          Richard Duffy of *Ainslee's*, who hires Dreiser as consult-
          ing editor. Continues to write articles for other maga-
          zines, and total earnings reach almost $100/week.
          Pleased when "On the Banks of the Wabash" is a huge
          success, but still angry with Paul. In Chicago, interviews
          Philip D. Armour and Marshall Field for *Success*, as well as
          Abraham Lincoln's son, Robert Todd Lincoln, president
          of the Pullman Company, for *Ainslee's*. Writes articles on
          writers and artists, including Alfred Stieglitz. Arranges to
          meet Sara, accompanied by her sister Rose, in Washing-
          ton, D.C., where they are married December 28.

1899      Dreiser and Sara move to 6 West 102nd Street. July,
          Dreisers join Arthur Henry and his wife, Maud, at their

large house on the Maumee River outside Toledo. At Henry's urging, begins writing short stories, one or more of four he will publish over the next two years ("McEwen of the Shining Slave Makers," "Old Rogaum and His Theresa," "Nigger Jeff," and "When the Old Century Was New"). The Dreisers return to New York in September with Arthur Henry, who lives with them. Begins writing *Sister Carrie* with encouragement and collaboration of Henry and Sara. ("I took a piece of yellow paper and . . . wrote down a title at random—*Sister Carrie*—and began!") "Curious Shifts of the Poor," Bowery sketch inspired by Stephen Crane's "The Men in the Storm," appears as lead article in November *Demorest's Family Magazine*. Accepts invitation to call on William Dean Howells and writes "The Real Howells" (*Ainslee's*, March 1900).

1900    Writes magazine articles. Finishes *Sister Carrie*, which is rejected by Harper & Brothers but accepted by Doubleday, Page on recommendation of editor Frank Norris ("it pleased me as well as any novel I have read in any form, published or otherwise"). Vacations with in-laws in Missouri. When Frank Doubleday attempts to reject novel, Dreiser insists Doubleday, Page honor its promise. Contract signed in August. *Sister Carrie*, published November 8, is distributed without publicity. Norris sends copies to reviewers. Reviews are mixed, but only 450 copies are sold; royalties total $68.40. Father dies on Christmas Day.

1901    January 6, begins work on *Jennie Gerhardt*. Depressed by reception of *Sister Carrie*. Has difficulty writing articles. Asks Henry to cut *Sister Carrie* when British publisher George Heinemann requests shorter version for Dollar Library of American Fiction. Summer, the Dreisers join Henry and his mistress, Anna Mallon, at her cabin on Dumpling Island off Noank, Connecticut. Quarrels with them, and returns earlier than planned to New York at end of July. Takes cheaper apartment at 1599 East End Avenue. *Sister Carrie* receives good reviews in England. Tries unsuccessfully to interest American publishers in reissuing it. Worries about money as income declines; sits in rocking chair, folding and unfolding handkerchief (a life-long habit). Signs contract for *The Transgressor* (*Jennie Gerhardt*) with J. F. Taylor Company, which agrees to pay him $100/month to finish novel by following summer. November, unable to write, decides to go with Sara to Bedford City, east of Roanoke, Virginia, for winter to improve spirits. Remains depressed over slow progress on novel. Spends Christmas and New Year with in-laws in Missouri.

1902     Dreisers travel through South. Goes alone to Lynchburg and Charlottesville, Virginia, in April. June and July, walks from Charlottesville to Philadelphia; joined by Sara in September. Consults Dr. Louis Adolphus Duhring, a dermatologist with a subspecialty in nervous disorders. For chest pains, headaches, insomnia, weariness, and inordinate appetite, Duhring prescribes experimental treatment for neurasthenia (analgesics and bromides taken in sequence) and for lethargy (tonic of small amounts of arsenic, strychnine, and quinine). Health fails to improve. Unable to complete *Jennie Gerhardt*; payments from J. F. Taylor cease. Writes occasional pieces for local periodicals. Sketch "Christmas in the Tenements" appears in *Harper's Weekly* in December.

1903     Sends Sara to her family in Missouri when money is almost gone. February, moves to cheap lodgings in Brooklyn. Suffers from insomnia, pain in fingers and toes, and has hallucinations. Lives on bread and milk; weight drops to 130 pounds. Refuses to seek help from family, although Mame, Paul, Ed, and Emma all live in New York. On city street, encounters Paul, who persuades him to enter former wrestler William Muldoon's sanitarium in Westchester County. After six weeks of rigorous exercise and regular meals, condition improves; records experience in sketch "Scared Back to Nature," published in *Harper's Weekly*. Paul pays $256 bill. June, gets job on railroad at Spuyten Duyvil shop on Hudson River. Lives in Kingsbridge, New York, and is joined by Sara in August. Receives occasional financial help from Paul. Resigns from railroad Christmas Eve.

1904     January, gets job with Paul's help as feature editor on New York *Daily News*, and takes apartment with Sara at 399 Mott Avenue in the Bronx. Writes a record of his psychological crisis, *An Amateur Laborer*. Quarrels with Henry about portrayal of him in Henry's memoir *An*

*Island Cabin.* Fall, takes job with Street & Smith editing dime novels for $15/week. With co-editor Charles Agnew MacLean, plans to start publishing company; MacLean buys plates of *Sister Carrie* from J. F. Taylor (which had bought them from Doubleday, Page) for $500, but venture collapses after they quarrel.

1905    Still unable to complete *Jennie Gerhardt*, owes J. F. Taylor $750 for advances. Writes poetry and articles for Richard Duffy, now editor at *Tom Watson's Magazine.* Becomes editor, with raise in pay, of new pulp journal *Smith's Magazine*, which appears in April. Begins lifelong friendship with Charles Fort, journalist and eccentric author of pseudo-scientific books. Marital difficulties develop in part over his unwillingness to have children. Paul, suffering from financial pressure and poor health, moves in with Emma; Dreiser visits nearly every day.

1906    Paul Dresser dies penniless January 30 of heart attack (family will later receive royalties from songs, including "My Gal Sal," which becomes a hit). After raising *Smith's* circulation to 125,000, takes new job as editor of the *Broadway Magazine* at $40/week. Uses generous budget to buy work from O. Henry and Kipling. Buys plates of *Sister Carrie* from MacLean for $550 and moves with Sara to 439 West 123rd Street, overlooking Morningside Park.

1907    Circulation of *Broadway Magazine* goes to 100,000; now earns $100/week salary. With investment of $5,000 becomes secretary and editor of B. W. Dodge & Company. Writes occasional poetry and sketches of New York City life. Dodge reissues *Sister Carrie*; receives good reviews and sells well. June, accepts offer to become chief editor, at $5,000/year, of the Butterick Company's "Trio" of women's magazines, *The Delineator*, *The Designer*, and the *New Idea Woman's Magazine*. In June, has appendix removed at St. Luke's Hospital. Starts campaign to find homes for orphaned children. Repays debt to J. F. Taylor for *Jennie Gerhardt.*

1908    Spring, meets and begins close friendship with H. L. Mencken. Invests in two lots near Nyack, New York, and a 150-acre tract near Nanuet, New York; buys ten-acre orchard in North Yakima, Washington, from

Arthur Henry's brother Albert. Grosset & Dunlap publishes inexpensive edition of *Sister Carrie* (5,248 copies sold by end of year). Recycles 20 chapters of *Jennie Gerhardt* written in 1901 to show publishers. Travels to Washington, D.C., and persuades President Theodore Roosevelt to support the *Delineator* campaign for orphans (forerunner of National Child Rescue League). Receives increase in salary when circulation of magazines goes up.

1909     July, with William Neil Smith, secures control of bankrupt magazine *The Bohemian*. Publishes O. Henry and his own sketches that later appear in *The Color of a Great City*. Fall, begins relationship with Thelma Cudlipp, 17-year-old daughter of Butterick assistant editor. Abandons *The Bohemian* in December.

1910     Attends social gatherings at home of Elias Rosenthal, wealthy attorney and admirer of *Sister Carrie*, and meets Rosenthal's daughter Lillian (who will become lover and lifelong friend). Spring, hires William C. Lengel, 21-year-old lawyer, as private secretary at *The Delineator*, beginning long friendship. Wants to marry Thelma and asks for divorce, but Sara, ill with rheumatic fever, refuses. Fired by Butterick Company October 1, after firm is threatened by bad publicity from Thelma's mother. Leaves Sara; moves to Park Avenue Hotel. Denied permission to see Thelma; angry, depressed, and suffering from insomnia, loses weight; writes her letters (which are intercepted by her mother). Dodge & Company taken over by creditors. Thelma sails with mother to England. Continues to see Sara, though they live together only sporadically. Attends Anarchists' Ball; sits with Sinclair Lewis and Emma Goldman. Sara helps edit first complete draft of *Jennie Gerhardt*, with "happy ending" in which Jennie marries Lester Kane.

1911     Revises ending of *Jennie Gerhardt*, with Jennie alone at death of Lester. Shows new version to Mencken, Flora Mai Holly, James Huneker, and other friends who admire the novel. Sara sails for England in January with copy to show Curtis Brown & Massie, London literary agency. July, moves to 3609 Broadway; joined by Sara on her return from Europe. Finishes first draft of *The "Genius"* by

August, but puts it aside to work on *The Financier*, first volume of Frank Cowperwood trilogy based on life of railway magnate Charles Tyson Yerkes. *Jennie Gerhardt* published by Harper & Brothers in New York and London on October 19. Novel is praised by Floyd Dell in *The Bookman* and Mencken in *The Smart Set*; Arnold Bennett visits America and says he knows little about American literature, but "I know there is one novel called *Sister Carrie*, by a man named Theodore Dreiser." Wants to travel to Europe to continue research on life of Yerkes, and is grateful when British publisher Grant Richards arranges luxurious European trip (in the style of Yerkes); Century Company offers $1,000 advance for three travel articles. Harpers advances $500 for *Jennie Gerhardt* and $2,000 for *The Financier*. Embarks November 22 on the *Mauretania* with Richards. Spends three weeks at Richards's country home at Cookham Dean, Berkshire. Visits Oxford, London, English countryside. Richards outfits him with expensive Bond Street clothes. Enthusiastic first encounter with painting of the European post-impressionists Cezanne, Van Gogh, Gauguin; responds strongly to Picasso's work.

1912    Visits the mills at Manchester and encounters strikers. Goes to Paris January 11. Joined by Richards, who shows him Paris night life. Goes to Monte Carlo and Cap Martin with Richards and Sir Hugh Lane, art collector and director of Dublin Municipal Art Gallery. February, stays two weeks in Rome at the Grand Continental Hotel. Worries about sales of *Jennie Gerhardt* and expense of trip. Sees Pope Pius X. Goes to Assisi where he visits the historical sites of one of his spiritual heroes, St. Francis. March, tours Florence and Venice. Travels through Switzerland to Germany, where he visits father's birthplace in Mayen, then to Amsterdam. Sails April 13 from Dover on the *Kroonland*; arrives in New York April 23. Stays at St. Paul Hotel. Relieved to find that *Jennie Gerhardt* has sold 12,717 copies since February. Meets Anna Tatum, who becomes his lover for a short time and later acts as literary agent. Moves temporarily to 605 West 111th Street. Late June, rejoins Sara at 3609 Broadway. Decides to remain with Harpers rather than sign with Richards. Completes *The Financier*, which is published in October by Harpers and receives good reviews. Works on travel articles. November, asks Mencken to be his literary executor. December, goes to Chicago for further research on Yerkes. Meets Edgar Lee Masters, lawyer and poet, to talk about Yerkes, beginning lifelong friendship.

1913 Introduced by Floyd Dell to Maurice Browne (founder of early Little Theater), actress Kirah Markham (with whom shortly after he begins an affair), and writers John Cowper Powys, Arthur Davison Ficke, and Sherwood Anderson. Urges Browne to bring theater to New York. On return to New York, works on *A Traveler at Forty*, account of European trip, and *The Titan*, second volume of Cowperwood trilogy. Worries about declining sales of *The Financier*. Summer, writes one-act play "The Girl in the Coffin" (*The Smart Set*, Oct. 1913). Begins living with Kirah Markham. *A Traveler at Forty* published by Century. Becomes member of Liberal Club in Greenwich Village. Attends Emma Goldman's New Year's party with Markham.

1914 Financial worries continue. Markham learns that Dreiser still spends time with Sara and returns to Chicago. Goes to Chicago for more research and sees Markham and Edgar Lee Masters. Hears from Anna Tatum that Harpers, after printing 8,500 sets of sheets, has refused to publish *The Titan*, claiming its realism is too uncompromising. John Lane Company, under direction of J. Jefferson Jones, accepts the book, giving $1,000 advance plus 20 percent royalty. Dreiser agrees to repay Harpers' $3,000 advance. Returns to New York in March and stays with Mame and husband, Austin Brennan, in New Brighton, Staten Island. Pays Sara $100 a month; keeps separation secret from friends. *The Titan* published by John Lane, May 10. Reviews are mixed (8,016 copies sold by year-end). July, moves with Markham to 165 West 10th Street (his residence for next five years). Revises *The "Genius"* and works on *The Bulwark*. In August, gives Mencken manuscript of *Sister Carrie* as gift. Tries to sell serial rights to *The "Genius"* (edited by Lengel). Writes five one-act plays: "The Blue Sphere," "In the Dark," "Laughing Gas," "The Spring Recital," and "The Light in the Window"; also writes a film scenario "The Born Thief," a philosophical essay "Saving the Universe." Completes first part of autobiography *Dawn*, but intimate revelations about living siblings lead him to delay publication.

1915    Unable to continue $100 monthly support to Sara, signs over land in Nyack, apple orchard, and furniture to her in lieu of 18 months' payments. Receives $1,500 advance from John Lane for *The "Genius"* and smaller advance for *Plays of the Natural and the Supernatural*. Tries to find publishers for Masters, Sherwood Anderson, Harris Merton Lyon, Charles Fort, and Benjamin De Casseres. Refuses request to write recommendation for Mencken's *The Smart Set* because he distrusts co-editor George Jean Nathan's influence ("too debonair, too Broadwayesque"). Sells story "The Lost Phoebe" for $200 (*Century*, April 1916). Gets a room in New York Public Library to study physics and chemistry, especially work of Jacques Loeb, scientist working in comparative physiology and psychology. Agrees to do book on Indiana with Indiana friend Franklin Booth, prosperous advertising illustrator, and in August drives with him to Warsaw, Terre Haute, Bloomington, Sullivan, Vincennes, Indianapolis, and Evansville, Indiana. October, *The "Genius"* published by John Lane; receives negative reviews, including attacks on Dreiser's German ancestry.

1916    Suffers depression and prostate trouble. Takes ship to Savannah, Georgia, and works on *A Hoosier Holiday*. Markham joins him after her play, Hauptmann's *The Weavers*, closes. *Plays of the Natural and the Supernatural* published by John Lane. Returns to New York in early April. Unhappy when Markham leaves because of his infidelity (she joins the Provincetown Players). Sends manuscript of *A Hoosier Holiday* to Mencken for editing. In July, learns that New York Society for the Suppression of Vice, headed by John S. Sumner, seeks to ban *The "Genius"* as blasphemous and obscene. Angry when Jones of John Lane agrees to withdraw the book (which has sold 8,887 copies) pending legal decision; begins campaign against Sumner aided by Mencken and Harold Hersey of the Authors' League of America. August, meets with executive committee of Authors' League, but its support is lukewarm. Ships plates of *The "Genius"* to New Jersey for safekeeping. Mencken and Hersey, with some help from Dreiser, collect 500 signatures in his support, including

Robert Frost, Ezra Pound, Mary Wilkins Freeman, Jack London, William Allen White, Sinclair Lewis, Willa Cather, John Reed, Max Eastman, Edwin Arlington Robinson, and Sherwood Anderson. Through Mencken meets Estelle Bloom Kubitz, who becomes secretary and lover. Begins lifelong friendship with Masters' friend, Dorothy Dudley. *A Hoosier Holiday*, published by John Lane November 17, sells 1,665 copies by end of year. *Laughing Gas* produced by Indianapolis Little Theatre Society December 7; runs for three performances. Completes play *The Hand of the Potter*, about sexually driven murderer, set against background of Lower East Side Jewish tenement life; it is praised in review by Abraham Cahan in *The Daily Forward*. Dreiser sends the play to Mencken, who tells him that he is ruining all efforts on his behalf in the anti-censorship campaign by writing it and warns, "Nothing is more abhorrent to the average man than sexual perversion." Feeling that Mencken has joined ranks of the conventional, Dreiser answers, "Tragedy is tragedy and I will go where I please for my subject."

1917    Along with other German-Americans (including H. L. Mencken), experiences anti-German sentiment as country comes closer to war. To address situation, writes article, "American Idealism and German Frightfulness," but fails to get it published. Meets Philadelphian Louise Campbell, who becomes his lover, editor, adviser, and typist. June, goes to farm near Westminster, Maryland, with Estelle Kubitz to work on *The Bulwark* and complete part two of autobiography (*Newspaper Days*). Has low blood pressure, and takes medication for nervousness and fatigue. Finds liberal publisher in Horace Liveright and permits him to reissue *Sister Carrie* (its sixth printing); discusses future publications. Revises stories for *Free and Other Stories*. November, buys Paul's piano from Mame and has it made into writing desk. Feels less pressure about money due to placement of stories in *Cosmopolitan* and *The Saturday Evening Post*. *The Girl in the Coffin* produced by Washington Square Players December 3.

1918    Obscenity case against *The "Genius"* dismissed on technicality by New York appellate court in May. Sells articles and stories to *Harper's Monthly, Metropolitan, Scribner's,* and *Munsey's*. Receives from Boni & Liveright $500 advance for *Free and Other Stories*, published in August. Sends essay "Hey Rub-a-Dub-Dub" and the play *Phantasmagoria* to *The Smart Set* in June but Mencken rejects them. Meets A. A. Brill, translator of Freud and founder of New York Psychoanalytic Society; reads works of Freud. Begins close friendship with San Francisco poet George Sterling. Plans *Twelve Men*, biographical sketches collected and reshaped mainly from earlier pieces.

1919   *Twelve Men*, published in April by Boni & Liveright, is praised by critics and sells better than expected. Threatens to leave Liveright unless they publish Charles Fort's *The Book of the Damned* (1920). In May, hit by car while crossing New York City intersection and suffers cuts in scalp and broken ribs. Spends night in Roosevelt Hospital; refuses to press charges against driver. Recuperates at apartment of Estelle Kubitz. June, goes to Indiana to visit former teacher May Calvert Baker and old friend John Milo Maxwell, now on staff of Indianapolis *Star* and at work on book attempting to prove that Robert Cecil wrote Shakespeare's plays (Dreiser later tries to find publisher for it). *The Hand of the Potter* published by Boni & Liveright. In September, visited by and falls in love with Oregon-born Helen Patges Richardson, 25-year-old aspiring actress whose mother was Dreiser's maternal aunt. Travels by ship with her to New Orleans and from there by train to Los Angeles. Accepts offer from Famous Players Lasky studio to write screenplays and Helen acts in movies. Boni & Liveright advances $333.33/month for one year on *The Bulwark*. Keeps address secret and uses post office box for mail. Moves to Highland Park in December. Takes trips to San Diego and Santa Barbara. His screenplays are rejected by studio.

1920   *Hey Rub-a-Dub-Dub*, book of philosophical essays and plays published by Boni & Liveright in January, receives negative reviews. Signs protest over suppression of James Branch Cabell's *Jurgen*. April, moves to Hollywood to be closer to movie studios. (Helen has minor roles as extra at $7.50, then $20/day; later gets supporting roles in *The Flame of Youth* and Rudolph Valentino's first film, *The Four Horsemen of the Apocalypse*.) Learns from Boni & Liveright that Anna Tatum threatens to sue if they publish *The Bulwark* (story based on her family). Writes movie scenarios but is unable to sell them. Begins work on *An American Tragedy*. Reads Poe and critical biographical works about him. Travels in October to San Francisco to see his friend George Sterling and begins another lifelong friendship with George Douglas, literary editor of San Francisco *Bulletin*. Pays for Estelle Kubitz's appendectomy in New York in December.

1921    Tries unsuccessfully to find a publisher who will issue all his books as a set. With Helen visits San Francisco, Portland, Seattle, and Vancouver in April. Enjoys drives in used Overland car bought by Helen. After several moves, decides in August to purchase cottage at 652 North Columbus in Glendale for $4,500. Sells articles on Hollywood. *The Hand of the Potter*, produced by Provincetown Players in New York City December 5, receives negative reviews.

1922    Hopes for reissue of *The "Genius"* and, despite distaste for an expurgated version, discusses cuts with Mencken, who negotiates successfully with John Sumner. Completes 20 chapters of what will become *An American Tragedy*, dealing with the history of parents of Clyde Griffiths; soon after abandons most of manuscript, feeling it is a false start. Drives with Helen in new Maxwell to San Francisco and Yosemite. Sells house in October and returns to New York with Helen to write *An American Tragedy*. Takes apartment at 16 St. Luke's Place in Greenwich Village. Sells manuscript of *Jennie Gerhardt* for $1,000 to W. W. Lange, admirer prosecuted in 1921 for giving *Sister Carrie* and *Jennie Gerhardt* to a minor. Receives $1,000 advance for *Newspaper Days*. Works on *The Stoic* (final novel in Cowperwood trilogy), two new plays, film scenarios, short stories, and sketches of women. A volume of autobiography covering his life as a newspaperman published under title *A Book About Myself* by Boni & Liveright in December; intended *A History of Myself* to be overall title of four projected autobiographical volumes.

1923    Meets Jacques Loeb, with whom he has been corresponding for several years, at Rockefeller Institute in January. Horace Liveright buys plates from other publishers and takes five-year leases on all books; in new contract,

signed February 7, agrees to pay Dreiser $4,000 a year
for four years, to reprint *The "Genius"* unexpurgated, to
publish book of poems and uniform collected edition of
Dreiser's works (starting Jan. 1927), and, after sale of
1,000 sets, to pay Dreiser $10,000. Dreiser agrees to de-
liver two novels in three years. Feels business affairs are in
order for the first time. Receives $900 first installment
from *Metropolitan* for serialized version of *The "Genius"*
edited by William Lengel. Sells various shorter pieces to
magazines. With Helen driving, tours upstate New York
in June, visiting scenes of Gillette-Brown murder case for
*An American Tragedy* in Cortland, South Otselic,
Herkimer, and Big Moose Lake in the Adirondacks. Suffers from chronic nausea and headaches. Moves to apartment at 118 West 11th Street in September. *The Color of a
Great City*, made up of earlier articles, published in December. By end of year *The "Genius"* has sold 12,301
copies.

1924        Modern Library publishes edition of *Free and Other Stories* with foreword by Sherwood Anderson. March, estranged from Helen, who returns to Portland. Interviews
Ty Cobb in Detroit ("The Most Successful Ball-Player of
Them All" published in *Hearst's International,* Feb.
1925). Helen returns in late October to support him in
writing of *An American Tragedy*. Finds work on novel
difficult, but continues, with Louise Campbell in
Philadelphia typing and cutting.

1925        Moves with Helen to apartment at 1799 Bedford Avenue
in Brooklyn to concentrate on *An American Tragedy*.
Takes office on Union Square; Helen types at home, and
Louise Campbell and Sally Kusell, his secretary-editor,
cut, edit, and retype. In August, he delivers setting typescript of Book One and Book Two; works on Book Three
in fall as he makes major corrections to galleys of first two
parts. November, asks Mencken to get him a pass to Sing
Sing prison's death row, for use in novel; later tells
Mencken "my imagination was better—(more true to the
fact)—than what I saw." Exhausted after completing
novel, starts on motor trip to Florida with Helen on
December 8 to rest and to avoid being in New York
when *An American Tragedy* is published December 17; en
route visits Mencken in Baltimore; inadvertently slights

Mencken who is grieving over his mother's illness and precipitates a nine-year break in the friendship.

1926 Researches real estate boom in Florida, puts $200 down on lot, and takes notes for articles (later published as "This Florida Scene" in *Vanity Fair*). Hears that *An American Tragedy* had sold over 13,000 copies in the first two weeks. Sails back to New York January 24 on *Kroonland*. Hurt by Mencken's disapproving review of *An American Tragedy*. March, moves temporarily to Hotel Pasadena; Liveright has commissioned Patrick Kearney to dramatize novel and Dreiser wants to be near production. Sells film rights for *An American Tragedy* to director and producer Jesse L. Lasky for $90,000; quarrels publicly over his share with Liveright, then pays $10,000 to Liveright as agreed in contract (Liveright had wanted more). Dreiser signs new contract with Liveright for 20 percent royalties on all subsequent works, $500/month on account, and invitation to sit on board of directors; Liveright is to begin publishing limited edition of collected works in 1927, followed by library edition in 1929. Resumes support to Sara Dreiser, sending $200/month. June 22, sails with Helen for Oslo to consult foreign publishers and collect further material for *The Stoic*. Prepares volume of poems, *Moods Cadenced and Declaimed*. Tours Norway, Sweden, Denmark, Berlin, Prague, Vienna (fails to meet Freud, though Brill has written a letter of introduction), Salzburg, Budapest, and Munich. Arrives in Paris early September. Visits Emma Goldman, now in exile. Goes to London in October and begins warm friendship with Otto Kyllmann, director of Constable, his British publisher. Visits George Bernard Shaw (later says Shaw is "witty, delightful, flashing with ideas. . . . He reminds me of H. L. Mencken"). Returns in October to Hotel Pasadena in New York. Patrick Kearney's adaptation of *An American Tragedy* opens October 11 at Longacre Theater on Broadway, runs for 216 performances, and grosses over $30,000/week. Dreiser moved to tears by performance. Grieves over suicide of friend George Sterling. Sells rights for novels to eight European publishers. Late December, moves with Helen to duplex apartment in Rodin Studios, 200 West 7th Street; buys Russian wolfhound, Steinway grand piano, Oriental rugs, and hires maid. Invites friends to call Thursday evenings. *An*

*American Tragedy* sells over 50,000 copies (royalties total over $47,000). Sets up corporation, Author Royalties, with Helen as president and himself as vice-president. Learns that brother Rome is still alive and destitute in Chicago; arranges to pay room and board for him as well as a monthly allowance.

1927 Introduces Louise Campbell to Helen. March, takes three-week walking trip for health from Elizabeth, New Jersey, through Pennsylvania, Maryland, and West Virginia, to the Shenandoah Valley and Virginia. *The Financier*, revised and shortened, with much help from Campbell, published April 16. Buys 37 acres with cottage near Mt. Kisco, New York. Agrees to visit Soviet Union on condition that all expenses will be paid and he be allowed to travel freely. Leaves October 19 aboard the *Mauritania*. Fellow passengers include publisher Ben Huebsch and painter Diego Rivera. Lands at Cherbourg, goes to Paris, where he briefly meets Ernest Hemingway. In Berlin sees Sinclair Lewis and Dorothy Thompson, also on her way to Soviet Union. November 4, arrives in Moscow, though ill with bronchitis. Stays in Grand Hotel near Red Square. Acquires services of American expatriate writer and translator Ruth Kennell as guide and secretary; together they travel and keep extensive diary. Attempts unsuccessfully to interview Stalin and Trotsky. Meets German writer Lina Goldschmidt, Konstantin Stanislavski of the Art Theater, film director Sergei Eisenstein, poet Vladimir Mayakovsi, Politburo member Nikolai Bukharin, and longtime correspondent Sergei Dinamov, state publishing house expert in American and English literature. Visits Tolstoi's country estate, Yasnaya Polyana, and meets his daughter and niece. Goes to Leningrad, and other major cities.

1928 Leaves Soviet Union from Odessa January 13; stops in Berlin to visit Lina Goldschmidt. Joins Helen in Paris and there finds Emma Goldman in destitute condition. London, interviews Winston Churchill, sees Kyllmann and George Moore. Sails from Southampton and arrives in New York February 21. Writes articles on Soviet Union for New York *World*, *The Saturday Evening Post*, *Vanity Fair*, and others; declares that it offers hope to the world. Because of interest in science, goes with Helen to Woods

Hole Marine Biological Laboratory at invitation of Boris Sokoloff, friend from Rockefeller Institute. Begins warm friendship with geneticist Calvin Bridges of Carnegie Institute at Washington, D.C. Oversees building of country house on property near Mt. Kisco, now called Iroki— Japanese for "beauty." Returns to New York, and with Helen dines with Thelma Cudlipp, who has married a wealthy attorney. Works on *A Gallery of Women* (collection of biographical sketches of women) and collects poems for volume *Moods*. With H. S. Kraft, arranges for John Howard Lawson to adapt *Sister Carrie* for stage, hoping to have Paul Muni play Hurstwood (project is never finished). *Dreiser Looks at Russia* published by Horace Liveright in November; sells poorly, less than 4,000 copies. Accused of plagiarism by Dorothy Thompson, whose book *The New Russia*, based on her newspaper articles, had appeared in September. Denies accusation (suit by Thompson eventually dropped). Writes to California governor C. C. Young on behalf of Thomas Mooney, imprisoned in San Quentin for 1916 San Francisco political bombings, arguing that he is innocent.

1929    *This Madness* (character sketches of women based on lives of Lillian Rosenthal, Anna Tatum, and Kirah Markham) serialized in *Hearst's International-Cosmopolitan*, February–July. Considers leaving publisher Horace Liveright because promise of collected edition has not been kept, but stays when Liveright offers larger advance ($50,000 for ten-year contract). April, attends trial on 1927 suppression of *An American Tragedy* in Boston; Clarence Darrow and Arthur Garfield Hays appear unsuccessfully for the defense. Continues work on Iroki with help of artist friends Ralph Fabri, Wharton Esherick, Jerome Blum, Henry Varnum Poor, and Hubert Davis. Hears from Lina Goldschmidt that she and others are trying to secure 1930 Nobel Prize for him. *A Gallery of Women* published by Horace Liveright November 30, in two volumes. Loses only part of savings in Wall Street crash.

1930    March–May, makes tours by train of Grand Canyon, Tucson, Albuquerque, Santa Fe, El Paso, and Dallas. Meets Helen in Galveston and drives with her to San Francisco. Visits Mooney in San Quentin prison and receives help for his defense from William Randolph Hearst. Brings brother Rome, now physically weak and mentally confused, to sister Mame in New York. Arranges to financially support Rome, Mame, Emma, and Sylvia. *The Hand of the Potter* produced in Hamburg, Germany. Is finalist for Nobel Prize; disappointed when it is awarded to Sinclair Lewis. Meets Indian poet Rabindranath Tagore. Negotiates with Jesse Lasky, now at Paramount, over production of *An American Tragedy*. Visited by Sergei Eisenstein and Ivor Montague at Iroki and is impressed by their scenario version of *An American Tragedy*; Paramount, however, decides it is too long and costly (a million dollars) and assigns film to screenwriter Samuel Hoffenstein and director Josef von Sternberg.

1931    January 2, signs contract with Paramount for sound rights to *An American Tragedy* for $55,000, with stipulation that he will see script and be allowed to suggest revisions. When he reads Hoffenstein's script, writes, "To me, it is nothing less than an insult to the book—its scope, actions, emotions and psychology." Slaps Sinclair Lewis at Metropolitan Club dinner, angered by accusation of plagiarizing Dorothy Thompson's book on Russia. March 22, flies to Hollywood to revise Paramount script. April, chairs meeting in his apartment of the National Committee for the Defense of Political Prisoners. Writes articles on arrests of Communists, and supports Scottsboro defendants. May 8, *Dawn*, second volume of autobiography covering childhood years, published by Liveright. Critics praise the book, but are amazed at frankness of revelations about himself and family; sisters are upset. June, investigates conditions of miners in Pittsburgh area at urging of Communist leaders William Z. Foster and Joseph Pass. Accuses American Federation of Labor and United Mine Workers of close relations with corporations and defends Communist-organized National Mining Union. After viewing film *An American Tragedy* in June, files suit to prevent distribution. Loses case in trial July 22, but Paramount adds eight minutes of film, following some of Dreiser's suggestions. Income declines; September, moves from 200 West 57th Street to Ansonia Hotel. November, visits Harlan County, Kentucky, with committee including John Dos Passos, to study plight of striking and unemployed miners. A night in a hotel room with a women makes the national news; defends himself by claiming to be impotent. Committee indicted in Kentucky on charges of "criminal syndicalism"; offense carries prison term of up to 21 years and/or $10,000 fine. Refuses to stop publicity in exchange for dropping of charges; collects relief funds for miners and publicizes conditions in newsreel and on radio. Attorney John W. Davis offers to defend him; governor Franklin D. Roosevelt of New York promises open hearing if extradition is requested. Senator George Norris calls for inspection of Harlan County situation. December 30, Liveright publishes *Tragic America*, a critique of capitalism that calls for an egalitarian social order modeled on that of post-revolutionary Russia; receives negative reviews.

1932    Redraws will, leaving Helen two-thirds of property. Saddened when Charles Fort dies May 3 ("the most fascinating literary figure since Poe"). Works on *The Stoic* with Louise Campbell's help. Liveright firm suffers financial setbacks and stops monthly payments. Dreiser reduces monthly support to sisters Emma and Sylvia ($100) and Mame and Rome ($80); continues payments to wife, Sara ($200). With George Jean Nathan, Eugene O'Neill, James Branch Cabell, and Ernest Boyd, becomes a founding editor of new literary journal, *American Spectator*. August, refuses to endorse Soviet statement condemning Dostoyevski ("he is a great artist"). Becomes interested in possibilities of Technocracy, Inc., group formed by friend Howard Scott of Columbia University Department of Industrial Engineering that believes government should be ruled and goods distributed by social engineers. First issue of *American Spectator* is successful and 20,000 more are printed. November, flies to San Francisco to visit Tom Mooney in San Quentin and addresses rally of 15,000. (Mooney is pardoned January 1939.) In Hollywood, sells producer B. P. Schulberg film rights to *Jennie Gerhardt* for $25,000 and seven percent of Schulberg's one-third interest in profits.

1933    February, goes to Nashville, Tennessee, and Hopkinsville, Kentucky, for research and interviews for film about 1906–7 rebellion of tobacco farmers against Duke trust; writes scenarios with Hy Kraft and Milton Goldberg, but film is never made. Lectures at colleges on problems in America. Though uneasy about suppression of Trotskyists in Soviet Union, refuses to make public condemnation. Delighted by film version of *Jennie Gerhardt* starring Sylvia Sidney. Visits old friends: poet Arthur Davison Ficke and his wife, artist Gladys Brown, and John Cowper Powys in upstate New York and the Eshericks in Paoli, Pennsylvania. Readers accuse Dreiser, O'Neill, and other editors of anti-Semitic remarks in *American Spectator*. October, begins correspondence and public exchange with Hutchins Hapgood on the "Jewish question" (Hapgood publishes "Is Dreiser Anti-Semitic?", *The Nation*, April 17, 1935). Visited at Iroki by Diego Rivera, Floyd Dell, Sherwood Anderson, George Jean Nathan, Lillian Gish, George Douglas, and others. Attends funeral of Horace Liveright, dead of pneumonia at 49. When Liveright's firm goes bankrupt, offers $5,250 for books and plates; receiver asks $25,000, dispute goes to arbitration.

1934        January, resigns from *American Spectator*. Sells stories to *Esquire* and *Scribner's*. Works on book of philosophy; parts appear as "The Myth of Individuality" (*American Mercury*, March 1934), "You, the Phantom" (*Esquire*, Nov. 1934), and "Kismet" (*Esquire*, Jan. 1935). Arbitration with Liveright firm settled in September; Dreiser buys plates for $6,500. Signs contract with Simon & Schuster, which pays $5,000 advance, promises uniform edition of his works, and gives large party at Iroki in October to celebrate. Almost 300 actors, filmmakers, dancers, artists, and writers attend. Article on Upton Sinclair, "The Epic Sinclair," appears in December *Esquire*. Renews friendship with Mencken in November after nine-year break.

1935        On Mencken's advice and because of his own lack of respect for most of the members, refuses Henry Seidel Canby's offer to join the National Institute of Arts and Letters. Suffers from grippe, bronchitis, and depression ("a sense of psychic earthquake as though something abysmal and final were first opening under or splitting once and for all the so-called conscious something which is me"). Works intensely on book of philosophy entitled *The Formula Called Man*. Corresponds with scientists on problems of chemical and physical processes and asks about order and chaos in universal laws. In Los Angeles, stays with friend George Douglas, who works with him on philosophy book. Returns to New York in October. Hires Harriet Bissell, a recent graduate of Smith College, as new secretary. Tries to sell Iroki; feels health will be better in Los Angeles. Urges Upton Sinclair to include Howard Scott's Technocracy in his EPIC (End Poverty in California) movement, but receives no encouragement from Scott or Sinclair.

1936    Continues study of science for philosophy book and writes Sherwood Anderson that science is "enormously rich, mysterious, varied, and in fact, entirely satisfactory in an emotional way." Saddened by news of death of George Douglas from heart attack, February 11. Rents out main house at Iroki for summer and lives in cabin until October 1. Late December, moves with Helen to Park Plaza Hotel.

1937    Loses suit brought by Liveright firm and is ordered in June to pay $16,394 for unearned advances and special editions of books purchased by him between 1929 and 1932. Summer, visits Calvin Bridges and researchers at Carnegie Biological Laboratory at Cold Spring Harbor, New York, and Woods Hole, Massachusetts. October, moves to 116 West 11th Street to save money. Exchanges visits with novelist Edward Dahlberg. Finds it impossible to pay Sara $200/month. Receives some royalties: $500 from Limited Editions Club for special issue of *Sister Carrie* and $200 from Czech publisher. Discusses Moscow trials with Dos Passos. Emma dies.

1938    January, learning that Eisenstein has resumed making films in Soviet Union, asks him to produce earlier script of *An American Tragedy* or to write one for *The Financier*. March, upset when Nikolai Bukharin is shot as traitor. June, leases Iroki. Stays at friend Marguerite Tjader Harris's beach house in Noroton, Connecticut; works on philosophy book with her and Harriet Bissell. Agrees to edit *The Living Thoughts of Thoreau* for Longmans, Green. Bissell researches the book for him. July, represents the League of American Writers in Paris at the International Convention for International Peace. Gives well-received speech. Feeling lonely, writes to Harriet Bissell: "My morning depressions are stupendous." Meets Louis Aragon ("one of those parlor radicals") and Paul

Blech, secretary of International Association of Writers. Gives talk on Spanish Civil War. July 28, goes to Loyalist-held Barcelona and meets with President Manuel Azana. Agrees to ask President Roosevelt for food and supplies. Visits close friends Otto Kyllmann in London and John Cowper Powys in Corwin, Wales. Sails for New York August 13. Stays at George Washington Hotel. September 7, discusses Spanish relief at lunch with Franklin D. Roosevelt on presidential yacht *Potomac* in Hudson River. Agrees to form Spanish relief committee, but is not successful (it is later formed by Roosevelt). Writes articles on Spain for North American Newspaper Alliance. Works with Harriet Bissell on Thoreau book; finishes introduction in November. Impressed by Quaker Rufus M. Jones when he visits him at Haverford College in Haverford, Pennsylvania, to discuss Spanish relief (later reads his book on Quakers). Attends farewell party at Sherwood Anderson's and has Thanksgiving dinner with Masters. Moves to California with Helen and rents apartment in Glendale.

1939    January, attends séance at house of Upton and May Craig Sinclair in Pasadena. Resumes work on *The Bulwark*. Lectures at various colleges. Dismayed by Loyalist losses in Spain; stops relief activities. Tries to sell *Sister Carrie* to movie studios; writes John Barrymore, "Live to present Hurstwood for me. I have, for so long, thought of you treading—in art—his sorrowful way. . . ." August, calls Britain worse than Hitler's Germany and approves of Nazi-Soviet pact. Fall, sees Sherwood Anderson for last time. Looks for new publisher because Simon & Schuster has not fulfilled agreement to bring out uniform edition of his works.

1940    Ill in January and February; feels neglected. RKO Studios buys option on *Sister Carrie* for $3,000. Dreiser actively opposes Hoover's Finnish Relief Fund (established after the U.S.S.R. invaded Finland in 1939), claiming Finland is being used by the British as a tool against Soviet Union. Accepts $5,000 from Oskar Piest of Veritas Press for book urging America to stay out of war and pays English novelist Cedric Belfrage $1,000 to assist him. Exhausted, works only three hours a day. Makes radio speech in support of the right of all parties to be on the ballot for Earl Browder, Communist Party candidate for president.

Elected a vice-president of American Peace Mobilization. November 9, makes radio speech and addresses mass meeting in Washington, D.C. RKO buys *Sister Carrie* for $40,000. Pays alimony owed Sara and buys six-room Spanish-style white stucco house at 1015 N. Kings Road in Los Angeles for $20,000. Brother Rome dies.

1941    January, radical press Modern Age Books publishes *America Is Worth Saving*, which argues that America should not enter war; takes strong anti-British stance. Has difficulty finding printer because of potentially libelous references. Sells story titled "My Gal Sal," based on "My Brother Paul" in *Twelve Men*, to Twentieth Century–Fox for $35,000, money to be split among siblings. March, in New York addresses American Council on Soviet Relations. Objects to Communist Party's use of his name without permission. Addresses American Peace Mobilization meeting in Philadelphia. Writes eulogy for Sherwood Anderson (appears in May *Clipper*). June 22, stunned by Nazi invasion of Soviet Union; now feels America must enter war against Germany. July, receives letter from closest English friend, Otto Kyllmann, expressing anger and pain over Dreiser's violently anti-British opinions in *America Is Worth Saving*; appeals to Kyllmann not to allow anything to interfere with their friendship. Fall, buys out contract with Simon & Schuster for $8,500. In New York signs agreement with G. P. Putnam's Sons to deliver *The Bulwark* by June 1, 1942.

1942    Work on *The Bulwark* hampered by arthritis in shoulder and intestinal flu. Decides to deposit his papers in University of Pennsylvania library. September 21, in Toronto, Ontario, for speech, denounces England in press interview for delaying opening of second front against Germany; says if Soviet Union should fall, he hopes that Hitler will invade England and oust the British ruling class. Speech is canceled by order of Ontario attorney general. Leaves secretly for Detroit, fearing arrest. Writes to George Bernard Shaw thanking him for public defense of his position. Sara Dreiser dies October 1. Works on *The Bulwark* and on film scenarios.

1943    March, stops work on *The Bulwark* and returns to the philosophy book, now entitled *The Mechanism Called*

*Man,* but finds writing difficult (work is never completed). Worries about money; still unable to sell Iroki. Suffers from colds, shingles, deterioration of one good eye, and weight loss. September, returns to work on *The Bulwark.* Conceives series for *Esquire* about "black sheep characters," in contrast to *Reader's Digest* series of "unforgettable characters." Invites Louise Campbell and others to write pieces for pay that he will revise and publish under his name.

1944      January, informed by Walter Damrosch, president of Academy of Arts and Letters, that he has won Award of Merit Medal, given every five years; prize includes $1,000 and travel expenses to New York (other awards go to Willa Cather, S. S. McClure, and Paul Robeson). Leaves on train May 10 for three-week stay. Sees family and old friends. Looks for new publisher to reissue works in uniform edition, but is told that paper shortage prevents it. Makes two recordings for Office of War Information to be broadcast to Germany and occupied countries urging the overthrow of Nazi leaders. May 19, accompanied by Edgar Lee Masters, receives award from Academy. Mencken refuses to join him, on basis of the Academy's early hostility to their work. Sells Iroki and half of land for $15,000, and makes last visit. Visits Mame in hospital before she dies; attends her funeral. June 4, sees brother Ed for the last time. Exhausted, cancels planned trip to Philadelphia to see Mencken, Markham, Esherick, and Campbell. June 5, takes train to Stevenson, Washington, to meet Helen. June 13, marries her there under his baptismal name of Herman Dreiser; only witnesses are Helen's sister Myrtle Patges and her fiancé. Invites Marguerite Tjader Harris to come to California to work on *The Bulwark.* August 20, celebrates birthday with 57 guests. Repays advance to Putnam's, severing connection. Renews work on novel, dictating to Marguerite Tjader Harris. Suffers from various ailments; finds work difficult. Sees friends Paul Robeson, John Howard Lawson, Charlie Chaplin, Clifford Odets, among others.

1945      May 6, finishes *The Bulwark* and sends it to Louise Campbell and to new publisher, Doubleday & Co. Upset by Campbell's cuts and changes, tells her to send manuscript to novelist James T. Farrell, author of recent two-part essay on Dreiser in *The New York Times Book Review*. Campbell's changes are restored by Farrell and Donald B. Elder, editor at Doubleday, before novel is published in March 1946. Receives $34,600 payment of royalties from Soviet Union for works published there. July, goes to Portland with Helen for several weeks. August, becomes member of Communist Party. Regularly attends church services of different denominations. September, sister Sylvia dies. Begins to have periods of disorientation and loses appetite. December 3, finishes all but last two chapters of *The Stoic* and sends it to Farrell. Responds to Farrell's comments about last chapters, "I simply stopped writing at the end because I was tired. . . ." December 22, reads proofs of *The Bulwark*. Spends Christmas with Lillian Rosenthal Goodman and her husband, and visits Clare Kummer (widow of Arthur Henry), who plays brother Paul's songs. December 27, rewrites penultimate chapter of *The Stoic* (never completed, book will be published posthumously in 1947). Drives to beach with Helen to watch sunset. Suffers intense pain 3:00 A.M., December 28; dies of heart failure at 6:50 P.M. Sculptor Edgardo Simone makes death mask and cast of his right hand. Buried in Whispering Pines section at Forest Lawn, Glendale, January 3, 1946. John Howard Lawson delivers eulogy; Charlie Chaplin reads Dreiser's poem "The Road I Came."

# Note on the Text

*An American Tragedy* is based on an incident that occurred in up-state New York in 1906, when a factory worker named Chester Gillette murdered a young woman on Big Moose Lake in the Adirondacks. The woman, Grace Brown, had been pregnant with Gillette's child. In a well-publicized trial, Gillette was found guilty of first-degree murder and sentenced to death. His conviction was upheld on appeal. After Governor Charles Hughes refused to grant a stay of execution, Gillette was put to death on March 31, 1908. He is mentioned in passing in Dreiser's essay "Neurotic America and the Sex Impulse," written sometime around 1917 and included in *Hey Rub-a-Dub-Dub* (1920).

In the summer of 1920, while living in Los Angeles, Dreiser began writing *An American Tragedy*. He worked steadily through the fall and felt confident enough about the novel's progress in December 1920 to tell his publisher, Horace Liveright, that he hoped to finish it by the following spring. But in June 1921 he stopped work on *An American Tragedy* and put it aside for two years. His early version, comprising 21 chapters, exists in two forms in the Theodore Dreiser Papers at the University of Pennsylvania Library: a 604-page manuscript and a 188-page carbon typescript typed by Estelle Kubitz. Dreiser revised the manuscript draft for the typescript, which included some changes suggested by Kubitz.

Dreiser resumed working on *An American Tragedy* in 1923. Now living in New York City, he researched the Gillette case extensively. In late June and early July 1923 he and his companion Helen Richardson traveled to upstate New York and visited key sites pertaining to the case, such as Big Moose Lake and the courthouse where the trial had taken place. Soon afterward he began rewriting Book One of *An American Tragedy* from the beginning, salvaging little from the 1920–21 version. He completed a manuscript draft of Book One in January 1924. Sally Kusell began typing this draft in the late summer or early fall of 1923; the following March, Louise Campbell began typing sections of the manuscript as well. Boni & Liveright received a complete typescript of Book One in June 1924. Although this document does not survive, a final revised typescript, presently in the Dreiser Papers at the University of Pennsylvania, includes revisions by Dreiser and Kusell. The other surviving documents for Book One—thc typesetter's copy, the author's galleys, and the revised page proofs—also contain alterations by the author and his typists. Boni & Liveright editor Thomas R. Smith and his assistant Emanuel Komroff made extensive changes of their own, as well as suggesting further revisions and cuts. Dreiser revised the galley proofs and the page proofs of Book One while working on Book Two and Book Three of *An American Tragedy*; the novel assumed its final form in the summer or early fall of 1925.

Dreiser began Book Two in January 1924 and finished a draft either in December 1924 or in January 1925. Kusell and Campbell continued to work as his typists, a role that also included editorial duties. Receiving the typescript in sections, Boni & Liveright were in possession of a complete draft of Book Two by March 1925. As with Book One, Liveright's editors Smith and Komroff revised passages and recommended changes that might be made for publication. The changes in the first set of page proofs were extensive enough to require the printing of a second set, which in turn were further revised by Dreiser. The revision of Book Two was completed in the fall of 1925.

Although Dreiser began writing Book Three with renewed vigor at the beginning of 1925, the book's progress was slowed by an attack of bronchitis in March and his continued work on Book One and Book Two. Dreiser's manuscript and typescript drafts were edited, cut, and retyped by Sally Kusell (until the late summer or early fall of 1925, when her relations with Dreiser were too strained for her to continue) and by Louise Campbell; Helen Richardson served as one of Dreiser's typists as well for Book Three, although it appears that she did not edit his work. By mid-August, Boni & Liveright, hoping to bring out *An American Tragedy* in October, was pressuring Dreiser to finish the novel. After submitting his complete typescript of Book Three at the end of September or in early October 1925, he made further revisions as it was prepared for publication. His final alterations were made on the page proofs on November 25, 1925. A few days later he toured Sing Sing prison with the intention of making additional changes to the book's final three chapters; after the visit, however, he decided that the novel was finished.

*An American Tragedy* was published in a two-volume set by Boni & Liveright on December 17, 1925. Dreiser made no changes in subsequent printings of the novel. The present volume prints the text of the 1925 Boni & Liveright edition of *An American Tragedy*.

This volume presents the text of the original printing chosen for inclusion here, but it does not attempt to reproduce features of its typographic design, such as display capitalization of chapter openings. The text is presented without change, except for the correction of typographical errors. Spelling, punctuation, and capitalization are often expressive features and are not altered, even when inconsistent or irregular. The following is a list of typographical errors corrected, cited by page and line number: 151.27, to that; 169.11, Griffith's; 172.24, clothes."; 236.4, to-night.; 249.16, Bridgeman's; 465.2, it's; 488.3, unforseen; 519.37, win to; 526.9, wier-wier; 527.38, Racquette; 541.31, Racquette; 554.28, may turn; 618.8, to Harriets'; 626.27, Baggotts', Harriets'; 659.4, all; 670.35–36, cathechize; 716.5, where-/ever; 732.35, afternoon.; 737.25, Green-Davidson.; 767.21, seem to; 783.23, enscorcelled . . . enscorcellor; 811.39, Sanders; 828.26, in any; 928.29, short?

# Notes

In the notes below, the reference numbers denote page and line of this volume (the line count includes chapter headings). No note is made for material included in standard desk references. Biblical quotations are keyed to the King James Version. Quotations from Shakespeare are keyed to *The Riverside Shakespeare*, ed. G. Blakemore Evans (Boston: Houghton Mifflin, 1974). For further biographical information than is contained in the Chronology, see *A Traveler at Forty* (New York: The Century Co., 1913); *A Hoosier Holiday* (New York: John Lane Company, 1916); *A Book About Myself* (New York: Boni & Liveright, 1922); *Dawn* (New York: Horace Liveright, 1931); *Letters of Theodore Dreiser: A Selection*, ed. Robert H. Elias, 3 volumes (Philadelphia: University of Pennsylvania Press, 1959); *Dreiser-Mencken Letters: The Correspondence of Theodore Dreiser & H. L. Mencken 1907–1945*, ed. Thomas P. Riggio, 2 volumes (Philadelphia: University of Pennsylvania Press, 1982); *Theodore Dreiser: A Primary and Secondary Bibliography*, ed. Donald Pizer, Richard W. Dowell, and Frederic E. Rusch (Boston: G. K. Hall & Co., 1975); Richard Lehan, *Theodore Dreiser: His World and His Novels* (Carbondale: University of Southern Illinois Press, 1969); Richard Lingeman, *Theodore Dreiser: At the Gates of the City 1871–1907* (New York: G. P. Putnam's Sons, 1986) and *Theodore Dreiser: An American Journey 1908–1945* (New York: G. P. Putnam's Sons, 1990); Ellen Moers, *Two Dreisers* (New York: The Viking Press, 1969); W. A. Swanberg, *Dreiser* (New York: Charles Scribner's Sons, 1965).

13.9–11    "WINE IS A MOCKER . . . WISE."] Proverbs 20:1.

13.22–23    AND IT SHALL MOVE] Cf. Matthew 17:20: "and it shall remove."

13.29–31    "LOOK, THEN . . . LIKE AN ADDER."] Cf. Proverbs 23:31–32: "Look not thou upon the wine when it is red, when it giveth his colour in the cup, when it moveth itself aright. At the last it biteth like a serpent, and stingeth like an adder."

15.29    Crœsus] King of Lydia (d. 546 B.C.), proverbial for his wealth.

51.36    Chesterfieldian] The reference is to Philip Dormer Stanhope (1694–1773), 4th Earl of Chesterfield, whose letters, published posthumously, became famous as expressions of aristocratic ideals and manners.

88.20–21    "The Corsair,"] Musical comedy (1887) by Edward Everett Rice (1848–1924).

142.16 "The Grizzly Bear,"] Song (1910) with words by George Botsford and music by Irving Berlin.

187.29–30 "Strong drink . . . mocker,"] Cf. Proverbs 20:1: "Wine is a mocker, strong drink is raging: and whosoever is deceived thereby is not wise."

188.24–25 what matter . . . soul?] Cf. Matthew 16:26: "For what is a man profited, if he shall gain the whole world, and lose his own soul?"

224.19 Beau Brummell] George Bryan Brummell (1778–1840), leader of London fashion.

236.13 "Brown Eyes"] "Brown Eyes—Why Are You So Blue," song (1925) with words by Alfred Bryan and music by George W. Mayer.

236.34 "The Love Boat,"] Song (1920) written for the *Ziegfield Follies*, with words by Gene Buck and music by Victor Herbert

307.3 "Sweethearts"] Song (1913) with words by Robert B. Smith and music by Victor Herbert.

321.29 orchestrelle] A reed organ, called a "one-man orchestra," mechanically operated by rolls similar to a pianola. The Aeolian Company in New York built the first 58-note player in the late 1890s, and by 1900 the Solo Orchestrelle using 116-note music was introduced.

374.21–22 fox-trotting type of the period] The foxtrot was introduced by Harry Fox in 1914.

425.24 "Thy desire . . . thy mate."] The command is to Eve in Genesis 3:16: "Thy desire shall be to thy husband."

526.9 weir-weir] In the first edition: "wier-wier." The bird's name is used twice in the novel, but the second time (565.30 in the present edition) it is called the "weir-weir." The discrepancy derives from a mistake in the transcription of the holograph manuscript. Dreiser had originally written "wier-weir" at this point, but the typist copied the metathesis in the first half of the name twice, a spelling that went unaltered through two additional revised typescripts, two sets of galleys, the first edition of 1925, and each edition since.

526.10 ouphe] Elf; sprite.

526.11 barghest] Ghostly spirit said to take the form of a dog and to foreshadow death or a tragedy.

550.10 Winebrennarians] Followers of John Winebrenner (1797–1860), a minister who broke with the German Reformed Church in 1828 and established his own denomination as the Church of God in Mechanicsburg, Pennsylvania. The Winebrennarians rejected all creeds and believed the Bible to be the sole source of faith and practice.

559.31    "Oh, the sun . . . Kentucky home."]  Song (1853) by Stephen Foster.

715.32    "Lord . . . trouble."]  Cf. Psalm 3:1: "Lord, how are they increased that trouble me!"

716.6–7    "By terrible things . . . O God!"]  Psalm 65:5.

716.13–14    'He leadeth . . . waters.']  Psalm 23:2.

716.17    'He restoreth my soul.']  Psalm 23:3.

716.22–23    Under his wings shalt thou trust.]  Psalm 91:4.

766.4–5    'Thrice armed . . . his quarrel just.']  Cf. Shakespeare, *King Henry the Sixth, Part Two*, III.ii.233: "Thrice is he armed that hath his quarrel just."

766.21–22    'Judge not . . . unto ye again.']  Cf. Matthew 7:1–2: "Judge not, that ye be not judged. For with what judgment ye judge, ye shall be judged: and with what measure ye mete, it shall be measured to you again."

852.35–39    "Thou art mighty . . . as wool."]  The prayer of Mrs. Griffiths has a number of Biblical sources; cf. Matthew 19:26, Deuteronomy 4:35, and Isaiah 1:18.

853.14    "the woman tempted me?"]  Cf. Genesis 3:12: "And the man said, The woman whom thou gavest to be with me, she gave me of the tree, and I did eat."

853.16    "His mercy endureth forever,"]  Refrain from Psalm 136; the phrase also appears in 1 and 2 Chronicles and in Jeremiah.

853.18    "If ye have faith . . . a mustard seed,"]  Cf. Matthew 17:20, Luke 17:6.

860.37–40    "Jehovah, jirah . . . Thou wilt not!"]  The passage incorporates echoes of several Biblical passages; cf. Genesis 22:14, Deuteronomy 23:21, and II Samuel 19:4.

875.6–7    "My God . . . me?"]  Cf. Psalm 22:1, Matthew 27:46, Mark 15:34.

875.18–19    'Behold, I will deliver . . . snares of the wicked.']  Cf. Jeremiah 15:21: "And I will deliver thee out of the hand of the wicked."

881.14    "abandon hope—ye who enter here."]  Cf. Dante, *Inferno*, canto 3, line 9.

892.17–18    St. Bernard . . . Hermit]  St. Bernard of Clairvaux (1090?–1153), Cistercian abbot and church reformer; Girolamo Savonarola (1452–98), Italian religious reformer whose attacks on vice and worldliness led him into conflict with Pope Alexander VI and the ecclesiastical hierarchy, and who was executed for heresy; St. Simeon Stylites (d. 459), Syrian hermit who lived for

35 years on a platform at the top of a high pillar; Peter the Hermit (c. 1050–1115), French religious leader of the First Crusade and founder of a monastery at Neufmoutier at Liège.

892.23–25     "He that . . . scattereth."]   Luke 11:23.

897.4–5     'The Lord . . . time of trouble.']   Cf. Psalm 9:9.

900.17–22     "Ask, and ye shall receive . . . a serpent?"]   Cf. Matthew 7:7–10, Luke 11:9–11.

901.27–29     "He hath said . . . hideth His face."]   Cf. Psalm 10:11: "He hath said in his heart, God hath forgotten: he hideth his face; he will never see it."

901.40–902.1     "The Heavens . . . handiwork."]   Psalm 19:1.

902.3–4     "For He . . . Days."]   Cf. Deuteronomy 30:20.

902.16–20     "Brethren . . . pure."]   Cf. 1 John 3:2–4: "Beloved, now we are the sons of God, and it doth not yet appear what we shall be: but we know that, when he shall appear, we shall be like him; for we shall see him as he is. And every man that hath hope in him purifieth himself, even as he is pure."

902.21–22     "Hereby know . . . spirit."]   1 John 4:13.

902.23     "For ye are bought with a price."]   1 Corinthians 6:20.

912.38–39     "Wide is the gate . . . destruction."]   Matthew 7:13.

922.29–31     "Ye are the salt . . . be salted?"]   Matthew 5:13.

927.39–928.1     "I know . . . against that day"]   2 Timothy 1:12.

928.17–18     'This day . . . Paradise.']   Luke 23:43.

930.6–8     "Humble yourselves . . . you.]   Cf. 1 Peter 5–6.

930.10–12     I am . . . by me."]   John 14:6

931.16     "I know my Redeemer liveth]   Cf. Job 19:25.

*Library of Congress Cataloging-in-Publication Data*

Dreiser, Theodore, 1871–1945.
  An American tragedy / Theodore Dreiser.
     p.  cm. — (The Library of America ; 140)
  Includes bibliographical references.
 ISBN 1–931082–31–6 (alk. paper)
  1. Triangles (Interpersonal relations)—Fiction.
2. New York (State)—Fiction. 3. Trials (Murder)—Fiction.
4. Social classes—Fiction. 5. Young men—Fiction. I. Title.
II. Series.
PS3507.R55  A7  2003
813′.52—dc21

                                              2002030168

# THE LIBRARY OF AMERICA SERIES

The Library of America fosters appreciation and pride in America's literary heritage by publishing, and keeping permanently in print, authoritative editions of America's best and most significant writing. An independent nonprofit organization, it was founded in 1979 with seed money from the National Endowment for the Humanities and the Ford Foundation.

*This book is set in 10 point Linotron Galliard,*
*a face designed for photocomposition by Matthew Carter*
*and based on the sixteenth-century face Granjon. The paper*
*is acid-free Domtar Literary Opaque and meets the requirements*
*for permanence of the American National Standards Institute. The*
*binding material is Brillianta, a woven rayon cloth made by*
*Van Heek-Scholco Textielfabrieken, Holland. The compo-*
*sition is by The Clarinda Company. Printing and*
*binding by R.R.Donnelley & Sons Company.*
*Designed by Bruce Campbell.*